Enter at your own risk – *Trust Me Too* is addictive reading!

Welcome to a feast of fiction, where thrills, spills, frills and chills await you. Visit other worlds – known and unknown, past and present – and inhabit other people's minds.

Fifty-seven Australian authors, poets and illustrators present a selection of their latest work for your reading pleasure.

Trust me – you won't be disappointed!

First published by Ford Street Publishing, an imprint of
Hybrid Publishers, PO Box 52, Ormond VIC 3204

Melbourne Victoria Australia
© this collection Paul Collins 2012
© in individual illustrations/text remains
with each contributor

2 4 6 8 10 9 7 5 3

This publication is copyright. Apart from any use
as permitted under the Copyright Act 1968, no part may be
reproduced by any process without prior written permission
from the publisher. Requests and enquiries concerning
reproduction should be addressed to
Ford Street Publishing Pty Ltd, 2 Ford Street,
Clifton Hill VIC 3068.

www.fordstreetpublishing.com

First published 2012

Reprinted 2018

National Library of Australia Cataloguing-in-Publication data:
Title: Trust me too / editor, Paul Collins
Publisher: Ormond, Vic. : Hybrid Publishers, 2012.

ISBN: 9781921665585 (pbk.)

Target Audience: For young adults.
Subjects: Australian poetry.
Short stories – Australian.
Australian literature.

Other Authors/Contributors:
Collins, Paul, 1954–

Dewey Number: A820.80994

In-house editor: Saralinda Turner
Cover design by Grant Gittus

Printed in Australia by McPherson's Printing Group

Contents

Judith Ridge
Introduction — x

Adventure

Kerry Greenwood — 1
The Calabar Crystal

Corinne Fenton — 25
Tin Horse Plain

Archimede Fusillo — 36
The Yard

Sandy Fussell — 45
Dingo Boy

Crime

Jack Heath — 53
Rats

Lucy Sussex — 62
The Thieftaker's Apprentice

Contemporary

Oliver Phommavanh — 71
The Reunion

Deborah Abela — 77
Don't Let Go

Phillip Gwynne — 88
Led Zep

Susanne Gervay *Boo*	100
Jen Storer *My Pop*	107
Hazel Edwards *Tag*	111
Mo Johnson *Red Rhino*	118
Susan Halliday & Phil Kettle *Why Me?*	128
David Miller *The Mysteries of Letterboxes*	136

Fantasy

Ian Irvine *The Harrows*	139
Gary Crew *Amanita Im*	149
Simon Higgins *The Woodcutter's Secret*	158
Wendy Orr *The Snake Singer*	169
Sean Williams *The Mirror in the Middle of the Maze*	177
Paul Collins *The Spell of Oblivion*	191

Science Fiction

Isobelle Carmody 206
The Journey

George Ivanoff 242
Gamers' Inferno

Michael Gerard Bauer 260
Oh Brother, What Art Thou?

Romance

Kim Kane 277
Scaffolding

JE Fison 290
The Bridge

Ghost

Kirsty Murray 300
The Night Swimmer

Janeen Brian 312
What Goes Around . . .

Bill Condon 322
The Girl in the Library

Horror

Justin D'Ath 333
Stilled Lifes x 11

Michael Pryor 344
Shop Till You Drop

Twilight Zone

Jenny Mounfield 356
Space Junk

Margaret Clark *A State of Rejection*	365
Sean McMullen *Running Invisible*	373

Historical

Sue Bursztynski *Call Him Ringo*	380
Sally Odgers *George and the Boat*	390
Dianne Bates *Child-slave Crusader*	398

Humour

Doug MacLeod and Mitch Vane *I am an Author*	411

Sport

James Roy *Free Billy*	416
Pat Flynn *King of the Playground*	434

Graphics

Shaun Tan	Frontispiece, Introduction
Grant Gittus	99, 148
Greg Holfeld *Zombie Salad Eaters*	239
Mark Wilson *Portrait*	326

Poetry

Leigh Hobbs — 449
Strange-headed Harry

Meredith Costain and Grant Gittus — 452
Shoefiti

Michael Wagner — 454
Various

Christine Bongers and Peter Viska — 456
Killer Stories

Sofie Laguna and Marc McBride — 460
My Boy

Steven Herrick — 462
There Are Worse Things Than Poetry

Lorraine Marwood and Judith Rossell — 464
Tour de Cycling

Gabrielle Wang — 466
Calling Me

About the Contributors — 467

Introduction

'I have made this letter longer, because I have not had the time to make it shorter.'

So wrote the French writer Blaise Pascal in the 17th Century – although if you go searching for this quote on the Internet you will find it attributed to many other writers, writers who were alive and working centuries before Pascal and centuries after. It seems that a good idea finds many owners, and if there's one thing that many writers agree upon, it's that 'writing short' is often much more difficult – and takes more time – than writing long.

In this collection, you will find a wonderful diversity of short works – mostly examples of the art of the short story, but also a readers' theatre-style piece with the kind of twist in the tale we often see in short stories, and some beautiful and witty examples of verse, both rhyming and blank. And while the collection doesn't have a specific theme, nor is limited to a particular genre, it's fascinating to see that a sort of loose theme has emerged nevertheless. Many of the pieces within these pages offer us glimpses into worlds – worlds known and unknown, worlds past and present and several that are a tantalising mix of the prosaic and the arcane.

In the stories set in a world that is entirely familiar to us, we meet people who might be just like us – if not on the outside, then in the heart, where it counts – experiencing things that many of us deal with every day. There's the unexpected hero of James Roy's 'Free Billy'; there's JE Fison's 'The Bridge', where the girl gets the boy not because of how she looks, but because of what she does. Jen Storer's 'My Pop' is a moving but unsentimental eulogy for a grandfather, while Phillip Gwynne's 'Led Zep' explores the generation gap with the kind of good-natured humour we are used to from his novels. Meanwhile, Mo Johnson and Susanne Gervay take us deep into the heart of the quest to find one's place in one's family in their stories 'Red Rhino' and 'Boo'.

Taking us completely out of our own world and into the world of the imagination are some of Australia's best and most highly regarded writers of science fiction and fantasy. The potentially short and brutish lives of young people forced into servitude to gods and dragons, and even the elders meant to protect them, is explored in Wendy Orr's powerful and visceral 'The Snake Singer', Sean Williams' gripping 'The Mirror in the Middle of the Maze' and Ian Irvine's, well, *harrowing*, 'The Harrows'. And the great Isobelle Carmody offers us a tantalising taste of a world known to many of her fans.

Yet other stories prove the maxim created by the writer LP Hartley in the opening line to his novel *The Go-Between*: 'The past is a foreign country – they do things differently there'. And not just the distant past of Lucy Sussex's 'The Thieftaker's Apprentice' and Simon Higgins' 'The Woodcutter's Secret' – tales set in distant times (times that, perhaps, never were) but also a past that is in living memory for your parents (well, your grandparents, certainly!) and many of your teachers. Sue Bursztynski takes us back to Melbourne in 1964 when there were five, not four, Beatles, and it seemed as if the entire city – the entire world – had gone Beatle-mad.

Some of the stories that most raise the hairs on the back of the neck are those where our known, 'safe', world collides with the 'other'. There are spine-chilling ghost stories and various tales of alien visitation – I dare you to read Michael Gerard Bauer's 'Oh Brother, What Art Thou?' and NOT wonder about your siblings as a result. Kerry Greenwood's 'The Calabar Crystal' warns us of the dangers of messing about with things we don't fully understand, while Janeen Brian's 'What Goes Around' tells us not to muck around with the wishes of the deceased. And I promise you will never again go for a jog, or contemplate getting a tattoo, or do the supermarket shopping without looking over your shoulder after you've read stories by Michael Pryor, Hazel Edwards and Sean McMullen.

If that all sounds rather dark and twisty, there are also plenty of laughs inside these pages as well, and not just in the short stories, but in some of the verse – check out Leigh Hobbs' hilarious and down-right weird 'Strange-headed Harry' and its accompanying illustrations. In fact, be sure not to overlook the illustrations accompanying some of the stories and poetry inside. Not only are they often strange and wonderful accompaniments to the writing, but some of them – the extraordinary Shaun Tan's illustrations in particular – are amazing short narratives in their own right.

A final word about the poetry – some of you may notice that a small sub-theme has emerged here as well. Several of the poems in the collection are meditations on the creative process of writing and of being a writer, while others simply enjoy exploring – and stretching – the boundaries of language.

There are many more stories and poems, and many more writers within the pages of this collection – too many to name all in this introduction, but all of which offer something to enthral and to entertain, to challenge and to inspire.

In short – if you'll pardon the pun! – if reading is something you do to find your way into the lives of other people, whatever kind of world they live in, you will find something to enjoy and ponder on within. Welcome. Have fun getting lost in these other worlds – but remember to come back again!

Judith Ridge

The Calabar Crystal

Kerry Greenwood

Liam is a nerd. Fortunately, I like him most of the time. We are in the same year at school. Girls have to fight tooth and nail to get any computer time – the hoons all crowd it, wanting to play Doom. You can see them sitting there, slavering as they kill things. It's revolting. Liam books two hours, and then splits it with me, which is nice of him and saves me having to enter into arguments with a lot of people who are bigger and stronger than me, even if they are dumber. I've got a small advantage. I've got red hair and everyone knows that redheaded women have fierce tempers. They don't call me by my name, which is Lydia. They call me Red. Fine with me.

Liam's fourteen and so am I. We hang around together because he's a historian and I'm fascinated with history, but even there we always disagree. I want to know what it was like to live in another time – what I would eat, where I would sleep, what I would wear. Liam wants to know about kings and emperors and politics, and I couldn't care less about them. They were all men, anyway.

He's the same height as me, but his hair is longish

and black, straight as a drink of water. He's short-sighted, wears glasses and hates sport, but he can run like the wind and dance like an angel. Running is a useful skill at our school and it gets the jocks off his back. And mine, because they assume I'm his girlfriend, though I'm not. I've never even kissed him.

His family are weird, not like mine, who are boring. His father is a physicist, his mother is a doctor and he has a collection of really strange relatives. So when he asked me to come and help him sort out his great-aunt Anne's goods and pack them for disposal, I agreed. We were getting paid for it, and I am always broke. I've got an mp3 habit. I calculated that I'd be able to buy at least ten new albums with the cleaning money.

We arrived at a seriously dilapidated house in Kew and Liam opened the door. A fog of dust and a strange, closed-in smell greeted us and we retreated, sneezing.

'She'd been in Africa for years and the house was shut up,' Liam explained, darting inside and hauling open a window. 'All her anthropological papers and specimens have been willed to the university, and they've collected them. We just have to pack up the clothes and things and give the house a clean. This might take longer than I thought,' he mused, dragging a handful of spider web from his hair.

'Courage,' I said. 'Think of all that money. Let's

get the stuff packed. It's easier to clean an empty house.'

The house was completely silent. Most houses have some noises – creaking boards, nesting birds, that sort of thing. But this place was dark and quieter than the grave. I wished I'd brought my mp3 player and speakers. The house was small, only five rooms, and two of the front ones were empty. The back bedroom was crammed with suitcases and trunks and all of them needed to be hauled out into the living room, dusted, and emptied into the tea chests that Liam's father had provided. Liam took the cases and I fought my way to the wardrobe and opened it. As I laid my hand on the door, I was suddenly afraid.

No reason for it. I struggled for a moment, bit my lip, told myself to not be a girlie, and flung it open.

Instead of the mummified corpse I had expected, there were lots of clothes. I pulled out an armload. Daggy. Tweed skirts and jackets, all baggy and dusty. Cotton shirts with beetroot stains. A pile of low-heeled shoes that had never been polished.

'Your aunt wasn't into clothes,' I commented, just to break the silence.

'My great-aunt. No, she wasn't. But she was a very eminent forensic anthropologist,' said Liam, annoyed. He brushed a cobweb from his glasses.

I heaved the load of dreck garments into a tea chest and asked, 'What's a forensic anthropologist?'

'She was an expert in the examination of bones. Working out how people died, that sort of thing. She took me to a leper's graveyard in Essex, once. The disease deforms the bones and she was interested in whether King Robert the Bruce was a leper. We collected skulls and upper thigh bones.'

'Weren't you scared?' I asked, shuddering slightly and piling up old shoes.

'Why would I be scared?' asked Liam seriously. 'They were only bones, and you can't catch leprosy from bones that old. In fact it's very hard to catch leprosy at all. It's a slow virus.'

'Never mind,' I muttered. Now I came to think of it, it was a silly question to ask someone like Liam. I had cleared the wardrobe of clothes. I dusted the empty wardrobe vigorously. Sneezing, I picked up a small, flat leather case marked 'specimens' and sat down on a trunk marked 'Not Wanted On Voyage' to open it.

'Liam, didn't you say the university had all of your aunt's specimens?' I asked. He didn't hear me. There was a crash as he tripped over a pile of empty boxes. I unclicked the latch and the case opened. There was a sheaf of scribbled notes and, hidden in crumbling tissue paper, something hard and cold.

I poked it and I must have gasped aloud because Liam looked over my shoulder.

In front of my eyes, I saw a forest. There was a great castle there, built of wood. I smelled smoke and a strange, spicy scent, hot and steamy. I heard a scream and there were eyes, I swear, eyes in the castle, and they were looking straight through me. I dropped the case and Liam caught it.

'What's wrong?' he asked, concerned.

I couldn't tell him. He took my hand and we went into the kitchen, where there was a working stove and two unmatched chairs at the wonky wooden table.

'Sit down and tell me what happened,' he said.

'There's something in there,' I said.

He took up my hand that he had been holding and turned it over. 'Where did it bite you, what was it? A spider?'

'Nothing bit me.' The picture was fading. 'I'm all right.'

He gave me a puzzled look and tipped the case's contents onto the table. Papers scattered, and the heavy thing clunked onto the surface. It was a round glassy pebble with two pinholes in it. Quartz, perhaps. Liam stretched out a hand to it.

'Liam, don't . . .' He looked at me again, and I realised I could not explain.

Liam picked up the crystal and held it in his hand. 'Pretty,' he said. I sagged with relief. Obviously I had been reading too much history and I was imagining things. 'I wonder where it came from?' he said, holding it as he ordered the pages. They were written in a spidery hand in pale ink and I couldn't read them.

'Part of a diary. Here's a heading. Africa. That's not a lot of help.'

'Let's get the house cleaned, then we can look at it properly,' I suggested cravenly. To my relief, Liam agreed, wrapped the quartz pebble in its mouldering tissue and closed it in its case. For some reason that made me feel much better.

It took us the rest of the day to sort the belongings and then to sweep the walls and finally the floors, clean the stove and the windows, but at six o'clock it was finished and we were filthy and exhausted. We each showered in the clean bathroom and dressed in the clothes we had brought, and phoned for a pizza. I decided that I had been overtired earlier when Liam sat down at the clean table and took out the diary pages.

'She's writing about some bones she found in Calabar that might help to explain some of the ethnic diversity in Ghana,' commented Liam, wiping melted cheese off his chin. His hair was wet and hung down like silk, marking his T-shirt.

I blinked spicy pepperoni tears out of my eyes and asked, 'What about the rock?'

'It's a seeing stone,' he answered. 'She says that she found it in a grave, a witch doctor's grave. He fled from the south, a year's journey, with the stone, a great treasure of Zimbabwe and . . . far out. The rest of the body is in the grave, but the head's missing. Anyone who uses the stone . . . here, see for yourself.'

He pushed the papers over to me, because he had fallen behind in his pizza-consumption and wanted to catch up. Once I got the hang of the script it wasn't so hard to read. It said, 'Anyone who deliberately uses the seeing stone will be cursed. His eyes will be dimmed. His blood will be spilled. His bones will be broken. He will be consumed in the unquenchable fire.' I read it aloud. Liam was unimpressed.

'Standard sort of thing. The Egyptians had much more complicated curses.' Then his hand fell on the stone and he stiffened. It should have been funny, Liam frozen in mid-chew with one hand on an ancient stone and one hand reaching for more pizza, but it wasn't. It was getting dark outside and the stone seemed to glow. He said something in a language I didn't know, and then I grabbed his arm and felt that he was shaking.

'You saw it too,' he whispered. 'You saw the stockade, smelled the cooking fires and heard the birds. That's what happened to you, Lydia.'

'Yes, I saw it too. I was scared. Are you all right?' I was rattled.

'Scared?' A beautiful smile broke on his face, the smile of a visionary or a saint. 'Scared, me? This is the greatest archaeological discovery since Schliemann found Troy. It's a window into the past.'

'Liam, what about the curse?' I grabbed his hand, which was about to touch the stone again.

'Just a way of keeping the peasants away from it. Nothing more. Let go of me.'

'No, I don't like this!' I cried.

'That's the attitude that held back science for centuries,' he snarled.

'I'm going home,' I snapped. 'I'll see you at school tomorrow.'

Then I walked out. The glow of the stone lit up Liam's enraptured face. I saw it as I slammed the door.

Liam, the next day, was pale, tired, and rapt. He sleepwalked through classes. He didn't even argue with the history teacher, and Liam and Miss Ellis had been sniping all year. She was surprised, too, and asked him if he was sick. He said he wasn't.

'It's amazing, Lydia!' he breathed when I got him to myself at lunchtime. 'I've seen the walls of Zimbabwe, heard the songs of the slaves cutting the trees.' He sang a snatch of something very weird. 'But it's tiring. It seems to take a lot of my energy to run the stone.'

'What happened to your glasses?' I asked. He was wearing his old pair, held together with duct tape. My father says that duct tape holds the world together.

'I broke them this morning,' he said dismissively.

'Liam, I don't think this is a good idea. Look at you. You're shaking.' He was peeling an orange with a pocketknife. Suddenly the blade slipped and cut his finger. He wrapped his hand in an ink-stained handkerchief and replied, 'I can't leave it yet, Lydia.'

'Yes, you can, if it's the greatest discovery since

Tutankhamen then you have to tell someone, take it to the museum, call the University,' I could hear myself babbling. I was seriously worried. Liam's eyes . . . didn't look like Liam anymore. They were alight with purpose, but vague. Vacant.

'Just another couple of days. I have to see. No one has ever discovered who the kings were who lived in those wooden castles. And the Queen is coming.'

'How do you know?'

'The workers. They talk. Now leave me alone.' Liam pushed me away. He had never pushed me before. Hurt and very worried, I ran after him.

'Liam, can I help?' I asked breathlessly. 'Give me the diary and I'll type it out. You know how you hate typing.'

He glared at me, then reached into his bag and handed over the bundle of pages. 'All right.'

'I'll call you tonight,' I said to his back as he sleep-walked away.

When I did, Liam's mother told me he couldn't come to the phone. 'He's had a little accident,' she said in her cool voice. 'Fell off the rock-climbing wall at the gym. I think he's broken a rib. Not a serious injury, Red, don't worry. I'll tell him you called.'

I went back to the computer and kept typing. Great-aunt Anne was a terrible gossip. A lot of the diary was about someone she was in love with who had married someone else and she was angry about it. I skimmed through and found the curse. As I typed it out, I noticed something. 'His eyes will be dimmed.' Liam's eyes were certainly dimmed when he broke his glasses. 'His blood will be spilled.' He had cut himself on the pocketknife. I had seen his blood shed. 'His bones will be broken.' Liam's mum had told me that he had just broken a rib. I went cold as I looked at the last line. 'He will be consumed in the unquenchable fire.'

It was late, but I rang again. Liam's mum was annoyed with me.

'He's not well, Red. He was in Thailand last year, he might have picked up malaria. He's a bit fevered, but it's nothing for you to be concerned about. Now, good night,' she said. The connection broke.

I woke in terror. Voices were all around me, chanting. I could understand them. 'The Queen! The Queen! The Queen comes,' they cried. The heat of a great bonfire scorched my face. All around the walls of the wooden castle loomed. On each of the stakes was a shapeless object. My sight cleared. They were skulls. Some old and grinning, fleshless and gleaming. Some fresh, sockets empty, mouths open, hair trailing or clotted, decorated with feathers. I was frozen with fear. I couldn't move. Liam was bound next to me. He was wearing pyjamas and his glasses. He did not look at me but rather at a tall man in the middle of the clearing. He was crowned with feathers, masked in white paint, and his hands were coated in red.

'Ewa!' he cried over the drums, and I knew somehow that Ewa meant death. I smelled blood strong enough to make me retch and cried, 'I'm awake, I'm awake!' and the vision blinked out.

A dream, perhaps, but Liam had been there, too. And Liam was in a fever, had shed blood, broken his glasses, broken a bone. The curse was coming true.

I considered how Liam would have poured scorn on the idea, and managed to get back to sleep.

Liam was not at school the next day. I cornered Miss Ellis and asked her about ancient Zimbabwe.

'Ah, another mystery. If you paid more attention to the places we know about you'd be easier to keep up with,' she sighed. 'Where's Liam?'

'He's sick. He broke a rib falling off a wall. What about Zimbabwe?'

'There are a lot of stories about the Land of Gold. You know, in the Bible, where the Queen of Sheba came from. Some people think it is Tanis on the Nile Delta. Others link her with the legendary Kingdom of Prester John, who was supposed to have lived in Africa.'

'Prester John?'

'He was a forgery – a bit of medieval wishful thinking. But archaeologists have found the remains of large temples or castles in Africa. They knew about iron and were rich in gold and bronze; but no one's really worked out who they were.'

'That's what Liam said.'

'Then you didn't need me to say it again,' she said sharply. 'What's the matter, Red?'

'Liam. I'm worried about him. He's . . . getting into Zimbabwe in a major way and I don't think it's such a good idea.' I wanted to tell her about the Calabar Crystal, but I really couldn't. Instead, I asked, 'Miss Ellis, do you believe in magic?'

She thought about it, then said, 'The definition of magic is "producing a change in the world by the action of the will". No, I don't. Why?'

'If . . . if you were writing about a curse, what would you do about breaking it?' She knew I was going to be a writer, and I could ask her about plotting. I couldn't tell her about the cause of Liam's illness because she'd never believe me.

'I'd write a curse that had an exemption clause.' I looked at her and she laughed. 'I mean, I'd make sure that the curse that said anyone stealing the sacred relic will be blinded or burned or whatever can be rescued by, I don't know, a maiden pure of heart who sheds three drops of her blood for him, or something like that.'

'Like a fairytale?' I asked, disappointed. She patted me.

'Fairytales are the oldest form of story we have. Even the Epic of Gilgamesh is a fairytale. That's the bell and I have to go and try and hammer the rudiments of classical history into 3B. What a life.' She walked away and I remembered that it was chemistry and I had better not be late.

'This is metallic mercury,' said Mr Foreman. We were all terrified of him. He had episodes of extreme rage that Liam had told me were pathological. The silvery metal ran into the chamber. He lit the Bunsen burner under it. It lost its sheen, turning into a crumbling red powder. 'This is mercuric oxide,' he commented, shaking the Pyrex beaker. 'Now we're going to burn it again. This is the experiment that the alchemists used to demonstrate the immutability of matter, should there be anyone in this class who is interested. Watch.'

The flame flickered. The red powder stirred. Then, miraculously, little beads of metal plopped up. Magic.

'Immutable, Sir?' I asked, greatly daring. He pinned me with a look and snapped, 'Unchanging.'

'No, Sir, I mean, I know the word, Sir, but is all matter immutable?'

'Ultimately, yes. We are all one,' he said gently. 'Star and plant and child and stone. All connected. Nothing in the known or unknown universe stands alone, unaffected.'

'Does that mean that nothing thinks or imagines alone?' I was waiting for him to bite me, but he didn't.

'The same thing. The act of observation changes the thing observed – chaos mathematics proves that. And in view of the requirements of quantum physics

I'd say that just thinking about something could change its state. But it's easier to heat it or cool it, and more repeatable.'

The lesson went on, but I had stopped listening.

That night when I rang Liam's mother she sounded a little less calm. 'He's really quite ill, but I have to go to casualty, there's been a horrific pile up on the freeway. Can you come and stay with him for a few hours, Red? I'll ask your mother for you and I can drive you home.'

Half an hour later I was sitting next to Liam.

'He's a bit delirious, nothing to worry about,' said his mother as she rushed out. 'Give him some barley-water if he asks for it.'

Liam was rolling his head on the pillow, humming or chanting some song. When I touched his dry forehead it burned me. Skin shouldn't be that hot. I raised his head and dribbled some water into his mouth and he swallowed, but although his eyes were open he didn't see me. He was looking beyond me, and he was afraid.

I wondered what he was holding in his shut-tight fist and tried to pry his fingers open, but they were locked together. I could see the malignant glow of the Calabar Crystal, shining red through flesh and bone.

'Liam, let go,' I begged. He did not react. 'Liam, come back,' I pleaded. 'Come back from the forest. I know where you are. I've been there.'

He lay curled around his closed hand, humming the distracting chant, 'Ewa! Ewa!' I thought about it, nerving myself. I was very afraid. Then I clasped my hand over his.

The fire beat on my face. I felt my hair begin to singe. The sightless heads glared at me. I smelt decay and wet leaves. Liam was bound to a stake and I was standing next to him. But the sorcerer was not there. Instead I heard a scraping noise as something crept over the leaves. 'Ewa!' shouted the unseen dancers. Feet thudded. Someone flung a handful of powder onto the fire and I winced away from the flash.

Then I couldn't move, because something heavy was on my feet. Scales, cold and dry as enamel slid across my shins as a huge snake inched effortlessly over my bare toes towards Liam. I screamed at him and he turned his head, eyes widening behind the glasses.

'Lydia, how . . .'

I shrieked, 'Never mind how! Let go of the crystal, Liam, let go of it!'

'The Queen is coming,' he said. 'I have to see . . .'

The snake rippled over me, raising its head as high as my shoulder. It flicked its tongue at me, tasting the air, marking its prey. I had time to scream, 'Liam! Let go!' again before darkness pulled me away from the fire and the forest.

I woke when Liam's mother shook my shoulder.

'Time to go, Red. Has Liam taken any barley-water?'

I nodded. She examined him briefly and shook her head.

'If he isn't any better tomorrow I'll get him into a ward, stabilise his fluids. His temp's too high. It must be malaria, but he hasn't got any other symptoms. And there's that death-grip fist while the other one is quite relaxed. Trust my son to have an undiagnosable pyrexia. Come along, nurse,' she said to me, and I went.

―――

My mother was surprised when I came straight home from school and went to the computer instead of demanding Coke and talking about our day, like we usually did. I told her it was urgent homework and she came up behind me and peered over my shoulder at the scanned yellowing pages.

'Copperplate,' she commented. 'My mother wrote like that. What are you doing, some history project?'

'It's pages from Liam's great-aunt Anne's diary. I'm typing it out for him.'

'Anne? I remember her.'

'You do?' I turned around on the typist's chair.

'Yes, she was a friend of my mother's. I didn't like her. Used to rush in and talk about the Importance of History – you know, with capitals.'

'She's talking about someone called Edmund,' I offered, and Mum coughed.

'I don't know if I ought to tell you about it – it's a

nasty story. And you don't look too well, Meggs.'

Mum calls me Meggs after a redheaded cartoon character. Usually it drives me mad, but I was willing to overlook it if she knew something about Great-aunt Anne that might help Liam.

I gathered up the transcription and the original and ushered Mum into the kitchen.

'I'll make the tea and you tell me about Aunt Anne,' I said, and she frowned.

'Like I said, she was a determined woman, a femocrat before her time. It must have been hard for her. A woman had to be twice as good as a man to get any recognition in those days, and she was good, I believe. Now, what did she say?'

'Come on, Mum!' I slammed the kettle onto the stove.

'Don't rush me. Mrs Brain isn't what she was. Yes. It was a man called Edmund North. Mum said she really was in love with him. But he was married, and he wouldn't leave his wife and two small children.'

'That didn't stop Dad leaving us,' I said, bitterly.

Mum gave me a startled glance. 'It was different in those days. You're really worried about Liam, aren't you?'

I nodded, blinking back tears.

'And you think that Anne Somers' life has something to do with his illness?'

I nodded again.

'Then I will have to remember. Make the tea,

Meggsie. Tea improves my thought processes.'

I dropped a teabag into a cup and poured boiling water over it in silence.

Mum said suddenly, 'Right. Edmund – he was an expert in tribal dialects – went with Anne to Africa and something happened to him.'

'What? Here's your tea.'

'He died,' said Mum. 'I remember now. They didn't find him for days and when they did . . .' She paused, looking at me.

'Yes?' I said impatiently.

'He had been dismembered – probably by animals. They never found his head. Anne was ill, they sent her home. She never spoke about him after that. Mum said she got stranger and stranger and then she went back to Ghana, I think it was, and she died there in March. Does that help?'

'I don't know.'

She stroked the hair off my face and said gently, 'Don't worry about Liam. People don't die of malaria anymore, you know.'

She meant well. I shook her off and went back to the computer.

I finished the diary that night. Anne Somers had fallen terribly in love with Edmund. She had taken him to Africa to get him away from his wife and they had been lovers, at least that's what I think she meant. But then he fretted, wanting to get home. She had sent him into the stone, knowing it was dangerous, and he had died.

The only clue I found that might have helped was a sentence at the bottom of the last page.

'If any are trapped in the stone, they can be redeemed by a strong heart who is willing to enter the forest and break off a branch of the sacred tree. Then with blood the captured shall be . . .'

The page was torn. The captured shall be what? Freed? Killed? And what of the strong heart – does she get out of the forest? And how could I do anything useful, assuming my heart was strong enough, when I was struck rigid with terror as soon as I got into the scene?

Before I lost my courage altogether, I rang Liam's mother. She said that she would put him in hospital tomorrow, but I was welcome to sit with him tonight. Mum let me go, looking worried. Fair enough. I was worried, too.

I smelled the spice again, felt the heat. Liam sagged in his bonds. The fire crackled. The skulls gaped lipless. With a great effort, I tried to move. I was helpless. The sorcerer approached and the chant was sinking into my bones, weakening me. 'Ewa! Ewa! Death! Death!' The painted mouth curved into a smile that chilled my heart. I was not strong. I was a coward. If he came closer, I was going to faint and then Liam's head would join the impaled skulls, his silky hair hanging down, his eyes pecked out.

A huge bird flew down and perched on Liam's shoulder. I could see its talons digging into his neck. Little trails of blood slicked his skin. It shook itself with a rattle of obscene, naked wings, and croaked, whetting its beak on the stake. A horror from an older world, pterodactyl or pteranodon, eyes glinting with intelligence and hunger.

It was too much. I screamed at it, waving my arms to scare it away, and did not realise that I was free until I stood next to Liam. I could move.

I moved into the darkness. I could feel the fire burning behind me. Sticks cracked beneath my feet. I blundered into branches as I ran, fell and skinned my knees, got up and ran again. It was not black night. There were stars, and the moon was full and huge, tinged red. I heard voices around me, chanting, calling. Something growled and something else hissed. I thought of that snake and kept going, driven at least as much by fear than by any remnants of reason.

I could taste brass in my mouth. I was winded. I stopped, panting, and looked around me. I had lost the fire and I could see little in the gloom. Leaf mould carpeted the ground. I made little noise as I trod among the biggest trees I had ever imagined.

'Which tree is the sacred tree?' I asked aloud. My voice shook. How could I find one tree among all these? It was impossible. Great-aunt Anne was laughing at me. I screamed, 'Where is the one tree?' and heard in the silence, 'All one, sky and plant and child and stone,' as though the forest was answering me. This world was all one. The trees were all one tree. The forest of trunks around me were a world tree.

I took a deep breath. I staggered to the nearest tree and laid a hand on the bark, and was instantly aware of the forest. A creature that lived nine hundred years, I felt its age. Old, uninterested. Human, it thought, also aware of me. A brief species. They hardly outlast a flower.

I cried, 'I need a branch for my friend Liam or he will die!' And the slow thought answered me, 'What is it to us if a human dies?'

'We are all one,' I said through numb lips. 'All one.'

It did not reply, but I felt it turn its mind away. Consent had been given. I grabbed a branch and hauled on it with all my weight. It broke, bark wrinkling and shredding like skin. I screamed along with the tree, but I did not stop even though I felt like all my limbs were being torn apart.

Then I ran, stumbling in the night, lost, until I realised that somehow the branch was pulling me, and I went where I was guided. The fire loomed up again in the clearing.

The sorcerer made a grab at me, but I ducked under his arm and dived for Liam, who lolled in his bonds like a scarecrow. Long wounds striped his throat and chest. The bird sprang up from its feeding, scolding, beak wet, and I hit it with the branch.

It flapped, knocked off balance. Smoke stung my eyes. The drums battered at my senses. The stench of blood choked me. I cried, 'Liam! Liam! It's me, Red, let go of the crystal! I have broken the branch for you! Oh, Liam, please!'

'Blood,' muttered Liam through the curtain of his black hair. I knew he was right. Blood was streaked across his chest, the reversal spell couldn't have required his blood. It had to be mine.

I found a splinter on the branch. The drums beat faster, faster, and I seemed to have slowed down. I watched my fingers as they picked clumsily at the wood, stopping to wave the branch at the bird. The sorcerer's hand closed on the branch and began to drag it away. He wasn't smiling anymore. Liam, awake at last, called, 'Lydia, no, get away!' then I heard him scream as the bird raked his arm with its claws.

The painted mask was close to my face. 'Ewa!' it screamed. I was fainting with horror. I thrust my hand, palm down, onto the splinter with all my force.

There was a tearing shriek and a snarling in the dark.

Someone was stroking my hair. It felt lovely. I was snuggling back to sleep again after my nightmare when Liam said, 'Lydia.'

He was sitting up. I gaped at him. His eyes were clear and when I touched his forehead it was cool. 'Liam. You're back.'

'You brought me back,' he said solemnly.

'Where's the Calabar Crystal?' I asked.

He opened his fingers. Coarse sand poured glinting onto the floor.

I tried to sit up but sank back onto his pillow. I hurt all over. I looked amazed at the red patches on my knees, which would colour into bruises. There was a bright mark in the middle of my palm and I could not close that hand. Had I slammed my hand down on the Calabar Crystal and broken it, braced against Liam's death-grip? Or had it been pierced with a splinter from the World Tree?

'It was a dream,' I said. It could not have been real.

'You saved my life,' said Liam, and opened his pyjama jacket to reveal the vertical slashes that the Calabar bird or my fingernails had left on his torso and neck.

'How do you feel?' I asked, lamely.

'All right. Bit battered. I wouldn't have come back, you know, I didn't want to at first, and then I couldn't. And I never saw the Queen . . .'

'If you'd stayed you wouldn't have seen the Queen,

they would have sacrificed you,' I snapped.

'There's Mum, I heard the door. You'll have to go home. Thanks, Lydia.'

He smiled his beautiful smile at me.

'My pleasure.' I got to my feet, biting my lip. I hurt. Had I really sustained these wounds rescuing my friend from the sorcery of Zimbabwe? Ludicrous. But painfully realistic.

'Lydia?' asked Liam, settling back on his pillows.

'Hmm?'

'I wonder what else Great-aunt Anne brought home from Africa?'

I should have left him tied to that stake. Really.

Tin Horse Plain
Corinne Fenton

Dan had set his alarm and placed it under his pillow so my dad wouldn't hear it. 'It'll be awesome, Josh,' he whispered. 'Just imagine. We'll have the whole place to ourselves. We can pretend we're the only people on earth. We might see some rare dragon lizards and we'll be back in bed before your dad knows we've gone.'

My friend Dan is reptile crazy. He has all sorts of lizards and even some snakes in a special enclosure in his backyard.

We dressed in jeans, T-shirts and spray jackets, threw water bottles, torches and a chocolate bar each into our backpacks and set off into the early morning darkness.

It was cold, and for a while I kept glancing back to see the lights of the motel behind us. We crossed the flat area that ran up to the expanse of desert known as Tin Horse Plain. Dan was ahead a little, his torch throwing a bright beam.

'Hey, what's the big hurry?' I called.

'You're the one who wants to get back to daddy,' he teased.

'Yeah, yeah, okay Lizard Hunter,' I said, laughing.

The red earth was rough and small rocks and stones tumbled underfoot as we walked. We could hear little desert creatures scurrying in the close-by bushes.

'Could they be dragon lizards?' I asked. But Dan's mind was somewhere else. He stopped, scratching his head then shining his torch over the map.

'So what's up, Lizard Hunter?' I asked. Dan scowled back at me.

Then we noticed the same group of rocks we'd passed half an hour before.

'We've been walking in circles, haven't we, Dan?'

'It seemed such an easy walk on the map, I can't understand where we went wrong,' he said.

We moved on towards a rocky ridge and as we looked down into the canyon below, in the early morning gloom Dan and I saw shadowy shapes rising from the dry cracked earth.

'Animals?' I asked.

'Don't know,' said Dan. 'But they're still as, so maybe they're only huge rocks, like pillars.'

In the distance, just for an instant, we saw an orange flash of light. While we were watching, the light moved. It seemed to bob up and down for a few moments before coming to rest very close to where we'd first seen it. Was there something or someone down there in the canyon among the shadows? Maybe UFOs?

Then it started raining and seconds later it was bucketing down.

'We have to go down there and find some shelter,' Dan yelled over the rain.

I nodded, not quite trusting my voice. Something about this didn't feel right. We pulled our jackets up tightly about our necks and then stepped onto a narrow path that wound down into the canyon. We walked along as fast as we could, treading carefully on the rough path. There were no trees to protect us from the pelting rain and soon we were drenched. Heavy drops stung our faces. We couldn't go on walking through this. We had to find shelter somewhere.

Around a sharp twist in the winding path we stumbled upon a rocky outcrop. We jumped over a muddy puddle at the entrance to a small cave. It was dark and the air was thick with a strange unfamiliar smell. My hands felt clammy and I could hear Josh's heavy breathing. We shone our torch beams along the ground, but as we moved slowly forward, something flashed over our heads.

'What the . . .?' Dan yelled.

I shone the torch's beam upwards, and there, hanging from the roof like little black umbrellas, was a colony of bats.

'Those things give me the creeps, big time,' Dan whispered.

'They're only bats,' I said, although my heart was thumping like thunder. 'At least it's dry in here.'

'I guess so,' Dan said.

We found a sheltered area up against one side of the cave and sat down with our backs against the wall. We watched the rain pelting down outside. It was as if the ground hadn't seen water for months, and was too dry to soak it up. Inside the cave, water was seeping down into the cracks, but the rest remained on the surface creating huge puddles and small rivers that had nowhere to go. The bats were dry as, hanging up there.

'Maybe we could be like the bats and hang from the roof,' I said, but Dan definitely wasn't in the mood for jokes.

'We can't stay here too long,' he said. 'Sooner or later the water's going to run right through where we're sitting.'

Dan sounded distracted. Was he scared? I tried not to worry. There was nothing we could do but wait.

―――

We were cold, wet and starting to shiver. Then as quickly as it had begun, the rain came to an abrupt stop. From the cave we could see the flashing light again; it was like a beacon, pulling us towards it. What could it be way out there in the middle of nowhere?

I loved sci-fi movies and reading about green creatures from other planets, but I knew, sure as anything, I didn't want to see one.

'We've got to check it out, Dan,' I said. 'It's the only thing that's not a bush or rock anywhere around.'

'Yeah, I know,' he said. 'We'd better get moving.'

We climbed to our feet and, stepping cautiously over puddles and gushing rivulets, headed back onto the twisting path. As we walked on, I thought about how and why we were here. I thought about how Dan had begged me to get up at 4 am to go out onto Tin Horse Plain. It had seemed like a good idea at the time. But right now, I couldn't quite think of it that way. If it wasn't for Lizard Hunter I'd be back at the motel sound asleep, not lost in a lonely desert in the middle of the rainy season. And why was there a bright orange light bobbing about in the middle of nowhere?

On top of that, the only animals we'd seen were the bats, not a dragon lizard in sight! But if I were honest with myself, deep down I'd wanted to go, too; I couldn't blame it all on my friend. But how would we ever find the way back? We had no idea at all which direction we were heading, only that we were going deeper into the steep canyon, towards an orange light. And once it was noticed we were missing, how long would it take Dad, and maybe even the police, to come looking for us?

Dad would be freaking out. I checked my watch. It

was six-thirty and almost completely light. Probably right about now Dad would be finding our empty beds. I imagined my little sister Ellie still sleeping. But my biggest fear by far was, out here in the middle of the desert, they'd never find us. Nobody even knew in which direction we'd gone. It would be like looking for two ants in a truckload of sand.

I jolted myself back to the present. Now that the rain and inky clouds had moved away, a pale sun was beginning to peer through the morning mist. Then Dan came to a full stop in front of me. 'What's that?' he asked.

Just then we heard a muffled groan. It sounded human and was coming from somewhere to our right.

'What the . . . ?' Dan said. I usually took no notice of Dan's favourite phrase, but this time his words sounded different. Panicky. He pointed ahead. I couldn't make out anything for a few seconds and then my eyes focused on a large grey-coloured object.

As we moved towards it we could see it was a car, an ordinary station wagon, but it was lying upside down.

Moving closer we saw that the sides of the car were bashed and dented and the back bumper was hanging off at a strange angle. Then we saw it, the orange flashing light that we'd first noticed from the ridge. An emergency lamp was lying on the ground next to the car and its orange light was flashing slow and steady. We both started to creep a few steps forward.

Then Dan grabbed my arm. 'What if . . . ?' he asked.

'You mean what if there's someone dead in there?'

'Yeah,' said Dan. 'What then?'

'I don't know, but we've got to look.'

We saw broken glass and battered metal scattered down a nearby embankment. The car had rolled quite a way before ending up here.

'There must be a road up there somewhere,' I said.

'Hello,' I called out, as we came up behind the car. 'Anyone here?'

For a few long moments there was silence. Then came a voice.

'I'm here . . . here . . . in the front.'

Dan and I moved forward and peered around the front door, which was bent and open. There was a man lying awkwardly on the inside of the car roof. Sticky blood was oozing from a gash on his head. He gave another loud groan, before looking up at us.

'Am I glad to see you two,' he said in a croaky, gravelly voice, looking at Dan and then at me. This guy thought he'd been rescued. How were we going to tell him that we were lost and didn't have a clue where we were?

'I was hoping . . . like crazy that someone would see my emergency lamp,' he said, slow pain-filled words, hiccupped with despair. 'I had it resting on the, the . . . window, but it fell and rolled out of the car. I didn't know if it was still working.'

I could see the man was in pain, bad pain.

'Can you move, Mister?' I asked. Then I realised how stupid my question sounded. If the guy could move he would have obviously been out of here long ago.

'Only my arms,' he said, 'but my legs are killing me.'

I didn't know much about people in car accidents, but I thought it was good that this guy could at least talk to us.

'By the way, I'm Mike . . . Mike Powell.'

'Hi, I'm Josh and this is Dan,' I said.

'Are . . . your parents around?' Mike asked, wincing with the effort of talking.

'Not quite,' I said. 'We got up early to go lizard hunting, then we got lost. We saw the orange light and walked down into the canyon when it started raining. We took shelter in a cave for a while but figured there must have been something down here.'

'We have no idea where we are,' Dan said.

'So . . . where are you staying?' Mike asked.

'At the Desert View Motel,' Dan replied. 'At the junction.'

'I think that's . . . about ten kilometres from here.'

'So you know where we are?' I asked.

Mike groaned. 'Yes, I know exactly where we are.' Then he became impatient.

'Look, my legs are totally . . . stuck, boys. I can't move them at all. There's a road up there behind us. The motel is probably about forty minutes walk to the right. It will be much faster that way than coming down the ridge.'

Then, like talking had been too much effort, Mike's eyes fluttered closed and his head slumped to the side. I checked the pulse in his neck. His heart was beating and he was breathing, but he was totally out to it. I looked at Dan. He'd gone stark white.

'Dan, listen to me. You run back and get help and I'll wait here with him.'

Dan seemed to snap out of it. 'Sure thing,' he said, with a look of relief on his face.

I watched him scramble up the steep embankment. He turned and gave a quick wave, then he was gone.

Time crept by. Mike didn't move or stir, but I kept checking he was breathing and I could still feel his pulse, although I thought it was weaker.

Finally, much later, I heard voices and then saw two police officers along with Dad, Dan and Ellie edging down the embankment. Dad gave me the biggest hug.

'The Royal Flying Doctor and the State Emergency Service are on their way,' said one of the police officers, as he checked Mike's vital signs. 'You boys did a great job.'

Minutes later the Royal Flying Doctor's Cessna circled low over us, and landed on the road behind. Then the state emergency crew arrived in a big response vehicle.

We watched as they cut away the damaged car door with the jaws-of-life, and in no time the Royal Flying Doctor people were freeing Mike from his car. He had IV tubes snaking into his arm and a bandage around his head as his stretcher was lifted into the plane.

Back at the motel, Dad looked at us. 'Well, you two. Do you know how dangerous that was? I was furious when I found what you'd done.'

Dan and I looked at each other. We knew what was coming and we knew Dad was right.

'Sorry, Dad.'

'Sorry, Mister B.,' echoed Dan. 'We know it was a dumb thing to do.'

'Yeah, especially in the desert,' Dad said. 'What were you thinking?'

There was a knock at the door. Standing outside were the two police officers.

'I thought you boys would like to know that Mike's doing well, and we wanted to tell you that if it hadn't been for you two we would never have found him in time.'

'Wow! So we really did save his life?' I asked.

'There's no question,' said the officer.

'But read my lips,' said Dad. 'No more exploring and lizard hunting without me knowing about it. Okay?'

'Okay,' Dan and I mumbled.

'And we'd like to second that,' said the police officer. 'You boys were also lucky you came across that bloke. The desert can be a dangerous place, especially when you're lost.'

'Don't worry,' I said, looking at Dan. 'I think we've learned our lesson.'

'How about some breakfast, a big breakfast?' said Dad.

'Awesome!' Dan and I shouted together.

The Yard
Archimede Fusillo

The Oakley yard was a scavenger's delight. It had bric-a-brac of assorted car parts, cannibalised engine blocks, rows of windscreens, roof-high stacks of bench seats, bonnets, and an assortment of tyres from the merely pedestrian, like you'd find on any family car, to the oversized monsters sourced from huge earthmovers. The Oakleys' backyard was a magnet to our curiosity.

No one was ever invited into the Oakley yard, and no one ever dared enter. It was a no-man's-land.

As Tom and I stood hesitating by the wooden fence over our next move, my knees went to water. 'We can get all the points we need by finding other stuff,' I tried feebly.

'You want to win this thing or not?' Tom asked me challengingly. 'I say we go straight for the big-ticket item and win the challenge outright. We've already wasted enough time looking for the other stuff. Now we do it my way. Okay?'

I narrowed my eyes. Winning the school's annual scavenger hunt by finding the number-one item and bringing it back would make Tom and me legends.

No one had ever dared put this one so-talked-about item on the list, ever. It was like the Holy Grail.

The entire town had heard about it, but no one had actually ever seen it. And now it was on the list as the most prized scavenger item of them all.

'What if she finds it missing?' I countered uncertainly.

'She won't miss it,' Tom said fixedly as he abandoned all caution and scampered up onto the fence. 'Trust me. It's not like she has any daily use for it, right?'

I hesitated. *Really?* I thought. *She won't miss it?* I doubted that very much.

'You coming or not?' he asked over his shoulder, his eyes challenging, one leg already dangling precariously into the Oakley's no-go zone.

I swallowed.

'Chicken!' Tom chirped and dropped out of sight.

I froze. He'd done it. Tom had talked about us going into Mrs Oakley's backyard, and now he'd actually done it.

'Tom?' My voice was a tiny squeal.

No answer. I swallowed again, licked my lips, and against a screaming voice in my head telling me not to, I scaled the wooden fence and . . .

Landed in a pool of stagnant engine oil, my brand new sneakers sucking up the black ooze like a thirsty sponge.

'Oh no!' I gasped, but didn't have time to think

about what I might tell my parents as Tom grabbed my shirt front and pulled me down behind a wall of crushed cardboard.

'There's someone in the laundry,' Tom announced out of the corner of his mouth.

Great, I thought. Maybe I could plead illiteracy as an excuse. Sorry, we didn't understand the signs: Do Not Enter, Trespassers Not Welcome, Stay OUT!

I lifted one foot then the other. Thick, sticky, black-as-night oil clung to them; splattered all over the tops.

'This better be worth it,' I protested. 'These were brand new and now . . .'

But Tom wasn't interested in my petty problems. When I looked up he was already across the yard, the spectre of whoever might be in the laundry not a deterrent to his ultimate goal.

Tom was going to recover the number-one item on the Scavenging List, and I was going to be a part of it.

'She keeps it in the shed,' Tom whispered as I came alongside him. 'I've heard her tell my mum. She keeps it on the driver's seat of Mr Oakley's old taxi, the one he apparently drove that celebrity around in.'

'If we get busted we're done for,' I offered, but now that we were in the yard I was actually feeling a little less fearful. After all, if we did manage to get the number-one item back to the school we'd be heroes.

I might get put under house arrest by my parents over the ruined sneakers, but I'd be a legend under house arrest!

I knew the house well enough to know that the laundry door faced the shed, and Tom and I had to get past the laundry to get to the shed. If there was someone in the laundry the way Tom figured there was, we would have to have our wits about us.

'Hand me those bits of broken tile,' Tom said, pointing at the jagged pile of roof tiles by my feet. I passed some to him and without a word he launched one huge bit high and fast into the air.

I held my breath as the tile tumbled and flipped and finally dropped on the corrugated iron sheeting at the rear of the roof.

The noise was piercing and sharp, the tile bouncing about wildly, clattering and tumbling with a racket that started the chooks in the henhouse squawking.

It brought Mrs Oakley out of the laundry, floral apron loose around her waist, one hand still clutching a wad of wet washing as the other shaded her eyes against the sun. She peered up toward the roof.

'Go on, get out!' she cried at what I imagined she thought had invaded the otherwise quiet of her afternoon. 'Go on . . . get!'

And that's when Tom launched the second missile.

It too clattered about and found its mark, only this time on the blind side of the roof so that Mrs Oakley tossed the washing aside, and with remarkable speed for an elderly woman, sped off round the side of the house to investigate.

'Come on!' Tom urged. We bolted across the yard, leaping over discarded car panels, outcrops of broken headlights and even the odd taxi dome littering the ground, and through a narrow metal door into the fabled shed.

Inside was just like I'd imagined it to be: close and dusty and cluttered, especially when Tom shut the door behind us. It was as though we'd entered another world.

Neither of us could speak. We simply gaped in awe at our surrounds. Besides the old cab we'd expected, its silver and black bodywork dirty under a patina of cobwebs, there were at least three other cabs, all sitting haunch to haunch and grill to rear end.

But it was what hung from the ceiling that really grabbed our attention.

It was Mr Oakley, his arms and legs splayed out like a cross, face down, eyes wide open as though protecting his precious collection of taxi cabs.

I gagged. So did Tom. But neither of us could move.

We had expected to find old Mr Oakley. He was supposed to be in an elaborate funerary urn his wife kept on the driver's seat of his last and favourite taxi, one of the original 1979 Holden Commodores.

We didn't expect to find him, mummified and

hanging from the roof of his shed, still dressed in the tattered remains of his taxi driver's uniform, guarding what he'd left behind.

'It's not real,' Tom managed finally. He prodded me gently and stirred me back to the present.

'It's a mannequin. Look, it's a female mannequin, like the ones in Hardy's Ladies Wear,' Tom continued. 'It's spooky, eh? Had you going though, buddy.'

'Like you didn't freak,' I spat back. I swallowed again.

Tom didn't answer. He was already climbing into the closest cab, prying the driver's door open just enough to squeeze through, leaving me still gazing up at the uniformed mannequin hanging like some otherworldly sentry over Mr Oakley's most treasured earthly possessions.

While Tom rummaged about inside first one cab then another, I took in the shed. It was a museum to Mr Oakley's time as the town's premier cab driver. There were framed photos, mostly grainy and some in muted sepia tones, of a youthful Mr Oakley standing beside the very cab Tom was pottering around in.

There was even a plaque commemorating the dead man's time as the only cab driver for the entire region, and a framed photo taken on the day he established his own taxi service, with a much younger Mrs Oakley standing just as proudly beside him.

'Found it!' Tom called so suddenly it startled me.

'Look,' he said, climbing out of the cab holding what looked to be a flower vase.

'Is that . . . Is that him?' I croaked.

Tom beamed. 'Yep. This is old Mr Oakley. And he was right where we'd always heard he'd be, on the front seat . . . As though he could still just drive off to work.'

Tom held the urn out to me, but I couldn't bring myself to touch it. I just nodded and cautiously followed him out the door, across the yard and out the back gate, which we unsnibbed from inside.

We didn't go far before we stopped and stood looking at the bronze-coloured urn Tom held out between us.

'We've won for certain. The number one, ultimate item on the scavenger list and we've got it.' Tom smiled and added, 'I told you to trust me on this.'

By the time we arrived at school, most of the other seekers were back, all of them carrying something or other from the list.

But only Tom and I had the major points earner. We had the urn containing old Mr Oakley's ashes!

We laughed as we made our way to the judges' table, high-fiving ourselves on being so daring.

A crowd gathered as we approached the table. Voices that had been raised in chatter hushed as Tom and I approached.

'Never doubt me again,' Tom gloated.

I winked and reached out to take hold of one handle of the urn so that we might place it together before the judges and claim victory.

And that's when we saw them.

Four urns. All identical in every way to the one we were holding between us like some revered trophy.

'The ashes I presume,' a Year Ten judge sniggered sarcastically. She reached for the urn.

Tom and I gave each other a quick glance.

And then, without a word, she unscrewed the lid and upended the urn on the table. Tom and I backed away from the expected cloud of ash that would come cascading out. I grabbed at the single small piece of paper that floated toward the table.

'Trust me,' the judge read without having to actually look at the note, 'don't believe everything you hear, and only some of what you think you see.'

And with that she put our urn alongside the others, so that there were now five identical urns sitting on the judge's table, a small note at the foot of each.

'Next!' the judge called and waved Tom and me aside.

We stood blinking at one another.

We'd been duped. I exhaled loudly and shook my head. I was about to suggest we go in search of the other listed items when there was a commotion over by the main door.

Someone walked in carrying an urn that was the exact duplicate of the one Tom and I – and obviously others – had brought back from our hunt.

Only it wasn't one of us.

It was Mrs Oakley. She didn't hesitate, but strode right up to the judges' table.

'Jack always loved scavenger hunts,' she declared through a chuckle that made my blood run cold.

'See?' she added, pointing at the urn. 'Here he is now. We caught a cab in.'

When she glanced back toward Tom and me, the old woman was smiling broadly, her aged eyes pressed into tiny dots that pinpointed us.

'Do we win?' She laughed, tossing back her head, her mane of frizzled grey hair catching the sunlight streaming through the overhead skylight.

Tom and I nodded in unison. Around us everyone else was doing likewise, even the judges.

Dingo Boy
Sandy Fussell

'Did you hear that?' Rua nudged her mate with a paw.

'I didn't hear anything.' Rrrk rolled away to face the wall of the den. It was an old abandoned rabbit burrow he had enlarged for the last litter of pups. The walls were still flecked with grey fur. Rrrk's stomach growled at the thought of fresh rabbit.

'Go to sleep,' he said and pretended to snore.

Rua was insistent. 'I heard something outside. It sounded like a pup.'

Rrrk grunted in irritation. Rua's mothering days were long gone and their den had been empty for five years now. But Rua often pined for the late autumn days spent nurturing newborns. Rrrk smiled. He missed it too. There was something satisfying about giving a fatherly nip to the rump of a wayward pup.

He turned and nuzzled the silver fur around Rua's snout. 'It's probably one of Urf's litter. She lets them wander all over the place.'

There was only one other dingo family in the area. Farmers had killed the male, Wuf, and Urf had her paws full with five rowdy little ones. Rrrk and Rua kept an eye on the pups from a distance, but Urf made sure they understood to come no closer. The protective instinct was strong in the young mother. She snapped and gnashed her teeth in mock defence whenever she saw the two dingoes watching her.

'It might need help. Come with me and look,' pleaded Rua.

Rrrk could not refuse his life mate and together they left the burrow and padded out onto the sandy soil. The moon was pearly white, draping the earth in evening shadows. Rua moved closer to Rrrk, touching his flank. Winter in the desert was especially cold this year and pain gnawed at their old bones.

Rrrk's ears pricked. He could hear the sound now. He was old and he could no longer run great distances, but his senses of smell and hearing were still keen. 'This way.'

The sound was coming from beneath a pile of freshly turned earth. Rrrk sniffed deep. Something was buried under the ground. It was making a noise like a pup mewling.

'I know what this is,' said Rrrk. 'It's a human burial ground. Wuf told me.'

Wuf had known a lot of things about humans. That was how the trouble started. He spent too much time poking his snout around the nearby farms. When he raided the chickens, the men hunted him down.

Rua bent her head closer to the dirt. 'Whatever the humans buried is not dead.'

'I'll dig it out and we'll see what it is,' said Rrrk.

'Be careful.'

'Stand back,' he ordered.

Rua didn't hesitate to obey. Humans were dangerous creatures and if they didn't want this, it might be even more dangerous.

It didn't take Rrrk long to dig through the earth. The soil was soft and his claws sharp. He dragged a wooden object out of the hole. Rrrk struck the box with his feet and it broke open.

'It's a human pup!' exclaimed Rua.

The box had an air of sadness about it that confused her. Rua's maternal heart could tell how much the parents had loved this child.

'It'll be nothing but trouble,' said Rrrk. 'I'll put it back.'

'No, you don't.' Rua turned to her mate and snarled. 'It's too young. And it's not dead.'

That was true. It was making an awful noise. Rrrk was the alpha head of the den in every respect except one. Rua was in charge of pups. Without even a yip of discussion, she lifted the child by its wrappings and headed towards the burrow.

Rrrk whistled softly to call her back, but she ignored him. He sighed, knowing it was a waste of dog-breath to argue about this and he was too old to risk having a patch of fur ripped out in the middle of winter. So he pushed the broken box into the hole and replaced the dirt.

'How will we feed it?' he asked when they were settled back in the den, the child curled between them.

'Him,' Rua said. 'I will ask Urf to help. She has enough milk for one more.'

Rrrk grunted and curled up like a ball of spinifex. The females were gathering against him and there was nothing an old dingo could do about it. If he were honest, he had to admit he liked the feeling of the child against his fur. It was warming.

Rrrk was nervous the first few days. He walked the ridges at dusk and dawn checking for anything unusual. He sniffed the length of his territory and re-marked it to keep other animals away. No humans came looking for the child. They thought the boy was dead. Urf joined his pack and he found new energy with two females, three pups and the boy to look after.

Rua named the boy Rlph and he grew quickly. Before long, Urf's pups were hunting and looking after themselves. Next summer, they would be leaving to find their own territory. But Rlph still needed help with everything.

When Rlph hunted with the pack he was always in the wrong place at the wrong time.

'It's your fault the rabbit got away,' his pup-brothers complained.

They laughed at his useless nose, his long arms,

and his skin that couldn't even grow fur to keep him warm at night.

'Leave me alone,' Rlph snarled. He waved a stick and threatened to throw it. Instead, he drew pictures in the dirt. His brothers couldn't do that with their paws.

But they came back later to dig holes and mark their territory over his artwork.

There was trouble coming. Rrrk could smell it on his whiskers. He would probably only survive one more winter. One of the young dogs would become the new alpha male. Probably Brr, the biggest and strongest of Urf's brood. He hated humans. Brr knew what the farmers had done to his father, how they had hung his dead body on the fence line. Rrrk told Urf not to tell him, but females never listened.

Often Rlph came home with bite marks on his rump. Rua was not happy.

'My pup-brothers said I don't belong here. I don't have a white chest like they do.' Rlph's chest was marked with a large reddish-brown blotch.

'Young dogs must learn their place.'

Rrrk cautioned his mate not to interfere. 'It is the rule of the pack.'

But Rlph was not a dingo. He was a boy.

One day he came racing into the den, Brr chasing behind him. Rlph hid behind Rua's back legs and covered his face with her tail.

'What's wrong?' Rrrk growled at Brr.

'He threw a rock at me. Look.' There was a deep gash in Brr's side.

'You shouldn't have done that, Rlph,' Rrrk said. 'Here in the desert wounds infect easily.'

'He was going to bite me. I haven't got sharp teeth like his to bite back,' protested Rlph.

'I haven't got arms or fingers. He poked me in the eye,' Brr whined.

That was even worse. A blind dingo would never survive.

'Go home, Brr, and get your mother to lick the wound clean,' said Rrrk. 'I will deal with Rlph.'

There was only one solution, and he had to discuss it with Rua first.

'The time has come for the young ones to go their separate ways. I need to show you something,' he said, when Rlph fell asleep. 'Come with me.'

Rrrk led Rua back to the place where they had found the boy pup. On top of the mound of earth was a bunch of grevillea flowers. They were fresh and Rua buried her nose in their sweet smell.

'The humans still come here regularly,' said Rrrk. 'Sometimes I see them on my dusk patrol. They will be here tomorrow.'

Rua said nothing. She pulled a stick of flowers from the bunch and trotted back to the den, the blooms between her teeth. When Rrrk returned, the den didn't smell like rabbit anymore.

The next night they took Rlph out with them.

'Where are we going?' he complained. 'It's too late for hunting and I'm tired.' He splayed his feet and refused to budge.

Rrrk nipped at his bottom and Rua pushed his legs.

'All right,' he said.

Rua and Rrrk settled down low in the spinifex. They motioned to Rlph to lie beside them.

'What are we waiting for?' Rlph whimpered. 'I'm cold.'

'Shhh,' Rua said. 'Someone is coming.'

They came hand in hand, the woman carrying a bunch of flowers. Yellow this time.

'They look like me,' Rlph whispered.

Without speaking, the man took the flowers from his wife and laid them on top of the earth mound. Rrrk pushed Rlph forward so hard he yipped in panic. The man turned and pointed. The woman hurried towards Rlph, who was too afraid to move. She picked him up and showed the man the large reddish-brown birthmark on Rlph's chest. Then she kissed him. Rlph struggled in the woman's grasp but she held him tight.

Rrrk and Rua stayed hidden in the grass. They watched the man and woman carry Rlph away. Rua sniffed.

'All pups have to leave eventually,' said Rrrk.

'I know. I wonder if we'll have any more?' Rua whispered.

'I hope not,' snorted Rrrk. 'I'm too old now. I just want to spend my last year with you.'

'Silly dog,' she said and snuffled against him.

Ralph hated the dingo fence but he knew it was necessary if the dingoes were to survive. Sometimes the dingoes managed to push holes through the wire mesh. Other farmers trapped any dingoes found outside the fence and hung the corpses on the wire to frighten those remaining on the other side. Ralph knew dingoes weren't that stupid.

The government paid Ralph to keep his section of the fence in order. It was the law and the best protection the dingoes had. So Ralph did his repairs late at night when the silver moon cast its shadows across the desert. If he was lucky he would see a dog silhouetted on the ridge. And when he did, he would tip back his head and howl.

Rats
Jack Heath

One cop, Detective Bromham thought. It's a crime scene – murder, no less. And how many cops do they send? Just one.

He eased the patrol car to a halt in the only available park, two blocks away from the source of the call-out. As the ancient brakes moaned and the engine shuddered, Bromham remembered a time when they used to send a six-man special tactics unit to the site of a domestic disturbance. Those were the days.

But as these disturbances became more common, they started sending these teams only to homicides. When homicides began to happen every other week, they sent cops in pairs instead. One to drive, one to shoot, his former partner had always joked – until his ear was shot off when they interrupted a video-store robbery.

And now, here Bromham was. Old newspapers crunching under his feet as he pushed through the fish stink of the alleyway, protected by nothing more than a Kevlar vest, a taser and a badge. Alone. It could be hours before the forensic team arrived.

He couldn't blame his bosses. Resources were stretched thin across this evil city. Last month an old warehouse had been quarantined when it was found to be full of dead cops, apparently killed by an unidentified bio-weapon. Those who were left alive were all busy searching for a perpetrator.

At least Bromham would have some company soon. When he got to apartment 303, he'd meet up with the officer who'd called in the homicide, and they'd investigate together. Bromham hoped Detective Simms would be an old man, like him, with stories of the glory days. Someone else who remembered how things were supposed to be.

There was no alarm when he wrenched open the fire door. Most of the apartments in this building had no registered occupants. They had been half-renovated when the credit crunch hit, and were left to fester in their patchy paint afterwards. Plain-clothes cops sometimes checked the building for vandals and illegal immigrants, but other than that, it stayed empty. Bromham didn't see a soul as he climbed the silent stairwell.

The third floor was a gallery of graffiti and burn marks. It was once a home for the wealthy, then for those who had nowhere else to go, then for no one at all. Some of the apartment doors were open, revealing yellowed mattresses lying on the bare concrete and cockroaches scratching across the ceilings.

The door for apartment 303 was closed. Bromham pressed his ear to it.

Silence.

He took a deep breath, thumped on the door, and shouted the words he'd shouted a thousand times before: 'Police! Open up!'

The noise boomed around the deserted corridors before fracturing into pieces too small to hear. There was no response.

Bromham tried the handle. It turned easily, but emitted a scraping sound that made the hairs on his arms stand up.

He saw the bodies before he saw anything else in the room – because there was nothing else in the room. Unlike the other apartments, which had a squalid, lived-in look, this one was eerily clean. It was like dust refused to cross the threshold.

The two corpses lay side by side in the middle of the living room, as though making snow-angels. They looked like a middle-aged woman and a teenage girl, although from this angle, Bromham couldn't see their faces clearly.

'Detective Simms?' he called.

There was no reply.

He stepped into the apartment, his hand sweaty around the rubber grip of the taser, peering left and right. There was no sign of anyone else. When he reached the bodies, he bent down to check the pulse of the older woman – and he froze.

Bromham had seen many dead bodies in his career. Sometimes they were sad, like the woman who'd been stung by a bee on her honeymoon and had gone into anaphylactic shock. Sometimes they were gruesome, like the man who'd been found in a sewer after drowning six months earlier, or the one who'd fallen onto the killing floor at an abattoir and been herded by the cattle into the bladed machinery before anyone could switch it off. But he'd never, ever seen expressions of horror like the ones on these two women.

The middle-aged woman's eyes were so wide that the whites were visible all the way around the irises, and her lips were drawn back to expose teeth that had been frozen mid-chatter. He found himself wondering if her hair had been grey before her death, or if fear had bleached the colour out of it.

Dried saliva was cratered around the teenage girl's mouth, and her face was as waxy as an old photograph. Her eyes were rolled back into her head.

Recovering his composure, Bromham touched their throats. No pulses, and each corpse was somehow colder than the room.

Leaving the bodies where they lay, he pulled on some latex gloves and went to examine the rest of the apartment. The bedroom had no bed, and the window was blacked out with tape. Inside the walk-in robe, he found no clothes, just rails from which they might be hung – and on the floor, eight dead rats.

At first he thought this might be the work of an exterminator, since there didn't seem to be any wounds. It was rare, he knew, to find dead rats in groups, because unless they all died at exactly the same time, the live ones devoured the dead. But as he bent down to look more closely, he could see that they were in varying states of decomposition. This one, with the pitted eyes and shrunken joints, had been lying there for weeks, but that one, still plump and furry, only days. Another looked like it could have been alive only hours ago.

One dies, Bromham thought. The smell draws another. That one dies, somehow, and the smell draws yet another.

He closed the wardrobe.

The bathroom was only identifiable as such because of the circular holes in the walls and floor. There were nooks for the vanity, the toilet and the shower, once the piping had been installed. Peering down one of the drains was like looking into a well. Bromham could faintly see his reflection in the distant water, and was surprised how unnerved he looked. As a teenager he'd visited a haunted house at a carnival, and been photographed just when a man in a rubber mask had grabbed his leg. He hadn't bought the photo afterwards, but he'd seen it on the flickering screen. His brows had been knotted together and his lips curled downwards at the edges in the same way they were now.

Keep it together, he told himself. The forensics team will be here soon enough.

He walked back into the living room.

He had three mysteries to unravel. Firstly, why had Detective Simms left the scene of the crime?

Secondly, what had killed these two women? There were no bullet-holes, no stab-wounds, no ligature marks. Their necks didn't look broken, and there was no vomit, which usually meant no poison. It looked like two simultaneous heart attacks.

Thirdly, why were there two bodies, when only one had been reported?

Very carefully, Bromham started going through the pockets of the teenage girl. No keys, no wallet, no phone. Her clothes had no labels; in fact, they looked homemade. The stitches were unwinding at the edges.

He expected to find the same thing when he searched the other body, but instead he found a wallet, a can of capsicum spray and a two-way radio. He opened the wallet, and found a police badge shining at him.

He looked at the ID. Name: Detective Rebecca Simms.

A chill crawled up his spine. That explained mysteries one and three. Simms had found the dead teenager and called it in, but she hadn't checked that the murderer was gone.

A dead cop needed to be reported right away. Bromham pulled out his radio.

'Dispatch, this is Detective Bromham. I'm in apartment 303 on the corner of Launceston and Callam, and I've got an officer down and a Jane Doe. Over.'

'Copy that, detective. Sending backup to your location. Over.'

Bromham hooked his radio back onto his belt, and thought again of the warehouse full of dead cops. What was this city coming to?

For no reason at all, he remembered the rats. One death lures another, which lures another . . .

The teenage girl sat up.

Bromham yelped, and jumped backwards, his brain rebelling against the sight. He'd checked her pulse. She was stone cold. How could she still be alive?

'Are you okay, miss?' he stammered.

The girl's head swivelled to face him. Her eyes stayed rolled back, but her mouth fell open like an oven door, revealing a thick, black tongue. She stood with unearthly grace, and before he had time to react, reached out and grabbed him by the wrist.

The pain was sudden and world-destroying, but it didn't come from his arm. It came from his chest where, after four decades of loyal service, his heart had suddenly stopped beating.

Bromham tried to scream, but his lungs were already growing too weak to push out the air. His head was spinning. Ice trickled through his veins, everywhere except where the girl's hand was sizzling on his arm like an oil burn. It was as though all the stored-up chemical energy in his body, all the glucose and fat and oxygen, was being incinerated and the resulting heat was being sucked out through his arm. His life force was being vacuumed up.

Bromham's vision was blurring, but he could see the room was swinging. He toppled over, fireworks bursting in his brain as the back of his skull hit the ground. The girl – the monster – maintained her grip, patiently.

He gripped the taser in his trembling hand. He doubted that it would work on the girl. But just maybe it would work on him.

He pointed it at his own chest and pulled the trigger.

There was a snap and a fizz and the monster yowled, tearing her hand away. Bromham barely heard the sounds over the renewed pounding of his heart. It was like stepping out of a meat-locker and plunging into a pit of hot tar. The blast of electricity to his core left him thrashing and twitching and not dead yet.

He couldn't stand, but he could crawl. He crawled towards the apartment door, cursing his shivering limbs for their weakness. His palms and kneecaps scraped the concrete. He dared not look back at the girl in case he lost his balance.

Three metres from the door. Two. One.

He reached up for the handle, as though he were a rock climber clawing at the precipice.

A hand closed around his ankle, and he felt the rest of his life slip away.

Detective Pravo pulled up a block away from the apartment building, and turned the key. The motor ceased its rumbling.

Two bodies. One of them a cop. Surely dispatch could have spared more than one detective to check it out? What was this city coming to?

Soon, she thought, they won't send anybody at all.

The Thieftaker's Apprentice
Lucy Sussex

Like all of Master Bath's adventures, it began with a summons at our lodgings in Fettler's Alley, beyond Covent Garden, London Town. I brought the message up to my master and pulled the curtains from around his bed; found his glasses as usual and his wig – without it he was bald as an egg.

As he read, he whistled.

'East India Company! Ever heard of them?'

Now I might be young, only a servant-lad and new in a thieftaker's employ, but even I had heard of the Company!

'All the riches of the Indies, sir.'

'Pouring into the coffers of dear old England!' he finished. 'And into ours, as well.'

'So a fat fee offered, then?'

A nod. 'Depending what's been taken. Some Maharajah's emeralds, slave girls, a boatload of elephant ivory.' He smacked his lips. 'So find my clothes, lad. We're off to the Old Bailey Courthouse!'

But when we presented ourselves, neatly dressed, and washed as much as my master does (a splash in a basin), the truth was less exciting.

'Only a trunkful of papers, Mr Fielding?' my master said.

Fielding was a magistrate at the Old Bailey, fat as butter, but with eyes as sharp and clever as my master's. He met us in his chambers, and being a man who liked his food and yet wasn't stingy, we both got a slice of his morning pie.

'A very large trunk, Mr Bath. Containing vital instructions for the company. Due to sail shortly. But someone thieved it off the coach, when the coachman had stopped to let out a passenger at the withered oak, outside Peckham. He noticed only when he stopped in Peckham proper.'

'You had it cried for?'

'Peckham might be neither one thing nor the other, like the fish or fowl-meat in this pastie – neither London nor country, but it does possess a town crier. "Oyez, oyez!" off he went, "trunk stolen, big reward!", ringing his bell, up and down the lanes around Peckham. But no result as yet.'

He took another bite of his pie.

'Time is short, Mr Bath. To work, to take the thief and earn your rich reward!'

Time being short, indeed, Master hired a horse, a skinny nag with a rolling eye and a hard mouth, but fast, guaranteed! I hopped up on behind Master. Off we went, through the crowded streets of old London, the crowds falling away as the houses became less dense, until we saw green fields. Peckham.

On the Gravesend Road we found the withered oak soon enough, near to death and the only tree for miles. Every other tree had been razed by London's thirst for firewood.

Master Bath dismounted, leaving me in charge of the nag. Master looked around with that hungry look he gets when he's thief-seeking, with hopes of the taking and a fat reward.

'What d'ye see from up there, lad?'

'Fields, sir. A cow or three. Some labourers, distant, mending a fence. And flatness.'

He rubbed his stubbly chin.

'Our scene of the crime. Imagine it, early morning, a brief stop, driver distracted with a call of nature I'll bet. A crime of opportunity. A passenger riding on the outside, doin' it cheap. Sees a trunk not well secured, gives the fastenings a little tweak with the pocketknife . . .'

His eyes were wide, gazing into the recent past as if it were a Bible-book.

'And then he hops off, taking more than his luggage with him.'

The horse let out a whinny, and we saw a donkey plodding towards us with a farmwife and her baskets perched atop, her skirts tucked up against the road's mud. Bath tipped his hat at her, she nodded her sunbonnet back.

'Busy road, ma'am?' he said, a question-greeting.

'Not at this spot,' she replied smartly, and urged the donkey onwards.

'What did she mean?' I asked Master Bath, but he was busy with the past again.

'A big trunk,' he said. 'No man, however strong, could tuck it under his arm and walk away. He had help! Another passenger, or the sight of a fellow miscreant on the road. Tips him the wink, stops the coach . . .'

He bent down, staring at the impressions of passage in the road's mud. I saw: our nag's big feet; the donkey's, daintier; several cows being driven to market and complaining with cowpats; but no other wheeled tracks over the ruts of the coach, nothing to help them get the prize away.

'Not even a wheelbarrow, sir.'

'See these?' he said, pointing at several footsteps, pressed deep. 'They were carrying weight. And they stepped up into the drier, grassy verge . . . But where did they put that trunk? They couldn't have got far, not without someone seeing them, on the road or in the fields.'

He was grinning now at the thrill of the chase, like a hound scenting a fox.

But my mind was elsewhere, worrying at the farmwife's words, and the sound of a faint buzzing. The nag was restive, too, tossing his head irritably, so that I had to hold hard onto the reins. Then I felt something alight on my neck. A flea? No, bigger! I swatted at it, and just missed. Something striped bright yellow shot between my fingers with a buzzing whine.

'Oh no!'

A wasp, and in the tree above it the London-town of its fellows, the reason why nobody had dared to take an axe to the withered oak.

'Oh no!'

The wasp landed on the nag's tender pink nose. As he tossed his head again, trying to dislodge the unwanted passenger, the wasp lashed out.

'Oh no!'

Stung and sore, the nag reared, while I hung on desperately. Then he shot down the road. I hung on as long as I could, but got shaken off on the verge. Down I fell, through grass and sedge into shallow, filthy, brackish water.

Silence, except for the nag's hooves galloping away. And then my master's face, looking down at me as I lay full-length in the roadside ditch.

'No broken bones, lad?'

I felt around, and shook my head.

He laughed. 'Well, you're a sight then!'

'Yes sir, and I think I know where the trunk might be.'

He pulled me out, dripping mud and leeches. The ditch was deep and wide under its thick grassy cover. We waited until the wasps calmed down, then we followed the line of the ditch past the oak. Some few steps onwards, covered with more grass and sedge, we found the trunk.

'The villains,' said my master, grinning. 'Clever, though, to stow the trunk out of sight where nobody would think of looking, thanks to the wasps. Planning to come back later I'll warrant, under cover of dark, with a handcart . . .'

It took three goes, in which we got even more muddy, but we hauled the trunk out of the ditch. It was a dead weight and the padlock was secure. We set the trunk down on the verge, and for somewhere to sit, sat on it. The nag was nowhere to be seen.

'What now, sir?'

He squinted at the fields, then dug into his purse.

'Take these coins lad, and hire those fence-menders to give us a helping hand.'

'Me, sir? I'm covered in mud!'

'But the coins aren't. Go on, stir yourself!'

Money greases all passage, and even though I looked like a beggar, Hodge and Will were happy to lay down their fencing tools and help us, for my master's pence.

Peckham village was half a mile away and even with the four of us, it was hard work carrying the trunk. Thirsty, too, and the first sight we saw was a glad one: the alehouse. Tied outside it was the farm-wife's donkey.

'Let me treat you all!' said my master, and still

carrying the trunk we waddled to the door. It slammed behind us and we set the trunk down; then looked up to see a roomful of patrons, gaping. At the nearest sat an old man with a great handbell in front of him. His jaw dropped like a hangman's trapdoor – he stood up and rang the bell loudly.

'Oyez, oyez, and if that isn't the trunk I was paid to cry for, with its thieves, too!'

Hands seized us, and the fence-menders, too.

'They paid us,' Hodge and Will protested, 'to do their dirty work. Said they were thieftakers!'

'A likely story, the filthy beggars!' said the Crier. From the back, a big man with a bigger cudgel pushed forward.

'I be the parish constable of Peckham. And who might ye be with this fine trunk, not your property?'

'I'm Mr Bath, thieftaker of London Town,' said my master.

'And I'm the Queen of Sheba!' said the farmwife.

So we ended up in Peckham's tiny watch-house, locked in one cell with the trunk for safekeeping locked in the other. We spent the night there, lying on flea-ridden straw with a thin blanket shared between us, and water and stale bread our food. But Master Bath always kept his wits about him, and had enough money hidden in his boots for emergencies. One bribe went to the parish constable for pen, ink and paper (even if it was the back of an old feed bill).

Another bribe went to the alehouse boy to carry a letter back to London.

And so it was, first thing in the morning we woke shivering to peals of laughter: Mr Fielding, leaning against the bars, all his double chins shaking like jelly. Although it hadn't seemed funny until that point, we joined in too. We got a ride back to London in Mr Fielding's coach, and cramped it was with the trunk safely inside with us, just in case. On a long rope, trotting behind us came the hired nag, with a swollen nose, but not the least sorry for leaving us in the lurch.

Mr Fielding, being Mr Fielding, had somehow found a fresh-baked pie in Peckham and so we showered crumbs all over the trunk on the way back to London. A quick wipe down and it was returned to the offices of the East India Company. We heard later it departed from Gravesend the next day, exactly as scheduled.

Back at our lodgings, Master Bath sat down and eyed me from behind his glasses. 'That was smart work, lad, to lead us to the trunk. So I'm thinking you've earned a small share of the reward.'

'Oh, I don't want money!'

He stared at me. 'In heaven's name, what do you want, lad?'

I had an armful of wood for the fire, and clutched it tightly, to get my courage up. 'I want to be more than your servant, sir!'

No one had ever heard anything of the sort before, Mr Fielding said, but he signed the papers and made an attested copy. And that is how I became not just a servant boy, but an accredited apprentice to Mr Bath, Thieftaker.

And one day, I'll be a Thieftaker, too!

The Reunion
Oliver Phommavanh

The empty car park was a bad omen. Kevin walked past the rusty gates of Gorgebank High, carrying second thoughts. He could still walk away and no one would ever know. No one would care. Who would go to a school reunion in the Facebook era? And a five-year reunion? It was too soon.

The hall still looked the same. The stench of the toilets nearby lingered in the air and revived Kevin's memory. There was nothing on the stage except a stereo coughing up some old music.

There were six large round tables surrounded by plastic green chairs. There was only one table with people at it. Kevin sat by himself, at the table furthest away from them.

Andrew waved at him. 'Come over, man.'

Kevin recognised that screechy voice and ignored it.

After ten minutes, Andrew and the others came over to him. Andrew was wearing his crinkled suit. It reeked like sour pasta sauce. He hadn't washed it since the Year Twelve formal. 'How's it going, Kevin Earnshaw?'

Kevin concentrated on the large banner stretched across the stage, under the faded green curtains. *Gorgebank High Class of 2007.* His mind raced down the list of better things to do on a Saturday night. An old man staggered in from the side door. He stood out the front of the stage, his face blending in with the cracked walls.

'Welcome to the reunion,' he mumbled. 'You may not know me. My name is Mr Tomly, I'm currently the Year Twelve advisor. None of your old teachers could make it.'

Kevin wished he were that smart.

Mr Tomly rubbed his hands. 'I'm sure more students will turn up. I'll go check on the sausage rolls . . . Help yourself to some cordial.' He shuffled back through the side door.

Andrew laid down his business cards like he was playing solitaire. He flicked one over to Kevin. 'If you want to claim compo, I'm your man.'

Kevin picked it up. 'You a lawyer?'

'I will be.'

Kevin looked closer at the card. *Andrew Carey, 2nd year Law student.* He pretended to stuff the card in his pocket, but dropped it under the table.

The girl beside Andrew smiled. 'Hi, I'm Millie.'

'Yeah, I know.' Kevin remembered her at their graduation day. She had lip-synced to the song 'Hero'. And it was still painful. Most girls Kevin knew from school had stacked on the kilos. Millie was an ugly duckling transformed into a slightly better duck. 'So, you and Andrew are together?'

'Nah, I've got a missus.' Andrew took out his wallet and showed them a photo. 'She gets her visa to come here next month.'

Millie went over to the drinks table and grabbed a jug of cordial and four plastic cups. She returned to the table, her face animated as she mimed to the song on the stereo. 'So what do you do, Kevin?'

Kevin shrugged. 'Um, stuff.'

'Oh, okay.'

The other guy snatched his drink. It spilled all over his shiny tracksuit. 'You remember me?'

Kevin looked at Andrew and Millie. They shook their heads.

'It's Phillip Bray.'

'Don't know, man,' Kevin said. 'I must have blocked it out.'

'Nah, it's all right.' He crushed his cup on his forehead.

Millie smiled. 'Well, I'm part of a girl band. It's called Desire.'

Andrew laughed until Millie's glare shut him up. 'We came fifth in the Gorgebank RSL talent quest.'

It was Phillip's turn. 'Um, I'm between opportunities. I'm taking care of my uncle. He got discharged from the army for being too fat. He got stuck in the tank's hatch.'

'I remember that,' Andrew said. 'He made the newspaper and everything.'

Kevin felt sick when everyone looked at him. Even the music stopped.

Millie played with her pigtails. 'Come on, Kevin, what do you really do?'

Her voice echoed in the hollow hall. Kevin's neck was sticky. They meant nothing to him, but he couldn't tell them the truth. Kevin thought about his stack of DVDs at home. He was in the middle of watching a reality series about celebrity funerals. He slouched in his seat. 'I'm a mortician.'

Kevin could hear their brains grinding. Why didn't he just copy Phillip?

Millie nodded. 'Sounds exciting.'

'Yeah it's, um, cool.' Kevin gulped his watered-down cordial.

Mr Tomly crept in with a plate of sausage rolls. 'Ah, still no one else?' He placed the plate on the food table next to the drinks. 'Help yourselves . . .'

Nobody moved. Mr Tomly sighed. He brought the tray of sausage rolls to their table.

Millie scrunched up her nose. 'I'm vegetarian.'

'I have some dim sims,' Mr Tomly said. 'They're just thawing in the microwave.'

'It's okay, I'm not hungry.' Millie poured some more cordial. She filled Kevin's cup, too.

Mr Tomly walked over to the stereo. 'Could have sworn I put in fresh batteries.' He shook it around.

Kevin bit into a lukewarm sausage roll. It tasted like cardboard and ice. Still, he was happy. This bunch of nobodies gobbled up his lie. He was better than them, even though he was a slacker. He couldn't wait to go home and write about it in his blog.

There was a loud thud. Everybody turned to see Mr Tomly lying awkwardly on the floor. Andrew rushed up and touched Mr Tomly's neck. 'Ohmigod. He's dead.' He put his hands on his head.

Millie shrieked. 'We gotta call the police!'

'If you call the cops, I wasn't here, okay?' Phillip said. 'I didn't even graduate here. I dropped out in Year Ten.'

Andrew picked up the battery from the dead man's hand. The tip was wet with spit. 'He must have licked it.'

Kevin studied Mr Tomly's face. He looked so peaceful. 'Let's just go.'

No one said anything for a while. Then Phillip stuffed the sausage rolls into his pockets. Millie tidied up the cups and cordial. Andrew and Kevin shut the doors and windows. Phillip found a cloth and wiped the tables and chairs down. Kevin switched off the lights. Any sign of life disappeared when they left the room.

'Are you on Facebook?' Andrew dug out his car keys.

'No,' Kevin said.

'Me either.' Andrew crossed the road to his car.

Phillip lurched away from them down the road, the stereo under his arm. Kevin went the other way. Millie walked beside him, breathing hard and fast. He glanced at her. 'I'm going to Maccas. Um, you wanna come?'

Millie nodded.

Kevin was in denial. He wanted to believe that he never ate that sausage roll. That he never met Phillip. That he never flicked Andrew's business card under the table . . .

Kevin stopped. Millie touched his arm. 'You okay?'

'Yeah, it's nothing.'

Kevin finished erasing the whole night in his head. But he held onto Millie. Maybe the night wasn't a total waste.

Millie twirled her hair. 'Hey Kevin . . . about Mr Tomly?'

'Yeah?'

'What kind of make-up would you use on him?'

Don't Let Go

Deborah Abela

I'm going to tell you exactly what happened. Others will want you to know a different story, but I guess everyone has their own version. Police, counsellors, family. Bits they need to leave out because they're embarrassed or wish they'd acted differently or because they were simply clocking up another shift and didn't care too much either way.

But I'm not any of those.

This story starts and ends in the same place, even though no one but me knows that. And now you.

I know why Rory did what he did and how much was my part. I'm tired of carrying it around and wearing it noosed around my neck. I hate what it's made me and that I've lied about it for so long, and nothing, not anything or anyone, is going to stop me telling you what really happened.

Mays Rock

A ritual of growing up in Hopetoun was a jump from Mays Rock. As a kid, it felt like standing on the tallest building above a city of trees, a jagged, snaking gully and a river that would snatch our breath away with its cold, black belly. Rory and I would ride our bikes along Beckett's fire trail, dumping them a few hundred metres from the end where we made our way on foot across the platform to the rock.

The first few times we went, we just sat and talked about jumping.

'I'd walk up to the edge, hold my arms out and jump.'

'Then you're an idiot, Superman,' Rory said. 'The best way is to take a run up, swing your arms out for momentum and launch into the air.'

'What makes you such an expert?'

'Natural smarts.'

'I hate to bring you back to reality, but smarts is the last thing that comes natural to you.'

That was it. Rory had me in a headlock. He looked puny, but he carried a lot of power in those skinny arms.

'Let me go,' I wheezed.

'Not until you admit you're wrong.'

'Never.'

'Then you're here for a long time. I don't have anywhere else to be.'

I tried to hold out, but I was starting to feel my head float from the rest of my body. 'Okay, you're right.'

Rory let me go. 'I knew it was only a matter of time before you realised my greatness.'

I laughed and nodded toward the edge. 'Does that

mean you're going to do it?'

Rory stared it down. 'Soon. Maybe next time.'

Next Time

We were standing near the edge. It was a perfect day for a jump. No wind, no one around, and with the early stirrings of summer and the climb on our bikes, the cool water would be welcome.

Rory stepped forward and looked over the edge. 'It's a long way down.'

'You're only working that out now?'

He turned to face me. 'Just letting you know in case you hadn't noticed, in fact . . .'

Rory's foot skated on a rock. It slid out from under him and he was going down. He twisted his body and reached away from the edge but his chest hit the platform. I flung my hands out and grabbed his wrists. The lower part of his body was dangling above the river.

His eyes met mine in quiet panic. 'Don't let go.'

'I won't.'

My fingers dug into his skin. I hauled him, inched him across the rock, until one final tug on the back of his shirt and he was safe.

I was panting, wrecked, my heart about to give out. Rory rolled flat on his back, his arms scraped and bleeding.

I turned to him. 'You need to practise your technique.'

Rory belly-laughed and said nothing.
We didn't jump that day.

The Jump

A few months later, we met one Saturday morning and did it. I know I should have built it up a bit more, but after years of thinking about it, planning it and backing out, it just felt right. For both of us. Without even speaking, we knew we'd do it. We climbed to the top in silence, swapped one brief look and nodded. We took a small run up (yes, Rory was right) and jumped. It was like riding bikes midair, legs circling and arms flailing. Rory let loose a scream. Then we were in the water. Bubbled beneath the surface, torpedoing down.

When we emerged, we didn't say much, just gulped deep breaths and laughed at the sky and the rock platform that was far above us.

We celebrated with a hamburger at Jules' Café. In between mouthfuls, we talked about the jump from every angle, talking loudly over each other while basking in how great we were. We were midway through congratulating each other, when this girl walked in from the kitchen. She was tying an apron around her waist and had a name badge that read, 'Mia'.

'You two look pretty happy with yourselves.'

'And you are looking at two of the bravest men in town.'

'Aren't I lucky? First day on the job and I meet the town heroes.'

'Any time you need rescuing, we're your men.'

I snatched a look at Rory who was staring at his plate. He wasn't good with girls. Tended to clam up. I'd asked him why in the past and he said he never had anything to say to them. I used to be the same, but lately I was finding I did. I could even make them laugh, and with Mia, I was starting to enjoy myself.

'I haven't seen you here before.'

'We just moved here. Mum knows Jules and she's letting me do a few shifts to see how I go.'

'Why'd you move to Hopetoun?'

'Same as everyone, the wide open spaces,' she said with a crooked smile. 'And all the heroes.'

She wasn't laughing at us. It was like she knew the joke between us and wanted in. I'm not sure why I did it, I'd never done anything even vaguely like it before and if I'd thought about it for even half a second, I would have silently yelled at myself for being a jerk and reconsidered. But it was too late.

'Would you like to go to the movies this Friday?'

Three things happened almost instantly. I can remember them as if I was still sitting at that table, beetroot-stained hamburger fingers, ready to yell at myself for being such a dreamy idiot.

1. She said yes.
2. Rory's head jerked up like I'd confessed to being a serial killer.

3. Rory's dad walked in, slamming open the door, swaying and screaming his name like he was calling for a dog who'd jumped the back fence again.

Rory flinched as if he'd been hit. His shoulders hunched and he mumbled that he'd see me soon.

Rory

Rory wasn't at school the next day. Or the next. I texted him, but he never answered. Finally, he wrote to meet him at the rock.

'What happened?'

Rory shrugged. 'Nothing.'

'To your eye? What happened to your eye?'

'I said . . . nothing.'

'Looks like something to me.'

'It won't be forever. Just for now until I figure a way out.'

I was quiet. I didn't know what to say. So I said nothing.

'Wanna try another jump?' He made a feeble attempt at his usual winning grin.

'Sure.' Looking at his eye, I didn't know what I wanted.

We stood near the edge. All the confidence from our first jump had been drained from him. Rory stood staring at the river below, shaking, as if he was eight years old again and the jump seemed almost impossible.

'Maybe another time, eh?' I asked.

He looked over the edge, his feet planted.

'Come on.' I slung my hand over his shoulder and drew him away.

Mia

After the movie on Friday, Mia and I had coffee. I'd been nervous all day about seeing her, worrying I'd have nothing to say, that that first day was a fluke, but the second I saw her, I felt calm and almost couldn't shut up.

'So what is there to do around this town?'

'Sightsee, eat at Jules' Café and watch out for all the heroes.'

'Anything else?'

'There's Mays Rock.'

'A rock?'

'Not just any old rock. It's sheer on one side all the way down to the river. It's a bit of a rite of passage to jump from it.'

'Okay.'

'Okay, what?'

'I'll do it.'

I scrambled. 'It's pretty high and . . .'

'Too terrifying for a girl?'

'No, it's just . . .'

'How about tomorrow?'

Standing on the Edge

We were looking down.

'How high is it?' Mia asked.

'About fifteen metres.'

'Looks higher.'

'When we were kids it seemed like a hundred.'

She kicked off her shoes. 'Shall we?'

'Now?'

'Sure.'

A twig snapped behind us.

'Rory?' It was good to see him. 'Mia's going to jump.'

There were times when Rory would get a look in his eye, like he was sliding away from you and if you couldn't grab him, he'd be hard to reach for the rest of the day. Maybe even longer.

He shifted on his feet. 'I can't stay.'

He mumbled something else that I didn't hear and walked back into the bush.

A Visitor

Mia jumped. Just like that. As if it wasn't something that had taken us half our childhoods to conquer. We stayed late and I walked her home.

When I got back to my place, Rory was sitting slumped against the side of the house.

'Can I stay here tonight?'

There was a red welt on his arm.

'Sure. Mum's cooking lasagne.'

'Why do you think I'm here?' He gave me a half smile. 'I could smell it all the way from my place.'

Dinner

Mia and her mum invited me over for dinner. Her mum was just as nice, like an older version of Mia and her dad welcomed me in like I'd known them for years.

My phone beeped. It was Rory.

> watcha doin?
>
> dinner with M
>
> have fun

The Next Day

My phone woke me early next morning.

'Wanna go to Mays?'

It was Rory.

'I'm taking Mia to the markets.'

'Oh.' There was a slight crack in his voice, a nervousness, like something wasn't right.

'How about this afternoon at four o'clock?'

He said nothing. I could hear his breathing, which seemed laboured and heavy.

I wanted to block it out. 'We'll do another jump and go for a burger afterwards. My shout.'

There was silence. A loud, ear-battering quiet that shouted at me, measured me up, looked me in the eye accusingly. It waited for me to do something but I did nothing. I just let it stumble between Rory and me, teetering and swaying like some careless, selfish drunk.

'Okay,' he said quietly. 'See you then.'

Missing

He was missing for days. He'd taken nothing from his room. His dad sat in the pub crying about how proud he was of his boy and how he wouldn't be happy until he came back. The cops searched the bush surrounding the town. Counsellors came to school, not sure what to counsel about. Some of them, you could tell, brought in from the city, thought it was just another runaway, especially after meeting his dad.

It was on the fourth day they found Rory. He was caught in tree roots at a bend of the river fifteen kilometres downstream.

The speculation was what drove me inside my bedroom, curled under the covers, not wanting to come out.

'He must have tripped and fell,' some said.

'No, he meant it. Must have.'

'Someone pushed him.'

In all the talk, no one guessed the real reason.

Me

I left six months later.

Dad thought a change would do me good, that I was too young to face a side of life that even adults struggle to deal with. I hadn't left our house except to go to school, and even then I was barely there.

An old relative in Europe had died, some great-aunt I never knew. Left enough money for an exclusive boy's college. I shrugged when Dad suggested it.

Mia stood on the front lawn, her face shiny with tears. I knew I'd miss her, but right then, I felt nothing. I didn't deserve to. I hugged her, told her I would write and waved from the car, all the things I thought I should have done. After a few months of not answering her emails, they stopped.

At school we have our own lake, boats, archery range, elite training gym. I fence, play water polo, ride horses, anything to leave me exhausted at night, so I don't dream and I can't hear the words in my head.

What Really Happened

He didn't fall, he wasn't pushed and he didn't jump. I did it.

I was late meeting him at Mays. Mia and I got caught up, talking. He wasn't there when I arrived. I texted him. I waited until it got dark. I called but only got his voicemail.

I let go when I told Rory I wouldn't. I said it like a promise, but it wasn't worth anything and now he's gone. Rory never asked me for much, all he asked was don't let go and I couldn't even do that.

Led Zep

Phillip Gwynne

'Can you keep the noise down a bit, please?'

Morry — my dad. Sometimes he drives me bonkers. He's the other side of forty and he thinks he's a rock star. Right now he's in the lounge with the amp cranked right up, playing 'Stairway to Heaven'. Cass — my mum — she's just as bad. I can hear her dancing around. She's singing too. I'm trying to practise, next week I've got a concert. How can I concentrate with that racket in the next room?

'Sorry, mate,' Morry replies, 'we got a bit carried away.'

I can hear them giggling. They're middle-aged and they carry on like little kids.

You wouldn't know it, but Morry used to be famous. For about a week. He was in a band called Crimson Viper. They had a couple of singles in the charts. They were even on *Countdown*. Molly Meldrum said they were going to be the next big thing. They weren't. Morry reckons it was bad karma, whatever that means. Their manager ripped them off, their drummer OD'd. The same sad old story.

That's when Dad met Mum. She was a groupie.

Well, she used to go to all their gigs anyway. Morry says she was always right up the front, next to the stage, throwing things at him.

'What things?' I asked.

'Roses,' said Mum.

'Knickers,' said Morry.

Mum was always trying to sneak backstage after the show. When she finally did, Morry fell in love with her and they've been together ever since.

Morry's never given up trying to be famous again. He's been in hundreds of bands. I'm not exaggerating, literally hundreds. They always start the same – all the members are really enthusiastic and practise a lot, usually at our place. Then they start playing gigs in scungy pubs way out in the sticks. There'll be about eight people watching. (My mum is always one of them.) They become more popular. Morry rings up all his old contacts – managers, DJs, producers, people from record companies. But just when they're ready to go into the studio, or play a really big gig, something happens. Something catastrophic. The bass player is offered a fortune to play in Slim Dusty's band, or the drummer OD's. Then the band busts up. After a while it starts all over again.

Morry still thinks he can make the big time. So does Cass. In her eyes he's never stopped being a guitar hero. I reckon he's got Buckley's. I'd never say that to him, I wouldn't want to hurt his feelings, but you've got to be realistic.

For a start there's his hair. Or lack thereof. Over forty bald blokes just don't become rock stars. Sure, singers like Elton John and Phil Collins haven't got much up top, but they went bald after they'd made it big, not before.

Another problem is Morry's musical tastes. Actually musical taste would be more correct, because really he only likes one band – Led Zeppelin, or Led Zep as they're known in this house. Led Zep hasn't made a record in twenty years. So what? They were the best. They invented heavy rock. Everything since has been second-rate. That's what Morry reckons anyway.

Everywhere you look in our house you see Led Zep. You can't even sit on the toilet by yourself. Led Zep is there, too, peering down. One corner of the lounge room is dedicated to the memory of John Bonham, Led Zep's drummer. He OD'd of course. There's an enormous poster of John, and underneath, a cross made from two drumsticks. When he died Morry was inconsolable. He moped around for weeks and weeks. He made a tape of all the Led Zep drum solos, and played it over and over. It drove us all bonkers.

Then there's my name – Robert (after Robert Plant, singer), James (after Jimmy Page, lead guitar), John (after John Bonham, drummer), Paul (after Paul Jones, bass player). I'm not joking, it's there on my birth certificate – Robert James John Paul Morrison. I suppose I'm lucky Morry's not a football fanatic.

Jimmy Page played a Les Paul. So Morry plays one. Jimmy Page played a Telecaster. So Morry pulls his out all the time. Jimmy Page played a twin-necked Gibson. So Morry went out and got one of those, too. When Morry sings, he almost sounds like Robert Plant. He's got the same stage mannerisms, too. If they ever make a movie about Led Zep, then Morry should audition. He'd have to wear a wig of course. Morry writes his own songs. They sound just like Led Zep songs, though.

'What Led Zep album's that off?' I'll ask when I hear him playing something vaguely familiar.

'Oh that's an original, one of mine,' he'll reply.

Yeah, sure thing, Morry.

Sometimes we'll go and visit Morry's mates. In the old days they used to play in bands with him. They live in big houses in places like Potts Point and Vaucluse. They're all bald, too, but at least they wear Italian suits and drive BMWs. As we drive home I ask Morry why he can't do what they do – write jingles for television ads and do stuff with computers.

'Sold out,' he'll say. 'They've all sold out. At least I've got my integrity. I haven't prostituted my talent to the corporate world.'

'Good on ya, Morry,' Cass will say.

In the meantime our beat-up old Kombi can hardly make it up the hill, we eat lentils at least five times a week, and the only way I'll ever get to the Conservatorium is by winning a scholarship.

I was playing guitar before I could walk. We've got the photos at home – me in nappies holding a baby Telecaster. When other kids were revving around the playground I was learning the chords to 'Stairway to Heaven'. By the time I was seven I was in Morry's band. I'd come on at the end and jam on the last couple of songs. The audience used to go wild. It's not as if he made me play. It wasn't like that at all. But there were always guitars lying around. People were either listening to music, talking about music or making music. It was natural that I should want to do it, too. I thought other kids were mad, kicking footballs or catching waves when they could be playing rock. Loud rock.

There's another thing about playing a guitar. It's to do with girls. They'd never been that interested in me. Not until we formed a band at school and played at a couple of socials. Then suddenly I was Brad Pitt. It was amazing. Girls would whisper when I walked past, there'd be all sorts of notes left on my desk, and Mandy McCarthy, the spunkiest girl in the school, asked me to go out with her. She dropped the captain of the football team to go out with me.

Not so long ago things were looking good as far as Morry was concerned. The latest band was tight. Morry was on vocals, I was lead guitar. The bass player hated Country music, the drummer was a Christian – he didn't even drink, so no chance of him

OD'ing. Morry had been on the phone non-stop for a week. To be honest, I think people were a bit fed up with him, all those producers and record-company types. They liked him, everybody liked Morry, but they probably thought like I did – the hair (or lack thereof), the Led Zep thing – this bloke wasn't going to make it big again. But somehow he managed to con them. We had studio time booked. We were going to cut a single. This was it. Morry had used up his favours a long time ago and if we blew this, there'd be no next time.

Then it all changed. Just like that. It wasn't the bass player. It wasn't the drummer. It was me – Robert James John Paul Morrison.

I was home by myself, playing around with the radio, trying to find something I liked. Usually I only bothered with the pre-programmed stations, the rock stations. But that day, for some reason, I started hitting the search button, seeing what it came up with. The radio locked into a strong signal. It was a classical station, I knew that, though all I knew about classical was that Morry hated it more than anything else, even more than rap, and that the kids who did it at school were all dorks.

I was just about to hit search again, but I stopped. I don't know why, but I did. I stopped, I sat down and I closed my eyes. The music didn't really sound like anything at first but after a while I started to hear things in it.

Bang! The door slammed, Morry and Cass were back.

'Wake up, Robby,' said Morry, changing the station, 'that nonsense would send anybody to sleep.'

I wasn't asleep. I wasn't really awake, either. I was somewhere else.

Morry picked up a mike, and threw me my guitar.

'Come on, Robby,' he said, 'lets practise the opening again.'

I thought that was the end of it, that it was just one of those strange little things that happens to you every so often. But that night, as I lay in bed, the classical music started playing again. The next day it happened, too. All I had to do was close my eyes and it began. I tried ignoring it. That didn't work. I tried to blast it out by playing 'Black Dog' at full volume. That didn't work. I tried not to like it. That didn't work, either. I did like it. I liked it a lot.

After that, when Morry and Cass were away, I'd tune into that station. Later I bought a little radio with earphones. I was listening to classical all the time now – on the school bus, during lunchtime, in bed at night.

What was happening? It had once seemed so straightforward. I loved Led Zep, I loved hard rock, I played electric guitar. I was good at it, it's what I'd do with my life. Now it wasn't so straightforward. For a start I was addicted to classical music. Worse than that – I wanted to play it as well. A musician can't just listen. Sure, Mozart didn't write a lot for the Telecaster, but I decided to learn another instrument, to ask somebody to help me.

The music teacher at school was always telling me not to play so loudly, but she was friendly enough. I asked her if she could teach me some classical on the piano. At first she thought I was joking, I was the school guitar hero after all, but then I started mentioning names – composers and pieces I liked. She was impressed. We arranged to have a lesson the next day. After that, it just happened.

At first I kept it secret from Cass and Morry. I was still playing in the band – not very well though. Try playing hard rock when your head's full of Beethoven. Then one morning Cass found my Chopin scores in my school bag. And didn't it hit the fan then!

'What's this?' said Morry, throwing the papers on the table. 'What the hell is this?' He didn't even give me a chance to answer.

'I'll tell you what this is. This is music written by old farts who died hundreds of years ago. This is music played by bloody robots. Old farts' music played by bloody robots. That's what this is.'

I explained the whole thing to him. How I felt destined to play this music. How my teacher said I had a 'natural aptitude', that maybe I could get a scholarship to attend the Conservatorium if I studied hard.

'Robby,' he said after I'd finished. 'Jazz or pop or techno or hip-hop or even rap I could understand, but classical? It's just not right, Robby. Bad karma. Bad karma.'

He walked out the door, still muttering, 'Bad karma. Bad karma.'

I suppose he's more or less accepted it now, weeks later, though things between us aren't great. Not like they were. We used to be more like mates than father and son. Probably because we played in the same band. It's hard to think of somebody as your dad when he's in the middle of a stage, legs wide apart, screaming into a mike about making mamas sweat and groove.

I had to stop playing in the band. He didn't say anything, not even 'Bad karma'. I knew he was cut up though. He cancelled the studio booking. I stopped playing in the school band, too. Mandy McCarthy, the spunkiest girl in the school, left a note on my desk – 'You're dropped, dork'.

Next week I'm going to play, all by myself, in front of the whole school, parents as well. Apparently somebody from the Conservatorium is coming. Cass says she'll be there. Dad doesn't think he can make it, he's got a really important gig with his new band. In some scungy pub out in the sticks, of course. Somebody from the record company might be turning up.

On the night of the performance my music teacher picks me up. I'm nervous as hell. I never felt like this playing in Dad's band.

'I can't go on,' I tell the teacher.

'Yes you can, Robby,' she says.

'No I can't. Morry's right — it's old farts' music played by robots.'

'What on earth are you talking about, Robby?' she says, and as my name is announced she gives me an enormous shove and I stumble onto the stage.

When I see the piano I feel okay again. I sit down on the stool and steal a quick glance at the audience. I can't see Cass, but it's hard to see anybody with the spotlights glaring in my eyes.

It doesn't go too badly, I only make a couple of mistakes and they're not really big ones. The audience is really clapping a lot. Maybe there's something else happening, like once when we played in a pub the audience was going wild and I thought, wow, they really like us, but it was the stripper on the bar they were cheering. (Dad made me look the other way.) There's no stripper here though, it's me they're applauding. Then I hear it, no mistaking it — it's Dad's whistle. I see him now, about halfway back, standing up. He's wearing his rock-star wrap-around shades, his best T-shirt and black jeans. He's stomping on the wooden floorboards with his cowboy boots. My mum's next to him, in a pink mini-skirt and shiny top. They're both clapping and yelling, 'More, more, *more!*' just like you do at rock concerts. I can't believe it. Of course all the kids start doing it too — stomping, clapping, yelling. Then the parents start as well, even these really straight people, stomping on the floor and yelling, 'More, more, *more*!' The noise is incredible. I play another piece. They all go crazy again. I play something else. More craziness. But that's it then, because I don't know anything else.

Mum and Dad come backstage.

'Great gig,' says Dad, slapping me on the back, 'For a robot.'

Mum plants a big kiss on my cheek. Then they go, because Dad still has to play and the pub is miles away. I have to hang around, to talk to the person from the Conservatorium.

I spend ages talking to him. He's pretty posh, but he's really friendly. He even knows who Led Zep are. He practically gives me the scholarship there and then.

I go out celebrating with my mates and by the time I get home Mum and Dad are already in bed. I walk over to Dad's amp, crank it right up. Then I strap his Telecaster on and start playing 'Stairway to Heaven'. It sounds loud, wild, out of control. The walls are shaking.

'What the . . .' Morry yells from the bedroom. Then he comes out in his pyjamas. The ones Mum made for him, with the little guitars all over them. He picks up a mike, cradles it in his hands, throws back his head just like Robert Plant (except the hair doesn't get in his eyes) and starts singing.

By this time Mum's out of bed, too. She's doing her spaced-out hippy dance, the one she always does to 'Stairway'.

Tell you one thing, I sure wouldn't want to be our neighbours.

Boo
Susanne Gervay

I'm thirteen and I want my name back.

Everyone is used to calling me Freddie. It's hard for people to change a habit. Boo runs into my arms and calls me Freya. No one notices because he's too little and they think he doesn't know how to say Freddie.

Boo looks cute with his red bow tie and navy jacket. He's dressed for his birthday party. Boo helped me decorate his train cake, although he ate as many of the chocolate buttons as he put on the icing.

My older brother Noah ran around the backyard with him on his shoulders as Boo tooted a train horn. We didn't have a birthday party for Boo when he was one. We didn't have a birthday party when he was two. But Boo is three now.

Mum's eyes shimmer with tears. 'It's time for a birthday party for Boo.'

Boo's sturdy build and strong legs make him look like a great bear when he runs. His dark brown eyes are always smiling and his three-year-old arms are like chubby chocolate. Fat, creamy brown, and delicious. I know that they are delicious because Mum always kisses them. Once, when Boo was sitting on her lap, I saw her gently bite his chocolate arms. My arms are white, with horrible scabby blobs on my elbows from when I fell off the swing. That really hurt. Noah was pushing the swing as high as he could and I was screaming for him to stop. But no. He just pushed higher and higher. 'Freddie fly, Freddie fly.'

Boo saved me. He kicked Noah so hard that he had to stop. But I still fell off. Right into the dirt. There was blood etched on my funny bone. Blood and dirt. I hate Noah sometimes. He said he was sorry, but he still flicks me under the table at dinner, saying under his breath, 'Freddie, Freddie Krueger.' He thinks it's funny.

I never cry in front of Noah, but I pinch him hard under the table. He just laughs and rubs his leg. It'd upset Mum if I complained. I haven't complained about anything for three years. Noah doesn't complain either.

Mum always has afternoon tea ready for us after school, even when she's tired from work. She helps Noah and me with our homework, reads books to Boo and tries to be happy. She is happy sometimes, but at night I hear her cry in her bedroom. I cry too. Noah doesn't cry. Boo sleeps quietly in his bed nestled in the corner of my bedroom.

Mum is going out with a man. She was nervous when she brought him home for dinner. 'He's not replacing your father,' she whispered anxiously. 'No one can.' He brought Mum daffodils and sweet plums for us to share. Daffodils are Mum's favourite flowers. How did he know that? How did he know that we like sweet plums? I didn't like him. Noah didn't like him. When the teacher phoned, Noah let him hang on the other end of the line for ages before he called Mum. The teacher said we could call him Jim. Boo held his hand.

He works with Mum at school. He teaches science. Mum teaches history. It's the first time she's dated in three years.

I remember that day in the hospice. I trusted that Dad would never die because he was my father and fathers don't die. His head was shaven so you could see the crooked cut across his skull. That's where they'd cut into his brain and made him into a different person. His brown eyes were too dark. I didn't want to look at them because I could see he was afraid. He didn't know where he was. He didn't know who I was. 'It's me, Daddy. It's me.'

I ran as fast as I could out of that ward, down the pathway, running, panting until I was gasping and sobbing, until I crashed into a huge old tree. I hung on, pressing my face against the rough bark. Mum was panting after me with her yellow daffodil dress flapping. She put her arms around me. They were cold. 'Daddy loves you, Freddie. Don't cry, Freddie. Don't cry.'

Daddy died that night.

Boo was born six months afterwards. Noah and I waited at home until Mum arrived with him from the hospital. She said he was born with his lips puckered in surprise, gurgling, 'Boo'.

I love the name Boo. It means precious. I hate the name Freddie, my baby nickname. But Mum can't call me anything else now. And I can't tell her not to. My real name is Freya. Mum and Dad told me that they called me Freya because when I was born I was beautiful and they fell in love with me. Freya is the goddess of love and beauty.

Dad had always been sturdy and strong, fixing everything in the house. He made me a wooden bowl to keep my necklaces and bangles in. My brother fixes everything in the house now, but he's never made me anything. Mum and Dad named my brother Noah because his birth was long and difficult – 'like weathering a storm' – but in the end it was safe, a resting place. Dad and Noah were great mates. They'd been working for months on their camping trip. Mum teased them that they were a double take of Indiana Jones. They had organised their two-man tent, sleeping bags, compasses and all the supplies they needed for a one-month trek into the mountains. They'd worked out depot spots to collect new supplies.

That was before. Afterwards, Noah sold all the camping gear. He doesn't talk about Dad much. Neither do I.

Now Noah hangs out with other sixteen-year-olds at the beach, checking out girls and watching the surf.

It's the Easter holidays and there's no school today. Mum's organised a picnic on the hill overlooking the beach. I don't go to the beach much anymore, but Mum wants me there. Noah's brought his board, so he can join his mates in the surf afterwards. Jim's carrying the rugs, the football and the picnic basket. Mum's wearing her yellow dress. My stomach twists. She's hasn't worn it since that day in the hospice.

Boo and I are running up the hill when we see tiny blue flowers hidden in the grass. Their yellow centres sparkle like golden treasure. We peer over the flowers and pick the forget-me-nots. I put them in my bag, then tickle Boo's tummy and he giggles. He puts his baby soft arms around me and I hold him so long that he starts to squirm away.

Noah checks out the surf, grunts at Jim. Mum's eyes cloud over. She wants us to like him. I say hello. Noah grabs the football and throws it to Boo who runs after it with his strong brown legs. I run, too, with my pasty white legs. Jim joins in and so does Mum. Her daffodil dress flutters in the wind and we're chasing the ball in the long green grass under the yellow sun.

Boo tumbles and cries and Jim races to pick him up. 'You're safe,' he says quietly. Tears come to my eyes. I brush them away.

The picnic rug overflows with food – roast chicken, potato salad, tomatoes and olives, bananas and blueberries. Mum's made my favourite strawberry sponge cake. It's a feast and we all eat too much. I lie on my back with the sun warming me and I can feel the rays colouring the tops of my legs.

Jim tells us about camping.

'My dad liked camping in the mountains,' I tell him.

Noah waits to see his response.

'I like the mountains, but I prefer the coast. The waves crashing on the sand, stars at night, sleeping in a tent, boiling water for billy tea, watching the wildlife at dusk. Do you like the coast, Noah?'

I see Noah struggle. He then nods. 'I like the ocean as well.'

I stare at my blotchy legs. Boo wants to go home.

Jim takes Mum out for dinner. He comes over to help Noah repair the ding in his surfboard.

'Do you like Jim?' Mum asks us.

I miss Dad, that's all. I want him back.

Boo sneaks into my bed. I put my arms around him. He looks up at me with his dark brown eyes. I gasp. I'd never seen it before. His eyes. Suddenly, I feel the rough tree bark under my face and hear my mother's heartbeat.

I play with the dried petals of the forget-me-nots in the wooden bowl next to my bed.

'Boo,' I whisper. 'Precious,' I whisper.

'Freya.' He puts his hand into mine. Suddenly I feel my father's hand. I feel him here with me.

I am going to ask my mother and my brother to call me Freya.

I want to be Freya.

My Pop
Jen Storer

If my family were dogs, Mum would be a greyhound. Not one of those sad, dumb, muscle-brains that chase a lure round a racetrack. No, she would be a graceful, leggy Royal Companion like the ones in medieval tapestries. Dad would be a scruffy mongrel of unknown origins (like Scuppers the Sailor Dog – that loveable mutt in the Little Golden Book). My little brother would be a pug because he's annoying and snot-nosed. And my big sister, well, she wouldn't be a dog, would she? She'd flatly refuse. She'd be a cat, a ridiculous puffball Persian the colour of pink champagne, with a sulky pushed-in face and a bad temper.

That leaves Pop. Pop would be a Labrador. A lazy, loveable golden lab who sleeps in the sun all day long and only gets up to eat and to chase the odd pigeon.

Pop used to live in a bungalow at the back of our house. He called it 'The Doghouse'. When Pop's wife died, Pop built the bungalow and then he gave the house to us. He never came into the main house again. Pop said he hoped we would be kind to the old house – and please could we paint it.

Pop also said that everyone should live in walking distance of a train and a butcher's shop. When I told Pop I was a vegetarian he frowned. Then he said, 'It'll pass.'

When I first brought Tiggy home Pop shook his head and said, 'Fancy keeping vermin for a pet.'

And I said, 'Every girl in my class has a pet rabbit, Pop.'

And Pop said, 'Do those girls know how to skin a rabbit?'

And I said, 'That's disgusting! You would never eat Tiggy . . . would you?'

And Pop said, 'Course I'd eat Tiggy. Just because it's got a fancy name doesn't mean it doesn't belong in a stew.'

Pop once told me that if it hadn't been for rabbits him and his brothers would have starved. He also told me that his family ate a lot of mushrooms, which they found in farm paddocks and around tree stumps.

One time his big sister picked the wrong mushrooms and everyone in the entire family went 'up the pole'. Pop said he saw terrible things during the war, but none so terrible as when he ate the poisonous mushrooms. (He swore he saw an axe-wielding gumtree striding across the backyard that night, and a headless cattle dog barking at the moon. He said you've never heard anything so frightening as the bark of a headless dog.)

Pop's little brother was the only one who didn't eat the mushrooms that night, and he had to drag the entire family (every one of them quivering and spewing and hallucinating) onto the back of the flatbed truck and drive them into town to see the doctor. Pop's little brother was eleven at the time.

Pop's bungalow had coloured light bulbs strung across the front. He turned them on at eight o'clock every night – so pretty on these dark winter nights – yellow, red, orange and blue, and every night he turned them off at eleven. That's how Mum knew something was wrong. When she got up at three o'clock the other morning, Pop's coloured lights were still shining.

Mum went down the garden path to check on Pop. She found him in his recliner with his feet up and his Western comic spread across his chest. The telly was on, but the sound was turned down. Pop never had the sound on. He said people on the idiot box are not worth listening to – which is why all TVs come with a mute button.

Mum shook Pop's shoulder but she knew he wasn't going to wake up. She knew Pop was dead.

Pop did not look scary or sad when he was dead; he just looked peaceful. The only difference was he looked a bit pale. Although somehow he looked smaller, too, which was odd. But maybe we have a spirit and when it leaves we shrink a bit. I don't know.

When we packed up Pop's bungalow we found all

sorts of stuff that we didn't know Pop had. There were finger paintings that us kids did in prep, and Christmas decorations we made in creche from wooden clothes pegs and green and gold ribbon. There was a plastic folder stuffed with magazine clippings of Princess Diana, and Masterfoods spices in glass jars with 1998 use-by dates.

There was also a small black-and-white photo of a handsome young boy in an army uniform. The boy's hair was blond and curly. Mum said, 'That was Pop when he was a teenager.' I had to look closely and use my imagination. I never knew that Pop had hair. I never knew he was a teenager, either. Somehow I always thought he was, well, you know, *Pop*.

They are coming to pull the bungalow down next week. It's okay, though. Pop always said, 'Get rid of The Doghouse when I'm gone. Plant yourselves a decent veggie patch.'

So that's what we're going to do. We're going to grow vegetables . . . and herbs . . . and a few flowers. But we will never, ever grow mushrooms.

The coloured lights are on our front verandah now. Every night at eight o'clock I turn them on – so pretty on these dark winter nights. I always look at the sky and wonder about Pop. Can he see the coloured lights from where he is? Does he know how much we miss him?

At eleven o'clock Dad turns the lights off.

But I'm asleep by then.

Tag

Hazel Edwards

'Is it a virtual-tag or a tattoo?'

I shrugged. 'Whatever.'

I never expected to end up in the International Rights Court in front of a judge and jury.

We don't even speak the same language. They were arguing about my chest art and who owned which words.

The interpreter shuffled some papers, then began to read:

'You are charged with being a Virtual Vandal. The band Hip-hop claims this song belongs to them. They own the rights. You had the lyrics tattooed on your chest. Every time someone looks at your chest and reads those words, you must pay a royalty fee to Hip-hop. You have outstanding debts of 2,371,977 dollars in your currency owing now. How do you plead?'

'Guilty.'

'Anything to add?' asked the judge.

'It was on my body. I'm the legal canvas.'

The courtroom was warm with afternoon light. Sunlight glinted on the designer watch worn by one of the jury members. Was that real or a copy watch?

'You copied lyrics illegally.' The judge looked at my face, not my chest. 'And then others copied you.'

'I was a fan, then.'

How could this dare get so out of control? It happened ages ago. Worst decision I ever made. It's ruined my social life. I can't get rid of the tatts. Can't afford the skin grafts. And girls won't come near me! I have massive debts. Please don't look at me!

I need to go back to the beginning. To my suburban high school, Greysville. I'll never forget Leb the 'Boss Kid' who tagged his territory. And the arrival of Picasso, the awesome art teacher.

Our school was one of those grey places. A bit run-down. Weeds. Peeling window frames. As if no one wanted to stay long enough to fix anything. Principals changed each term. In the streets nearby, any abandoned house was graffiti-covered within days of the tenants leaving.

Leb's gang would tag any walls or even bumpy fences to mark their territory. Sometimes the estate agents would repaint fast if they had tenants coming. They tried dark blue and Leb used white spray. They tried light paint and he used dark spray to tag. But after a while, they gave up.

Greysville became Graffiti-ville. But tags weren't the only kinds of branding.

Tatts were skin graffiti, a different kind of tag. Leb had a few.

In between school races at the pool, I was trying to work out a row of Roman numerals just above the back of Leb's bathers. His swimsuit featured school colours because the squad had to wear them.

Leb noticed me staring.

'Like my tatts?'

'Er . . . what are they for?'

'My year of birth. In Roman numerals MCM.'

'Can't you remember how old you are?' His eyes narrowed and I quickly added, 'Hey, we're on. Let's go.'

Leb couldn't see those numbers, even doing a back flip. Unless he looked at himself in a double mirror, and then they'd be back to front. Or would they?

We won the relay, due to Leb. He was a splashy swimmer, but fast.

Then Picasso arrived as a relief teacher. That wasn't his real name. Picasso was what we called him. He was small, round, and loved fine art. In our school, that was a first.

'Graffiti is like a tattoo for a building, but the owner and the wall have no say in it,' said Picasso. 'Graffiti was in Ancient Rome and Greece, too.'

'Awesome,' said Leb. 'I'm part of history.'

'They were Vandals,' said Picasso. 'They destroyed cities like Rome. That's where the name vandal comes from.'

'I knew that,' said Leb, who didn't.

Picasso suggested we Google graffiti. He wrote the spelling for us.

'If you're going to be a street artist, let's go for quality. Write something others will notice, something that matters. A tag is a keyword for information. Like a meta-tag.'

'A tag?' Leb thought he was the expert.

'You should specialise.'

'Duh?'

'Saw your tag on the railway fences.'

Leb smiled. 'Yeah, I'm a bit of a celeb.'

'Celeb scribbler.'

'Scribbler?'

'Just like pre-schooler scribble. No message for change.'

'Don't do politics,' said Leb. 'Nothing to say.'

Picasso smiled. 'You're wrong there. Paint something others will think about. Try a mural.'

'A what?'

'A story in pictures on buildings. And on roofs. Tourists still pay a fortune to visit some famous murals.'

Leb Googled **murals +tourists +visit**.

Later, supervising our swimming squad, Picasso noticed Leb's tatt.

'MCM means nineteen hundred. When were you born, Leb?'

'Two thousand.'

'That's MM. You're a century out.'

'Short-term memory, Leb?' someone called.

But street-smart Leb said quickly, 'That 'C' stands for my dog's name.'

'Lucky the tatts aren't on your elbow. No one can lick their own elbow,' joked Picasso.

We tried. He was right. It was the quirky stuff that Picasso knew that got us interested. Took us on a virtual tour of these old galleries online. Leb was keen on the 'Loo', as he called the Louvre, the famous place in France.

'Tatts are your choice at the time. They're permanent. Later you may regret them. Temporary graffiti is on walls owned by others. They have no choice. The third option is quality work on a legal canvas.'

Picasso got us painting murals on the sports store walls. We did space footy figures, and cyber-scooters and stuff.

'Mural is history in paint,' he said.

The store became our legal canvas. We put up cool designs with bright reds and yellows and lots of black.

I was a fan of Hip-hop's lyrics. So I drew them, too, to music.

'We're going into the adoption business,' Picasso said as he unpacked boxes of art supplies.

'What's that?'

Picasso suggested each of us 'adopt' a local wall or even a street to repaint immediately after tags were sprayed on them.

He looked directly at Leb when he said that. 'Choose.'

Picasso held up spray cans and brushes. 'Practise.'

'What do you mean?'

Then Picasso told us about Intergalactic Central. 'This Exhibition requires artists to submit under their real names. Not just a tag. Or you can Photoshop graffiti online, instead of just photographing street art for an entry.'

'Why do that?' asked Leb.

'So your parents can see your work exhibited internationally.'

'I'll think about it,' said Leb. 'My mum might come.'

I never remember whether there are two f's or two t's in graffiti. Leb used spell check for his entry. And he always wore a belt now, to cover his Roman numerals.

I started thinking about another legal canvas, once I was old enough. As a fan, I could advertise for them, like a T-shirt.

'Lyrics belong to the creator who wrote the song, not to you,' warned Picasso.

After the exhibition, Leb's graffiti wallpaper designs sold online, and 'Sew Trendy' was a sell-out in temporary tattoo lip stickers.

Leb dared me. 'You say words matter, Wimp. I dare you to get Hip-hop's lyrics on your chest. Skin words are better than wearing a fan T-shirt.'

Leb was wrong about that. Tatts are forever.

Images of my chest art went on viral-cam. Someone uploaded pics of my tatts online and the pictures went viral. And then along came the copyright issue. Hip-hop owns those words in that sequence.

Now I have to pay every time someone looks at my chest, anywhere in the world.

I've been sentenced to wear skivvies for life.

Red Rhino

Mo Johnson

It crouched scarlet and shiny on top of the slope that led downhill to the paddock. Its front was rounded and bug-eyed, like a massive lady beetle, but its sleek jutting bits made it look squat and fierce. A rhino. A red rhino at rest.

Of course I didn't notice any of this. Pip did. He said every word out loud to Mum as we sprawled on the day bed on the back deck, like sleepy cats. The midday sun was too hot for the real sleepy cats. They'd disappeared ages ago.

'They're going to dream about milk pools in the cool part of the house,' Pip commented as we watched them slink away.

'There is no cool part,' I grumbled.

He screwed up his nose and his big ears wiggled. He looked like the gingerbread goblin from one of the books he loves reading.

'It's cool in the fridge,' he said. Mum snorted. I closed my eyes and began to count to ten. It was something I did a lot now.

When I opened them, he was still sitting in his favourite spot at the edge of the deck, his long pins swinging to and fro, intent on things that only he seemed to see.

Mum gave me a smile.

'Shall we tell Dad about the Red Rhino, Pip?' I said, brightly.

'Dad won't get it. He's not very good at describing stuff.' Pip's look was scornful. 'I mean, the last mower didn't look a bit like a lemon to me. It wasn't even yellow.'

Mum laughed and this time I joined in.

Suddenly Pip fixed his eyes on Mum's teacup.

'Why do people drink hot stuff on boiling days?' he asked, still staring. I made a face at Mum. This one was all hers.

Before she could answer, a shuddering rumble cut through the air. The whole house shook. I jumped up so fast I almost knocked Mum's cup out of her hand.

'He's started! He's started!' Pip yelled above the roar and pointed excitedly across the lawn. 'Quick! Come and see,' he insisted and hauled himself to his feet.

A few metres beyond the deck, Dad sat astride the Red Rhino. He was dressed in the clothes that Mum made him wear in the garden. His gardening pants – torn blue denims – a T-shirt that might have been white once, a hat with a mullet like the ones kindy kids wear, and his stinky, brown work boots.

Dad snapped on his earmuffs and positioned his

goggles. Mum had no control over those. He kept them meticulously clean, swaddled in soft cloth, in their boxes in his neat shed. They made him look like a model, sort of . . . like the kind of dads you see in hardware-store catalogues. I said so. Pip looked puzzled. 'But he's not in a catalogue, he's right there.' He pointed.

'You're right, Pip,' Mum reassured him.

Maybe I should write a rulebook for Pip and me. I don't know what the rules are for us lately, but I always feel like I've broken them anyway.

Pip's not good with rules either unless they're painted on clowns as questions, like in the fun park near Grandma's house.

Are you as tall as me?

He was thrilled to find that he was tall enough three summers ago. He squealed with delight and tried to hug the wooden dodgem clown. But he didn't go on the ride. He always shied back at the last moment and refused to get in the car with Dad.

It was different this summer. We went to the park without our parents. I was in charge. I took him to the dodgems and ordered him into a car.

'Noooh, Sara,' he shouted, stamping his foot.

'Don't be a baby, Pip.'

'I don't want to.' His eyes were wide, his eyelids blinked rapidly.

'Baby, Baby, Baby,' I taunted.

Finally he allowed me to push him into a car.

The music thumped, the ride started and I was exhilarated.

It took me ages to notice Pip was holed up in the far corner of the rink, unmoving. Petrified. I looked over at the ride supervisors. They were in confab. I put my foot down and crashed into two cars at once, trying to make the most of those last precious seconds. As expected, the power to all cars was cut abruptly and Pip was surrounded by concerned staff. Eventually I broke my way through the gawping circle. Pip was making the little mewing sounds he resorts to when he's super-stressed. His fluttering eyes landed on me and focused. He held out a large trembling hand. I snatched it and we were out of there fast as.

'Can we go on the little cars?' he asked, the minute we put space between the dodgems and us.

'No. We're going back to Grandma's,' I snapped.

'Please, Sara.'

I didn't answer and half dragged him out of the park. Good job I didn't have to take him with me in the evenings when all my mates were there. At one point he stumbled over his own boat feet and clutched at my elbow.

'You're walking really fast, Sara,' he panted.

I looked up into his eyes and saw bewilderment and fear. I felt sick. 'Grandma's got ice-cream,' I said.

'Really? Will she give me some?'

'Definitely,' I said.

He beamed, rides forgotten.

I wish I could forget stuff as easily as that. If I could, I'd never remember the dodgems day again.

'Is the Rhino different from the lemon?' Pip asked Mum. 'I was never allowed on the lemon.' He mimicked Dad's cross voice so perfectly that Mum and I doubled up.

'You're not old enough, Pip.'

'You're not coordinated enough, Pip.'

'You're too tired, son.'

'I'm just finishing up, son.'

'Your mum needs your help with something.'

'Stop it, Pip,' Mum snorted, fanning her face with her hands.

He giggled.

'Do the Tupperware story, Pip,' I urged him.

'What Tupperware story?' Mum asked.

Pip grinned at me. He began to mime a perfect picture of Dad opening an overhead cupboard and being attacked by falling plastic – a weekly occurrence in our house.

'What the hell is going on with these containers?' Pip roared and I swear Dad's voice was coming out of his mouth.

'Stop buying the stuff then. There's nothing wrong with Glad Wrap and a bowl.' He'd switched to the best version of Mum.

'It messes up my stacking system in the fridge.' Now he was Dad again.

Tears were running down my face. 'Good tears,' I said, hurriedly, and Pip's frown disappeared.

'I like it when you laugh, Sara,' he said.

'You two,' said Mum, trying to sound insulted but failing.

'Look,' said Pip. 'The Red Rhino knows how Dad mows the lawn.' He pointed and I followed the line of his finger. Dad and Rhino were making giant figure eights in the paddock.

'Dad is Red's master and Red loves him,' Pip informed us. 'Not like the lemon. The lemon always back-chatted, even if Dad said nice things to him. The lemon was lazy.'

'He sure was,' said Mum, as Dad and Red flew down the left side of the field, curved wide around the black rock, and charged back up the hill in seconds. Every time they got to the top, Dad gave us a salute.

'We are the kings and queens of the land. They're mowing the lawn for us,' Pip yelled.

When Dad next came up the hill, he pulled Red to a stop and climbed off, wiping the grass from his pants. He stomped up onto the deck.

'Drink, mate,' he said and Pip lumbered off.

My parents perched side by side on the edge of the deck, their legs swinging with mine.

'You should give him a go,' Mum said.

'It's too powerful for him,' Dad argued.

'Then walk beside him. It's got a safety cut-out, hasn't it?' Mum asked.

'He won't be able to mow in straight lines,' Dad said and Mum sighed.

'I will, I will,' Pip cried, sluicing the wooden floor with Coke as he rushed over. 'Please give me a go on Red Rhino, Dad,' he pleaded.

Dad looked at us. 'Who?'

'The mower looks like a rhino,' Mum explained.

Dad looked at me.

'And it's red,' I added.

Dad shrugged and took out his hanky to mop up the drips of Coke. Finally he said, 'Right, Pip, you can have a ride, but you have to really listen and concentrate.'

Pip whooped in agreement and tumbled off our deck, but he still managed to land on his feet.

'No superheroes, kings, knights or alien nonsense,' Dad said.

Pip agreed.

'No looking at clouds and insects. You've got to keep your eyes up front.'

Pip agreed, jumping up and down on the spot.

'And mow in a straight line, son,' Dad added, beckoning him to climb aboard. Pip's last response was smothered by a gulp of excited air. He bounced on the seat and placed his massive hands on the thick, black steering wheel. When Dad turned the key, Red rumbled and Pip yelled, 'Sara, it's like a space rocket going . . .'

'Pip, concentrate,' Dad snapped.

'I am,' he shouted.

'These are the blades so you switch this down to lower them and up when you stop. If in doubt, hit this. It's the engine safety switch.'

Pip nodded.

'Hang on,' Dad said, stooping to pick up a large branch that had fallen from a nearby tree. 'I'm going to walk with you. Always keep your left front tyre on the line that I've already cut.' He pulled Pip's goggles into place, plopped the earmuffs over his ears and eased off the handbrake.

'We're moving! Red is mine now,' Pip squealed.

Dad ran ahead and snatched up some more branches.

'Throw down your lances!' Pip screamed.

'Oh, no,' Mum whispered.

Dad's head whipped around. 'What? Slow down, Philip!' he yelled. His lips were moving, but I expect Pip couldn't hear through the earmuffs. Dad was waving his hands. Pip eventually slid the earmuffs down round his neck.

'Concentrate! Straight line! Straight line,' Dad screamed. 'Where's your left wheel?'

Pip looked. His left wheel was creeping away from Dad's next line, taking Pip and Red with it. He tugged on the steering like one of those actors in a movie car chase.

'No!' Dad's hands sliced the air, doing karate

chops round his head. 'Straight!'

Mum clutched my arm.

I sucked on my cheek. It was pretty hard to know what straight Dad wanted from Pip with those jelly arms waving. Good job he wasn't a traffic cop, or a guy who brings in planes.

'Pip!'

Pip adjusted the wheels again, quite quickly I thought, and headed back up the slope. I didn't dare look at Dad, but at least he'd stopped yelling. Mum loosened her grip and the blood ran back into my hand.

A breeze picked up and the smell of mown grass tickled my nostrils. Halfway up the hill a flurry of small white butterflies flittered from the lawn, cutting each other off in their hurry to get airborne. Did they enjoy it when the lawn was mown? Was it like a council clean-up for their houses, or did it leave them homeless? I lifted my eyes as they clouded above Pip's head. Beside me Mum was waving hard and smiling. Her blonde hair crinkled around her head like a monster sunflower. It always went curly on humid days like this.

Pip pushed down hard on Red's pedal, picking up speed. His back was ramrod straight and somehow he'd now acquired a long stick.

'Take me to the queens, Red!' he cried, flourishing the branch. There was a shout behind him. He didn't seem to hear. His face was radiant. It was impossible for his smile to get any wider as he tore up the hill towards us. I held my breath, but Mum was cheering.

'Come on, Sir Pip,' she cried.

When he reached the top he took his foot off the pedal, lifted the blades, then switched off the engine just like Dad had told him. I let out a long hiss of air. Mum didn't seem to notice.

'Did you see me?' he asked excitedly, leaping off Red.

'Of course. Come up here and look at what you did,' Mum said.

Dad came jogging, pink-faced, to meet us.

'Didn't you hear me shouting, Pip? You were going too fast,' he panted, and then he looked anxiously at Red. He seemed a little disconcerted on seeing his precious mower still in one shiny piece. Recovering himself, Dad joined us on the deck to observe Pip's work: a massive shape, carved into the paddock.

'It's like Zorro's sword,' Pip murmured. 'It's amazing.'

'Pip,' Dad began.

'That's the straightest Z I've ever seen,' Mum interrupted.

'I'll do your initials next time, Sara, and they'll be straight, too,' Pip promised me eagerly.

Dad ruffled my big brother's hair and gave me a wink.

Below us, Red Rhino creaked, content with a job well done.

Why Me?
Susan Halliday & Phil Kettle

Monday: 3.35pm

Cam: Why me?

What did I do that caused Cranny to spin out and slap me with a detention?

Maz: Oh come on, it's got to be obvious, even to a brain dead loser like you. Surely?

Cam: Brain dead? Loser? Me a loser?

Well, I suppose you're right, if being a loser means being stuck here with you doing detention. I should be out doing something constructive with my friends.

Maz: Constructive? Other than stuffing your face with canteen food that's half price because no one else wants it, you've never done anything constructive in your entire life!

Don't you mean off doing something DE-STRUCTIVE with your friends; assuming that you know the difference!

Cam: Might I remind you that my friends are far better friends than those *precious little princesses* that you hang with.

Maz: At least my friends don't walk around burping, picking and flicking.

Cam: Nope! Your friends don't walk around at all. They're too busy in the toilet block checking out their new boobs and bleached hair in the mirrors.

Maz: As if!

You know, one way or another, I'll get you back for this. After all, it's your fault that I'm here doing friggin' detention.

Cam: It's not my fault!

Maz: Oh come on. Did you *really think* that Ms Cranny wouldn't work it out, or was it that you just didn't *think*?

Cam: Well, she's not that bright. She's just a history teacher who catches a bus to school.

Maz: Trust me – it's not Ms Cranny that's suffering from *not that bright* syndrome!

Now why don't you do something constructive seeing that you're here, and stop bugging me? Give your mouth a rest, your brain a workout, and say *heelllooo* to your science homework!

Cam: Started yours yet? So what's the answer to the first question?

Maz: Like I'm going to tell you! I've got an idea – how about you let me finish it, then I'll leave it on the table so that you can copy it. Sound familiar?

Cam: Build a bridge and get over it. I didn't copy

your history homework. It was just sitting there on the table so I had a quick look.

Maz: Jeez, Cam. I can't believe you copied my answers.

Cam: Look, I was doing you a favour – I was just checking to make sure that you had the same answers as me. You know what I mean? The correct answers!

Maz: Yeah right! I bet you didn't even read the questions. You just came to school, handed your stuff to Ms Cranny and pretended that my answers were yours.

Cam: Okay. But I *am* really good at history.

Maz: So then, tell me who Tasmania was named after?

Cam: That's easy! Mr Tasmania of course!

Maz: Oh, *haa! Haa!* Yeah right, you know heaps about history. Cam, Tasmania was named after the Dutch explorer, Abel Tasman.

Cam: Well, for your information Abel Tasman changed his name by deed poll to Mr Tasmania. So there. Stick that in the rear end of your history book.

Maz: Good-o then! So what was Tasmania called before it was called Tasmania?

Cam: That's easy, too! It was called Tasmanian Tiger Land. And then when those tigers became extinct the only thing left to do was to call it boring old Tasmania.

Maz: Your history is *pathetic*. In fact you're pathetic. Not funny, pathetic! It was called Van Diemen's Land.

Cam: No way! How the crap did they get the word Tasmania from Van Diemen's Land?

Maz: Uugh! And what year did they change the name from Van Diemen's Land to Tasmania, *oh wise one?*

Cam: Who really cares? It was *sooo* long ago, even Cranny wasn't born. But what I do know is that it's really important to know about sporting history, like that Collingwood won the AFL Premiership in 2010.

Maz: And like you'd need to know that bit of useless information to blitz a history test! The year was 1856, Cam – it was renamed Tasmania in 1856!

I bet you didn't know any of the history homework answers, did you? You just helped yourself to mine; copying each and every one of them down, like the lazy little cheat that you are!

Cam: Maybe I did, maybe I didn't. Either way the history *I* know comes in pretty handy at our sports trivia nights, unlike the useless crap you know.

Maz: It might come as a shock to you – but sports trivia isn't going to help you pass the history exam at the end of the term – and nor am I!

Cam: Who cares? I'm only interested in what's happening today, not what happened a million years ago.

Maz: It was only 1856; you should be looking forward to failing maths, too!

Cam: Ahhh – whatever!

Maz: Well, so you're only interested in what's happening today, and what's happening today is that you've got a detention, and the reason that you've got a detention is that you don't know anything about history, and because of that you had to copy my history homework – so history is important today! Get it?

Cam: Enough already! You're driving me nuts! You're like a crazy dog with a bone!

Maz: I'm just making my point. And if I was a dog, and I had a bone, you'd be following me around to see where I buried it because you, the lazy little cheat that you are, would be too lazy to find your own bone.

Cam: Sure. That makes sense. Why would I bother trying to find my own bone when I could just as easily have yours, chew on it for a while, and then bury it back where I found it?

Maz: So, why would you bother finding your own history homework answers, when you could just as easily have mine? Sound familiar?

Cam: Oohhh, okay! So what do your reckon Miss Nook-n-Cranny is going to say when she gets back?

Maz: Time to find out, cause here she comes.

Ms Cranny: Ahhh – here we are. The class clown

and the bright girl who knows nothing – ironic isn't it?

Well, at least it's good to hear that the two of you are getting along – in fact everyone down the hallway can hear that you're getting along!

Now, hopefully you've spent the last thirty minutes wisely and have decided to explain how you ended up with exactly the same history homework answers. One hundred questions and one hundred identical answers!

Cam: (silence)

Maz: (silence)

Ms Cranny: I take it that you are not ready, or probably more to the point, simply not going to try and explain anything?

So Cam, who discovered Tasmania?

Cam: Dutch explorer, Abel Tasman, Miss.

Ms Cranny: All right then, Maz, what was Tasmania first called?

Maz: Van Diemen's Land.

Ms Cranny: And when was the name changed to Tasmania, Cam?

Cam: In 1856. And that was less than a million years ago. So when were you born, Miss?

Ms Cranny: I'm very suspicious about you two ending up with exactly the same answers and each scoring one hundred per cent. *I smell a rat.*

Cam: No Miss, that's not a rat, that's the canteen. Marge and Betty Large are cooking today's leftovers for tomorrow's lunch!

Maz: Oh please – like you're helping. Will you shut-up, Cam!

Ms Cranny: That's enough. Be warned, there will be letters going home to explain my concerns, detailing the reasons why you were given detention.

Cam: Great! But can you explain to me why I'm on detention first, Miss?

Ms Cranny: This detention was given to you, Cam, so that you had an opportunity to reflect on how it was that you achieved a one hundred per cent score for your history homework, when it is a subject that you pay zero per cent attention in.

And Maz, you're on detention because I believe you know the answer to the unanswered question – but you refuse to enlighten me.

You two have left me no alternative other than to find my own solution to the problem.

You both submitted history homework answering one hundred questions – so you both deserve a mark. You both achieved a one hundred per cent score for the same work – and by that I mean, homework that appears to belong to one person, despite the fact that it was presented by the two of you.

So to solve the problem I'll be dividing the one

hundred per cent by two, which leaves you each with a pass mark of fifty per cent.

Maz: That's *sooo* not fair!

Cam: Passing is better than failing!

Maz: I don't fail history!

Cam: Well, clearly, neither do I, because I just passed with fifty per cent!

Three hours later at the dinner table

Cam: Maz, *Maz*! Have you done your science homework yet?

Maz: Yep! And it's locked away in my desk drawer. Having to share my good looks with you is more than enough! So from here on, *my dear twin brother*, unless you're going to pay up, I'm not going to share my brains.

Cam: Okay then. Here's fifty per cent of my allowance. That should get me a pass for the science homework.

Maz: Fifty per cent of your allowance? I'll take that as payment for the fifty per cent you scored on last night's history homework.

As for your science homework, that'll cost you one hundred per cent of next week's allowance, and that'll get you fifty per cent of the answers.

Take it or leave it!

The Mysteries of Letterboxes
David Miller

On a country road intersection I pass from time to time there is a large collection of letterboxes. They start me thinking.

Why won't the postie go down the road?

Is it dangerous?

Does a monster live down there?

Is the postie very fussy about keeping his car clean and won't go down a dirt road?

Is it too far to the end?

Are the people who live down there horrible?

Do the letterboxes match the houses? Do the letterboxes match their owners?

What do the people who live down the road do? Are they friendly with each other? Do they play and work together? Or are they grumpy and keep to themselves?

What is in the letters that are in the boxes as I pass? Good news, like invitations to parties and prizes won, or bad news like speeding tickets, bills, death notices?

These are all beginnings for stories, which I begin to think up as I drive past.

Then another idea occurs to me. I could tell a story about each letterbox and the family that collects the letters from it. So there could be a story about . . .

No 1. Pink, with a pointy roof and a tube for the paper. There are three girls in this family, two will only wear pink and are very good ballet dancers. The other wears blue jeans and keeps ferrets. They are entered in a ferret show next weekend, but there is also a ballet exam on then, and the car has broken down.

No 2. Rusty red box welded to an old crankshaft and on a bit of a lean. Bert and Hilda live at that address. Bert was a boxer and loves making things out of old stuff. Hilda came from Holland when she was little. They met in a Heidelberg hotel.

No 3. The letterbox has come off its post and has a brick on top of a board to keep the rain out. No one has collected the mail for some time.

No 4. This letterbox is big and new on a strong post. It has a sparkling coat of white paint and someone has planted geraniums all around. The house belonging to this letterbox is also new and painted white. There is a team of gardeners putting down perfect lawns and perfect gardens surrounding a swimming pool and a tennis court.

No 5. This one is a fuel tank from a motorbike. It has a chrome lady on each side.

I'm still thinking up stories as I drive through the

next town. One day I might use one or two of these ideas to write a book.

That is, if you don't first . . .

The Harrows
Ian Irvine

'Why does it have to be me?'

An icy wind whipped Lita's blonde hair around her tear-streaked face; her green eyes were wide with fear. She pulled the cloak around her small frame but could not stop shivering. Beside her, the waterfall roared. The drop was dizzying, the rocks at the base jagged. She could not do it. She wanted to run back to the safety of her clan but there was no choice.

'Because the other ten girls failed,' said Horler. The old wisemon was gaunt, fleshless, yet she seemed immune to the cold, the drenching spray and the fatal plunge two feet away.

'They didn't *fail*. They died, broken on the rocks.'

'They let the clan down.'

'You made them dive for the pool. It's your fault they died.'

Horler was relentless. '*You* won't fail our people, will you?'

Sickness churned in Lita's belly. The rocks seemed to be reaching up to her. *Jump, jump!*

'You're the last – *except for your little sister,*' said Horler. 'Would you prefer I used her?'

The threat silenced Lita, as always. Tissy was special. She had to be protected.

'What if I don't have the gift?'

'I think you do.'

'Why can't I climb down to the pool?'

'It's protected.'

Lita swallowed. 'What if I can't find my gift in time?'

'You must.'

'Why me?' Lita repeated.

'To atone for our clan's shame.'

An unknown woman of the clan had meddled where she had no right, letting loose the harrows. Lita looked down. A series of odd streaks, like scorch marks, ran across the algae-covered rocks. How could that have happened when the rocks were drenched by the falls? She counted the streaks. Ten. One for each dead girl.

The wisemon drew a glitter-blade. Its edge twinkled in the dawn light. 'Hold out your left hand.'

From here, the pool Lita had to dive for was the size of a coin. She could not do it. No one could.

She hugged her arms around herself, shuddering. 'W-what's the knife for?'

'Price to air, price to water.'

'What?'

'You have to pay both, or neither will support you.'

'The air won't support me. I'll be smashed to bits on the rocks.'

'You will fly to the pool,' said Horler. 'You will dive to the bottom. You will find the box, and open it, and bring back the cure, and save your clan from the harrows.'

Lita rubbed the swellings that ran across her shoulders and down her arms. 'I have no gift,' she lied. 'I can't fly.'

'Everyone in our clan has the gift.'

'I'm not allowed to try. The more the gift is used, the quicker the Change when we grow up. The quicker the Change, the worse the harrows.'

Horler curled her wrinkled lip. 'And you think, if you don't use your gift at all, you'll be spared the harrows?'

'Papa said –'

'He's a fool. The harrows will get you, gift or not. My way is the only way, and you're the only one left who can save the clan. Hold out your hand.'

Cringing, Lita extended her small hand. Horler grabbed it and thrust it out over the water. She slashed the glitter-blade across Lita's palm, then shook her wrist violently. Blood sprayed through the air, spilled into the water.

Horler's eyes went a smoky, malevolent black; her lips pulled back to reveal yellow teeth. She dropped the knife and reached out to grab Lita, who suddenly realised that she wasn't meant to be a saviour, but a sacrifice. Horler was planning to hurl her over the edge to die, like the ten girls before her.

Her hand was slippery with blood. She wrenched free, hurled her cloak in Horler's face and ran. But not back towards clan-hall. She would find no shelter there – only the burden of all those who had grown up, gone through the Change, lost their gift and had been struck down by the unbearable wasting of the harrows. Horler was right about that. Lita was the only one who could do it. She had to save her clan.

As she ran, she reached inside herself for the gift she had been told never to use and, perhaps because it had been suppressed so long, it rose in a scalding tide. Her face was burning, her vision blurring, the strength draining from her legs as the swellings along her shoulders and arms throbbed and grew. The gift was working. Go, while you still can!

Lita shot past the wisemon, whacking her clawed fingers aside, bolted towards the edge of the falls and, sobbing with terror, hurled herself out and over, towards the pool.

Behind her, Horler howled with fury. Lita plunged headfirst down the cliff, faster and faster. The rocks were ferocious, the pool tiny. The swellings were opening, the leathery glide-wings she had never used extending behind her outstretched arms. But slowly. Too slowly to save her. She was going to smash into the rocks …

The glide-wings snapped open with a wrench and a burning pain in her shoulders, as if the shock had torn her arms out of their sockets. Had it? What if her wings collapsed? It felt as though they were going to. They thrashed, shuddered, held. Then she caught the updraught, lifted, and she was soaring, weightless, free for the first time in her life. And oh! The gift was wonderful. It was worth all the pain, even the cost when the harrows eventually wasted her.

As she turned in a wobbly, rising spiral, Lita realised that she could finally escape the burden of guilt that had suffocated her all her life. Escape her dying clan that nothing could save from the harrows. Escape the murderous wisemon.

But flying was much harder than she had expected. Every flap made her shoulders throb and her muscles burn. As she circled, the streaks burnt across the rocks caught her eye. Could they be —?

Crack-crack. Horler's cloak was streaming out behind her, firming and taking on a wing shape. The wisemon took three steps to the brink, lowered her head and shoulders into the updraught and the wind lifted her straight up. She side-slipped left, then right, then dived. Lita's mouth went dry. Horler was an expert flier.

She came hurtling down, so fast that the wind hissed over her wing. Lita tried to get out of the way, but she was tiring rapidly. Horler's teeth were bared, her fingers hooked as if she wanted to tear out Lita's heart.

Lita flapped her wings, but could not get out of the way in time. Horler shot past, caught her by an ankle and heaved her upside-down. Lita felt a burning pain in her head, and her wings were shrinking back into her arms. Her gift was fading – no, it was being drawn out of her, stolen from her. She tried to push Horler away, but the short flight had exhausted her.

Horler swung Lita around by the ankle until the sharpest rocks were below her. The wisemon wore a look of wicked triumph, and only now did Lita understand. Those streaks must have burned across the rock when the dying girls' gifts had been brutally wrenched from them. But where had their gifts gone?

Lita had to stop this. She had to get the panacea from the box. She kicked upwards with the last of her strength. Her left heel caught Horler under the jaw, snapping her head back, and the wisemon lost her grip. A little of Lita's gift came back and she dived away, praying that she could glide to the pool on her wing stubs. But she was falling like a brick, arcing over and down. She was going to slam headfirst into the rocks.

She flapped furiously, churning the air with her useless winglets, and gained a little forwards motion. Was it enough to reach the pool? She dared to hope.

But Horler was again diving after her. Lita scooped the air with her arms, slipped sideways, shot over the edge of the pool and plunged in.

The shock almost stopped her heart – the water was icy. Lita plunged all the way to the bottom, sending up swirls of grit that scratched her eyes. She blinked them clean and there it was – a small brown box on a bed of fine white sand.

And the box was calling to her.

She clawed at the lid, wrenched it up and felt inside for the cure.

The box was empty.

Horler's story had been a lie.

There was no way to save her clan from the harrows.

Lita shrieked underwater. She pounded the sand until it whirled up in clouds around her. Then a shockwave passed through the water and her ears popped. Bony hands closed around her throat from behind and squeezed.

She panicked, thrashed uselessly. The hands tightened, choking her, Horler's ragged nails tearing her skin. Lita's head spun. Her vision blurred. She had to act now or die. She slammed the back of her head into Horler's nose, then scrunched down into a ball and rolled forwards.

Horler went tumbling over her, nose trailing blood, and her head smacked into the open box. The water seemed to boil around her. Yellow rays – eleven of them – were drawn from Horler into the box, then she slumped sideways and the lid fell shut.

The rays faded. The sand settled. Horler lay on the sand beside the box, motionless.

Now desperate for air, Lita churned up to the surface. She wanted away from here, but first she had to understand. After taking three breaths, she dived again. The box seemed to be calling her again, and she wanted to open it. She felt sure the cure was there now.

But there was no time. She bore Horler up. The malevolence was gone from her eyes; she was just a bony old woman, close to death.

'What happened?' Lita said, panting.

'Harrows lifted. Clan saved.'

'How?'

'You – the cure.'

Lita no longer wanted to escape. It was over and she ached for her clan. 'I don't understand.'

'But you – can never – go home,' croaked Horler, sinking beneath the water to her chin.

Pain, worse than being slashed with the glitter-knife. Lita hung on to the rock with one hand, Horler with the other. 'Why not?' she said hoarsely.

'Work . . . it . . . out.'

Lita stared into the old woman's eyes. 'It was you! You opened the box, ages ago. You released the harrows.'

'I was the fool who opened it,' Horler said bitterly.

'But I did not release the harrows – I became the harrows.'

'Then why – why did the other girls have to die? Why try to kill me?'

'I'm old. Fading. Harrows failing with me. It needed to feed on their gifts.'

'But if it's gone, why can't I go home?'

'Harrows gone back – into box. And you've opened it.'

'But the box was empty,' said Lita.

'Not empty now. Harrows has fed. It's waiting. For you to open the box.'

Lita closed her eyes. The pain was getting worse.

'Go! Fly!' said Horler.

'Where can I go? I'm only fourteen.'

'Too bad!'

'Tissy won't understand. I've got to see her first.'

'You can't. Never come back or you'll open the box. You'll become the harrows.'

Horler's eyes went blank, she slipped from Lita's grasp, the water closed over her head and she was gone.

Lita lifted off, but as she laboured up past the falls, she heard the box calling again. What was worse – to spend the rest of her life in bitter exile, or rejoin the clan she loved, only to harrow them again?

High above the pool she circled. Tormented. Tempted.

She had to say goodbye. If she opened the box, just a crack, could she see Tissy one last time?

Lita was strong.
Surely she could close it again?

———

Thanks very much to Lisa Leigh for the seed from which this story grew.

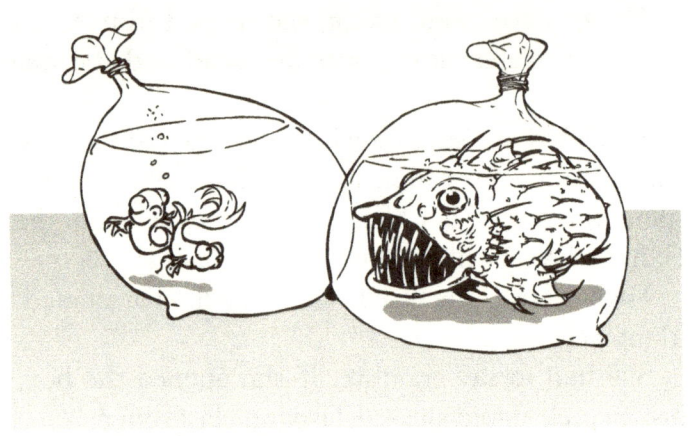

Amanita Im
Gary Crew

Legend tells that gypsies abandoned the boy at the gates of the monastery. Perhaps this is true, perhaps not. But one thing is certain: having found the child shivering in the snow, the friars of St Benedict took him in.

Martin, they called him, and raised him as one of their own.

Being worthy men, and devoted to their garden, they taught the boy all that they knew. Of rue and rosemary, liquorice and lavender, cloves and comfrey, and every healing herb whose root or branch or bud or flower flourished within those grey stony walls.

Nor was the garden the only place where Martin learned.

When evening fell, the boy could be found, candle in hand, poring over ancient manuscripts in the monastery library, gleaning all that he could of field and forest, hill and vale in those distant lands where mystic remedies grew wilder than his imagining.

One night, as Martin sat reading in a secluded alcove, he spied a manuscript secreted in a dusty recess. *Now there is a strange thing*, he thought, but as he reached for the document, a sudden shiver passed over him and he drew back, afraid.

Next morning, he hurried to the library, took down the manuscript and hid himself away to read alone.

When he had unrolled the document, he saw it was a map. 'The Kingdom of Darcia . . .' he whispered. 'They say it is a dreadful place. Its people bewitched by a shaman. Its caves the abode of lizards so huge they might, perhaps, be dragons. But why should a map be hidden . . .?'

Though the ink was faded, and difficult to read, he examined the map until finally, he cried, 'Here is a word that I recognise. *Amanita*, the name of a mushroom.'

True, the word following was almost indecipherable, but at length he made out the first two letters: *Amanita Im* . . . And after, Whosoever shall eat of it shall be made whole, and live like . . .

'Live like what?' the youth wondered. 'Like kings? Surely that is the answer! *Amanita Imperialis.*'

At this, Martin fell to thinking. If only he could find this mushroom, what medicines, what healing balms and poultices the friars might make from it. Yes, he would travel to Darcia to find it. Yes, he would risk his life for that!

And setting aside his fears, he hid the map in another place until he was able to study it at will. Which he did, daily, dreaming always of his *Amanita Im* and the salvation it might bring to humankind.

So it was when Martin reached the age of seventeen and the friars invited him to join their order, the youth graciously declined. 'I thank you,' he said, 'but I would rather pursue the studies of moss and herb and root-of-fern that I have learned while in your care. I have long desired to discover more. Please, I mean no disrespect, but grant me my liberty.'

Heartened by the good friars' ready blessing, Martin happily set out upon his long-dreamt of quest.

He crossed boundless oceans.

He climbed the Mountains to the Moon.

And finally, on the very morning of his eighteenth birthday, he reached his goal.

The Kingdom of Darcia was all that rumour had warned it would be. A land pocked by hail and parched by sun, of will-o'-the-wisps and whirlpools, of rain and mist and dreary desert, and though Martin saw no sign of herb or grass, or flower or fern, he trudged on, his dream glowing bright with faith.

One evening, more dead than alive, he entered a cavern whose steep descent and tortured wall caused him to cry, 'Surely, I have died and entered Hell! Now I know why the map was hidden. In their wisdom the good friars would have kept me from this path.' And only through pure valour did he keep on.

The creatures that inhabited this place lay resting

in their caves. Such was their astonishment at seeing a man, one called, 'Ho, Pilgrim, what has brought you to this fearful land? We have not seen the likes of you for many a year.'

And Martin, being a worthy youth, answered boldly, 'It is indeed a fearful place, and though monsters you be, I do not envy your habitation. I have come in search of a humble mushroom. A plant by whose good grace the poor and needy might live as kings. It is known to us as *Amanita Im . . .* '

Before he could finish, a lizard – a dragon? – slipped from its lair and came towards him, its great wings folded, its fiery mouth extinguished, its sinewy neck stooped low and supple in courteous greeting. 'There is another like you in the distant mountains,' the beast whispered. 'His hut is a good day's journey north from here.'

'And what have I to do with him?' Martin asked.

'He is an old man, and solitary. A shaman. A tender of herbs and cure-alls. Perhaps he knows of the plant you seek, this *Amanita Im.*'

'Perhaps he does,' Martin agreed. 'How should I find him, since he lives so far?'

'If you would spend the night among us,' the beast graciously replied, 'I would take you there in the morning.'

'You are a monster,' Martin answered. 'Little of me though there is, and so near to death as I am, surely you would devour me while I sleep.'

At this the beast turned aside, its eyes downcast. 'And surely you are a man, and ignorant of courtesy. If I had so desired, I would have eaten you already.'

Humbled by the truth, Martin regretted his words. 'Forgive me. I forget myself. What might I offer for your kindness, seeing my scrip is empty.'

'Why,' the beast replied, delighted, 'a simple story.'

'A story? And if I should tell you one, you would be satisfied?'

The beast laughed. 'How else might a dragon survive? Since by story we were imagined into being, by story we live.'

Upon hearing this, Martin followed the dragon deeper into its cave, and when he had kindled a fire and settled to rest upon a bed of rushes, and when the creatures from without had curled quiet and cosy round about, he wove a tale of knights and maidens, lilies and roses, chivalry and kind courtesy (in which he had been sorely lacking), until all fell deep into a joyful slumber.

In the morning, having woken to the delight of finding himself refreshed, Martin set out, the dragon his companion. Again the land was raw and barren and, tired after his arduous journey, the youth all but yielded to despair. 'I will abandon this foolish quest,' he moaned. 'It is better that I return to the friars and spend my life in prayer and penitence.'

'For the second time you insult me,' the dragon remarked. 'I have told you that the old shaman lives beyond those distant hills, and that he keeps a garden rich and rare. When will you learn to believe in what you must, meanwhile, imagine?'

Humbled again, the youth went on.

At length, true to the dragon's words, a single buttercup appeared and then sunflowers and violets and forget-me-nots, and by twilight a view of a valley so patterned with fields of azure and yellow, emerald and scarlet, so brushed with silver and spangled with gold, that it might well have been a scene illuminated upon a manuscript – not a land of the real and everyday.

'Let us wait until morning,' the dragon advised. 'Then we will descend at our leisure.' So Martin slept upon the hillside, wrapped in the warm promise of the morrow.

No sooner had the sun lit the valley than the dragon woke, and having yawned and flexed its steely scales, it said, 'Since the descent is steep, I will fly us down, if you would but climb upon my back.'

Disbeliever though he was, Martin did as he was asked, and withal the dragon spread its wings and glided slow and easy into the painted valley to land, soft and safe, in a garden by a cottage.

As Martin stepped down, an old man appeared. 'Ho, good dragon,' he called. 'I have not seen you in many a year.'

'Greetings, old man,' the beast replied. 'I have brought a friend to speak with you.'

'Pardon my intrusion,' Martin begged, bowing and offering his name. 'I have been ward to the friars of St Benedict, who are herbalists all. I come in search of a mushroom, *Amanita Imperialis.*'

'You are most welcome,' the old man answered. 'But no such mushroom grows here. No. Not *Amanita Imperialis.*'

Martin paled, fearing his quest had been in vain. 'But I have seen it named upon a map,' he replied. 'Or the words *Amanita Im*, at least.'

'We must talk,' the old man said. And while the dragon remained in the garden, preening its wings, the youth followed the old man into the cottage where they sat down to eat a humble meal of bread and honey, nuts and mead.

'I see in your face that you are an honest lad,' the old man began. 'For that reason I will trust you with the truth. The mushroom you seek is not called *Amanita Imperialis* . . .'

'Why, it is the food of kings,' Martin broke in. 'I have read that "Whosoever shall eat of it shall be made whole and live like kings . . ."'

'I think not,' the old man replied. 'The truth of the writing is, 'Whosoever shall eat of it shall be made whole and live like gods . . . '

'Like gods?'

'Indeed. The name of the mushroom is *Amanita Immortalis*. And those who eat of it shall live forever.'

'*Immortalis!*' Martin gasped. 'Truly, that is the

desire of the ages. The Secret of Eternal Life! We must gather this wonder. Come quick!'

But the old man did not move.

'What is the matter?' Martin asked. 'Would you keep this wondrous secret for yourself?'

But the dragon overheard and shouted from the window, 'Leave off, foolish boy! I have tried to teach you the power of imagining, but you have learned nothing. Leave off!'

At this the old man raised his hand for silence. 'Martin,' he said, 'our friend has spoken the truth. Imagine what might come of taking this wonder to the world. You speak of the desire of the ages, and marvellous though this plant may be, imagine the horror it might carry in its wake. Consider for one moment, if humans kill for wealth, what might they do for this? Imagine . . .'

'But it would end all suffering,' Martin moaned. 'How can I leave such a thing? Tell me, how?'

'I am a shaman,' the old man answered. 'I grow herbs that you know nothing of. Benlack for the cancer. Mendane for the plague. You must not take the *Amanita*, but you will not leave Darcia empty-handed.'

And though Martin wept bitter tears, he could not rid his head of the image of a world gone mad for his *Amanita Im*. At last, seeing all his pleading was in vain, he said to his companions, 'You have shown me the truth and I thank you. Old man, I readily accept the gift of your herbs. But not, as you say, the false promise of your precious mushroom. So come, my dragon friend, and carry me away. Thus I will share your bounty with my brothers and they, in their turn, will give them to the world.'

Legend tells that a dragon set Martin down at the gates of the monastery. Perhaps this is true, perhaps not. But one thing is certain: his scrip was laden with healing herbs the likes of which the friars of St Benedict had never seen before. Benlack to heal the cancer. Mendane to cure the plague. And having distributed his gifts, the youth once more clambered upon the dragon's back and departed for the land of Darcia where, to this day, he dwells among those mystic hills, the guardian of his *Amanita Im*, a plant so wondrous that to eat of it would bring the ending of the world.

The Woodcutter's Secret

Simon Higgins

Let me tell you of the strangeness of life. It was well after midnight when my father shook me awake, one finger pressed to my lips. I forced open my eyes to see that he had rekindled our night lanterns. That always meant trouble.

Driving autumn rain had lashed our lonely inn for hours after sunset, making the ceiling of my tiny room leak, and forcing me to once more drag my rope bed to our entrance room, where the roof was sound and all below it dry. Now the world had fallen silent again, and mist shrouded the sky and the full moon's light. I clambered from my bed, shook my head, then listened. From the old Roman road outside our small lodge came the *clop* of hoofs, that breathy sputtering of weary horses and the *clink* of gauntlets brushing chest armour.

'War mounts?' I rubbed my sleep-heavy eyes. 'What sort of knight travels at this hour?'

'Whoever is out there,' my father's good eye flicked to the door, 'they didn't ring the bell on the gate post as they passed it.' He gripped my shoulder hard. 'Perhaps they intend to surprise us.'

As we both glanced at the chest in the corner where our sword lay hidden, there came a thunderous *crack*! The door burst apart, its solid cross brace snapped effortlessly. Night air surged into the room and broken planks wheeled through its chill to clatter at our feet. My father and I stared in disbelief.

A great grey form appeared: the hindquarters of the huge horse that had just kicked our door in. A caped knight, armoured neck to toe, but helmetless, straddled the beast's back, peering over his shoulder at us. A taller, identically suited figure loomed behind him, clutching the reins of his own mount. My father took a stride for our hidden blade, but I lunged, grabbing his arm.

'No!' I tugged him back against the wall. 'You have no chance! Wait, they may not harm us!'

The horse vanished and the tallest knight filled the doorway, sword drawn and brandished. Was he just cautious . . . or murderous? My blood ran cold as he shuffled into the room, head turning left and right. I flinched when he pointed his blade straight at my father.

'You there, in shadow! Step closer! Show me your face.' My father obeyed. The knight lowered his steel. 'No. Aliforde the Woodcutter has two good eyes.' He sheathed his weapon.

His shorter companion, sword undrawn, appeared at his side. 'Who shelters here this night?' he demanded. 'Speak, man! Is it merely you and the boy?' My father nodded quickly.

'We . . . we will pay for the door, and for information.' The tall knight sighed. 'Since clearly, at least some of ours is wrong.' I traded stares with the man. He was not that old, sharp-eyed, obviously the leader.

The fighters exchanged a glance, then the tall fellow spoke earnestly. 'I am Sir Gareth Colver. My aide here is Sir Lionel Shelton. We were told that the man we seek, one Aliforde the Woodcutter, lives on this mountain. In the shifting mist that has followed the rain, we took your small inn for his hut.'

My father protectively encircled my shoulders. 'Sirs, we cut no timber, making our meagre living instead by lodging a few travellers at a time, pilgrims and monks moving between the remote abbeys . . . though these days, with that new road cut to the north, less are coming.' He paused; no doubt reminding himself that, money aside, withholding information from a knight could lead to death. 'We do know of your Aliforde, however. Indeed a woodcutter, he lives higher up the mountain, by a track that rises behind this lodge.'

Sir Gareth Colver edged forward. 'Can you lead us to his hut? I would risk no more mistakes.'

Worried glances passed between my father and me. While little more than an acquaintance, Aliforde was a local, a neighbour, and had caused us neither offence nor harm. Colver saw our looks. Immediately, he pulled off a gauntlet and reached for a pouch tied to his belt. My mouth fell open when he held up a gold piece with the king's head on it.

'If your flow of lodgers dwindles, best you look to the future, old man.' The knight nodded my way. 'Think of the boy.' Narrowing his eyes, Colver turned the coin so that it caught the light. 'Could your tiny inn make such as this in a year?'

My father bit his lip then looked down at me. His lined, tired face displayed his thoughts: whether these intruders proved to be robber-knights or men of honour, we had little choice. They seemed young, inexperienced, but were men-at-arms nonetheless, and they would get their way. Besides, the incentive they were holding out was, put simply, every commoner's dream. Yes, we would help them. Then I pictured my father actually going up our mountain with them, *in the dark*.

'I could lead you,' I blurted. I heard my father gasp, felt his grip on me tighten, but still I went on. 'My father has but one eye, its vision poor, and his back is often disagreeable to riding or climbing. But I too know your man by sight. We last traded with him for cut wood only a moon ago.'

'Come then.' Colver tossed my father the coin, raised a gauntleted hand and beckoned me.

'This Aliforde.' My father swallowed hard. 'You . . . you're going to kill him, aren't you?'

'His fate,' Sir Lionel Shelton replied coolly, 'is tied to the king's own business, good fellow.'

I offered the warriors a compliant bow. 'Ready, sirs. But forgive me, I have never ridden.'

'Fear not,' Shelton grinned. 'As long as you know how to grip tightly.'

My father passed me my boots and a rough-weave cloak. 'Sirs,' he said meekly, 'the boy is but fifteen, and all the family I have left. I depend on him for so much. If he should come to grief –'

'I will protect him,' Colver said. 'You have my word.' He looked me up and down. 'Courage, lad. Seems you are about to enter royal service.'

'Andrew –' My father brushed the back of my hand. I paced to the horses, fighting a wave of fear. Then I glanced back once, a lump in my throat, trying to look confident. My father stood in the doorway, his one good eye on me. It was empty; his heart bleeding. Would I return? Most likely these warriors *were* here to slay Aliforde, and if there was to be combat, could Colver truly guarantee my safety? Why kill a woodcutter? A quiet, honest, unremarkable, middle-aged hermit. What had he done?

Colver helped me onto Shelton's horse. Nervously I leaned back against the knight's chest armour. Giving my father a final nod, I indicated the way to the track. Shelton took the lead and we started uphill through the dripping forest.

We rode for some time, the moon bright through the trees, the only sounds the clinks of armour and the muffled steps of the horses. But as we climbed higher, I heard the distant, echoing shriek of a hunting owl and, though I tried not to, I took it as a bad omen.

At a familiar fork, I gestured to the right. Shelton nodded. The horses slowed and we entered a half-hidden clearing, a lone hut in the centre of it.

The knights dismounted and I awkwardly slid from Shelton's beast. Colver studied the approach to the woodcutter's hut. In the moonlight, his breath plumed into steam as he whispered, 'We will try for a *quiet* surprise this time. Stay back with the horses, boy.' He thrust their reins into my hands. 'If they react, hold firm. Anything could happen. I know not how much of our briefing to trust, but it is said that this Aliforde suffers from a peculiar madness. It causes him to flee or attack at the mere sight of a man in armour.'

I blinked, weighing his words. This grew stranger! If they held Aliforde to be a lunatic who would either run or fight them, and their goal was to capture him, their sudden, violent entry to our inn made sense. But was the story true? I had never seen Aliforde behave oddly, but to be fair, I had also never seen Aliforde in the presence of a knight.

The pair crept forward, perhaps five strides apart, each angling for the door of the hut. Only paces from it, Shelton stepped on a twig that snapped noisily. Both men froze, gripping their undrawn swords. Colver waited then made a hand sign, and he and

Shelton moved on with ever more careful stealth. I drew in the smell of wet leaves and night flowers, felt the pre-dawn chill on my face, but my eyes never left the door of that hut. What would I see? Combat, flight or murder?

With a sharp creak the door flew open and I caught sight of Aliforde the woodcutter, though as I had never seen him before. He wore the usual woollen cape, but now he stood tall and strong like a knight, braced for action, a sword in his hands. His head snapped in the direction of each intruder, then, to my amazement, he rushed Colver. The knight shouted something, but the sudden anxious neighing of the horses smothered his cry. Colver leapt back and drew his blade with desperate haste as Aliforde closed with him. Shelton let out a muffled curse, unsheathed his weapon, and charged for the woodcutter.

It all happened at blinding speed, swords gleaming in the moonlight, moaning as they cut the still, cold air. The woodcutter hacked at Colver, who barely blocked his strong descending cut with a ringing blade. While the knight was still off balance, Aliforde bobbed low with surprising agility to slice at Colver's armoured leg. The blow glanced aside but sent the knight tumbling to the ground. Shelton tried to ambush Aliforde from behind, but the woodcutter spun round in a low stance, bounded to one side then swatted hard at Shelton's forearm guard with the flat of his blade. With a cry Shelton stumbled, the sword whirling from his hands. The tip of Aliforde's weapon darted straight to the fallen knight's throat.

For a long moment, nobody moved. My heart stalled in my ribs. If Aliforde slew a high knight, whether acting in self-defence *or* out of madness, furious royal vengeance might find us all.

'Woodcutter!' I bellowed. 'Don't kill him! They are the king's men!'

Aliforde looked round at me then stepped back and studied his assailants carefully. Colver struggled to his feet. Propping himself up on one elbow, Shelton stared warily at Aliforde's sword.

'Prove his claim, you puppies,' the woodcutter said. 'Or this old wolf will bury you both, right here, before dawn's first light.'

Sir Gareth Colver dropped his sword and limped to Aliforde. 'Here,' he said painfully. He took off a gauntlet once more, freed the leather pouch from his belt and held it out. Its coins jingled. I couldn't see the pouch's markings then, but later I learned that it was adorned with the royal crest.

Aliforde stared hard at it, then motioned to me. 'Let us all go inside.' He pointed at a sapling, 'Tie the horses there, boy.'

Within the hut he took up a flint kit and fired his candles. As the smell of their wax filled the little room, Aliforde looked the knights over. 'You are not wounded?'

'No,' Colver replied, 'merely bruised. Our apologies for startling you. I tried to shout that we were on royal orders, but as things turned out, my cry was not heard. Thankfully, no one fell.'

The woodcutter gestured at me. 'You have this one to thank. He called out just in time.'

'Who are you, sir?' I smiled with shameless admiration. 'Surely no simple woodcutter.'

'Oh, I am a woodcutter now,' Aliforde said wearily. 'But as you say, it was not always so.'

'This man was the king's own champion,' Colver said, bowing low to Aliforde. 'I'm told that once, none could match him with lance or sword. It seems that second skill has not faded with time.'

'Good sir,' Shelton said gently, 'it is a relief to see that much we were told about you proves untrue. Please, end your self-imposed exile. We are sent to compel you thus.'

The woodcutter turned away to stare at a lantern. 'How?' He angled his head. 'What has changed? Can you turn back time? Give the dead new life?'

'What happened?' I said, instantly realising that it was not my place to ask. Nonetheless, Colver saw fit to answer me. In hindsight, I now think he was actually speaking to Aliforde indirectly.

'Aliforde the woodcutter is in truth Sir Alfred Pierce, King's Champion, as you have heard. Three years past, after the death of his son by the plague, he accidentally slew a respected rival during the annual Great Joust. All judged it but cruel fate and forgave.' Colver fixed his gaze on the back of Aliforde's head. 'All but Sir Alfred. Holding himself accountable, he withdrew from royal service. Begging the king to discharge him, he left court and hid himself, out here in the world.'

'Huh!' The woodcutter turned, eyes bleak with painful memories. 'Hid myself? Not well enough, it seems.' He folded his thick arms. 'So tell me then, what could possibly tempt me to return?'

Colver smiled. 'The king has a new son, whom he has named Myles, after your lost boy and in his honour. Our liege was told you had succumbed to madness born of grief, but given his affection for you, I doubt he ever really believed it. His heartfelt dream remains that you return to court, to accept a post as the lad's fencing instructor. His majesty says that if you do, his own wound at your loss shall be healed, his recent joy made all the more complete. He would have you become, as it were, an uncle to the new prince.'

Sir Alfred turned away. 'Myles,' he whispered. 'A new Myles.' He looked around his squalid hut and sighed piteously. 'Perhaps it is time for renewal.' The woodcutter-champion eyed me thoughtfully, and then rounded on Colver. 'I will accept on one condition. Any knight at court, regardless of role, needs both squire and groom.' He motioned at me.

'This plucky boy and his honest father are surely fit to serve me as such. What say you?'

'My orders were to capture you if mad, and if sane, to convince you by any means,' Colver said. 'So, on behalf of the crown . . . yes!'

And strange as the whole affair was, that was the start of *my* renewal. I, but a peasant, became a squire and, after two battles and my nineteenth year, a royal knight whom his majesty named Sir Andrew Inman. My widower father met a widowed cook after we joined the court and is now happily remarried. He still loves to say that Lady Destiny is a trickster who can lay her ambush anywhere.

Even on a lonely mountain, wrapped in a woodcutter's secret.

The Snake Singer

Wendy Orr

Aysha is always hiding, always spying. That's what the temple servants say, and it might be true. When you fall between two worlds, hiding is the safest thing to do. And when you're hiding, spying is what you do.

Her favourite place is in the window alcove of the temple, sitting still as stone in the shadows behind the screen, while her mother sings to the snakes. The halls are cleared and hushed just before the priestess enters: it only takes a moment to jump, grab the ledge and swing herself onto it. There's a split second of fear as she balances and pulls herself up to the window, then an easy wriggle through the gap between the latticework screen and the edge of the windowsill.

Her head resting on her knees, she crouches on the cool stone watching the asps slither from their pots. One by one, they come to the priestess's call, twining around her arms as she dances the secret, sacred rites. Watching and listening, as mesmerised as the snakes themselves, Aysha used to pretend that her mother knew she was there, and was singing for her, too.

She can't pretend any longer, because at the last new moon, the priestess began initiating Fila into the mysteries. Aysha should have been struck deaf already for listening. But Fila, Aysha's beautiful, sweet-natured younger sister, has a voice to scare toads. The snakes do not come to her; they become agitated and hiss, and if the priestess didn't sing them away, her favoured daughter would die a swollen, painful death twenty times over.

Aysha is the unfavoured daughter, the dark and bony girl with a twist to her mouth, the baby who should have been abandoned at birth if her father, with tears in his eyes and a sharp knife in his hand, had not sliced off the limp sixth finger budding from the little finger of each hand.

The gods were not pleased. Aysha's father, the strongest diver on the island, was swept off his boat and swallowed by the sea the very next day. The priestess gave the baby to a temple maid to rear, and never spoke to her again.

Now all that remains of those unlucky digits are their two silver snips of scar – but the islanders have long memories. At the sight of Aysha they turn their heads to spit her evil luck over their left shoulder. She'd never thought it could be any other way until Luki stopped doing it. Maybe that's why she's curious when she notices him now. He's slipping out a side door as she returns from the woods with her basket full of dew-wet herbs. He doesn't see her, and she can tell by the hunch of his shoulders and the softness of his step that he doesn't want to be seen.

Luki is not an outcast. Luki is loved and adored, because his life and death will keep the island safe. He is one of the two boys and two girls, born the same year as Aysha, who will leave to dance for the Bull King in the spring.

The deal is simple: the King in his distant palace needs fresh blood for his bulls; Aysha's small island needs the protection of his ships. So four youths are sent every two years, and four thousand islanders are kept safe from being invaded and sold into slavery.

That's the promise, and it's held true for generations. The other promise is that anyone who survives the bull dancing for two full years will be free to return to their own home. No one alive has seen that promise tested, but the grandmothers remember a man who was old when they were young, who was said to have come home at the end of his two years covered in gold.

So the bull dancers leave their families at seven summers to live in the Temple compound and learn all they can about dancing with the bulls. Maybe, just maybe, each of them thinks, I'll be the one to survive.

But sometimes Aysha thinks that being worshipped isn't so different from being outcast. Girls giggle and call out to Luki as he passes, boys mimic the way he tosses his hair out of his eyes, but he has no more true friends than she does.

She goes on into the kitchen, carrying her basket through to the cool cellar of the wise women's larder. The cooks are clattering and calling, but she is, as usual, invisible. No one asks where she's going as she heads down the winding lane in the direction Luki's gone. More importantly, no one else has seen him leave. As the lane ends in a field of sprouting corn, she spots a lone figure, already far in the distance, heading into the woods.

Aysha skirts wide and follows. She has to remind herself not to hum. Whenever she's alone, she sings, as naturally as breathing. Sometimes it takes her by surprise when she hears it in a sudden silence, when the flight of a hawk stills the small birds' chirping, so that only Aysha's throbbing hum rises into the still air. If she didn't keep her mouth against her knees when she hid in the temple, she's afraid she could commit the greatest sacrilege of all and sing for the snakes.

The path climbs steadily up a hill; Aysha picks her way through the undergrowth beside it until suddenly she comes out blinking into sunshine. She's at the top of a steep, rocky slope. At the bottom of the slope is a wide green field. Even before she sees him, Aysha understands immediately why Luki has come here so secretly.

Powerless to stop him, Aysha slips silently across to a thicket of wild roses and huddles behind their prickly screen.

Luki is not alone in the field: he's facing a large, angry billy goat. The boy is bouncing on his toes and raising his arms to the sky; the goat is rearing, dancing on its hind legs.

The goat lowers its head and charges. Luki grabs the horns, flips into a handstand, and throws himself over its back.

Aysha holds her breath. This is exactly why bull dancers are forbidden to leave the temple compound on their own: they need to be alive and healthy when the ships arrive.

Luki lands on his feet. He claps his hands above his head, taunting the big goat. The animal is only confused for a moment; it spins around and charges again. The boy grabs the horns – but his timing is out. He starts to leap too soon, the goat swerves as Luki starts to pull himself up.

Suddenly the bull dancer is on the ground with the goat above him.

Aysha bites her fist to stop from screaming.

Luki doesn't move.

Aysha scrambles out from behind the roses, thorns tearing at her skirt and arms. Rage fills her; she's ready to punch the goat between its horns, chase it through the field all the way down to the sea.

The goat, however, has lost interest now that its

enemy is flat on the ground. It butts the bull dancer's thighs half-heartedly, then trots away.

Luki still doesn't stir.

Aysha hesitates. A moment ago she'd been afraid he'd know she was spying – now her heart is clenching with true, white terror. She wants to run for help; she can't, won't, be the one to find him dead.

Blood dripping from her scratches, she runs, leaping, skidding, down the rocks towards him. 'Luki!'

His name freezes on her lips. Slithering towards the fallen boy is an asp, quick and lively in the noon warmth. Full of venom after its winter sleep.

Time stops. Blues of sea and sky, greens of grass and shrubs, shadows of forests, sharpen and then blur into background; Aysha can see nothing but the boy lying on his back, one arm thrown above his head, and the snake sliding closer to that outstretched hand.

It's nearly there. She can't rage or chase or sacrifice herself; anything she does now will only drive the serpent faster towards the bull dancer's death.

Then the fluting Snake Song of the high priestess wafts through the air. It's high and pure: a new song especially for this snake, on this day in this field.

The asp raises its head. Aysha's vision is so sharp now she can see its long tongue flickering.

The song continues.

The snake veers away from the boy's hand. It

curves and slithers back the way it came, moving steadily and calmly towards Aysha.

Luki sits up, rubbing his eyes. He stares at Aysha, at the snake, and back at her.

The singing stops. Time moves again; the air blows fresh against her cheek. The snake disappears under a rock. Aysha looks around but the priestess is nowhere to be seen.

'It was you,' Luki says.

'But I can't! I couldn't . . .'

'You did,' says Luki, walking towards her. 'You're the snake singer.'

'I'm forbidden!' Aysha holds up her hands, as if the bull dancer might be the only person on the island not to know their history.

'Forbidden by priests, not the gods,' says the bull dancer. 'Like my practising today.' He takes her imperfect hands in his, rubbing his thumbs along the silvery scars. Aysha can hardly breathe for the song rising in her heart.

Luki looks away awkwardly. 'I have no right to ask, but . . .'

'You can trust me to keep your stupidity secret!' she snaps, jerking her hands free.

'How could I not trust you?' he asks. 'I owe you my life. But while I'm away, would you sing for me sometimes, so I can think of you out here, where your song can carry across the sea?'

'I swear by all the gods,' says Aysha. 'I'll sing here at dawn every morning until you return.'

'I swear by all the gods,' he replies, taking her hands again, 'that I will return.'

The Mirror in the Middle of the Maze

Sean Williams

The walls of the maze were made of rough-hewn yellow stone. The floors and ceilings, too. Occasional gleams of quartz threw Ros's clear yellow light back at him, like the eyes of spiders at night, as he faced another difficult choice.

The tunnel he had been following terminated at a crossroads. There were no scratch marks on any of the walls, indicating that he hadn't come this way before. Of the three paths ahead of him, two of them likely went nowhere, since there was only ever one way into the centre of a maze. Possibly all three were dead ends.

Ros played with the scant wisps of hair on his chin and thought hard.

He wasn't afraid of mazes *per se*. He had escaped from several over the years, all of them set by his teacher, Master Pukje, as tests of his ability to navigate, to reason, or to run. This maze, however, contained no swirling, tantalising lights to distract him, no puzzles to solve – apart from the maze itself – and no sharp-toothed creatures snapping at his backside to make him hurry. This maze was something entirely different.

He considered his options. The air from each of the tunnels smelt and felt the same. Each path seemed equally curved as far as his eye could see. None of them gave any sign that it would lead to the centre of the maze.

Giving up on reason, Ros tried chance instead. He gritted his teeth, gripped his chin-hairs tightly, and pulled.

Two came loose. By a code he had determined earlier, that meant he should take the second entrance on his left. Straight ahead, in other words.

It had better be the right one, he told himself, or he would soon run out of bum-fluff.

That was the least of his worries.

He scored a notch in the yellow wall and set off down the new tunnel. It wound left, then right, then left again. No junctions, no tempting passageways to either side. Was he imagining it, or did the air smell fresher? He put on speed, beginning to hope that this time he had found the one, that he was at last about to reach the centre . . .

Ros ran around the third bend and skidded to a halt.

Ahead of him was nothing but yellow stone and gleaming quartz.

Another dead end.

He took a deep breath, telling himself that he

wasn't scared – not of a maze, no matter how strange it might seem. No matter how deadly.

The floor vibrated underfoot. Dust rained from the ceiling above. The candle burning in his palm began to dance as though in a fitful breeze.

Instinctively, Ros crouched down as the maze *contracted* around him, growing fractionally smaller in less time than it took to turn in a circle, twice.

When he stood up again, the tips of his dusty hair brushed the ceiling of the maze.

He dusted himself down, resolved not to think of how many more dead ends he could afford, and turned back the way he had come.

It had started innocently enough, with quite understandable curiosity.

'What happened to your last apprentice, Master Pukje?'

'You don't need to know.'

He had been twelve years old the first time he had asked and, unsatisfied with his teacher's dismissive answer, he had repeated the question at every opportunity. Now he was fourteen and in all the time between, Master Pukje had never once mentioned another student. Not specifically, although Ros knew he wasn't the first. It was only natural that he wanted to know more about the ones who had come before him.

'I don't understand why you won't tell me about

them. Did they grow up to be famous Changeworkers, or did something horrible happen to them?'

'I told you. You don't need to know. Something horrible will happen to you if you keep asking.'

Ros wouldn't take no for an answer. If he asked once, he asked a thousand times – in hope of a reward when he did well, and when he did badly because he knew he couldn't get in any more trouble.

And then, just a week ago, while setting camp in the hollow of a stony outcrop, his back carefully turned while his teacher changed from dragon to imp form, 'Please, Master Pukje. Won't you tell me what happened to your last apprentice?'

'You don't want to know.'

The slight difference in wording caught Ros's ear immediately.

'I do want to know, Master Pukje. Why would I ask you so often if I didn't?'

His teacher came around to face him. There was no mistaking the mischievousness in his tilted, glittering eyes.

'You only *think* you want to know,' he said, 'because you don't know anything, really.'

'That's true, Master Pukje,' said Ros, trying humility where all else had failed. 'But if you won't tell me, how will I ever learn?'

The imp barked a laugh.

'All right, but I need you to fetch some things first. There are particular plants that grow in the shadows around here, deep in the cracks where the sun never shines. We'll want water, too, and a fire.'

Ros wondered why all this was necessary just to learn a little history, but he did as he was told and, come nightfall, as the fat moon rose up in a bright starry sky, he got his answer.

'You want to know what happened to my last apprentice?' Master Pukje held out a stone beaker containing the potion he had made. 'Drink this.'

Ros took the beaker and studied its contents. The potion was thick and greenish, with numerous black dots floating on its surface like pimples. As he stared, one of the dots popped, emitting a puff of mist that stank of ancient swamps and underpants.

'What is it?'

'You see what it is.'

'I mean, what does it do?'

'It does what it does.'

Ros rolled his eyes. Sometimes having a conversation with his teacher was like being tied up in knots.

'I *mean*, what does this have to do with your last apprentice?'

'Drink and find out.'

'It smells like poison.'

Master Pukje squatted in front of Ros so the fire was at his back. A falling log sent out a spray of golden sparks that rose up above his head like a halo. He folded his hands and settled down, as though to watch Ros's internal struggle play out.

'Don't you trust me, Ros?'

Ros didn't know how to answer that question. He had entered his apprenticeship willingly, even though he knew next to nothing about the creature who would be teaching him. Sometimes he felt as though he were learning matters of great profundity, but other times he felt that Master Pukje was toying with him, keeping him busy so he wouldn't learn anything important on his own. He didn't know if this was one time or the other.

'*Should* I trust you, Master Pukje?'

'I don't know. *Can* you?'

Ros agonised for a dozen breaths. If he didn't drink the potion, he would always wonder . . .

Raising the beaker, he knocked back its contents in three gulps, willing himself not to taste the potion as it slid down his throat.

'There,' he gagged, handing his teacher the empty beaker. 'So what's the big secret?'

'Wait and see.'

Master Pukje leaned close to catch him as the fire went out and the world fled.

When Ros woke, he was in darkness, lying limp on his side with his mouth full of dust. It took four attempts to get to his feet and two to conjure a small amount of light. Only then did he learn that he was in a vaulted hall, the ceiling of which hung far above his head, just out of reach of his tiny flame.

He didn't know about the maze until he followed the hall to the first intersection and learned that it was just one of many such tunnels, wending and winding through unknown depths. He knew all about mazes – specifically, that they had centres. Hard experience had taught him that if he could find the centre, Master Pukje would let him out, and not before. He had no reason to believe that this maze was different to any other.

Then he took a wrong turn and met his first dead end.

With a shudder like one of his teacher's dragonish late-night shivers, the maze shrunk around him and suddenly, where once had been only shadow, he could see the yellow ceiling.

That was weird.

Two more dead ends and the ceiling came within reach of his questing fingers.

That was worrying, given he still had no gut feeling on how to navigate the maze. The skills Master Pukje had taught him were no use to him in here: he had tried to get his bearings that way and failed many times. He might wander at random for days, hoping for a lucky break but never finding one.

He didn't let that deter him. If anything, Ros's determination grew stronger. He would find the centre somehow and make the maze his own, and show Master Pukje that he wasn't so easily cowed.

Two more dead ends and two more grinding,

unstoppable contractions crushed his certainty somewhat.

Using his bare hands, he tried digging his way out through the ceiling and nearly brought a landslide down upon him.

'Was this what happened to your last apprentice?' he shouted at the yellow walls. 'Did you put him in here, too?'

There was no answer but a distant rumbling, as though of mocking laughter.

If talking to Master Pukje was like being tied up in knots, his silences were like being tied up and rolled off a cliff.

———

Ros walked carefully back to the crossroads and took the left path, ducking his head to avoid banging it on rocky outcrops. The risk of taking a wrong turn was undiminished, but he would rather fail by trying than by sitting in the dark, empty of hope.

Inaction was for the wise, his teacher sometimes said. And for the old, Ros always replied.

At the next dead end, he was forced to crouch back the way he had come.

This time he went straight across the intersection to the one tunnel he hadn't followed, another curving, sweeping route that led to a T-junction. He went right, feeling the awkwardness of his hunched posture in the muscles of his back and thighs.

The dead end he found there reduced him to a

crawl. And crawling meant no light, because both his hands were busy.

But he didn't complain. He said nothing at all. The only thing he could do was retreat and press on, feeling for the notches he had left and hoping the maze would make sense sooner rather than later. Because at this rate, there might not be a later before long.

Another intersection and then another. His knees were bruised and raw by the time he found himself nose to stone at another dead end. He wrapped his arms around his head as the tunnel shook and shrank. He hacked and coughed in the rising dust. Afterwards, there was barely sufficient space to turn around.

Ros fought a rising panic. He wasn't ordinarily afraid of small spaces, but this was different. This was a nightmare. Who knew how much further he had to go before reaching the centre of the maze, crawling on hands and knees until they were bloody to the bone? Who knew how many more dead ends he could endure? He didn't dare imagine what it would be like to be trapped down here forever, lost like a rat in a snake warren with no end.

He kept fear at bay, barely, by telling himself that Master Pukje never did anything without a purpose, even if it was at first inscrutable. He wouldn't throw away the life of his apprentice on a whim, even if Ros was just the latest of many.

But what about a *failed* apprentice . . . ?

Shut up, he told that treacherous part of his brain. I've beaten everything else he's thrown at me, and I'll beat this, too.

After the next dead end, he couldn't turn. He had to back up awkwardly to the last intersection and twist until his spine almost snapped to fit into the next tunnel.

And then, when that tunnel also turned into a dead end, he found that he could no longer crawl at all. He could only creep along by flexing his toes and his fingers like some ungainly human earthworm, unable to see anything, unable to hear anything but the desperate rasping of his breath. *Please*, it sounded like – and the rhythm of his flexing limbs went *what happened, what happened . . .* ?

They couldn't all be dead ends, could they?

He almost wept when the tunnel he had been painfully inching along concluded in, not the centre of the maze, but one more blank yellow wall.

The maze pressed close around him, gripping him as tightly as a stone coffin. And so it might as well have been.

'Master . . . why?' he asked, unable to move even a fingertip. 'What did I do wrong? How did I fail you?'

His voice sounded very loud to his dust-plugged ears, but no one answered.

There was nowhere else to go. He was trapped. The air was already growing stale.

Ros sagged in defeat, wishing he had never wondered about the apprentices that had come before him, boys he had never known and should have cared less than nothing about. Maybe their skeletons littered corners of the maze he hadn't reached yet, and now his would join them. He could go no further, no matter how much he might want to. His journey was over. He would die ignorant, denied the future he had dreamed of.

I'm sorry, he whispered to the girl he had promised himself to long ago, even though there was no possible way she could hear him.

He had reached the end.

In the lightless coffin, Ros's eyes suddenly shot open. The darkness looked the same to him, but everything was suddenly different.

He had reached the end.

Could it be so simple? He didn't dare hope, but hope blazed in him anyway. There was nowhere left for him to go, so couldn't it be said that he had, in a weird way, reached the centre of the maze? It was exactly the kind of riddle his teacher might call education.

'Master Pukje, I get it,' he croaked. 'I am the centre. Now let me out of here before I choke!'

Through layers of stone, like a distant earthquake, came the same mocking chuckle as before, and for a terrible moment Ros feared that he was wrong, that the end of his subterranean struggles really did mean the end for him, too.

But then the stone flexed around him, bucking and buckling his body into a series of unnatural and painful shapes. His skull was squeezed so tightly he saw tiny lights in his eyes.

Then all the lights coalesced into one, growing brighter and brighter and he was moving, surging forward as though on the back of an avalanche, tumbling, turning and falling heavily to the ground at the feet of an open-mouthed dragon. A dragon who had coughed him up like a fur-ball from depths he couldn't fathom.

'Welcome back,' said Master Pukje. 'Have a nice trip?'

Ros laughed, coughed, then laughed some more. The stars were impossibly clear. The air smelled sweeter than he had ever known it before. He was alive.

'Did I imagine all of it?' he managed to say. 'I can't *really* have been inside you, can I?'

'What difference does it make? The important thing is that you learned your lesson. Tell me what that was.'

'I am the centre of the maze,' he repeated.

'I think you can do better than that.'

Ros composed himself, forcing his aching limbs into a sitting position and raising a small cloud of yellow dust as he did so.

'I am the architect of my own confusion?'

'Could be.'

'Being with you is making me more lost than ever?'

'Now you're trying too hard.' Master Pukje grinned. 'Maybe I just want you to think twice before accepting a potion from someone, no matter how trustworthy they might seem.'

'So I *shouldn't* trust you?'

'I don't care if you do or do not, Ros. Just trust yourself more.'

Ros thought all this through, wondering if he was dreaming this conversation, too. The scabs and scrapes *seemed* real. He was thirsty and tired and, judging by the stars, some hours had passed. The *experience* was real enough. The lesson, too, whatever that was supposed to be.

He felt a rising dizziness: the after-effects of the potion, he assumed.

'You said I'd find out what happened to your last apprentice.'

'And you did, Ros. She went into the maze, just like you.'

'But did she pass the test?'

'No. I ate her.'

'I don't believe you,' he said.

'All right, then. She was smarter than you and got

out within half an hour. Does that make you feel any better?'

Ros lay down on the ground and closed his eyes, which did nothing at all to quell his vertigo. Real or hallucinatory, the world was fading again.

'I don't think either of those stories are true, Master Pukje.'

'I don't think that really matters.'

Ros's teacher curled around him in dragon form, like a giant leathery dog, and gently covered him with one expansive wing.

'You're here. Let that be enough, for now.'

The Spell of Oblivion

Paul Collins

Of all the girls in the port city of D'loom, nobody knew better than Jelindel how far or fast Lady Fortune could cast a person down. She had been in the garden of her prosperous father's mansion one night, gazing up at the night sky and escaping the noise and bickering of her family. That very night the dark, deadly figures had struck, slaughtering everyone in the house, then burning the place to the ground.

Jelindel alone had escaped, but because she could read and write, she soon found work as a scribe in the market. She dressed as a boy and called herself Jaelin, because if someone had wanted her entire family dead, they would now be looking for the one girl who had escaped. If the murderers had done a body count before starting the fires, then she was definitely being hunted.

The day had all started like any other, and by the afternoon she found herself making a little more money than usual. The D'loom market was always crowded with buyers and sellers, the latter hawking their wares at the top of their voices, the noise indescribable.

Jelindel had been sitting cross-legged beside the scribe's stall she shared with Bebia, though just then the old man was off fetching his afternoon cup of teblith – a drink brewed from dried beans, and that seemed strong enough to make the dead sit up.

'I'm alive and things can't get any worse,' was what she whispered to herself every day, every hour, and sometimes every minute. She was whispering it when a sudden quiet made her look up.

Coming towards her, swathed in their distinctive maroon-coloured robes, was a clutch of Maelorian monks. She looked to her left. In the distance, rising grandly above D'loom's smog, were the towering walls of their temple fortress, Maelor, named after the god they served.

Only moments before, the marketplace had been a seething cauldron of noise and activity. Now it was silent, and a large space had opened up around the monks to let them through unhindered.

Jelindel wondered what was happening, because the monks of Maelor seldom left their temple fortress. Although powerful and dangerous, they rarely interfered with those in D'loom. It almost seemed as if the citizens of the port city were not important enough to murder.

'Get an eyeful,' muttered Barbar, the one-eyed salt

seller in the next stall. 'Pity them as have business with that lot!'

'Keep your gaze and voice down!' Jelindel hissed back.

'Trouble's brewing.'

'What now?'

'You have customers.'

The monks weren't passing by, they were coming straight for Jelindel's stall. She swallowed, and noticed that Barbar was sidling away from her.

The monks came to a stop in front of the stall, as perfectly synchronised as a squad of soldiers. They parted, and a senior monk stepped forward. He was short, well-muscled, and utterly expressionless.

Jelindel stood, trying not to let her legs shake. She gave the monk a small bow, unsure of the proper etiquette for greeting killer monks.

'Welcome, exalted one,' said Jelindel. 'My master, Bebia Ral'Vey, greets thee through this junior one, and sends his apologies for being absent at so auspicious a time. May this unworthy one bear a message to his master?'

The short monk gave her a curt nod. 'I am Stands Waiting. I serve at the feet of my master, who is called Benign Fist. I am here to engage your services, Jel – Jaelin.'

Jelindel gasped inwardly. Stands Waiting had all but told her he knew her real name. How could that be? Jelindel dek Mediesar was supposed to be dead, butchered and burned with the rest of her family! So, the murderers had indeed counted the bodies, and had noticed that they were a body short.

Had the monks killed her family?

She kept any hint of her inner turmoil out of her voice as she answered. 'This unworthy one is honoured beyond words for such unexpected benevolence.'

Stands Waiting regarded her for a moment, then stepped closer. Jelindel tried not to flinch. Maelorian monks could move so fast that their movements were a blur. Even Zimak, considered one of the finest Silurian kick-fist fighters in D'loom, would have turned and run if Stands Waiting had stepped into the ring with him.

'Let us speak plainly . . . Jaelin,' said Stands Waiting, lowering his voice to almost a whisper. 'Let us also speak very, very quietly.'

He raised a hand, palm up. From behind him a monk placed a bamboo tube into his grasp. Stands Waiting removed a scroll and spread it on the stall in front of Jelindel.

'This is the Star Testament. As you see, it contains writing in the ancient language of Astradis. I know that you have been taught it, no need for silly games of deception.'

'But many scholars know Astradis.'

'True, but the person who wrote the testament was killed by her captors as soon as it was finished.

Only then did they discover that it had been a subtle code, woven within the astrological text and pictures. We want you to decrypt it. Many have tried. All have failed.'

'But master, why me?'

'Because you are one of the speakers of Astradis who has not been given a chance to decode it. Take care and be diligent, because we kill every fifth scholar who fails, just to give the others some incentive.'

Jelindel gulped. There had been the slightest emphasis on the word 'fails'. It told her that there was a fairly good chance that the previous four scholars who had disappointed Stands Waiting were still alive.

'We will return in forty-eight hours,' said Stands Waiting, who then turned and strode away without another word.

'Wait!' called Jelindel.

Stands Waiting stopped and turned, regarding her with a cold, blank expression.

Jelindel gestured at the scroll. 'Forty-eight hours isn't enough!'

'Is forty-eight years enough?' asked Stands Waiting. 'You have forty-eight hours, use them wisely.'

'But I'm not certain I can do it!'

'Then the scholar who follows you will have your fate to inspire him.'

There was that threat again, though less veiled than before.

'What if I can't do it?' asked Jelindel, desperate to

find some trapdoor to escape this mad commission.

'Then here is a little more incentive,' said Stands Waiting. 'We know who killed your family. If you fail, we will tell them where you live. If you succeed . . . we know where they live.'

'But –'

'And if you succeed, do not think about using the secret of the Star Testament on us. The followers of Maelor are shielded by an anchor spell. It protects us from even the intention of attack.'

And with that, the monks of Maelor were gone.

Jelindel stared after them, shifting rapidly from one mood to another: anger, relief, fear, and then back to anger. She sat down hard and stared at the scroll.

From nearby came Barbar's voice. 'My deepest condolences, Jaelin,' he began, but she waved him silent.

Moments later, Bebia returned, looking pale. 'Is it true? Were they here?'

Jelindel nodded. Bebia sat down, pressing a hand to his chest. 'May the gods protect you.'

'Should I start running or decoding?' Jelindel wondered aloud.

'Nobody can run faster than the monks,' said Bebia.

If running and decoding were not options, that left hiding. The youth Zimak was good at hiding, especially when he had just thrown a kick-fist fight, and angry betters were looking for him and waving cudgels.

'I need to see Zimak, do you know where he is today?' asked Jelindel.

Bebia nodded. 'He's in the stocks for a week, for throwing a fight.'

Jelindel closed her eyes tightly for a moment. Zimak was not so much her best friend as her only friend. She was in hiding, pursued by criminals, so she needed criminal skills. Zimak had been the perfect teacher for anything criminal, but now he was no help to anyone.

'I fear, boy, that you are too good at what you do,' said Bebia. 'Word has spread.'

'Cursed by competence,' muttered Jelindel, picking up the scroll.

Jelindel didn't sleep that night. Even as the noise in the marketplace died away with the coming of darkness, she sat poring over the testament by the light of a lamp burning discarded cooking oil. It did not take long to translate the testament, but the words told her nothing. She studied the pictures from every angle, even upside down. But it was all to no avail.

Jelindel threw her hands up in despair and slumped across her work bench.

Dawn came, and the D'loom market lurched into life again, unsteadily, like a soldier forced to wake up and start marching after a night in the taverns.

Today something was different, however. It was as if everyone – buyers and sellers alike – was avoiding the scribe's stall. Even Bebia managed to make himself absent for long periods.

In a way, this helped. Jelindel had slipped into the world of code breaking, searching for subtle patterns, recurring motifs, analysing the spacing between words and letters, the orientation of pictures and script, always seeking symbolic meanings . . .

By late afternoon Jelindel had used up her first twenty-four hours. When the sun set she had less than twenty hours until the deadline.

Jelindel began to panic. There was nothing in the testament! It simply told the myth about a witch who had made a journey to the stars and returned with a terrible spell, one so powerful it could not be shared. The witch had been forced to write the testament, but she had probably known what was going to happen to her. She had also been gagged, so that she could not use the spell on her captors. Had she used a code too clever for her stupid captors, or had she written gibberish? Were the monks wrong? Was there no secret message?

Jelindel had examined the other side of the scroll, which was blank. She had cast some simple spells, toy magic used by teenage scholars to pass invisible messages to each other. They revealed nothing. The parchment itself was very old, and had been inscribed with a pen using an expensive metal nib.

At various points the nib had pierced the parchment, as if the writer had paused as she wrote, perhaps lost in thought.

Midnight came, and Jelindel slumped back in her chair, defeated.

'Were I the witch, what would I do?' she muttered, her mind exhausted.

It would be simple enough to write nonsense, knowing that her captors would not know the difference. On the other hand, what if there was an important message to pass on to someone who was less stupid than her captors?

Jelindel wondered why the document was called the Star Testament. True, it was the testament of a witch who had visited the stars. But what did that mean? Jelindel glanced up at the night sky. The diamond-bright pinpricks of light reminded her of something she had seen recently . . . very, very recently. She caught her breath.

There was a secret code after all! She held the scroll up to the meagre light issuing from her foul smelling lamp. The places where the quill had punctured the parchment formed a diagram cipher. The long-dead witch had been smart. There was just a bunch of random-looking holes, the kind of mistakes one always found on parchments! The difference was that these mistakes had been made with exquisite care.

Jelindel began to read what was woven into the

words, rather than the words themselves. What she saw filled her with horror.

It was a spell that travelled through time, erasing whatever you wanted to erase. Don't like somebody? Send the spell back through time and stop them from ever being born. Detest an entire town, guild, a country? Erase it from history, as if it had never existed in the first place! If you didn't want to annihilate it completely, you could just sponge away the memories of the people.

The more Jelindel thought about the spell's power, the more frightened she became. She felt as if she'd removed the lid from a basket and discovered an angry snake that was about to leap up at her face.

But she'd discovered something else, too. Slowly, fearfully, Jelindel began to whisper the spell of oblivion . . .

Tired yet invigorated, Jelindel arrived at the stall where Zimak slept. She roused him by snatching his blanket away. The youth bounded to his feet, assuming that someone was attacking him.

'You owe me a favour,' said Jelindel, tossing the youth's blanket back to him.

'Favour? What favour?'

'I rescued you from a week in the stocks.'

'What do you mean? Why would I be in the stocks?'

'You're not in the stocks because I erased the memories of some very angry men who bet lots of money that you would win today's kick-fist fight – the fight that you threw.'

'I never threw any fight!'

'Keep your voice down and only we two will know. Get dressed, then come with me.'

'Where are we going?'

'I need a criminal, someone good at lying. You have the right qualifications. Oh, and best you act like an oaf for the rest of the day. You'll enjoy that.'

Zimak approached the fortress temple. He had Jelindel in tow. She was clutching a scroll and a sheaf of other papers, and looked confused. As expected, the guards challenged them.

'I'm his bodyguard,' explained Zimak. 'I received instructions to bring him here and ask for Stands Waiting if something went wrong. Well, something did.'

'What went wrong, Zimak?' asked Jelindel. 'Why are we here? What are these papers?'

'Simpletons,' growled one of the guards, but his companion noticed the Maelorian royal seal on the scroll.

'I'll fetch the master.' The guard glared at Jelindel and Zimak. 'Be it on your heads if this is a lark.'

Stands Waiting arrived moments later. His usual passive expression seemed feverish with excitement.

'You have accomplished your task?' he said to Jelindel.

'Yeah, well, me scribe friend said he's worked out a secret,' began Zimak.

Stands Waiting turned to Zimak. 'Continue,' he said impatiently.

'Well, I asks Jaelin what he discovered, an' he says some words that sounds like a goat being sick. Then he says he wishes he could forget about the past two days, and then wham! He's forgot the past two days.'

'It's the spell, you blithering fool!' exclaimed Stands Waiting. 'Guards, keep this boy here at the gate. Scribe Jaelin, come with me.'

Benign Fist was meditating on a balcony of a tower facing out to sea when Stands Waiting entered with Jelindel. 'Ah,' he said, standing. 'Our young market scribe whose life hangs in the balance. Welcome, child.'

'She has suffered a foolish accident,' Stands Waiting offered. 'Perhaps a failed experiment with the Star Testament.'

'Has she now?' Benign Fist said. He cupped Jelindel's head with his hands and performed a probe spell. Shortly he stepped back from her. 'Nothing,' he said. 'She has indeed had the memory of the two days past sponged away.

'And what are the papers that she carries? Let me see . . . notes, scribblings, words crossed out. Here! This passage here. Words in the ancient Yurlish tongue – no, this second last word is *loksig*, the *Astradis* word for *anchor*.'

'From what her monkey of a bodyguard said, you speak these words, then say what you wish to have obliterated.'

Benign Fist looked up from the parchment. 'Then let us perform a test. That filthy port city of D'loom is an insult to my eyes. I would have it sponged from history.' Benign Fist held the page up to the lamplight then began reading. '*Qellio innaculus d'arthier . . .*'

Stands Waiting had a feeling that something was not quite right, but Benign Fist demanded absolute obedience, so he held his tongue. The only problem with having followers with absolute obedience is that you must always make good decisions. In his eagerness to use this doomsday weapon from the dim, forgotten past, Benign Fist had allowed himself to be swept away. He had made a bad decision.

Benign Fist reached the end of the spell.

'. . . *vati kel loksig slarsh.*'

He never got a chance to say '*D'loom*'.

For one terrible, terrible moment Stands Waiting realised what had happened. *Vati kel* was 'this thing' in Yurlish. *Slarsh* was Yurlish for 'obliterate'. Benign Fist had just obliterated the Astradis word for anchor, and the anchor spell that protected the fortress temple was in Astradis. Deprived of the word *anchor*, the anchor spell that had protected Maelor for centuries collapsed.

An attack by Katrusi brigands many centuries ago had not been beaten off with the aid of the spell for it had now never existed. The temple and what was then the new sect of Maelor had been wiped out in the attack.

Jelindel found herself falling, and before she even had time to be afraid she crashed into thick bushes that were growing in the ruins of the ancient fortress temple of Maelor. Hearing the noise, Zimak came hurrying across the piles of overgrown rubble. Jelindel was not hurt, apart from cuts and scratches.

'At the risk of sounding a bit simple, what are we doing here?' asked Zimak.

Dazed, Jelindel looked about. 'It's the ruins of the Maelor temple.'

'I know that. But why are we here?'

'Well, I don't know, Zimak. Maybe you were teaching me to climb walls and burgle buildings.'

'Out here?' exclaimed Zimak.

'Makes sense. If we practised on buildings with people in them, they'd set the city guards after us.'

'Look, answer me one thing,' said Zimak. 'You fell into those bushes, right?'

'I think so,' Jelindel agreed.

'From what? This tower was destroyed hundreds of years ago. It's no higher than a midget's gallows.'

'Maybe some ancient magic lingers here, and it threw me up into the air,' suggested Jelindel. 'Maybe it plays tricks with our memories, too.'

'You know what?'

'What?'

'I think coming here was a bad idea. We should go back to the market and get some sleep. It's Haggling Day tomorrow.'

'Haggling Day is still two days away,' said Jelindel firmly.

'You like to bet on that?' asked Zimak, tossing a coin in the air.

And so the two young heroes returned to D'loom, unaware that they had saved the city, the past, the future, and the world. Behind them some sheets of paper that had fallen with Jelindel had been found by a rat that lived among the ruins. It began shredding them to build a nest.

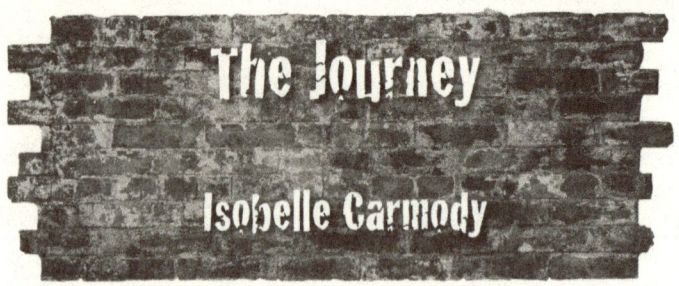

The Journey

Isobelle Carmody

She recognised him from the holovids and nuscan bites as soon as she was ushered into his office. Tall and handsome, electric blue eyes, a great eccentric mane of white-blond hair and a smile that seemed just a little too bright and wide in real life. William Reichler was fleshier than in the vids, but the visual slimdown might not be vanity. Cam crews always shaved off podge, claiming it was aesthetically unappealing and therefore bad for ratings. When he rose and held out his hand to her, she noted his pupils were dilated. She told herself hers were probably dilated, too, after the stimutabs and coffee, and so what if he had slipped a couple of uppers? Everyone used them in corporate cities. Her parents disapproved of using drugs to pep up or calm down, yet current thinking said it was savvy to make your mind and body serve your will and needs. Her parents were old-fashioned in their attitude to chems, but she suspected she had absorbed their bias, because she always found herself making excuses to rationalise why she would not take a pill or a hotshot.

You can take the girl out of a Tipodan freetown,

but you could not take the freetown out of the girl, she thought wryly. That was what her friend and co-worker, Eva, had warned on the way to the airport.

Eva had also told her she was a fool to give up her apartment, sell off her furniture and books and shift halfway round the world to Uropa to take part in research so new it was on the crackpot edge of science, all on the say-so of someone she had never met. But William Reichler had not been a stranger. Discovering his book had changed her life. Before reading it, she had thought of herself as a lone freak. For all their liberal inclinations, her parents' minds had been full of blind spots and guilt because she had been a very late child conceived by in vitro fertilisation. They never openly acknowledged what she was, and for a long time she had tried desperately to change herself, to be normal. Then a day came when she had accepted she could not stop being what she was. So she had made an art of hiding it.

Then William Reichler's book made her see she might not be an aberration, but the next tentative step in human evolution. Her first e-send to him had been a girlish outpouring of admiration and excitement, and she had received a polite note from his personal assistant acknowledging it. Soon after, she stumbled onto an article whose author observed that humans co-evolved with their technology, and this had given her the focus for her own work. Years later when she had sent articles about her work, published in *Tipoda Tomorrow*, to William Reichler, he responded personally with interest and encouragement. After that they had corresponded intermittently until his offer of an internship at the Reichler Clinic.

His letter did not say there would be a job at the end of the unpaid internship, but it was implied. And Hannah was good at what she did. Better than good, according to her workmates and supervisors, though their opinions mattered less to her than her own feelings. You had to have a realistic idea of what you were worth or else you would be forever at the mercy of other people's opinions, which most often would depend on their level of liking for you. You had to know yourself and, above all, you had to be honest with yourself.

'Ms Seraphim, it is a real pleasure to meet you in person, at last,' William Reichler said, his big pink manicured hand encompassing hers in a warm, slightly clammy grip. 'Your last paper on the way some humans adapt to the speed of technological development was very fresh. Young woman, you have a brilliant mind, though I must say it is a shock to see how very young you are.' He gave an avuncular chuckle.

'My age . . .' Hannah stammered, overwhelmed by the way he had leaned towards her, still holding her hand.

'Is no problem,' he concluded firmly. He sat on a soft fat sofa, drawing her down with him, and shifted smoothly to talking about the work of the Reichler Clinic with an easy familiarity that made him sound glib. It was a natural consequence of him having to say the same thing over and over, she supposed, and she told herself it would be no surprise if his brain just wandered off in another direction completely, leaving his mouth to run on auto-pilot.

It was a mistake to think about his thoughts, she realised a split second too late as her mind peeled open.

. . . like them young . . . good hands and legs and great hair . . . probably reach her waist if she let it down . . . like a woman with a good head of hair . . . pity about the neck to knee retro-frump freetown threads . . . transpo gel tube would make the most of her breasts . . . too small, but bump them a size or two and she'd be specky . . . give her a year or two and she'd get over her outmoded freetown attitude to augmentation . . .

For one shocked and disorientated second, Hannah thought she must be picking up the mental thread of the only other man in the room, an older, white-coated scientist who had yet to be introduced, except her mind was too well disciplined to open itself to more than one thread at a time and risk being mentally bludgeoned. No, the stream of crude speculation was flowing from William Reichler's mind. The physical contact and the eager razzle-dazzle of his personality, combined with the dual hype of nerves and stimutabs, had broken through her carefully constructed mind-shield.

Ordinarily her ethics would have made her withdraw immediately, but William Reichler's thoughts made it all too painfully clear that Eva had been right. Hannah had not known him. The revelation of his arrogant disrespect for her dispelled any guilt she might have felt as she delved through what transpired to be a superficial, atavistic sensuality crusted over a vast and rapacious, self-centred hunger for glory and the social power that came with it. Her heart sank into her new gel boots, for not only was William Reichler a lecher, he was a liar. One look into his deeper mind made it clear he did not have the ability or knowledge to have undertaken the research upon which his book and articles were based. He had cribbed the science from raw data, spinning it into brightly accessible rhetoric.

It did not comfort Hannah to find he had every intention of offering her an employment contract at the end of the internship. The only reason he had not done so already was because he believed an unpaid internship would establish an advantageous power structure between them, ensuring she was locked into a subordinate and subservient role. He had no fear she would go elsewhere because of her blatant hero worship of him.

How it rankled to remember she had gazed into those brilliant blue eyes in vids, reading in them sincerity, intelligence and sensitivity. She felt ashamed because she ought to have known better than to expect truth from vid and nuscan spinners, or even to take the things that William Reichler had written in e-notes to her, as any indication of his character or ethics. How many times in life had her abilities revealed that a bland or smiling face could hide anything from deep neurosis and fear to loathing or boredom? It was the bitterest kind of joke that these abilities, which had brought her halfway round the world to this meeting, now revealed the brilliant, charismatic William Reichler as a charlatan.

Her disappointment and despair did not show in her expression or manner any more than her shock and outrage had done. She had learned the hard way not to react obviously and openly to the things she learned from people's minds, and in this case, she was very glad because a man with an interest in paranormal abilities might very well jump to the right conclusion. Instead, she managed to nod and smile as the interview progressed, and even to talk enthusiastically about working at the Reichler Clinic; though the second she left the building she was determined to return to the hotel, pack and leave, after dispatching a bland little e-note expressing contrition and regret at her decision to refuse the internship because she was homesick for Tipoda.

Then William Reichler introduced the other man in the room.

'This is my cousin, Axel Reichler,' he said. 'He is the head of the laboratory here at the Clinic and he will conduct you on a tour of the facility so that you can see what you will be getting into.'

The white-coated man rose and bowed slightly from his waist. He was older than his cousin by a good decade and as strikingly ugly as William Reichler was handsome. That he should remain so in a world where no one had to be ugly intrigued Hannah, despite herself, as he ushered her, with William trailing behind, from the reception room. She did not hesitate to access his thoughts. She almost gasped in relief to discover that *this* was the mind behind the research, though she had never heard Axel Reichler's name anywhere in the publicity about the Clinic, or seen it on the articles or books it had produced. Delving deeper as she followed him from laboratory to laboratory and through rooms full of the latest technological tools for brain and mind research, she was looking for the hold that William Reichler had over him, that had allowed the theft of his work. Instead, she was astonished to learn that Axel Reichler had no objection to William absorbing the limelight by putting his name and face on the books and articles that had resulted from his work. He knew his cousin craved power and visible success and appreciated the social skills that were honed and sharpened by that hunger because they served his own ends. He did not care at all that his name was unknown. He cared nothing for fame or power, or for money, save that it would buy him the equipment and materials he needed to continue his research.

Hannah might have admired his single-mindedness, except that he had no more notion of what it would be like to be a person with the abilities they were so hungrily researching than his cousin. To Axel it was all theory and to William it was an angle to be played out like bait on one of those ancient fishing poles that people used to dangle in water. William didn't even believe paranormal abilities existed. It was all smoke and mirrors to him. What he did understand was that people wanted to believe their minds held a potential that might be woken. There were dozens of sponsors paying good creds to the Clinic, in the belief that when the breakthrough came, they would be first in line to receive the serum or pill that would unleash that potential.

Both men wanted Hannah to join the Reichler Clinic, though neither guessed her groundbreaking work was the direct result of her possessing the very abilities of mind they were trying to document. Axel believed the direction of her research would lead him to a breakthrough in finding a means of creating a machine capable of isolating and identifying people with fledgling paranormal abilities. Hannah shifted to William Reichler's mind, wanting to learn if his motivations were the same, but he was thinking about a meeting that morning with a couple of government men interested in the possible uses of paranormal abilities in conflict. The govogeeks had indicated they were prepared to pay well if the work at the Reichler Clinic could be shaped to serve their ends.

Hannah slipped back into Axel's mind. He might be cold, but he was brilliant and in his own way, honest. He believed in paranormal abilities, though her probing showed his certainty they would only manifest after chemical or genetic intervention upon people whose minds were receptive. He actually conceived the possibility of breeding them, like to like, to improve the paranormal strain. He had not once, she saw, considered how a paranormal might feel about being used in this way. To him they were merely hypothetical experimental subjects.

It hurt Hannah that she had believed in their research, had set so much store by it.

The tour through the Clinic ended and as they made their way back to his office, William began to speak of a future in which mobile testing units would allow people to self-test to discover if they possessed any paranormal tendencies. This would offer a far greater sampling than they had been so far able to assay, he pointed out enthusiastically. Hannah read Axel's surprise in his mind. He and William had discussed the need for the development and creation of equipment to provide proof of their theories, she learned, but they had never spoken of mobile testing units. Axel was no fool and was already wondering what angle his cousin was playing, and why. He did not know William had met with the govogeeks or that he was calculating how much he could dun them for the money to set up mobile test units that would enable the compilation of a list of suitable candidates.

Candidates for what? Hannah wondered uneasily, but Axel was asking what sort of research she might be interested in pursuing. His mind told her he was genuinely interested, but he was distracted wondering what his cousin was up to. He needed to find out and to be sure it would help, rather than hinder, his work. Hannah withdrew from his mind as she began to talk. She was very careful because she was aware that the truth about her abilities was woven into her research. She would have spotted it. Maybe, she thought bleakly, *only* someone like her would have spotted it: a lone freak of nature; the exception to the rule of normality.

When she stopped talking, both men were smiling. William produced a contract and pressed it into her hands, suggesting she take it away and return later in the week to discuss it. He spoke as if her employment was a fait accompli, the contract a mere formality and not, as she ascertained from a swift dip into his mind, a binding intern contract connected seamlessly to an agreement to be employed at whatever wage was offered her, for a period not exceeding five years. He must think her a fool or perhaps he counted on her being overawed. Hannah cared too little to discover which. Indeed, her first impulse was to throw the wretched contract into a passing trash unit as she left the building. But she stuffed it into her document case and slung it over her shoulder before setting off for the glide stop where she had been set down two hours earlier with such high hopes.

Half an hour later, Hannah gazed out the window of the glide, her eyes slipping over the enigmatic surfaces of the gleaming splinter towers with their mirror-coated glass that reflected everything and revealed nothing of what lay within. Everything offered you back to yourself in the corporate city of Londo-Arko, which was sprawled along both sides of the river that bisected it. You would never know it was an ancient city, looking down at it from above. You had to get on the ground to see beneath its shiny skin and, even then, in many places, genuine age had been replaced by faux age dens catering to the growing New Luddite movement spawned by those for whom technological advancements had not answered. It was a potent minority giving rise to a multitude of offshoots from radical fundamentalists to conservative ecolniks like her parents. Still, ultimately, it was a minority because in corporate cities, the culture tended to be middle-of-the-road conservative. But even in a freetown in Tipoda, people were content with technology and happy with where it was leading them. Happiness was the accepted proper goal of life, though that had never seemed enough to satisfy her own restless intensity of yearning. It was odd how her refusal to worship at the altar of happiness angered and irritated people. When she was six a teacher had become infuriated because instead of painting something that had made her happy at home, as instructed, she had painted a city as a bleak and smoking ruin over which loomed a dark, bruised-looking sky, the only visible thing a great green smiling neon face at the apex, one eye gone dark and dead.

She had listened, head hung, as the teacher ranted at her for egoising, too ashamed to explain she had been unable to think of something happy at home so she painted what she dreamed the night before instead. She had already learned never to talk about what she saw in her dreams.

The endless mirroring of other buildings, the sky and clouds was oddly hypnotic and she let their motion soothe her jangling nerves. The coiling flow of the segmented public glide and the quick darting movement of the small private glides reminded her of fish and sea snakes weaving through the waving fronds of a submarine forest of seaweed floating and undulating upward.

Diving was one of the things she had left behind in the remote freetown on the northern part of the west coast where she had grown up, and where there were still places you could dive and actually catch sight of fish. Not that you killed them as divers had once done. That was illegal in all countries now. Not just the killing of the big sentient cetaceans, but all remaining wild sea life. The five big governments and the powerful corporations running all but a few of the biggest cities had agreed it was a bad idea to kill off all life in the sea and a pact was made to leave it alone for a millennia or so. All the fish people ate was now either flavoured soy substitute or tank grown if you could afford it. The sea was totally out of bounds save for harmless recreational activities in closely monitored areas.

She could dive in Londo-Arko. Not in the deadly matte-black Thames or even in the sea, because that would require a contamination suit and there would be no marine life to see in any case. But Eva had told her of a public aqua park where you could do bare skin dives, when Hannah revealed her intention of using the remainder of her scholarship grant to travel to Uropa rather than trading up to a government research facility fellowship or a grant with one of the big corporate entities. Knowing Eva, Hannah had taken a look, only to discover the so-called dive haven was really just a big fish tank sunk into the ocean to produce the illusion that you were swimming in the open sea. It was so crowded it might as well have been called people soup.

Glumly, Hannah accepted she had been naïve

on all fronts. Certain the Reichler Clinic internship would result in a proper work contract, she had been cheerfully prepared to live carefully on the remainder of her grant and to take any work she could get to eke it out, no matter how menial, until she had proven her worth. She even accepted she might need a part-time job to supplement the startup wage, because she would be working with someone she admired on research in an area that mattered to her.

She had said that to Eva.

What she had not said was that somewhere in Uropa was a place she had been dreaming about her whole life – not an ideal, but a real place with a name, that had somehow become the shape of her deepest unnamed desires. She didn't know why it was so important to find it, except that when she dreamed of it, a great sense of calm purpose unfurled in her. Somehow she knew that when she found it, she would have found herself. She would be home. For that reason, she had always known that sooner or later, she would travel to Uropa. She had already looked for her place using the worldweb, but so far, to no avail. But it was here, somewhere, and she was determined to find it. In the meantime, she would have her work.

Or so she had thought.

She sighed, feeling as if years had passed since she had woken too early that morning, still jet-lagged from the long flight from Tipoda two days before, but wired with anticipation. She had slept a lot since landing, but the time change had not got through to her on a cellular level and she had been forced to indulge in a face-brightening session in a Spruce kiosk to get rid of the bags under her eyes, knowing how much face mattered to people in corporate territories. She could have flown a rocket plane and done the trip in four hours, hence avoiding the dehydration and body stress that were the main components of classic jet lag, but the price would have taken a hefty bite out of her grant. Once she dealt with her external appearance, it had taken two stimutabs for her to feel halfway alive mentally, and a big cup of black coffee to complete the process. The trouble was that all that false adrenalin and hype took its toll when the caps and caffeine wore off.

She debated nibbling another stimutab to head off the downer. They were a herb-based chem and basically harmless in the short term, but too many would give her the jitters and she didn't like that feeling. Even less did she like the way chems messed with her mind. Besides, she was so thirsty she didn't think she would be able to swallow anything. She was sorry she had not stopped at the Javabooth by the glide stop for a tube of aqua, but she had just been too devastated by what had taken place in the meeting to do more than stumble aboard the first glide to set down.

Hannah shifted on the gel seat, which moulded

warmly and somewhat obscenely to her buttocks, wondering what it was about this whole city that seemed too grabby, too intimate, too personal, for all its coldness and superficial glam and glitz.

'What now?' she muttered. 'Do I go back to Tipoda with my tail between my legs or go on, and if I go on, what do I go on to?'

'Hah?' muttered an old woman seated next to her.

Realising the woman was unsmoothed, Hannah had to suppress the urge to reach out and squeeze her hand companionably. The trouble with the smoothing process was that while the people who had it done sure looked smooth, at some point they stopped looking real and started looking like those lifelike clone-bots some of the android companies were trying out. But maybe she was just more sensitive to it, having been raised in a freetown community, by people who would not have thought of smoothing their faces even if they had the money for the procedure. She had not seen too many young smoothies here yet, but according to the holos the trend was all the rage in face-conscious Mericanda where all cities were corporate-owned, and what happened in Mericanda, so the saying went, ended up everywhere. Though her father always said this was a saying begun by Mericandans, who had a tendency to believe their own spin.

She had smiled involuntarily at the old woman, whose eyes now narrowed suspiciously. Hannah heard her wonder if she was one of those pet snatchers who stole your beloved and sold it to the illegal fur traders. To her surprise what Hannah had taken for a faux-fur purse clutched in the woman's gnarled hands on her lap suddenly lifted its head and looked at her. It was a lap fox, bred to be small enough to fit into a handbag. Amused, Hannah projected warmth and non-aggression at it. She felt its curiosity spike, and when it craned its neck, she obligingly held her hand out for it to be sniffed.

The old woman looked startled and drew the little beast protectively closer to her. 'Could give you a nasty nip,' she said hopefully. She was wishing she had not forgotten the mugger spray her son had given her. The little creature merely wagged its bushy tail and projected firmly that it was hungry and wanted to get down to pee. It had figured out in the way animals always seemed able to do, that Hannah could understand it better than other humans. She debated passing the message onto the old woman but thought better of it.

Turning again to gaze out at the city, she told herself that there would be no shame in returning home. It would be downright foolish to remain in Londo-Arko simply to avoid the so-called humiliation of admitting she had made a mistake. Her flat back home would be gone, of course, but since she had refused the facilities that might have taken her on, she would have to wait for the midyear intake to get a place anyway. In the meantime, she could go home and have a holiday, do some diving. She rejected this thought as soon as it formed, for while she did not doubt that her parents cared for her, she was the cuckoo child they had brought up gently and with real affection, but whom they had never been able to regard as their own. Their thoughts had told her too brutally that neither could believe such an abnormal child had come solely from their genes. Something had gone wrong and though they would never stint on her, neither could they truly love her. No, she could not return to their gentle bafflement and determined kindness, which had cut her so deeply that, at some level, she was still bleeding.

To go back to her parents would be to return to the drowning loneliness of her childhood. Indeed, she might truly have drowned had she not happened on William Reichler's book, which had made her wonder if there might be others like her, alone and isolated inside their caution and secrecy. She had resolved to find them and no matter what she now thought of William Reichler, she had to acknowledge that his words had given her direction. She had ceased trying merely to exist, unnoticed, and had begun actively to pursue studies and subjects that would let her examine research into the mind and evolution. She had taken her first degree in anthropology and her second in nano-biology. She was now on the final year of her third degree, hence the grant. She had made an agreement with the educational facility to produce her final thesis based partly on the work she had expected to do with the Reichler Clinic and there was no doubt the grant body would take a dim view of her refusing the offer she had courted. At the least, she would have to find something to do that would be equally worthy and relevant to her studies. Her parents would pitch in financially if she was fined, but they were older and their earnings had never been great. The small biofarm where she had grown up was self-sustaining, but there had been nothing extra to stash away in a bank, even if her parents hadn't regarded bankers and stockbrokers and all money manipulators as the ultimate pornographers. Of course they had chosen to live where they had because of her. Funny how you could think of your life as so normal, and then look back and see how strange and eccentric it had been, only finally coming to understand that even while you were the result of all that strangeness, you might also have been the reason for it.

She sighed, and closed her eyes.

When she woke, she had missed her stop. She didn't recognise the part of the city she was in, but she got off at the next stop. It was not until the glide had taken off that it occurred to her she didn't know the location of the return stop. Feeling better for her sleep, she decided it would not hurt her to walk a little. She knew her hotel was north and she could call up a cab if she got tired before she found another public glide stop. The truth was she needed to walk off her weariness and her disappointment.

She had gone some way before it struck her she had entered one of the old districts. In general they were densely populated, but she seemed to be alone. That made her uneasy until she woke to the fact there were other people around, lurking in shadows or doorways, staying out of sight, and unease racheted up into anxiety. As she continued, buildings and pathways became more and more dilapidated, and then she noticed with a little flip of fear that someone was following her. Maybe they were just curious, but worrying, given she was definitely not in one of the trendy retro-age precincts. This was a genuinely run-down area and her sneers at the shiny faux newness of the city came back to haunt her as she yearned for a brightly lit mall zone full of shopping smoothies. She thought of the holo on trashers she had seen on the plane – people who lived in the so-called 'rim'; poor people, angry people, radical dissidents, without the disposable creds to interest corporate bosses in providing resources.

She lifted her wrist to summon a cab but the reception was full of static. She must be too close to a junction in the power grid. She would have to keep on walking. She tried to walk confidently in the hope that whoever was following would assume she had a weapon, until it occurred to her that her stalker might also have a weapon. The next time she caught a glimpse of her shadow, she sent her mind arrowing out, and was chilled to learn that although the man had no weapon, he was a detoxing chemhead hungering for the wrist unit he had spotted when she got down from the glide. He figured on bartering it for a hotshot. She considered knocking on one of the doors, but when she glanced up at the windows, she saw most of them were blank and dark, the glass in them long since smashed and fallen away. The inhabitants, if there were any, were as likely to attack her as the man following.

Hannah licked her lips and tried to calm down, but her heart was galloping because now the chemhead was trying to work up the courage to attack. Only paranoia had held him back so far, the possibility she might have been set down as a police lure. It was actually a rational speculation, she thought shakily, because what sort of idiot would come wandering alone and unarmed into a rim area? Tourists were warned of the danger of areas not patrolled by the corporate police, and indeed she had been cautioned in the pre-landing holo, but she had been too preoccupied worrying about her meeting at the Clinic.

She dared not stop and figured if she could put a little distance between her and her stalker, she would try her wrist unit again. She wanted to be out of sight of the chemhead to do it because he was watching for a sign that she might be summoning back-up. He was panicky and desperate and would not hesitate to kill her. He had killed before with his bare hands, she saw, because he was thinking about the kill. She wondered what he would do if she took the unit off and left it on the cracked sidewalk. It was a graduation present from her parents, but she thought they would prefer a live daughter without a wrist unit to a dead daughter with the proper urban accessories.

She came round a corner and her heart leapt at the sight of a corporate road beyond two tumbledown buildings. The ground level stream was close enough to take in her plight but most vehicles would be delivery and service glides, and even if they had human drivers, it was unlikely they would open and take her in in this area. On the other hand, she was clean and unarmed and young enough that they would surely ping the pollys and make a report. She didn't run, but she walked faster – aware her stalker had developed an entourage and they were all speeding up.

She was within a few steps of the road and on the verge of breaking into a run, when a man dropped down from the building to the left to block her way. He was wearing what she recognised as the latest in urban combat, complete with the little antigrav pac that had let him make his dramatic entrance without straining an ankle. He had plast body armour moulded into an exaggerated pectoral frieze and she stared at him in confusion, not knowing if this was a rescue or a new threat. She tried to penetrate his mind to find out, but the helmet he was wearing had some sort of tronics that blocked her.

'Hile woman,' the man said, his voice distorted by the tronics.

'Uh, can you help me?' she gasped. 'I got off the glide at the wrong stop and I'm lost.'

'You sure are, Doll, but N'zo found you and now you gone be saved.'

'Oh, that's great. Thank you,' Hannah said stiffly. She couldn't see the man's face or read his mind, but there was a gloating cadence in his voice and her erstwhile stalker was withdrawing, his mind revealing that he had recognised her rescuer as a nunazi ganger whose favourite recreational activity was to laser-graffiti his gang sigil between the eyes of trashers. She was no trasher, but her every instinct told her to run. Hannah's eyes darted past the man to the road as she calculated how much time it would take between breaching the seal on the road and the arrival of a police pod.

'Actually, I just need you to point me to the nearest glide stop, or wait while I call a cab,' she said, adding absurdly, 'I'm late for a meeting.'

'Don' worry, Doll, N'zo gone take you to a meeting that will change your life,' the man said and this time he gave a creepy skittering giggle.

Hannah saw the man's intention to lunge in the

shift in his stance and she leapt left, as he lunged right. The result was that he was wrong-footed, but he spun on his heel with swift grace and lunged again. Fortunately Hannah was quick and she had got past and set her gel boot triumphantly down on the smooth blue-sheened tarmac. Her attacker froze and glanced up and around, as she did, looking for a polly pod, but there was only one sleek private glide in the highest stream and no siren to announce that help was on the way. Hannah's heart sank.

'Pollys doin' their thing elsewhere, Baby Doll,' crooned the man. 'Lucky fo you, N'Zo here to take care of ever' little thing.'

But even as he stepped towards her, Hannah heard the sound of a glide in descent and she looked up in time to see the silver highflier doing a swift vertical drop.

'Don' fight me, Baby Doll,' the man snarled as he closed his arms around her in a bear hug. Before he could tighten his grip, she dropped to her hands and knees and rolled sideways, snapping out a kick at the unarmoured side of his knee. He gave a grunt, but he had thrown out a hand and, catching her by the hair, he hauled her up. The pain was excruciating as he lifted her off the ground. She clawed desperately at his hand. Too late she remembered his free hand and he punched her in the side of the head, turning out the lights.

She woke to someone touching her cheek and murmuring her name. 'Hannah? Hannah?' At first she thought it was Eva's brother, but then a face swam into focus and she realised it was a stranger with a kind face, in whose lap she seemed to be lying.

'Who . . . who are you?' she asked. 'How do you know my name?'

'I'm Jake and your name is coded into your wrist link.'

'It's encrypted,' Hannah said, noting that her voice slurred. She was having trouble remembering what had happened, but it seemed to her she could see out of one eye a good deal better than the other.

'Yes,' he said with a mild smile. 'I apologise for hacking you, but I needed to know if you had any medical conditions before I let Wu administer a revival shot.'

'Someone was chasing me, then a moron in combat gear leapt down from the building and knocked me out,' she answered indignantly, as things began to float back. She felt her temple and winced at the size of the swelling.

'So we saw,' the man said. 'You have an impressive black eye, but your assailant was limping badly when the pollys led him off.'

'Good,' she muttered wrathfully. 'Who was he?'

'A ganger,' he answered. 'The nunazi are anti-technology, with a chaser of archaic notions about purity of race taken from an ancient cult. Somewhat difficult to put eugenics into practice in this day and age so the nunazi base their credo on appearance. You have pale skin, therefore you qualify as a potential recruit. As would I. Whereas my driver, Isah, or my assistant, Wu, would be considered sacrifices, as they term their victims.'

'They practise sacrifice?' she asked, aghast.

'I daresay they dream of it, for their rhetoric and literature is very violent, but as far as I know, the sacrifices are merely shaven and tattooed with a symbol used by the antique Nazi cult from which the nunazi take some of their less charming practices. The so-called sacrifices are ritually humiliated before being turned loose, naked. As a recruit, you would have been required to do the shaving and engage in the ritual humiliation before being tattooed yourself, on the arm.'

'He said he was going to save me and take me to a meeting,' Hannah murmured. Then she looked at her rescuer. 'You seem to know a lot about them.'

'Whereas you appear to know remarkably little and yet I understand the cult is gaining popularity in Antipoda,' he said gently.

'I didn't live in a city in *Tipoda*,' she said, stressing the preferred freetown term. She was beginning to take in her immediate surroundings. She was lying along the back seat of a large glide with the sort of luxurious appointments ordinary human beings did not warrant. She noted the man wore a beautifully-fitted grey suit and his hair and hands were perfectly groomed. In the background his assistant, Wu, a ravishing Asiatic-looking woman with dark skin, was tapping into her wrist unit.

'Where are you taking me? Hannah asked, struggling to sit up.

'To your hotel, which is where I assume you were headed when you decided to take a stroll through one of the worst districts in Londo-Arko. The name of your hotel was in the link, too,' he said apologetically.

'How come there were so few people in the area where you found me?' she asked. 'I thought rim districts were packed.'

'They are,' he said. 'Except when they have been evacuated for redevelopment. That one is situated right between two rim slums whose residents fear their areas will be next, and who are determined to frighten off investors. The clearances are scandalous and brutal and verging on illegal even in a corporate city, but there is no profit in defending rim dwellers so no one does anything. Your ganger belongs to a group inhabiting one of these, with ties to a new Luddite fundamentalist group called the Shepherd Faction.'

'Them I've heard of,' she said grimly. 'Strange bedfellows.'

'Indeed,' Jake said, giving her a thoughtful look. 'In any case, there are rather more pleasant places to walk than rim sectors, even in a corporate city.'

'I fell asleep on the public glide and when I got off to backtrack, I couldn't find a stop. Thought I'd walk until I came to one. Dumb, I guess,' she said, depressed because now she was remembering what had preceded the glide journey. 'You don't need to take me all the way to my hotel. Just drop me at a glide stop.'

'It will be no trouble,' he said smoothly.

'You have an accent,' Hannah said. 'I noticed it when I first woke, before I was properly awake.'

'Everyone talks like that in New Scotia and we are resistant to the nuspeek of the corporate cities, as you will have noticed,' he said wryly. 'I have lived away some time now, but the accent gets stronger when I am agitated. As I was at seeing a young woman attacked by a much larger man. You were brave to fight back.'

'Brave on top of stupid might just equal stupid.'

'Courage is worthy of honour wherever you find it, no matter the circumstances,' the man said, sounding for a moment like her father, who had also eschewed nuspeek, saying he preferred his language straight up. But then again he had been a teacher. She remembered all at once that she had not thanked her rescuer. She remedied this and he smiled. It was the kind of smile some people have that starts out in their eyes and flows out to light up their whole face. It turned her rescuer's nice ordinary face into something special. Then he had his assistant prepare a pain blocker. Her head was throbbing badly enough that she gave in, after being told the coffee and stimutabs she had consumed would not affect it. As his assistant administered the shot, Hannah watched her rescuer covertly, resisting the temptation to violate her own code and probe him. He was a good seven years older than she, but still young, and yet he had the gravitas and polish of an older man. Power and money, she diagnosed, and that took her thoughts the full circle back to William Reichler.

'What is it?' Jake asked.

Hannah shrugged. 'I came to Londo-Arko for a research internship and the interview was this morning.'

'It didn't go well?' He actually sounded as if he cared, but maybe that was just the lack of nuspeek, which always sounded too cool and slangy to be sincere.

'They offered me the position only . . . only the company was not what I had thought it was. They want different things than I want.'

'It is often the case when an individual wishes to join a group,' he said. 'The individual has to choose whether they can work within the group agenda or if they would be better to go their own way. What you must ask yourself is if there is any advantage to doing your work with these people.'

His words forced Hannah to think about her own agenda. Before the meeting, it had been her desire to come to Uropa and work on research that might help her better understand her abilities, and which might bring her into contact with others like her. Of course she could go back to Tipoda and eventually continue her own research, but she could not deny the Reichlers had shown her the way in the first place, or that their facilities were beyond impressive. Despite knowing what they were really like now, she could pursue her agenda far better working for them than in returning to Tipoda, so long as she kept her secrets. And if she didn't work with them, Axel would go ahead with his research anyway. He was certainly brilliant enough to succeed in finding a way to identify people with paranormal tendencies. If Hannah took part in the research, she would be able to guide and protect them, and perhaps teach them what she had learned.

'Hannah, we are about to set down on the pad atop your hotel,' Jake said. 'And I apologise for silencing you with a lecture. I am afraid the tendency to pontificate is part of being an ethno-sociologist.'

'I wasn't silenced, just thinking,' Hannah assured him. 'In fact I think you have just helped me to make up my mind to take the position. I don't like the company, but I can work with them. At least for the time being.'

His brows lifted, and there was approval in his eyes. 'Then you will be staying in Londo-Arko rather than returning to Tipoda?' Hannah nodded, pleased at his careful use of the freetown term. Jake glanced at Wu, who passed him a holocard. He gave this to Hannah two-handed, bowing a little over it. 'Perhaps you will allow me to show you a more pleasant route to walk, one afternoon next month. I have to go off planet for some time, but I will be in Londo-Arko upon my return.'

'You don't live here?' Hannah asked.

He shrugged. 'I'm afraid the corporate cities are not for me. Nor even a corporate town where there is somewhat more autonomy. But I travel here regularly as part of a liaison committee between the corporate committee and the Uropan government.'

'Is that why you are going to the moon?' Hannah asked, fascinated, for while there was some exploration and tentative settlement on Mars, it was primitive and not open for general settlement. The Moon base, on the other hand, was a small government city, though there was talk the corporations were slavering to get a foothold.

'I am travelling to the moon, but on another matter,' Jake said. 'My construction company is involved in some work for the World Council.'

'How does an ethno-sociologist come to have a construction company?' Hannah asked then flushed at her rudeness. 'I'm sorry. That is none of my business.'

He smiled that warm smile. 'It is a family business

that I inherited by default. As to where I live, I have an apartment in Newrome.'

'Newrome is the free city under the ground,' Hannah said in wonderment, remembering with a little start that one could not travel there without the endorsement of a resident patron.

Jake's smile broadened. 'Strictly speaking it is a city built within a series of vast linked subterranean caverns. It is a free city though the corporations have their feelers out and would move in at once if those of us who have the power and the money to stop them falter in our vigilance.' The door to the glide slid open and he stepped out and handed Hannah down. He was very tall, she noted as she thanked him again. 'My name and address in Newrome are on the card, as well as my contact details. Ping me if you would like to take that walk. Or if you plan on visiting Newrome.'

Hannah glanced down at the card and suddenly she had trouble breathing. She gaped at the vivid little holo of the mountain valley pictured on the card, the shape of the peaks as familiar to her as her own eyes.

'Obernewtyn,' she breathed.

'Yes,' the man said. And only then did she take in the name in raised type above the image of the valley: Jacob Obernewtyn. She looked up into his face and saw his smile fade, a little ridge of puzzlement forming between his brows. 'Is something the matter?' he asked, and Hannah heard his clear thought that her green eyes were the saddest, deepest eyes he had ever seen. Eyes that would see things other eyes did not. The thought was so close to the surface that she was not sure he had not spoken it aloud.

'You . . . I . . . I was just –' she stammered. Then she stopped, took a breath and asked more calmly, 'What is the place in the holo? Where is it?'

He smiled and there was pride in his expression. 'It is a property I own in the mountains outside Newrome. At the moment I am simply calling it Obernewtyn, but I will give it a proper name once I have built there.'

'You . . . you're going to build there?'

'I had always thought to build a refuge there. A place to escape to when I need it,' he said.

She swallowed hard, and looking back down at the place of her dreams, said softly, 'I am sure you will build something special in this place. And Obernewtyn would make a perfect name for a refuge.'

'You think so?' He looked half amused, half pleased.

'I know so,' Hannah said.

ZOMBIE SALAD EATERS
WORDS AND PICTURES • GREG HOLFELD

Gamers' Inferno

George Ivanoff

Raph ran down the cobbled laneways, the grey haze occasionally making a brief appearance in his peripheral vision. He shook his head in an endeavour to get rid of it.

Sandstone buildings rose high on either side of him, their doors and windows firmly closed. As he looked up, he glimpsed a curtain shift, a pair of wary eyes watching him intently.

In the distance, Raph heard the sound of bells ringing out from the highest spire in the city, warning the residents that the Inquisition's militia were searching for someone. Him! The orphan boy from the slums. The boy who had been turned in by the Physician General.

Raph remembered how the middle-aged man with the neat goatee and expensive clothes had suddenly taken an interest in him. The Physician General had been inspecting the public infirmary, distaste obvious in every aspect of his countenance. Raph had been trying to explain to a student physician that he kept seeing things, like an encroaching greyness, when the Physician General was at his side, talking to him about 'perceptions of reality'. And then the physician was gone, racing from the building as if his life depended on it. Raph was leaving, finally fed up with trying to explain his visions, when the bells began and the militia arrived.

His mind returning to the present, Raph ducked down a small alley and allowed himself a moment to rest. He doubled over, leaning his arms on his knees, panting heavily. Staring down at the stones beneath him, he noticed that one of them was shimmering, as if it might not be real. 'Not now!' He quickly closed his eyes, blocking out the vision.

'That way!' he heard a distant voice calling. 'I saw him go down there.'

Raph cursed silently and took off. Right, left and another left and then he was out into a deserted square.

'Boy!' screeched a shrill voice.

An old man stood by a narrow opening between two buildings. Dressed in rags, with a scraggly white beard and wrinkled face, he was hunched over and leaning heavily on a walking stick. He lifted a skeletal arm and beckoned to Raph.

Raph approached cautiously.

'Nuthin' ta be a fearin' from me,' said the man. 'I is Raphaello the Sighted.'

Raph looked into the old man's eyes and saw nothing but a dull grey. 'But . . . but you're blind.'

'I sees the truth o' the world around us,' said the

old man. 'For that I does not need eyes. But you, my lad, you has the Sight and the eyes.'

'What do you mean?' whispered Raph.

'I does mean many a thing.' The old man nodded knowingly. 'What is your name?'

'Raphael,' answered the boy. 'But people call me Raph.'

'Does they?' The man chuckled. 'Of course they does. You has the Sight. You has the Name. Linked, they is.'

The bell rang again in the distance and Raph made to go. 'I've got to get away.'

'Wait!' hissed the old man. 'Away you has got to get. But to get away you must be caught.'

'What?'

'But not yet.' Raphaello shook his head. 'Others you must first meets. Sisters who can explain things. Paradise and Inferno and Inquisition.'

Now Raph could hear approaching voices. He made to leave, but the old man grabbed his arm in a vice-like grip that seemed impossible for his age and frail appearance.

'No,' he said. 'Through there.'

He shoved Raph behind him, into the space between the two buildings.

'There's not enough room,' complained Raph, trying to get back out.

A shout made him look out over the old man's shoulder. A squad of soldiers was heading his way.

'Hurry!' The old man's voice had an edge of desperation. 'You is this city's last hope.'

Raph breathed in and squeezed himself further along the narrow space. With a bit of effort, he found he could move forward.

'You has to embrace the visions,' the old man shouted after him. 'They will show you the Oracle. You must –'

The man's voice cut off with a strangled cry. Raph glanced back to see a soldier, his large frame and broad shoulders preventing him from following. He had his spear aimed at Raph.

Panicking, Raph scrabbled on. But the passage was narrowing further and he found himself wedged between the buildings. Looking around, he saw the soldier draw back his arm, ready to launch the spear. Raph closed his eyes tight and prayed to the Designers.

And then he fell backwards, the wall behind him giving way with the grinding sound of stone on stone. He hit the ground hard. Opening his eyes, he saw the wall slide back into place. Then all was dark.

Slowly, a soft glow took the edge off the darkness.

'Follow me!'

Raph jumped to his feet and came face to face with a girl holding a lantern. Long blonde hair, straggly and matted, framed a round face, the lantern's soft glow giving her an angelic appearance. Her eyes were large and dark and a little bit watery. She wore dirty grey robes that may have once been white. She turned and took off down a dark passageway.

Raph followed as she led him through the darkness – along twisting and turning tunnels, down steps and through the sewers, until they finally came to a doorway. She stared at him with her disconcerting, watery gaze, indicated that he should enter, then turned and left.

Raph looked at the doorway but could see nothing but darkness. He took a deep breath and stepped in.

The darkness parted like a curtain. Raph blinked in surprise, barely noticing the greyness in his peripheral vision. He was in a room full of candles – free-standing candelabra and tiered arrangements, wax dripping from shelves set into the stone walls, spilling down onto an elaborate parquet floor.

A figure in dark brown robes sat on a high-backed stone chair in the centre of the room. The chair was intricately carved with criss-crossed lines, each inlaid with a fine thread of copper. The metal reflected the flickering candlelight, making it appear as if the light travelled along the copper.

A large cowl concealed the face of the seated figure.

'H . . . hello.' Raph's voice sounded small and timid.

The figure shimmered slightly. Then it moved, lifting gloved hands as it pushed the cowl back just enough to reveal a face.

It was an ancient face, so deeply lined that Raph couldn't tell if it was a man or woman. Dark eyes, sunk deep into the flesh, looked odd without eyebrows or lashes.

'Welcome, Raphael.' The voice was soft and feminine and surprisingly youthful, coming as it was from a wizened, toothless mouth. 'I am the Dama Sebastiana Annunciata.'

Raph inhaled sharply.

'Yes,' the woman continued. 'You believed me to be but a story, a legend – the fanciful musings of weak minds. Not so. I am as real as anything in this world.' The corners of her mouth pulled up slightly in an approximation of a smile.

Raph dropped to his knees and lowered his eyes.

'No. Do not kneel to me. Do not avert your eyes. Always look. Always observe.' She drew a rattling breath. 'See the candles.'

Raph lifted his gaze to the candles.

'Do more than look. You must see!'

Raph picked out one candle and stared at it intently. He gasped as he realised that the light dancing around the wick was not a flame. It was a sizzling greyness, like that which taunted him from his peripheral vision. He felt as if he were being drawn into that grey light, falling through a boundless nothing filled with apparitions of things he could not comprehend.

'You have Sight,' said the Dama. 'You are the one

to return things to the way they should be.'

A muffled shouting drifted in through the doorway. Raph stood up and looked back over his shoulder, but all he saw was darkness.

'Once upon a time . . .' began the Dama, 'there was no Inferno. People came to the Designers Cathedral to request Paradise. I would introduce them to the Oracle, palm to palm. If they were deemed worthy, they would be granted entry.' She sighed, long and heavily.

'But then the Inquisition came. The triumvirate lords and their militia took the cathedral. The sisterhood saved me and hid me down in the bowels of the city. And so I have waited for one who can see the truth and who will be unafraid to embrace it.'

More shouting. Closer now.

'See the Inferno for what it is. Find the Oracle. Redeem our city. Return its access to Paradise.'

The militia burst through the darkness of the doorway – four men with sheathed swords.

'You have much potential. Trust in yourself.' The Dama stared intently at Raph. 'Fear not for me. I am not important.'

'Indeed, you are not.' Another man had entered the room. Tall and imposing, with black hair and cold eyes, he wore the insignia of a captain. 'Take the boy.'

One of the soldiers grabbed Raph's arm and

twisted it behind his back. The boy gritted his teeth to stop himself from crying out.

The captain pulled back the Dama's cowl. Her head was bald, and from the back protruded a mass of silver threads, sparking with light.

'Black magik,' spat the captain, drawing his sword.

The soldier gave Raph's arm a painful twist and shoved him through the doorway.

Out in the passageway, Raph saw the girl who had brought him here. Eyes wide and watery, hand clutching a gold coin, she watched him being dragged away.

Raph was hauled through the underground passageways, out into the streets and straight to Designers Cathedral. It was an imposing building, constructed with large stone blocks formed into arches, spires and towers, around an enormous central dome.

Raph gasped in awe as he was shoved through the door. He had never been inside before. The domed ceiling rose high above him. Light flooded through dozens of intricate stained-glass windows, overlaying coloured patterns on the faces of the people gathered there. The far end was dominated by a large marble statue of a woman in robes, one hand held forward, palm out as if warning those approaching to halt, the other raised skywards as if in praise of the Designers.

Raph stared at the statue, as it appeared to shimmer around the edges. Waves of sparkling greyness washed over the cool marble-cream surface.

'Get moving,' snapped the captain, pushing him forward through the crowd of richly dressed people – the wealthy and the powerful, gathered in subservience to the Inquisition.

At the head of the cathedral, three men sat in ornately carved stone chairs, like kings on thrones – the Lords of the Inquisition. They were dressed in the finest of clothing, rich reds and purples the dominant colours. Each wore a sapphire pendant and the man in the centre held a jewelled staff with the bluest of blue sapphires mounted on top.

A woman in plain dirty-grey robes stood on a small circular podium.

'It is time for judgement,' said the lord with the staff, getting to his feet. 'Paradise or Inferno?'

He raised his staff and brought it down heavily onto the flagstone floor, three times. The sound echoed through the cathedral.

And then there was silence as everyone waited. Raph watched expectantly, unsure of exactly what he was waiting for.

A scream broke the silence. It was the woman on the podium. Flames appeared around the edge of the raised circle. The woman tried to back away, but there was nowhere to go. The circle's diameter was barely an arm's length.

The air was filled with the grinding sound of stone on stone. Raph was reminded of the sound he had heard when the secret door leading to the underground passages had first opened.

Suddenly the woman was gone, massive flames leaping into the air where she had been. The great staff hit against the flagstones three more times, and the flames receded.

'Designers Inferno!' the lord's voice boomed through the cathedral.

As he sat down, the captain shoved Raph forward. Raph stumbled out before the three men.

'What have we here?' said the lord with the staff.

The captain dropped to one knee. 'It is Raphael, the orphan, Lord Dante.'

Lord Dante inclined his head towards the man at his right. 'Lord Brimstone.'

Lord Brimstone stood. 'This boy claims to have Sight, a legendary gift from the Designers. But we know the truth to be black magik.'

'I haven't claimed anything,' Raph protested.

The third lord rose to his feet. 'The boy was overheard boasting about his Sight at the public infirmary. There is a witness?'

The Physician General stepped forward. 'Yes, Lord Blaze. He made these claims to me.'

Lord Dante stood. 'The claims are a blasphemy. Only the Lords of the Inquisition have the blessings of the Designers.'

'What about the Designers Oracle?' Raph shouted in a moment of defiance. 'What about the Dama?'

'The Dama no longer exists,' said Lord Brimstone.

'And there is no Oracle,' added Lord Blaze.

Raph's eyes darted to the statue, a greyness swirling through the marble like gathering storm clouds, the outstretched hand shimmering.

'It is time for judgement,' said Lord Dante.

The captain drew his sword.

'No need,' said Raph. 'I welcome the judgement of the Designers.' He walked past the lords, trying his best to look confident, and approached the podium. He noticed the recesses, spaced at regular intervals around the edge of the dais. Carefully, he stepped up and immediately felt the heat through his worn shoes. He looked down at his feet and at the circle of stone beneath them. A concealed hatch, he was sure of it.

Lord Dante raised his staff.

'Wait,' called Raph. He licked his lips nervously. 'This is just a trapdoor with a fire below, controlled by the three of you. I would prefer to seek the judgement of the Designers through their Oracle.'

As Lord Dante brought his staff down onto the flagstone floor, three times in quick succession, Raph jumped.

Flames appeared around the dais, and Raph watched the stone circle drop down into the podium and slide back, allowing more flames to shoot up into the air. The gathered crowd gave a collective gasp.

Raph ran to the statue and stopped beneath its hand, hoping desperately that he was right. Standing on tiptoes he reached up and placed his open palm against that of the statue's.

His stomach lurched as his surroundings disappeared.

Swirling, sizzling greyness surrounded him in a disorienting static fog. Raph closed his eyes tightly, took a deep breath and opened them again. It was still there.

'Bit like an analogue TV channel that's lost its signal, isn't it?' The voice came from nowhere and everywhere.

'What?' Raph looked around, trying to find the source of the voice.

'Yeah, well, you wouldn't know what a TV is, let alone an analogue one.'

Raph still couldn't see anyone.

'You looking for me?' A figure materialised in front of Raph. The tall young man wore colourful baggy shorts and a shirt, with a cap firmly planted backwards on his explosion of dark curly hair.

Raph gaped at him. 'Who are you?'

'Dude!' said the man, spreading his arms. 'I'm like . . . the Oracle. But you can call me Orry.'

'What's going on?' asked Raph.

'Well, Raph-dude, not that this is gonna make much sense to you, seeing as you come from an environment that's not at all techno-savvy, but . . .' Orry took a breath. 'Here goes. You are in the Interface between environments, within the great and glorious Game, which the Designers have created and peopled. You got here by making contact with the Oracle Statue, which is kinda my window into your world. Your environment has a glitch – well, three glitches to be exact – and things have sorta gotten out of hand. It used to be that people came to me for access to Designers Paradise, and assuming they had done enough good deeds, or had enough cashola, I'd facilitate their visit to whatever their vision of paradise happened to be. But then along came the three glitches and they hijacked the environment. I call them Larry, Moe and Curly, but they like to refer to themselves as Lords Blaze, Brimstone and Dante.' He shook himself theatrically. 'Sends a shiver up your spine, don't it? Their collective noun of choice is Inquisition. An Inquisition of Glitches! Kinda has a ring to it, don't you think?'

Raph didn't respond. His mind was whirling, his stomach was churning and he understood very little.

'Not very talkative are you?' Orry frowned. 'Stuck here all on my lonesome for . . . for a long time – and I get a real conversationalist as my potential saviour. You know, I'm teetering on the edge here. I've been talking to myself for way too long . . . I'm fairly certain I'm developing OCD and then there's the whole multiple personality thing. I used to look like the statue – you know, robes and female bits – but I've been mixing things up a bit just to stop myself from self-destructing.' He took a deep breath. 'Is any of this getting through to you, dude?'

Raph stared at the Oracle, bemused expression firmly in place. 'Um . . .'

'Okay.' Orry sighed. 'Let me try and give you the basics in terms you might understand. I'm the Oracle – your link to the will of the Designers. The three lords are . . . well, let's call them evil spirits. Okay? With me, so far? Good! They've dug a pit, loaded it up with combustible materials, and are regularly dropping innocent players . . . ah, people, into it. I can't stop them 'cause I have no physical presence in your world. So, what I need you to do is to get them to touch the statue. Then I can deal with them.'

'Umm . . .' Raph was still staring blankly at Orry. 'How?'

'Well, that's up to you,' said Orry. 'But I'm sure you'll put your finger on it. Or mine.'

'Huh?'

'Never mind,' said Orry, rolling his eyes. 'Time for you to get back out there and right the wrongs, fight the good fight, play the game, defeat the glitches and ensure that happiness prevails. Ciao, Raph-dude.'

Raph was standing back in the cathedral, arm outstretched to the statue, his palm touching the marble hand. The crowd made urgent but hushed sounds.

'Black magik!' Lord Dante's voice boomed through the cathedral. 'Execute him!'

The captain stepped forward, sword drawn and at the ready. Raph rushed back to the podium, making sure the belching flames separated him from the captain. They circled, eyeing each other through the fire.

'Men!' Four militia soldiers stepped forward at the captain's call. 'Get him into the open, but don't kill him. He's mine.'

As the soldiers approached, Raph made a dash back to the statue, the captain on his tail. He ducked behind it as the captain swung his sword. The sharp metal connected with the stone. A small chip broke away with the impact and fell to the floor. But the sword held fast as if glued to the marble. The captain heaved with all his might, but it would not budge. Reaching out a hand to steady himself, the man touched the statue . . . and was gone.

The sword clattered to the floor.

The hushed voices of the people gathered there rose in volume and pitch, a note of panic working its way through the crowd. But still they stayed in place, more fearful of the Inquisition than potential black magik.

Raph stepped out from behind the statue and knelt to pick up the sword, his confidence growing by the second.

'Execute him!' the three Lords of the Inquisition shouted in unison.

One of the soldiers tentatively approached. Raph pointed the sword at him. 'If I'm using black magik and I just made your captain disappear . . . what do you think I'll do to you?'

The soldier backed off.

Raph was now definitely feeling more sure of himself. He turned to the Lords. 'The Oracle would like to speak to the three of you.'

Lord Brimstone removed his pendant and brandished the sapphire. A crackle of blue energy, like directed lightning, sizzled from the blue jewel towards Raph. The sword was blown from his hands, and Raph was thrown to the floor. He scrabbled backwards, his fingers brushing the chip of marble that had broken from the statue.

Raph's hand closed around the small piece of stone. Murmuring a quick prayer to the Designers, he jumped to his feet and hurled it. The chip connected with Lord Brimstone's forehead.

The lord's pendant hit the floor, the blue jewel shattering as he flung his arms out wide. His mouth gaped in a silent scream as he disappeared – not in a single instant like the captain, but slowly, painfully, piece by piece.

All eyes were on Lord Brimstone's disintegrating form. Raph tore his gaze away, knowing that he had to act fast. Scooping up the sword from where it had fallen, he swung it at the statue's outstretched hand. Two marble fingertips fell to the floor. Dropping the sword, Raph snatched them up and threw the first at Lord Blaze.

The Lord lifted an arm to shield his face. As the marble fingertip touched his hand, the second Lord began to disperse.

Raph tossed the second fingertip, but Lord Dante raised his staff and blasted it away with an arc of blue lightning. His face distorted with rage, the final Lord strode towards Raph. Energy flashed from the end of his staff.

Raph flung himself to the floor, narrowly escaping a bolt of blue, then rolled to dodge another, and jumped to his feet. As Lord Dante took aim again, Raph dashed to the statue and tried to conceal himself behind it.

'The Oracle cannot protect you,' snarled Lord Dante. He thrust the staff forward and a blaze of energy erupted towards the statue, hitting it square in the chest. Raph was slammed into the wall by the force of the explosion, which shattered the marble into thousands of tiny pieces, scattering in all directions.

As Lord Dante threw back his head to laugh, a miniscule fragment of marble flew into his mouth and lodged in his throat. His laughter choked and his expression turned from victory to defeat. And then he too was gone.

Raph rubbed the back of his head as he walked through the rubble. He looked around, amazed that the people had remained, stunned into silence.

Behind him, the fragments of marble rose up and reassembled themselves. When the statue was again complete, the captain reappeared beside it.

At first bemused, he looked at Raph, then dropped to one knee. 'Lord Raphael.'

Raph turned to the captain. 'Lord Raphael?' He said the words tentatively, as if trying them on for size. 'Lord Raphael. I think I like that.'

He looked at the statue, trying to make sense of what Orry had said. Interfaces. Games. Environments. Glitches. It did not make sense.

He turned to face the people. This is what made sense. They were all gazing at him in awe. Him? An orphan boy? Except that he didn't feel like a mere boy anymore.

Possibilities rushed through his mind as he strode over to the three stone chairs. The Inquisition was gone . . . but so was the Dama. After a moment's hesitation, he sat in the centre chair.

One by one, the people dropped to their knees.

And Lord Raphael smiled.

Oh Brother, What Art Thou?
Michael Gerard Bauer

Get this. You are so not going to believe it. About twenty minutes ago Mum calls me for dinner, see. So I go out and everyone's at the table because Nan is visiting us, which means we're having one of those special sit-down, can't-have-the-TV-on-under-any-circumstances, forced-to-listen-to-boring-conversation kind of meals together.

Anyway, Nan's grabbed the spot at the head of the table, so I pull up a chair across from Mum and Dad and the first thing I notice is the number of places set. I'm about to say something but Dad calls out, 'Jason! Come on, matey. We're waiting to eat here.'

Then Mum rolls her eyes and asks, 'What does that son of ours *do* in his room all day, anyway?'

Well of course I go to say something *again* but Mum beats me to it. 'Finally!' she says looking behind me. 'Come on, Jason, hurry up or it's going to get cold.'

And before I know it, the chair next to me gets yanked back and I hear, 'Shove over, Sis. We all know your bum is enormous but you don't need that much room.'

Now I guess that sounds fairly normal right? Just

the sort of thing a pea-brained, pain-in-the-butt brother would say to his amazingly beautiful and absolutely average-backside-sized sister?

Sure. Except for this one teensy-weensy detail:

I DON'T *HAVE* A BROTHER!

In fact, I'm an only child. That's right. Thirteen years ago when my parents copped an eyeful of their cute-as-a-button new-born baby girl, they obviously thought, 'Well, you can't improve on perfection, so we might as well give the whole breeding thing a big miss from here on in!'

So let me just repeat – I DON'T *HAVE* A BROTHER!

What I *did* have however, was some strange kid with freckles, a mop of messy hair and an expression like a bored zombie, sprawled beside me at the dinner table, chewing with his mouth open, *claiming* to be my brother, while my parents and my nan just sat there as if this was all perfectly normal!

I must be dreaming, I thought. So I just did what I normally do to jolt myself awake. I closed my eyes, pictured myself in bed and shook my arms and legs about madly.

When I opened my eyes I was still sitting at our dining room table, but now three members of my family plus one complete stranger were gawking at me as if I was an escaped lunatic.

'Teagan, what in the world's got into you?'

That was Mum.

'You're not coming down with something are you, sweetie?'

That was Dad.

'Gee T-bum, just when I thought you couldn't possibly get any weirder, you go and prove me wrong.'

That was my obnoxious, never-seen-him-before-in-my-entire-life brother.

'She's having a fit! And no wonder. Spends far too much time camped in front of a computer screen – it fries the brain cells!'

And *that* of course was my nan who spends far too much of *her* time telling me about the dangers of computers and warning me all about *me*.

For example:

'Teagan, you're too pig-headed for your own good!' And you're too kind, Nan!

'Teagan, if someone tells you to do one thing, you go and do the exact opposite!' Got me in one, Nan!

'Teagan, you mark my words, that stubborn streak of yours will land you in trouble one day, my girl!' Gee thanks for the pep talk, Nan!

I stared back at the four sets of eyes that were now zeroed in on me. It was definitely time to put an end to all this craziness.

'Okay, well I give up then,' I said jerking my thumb at my non-brother. 'Who is this guy and why is he pretending to be part of our family?'

Stranger boy next to me stopped eating for a moment and sat there with his mouth open, displaying a lovely gob full of half-chewed food. Mum and Dad glanced at each other briefly, then back at me. Nan jabbed a finger my way.

'I knew it! She's contracted an Internet virus and now she's delirious!'

Beside me, my mystery-guest brother grabbed his head, rolled his eyes back and let out a long groan. 'Awww, you can *not* be serious. You're not *still* going on about that stupid camera thing are you, Sis?'

'What stupid camera thing?' Mum wanted to know. Me too.

'*Apparently* her camera's not working properly so *naturally* I get the blame. Says I borrowed it without asking and then reckons I broke it somehow. I told you a *million* times, Sis, I *never* touched it.'

This was getting way too weird for words. I swung around to face the ring-in at our table.

'This has *nothing* to do with you – *whoever you are* – borrowing my camera. *AND STOP CALLING ME "SIS"*! I am *not* your sister. And you are *not* my brother. And you know why? Because I don't *have* a brother. And if I ever *did* have a brother, you can bet your life it wouldn't be a drop-kick like *you*!'

But I didn't seem to be getting through to any of them. Nan just sat there making annoying tsk-tsking noises at me, while my 'brother' stuffed his face with food (occasionally finding his mouth) and Mum rabbited on to Dad.

'I really don't know what's got into the two of

them lately, do you? They used to be best mates. Remember all those beautiful sandcastles they spent ages building together at the beach?' Mum said.

Now my head was beginning to spin.

'What are you *talking* about? They were *my* beautiful sandcastles. Nobody helped me! I made them all my . . .'

I jumped up from the table, raced into the lounge room and grabbed the big digital photo frame off the TV cabinet. I'd figure out how I could put a stop to all this madness. I clicked through a few images until I found the one I wanted.

'There!' I said placing it on the table in full view of everyone. 'All my own work!'

It was a photo of me – just *me* – sitting proudly behind a huge sandcastle stunningly decorated with driftwood, shells and seaweed.

'Hey, come on, Sis,' my non-existent brother whined, 'be fair. *Your* design maybe, but *I* did most of the muscle work. Look,' he said poking his finger at the empty patch of sand beside me on the screen, 'I've got my trusty spade in my hand.'

'Yes,' Mum said with a frown and pointing to the same vacant space, 'but just look at the colour of your shoulders and face, Jason. You were always a devil to keep sunscreen on!'

I squinted at the photo until my eyes stung.

'Wh . . . what are you looking at? There's noth . . .' But Mum was already busy clicking through more pictures and everyone else was ignoring me and crowding in to get a better look.

'Awww, now *that's* one of my absolute favourites,' Dad said. 'A terrific shot of the both of you. Love those big smiles!'

'*Both* of us?' I said peering at an image of me on a horse. 'It's just *me* in that photo. It's just me in *all* these photos!'

'Come on, Sis. You're taking this stupid "my-big-brother-doesn't-exist-anymore-cause-I'm-really-mad-at-him-even-though-he's-done-*nothing*-wrong" thing a bit far, aren't you?'

Everyone's eyes were now directed my way like I was the odd one out, like I was the one spouting crazy-talk. I began edging away from the table. This wasn't just weird anymore. It was getting scary.

'I haven't got a clue what's going on here,' I told them, 'but I want you all to know that it's SO. NOT. FUNNY!'

I spun around and stamped down the corridor to my room. When I got there I slammed the door behind me, threw myself on my bed and hugged a pillow to my chest. This had become just too freaky for words. I wanted my normal, boring, predictable life back! I decided to go over everything that had just happened to see if I could find some answers.

From the bottom drawer of my bedside table I dug out an old Dictaphone that I'd borrowed from Dad ages ago to record and store all my brilliant world-shattering ideas. Of course that was before I discovered that I didn't actually have any brilliant world-shattering ideas. Now maybe it was finally going to come in handy.

I sat up in bed and propped a pillow behind my back. I pushed the 'power' button and watched the little Dictaphone light glow green. Then I hit 'record' and held it close to my mouth.

'Get this. You are so not going to believe it. About twenty minutes ago Mum calls me for dinner, see . . .'

I'd only just finished recording what could have been the pilot episode for 'When Normal Families Turn Nuts!' when a single thump shook my bedroom door.

'Sis, it's me. Can I come in?'

The door started to open so I quickly pressed 'stop' and shoved the voice-recorder under a pillow on my lap. Then my make-believe brother wandered in, spun my desk chair around and plonked himself down on it.

'Hey you're not *still* mad at me are you, Teags? Look you gotta believe me I . . .'

'You stop right there, mister!' I told him pushing myself back against the bed head.

'But Sis . . .'

'I mean it! STOP!' I held up my hand like a traffic cop. 'Let's get one thing *perfectly* clear. You are *not* my brother and I am *not* your sister . . . well . . . okay . . . that's really two things . . . but I don't care. It's still *true*. You know it and I know it, and if you don't stop *pretending* that you are my brother immediately then I will start screaming my lungs out until my parents are *forced* to call the police and have you arrested just to shut me up! Now tell me the *truth*. Who are you really?'

It took my fake-brother a while to answer me.

'I can't.'

'Why not?'

'Because it's against the rules and anyway you won't believe me.'

'Try me.'

'Okay, I'm a visitor from another planet.'

'Ha! Garbage!'

'Told you.'

'Well alrighty then, ET. Why don't you just *prove* it to me? Like how about you use your super-duper, extra-special, whiz-bang, inter-galactic, magic powers to . . . let's see . . . um . . . oh, I know, levitate my iPod off the desk.'

My iPod instantly levitated off the desk, rotated every which way, separated into a hundred different bits and pieces, then reassembled itself, played a blast of 'Ta-daaa!'-type music and returned exactly to where it had been.

I screamed. Loud and long.

Dad's voice drifted in from the lounge room. 'Come on, you two. That's enough now. Sort out your differences. No more fighting. I mean it!'

I had a feeling our *differences* might be more humungous than my father could ever imagine.

'But . . . but . . . how . . . how did you . . . *do* that?'

'Easy. I just used my super-duper, extra-special, whiz-bang, inter-galactic, magic powers.'

My brain felt like it was about to pop. A visitor from outer space? That was just too corny and too way out to be true. Wasn't it?

'You . . . you don't . . . *look* . . . like you're from another planet.'

'I'm wearing a Subatomic Molecular Image Refraction and Distortion Shell.'

'Of course you are,' I said in a daze. 'I heard they're all the rage this summer.'

'Perhaps if I disengaged it for you?'

The would-be alien closed his eyes and his whole body glowed and shimmered. His messy hair morphed into a smooth, neat covering like velvet, his cheeks rose, his nose shrank, his ears pushed close against his head and his freckled skin became as flawless as an air-brushed supermodel's. He re-opened his eyes. They were larger than before and a deeper bluey-green colour. He smiled. His teeth were perfect. Then I noticed that a skin-tight material that clung to every curve of his body had replaced his old T-shirt and jeans. A single thought floated around my head.

He's hot as!

(Of course it was perfectly okay for me to think

this because, remember, he wasn't *really* my brother, he was just an alien.)

Then he spoke with a voice as smooth and sweet as honey.

'In your language my name is pronounced Darvan. I hope we can be friends.'

For a moment I thought I was going to pass out or be sick or possibly both. My imposter-brother was actually from another planet! Aliens had landed! We were being invaded! I had to tell someone, but even if I did, who in their right mind would believe me?

That's when I remembered the Dictaphone I was still clutching under the pillow on my lap. I ran my finger over the buttons and selected what I knew was 'record'.

'Well, go on,' I said, 'if you really want us to be friends, you have to tell me the truth. All of it.'

Darvan studied me closely like he was making up his mind. Then he spoke.

'Fine. If you want the truth, then this is it. You were right of course about me lying. I am not your brother. I come from a planet not unlike your own, but many galaxies away. My people have come here in peace. We wish only to learn about your civilisation, so that we can better help and protect you.'

'Help? What makes you think we . . . ah . . . earthlings . . . need *your* help anyway?'

'Global warming? Hole in the ozone? Species extinction? Pollution?'

'Oh yeah, right.'

'We are far more advanced than you and have the technology to fix those problems. We can secretly guide your top scientists and innovators in the right direction.'

'But wait on, my parents aren't scientists or innovators. Mum's an accountant and Dad's a counsellor. What big discovery could you possibly be "guiding" them towards?'

'I am not an Advanced Technology Facilitator yet, but I hope to be. I am only young – like you. This is what we call an *imbedding*. I am in your family to learn as much as I can about your race and your customs. You have nothing to fear from me.'

'So you're here like . . . on work experience?'

Darvan smiled and nodded.

'But you also said something about protecting us. Protecting us from what exactly?'

'Attack. Invasion. Not everyone in the known universe is friendly.'

'You're telling me that there are some bad guys out there?'

A corner of Darvan's mouth twitched slightly. 'Oh yes. *Very* bad.'

'Well, protecting and helping *sounds* okay, but what about Mum and Dad and Nan? What have you done to them?'

'They have undergone a Temporary Reality Adjustment. I assure you, the procedure is completely safe and reversible. They now believe they have a son and grandson called Jason and everything they see and hear will always conform to that reality.'

'So how come I didn't get the adjustment thingy, too?'

'You did. But you have obviously resisted and rejected it. An extremely rare thing. You must have a *very* strong mind.'

Woohoo! Chalk up a win for Team Pig-headed! Take that, Nan. Looks like it pays sometimes to do the opposite of what you're told. I restrained myself from pumping a fist into the air, but I couldn't stop myself from blushing, just a little.

'So what do you alien types do when the old Temporary Memory Adjustment has an epic fail?'

Darvan smiled.

'We do a one-on-one,' he said and his beautiful eyes met mine.

All at once all the confusion, anger and fear I'd been feeling just evaporated and I was completely calm. Darvan's pupils were shining back at me like opals, full of light and fire and hidden layers. They were drawing me in, leading me gently but firmly further and further down a long hallway deep into his mind.

A thousand memories began to fill my head and file themselves away like books in a library. Birthday parties. Holidays. The beach. Sandcastles. Me and my brother playing together. Jason laughing at me and digging in the sand with his spade.

But I wasn't about to be sucked in by the old Temporary Reality Adjustment trick. No way! I had a 'very strong mind', remember. Darvan had no idea who he was up against!

Concentrating with all my strength I pulled back against the force that was trying to suck me in. Too easy! I was beating it! I could feel my real memories returning as I withdrew more and more from the grip of Darvan's mind.

I was almost totally free when I saw it – or rather sensed it.

It was like a wormhole or a doorway to another part of Darvan's consciousness, but it was locked and bolted with a big STAY OUT! THIS MEANS YOU! sign nailed on the front. I hesitated for a moment then moved my own mind towards it. It pushed me away. Something was hidden in Darvan's alien mind that he definitely didn't want me to know about.

Maybe Darvan wasn't all he seemed? Maybe there was another layer to his Subatomic Shell thingy and he wasn't so hot-looking after all? Maybe he and his 'people' were really scaly lizard creatures with gross, pointy teeth, beady eyes and ugly flicking tongues?

And what if he'd lied and he and all his mates weren't really here to *learn* and *help* like he claimed? What if they were here for lunch and to help themselves – to us! What if *they* were the bad guys we needed protection from?

The truth had to be hidden somewhere behind that imaginary door in Darvan's mind, but he was holding me back and forcing me away. He was telling me I had to leave. He was *telling* me I was forbidden to enter.

Well, hard luck, Space Boy. Like Nan will tell you, no one makes Teagan Carter do something she doesn't want to do!

I summoned all my powers of pig-headedness and in one final effort, willed myself forward. Just as I did, all resistance gave way and I plunged through the door and deep into Darvan's mind.

Suddenly everything was revealed to me and I finally knew the truth. I had been right all along. He was lying!

It was Dad's voice that finally brought me back to the bedroom.

'What's this then? A good old-fashioned staring competition or are you two just giving each other the silent treatment?'

I turned away from the freckled face and the mop of hair I'd been gazing at to find Mum, Dad and Nan all squeezed around my doorway.

'Here,' Mum said stepping forward and placing a plate on my desk, 'these are guaranteed to help bring about a truce. A bunch of Nan's homemade gingerbread men for both of you to share nicely.'

'Gingerbread men and *women*,' Nan added. 'I

didn't burn my bra back in the sixties for nothing.'

'Just hope you remembered to take it off first, Nan!'

Everybody laughed.

I laughed, too.

'Yeah, good one, Jason . . .' I began to say, but stopped. I turned back to the dopey face that was grinning back at me. And I remembered. He was a liar. And soon his own words were going to help me prove it!

I whipped the Dictaphone out from under the pillow on my lap and rewound it to just the right spot. I smiled up at the confused face sitting opposite me.

'Thought you were going to get away with it, didn't you?'

After turning the volume up high, I held the Dictaphone towards my parents and Nan.

'Listen up everyone,' I said and stabbed 'play'. The Dictaphone crackled into life. My voice came on first.

'Well, go on,' I heard myself say. *'If you really want us to be friends, you have to tell me the truth. All of it.'*

I waited eagerly for the reply that I knew was coming.

'Fine. If you want the truth, then this is it. You were right of course about me lying.'

I beamed a triumphant smile around the room. 'But wait, there's more!' I said and the confession on the voice recorder continued.

'I did break your camera. But it was an accident, Sis. I borrowed it to take some shots for my Facebook profile and sort of dropped it on the floor. I didn't tell you because I knew you'd go nuts about it. But I thought it would be okay, honest.'

A deathly silence settled around the room. I was the one who shattered it.

'See! I *told* you he took my camera, but you wouldn't believe me! I *told* you he broke it! I *told* you he was lying!'

Mum and Dad and Nan were now all frowning daggers at Jason. It was awesome! Dad looked grim.

'Well, mate, on the positive side I suppose you *did* 'fess up . . . eventually. But I'll still expect you to pay for the repairs out of your own pocket money and as for the lying part – consider yourself grounded for two weeks.'

Jason groaned and slumped down in his chair.

'Now, no more fighting, you two,' Mum said as she and Dad and Nan filed out of the room. 'It's about time you showed a bit more maturity – *both* of you.'

When they'd gone I looked at my brother. You know, maybe Mum was right. Maybe it was time to show some maturity. I moved to the edge of the bed and reached out to Jason. Then I punched him hard on the arm.

'Grrrounded, suckerrr!' I laughed. 'That'll teach you to mess with me.'

Jason held up his hands in surrender as he leaned back on the chair and stuck his dirty feet on the end of my bed.

'All right T-bum, you win – this round at least. You really got me with that recorder thing.'

'Tell me about it. Sucked. You. Right. In!'

That made my brother laugh for some reason. Then he gave his shoulders a shrug and grabbed one of the gingerbread women from the plate and looked at it closely.

'Oh well, it's only for two weeks. I'll survive. After all,' he said with a typical, Jason Carter know-it-all smirk, 'it's not like it's . . . the end of the world.'

Then he chomped the head clean off his gingerbread biscuit and shoved the rest in his mouth before adding, 'Not yet, anyway.'

I shook my head as Jason munched away loudly. When he saw me watching he narrowed his beady eyes and flicked a revolting biscuit-covered tongue my way.

My brother can be so weird and disgusting that I find it hard to believe that we're related.

Sometimes I wonder if we're even from the same planet!

Scaffolding

Kim Kane

'How much is the concert?'
'Eighty-five dollars.'

'Eighty-five dollars?! It's not priced for us then.'

'It's not meant to be – it's to raise money for the new pool.'

The five of them sat on a bench in the courtyard watching the choir adjust their robes. They were a real gospel choir from a real church in Harlem and their accents slapped the night. Katya studied the skinny ankles of one woman; so skinny her pale tights bagged about them and her too-big shoes were like dress-ups. While other people noticed the whole picture, Katya was only ever interested in detail. It was why she could never describe her response to a book or a film or even a football game properly. Everyone else could talk about the storyline and the themes, but Katya would focus on something tiny and insignificant, like the lead character's hatpin. Her best friend, Priyanka, had become quite skilled in interpreting the detail for a broader audience. Katya looked around the circle of fair-haired, light-eyed kids.

There were no girls called Priyanka here.

The choir had filed indoors, and the organ started to play, muted through the solid stone.

'Another heady Saturday night in rural Victoria. We're even barred from the school chapel,' Lilly said.

Through the walls they could hear voices and clapping. Just. Everything was overpowered by the organ, which was flush against the Quad wall. However it was hard to feel anything other than mild irritation, for it was a warm night, thick with the scent of jasmine and the promise of summer. Katya pulled her feet up under her skirt. Her good shoes pinched, but they dressed up for dinner on Saturday nights. They also got ice-cream for dessert and that called for some sort of recognition. Across the Quad, the clock chimed seven times, one gong short.

'Come on,' said Will. 'This is tragic, we can't even hear from out here.'

'If we climbed the scaffolding on the other side we'd hear better,' said Sam.

'If we what?' Lilly voiced what everybody was thinking.

'If we climbed up on the other side of the chapel where they're doing the restoration work we'd get a better view. We'd get to see in through the windows and hear the choir rather than the organ.'

Sam had leapt up and was bobbing around on one foot. Sam was bright, but too bouncy to concentrate in his seat for long. Even as he spoke he was stripping leaves from a piece of ivy and whipping the stalk through the air until it hummed. He looked around the circle, eyes shiny gold and excited.

'Nahh,' said James.

'Nahh,' said Will.

'Nahh,' said Lilly.

This was the group's dynamic. Sam suggested things, and James, Will and Lilly rejected the suggestions (at best) or ridiculed them (frequently). Katya was new and still quiet.

'Oh, come on guys, it will be amazing. We'll climb up the scaffolding and peek through the stained glass. House seats.'

'Until they collapse. It's a building site, Sam, not an adventure park. You'll be chucked out if you're caught.'

Sam tugged at the brim of his cap, pushing his fringe up under it. He did this when he was thinking.

James picked at a loose stitch on his cricket ball. 'Don't forget the CCTV cameras. The porters will have the whole thing recorded.'

Sam slunk back onto the seat next to Katya and stretched out his legs. He was wearing shorts and the hairs on his legs were exactly the same colour as his skin. He was gilded; he shone in a way that Katya had never seen a person shine before. There was vim and irreverence to Sam that made him the sort of person people warmed to immediately. He energised a room through his sheer exuberance; people could even overlook the fact he wore a cap backwards at night.

'Forget it.' James stood, scooping up his bat. 'Hey, Willo, you up for a hit before it gets too dark?'

'Sure.'

James and Will wandered off, tossing a scuffed ball between them. Lilly started drawing a pattern on Sam's hand with a black biro. Katya admired Lilly's ease. There was a stiffness in herself she couldn't overcome. A formality. Katya was not the sort of girl other girls threaded their arms through. People kept their distance. She noticed it most acutely when people pulled out their cameras. There she would be with her fingers and jaw clenched, smiling, but isolated while everybody else slung their arms about each other – as loose and casual as jumpers on the shoulders of Country Road models.

Katya's gloom was interupted by the porter passing them on his nightly circuit. 'Evening,' he said. He had a thick face and a thicker stomach from too many Butternut Snaps dunked in instant coffee.

Sam extracted himself from Lilly and her biro. 'Whistle when he passes again.'

'What?'

'Whistle when he comes back.'

'Why?'

'I'm going into his office to check out the CCTV monitors. If the cameras aren't beamed onto the scaffolding, I'm going up.'

'You're mad.' Lilly stopped clicking the nib of her pen. Silence made the still evening tense.

'Oh, come on, help me out here.'

Lilly had switched pens and was drawing on the instep of her black boot. The ink was strangely pink and iridescent where she coloured. She didn't look up. 'Okay, but hurry. This is your plan and I don't want to be part of it.' For someone so relaxed, Lilly sounded uptight.

Sam sprinted off around the Quad. Katya watched his calves split into upside-down hearts with each step.

'He's mad. One of these days he's going to get busted and he'll be thrown out of school. Life in Staircase Seven may not be fancy, but it's got to be better than Melbourne High.'

'Where?' Katya made herself look back at Lilly.

'Melbourne High. It's one of those elective high schools. Mum's always threatening to send me there whenever I complain. It's her version of a State school but I don't think she realises I couldn't actually get in.'

'Why couldn't you get in?'

'I don't meet either criteria: I'm no brain and my voice hasn't broken – and isn't going to. I hope.'

'Sheesh, Lilly, look!'

Lilly was interrupted by the sight of the porter rounding the corner on the other side of the quadrangle with a bar of chocolate and a steaming mug.

A wad of keys jangled against his belt.

Lilly pulled her fingers to her lips to whistle and then laughed. Katya looked at her in horror: the porter was almost back at the entrance to his surveillance room. Katya tried to whistle too, but her tongue jammed. She looked over her shoulder. Sam was walking towards them, jauntier than usual, hands deep in his pockets. 'Thanks for your help. You guys left me high and dry.'

'We told the porter what you were up to.'

'I'd believe it. Well I could believe it from you, Lilly Hanson, but I expect more of Katya.'

Katya blushed when he said her name. He said it nicely. Not quite as Russian as her mother, who rammed her tongue against the back of her front teeth, but he'd made an effort with the pronunciation and, well, it was charming.

'Okay, so here's where we're at. I've done recon. There are four TVs in the porters' bolthole and eight cameras. There is a camera in the back courtyard right near the scaffolding, but it's focused on the fishpond.'

'So what are you going to do, GI Joe? Pause the video?'

'No, I'm not going to pause the video.' Sam rolled his eyes. 'If we walk across to Stairway Nine and then duck off near the bikes we should be out of sight.'

'Well that's fine, except you've managed to forget

that your plan does not involve us. The only one of us in "we" is you.'

'Oh, come on. Don't be such a spoilsport. This is culture, Lil. Imagine how amazing it will be to see them. Listen to it.' In all of the tension they had managed to forget about the gospel music. Behind them the choir's song rose. Katya suspected that for Sam, the music was secondary to the exploit.

Lilly stood up. 'No way. I'm not coming. I got enough detentions last time you had a great idea. Big Sam and his Big Plans.'

'What idea was that? I have no idea what you're talking about.'

'What was it, Lil?' Katya liked hearing about Sam. She stored the anecdotes like her mother stored recipes — somewhere between her heart and head, rather than on files or cards.

Lilly started on the other boot. 'Sam got us to sneak into the Harry Potter movie without paying. He walked ahead and I got sprung. I can't believe you've managed to forget, Sam. If only my parents had your memory.'

'Whatever.' Sam looked at his chunky sneakers and then at Katya. 'What about you?' The question sat there, quivering on the palm of his outstretched hand.

'Gallant.' Lilly poked Sam with the nib of her biro.

'Ow, don't. I'm waiting for an answer.'

The problem with being new, thought Katya, is that she didn't have good-behaviour credits. Nobody knew Katya from the next delinquent or the next prefect. There was a freedom in that, even if on appearance, Katya was heading towards prefect. She was quiet, neat, elegant in her casual clothes. She wished she could look fit-cool in a rowing hoodie and faded trackies like Lilly, but it didn't work like that. It was the formality thing and Katya could feel herself being shut into a box in which she was not particularly comfortable. She wanted to be funny, spontaneous, bold – 'Okay.'

'Are you serious?' Lilly stopped drawing on her boot.

'Wooohooo!' Sam clapped.

'Why not?' Katya savoured the freedom-surge.

'You don't have to do this. It's the fast track to suspension.' Lilly looked worried.

'Yes she does. She's my partner in crime.'

Katya shrugged, embarrassed by the attention. The freedom was souring. She turned to face Lilly, ignoring Sam. It was an unfortunate habit. The people Katya liked the most, she ignored. Lilly would never make that mistake. Lilly liked Charlie Britcliffe in Year Eleven. Did she ignore him? No, she flirted with him, taking provocative bites of his muesli bar, looking at him intensely while she stretched after cross-country, responding to things he offered with

American superlatives: *Super*, *Awesome* and *Teeerrific*. She was a natural.

Lilly rubbed at a biro mark on her thumb until it smeared. 'Well, if you're going to go through with this, at least take off your cap or turn it the other way. Nobody else wears a cap like that. And here, put this on.' Lilly tossed Sam her hoodie.

Sam smiled. 'They'll blame a rower.'

'Bingo.'

Katya looked down at her tulle skirt and ballet pumps. She looked more ballet than burglar. 'Hang on a tick. I'll just nick up to my room.'

'Put on something dark,' called Sam.

'And tight,' giggled Lilly.

Katya trawled through the contents of her wardrobe. She put on a pair of cords that hung low on her hips and a loose top that sat nicely on her breasts. She covered it with her denim jacket, which she buttoned all the way to the top and tied her hair back in a pony-tail. When Katya got downstairs again, the choir was in full force. Light shone from the windows of the chapel in red and orange and yellow. The sky was dusky and the edges of the Quad had smudged.

Sam stood at the bottom of the chapel wall near the cyclone fence. He had lifted the metal pole out of its plastic base. 'Okay, let's go. Stick to the side – this is the risky bit. Once we're inside the scaffolding we should be hidden by the green mesh.'

They ran to the ladder, faster than kids coming-ready-or-not.

Sam started climbing. Katya put her head down and climbed behind him. The scaffolding was dusty but stable, and her sneakers squeaked on the rungs.

Sam looked down and winked. 'Squealers,' he whispered.

When they got to the top of the first storey Sam clambered out onto the platform. The boards shook. 'Crap,' he hissed. 'They're not nailed down.' The crack of wood on metal reverberated around the courtyard. Sam thudded across to the next set of stairs like a walrus. Suddenly everything was lit, bright and white.

'Jeeez.' Katya stopped.

'Crap. The security light.'

Katya squinted. The glare was so harsh she couldn't see her hands.

'Hang on, hang on. I didn't think about that.' Sam thundered further across the ledge. 'Don't move.'

Don't move, thought Katya. Nothing was moving, not even vital organs like her heart. Katya was scared, really scared. The building site was so obviously banned that they had not even mentioned it in assembly. It was just assumed that Year Tens knew not to muck around on building sites on which there could be dangerous machinery, loose scaffolding and, well, buildery things that caused long and painful deaths – like cement and asbestos. Katya perched on a rung between the first and second storeys, hunched down. She heard a click and everything went dark again. As her eyes readjusted, she made out the school crest on Sam's top, just above her. He put his finger to his lips in a *shhhh*. Below, the garden was still.

Sam crept back over to the ladder. 'Disabled it. Sorry about that.' He pulled Katya up onto the next landing. 'You okay?'

Katya nodded and clutched his arm just longer than she needed. The climb was steep and her heart thumped. Sam pushed on.

They climbed another storey, and then another and another. They fell into a rhythm; there was no sound but their breath and the squeak of sneakers on iron – the latter somehow reminding Katya of the feel of soggy lettuce on her teeth.

When Sam reached the next storey he stopped. They were about half way up the enormous sandstone wall at the foot of the great windows. He crawled over the landing to the chapel; Katya followed. They sat with their heads tipped against the wall, side by side in silence. The stone at their backs still held the afternoon's warmth and Katya could feel vibrations from the music that roared up behind them.

Sam stood and motioned to Katya. They peered though the window, which started at waist height and shot up fifteen metres above – brighter than any epiphany. The glass was wonky – alive with tiny bubbles, perfect in its imperfection. Through the window, Katya could see their housemaster with his bent head swaying. She could see Ms Buchanan texting under the pew.

Sam looked down at her and smiled. 'It's amazing, isn't it?'

And it was. It didn't even need an answer. The choir swung, clapping, heads and hands raised and their song shot up, up, up, joyous and holy.

One of the men at the back of the chapel caught Katya's eye. He frowned, tugged at his cufflinks and looked confused. Sam ducked, pulling Katya down beneath the window.

'Who was he?' Katya giggled.

'No idea. A pool-paying guest.'

'Do you think he saw us?'

'I doubt it. We're quite far back. The windows will be black to them.'

'So we'll look like the devil?'

'Or angels.'

Katya turned to Sam. They had jumbled on landing, and were closer than before. She was pressed against Sam's side; he didn't move. She left her arm where it was, aware of the warmth of his. Light from the window fell down across the dusty platform in pretty lolly-coloured streaks. Sam stared at her. His eyes were shiny in the glow, his lips full. He pushed his fingers through his hair which sat back on his head, moulded by the cap. Then he smiled and leant across, slowly.

Katya's heart was pushing blood. Everything was bold, exaggerated. Her stomach fluttered and she pressed a hand to her tummy to stop the butterflies. Sam took a breath and just as she looked up, he reached in under the light and kissed her. Just a small kiss, but it sat on her lips, tiny and buzzing. He reached in again and kissed her slowly again on the top of her lip. He ran his finger over her eyebrows, tracing them.

'You have lovely eyebrows, too,' she blurted and felt like an idiot. An arrogant idiot because he'd never even mentioned hers and it was possible he thought them too thick, too woggy.

Sam laughed. 'Um, thanks.'

Katya could smell Sam's deodorant, and sweet milk from the evening's ice-cream faintly on his breath. She could see the flutter of their hearts in his neck. Sam kissed her again. They sat under the light, hugging against the warm wall of the chapel as the music arched above them.

'I like you, Katya Solovyov,' whispered Sam and kissed her forehead.

Katya felt his name roll in her mouth like a plum pip. She liked him too much to say it back. But there was no need. She trembled. In the thick spring air, embraced in song, there was no need to say anything at all.

The Bridge

JE Fison

'Dora the Explorer or Snow White and the Seven Dwarfs?' I ask myself, peering into the bottom of my little sister's underwear drawer. It's a choice no self-respecting thirteen-year-old wants to make. But ever since Mum started her own business, the options for clean underwear on a Friday morning have been basically non-existent. Today, of all days, when my insides are so knotted I want to vomit and my head is so dizzy I feel like fainting, I could do with some comfortable, cartoon-free underwear, but sadly that's not going to happen.

'Ellie, you're just about to miss your bus!' Mum shouts from the kitchen.

I squeeze into the Disney undies, throw on my uniform, grab my bag and run for the front door. Late again.

'Relax. Just be yourself,' my mother says, giving me a kiss as I rush out. 'And don't play with your undies, it looks like you've got worms.'

I groan. As if any of that's possible. How can I leave my undies alone when they're designed for a six-year-old? How can I be myself when I've got a special session with the boys' school today? And as for relaxing – I haven't been able to do that since the start of term. That's when I accidentally caught the wrong bus home. And because I didn't know the route, I wasn't holding on when the driver took a sharp right turn. And when I lost my balance, I grabbed the only thing available – a guy with floppy blond hair.

As he turned to see who was swinging off the back of his shirt, the bus pulled up. I released my grip and for a moment we stood facing each other – his brown eyes, wide with surprise at first, suddenly got intense. I should have looked down at that point. That's what I normally do when I see a cute guy. But this time I couldn't. I was trapped. And I didn't want to escape.

I don't know what happened next, and maybe it was nothing, but it felt like something passed between us. And I think I saw . . . a *possibility*.

Then he looked away and swung his school bag over his shoulder. As he headed towards the back door, I saw the name on a book that was hanging out of his bag. Gabe Cartwright. I haven't stopped thinking about that name ever since and I can't help dreaming about the possibility.

Today I'm not just going to meet him, we're going to spend the whole morning together. We've been assigned to the same group for our inter-school bridge-building session. I'm so nervous about it my palms are sweating. The sight of Steph Mason, standing beside my locker, makes me feel even worse. Of all the girls in my class, why do I have to share Gabe with her? It's not that I hate Steph, it's just that I know – when we're side by side, Gabe will definitely prefer her.

'Excited to be finally meeting Gabe?' Steph says, opening her locker and taking out a tube of lipgloss.

I shrug, wondering why I ever told Steph about Gabe. But a smell coming from my locker distracts me – in fact it's so bad, it almost knocks me out. Has someone rerouted the sewer in there?

I rummage through my books with one hand over my nose, trying to uncover the source of the foul odour. Unfortunately I feel it before I see it – my fingers sink deep into a squishy mess that's wedged in the middle of my history book.

'Gross!' I say, wiping my sticky fingers on my skirt and inspecting the contents of my textbook from a safe distance. 'It looks like it used to be an egg sandwich.'

I turn to Steph. 'Know anything about this?'

'I didn't put it there!' she shrieks, stepping away from the smell and stifling what looks a lot like a guilty smirk. 'I don't even like egg!'

'Exactly,' I grumble, flinging the sandwich out of my book.

'Come on,' Steph says, stepping around the sandwich. 'You don't want to keep Gabe waiting.'

But by the time I've cleaned the egg out of my

locker and we've made a trip to the toilets to check our hair, returned to our lockers to get breath mints, then gone back to check our teeth in the bathroom mirror, our whole class along with a group from the boys' school are waiting for us. Everyone is already seated as Steph and I file into the classroom. I try to keep my eyes down, but I can't help noticing Gabe, sitting beside an empty seat. He leans back in his chair and I see him glance at me from under his long fringe. My heart thumps as I walk towards him, wondering if he remembers me, wondering what to say. I snatch another look at his face. His eyes are totally dreamy, but they're not on me anymore, he's staring straight at Steph. She's dancing more than walking and laughing loudly, even though there's nothing even remotely funny about walking into an art room. And it's not just Gabe that has his eyes on her – pretty much every guy in the room is looking at her. I have slipped into the classroom under the radar. As usual.

'He's pretty hot,' Steph whispers – not to me, more as a note to herself.

That's when I feel my chances with Gabe being suffocated – by Steph's freshly glossed lips, her perfect skin, her shiny black hair. And I know I have to act. I have two hours to build a bridge to Gabe Cartwright and if I want to get there before Steph does, I need to change. I need to get noticed and I need to do it now.

I casually (but very quickly) make for the chair beside Gabe. But Steph has the same idea and for several ugly moments we scramble over the chair while trying to look like we are both just holding it (really tightly). And right when I think I'm about to win, Gabe starts waving his hand across his face. 'Can anyone smell rotten eggs?'

The chair war ends right there. I back away, trying to flick the egg off my skirt, and pull out a seat on the opposite side of the bench. I watch as Steph sits down next to Gabe, giving him a shy smile (even though she's not shy at all) and shrugging at me (as if it's some complete accident that she's sitting beside the guy that I like). I look away, sucking up my disappointment. And I wait for my chance to get even.

My opportunity comes a short time later when Mrs Garfunkel explains the basics of bridge design and cracks a joke. I'm not really listening so I don't know what the joke is, I just hear Steph giggle. She gets a predictable reaction from every guy in the room.

And that's when I strike. I take a page right out of the Steph Mason *How to Get Attention* manual and laugh – not just a little, girly snigger, but a loud, belly-rumbling roar. I toss my head back so that everyone looks my way – even Gabe, which is a shame, because it's just as I have Gabe's attention that a fly buzzes past and, finding my mouth open, decides to go in.

I stop laughing and start choking. Steph gives me

a slap on the back (about twice as hard as she needs to) and with a violent hack the fly is dislodged from my throat. It soars out of my mouth and lands right in the middle of Gabe's desk. Gabe stops looking at me and stares at the dead fly.

'Sorry,' I splutter, getting to my feet.

I'm coughing so much I'm about to wet my pants. I rush off in the direction of the toilets. My bridge-building plan is looking a bit shaky at this point, but I'm not beaten. Yet.

I admit that many girls would take a long hard look in the mirror after coughing up a fly in front of a super-hot guy, accept defeat and go back to a life under the radar (or off it completely). But something is pushing me on and I know it sounds insane, but I think it's Snow White. I feel strangely driven by a girl in a red headband. By the time I leave the toilets, my undies are feeling more uncomfortable than ever, but I'm certain they're bringing me luck. Instead of giving up on Gabe, I'm even more determined to impress him.

As I walk into the classroom, I realise I have returned just in time.

'Do I have a volunteer to sketch a bridge on the white board?' Mrs Garfunkel asks.

I don't hesitate. I don't wait to be asked, I just march straight up to the board to accept the job. Mrs Garfunkel, apparently too stunned to argue, hands me a pen. At last – my chance to show Gabe my talents.

Within seconds I've drawn the Sydney Harbour Bridge — and it's a pretty good likeness, even if I do say so myself. I'm not surprised that girls are whispering behind my back — I expect they're just as impressed as I am. And I'm not even worried when the class starts sniggering, because under the bridge I've drawn a ferry being chased by a shark and it does look pretty funny. The shark is standing on its tail, snapping at the boat.

But it's only when I glance over my shoulder to see if Gabe is paying attention that I notice his eyes aren't on my picture — they're on my bottom. I look down, hoping I've just got some sticky tape on my uniform — but, no, it's much worse than that. The back of my skirt is tucked into my undies. Snow White and her seven dumpy mates are waving at the class. A few of the guys are waving back, then someone who looks a lot like Dopey starts whistling. *Heigh ho, heigh ho, it's off to work we go.*

Suddenly, the bridge that was looking so sturdy just seconds ago collapses in a pile of burning rubble and a ball of fire starts working its way up my body until I feel my face being licked by the flames. Snow White hasn't helped me get to Gabe — she's burned down the bridge and basically ruined my life.

I wrench my skirt free and slink back to my seat, hoping for some sort of minor natural disaster — anything to distract Gabe from what he's just witnessed. It doesn't have to be an earthquake, a nasty thunderstorm would do, even a swarm of bees would probably be enough.

But nothing comes to save me. Not even a fly.

'Shame about your choice of knickers,' Steph says, not helping at all.

I don't even try a comeback line. I just open my art book, put my head down and shut my mouth. For the rest of the session I let Steph do all the talking and the giggling. While she and Gabe work on their bridge design, and then a paddle-pop-stick construction, I disappear into a drawing – creating a mythical forest inhabited by owls, wolves and a one-eyed dragon, then I put Snow White right in the middle of it. I know it sounds cruel, but I think she deserves it.

And even when the bell rings, finally bringing an end to the bridge-building session and the most humiliating episode of my life, I don't even look up from my art book. It's only when the room goes quiet and Mrs Garfunkel insists that I leave, that I close my book, wondering why I ever thought I had a chance with Gabe Cartwright.

But when I get to the door someone is waiting for me. And all I can do is stand and stare.

'Can I see what you've drawn?' Gabe says, breaking the impasse.

I shake my head, unable to say anything.

'Please . . .' Gabe insists.

I flash the page at Gabe and then close the book.

'Please . . .' Gabe repeats, his hand outstretched.

Further down the hall I can hear some girls laughing. I can tell without looking that Steph is one of them, but Gabe doesn't seem to notice – his eyes are focused on my book.

'Okay.' I shrug.

Gabe takes my art book like I've just handed him a folder of Van Gogh's long-lost sketches. Slowly, he thumbs through the pages, taking everything in, pausing to 'ahhh', stopping to 'ohhh', until finally he meets Snow White's terrified eyes.

'Awesome,' Gabe whispers, studying the picture.

'You think so?' I say. 'Kind of freaky, really.'

'I wish I could draw like that.'

I take the book from Gabe and tear out the picture of Snow White, then hand it over. 'It's yours.'

'Thanks,' Gabe says, staring at Snow White. 'Thanks, Ellie.'

His eyes flick up to mine, and that's when things start falling apart again – I feel my pulse pounding in my ears, my face is on fire and my brain goes on lunch break. I'd like to respond to Gabe. 'You're welcome,' would be a good start, but apparently my tongue and vocal chords are no longer on speaking terms. Gabe's eyes are paralysing me.

'Ellie . . .' Gabe says, finally breaking the silence. 'Will I see you on the bus again?'

I shake my head. 'That time I caught your bus was . . . an accident,' I manage to say.

I'm so shocked that Gabe remembers me I can't even make up an excuse.

'Oh,' Gabe says. His eyes find Snow White again. He studies her for what feels like several minutes before he finally goes on. 'Do you think I could have your . . . number . . . so I could . . . we might . . .'

Gabe doesn't finish the sentence, he just hands me a pen and his book. I'm so excited that I might see Gabe again that my hand shakes as I write out my number. When I hand the book back I feel like the whole world has gone quiet, watching and waiting to see what will happen. I look down the hall and notice it has. Steph has stopped laughing with her friends. She's just staring at Gabe's book with her mouth wide open.

'Gabe!' Steph calls. But Gabe doesn't look up; he doesn't seem to hear.

'I'll call you,' he says, slipping my picture into his book and turning to leave.

'Gabe!' Steph calls again from down the hallway. But Gabe just walks off in the opposite direction.

That's when Steph laughs her loudest, most attention-seeking laugh ever and this time Gabe does turn round. But his eyes don't go to Steph, they rest on me. And once again I see the same intensity I noticed on the bus. But this time I don't just sense a possibility. Now, I can see the bridge.

The Night Swimmer

Kirsty Murray

The nights Blake spent with Miranda changed everything. He could never forget how cool her skin had felt against his chest as they rode the crest of the black waves together.

Blake hadn't wanted to go on holidays during term. It had been fun when he was a little kid in primary school, when he didn't care about school. But now that he was in Year 9, he hated missing the beginning of term.

Caravans, pop-tops and campervans pulled out of the driveway of the Clifftop Holiday Park as Blake's family parked their caravan outside the front office.

'Looks like we pretty much have the whole place to ourselves,' said Dad.

They cruised slowly through the park, past the bouncy castles and the kids' club corner, past the cabins and the pool and the kiosk and the tracks down to the beach, right up to the top corner where huge fig trees spread deep shade across every site. In some places the grass was completely dead – brown squares where tents had sat all summer, yellow where caravan annexes had been set up for months. Dad picked a site far away from the last two remaining campervans.

Blake had his tent up in five minutes. At least he'd won the argument about having his own space on family holidays. His parents and kid sister, Sophie, slept inside the caravan while Blake had a tiny two-man tent all to himself. He slipped into his board shorts, grabbed a towel and headed for the beach.

'Wait for me,' called Sophie.

'Don't you let your sister out of your sight,' said Dad. 'Don't wander off and leave her or let her swim alone. I want you both back here for a barbecue in half an hour.'

'She's nearly thirteen, Dad,' said Blake. 'She doesn't need a babysitter.'

'She needs her brother,' said Dad.

Later that night, Blake was glad to crawl into his tent. There was nothing much else to do in a semi-deserted caravan park after dark and he was bored of playing 'Spit' with Sophie. He fell asleep over the pages of a manga and woke in the middle of the night busting for a piss. He grabbed his torch, stumbled out of the tent and walked through the shadows and flat white glare of the caravan park lights to the amenities block.

Even before he reached the green and white building, he heard music. It sounded as though someone was throwing a party inside, but when he stepped into the men's shower block it was eerily empty.

AC/DC's 'Highway to Hell' pumped out through the loudspeakers, echoing against the tiles.

When he turned the corner of the amenities block and passed the entrance to the women's showers, he saw Miranda for the first time. Her long blonde hair gleamed beneath the fluorescent light. She was dancing, flitting past the entrance and back again as she pirouetted across the tiled floor.

The next morning, Blake and Sophie walked down the cliff track to the estuary, where the swimming was safer than the main beach. The water filling the inlet was absolutely still, without a lick of surf.

'Hey, Soph,' said Blake, trying to sound casual. 'Have you seen that girl with the long blonde hair?'

'What girl? You mean that little four-year-old whose family is next to the bouncy castle?'

'No, this girl's about my age. I saw her in the women's toilets last night.'

'What were you doing perving on the girls' toilets?'

'I wasn't perving,' said Blake. 'I can't help it if you can see in when you walk past. In the middle of the night, last night, there was this girl with long blonde hair dancing in front of the mirrors.'

'In your dreams,' said Sophie. 'There are no other teenagers in the whole caravan park. Only teeny tiny kids. Trust me, I've checked.'

Blake watched the ocean and the line of white breakers beyond the reef. Sophie was wrong. That girl had to be staying somewhere in the caravan park. Why else would she be in the amenities block at 2 am? He dusted the sand from his legs, threw the towel over his shoulder and started back towards the road.

'Where are you going?' called Sophie. 'Don't leave me. I don't want to hang out here alone.'

'Just stay by the estuary and you'll be okay. I'll see you back at the caravan,' he called over his shoulder.

Blake followed a narrow track through the scrub and up to the caravan park to search for the girl. A flock of grey nomads in white rigs were parked in one corner. Camped next to the pool area was a French family with a couple of little kids. Blake picked up his pace and turned towards the far end of the campsite where a row of small tents was pitched overlooking the sea. But there were no teenage girls on those sites either, only three English men sitting in deck chairs, their thin white legs patchy with sunburn, and a couple of Aussie blokes with a litter of tinnies outside their tent.

Blake walked slowly past the cabins, looking for the girl. But why would anyone from a cabin use the shower block if they had a bathroom of their own?

A gentle rain fell as Blake crawled into his tent that night. He was glad to get away from his family. His parents had been furious with him when Sophie came back to the caravan alone. Sophie just shrugged and tried to cover for him but Dad gave Blake a full-on lecture.

Blake drifted off to sleep to the sound of rain on nylon. He didn't know what woke him. The rain had stopped. He lifted the tent flap and stared out into the night. He could hear music from the amenities block. It seemed louder than the night before. He didn't really need to get up, but the longer he lay listening to the music, the more awake he felt. His mouth was dry and fuzzy. He reached for his toothbrush and stepped outside.

The girl stood alone, leaning across the bench, staring into the bathroom mirror, studying her reflection. As Blake watched, she started to dance, studying her moves in the mirror. Blake hadn't meant to stare but the girl's movements made him feel as though he were hypnotised. Suddenly, she stopped midway through her dance and turned to him and smiled. Blake raised one hand to wave and then hurried into the men's. He stood at the sink nearest the wall. She was just the other side of the breezeblocks.

On the third night, when he woke, it was as if she were calling him. He stopped outside the entrance to the women's shower block. At first he thought she wasn't there. Then he heard a door bang and the girl stepped into the light. She stared at Blake.

'I was wondering if you'd be here tonight,' he

said. 'My sister reckons I'd imagined you. She thinks I'm crazy.'

'My brother couldn't care less about me,' said the girl. 'You're Blake, aren't you? I'm Miranda.'

Blake smiled. 'Do you want to go for a walk? It's a little uncool for me to be caught standing around outside the girls' shower block.'

Miranda hung her head, her long blonde hair framing her face. 'Someone might see me. I'm not really meant to be here.'

'Where's your campsite?'

'I don't have one anymore. My family went home without me.'

'You're kidding? You mean you're here on your own?'

Miranda ran her hands through her hair and sighed. 'It's not so bad, so long as no one else sees me. No one except you. You want to swim? I love this end of summer, when the water's still warm enough for night swimming.'

'What? Now? The moon's not even up yet. It's pitch dark down there.'

'Who cares? Haven't you ever been night-swimming before? I love it. I go every night.'

'My parents will kill me if they find out,' said Blake, already knowing he was going to follow Miranda.

'Mine didn't care what I did,' said Miranda as they walked through the sleeping caravan park. The white glow of the security lights fell in pools across the roadway. 'I slept on the beach the last night they were here and they didn't even notice. Then they left without me. They were only interested in my brother and he was only interested in himself. No one worried about me.'

As they turned onto the narrow track to the beach Blake could just make out Miranda's pale hair swaying in the dark ahead. The moon began to nudge its way over the horizon, a tiny crescent of light, small and sharp as a fingernail. The crests of waves glimmered silvery white against the black water and the night sky was ablaze with stars.

Miranda slipped off her clothes and walked into the surf.

'Follow me,' she called, as the sea washed around her legs.

For a split second, Blake hesitated. Beyond the breakers, the water was as black as ink. Miranda's body was swallowed up by the waves. Blake tore off his clothes and followed her into the sea.

Blake slept in late. His head felt heavy when he woke. Miranda. It was the first word that came to him when he opened his eyes.

'Blake,' called Mum, from outside his tent. 'Where's Sophie?'

'I don't know,' said Blake, covering his head with a pillow.

'She was waiting for you to wake up. She must have gone down to the beach. I don't like her going alone, Blake. Can you run down and check on her?'

Sophie, Sophie, Sophie. Always Sophie. Blake jogged down the track to the wide curve of the bay. Sophie wasn't sitting in their usual spot by the estuary. He shaded his eyes and scanned the water. For a moment, he felt a little clutch of panic. Then he saw her, at the far end of the beach, clambering over rocks. He ran along the sand, cupping his hands around his mouth and calling her name.

'Where the hell do you think you're going?' he said, when he finally caught up with her.

'There's a cemetery up there,' said Sophie, pointing up the cliff. 'I just thought I'd check it out.'

'Mum was freaking. She thought you'd drowned.'

'Sorry,' said Sophie. 'I just want to see the cemetery. Will you come with me?'

Blake shrugged. What choice did he have? If he went back without Sophie their mother would go berserk.

They clambered over black rocks, searching for handholds, until they found a path carved into the cliff. When they reached the top they climbed over a wire fence. The cemetery was tiny – two small fields of grass with a smattering of low tombstones. Further back, sheltered from the sea winds, was an obelisk with the names of the men from the town who had died in the wars of the 20th century.

'Hurry up, Sophie,' said Blake.

'Come and see this one,' said Sophie. 'It's so sad.'

Grudgingly, Blake made his way over to the corner of the graveyard. It was the last grave, on the very edge of the cliff top, facing the ocean. A simple headstone with a picture set behind glass embedded in the white marble.

'This girl was only fourteen,' said Sophie. 'Don't you think that's tragic?'

A stoneware vase full of fresh flowers had been placed on the grave and beside the headstone stood a figurine of a dolphin rising out of the water.

'Someone takes really good care of this grave,' said Sophie. 'You can tell.'

Blake simply stared at the inscription.

In loving memory of Miranda, our darling daughter and beloved sister, a free spirit. The wind and sea cried out to her and she answered.

Blake felt all the blood drain away from his head. He turned and stared out at the white-capped ocean. The wind whipped his hair off his face. He took a deep breath.

'C'mon,' he said, taking Sophie's hand. 'Let's get out of here.'

Mum and Dad were already down on the beach. They looked relieved when they saw Sophie and Blake waving from the cliff path.

'Sophie,' said Mum. 'You mustn't head off on your own like that. Ever. Wait for Blake.'

'Blake doesn't want to hang out with me,' said Sophie. 'He doesn't care anymore.'

But Blake didn't hear her. He was already running along the beach, straight back to the caravan park office.

'Miranda Prosper,' he blurted at the receptionist. 'There's a girl called Miranda Prosper buried in the cemetery on the headland. Was she a local kid? Do you know how she died?'

The receptionist turned pale. 'It was nothing to do with us. We put up warnings.'

'What happened?' asked Blake.

'If you must know, she drowned. We warn everyone about not swimming at night and not swimming alone. She did both. She went down to the back beach at night and was swept out to sea.'

Blake could only nod, as if he'd known all along.

That night, as he walked through the darkened caravan park to the shower block, he knew what he had to say to Miranda.

'Hey Blake,' said Miranda, smiling and flicking her silky hair over her shoulder. 'I was hoping you'd come back. It was fun last night, wasn't it? You want to go swimming again?'

'No,' said Blake. 'There's something I want to show you.'

Miranda didn't show a flicker of hesitation as Blake led her up the cliff track to the cemetery. A crescent moon had risen and faintly lit their way. Blake looked back into Miranda's upturned face as she followed him. How could she not know? He gripped her cool hand tightly.

When they reached the top he helped her over the wire fence and led her to the grave at the tip of the headland. He'd brought his flashlight but he didn't need it. The gold lettering of Miranda's name glittered in the moonlight. Her face smiled out from the framed photograph. He heard a sharp little intake of breath.

'But they didn't care,' said Miranda. 'After I died, they just left me.'

'No, Miranda, they buried you here. Someone comes and tends this grave. Someone lays fresh flowers on it.'

Miranda bent down and picked up the blue dolphin. 'This was my brother's favourite. He loved dolphins.'

She turned towards the cliff's edge and stared out to sea. 'When I was alive, they never told me how they felt,' she said. 'I guess only the living can truly change.'

'I'm sorry, Miranda.'

'It's okay, Blake. Don't follow me this time.'

She leapt into the moonlight. And then, she was gone.

In the car driving back to the city, Sophie sat looking glumly out the window. She ran her hands through her long blonde hair and sighed.

'What's up, kid?' asked Blake.

'I don't want to go home. I don't want to start high school. I'm scared. We'll be getting back late and everyone will already be in some cliquey group and no one will want to know me.'

Blake took her hand and held it tightly. 'I'll *always* want to know you, Soph,' he said. 'Don't you ever doubt that. I'll always be there for you.'

What Goes Around...
Janeen Brian

'Hey, Sam! *In here!*'

'Okay.' Sam walked around the bulldozer that sat in the middle of the lawn and kicked at bits of rubble and guttering from the semi-demolished house. He then picked his way over brick stacks, foundations and random flooring boards.

'Where?'

'Here.'

Kon was kneeling in the corner of a room that must've once been a bedroom. Maybe Mrs Martin's. Because the room was now open to all weathers, the pink rose wallpaper was faded and peeling. With a smirk, Kon turned towards Sam and jabbed his finger towards a hole in the floor and then at a pile of short, even floorboards.

Sam raised his eyebrows. 'So what?'

'Mate, it's a hole.' Kon enunciated the words slowly, as if to a toddler. 'Note the floorboards have been cut. *And* replaced.' His smirk broadened. 'That is, until I got to them. But, hey, you may ask, why would anyone, especially an *old lady* like Mrs Martin, do that, eh?'

Sam leaned against the wall and shrugged. 'White ant treatment?'

Kon pulled a face. 'That is a such a crap answer.'

'It is not. We had it done at our place, in the kitchen, and that's exactly what happens. Next time you're –'

'Okay! Okay!' Kon pushed his palms upwards. 'But, mate, in my humble opinion, this hole was not cut for any white ant treatment.'

'So? It's a hole.' Sam gave a deliberate, disinterested yawn. It was obvious to him that Kon had something up his sleeve. His friend was holding back, baiting him. Kon liked nothing better than a bit of showmanship – especially when he was the main act.

Oddly enough, this time the play took a different turn. Kon didn't jump in, drums thumping and flags waving. Not straightaway anyway. Instead he paused and muttered, 'Geez, Sam! What if Mum and Dad had built our new house right on this spot?'

Sam continued to scratch at a piece of peeling wallpaper. He had no intention of asking Kon what he was on about. His mate was probably still baiting. But he was about to lose his audience. 'I reckon I'll head off,' Sam said, 'and leave you with your hole.'

Kon blinked, as if suddenly brought back down to Earth. 'No, hang here, mate.' His dark eyes shone with urgency.

'Nah.' Sam flicked a scrap of wallpaper in Kon's direction. 'Not unless you've found treasure or something.'

Kon's expression remained blank, but his mouth opened and shut, goldfish style.

It took Sam by surprise. Had his offhanded comment hit some kind of mark? 'You haven't, have you?' he said, his voice rising.

The corners of Kon's mouth curved upwards and he edged closer to the hole. 'Well, have I got a story to tell you, mate. Listen to this. I pulled up those boards, right, and I was feeling around underneath, like this, and the next thing . . .' He paused, leaving the rest of the sentence dangling mid-air.

'So did you or didn't you?' said Sam.

'Did I or didn't I *what*?' repeated Kon, rolling his eyes and reaching into the small, square recess. 'Mmm. I wonder what's in here?'

Sam sank back against the wall. Damn Kon. It was a set-up. Showmen had their practical jokes and Kon was no different. It'd be just like his friend to produce a large fistful of dust and hurl it at him with a loud, *gotcha* laugh.

But he didn't. With a flourish Kon drew from the hole an old-fashioned tin, its gold pattern scratched and worn. He offered it to Sam.

'Open it,' Kon said.

Sam laughed, now totally wised up. 'Nup. Not falling for that one. You open it.'

'Ah.' Kon sighed with mock resignation. 'You're a sad case, Sam. Okay, if I *have* to.' He prised open the lid and casually held the tin at arm's length. 'Check it out yourself.'

Sam rolled up on the balls of his feet, head tilted. He was primed and ready to back off fast if necessary.

He peered at the contents.

'Man oh man!' he whispered. 'Is that for real?' This kind of thing didn't happen to ordinary kids like him and Kon, living in an ordinary suburb in Adelaide.

'Course it's real!' Kon's laugh barely concealed a note of triumph. 'What did you think it was? Monopoly money? I found it right there, in that hole, like I said.'

Sam clasped his hands on top of his head and breathed out noisily. 'How much?'

Kon flicked at one bundle and twisted his lips, considering. 'I reckon . . . about five hundred.'

'Five hundred dollars,' sighed Sam, sinking down onto the floor. 'That's one helluva lolly tin!'

'I know. Sweet as!'

'Now what?'

'Now what, *what*?' Kon gaped as if confused.

'Come on. Do I have to spell it out? What's going to happen to the money?'

Grinning, Kon hammered the lid back on with his fist. 'Finders, keepers,' he said as he attempted to push a piece of paper into his jeans pocket.

Curious, Sam snatched it out of Kon's hand and

waved it aloft. 'Caught out, mate. This was in the tin as well, wasn't it?'

Kon made a grab for the paper. 'It's nothing!' he cried. 'Nothing. Like it's so hard to read, I dunno what it says.'

'Okay,' said Sam. 'I'll try and decipher it. "*I, Josephine Martin,*" he began slowly, '"*being of sound mind, bequeath the contents of this tin to the Stirling Dogs' Home. In the event of my death, I trust my savings will be delivered to the Home to help care for the animals I love so dearly. Yours sincerely . . .*" and signed by Josephine Martin.'

Sam looked up. 'Old Mrs Martin. Remember her, Kon? She used to bake biscuits for us and let us play on her trees. Grew veggies for people even though she could hardly use her hands. Remember the accident she told us about? When she fell in a campfire as a kid and burned them.'

'Yeah, course I remember,' said Kon. 'And I remember the white gloves she always wore. But mate, what's all that got to do with this?' He rapped his fingernails on the tin. 'Like, the old lady's dead. I'm sorry about her burned hands and I'm sorry that she died, but none of that's my fault.'

Sam turned away from the steely look in Kon's eyes. 'Finders, keepers, eh?' he said, feeling disgust rise in his throat. 'I reckon you'd better think again, Kon. That tin goes to the dogs' home.' Sam was surprised to feel his heart thumping so hard.

Kon stood. 'You're joking, right? If I hadn't found this tin, guess what would've happened to it? The bulldozer would've come in and buried it under all this crap.' He gestured at the ruin around him. 'You don't like finders, keepers? Mate, what if *no one* had found this tin? Then *no one* – not you, not me, not even one little four-legged terrier at the dogs' home would've got a cent of this money. So, all I'm saying is that the lady's dead and I found the money. Simple.'

Sam stood and faced him. 'You're right, Kon. It is simple.'

A smile spread over Kon's face and he punched Sam's arm. 'That's my man.'

'Because it's all going to the dogs' home.'

'Sam!' Kon took his friend by the shoulders. 'Listen. The old lady said in the note that she was of *sound mind*. Well, if you're of sound mind, you don't go burying your money, do you? Besides, I'm not going to keep it all for myself. You were here when I found it, so there's a share in it for you, too.'

'I don't want a share.'

'That's very generous, but we're mates and mates share. So I'm telling you we'll split. No questions asked.'

'And you're not listening to me. I don't want any.' Sam turned to go. 'You found it,' he said over his shoulder, 'you keep it.'

Kon put his hand on Sam's arm. 'Hey, we're not doing anything illegal. If you found a five-dollar note on the footpath, what would you do? Try and find the owner? Course not. You'd keep it.'

'Yeah. I would.' Sam pulled free from Kon's grasp. 'But this,' he said, 'is very different. See ya 'round, Kon.'

―――

Kon's new family home was built on the spot where Mrs Martin's house had once stood. One blowy day Kon noticed something odd from his bedroom window. He'd just unpacked some sound equipment and happened to glance at a large gum tree swaying in the wind. He'd never noticed before but when he lined up the tree and a neighbour's fence, he discovered that his bedroom was roughly in the same position as the old bedroom with the pink rose wallpaper. How was that for weird?

The brand new sound system looked great and had only cost six hundred dollars. 'Wicked,' Kon murmured, fixing the last speaker in place. He'd told his parents he'd saved his pocket money and earned more by doing odd jobs around the neighbourhood. He figured it wasn't really a lie. It had been *odd* that he'd found the money tin in the first place; it had been a hard *job* to get the floorboards up and it had all happened in the *neighbourhood*.

Not only had his dad bought the white lie, he'd even praised Kon for what he called 'his effort', adding, 'What goes around, comes around, son. It's the nature of the universe. You worked hard to get the money and so the sound system is your reward.'

Kon stood back now to admire it. Pity Sam wasn't here to check it out with him. But then, he and Sam didn't hang around much together anymore.

By nightfall the wind had died down, and all Kon heard was a gentle rustling in the trees. Some time later, however, he was woken by a strange scratching noise. Sleepily, he turned on his bedside light, but after checking the room, he turned it off and went back to sleep.

Next evening, the same sound woke him again. It was a clawing, scraping sound, the kind a rat might make. Kon checked the room once more. Still nothing.

The following night, the sound was there again. Kon grabbed a torch and shone the beam out the window just as a sudden gust of wind sprang up. Something thin and spiky flicked into view and Kon's heart leapt to his mouth.

It was one of his mum's outdoor potted plants.

'Great,' he mumbled and snapped off the torch. Relieved, he dragged up his bedclothes and was asleep in minutes.

But the next morning he sat up in bed, his face crumpled with shock.

On the wall in front of him was a large crack. It zigzagged right above his sound system.

Kon's dad was even less impressed. 'A new house, and this is what happens. I'll get on to the plasterer today and he'd better have some answers.'

But all Kon could think about was how the ragged snaking line spoiled the look of his new equipment.

When the noise came again that night, it didn't come as a rasping, scratching sound. It exploded like a crack of thunder. Kon sat bolt upright in bed, wide-eyed. After fumbling for the light switch, he gaped, terrified, as the crack slowly widened like the mouth of a large creature. Then from somewhere came a voice. '*Give me back my money,*' it wailed. '*It was not yours to have. It was for the dogs. Give it back. Give it back.*'

Next, from the great yawning gap, appeared a pair of hands. They were wearing white gloves and they flew, flapping, towards him.

Kon screamed. And he kept on screaming as he fled from the room, batting his hands at the gloves that refused to be knocked away.

The plasterer was completely baffled. But he and the brickie repaired the damage at no extra cost and assured Kon's parents that it was unlikely the problem would return.

Later Kon's dad said to Kon, 'Sorry about your new sound system, son. Such a terrible shame all that rubble falling on it. We'll claim insurance of course, and get you another one.'

Whitefaced, Kon nodded. His mum put her arm

around him. 'Fancy a nightmare and the wall cracking at the same time. Not much fun. Come and I'll make you a Milo.'

That night Kon chose to sleep in the small, spare bedroom. Weeks later, his mum said to her husband, 'You know, Steve, Kon hasn't really settled since that night, has he? What do you reckon about getting him a pet? He's never had a dog and they've got plenty at the Stirling Dogs' Home.'

'Yeah. Good idea, love. Let's go and tell him.'

But Kon wasn't in either of the bedrooms. He was already at the Stirling Dogs' Home.

'I can come after school to help,' he said. 'I'll do anything.'

'We can't pay you,' said the woman behind the desk.

'I don't want money,' said Kon as he tried once more to push away the image of the white gloves that still haunted his days and nights – that hovered like giant moths around a flame.

The Girl in the Library

Bill Condon

My life got tipped upside down in the library. I was sitting there with a book, when I became aware of a stare burrowing into me. Yes, burrowing is the right word – it was that intense. I glanced up and saw the culprit was a beautiful vision in black – a girl vision. There had to be some mistake. Girls didn't look at me. They didn't even see me, or if they did, they quickly looked the other way. Fat guy, that's me. But this girl's eyes were locked on tight. Strangely enough, I didn't feel annoyed about it or uncomfortable. I felt peaceful.

Then something truly amazing happened. She came over and sat down beside me.

'Hi,' she said.

'Um,' I replied.

It wasn't up to my usual witty standard, but you have to remember, I was in shock.

'I've seen you here before,' she said.

That was odd. I hadn't seen her – and believe me, a Goth girl stands out in sleepy Canleytown.

'I noticed that you're nearly always in the same section of the library,' she continued. 'Non-fiction –

literary stuff. That's why I came over. I got curious.'

'About what?'

'The whole deal – who you are, what you do.' She gestured at the book beside me: *The Lives of Writers*. 'Why do you read books like that?'

I've got this theory that sometimes the words that fall from our mouths are chosen by someone else. I never would have been brave enough to say, 'I want to be a writer.' But those are the words that tumbled out.

'Are you sure?' She leaned in closer. 'I know a lot of people say that, but it's not easy. Hardly anyone makes it.'

'I don't care. That won't stop me.'

Someone else had picked out those words for me, too. I didn't share my crazy secrets with strangers – until now.

'Wow . . . what do you want to write?'

'Poems. Stories. Anything. Everything. I'm into writing. Full stop!'

Her chalk-white face lit up. 'Yes, you are a writer, I can tell. And you're really passionate about it. That's so cool.'

Those words went straight to the framers. In my mind I have a shop that frames good things that have been said about me. It doesn't get a lot of business. No one had ever thought of me as 'passionate' or 'cool' before.

I tried to nod in all the right places as she raved

about books and her fondness for words.

'My faves are true stories,' she said. 'That doesn't mean they can't be fiction, but they have to ring with honesty and be written from the heart. Good writers can transport me to another world.'

I was having trouble finding any words at all. My brain was in meltdown, possibly because I was daydreaming about kissing those red, red lips. But I was able to conjure up one small slice of conversation.

'Are you interested in angels?'

The book she was clutching hinted that she was.

'Not this kind. This is silly stuff. I only flicked through it to see if they got it right.'

'And did they?'

'Nope.' Her eyes were the colour of clouds. 'They never do.'

That was too good an opening for me not to dive in.

'So you know about angels, do you?'

I said it in a jokey way, hoping it might score a grin. But she looked back at me very seriously and said, 'I'm learning.'

There was an uneasy silence after that. I didn't know what to say next, apart from, 'You're really weird,' which didn't seem like a good idea.

Thank god she laughed. Not a rattle-your-bones kind of laugh or a cute chuckle, but enough to let me know she wasn't so strange after all.

'It's good to talk to you,' she said.

I shrugged as if this was nothing to me, as if I regularly got chatted up by drop-dead gorgeous girls. I did, too, though not in my waking hours. But this girl was definitely not a dream, and I didn't even know her name – so I asked her.

'Shari,' she said.

I told her mine – Andrew – and as I did, I took a huge risk. I smiled at her.

My smile hadn't been used for a long time so it probably wouldn't have won any awards, but if it was lame she didn't say so. Instead, for the first time in my life, a girl looked at me as if I was more than a fat boy.

It was all going so well, until she crushed me to a pulp.

'This place is way too cold for me,' she said. 'I'm out of here.'

But then, in her very next sentence, she un-crushed me. 'There's a cosy coffee shop at the mall. We can talk some more there – if you like?'

I managed to restrict myself to only two nods, in case my head got up momentum in the excitement and couldn't stop.

I was worried. The mall was more brightly lit than the library. Perhaps Shari hadn't really seen me properly before. The subdued lighting might have made me look slimmer; that and the fact that for most of

the time we talked, I'd sucked in my breath to shrink my waist.

I couldn't go on doing that forever or I'd need major surgery. Take me as I am, or don't take me. That's what I decided.

Relax. It's okay.

Shari didn't say that out loud, but as we sat down, her facing me and looking happy to be there, I heard those words in my head. It was her voice that said them. Most probably I imagined it, but whatever, it worked.

We drank hot chocolate and ate raspberry muffins. And took turns at talking. Shari went first.

She had two sisters, both older than her.

Rachael was getting married next year.

Emily was in a convent training to be a nun.

There was a mum and a dad, and two cats.

'But what about you?' I asked.

'Oh, I'm not very interesting.'

'Tell me anyway.'

'Okay. You've twisted my arm. But where do I start? Well – I love acting. From when I was little I was always doing a drama class. I've been in four plays. Never the major role. I was the girl in the background who screamed or giggled – they were my best acting qualities. Ummm – my best friends are Amy and Kendall. They're Harry Potter experts. You can ask them anything – they'll know it . . . I miss them.'

'You don't see them anymore?'

'No, wish I did. We were at Saint Brigid's together. But then – almost a year ago now – I had to move on.'

'How come?'

'Don't ask.' She rolled her eyes. 'For a while I didn't think I'd survive, but I did. I'm doing okay now.'

The words that had evaded me when we first met were now lining up eagerly and clamouring to get out. I had heaps of questions.

Where do you live?

Why haven't I seen you before?

And what does 'doing okay' mean?

But Shari got in first.

'That's enough about me,' she said. 'What's your story?'

I wanted to make it sound riveting, like a book you can't put down. But my life wasn't that kind of book. Sticking to my plan about taking me as I am, I blabbed out the boring truth.

'Since I was twelve,' I began, 'I've helped out at the family servo. Mum does the accounts and works in the shop. I've got a little sister, Karen. She goes to the shop, too – but only to be annoying. Mum says that's her job. Dad's the mechanic. When I leave school – which is any time soon – he wants me to come work with him. Says he'll teach me the trade.'

Shari folded her arms. Her sunny face became a stern, no-nonsense one.

'Is that what you want, Andrew?'

'No way. I don't know about cars – don't *want* to know. I want to write.'

'Exactly,' she said. 'So it's all settled. Just tell him that. Problem solved.'

Shari didn't know my dad.

'Thanks,' I told her. 'I'll give it a try.'

'You better.' She wagged a finger at me. 'I'll know if you don't.'

Soon our drinks and muffins were only a fond memory. Shari looked at her watch, confirming my fears – it was time for her to go.

'I'm sorry I can't stay longer.' She pushed back her chair and stood. 'This has been fun. But you know how it is – things to do, people to see.'

'Maybe we could meet up again some time?' I tried to say it as casually as I could, as if it didn't really matter to me.

Her answer wasn't made of words. She took my hand in hers and squeezed it tightly. I swear, in that second, there was no one else in the mall, in the country, who felt what I did. It was like my heart lifted up, and all the drudgery that had been my life, was swept away.

She strolled off, and less than a minute later I wanted to kick myself for not at least asking for her mobile number. I had no way of contacting her. I asked around at school the next day, but drew a blank. A mystery girl; that was Shari.

All the same, in the weeks that followed, I felt that

she wasn't far away. I sensed that she was with me when I dyed my hair jet black, to match my new clothes.

Also, I think it might have been Shari's idea for me to have one thick and dangerous lock draped across my forehead. It looked like a monster's claw emerging from primeval slime. The slime was hair gel. I was considering getting a lip-ring, too, but the body piercing shop wouldn't give me a general anaesthetic.

And I was sure Shari was right beside me, nearly a month later, when I at last found the courage to tell Dad that I wouldn't be joining him in the servo, because I was going to be a writer.

'Writer? You gotta be jokin'!' That was his response.

'Andrew's always talked about writing, George.' Mum was in my corner, as usual.

'My point exactly.' Dad jabbed a hole in the air with his finger. 'All he ever does is talk. This is twaddle, Dorothy. I've never seen anything he's written yet.'

'He's done plenty,' Mum said. 'All sorts of stuff. But he's only ever let me see one thing.'

'Is that so?' Dad turned to me. 'Well how come I haven't seen this masterpiece, then?'

'It was nothing.' I shrugged. 'Forget it.'

'It was a poem.' Mum straightened her back as she said it and stood up tall. Like she was proud. 'He didn't show it to you, George, because it was *about* you.'

'A poem?'

He looked at me, scratching his head and seeming perplexed.

'You wrote a poem about me?'

'Yeah, Dad.'

'That's about the dopiest thing I ever heard.'

Mum sighed, loudly. 'Andrew knew you'd react like this.'

Dad slumped deep in his chair and scraped a hand up and down his chin. I'm pretty sure I know what he was thinking –

Gawd! Cars aren't as much trouble as people!

'All right then,' he said finally, 'give me a look at this flamin' poem.'

'I tore it up, Dad. It was garbage.'

'It wasn't garbage.' Mum's arm circled my waist. 'It was about a boy who believes his father doesn't know the first thing about him – doesn't care about him.'

Dad grimaced.

'You don't see how sad he gets, George. It's right there in front of you, but you never see it.'

I tried to stop her.

'Please, Mum. Drop it.'

She didn't.

'He's like that because he can't get close to you;

can't talk to you. He's different, so you've shut him out, but he's still your son, and he still loves you.'

Dad's eyes moved slowly from Mum to me. He gulped and for a second I thought he might spill a tear. But he huffed, and blinked it away.

'Was it any good, this poem?'

'It was very good,' Mum said.

'Really?'

'Yes, George. Really.'

Dad clicked his tongue. His brow was deeply furrowed. It was an exact replay of how he looked when he first saw my dyed hair and Goth gear.

But this time he wasn't angry.

'I don't care about ya, eh?' he said to me. 'You big hairy galoot. Come here.'

My dad was big like me, but where I had flab, he had muscles. He was bald and his nose was bent and he stomped more than he stepped. He looked like a wrestler who'd overdosed on head-butts. But when he hugged me, he was just my dad.

I never saw Shari again. Didn't expect to, really. But to this day I still spend an awful lot of time in libraries. Just hoping. Hoping and writing.

Stilled Lifes x 11

Justin D'Ath

#1 'Butterfly and Ant'

'Eeew!' said Angel Divine's mother. 'You're supposed to eat your breakfast, not draw with it!'

Hannah had only left the room for two minutes. Long enough for thirteen-month-old Angel to smear pureed apple and mushy Weet-Bix all over the tray of her highchair. Hannah took her daughter's spoon and bowl to the sink and returned with a damp tissue. But she only got as far as wiping her daughter's hands.

'Edward!' she called, the tissue clutched forgotten in her hand. 'Edward, come and look at this.'

Her husband bustled into the kitchen, doing up his tie. 'What a mess!' he said. 'I told you she's too young to feed herself.'

'I didn't call you in here to have an argument,' said Hannah. 'Look at what she's drawn.'

Edward studied the highchair's food-smeared tray. 'What's it supposed to be?'

'A butterfly.' Hannah pointed. 'Look – those are the wings. There's the body and head. It's even got eyes!'

'If you say so,' Edward said, turning to his wife. 'Could you straighten my tie, honey? I've got a meeting with some new clients in half an hour.'

Neither parent noticed that there was more than just pureed fruit and cereal in Angel's artwork.

One of the butterfly's tiny black eyes was moving.

#2 'Flower and Fly'

At lunchtime three days later, Angel made a flower with a bee on it. She used mashed banana, yoghurt, and something that her mother didn't notice. Hannah took a photo with her mobile phone and showed it to Edward when he got home.

'That's not bad,' he said.

Hannah's eyebrows shot up. 'Not *bad*?' she cried. 'Darling, our daughter's only thirteen months old!'

'And obviously too young to be feeding herself,' said Edward.

#3 'Spiderweb with Beetle'

Angel's 'Spiderweb with Beetle' was her breakthrough work.

It was a Saturday afternoon and the Divines had friends over for a barbecue. Someone bumped the food table, knocking a squeeze-bottle of tomato-sauce onto the lawn. Nobody noticed until Angel had emptied most of it across the patio.

'My goodness!' cried a woman called Chloe. 'Did you do that, Angel?'

'Uh-oh! What's she done?' asked Edward, hurrying over from the sizzling barbecue. He stopped in his tracks.

'Holy smoke!'

A minute later, everyone was gathered in a circle around Angel's creation. It was a huge, intricately drawn spider-web, all done in tomato-sauce.

'Look, there's even a fly!' said Chloe's husband, Josh.

The fly was done in tomato sauce, too. Or most of it was. Its legs were black, and they were moving! Angel had pushed a large black beetle upside-down into the fly's tomato-sauce body to make its legs.

'Did *Angel* do that?' asked a friend who had just arrived.

Edward beamed with pride. 'We think she's going to be an artist, don't we, Hannah?'

#4 'Poodle and Snail'

Edward made a movie of Angel and her tomato-sauce spiderweb. He put it on YouTube. There were 523 views in the first twenty-four hours. Within a week, more than four thousand people had looked at it.

Word spread about the little girl in nappies who made amazing pictures with food. People compared her to Picasso, to Van Gogh, to a young Michelangelo. The local newspaper sent a reporter and a photographer. They brought some butcher's paper and non-toxic crayons, but all Angel would do was chew on the crayons.

'She usually draws with food,' explained Edward.

Hannah got a selection of things from the fridge and put them on the floor next to their daughter. Then she pointed at the butcher's paper.

'Draw something, darling.'

Angel got to work. She made a poodle out of leftover spaghetti and dollops of mayonnaise. It had a pickled capsicum for a tongue and a black-olive nose.

'Extraordinary!' said the reporter, madly making notes.

The photographer took about fifty photos.

When the poodle seemed to be finished, everybody clapped.

Angel looked up at them, frowning. 'No fin,' she said, shaking her head.

'She says it isn't finished,' Hannah translated.

Angel got up and toddled over to the sliding doors. It had rained overnight and a big garden snail was sliding up the outside of the glass. Angel pointed at the snail and looked back at her mother.

'Ta,' she said.

Hannah shook her head. 'It's yucky, darling.'

'Ta!' Angel repeated, louder this time.

'I think she wants it for her picture,' Edward said.

He opened the door and got the snail for Angel. She waddled back to her artwork, plopped down on her nappy-padded behind and pushed the snail into the poodle's spaghetti-and-mayonnaise head. Now it had a big, round eye.

'Fin!' Angel said.

And the photographer took a photo that would appear on the front page of the weekend newspaper.

#5 'Giraffe with Worm'

Channel Nine got in touch. Angel went on *Sixty Minutes*. They filmed her in the Divines' backyard making a giraffe out of bread slices, yo-yo biscuits and chocolate ice-cream topping.

It wasn't 'fin' until Angel found a fat, pink worm under a flowerpot and used it for the giraffe's tongue.

#6 'Coral Reef with Crayfish'

Late one night there was a phone call from America. It was the producer of *The Ellen DeGeneres Show*. They offered to fly Angel and her parents to Los Angeles, all expenses paid, so Ellen could have Australia's young food-artist sensation on her show.

Edward took a week off work, a limousine drove them to the airport, and forty-eight hours later Angel Divine was on live television in ten million American homes.

The show's production team had spared no expense in providing Angel with art materials. There was every sort of food you could think of, even a tank with a live crayfish inside.

Angel had watched *Finding Nemo* five times on the

flight from Australia. She made the studio floor into a huge coral reef. All the fish and the colourful coral and the seaweed were created from food.

It was spectacular.

Ellen was amazed. 'How *old* is your daughter?' she asked Angel's parents.

'Fifteen months last Saturday,' Edward said proudly.

'She is an absolute prodigy!' Ellen said, bringing her hands together in a show of amazement.

That started the live audience clapping. But when the applause died down, Angel frowned at the audience.

'No fin,' she said, shaking her head.

'What are you saying, sweetie?' asked Ellen.

'She's saying it's not finished,' Hannah translated.

Angel pointed up at the crayfish tank. 'Ta,' she said.

Ellen smiled. 'That's a lobster, sweetie.'

'She wants it,' said Hannah.

'She always has something alive in her collages,' explained Edward.

A stagehand wearing rubber gloves netted the crayfish and took it to Angel. Holding it against her jumpsuit to stop it wriggling, the tiny artist toddled over to her coral reef scene and carefully placed the crayfish next to the bagel-and-licorice octopus.

'Fin!' Angel declared, smiling in satisfaction.

And everyone clapped again.

#7 'Garden with Caterpillar'

Something happened after *The Ellen DeGeneres Show* that changed the Divine family's lives. They were talking backstage to Ellen when one of her personal assistants came over with a phone.

'Excuse me, Ms DeGeneres,' she said. 'I've got a New York art collector on the line. He's offering fifty thousand dollars for the little girl's reef painting.'

Ellen laughed. 'Tell him it's not a painting – it's made of food. You can't hang food in an art gallery!'

That started Edward thinking. If there was some way to preserve Angel's artworks – some way to keep them fresh so they could be hung on art gallery walls – people might buy them!

As soon as they got back to Australia, he phoned his friend Josh, who was an industrial chemist. When Edward told him what he had in mind, Josh said he'd work on it.

A month later, Josh came to visit. He had a bottle of pale yellow liquid and a small pressure sprayer.

'I think this'll work,' he said.

They sprayed it on Angel's latest artwork, a fruit and left-over-pizza creation called 'Garden with Caterpillar', and the result was perfect. When the spray dried – it only took a few minutes – the collage set rock-hard, as if it was made of china. But the food still seemed fresh and lifelike. Even the frozen caterpillar looked as if it was still alive.

Edward put the finished collage on eBay and the

bidding was fierce. His auction finished at $12,466.

#8 'Balloon with Budgie'

Thanks to Josh's preservative spray, Angel's artworks could now be sold.

Edward hired an agent. His daughter's collages went to art galleries and private collections all over the world. Within fifteen months, before she had turned three, Angel Divine was among the top ten most successful artists in the world.

One of her works, 'Balloon with Budgie', sold for $3,000,000 at a New York art auction.

#9 'Me and Daddy Fishing'

The Divines moved house. They needed somewhere bigger. Angel wanted her own studio and her mother was expecting another child.

With the money from Angel's three latest collages, they bought a huge mansion on the Sydney foreshore. The views were magnificent. There was a lovely nursery for the coming baby and a spacious detached studio at the bottom of the garden where Angel could work without being interrupted.

Hannah bought a new budgie and put a lock on its cage door.

Living on the seashore provided the artist with a whole new range of art materials. Crabs, scallops and sea anemones began appearing in her collages. She learned how to catch fish.

#10 'George Crossing the Harbour Bridge'

They hired a live-in housekeeper. She also cooked meals when Hannah was feeling a bit tired, as she often did lately. The housekeeper's name was Mrs Piperidis and she lived in a little unit behind the main house. She had a fourteen-year-old Australian terrier called George.

One day Angel came up from the beach in a bad mood. She needed something to finish her latest collage, but it was high tide and the rock pools were underwater.

She was heading for her studio when she noticed old George waddling slowly across the yard.

'Come here, George!' Angel called softly.

Several hours later, Angel, Mrs Piperidis and Hannah were gathered in Angel's studio. All three of them were crying.

'Angel, how *could* you!' sobbed Hannah.

'Sorry!' sobbed Angel.

'Say sorry to Mrs Piperidis,' Hannah sobbed. 'Not to me.'

'Sorry, Mrs Pipi,' sobbed Angel.

Mrs Piperidis was crying without making any noise. Tears streamed down her face as she stared and stared at 'George Crossing the Harbour Bridge'.

Finally she spoke. 'Can I buy it?' she said softly.

'What do you mean?' asked Hannah.

'Can I buy the art?' Mrs Piperidis said, pointing at Angel's latest creation.

'You can have it, Mrs Pipi,' Angel snivelled, 'for free.'

Then the housekeeper did a strange thing. She bent and gave Angel a big kiss and a hug. 'Thank you, thank you, thank you!' she said.

'George, he was very very old,' Mrs Piperidis explained to Hannah. 'He would have died soon anyway. But now, because of your little Angel, I will have him with me always.'

#11 'Untitled'

The next day Hannah had a car accident. She almost lost the baby. The doctors had to perform an emergency caesarean.

Michael Divine was born six weeks early. He was tiny. And something had happened to him in the accident. Nobody thought he would survive.

But after three weeks in hospital, the doctors said he should go home.

Angel loved her new baby brother. He was like a living doll. But he just lay in his crib, staring up at her. He hardly moved. A doctor came every day to check on him.

One day Angel overheard the doctor and her father speaking quietly in the passageway outside Michael's nursery.

'Is there any chance he's going to make it?' asked Edward.

'I'm afraid not,' the doctor whispered. 'It's a miracle he's survived this long.'

Early next morning, when Hannah went to check on Michael, she found his crib empty. She rushed to get Edward and they searched the whole house. They looked in Angel's room, and she was gone, too.

'The studio!' said Hannah, and they both started running.

Angel met them at the studio door. She was just coming out. Her sleeves were rolled up and there was a big smile on her face.

'Fin,' she said.

Shop Till You Drop

Michael Pryor

Tom should have said no. He could have, but he didn't. When Kyle and Amy pointed out that the party was running short of chips and Coke and suggested that Tom go and get some more, he could have said, 'No, I'm having a great time. I think I'll just hang around here.'

Instead he grinned like an idiot and said, 'Yes.' That's what he always did, and he was sick of it. Agreeable Tom. Nice Tom. Dependable Tom. Tom, the guy who won't be missed if he has to duck out and do some shopping for everyone.

One day, he'd like to use that word 'no' he'd heard other people use. It seemed to work for them.

He trudged down the road at 11.30 at night, heading towards the supermarket, with the small comfort of enjoying his own music instead of the gut-turning stuff they were playing at the party.

The supermarket was new. It was one of those buildings that had gone up almost overnight. A vacant lot one day, a sign saying 'Coming Soon' the next, and then, *pa-zow*, a supermarket. It was probably built of plastic, Tom decided, as he made his way through the deserted car park. A few abandoned trolleys huddled, looking as if they wished they were somewhere else.

Once inside, Tom shuddered. The supermarket music was sweet, soft and absolutely awful, worse even than the music back at the party. He fumbled for his earbuds and made sure they were well and truly jammed in. The soothing sounds of extreme thrash metal neatly drowned out the supermarket pap.

A large, hungry-looking woman barged past him as he stood in front of the turnstile. She paused, shook her head slowly and stared around. Tom frowned as her gaze slipped over him and kept moving. Her eyes were strange. No, scratch that, her whole face was strange. Saggy, as if all the muscles had decided that it was all too much effort and it was time to give up. He shrugged. She probably just needed a couple of kilos of corn chips really bad.

Then she grunted, loud enough to make Tom jump. She shuffled off, banged through the turnstile, eyes vague and glassy – a real supermarket-shopper stare.

Tom waited a moment, giving her plenty of time to get well away, and then he picked up a carry basket, eased through the turnstile and went in search of supplies.

He went past displays of dog biscuits and chocolate biscuits, tinned spaghetti, fruit, cereal and coffee.

As he made his way to the central intersecting row, he started to grow uneasy.

At first he couldn't put his finger on it. The place was nice and clean and all the shelves were well stocked; nothing wrong there. Then he realised what it was. He couldn't see anyone else. From his position in the central row, he could see up and down each aisle. They were all empty. Plenty of orange juice, paper towels and cheese, but no customers and no staff. No cleaners. Even the woman he'd seen earlier had disappeared.

'Come on,' he muttered to himself. 'How many people do their shopping at midnight?' Then he started to imagine the sort of people who would. Loners. People who didn't like mixing with others. People who preferred the night . . .

He shook his head. 'Cut it out, Tom,' he told himself. 'You've been reading too much. You should be spending more time in front of the TV.'

He snorted, upped the volume on his music, and marched to the chips aisle. He filled the basket, remembered he had to get soft drinks, too, put a few packets of chips back and piled the basket with Coke and lemonade. The bottles made the basket heavy and he had to use both hands to lug it along.

Tom's eyes opened wide when he reached the front of the supermarket. It was totally deserted. No bored workers at the cash registers. No customers standing waiting for help. 'Hello?' Tom called, wondering if he'd stumbled on a mass kidnapping. 'Anybody there?'

Tom was no fool. This wasn't safe. He wasn't sticking around in a place like this. First step was to get out of the place, then ring the police. Let them handle it.

He left his basket at a checkout, wiped the palms of his hands on his jumper, bit his lip and hurried towards the doors.

He nearly broke his nose when they didn't open.

He staggered back, swearing. His eyes were full of tears. Gingerly, he smeared the tears away with one hand, and tried the doors again, approaching very, very slowly this time.

They didn't move.

Tom looked around. This wasn't good. Bright lights, lots of colourful packaging and 'Sale' signs everywhere, but the supermarket had started to feel like a prison rather than a retail outlet. A very strange prison.

He hammered on the doors with his fist but they didn't budge. He groaned. This wasn't the sort of shopping expedition he'd been planning. Trapped in a supermarket? It sounded like the start of a bad joke.

Tom felt a soft touch on the back of his foot and he whirled, forgetting about the pain in his nose – and saw nothing. Panting, his heart racing, he lowered his gaze and saw a lonely can of air freshener lying on its side, next to his sneaker. He stared, open-mouthed. Where had it come from? The laundry and bathroom aisle was on the other side of the store!

Tom scanned the empty checkouts, then shot a glance at the aisles. The pasta aisle was shuddering, as if an angry shelf stacker had shaken it. Then an aisle-end display of chocolate biscuits toppled and sent packets skidding across the floor.

Someone was moving. Someone, or something.

Tom wiped his sweaty palms again as a scatter of tuna tins rolled and skated out of the canned food aisle. His heart hammered and he backed against the stubborn doors.

Out of the 'Cake Mix and Sugar' aisle lurched a tall, lanky figure – a man with a long, grey beard pushing a shopping trolley. 'Hey,' called Tom, and his heart backed down out of his mouth and reassumed its position in his chest. 'Am I glad to see you! I thought I was the only one in this place. Can you give me a hand with the door? It seems to be stuck.'

The old guy stopped. He turned his head slowly in Tom's direction – and Tom stared. The man's mouth was hanging open, and his chin was slick with drool, which matted his beard. Even worse were his eyes. They were the stuff of nightmares. They were wide open, as if the lids had been stretched, and so bloodshot the whites were pink.

Tom started to pull his earbuds out, but the awful supermarket music seemed even louder than before so he jammed them back in. 'Hey, mister, I . . .' Tom gulped. The old guy was moving faster, building up a bit of steam as he pushed his trolley, but his gait was unnatural. He was walking strangely, all stiff-legged, almost rocking from side to side.

Strange though his movements were, the old guy began to move faster and faster. Tom blinked as the trolley thundered towards him, clashing and snarling as it rattled along. 'Hey! I mean, hold on a second!'

The old guy didn't stop. He rammed the trolley directly at Tom, never changing his vacant, drooling expression.

Tom yelped, hurling himself to one side and sliding across the slick new floor. The trolley crashed into the door and bounced back, leaving a crack in the glass that snaked from corner to corner. The old guy staggered a little, but he didn't let go. 'Hey!' Tom said as he picked himself up, anger replacing his fear. 'You could have killed me!'

But the old guy didn't seem to hear. He moaned a little, gave the trolley a few half-hearted shoves, then tried to back it away from the door, ignoring Tom completely.

That was when Tom saw the others out of the corner of his eye. He turned and his stomach caved in. What had been an uncomfortable situation had just become a distinctly terrifying one.

A squad of shopping trolleys was grinding towards him. Each one was pushed by an open-mouthed, drooling, pink-eyed zombie. Some were wearing staff uniforms, some looked like typical customers. Tom blinked when he saw the front of some of the trolleys were stained a dark red. *It's not blood*, he told himself as he backed away. *Not blood. Tomato sauce. Sweet and sour. Anything but blood.*

The old guy behind him was still trying to back his trolley out, still with the vacant expression on his face. Tom darted around him, took two long steps, and vaulted over the turnstile – only to find himself on the same side as the approaching zombies. They shuffled to face him, but he was already moving toward the closest vacant aisle, panic adding to his speed.

He ran past the soup, while behind him a massive trolley snarl erupted as the zombies all tried to ram through the same checkout. Tom knew that wouldn't hold them for long, and he frantically searched for a way out. As he ran he dragged cans and bottles off the shelves, hoping to slow his pursuers down. Oil, flour and sugar crashed to the floor, but he didn't stop to see the results.

Sliding around the end of the aisle, Tom lost his footing and slammed against the bread rack. Crumpets and multigrain bread rained around him, and at that moment one of his earbuds popped out. Immediately, the awful supermarket music poured in, rich and sweet and sickly. He staggered away, panting, putting a hand to his head. He tried to run, but his feet felt as if they weighed a few tonnes apiece. He slowed. He shook his head and tried to clear it. His eyes were sore and itchy, and his mouth started to droop.

He shook his head again, wondered where the fog had come from and numbly decided it was inside his head rather than outside. Then, with a huge effort, he raised a hand and slapped himself. The pain was sharp and stinging, but it worked. His head cleared a little and, automatically, he jammed his dangling earbud back in his ear.

He straightened. The fog disappeared. His eyes stopped itching. He could move again.

The shopping trolleys were getting closer, but Tom knew what he had to do. He braced himself and pulled out an earbud. Immediately, worse than ever, the music flooded into his head, numbing his thoughts. He barely had enough will to slip his earbud back in, but once it was in place he was normal again.

It was the music. Something in the music was turning people into zombies. He knew supermarkets tried to control their customers, but this was ridiculous! Just to be on the safe side, he turned up the volume on his life-saving music player to make the most of a fifteen-minute guitar solo.

A trolley rattled out of the end of an aisle. A man in a boiler suit – or what had once been a man in a boiler suit – was pushing it. When he saw Tom, he moaned loudly and others picked up the sound. It echoed from aisle to aisle, penetrating Tom's earbuds. A hunting call.

Tom backed away, turned, and sprinted.

At the back of the store, he found a door. STAFF ONLY. Without thinking, he raced through, slammed it, hit the lock and stood with his back to it. A few dirty mugs and a half-eaten pie sat on the grey table. No other doors. A blue couch beneath a small, locked window with no key. He leapt on the table and peered through the glass. The carpark.

He glanced back at the door and saw it shake on its hinges from a massive blow on the other side. He swallowed and fear was a tight knot in his throat.

He was trapped.

The door shook again, but Tom hardly saw it. Instead, his gaze was locked on the rack on the wall next to the door – a rack of keys.

He leaped off the table and bounded toward the door, which burst open as he grabbed the keys. He screeched when a mob of zombies stumbled through the doorway, tripped, and sprawled on the floor. Tom had to prance and hop to avoid their clawing hands, then he danced around the table while trying to sort through the tags on his handful of keys. He was torn between this task and keeping an eye on the zombies who had blocked the doorway in their clumsiness, tangling themselves up in their efforts to get to him. Tom spared a second to kick a mop and bucket at the zombie jam, and then he found the tag marked 'Window'. He snatched a sugar bowl from the table, bounded for the couch and was grateful when the key worked smoothly. A split-second later he was outside. Gasping, he turned and flung the sugar bowl at the window. The glass shattered and the mad ringing of a burglar alarm cut through the night. 'Perfect,' he said, and he disappeared into the night.

Tom had to drag the others back, even after he told them everything. 'You have to come,' he said. 'You'll kick yourself if you don't.'

As they drew closer, the blue and red flashing lights of police cars made the parking lot look like a theme park. Tom noticed a few ambulances. He wasn't surprised.

'What's going on, officer?' Amy asked.

'Nothing much. Just a break in.'

The officer went to move off, but Tom wasn't going to let him get away that easily. 'Can we see?'

'No,' the police officer said quickly. 'There's been a gas leak, too. It's dangerous. In fact, they're going to have to do some work on the whole building. It's a real problem.'

'No zombies, then?' Kyle said, grinning.

The police officer narrowed his eyes. He moved closer. 'And who said anything about zombies?' he said softly.

Tom took a step backwards. Behind the police

officer he could see a handful of paramedics talking seriously and pointing at the supermarket. Two workers were nailing a 'Closed for Renovation' sign across the entrance. Watching them were two men in suits, both carrying briefcases, standing next to a black van with ACME SUPERMARKET MUSIC CO written on the side. The cool, business-like attitude gave him the chills. Where were the screams? The panic? The shouts of 'Look out! Zombies!'

Something was wrong.

Tom took Kyle's shoulder. 'Don't worry about him, officer. He thinks he's funny when he's not.'

The police officer studied them carefully. 'I see.' He reached out. Tom flinched, but all the police officer did was brush his shoulder. 'A bit of broken glass. Could have been dangerous.'

Tom nodded, but wondered if the police officer knew just how dangerous a time Tom had had. 'Thanks.' He turned to his friends. 'We should be going. Come on, guys.'

He herded them off. Tom looked over his shoulder to see the police officer had gone to the black van. He was talking with the briefcase men, and Tom felt cold when the police officer pointed directly at him.

'Come on, guys,' he said urgently. 'We'd better go.'

'What?' said Kyle. 'Don't you want to stick around and see what happens?'

Tom looked at the supermarket, then at the hard-faced men in suits. 'You'd better believe me when I say no.'

Kyle and Amy were puzzled, but Tom wouldn't argue. He led them away, making a long detour around a solitary shopping trolley abandoned in the gutter. A shopping trolley with a large red stain on the front wheels.

Space Junk
Jenny Mounfield

Jarn is yanked from sleep by the sound of his phone.

'Whoisit?'

'It's Hari. You awake?'

'No.'

'Guess what?'

'Can't this wait till after the sun comes up?'

'Leni rang. He's gone fishing with some mates. Says he saw a UFO.'

'Your brother's full of it.'

'Serious. He said it fell into the trees out past the recycling centre. Reckons it's either space junk or a meteorite. Either way he can sell it for heaps on eBay. He'll cut us in if we go find it.'

Fully awake now, Jarn sits up and rubs his eyes. 'That's a pretty big area to search. Even if there is something there, we'll probably never find it.'

'Leni knows where it went down. 'Sides, got anything better to do?'

Jarn has to admit he doesn't.

'It's just after six now,' Hari goes on. 'Meet me outside the recycling centre at eight.'

'I'll give Adam a call. He'll –'

'No way!'

'Adam's all right. You just need to get to know him,' Jarn says.

'Forget it.'

'If Adam can't come you can search for the UFO by yourself.'

'Aw man! Okay. But he's not getting a cut of the money.'

Jarn has been trying to get Adam and Hari to like each other since Adam moved to their school two months ago. But for some reason putting his two mates within sight of each other has them facing off like a pair of pit bulls.

Jarn hangs up and rings Adam.

The recycling centre is a five-kilometre ride from town. Despite the cool autumn morning, Jarn is lathered in sweat by the time he gets there. Adam and Hari are already waiting, trading insults and air punches.

'What took you so long?' Hari snaps as Jarn's bike rolls to a stop.

'Get off his back,' Adam growls.

'Make me!'

Adam takes a threatening step towards Hari.

'Bring it ON!' Hari bounces on his toes, fists up.

'Stop it!' Jarn yells. 'Or I'm outta here!'

Hari drops his fists. 'Leave the bikes. We'll walk

from here.' He shoulders his backpack and stalks towards the scrubland bordering the recycling centre. The land has been earmarked for a housing estate. For now, though, it's home to nothing but insects, reptiles and a roo or two.

The boys enter the scrub, dodging felled trees and densely grassed patches that might conceal ankle-snapping holes or worse. Everything here is dying of thirst. Sticks and dead grass crunch beneath their feet. When a stray breeze stirs, the sparse foliage topping the gum trees rattles like bones.

After twenty minutes, Adam says, 'How much further d'ya reckon?'

Hari looks over his shoulder. His top lip lifts in a sneer. 'Aw, is Addie-waddie getting tired?'

Holding Adam back, Jarn says, 'It's a good question. Do you know where you're going?'

'Course. For your information, we're more or less in the right place.' Hari points to a downed gum tree lousy with termites. 'We'll make that our base and each search a couple hundred metres in a different direction.' He drops his pack beside the tree.

'Might want to check for snakes before you sit on that,' Jarn says.

'If I find one I'll let Addie have it.' Hari smirks.

'And maybe I'll wrap it round your pencil neck and strangle you with it,' Adam says.

'Not if you're dead from a poisoned bite, you won't.'

'I'd strangle you before I die.'

'As if. You couldn't strangle a budgie with those girly arms.'

Jarn refuses to listen to any more. He storms into the trees, kicking rocks and leaves and whatever else gets in his way. He shouldn't force his friends together. It's obvious they'll never get on.

After a few minutes, Jarn stops to shake off a spider's web he's walked through. When he's done, he looks up and sees a charred patch of ground up ahead. Without a second thought, he hurries towards it. The patch is a crater several metres in diameter. The trees encircling the crater are all burnt. Jarn's nostrils twinge with the smell of smoke. The air tastes of ashes and metal.

He walks to the edge of the crater. It isn't very deep, maybe half a metre at its centre. It might have contained a bonfire made by human hands, but Jarn doesn't think so. A fire this large and burning as hot as it must have burned to blacken the earth that way should have set the bush alight for kilometres around. Yet apart from the first row of trees, the surrounding scrub remains untouched.

Jarn paces out the circumference of the crater. It appears to be a perfect circle. As he completes his circumnavigation, sunlight sparks at the crater's heart. He jerks to a stop, slaps a palm to his eyes, and then peers between his fingers. His heart leaps. There is something metallic down there.

Jarn steps into the crater. Clouds of fine, black ash puff up with each footfall. Reaching the centre of the charred circle, he squats and stirs the ash with a hand. His fingertips brush a solid object. Grasping it, he lifts it into the light. It's a black cube roughly the size and weight of a golf ball. Jarn palms the cube and walks out of the pit.

Hari and Adam emerge from the trees. 'Phew, I smell barbecue,' Hari says. Then spotting Jarn adds, 'Find anything?'

Jarn stamps the dust from his feet. His jeans are black from the knees down. He opens his hand to reveal the cube resting on his palm. 'What do you reckon this is?'

Hari squints at it. 'That's just a lump of charcoal.'

Jarn turns the cube over and looks at the silver patch on one corner. This must have been what caught the sunlight. He spits on the cube and rubs it with the tail of his T-shirt. The soot wipes away easily to reveal a strangely cold cube of dull silver metal.

'Never seen nothing like that before,' Adam says. 'Think it fell off a satellite or something?' He looks at Jarn.

'How the frig would he know?' Hari snaps. 'Geez, you say some dumb things.'

Jarn rubs the pad of his thumb over each one of the cube's faces. The metal is as smooth and seamless as an ice cube.

'I'll take your word for it seeing as you're the expert on dumb,' Adam shoots back.

'You're one clever comment away from living on soup for the next year!' Hari warns.

Beneath Jarn's thumb the metal grows noticeably warmer. Before he even has time to wonder about this, the cube emits a burst of brilliant white light which strikes Adam square between the eyes. Jarn drops the cube in shock.

'Holy mother of mayhem!' Hari yells.

For a drawn-out moment all is silent. Then a bird squawks and the wind rattles the leaves.

Finally Jarn's jaw unlocks. 'Adam, mate, are . . . are you okay?'

Adam stares vacantly, mouth ajar. Then a big dopey grin breaks his face in two. He leaps at Jarn, throws his arms around him and squeezes hard enough to crack ribs. 'I love you, man.'

'What the . . .?' Hari says, and then Adam falls on him.

'I love you too, mate. You're tops.' Adam follows this declaration with several hearty whacks to Hari's back.

'Get OFF!' Hari gives Adam an almighty shove.

Adam thumps on his backside in the dirt, teeth snapping together. Jarn holds his breath, waiting for the all-in brawl that is bound to erupt any second. But all Adam does is paste that stupid grin back on his face, get to his feet and say, 'No worries. Whatever you want, mate. All you gotta do is ask.'

Hari watches Adam the way you'd watch a mad dog. 'Yeah? Well, go sit over there.' He points to a spot a safe distance away.

Without a word of complaint, Adam does as he's told.

'Whoa, that was weird. Do you reckon that thing scrambled his brainwaves or what?' Hari says.

Jarn picks up the cube and examines it.

'Hey, don't point it at me!' Hari dives out of the line of fire.

'Adam hated your guts then he got hit by some sort of laser beam and all of a sudden he loves you,' Jarn says.

Hari's eyes widen. 'Geez, man, you've gone and found an alien love machine!'

Jarn looks at it. 'Nah.' Then at Hari. 'You think?'

'Must be. Hey, Leni will get a fortune for it on eBay, which means we're gonna be rich!' Hari glances at Adam standing under one of the scorched trees, humming to himself. 'Stop staring at me, you freak!'

'Forget about eBay,' Jarn says. He can barely contain his excitement. 'If this is an alien love machine, do you have any idea what it could mean? Imagine if everyone loved everyone. There'd be no more wars. No more suffering. Only peace. Forever. This metal block could change the world. We'd be famous for finding it. We'd probably even get a Peace Prize.'

Hari frowns. 'Yeah, but if there's no wars, who's gonna make those games you love so much?'

'Hey, guys, do you think I can have another hug?' Adam calls.

'NO!' Hari yells. He turns back to Jarn. 'Do you really want a world full of people acting like *him* 24/7?'

'But if everyone's the same then it wouldn't bother ...' Then something occurs to Jarn. Who would have control of the cube? And could they be trusted not to use it for their own gain? One country might use it on every other country then make the others do whatever they wanted. Jarn knew enough of human nature, not to mention history, to know that this was a definite possibility. One government alone could control every resource on the planet; make people into slaves – anything.

'Argh!'

Adam sneaks up behind Hari and locks him in a bear hug.

Jarn looks at his friends wrestling in the dirt. He strokes the ice-smooth cube. The alien love machine could be the most powerful and terrible weapon the world has ever seen. But it could also solve his biggest problem by making Hari and Adam friends.

The cube grows warm in Jarn's hand and then a beam of light shoots across the clearing. It hits Hari in the chest. A slow grin spreads across his face. He looks at Adam and spreads his arms wide. 'C'mere, maaate!'

Jarn leaves Hari and Adam to trade hugs and compliments. He crouches in the ashy crater and digs a hole. When it's more than deep enough, he drops in the alien love machine.

The world may never be ready for that much love.

A State of Rejection

Margaret Clark

This afternoon when I got off the school bus I had a strange feeling that I was not alone.

I turned my head quickly, but no one was there. In fact the nearest person to me was a little old lady pulling her shopping jeep behind her, and she was on the other side of the street.

It must've been too much stress. The teachers have been giving us loads of homework and I've been struggling to get it all done in time. Usually school's easy for me and I'm always near the top of the class. But recently I've been unable to cope or concentrate, as if I'm operating in a thick fog.

It isn't just schoolwork. It's Ben Jardini.

Lately, he's turned really nasty because I won't go out with him. Girls are falling all over themselves to get with him, but because I'm not interested it's made him ridiculously over-the-top determined. Apparently I'm the first girl who's rejected him and he doesn't like it.

Right now I don't want a boyfriend to complicate my life. My best friend Evie's just been dumped by Silas, who just happens to be Ben's best mate, and she's a mess, crying and texting, totally out of control, making an idiot of herself. And rumour has it that Ben told Silas to dump Evie as payback, so now she's not talking to me. It's all one big mess. Hell would freeze over before I'd go out with Ben Jardini and the whole school knows it.

Suddenly I felt the softest breath on my neck.

I swung around. No one. Just a little breeze, a puff of wind from the sea.

Then I heard a sigh. This was scary. I started to walk faster.

'You can't escape from me, Amelia,' said a reedy voice in my ear.

I stopped. 'I know this is some kind of a trick. Ben Jardini, I'll bet it's you. Where's the hidden gadgetry? In my bag?'

'Amelia.'

The voice sounded sad.

'Go away, Ben. I don't know how you're doing this, but you're being a real pain.'

'Why are you so cruel and heartless?'

'Me? Cruel and heartless? I don't think so. It would be cruel if I led you on, let you think I liked you then dumped you, like Silas dumping Evie. That's cruel.'

A man carrying a toolbox and dressed in overalls was walking towards me. He must've thought I was a raving lunatic, talking to myself.

'Are you all right?' he asked as he drew closer.

'Yes. I'm just rehearsing for my school play.'

'Good answer, Amelia,' breathed the reedy voice in my ear. 'I've always admired your intelligence and wit. I trusted you. And you broke my heart.'

'Look,' I said, stopping short. 'I don't know how you're doing this, but it's not funny, Ben. Just go away!'

'I'm not Ben.'

'If you're not Ben, then who are you?'

'You know who I am, Amelia.'

I paused by Judy Bromley's gate. I babysat for her sometimes and knew she was inside because her car was in the driveway.

'If you don't stop pestering me, I'll go in here and ask Judy to call the police.'

'Pestering? You don't know the meaning of the word.'

Suddenly I felt a sharp stinging sensation on my cheek. It hurt, as if someone had slapped me hard. Was it a stone from a slingshot? I jumped away, really scared.

'Don't do that.'

'You ruined my life.' The voice sounded bitter and callous.

I felt a breath on my cheek. To my horror, dry, cold lips kissed the spot that was still smarting.

Somewhere in the deep recesses of my memory there was a faint stirring as if my subconscious was struggling to remember an event in my past. No, not my past, it seemed like someone else's, many, many years ago, mistily just beyond my reach.

My legs had gone wobbly so I sat down on Judy's brick fence.

'Honestly, I don't know who you are. I thought you were Ben from school giving me payback, but now I'm not so sure. If it's a joke to scare me, then you've won, so go away.'

'I'm not trying to scare you, Amelia. I love you. Trusted you. And you left me high and dry at the altar and ran off with the coachman.'

This time the blow to my cheek almost knocked me to the ground.

'Oh. My dreadful temper. But then if you ruin someone's life, if you rip their heart out and toss it aside, you should see how that feels, too. You should be punished.'

By now I was really scared. With a lurch I heaved myself off the fence and ran up Judy's driveway as if all the hounds of hell were after me. I pounded on her door.

She opened it with Harriet on one hip and Jeremy clinging to her legs.

'There's a man,' I choked. 'He scared me.'

Judy gave Harriet to me to hold, peeled Jeremy off her legs and marched out into the street, looking up and down.

'I can't see anyone. What did he look like, Amelia? Do you want me to call the police?'

I realised that I couldn't describe my attacker and

that if I couldn't see him maybe no one else could either.

'No, it's all right. He just seemed a bit weird. I probably overreacted. I'll be fine now, I'm nearly home.'

'I'll come with you.'

So Judy and I walked to my front door.

'Phone if you need me,' she said as I inserted the key into the deadlock.

'It's okay, Dad will be home soon.' I tried to sound more confident than I actually felt. 'He's on early shift and finishes at four-thirty.'

I could hear the wail of an ambulance as I quickly went in, locked the door and put the chain on. Once in my bedroom I looked in the mirror. My left cheek was slightly redder than my right, but not too noticeable. Gingerly I touched my sore head where his fist had connected. I felt angry. Very angry. My parents had never slapped me. How dare some weirdo stranger do this? Wait a minute, what if he'd somehow followed me inside?

I went to the kitchen and scrabbled in the second drawer for a sharp knife for protection.

'Show yourself, you coward,' I yelled, brandishing the knife.

Nothing.

I heard the key rattling in the lock. Him! I crept up the passage.

'Amelia. Are you in there? You've got the chain on.'

'Dad!'

I dropped the knife, opened the door and hurled myself into his arms. To my horror I started crying and couldn't stop. Eventually I calmed down enough to tell him what had happened.

'You felt a sting on your cheek then someone hit you hard on the side of the head? Yet no one was there? It doesn't make any sense.' Dad looked sceptical. 'It's windy outside. You might've got hit with some flying debris.'

'But what about the voice?'

'Have you looked in your bag? Perhaps someone's playing a prank on you and put one of those mini tape-recorders in there to frighten you.'

Together we upended my bag on the bed. Just the usual jumble of books and my lunch box. No hidden paraphernalia.

Next thing Mum was home and of course she had to hear the whole story.

Dad looked at Mum. 'Maybe she needs to see a doctor. She's been overwrought lately, not concentrating. Maybe . . .' he let his voice trail away.

'You mean I need a shrink?' I yelled. 'You think I'm a nut-bag, gone schizo, imagining voices in my head? Well, I haven't. What about this red mark? Do you think I slapped myself? This really happened. Trust me.'

Mum was frowning. 'This voice said you'd run off with the coachman?'

'Yes.'

'Your great-great-grandmother jilted her fiancé on her wedding day and ran off with the coachman,' she said slowly.

Dad just stared at her.

I went cold. 'What was her name?' I said shakily.

'Amelia.'

Mum found an old album. The photos were faded, brown-and-white sepia. My own face stared back at me.

'Amelia's fiancé,' Mum pointed, 'Lewis Harper.' She turned the pages. 'And there's the coachman, your great-great-grandfather.'

It made no sense. That night Mum slept in the spare bed in my room. I tossed and turned, frightened to close my eyes, but there was no soft breath on my neck, no sharp slap on my cheek.

The next day while we were having breakfast, I heard the news on the radio. At around 4 pm the previous day, Ben Jardini had been knocked down by a hit-and-run driver and died later in hospital. I felt sad. I'd never liked him; in fact I thought he was totally gross as a human being, but I didn't want him to die a horrible death.

Strangely, though, I knew there was a connection between his death and what had happened to me.

Somehow Ben's spirit had become enmeshed with Lewis Harper's. I believe that in their mutual rejection by Amelia from the past and Amelia from the present, Lewis had briefly gained energy to confront me, who in his mind was the old Amelia.

Sadly, Ben Jardini is gone.

Not so sadly, the revengeful Lewis Harper is gone, too.

Forever.

I hope.

Running Invisible

Sean McMullen

A lot of people think going for a run is pretty boring, but they're wrong. It's only boring if you run at the wrong speed.

I started running at school. I had dreams of being a champion runner and winning lots of medals. Trouble was, even if I trained really hard, I only got a little bit faster. I was never fast enough to win medals.

But at least it got me out of the house, so I didn't have to listen to the rest of the family arguing, or play loud music to drown out the sound of shouting. Most of the arguments happened at night, so that's when I did a lot of my running.

Pretty soon I couldn't get along without going for a run every night. It was like an addiction, but one that made you better instead of trashing your body and twisting your mind. I went out in all weather, cold, wet, hot and windy. I preferred bad weather, because it kept other people off the streets.

I like to be left alone when running, so I can relax and think. That was a bit hard when people threw cans from passing cars or jeered at me from balconies. Sometimes drunks would jog along with me. I'm not sure why. Other times the police would stop me and make me turn out my pockets. I only ever carried the front door key and my phone.

One night I realised that I could do something so strange that it made me feel as cool as a movie star who had just been given an Academy Award. If I ran at a particular speed, people didn't notice me.

I experimented to prove it. Run too fast, and it's, 'Wow! Look at him go.' Run too slow, and they try to talk to you. Run just right, and you're fast enough so people don't bother you, but slow enough so they don't pay attention to you. You're something they don't notice, so you're outside their world. You're invisible.

When you're invisible, people do things without realising that you are there. One night I jogged past three guys breaking into a house. I called the police from around a corner. They were being arrested as I ran back, but nobody noticed me then, either.

Animals see right through me as well. People know that a lot of possums live in the suburbs, but I discovered that there are lots of foxes and owls, too. When I run invisible, they don't bother to hide.

I was surprised when some really odd people became visible who hadn't been before. They didn't notice me, but I could see them. It was just like the foxes, possums and burglars. If I stopped running, they vanished. So I kept running.

Some of these people looked a little weird, and most of them looked seriously weird. Quite a lot of them were not even people. In fact, I'm not sure what they were.

There was one guy who rummaged in the garbage bins along the beach every night. He had a door open in his chest and a fire was burning inside. As far as I could tell, he was tossing garbage into the fire like the rest of us eat food. Smoke was coming out of his nose.

I'll admit I was seriously weirded-out the first time I saw him. Then I discovered that he was one of the more normal ones.

On Saturday nights I always saw a couple made of gold, walking along the esplanade. They looked like Oscar statuettes, because they wore no clothes and had no faces. They talked to each other by playing tunes on trumpets that came out of their bums. When a vampire leaped out of the bushes and bit one of them he broke a fang.

At first I thought I was just seeing things, like dreaming but awake, but then I had to do Art Appreciation at school and that changed everything. There was this painter named Pieter Bruegel who lived over four hundred years ago, and he painted some heavily weird stuff. The funny thing was that his paintings looked quite a bit like what I saw when I went running.

The teacher asked the class where we thought

Bruegel got his ideas. I said he probably thought of them while jogging. The teacher said people didn't go jogging back then. Oh well, you can't tell a teacher anything.

The drop bears were a worry. I could see them waiting in the trees. They only dropped onto werewolves, and would cling onto their heads. Apparently the only way to get rid of them was to go to another tree, where they would get off. They never dropped on me, but I still worried about them.

One time I saw a werewolf trip, and the drop bear fell off his head. A little dinosaur with lots of sharp teeth and long claws like sickles ran out of a storm water drain and ate the bear. That explained why drop bears don't do their own walking.

When I ran back, the werewolf was buying the dinosaur a takeaway coffee from the man with a fire in his chest. He now had a sort of coffee machine backpack with tubes coming from his chest to heat it. Maybe he was trying to improve himself.

At first I could hardly believe what was going on around me, all invisible unless I ran at invisible speed. I really looked forward to going for a jog because it was so much more interesting than the real world.

At school my results in maths and science were still so-so, but in English I started to do brilliantly. The teachers said I had such a wild and wonderful imagination, and everyone kept asking me where I got my ideas. I just said it was pretty strange inside my head. I never told them it was strange everywhere else, too. All you had to do was go for a run, late at night, at the right speed.

Most of the humans in the invisible world dressed in black, and wore little clockwork machines on silver chains. I think they were sort of weird iPhones, because they stared at them closely and tapped at them. The Goth motorcycle gangs rode black horses that drove steam-powered sports cars. I always wondered why they didn't just drive the cars themselves, and forget the horses, but maybe they didn't think it was cool.

The Goths seemed very peaceful, but then all of them wore rings with little cannons mounted on them. They were only as big as pen tops, but I think they worked. Everyone was armed, so it was too dangerous to start a fight.

The only police I ever saw were police dogs wearing top hats and carrying whistles around their necks. The cats all wore masks, so I presume they were cat burglars. I only ever saw them lying about and drinking coffee from saucers, so maybe the masks were just a fashion statement. Or maybe they were just to annoy the police dogs.

Out on the water there were always pirate ships with paddle wheels and steam engines. On the decks were lots of girls wearing black body-stockings and floppy hats with feathers. Some of them were fencing with silver swords, but most were doing Pilates.

There were always plenty of buskers. I rather liked the gorilla belly dancer, but when I tried to toss her a coin as I jogged past it just vanished. Her music was supplied by an octopus playing a steam-powered organ. It was breathing through a long pipe that led to the sea.

All that was long ago when I was still at school. I know what you are thinking. You think I'm going to say that I grew up and stopped seeing really weird stuff, and that I don't even jog any more.

You're wrong. When I got home I started typing what I saw into my computer. At first I used all that weird stuff in English projects. Then I wrote stories. The stories got published. I earned lots of money. I was flown all over the place, appeared on TV, and got to meet lots of really famous people. It was a seriously cool way to earn a living.

My life is very busy these days, but when the pressure gets too much, or when I need some new ideas I go for a run. I can always be sure of relaxing when I am running invisible because I am, well, invisible.

Until tonight. Tonight I am not very relaxed at all.

Sometimes I run past a lady dressed in a black cloak and black leather jacket, and wearing so much clockwork jewellery that you'd think she had just mugged a watchmaker. Her fingers are tipped with silver claws, and they look sharp and pointy. A chain is attached to her belt, and at the end is a tiny stove on a trolley. Gathered around this are six possums wearing black chef hats. They always seem to be making tea and scones.

Last night I noticed that the lady was reading one of my books. That was a bit of a shock. Nothing I do ever gets into this world.

Tonight the cloak, jacket, clockwork and chain are draped over the bench, and the possums are standing guard with a little cannon. The lady is nowhere to be seen . . . but I can hear another runner closing in behind me.

Call Him Ringo

Sue Bursztynski

Rachel woke from a dream in which she had been called on to cover for Ringo Starr at the Beatles concert. She sighed. If only. Ringo *was* sick, but his cover was some guy called Jimmy Nicol, not a girl called Rachel Silverstein. Pity. Still – she had her ticket.

Mum bustled into her room, opened the blinds and bent over to give her a kiss. 'Sorry to wake you, but you really need to eat before you go to school.'

Rachel stroked her mother's huge belly. Mum was due any day now. 'Call him Ringo, Mum? Pleeease?'

Mum laughed. 'No. Not even if it *is* a boy. Now get up.'

In the kitchen, the radio was advertising free Beatles beakers with every thirty shillings spent at Spotless Dry Cleaners. Rachel, whose school uniform had to be drycleaned, had been nagging Mum, but there was only one uniform to clean at a time and it would take a lot of drycleaning to spend thirty shillings.

Dad looked up from the *Sun*, which had a front-page picture of a girl who had written an eighty-thousand-word letter to the Beatles and was being flown to Melbourne for their concert. *If only I'd done that*, thought Rachel sourly. *All I did was save up my paper-round money . . .*

'Good morning, love.' He smiled.

Rachel smiled back and poured cereal and milk into her bowl. 'Dad, Mum, there's a Beatles rally at the Southern Cross Hotel this Sunday. Can I go?'

'Not by yourself,' Mum said firmly. 'There'll be thousands of people. You could get lost, knocked over, hurt.'

'So I can go if I'm with someone?'

'We'll see,' said Dad. ' Depends who. Now eat – you're going to be late for school. You were up late last night.'

'Rehearsing for the school social,' Rachel pointed out. 'It's my first gig. Only two weeks away; we have to get it right.'

'Darling, what if that girl Hannah comes back from hospital?' Mum said. 'The band will want her, not you. You'll have done all that rehearsing for nothing.'

'Not for nothing, Mum. The Commas are a terrific band and I've learned so much from them. *Please*, can I go to the rally?'

'I don't know why you want to go anyway,' Rachel's older sister Beck said, looking up from her politics textbook. Beck was in her first year at Monash University. She went on a lot of protest marches. 'If you're going to go crazy over a musician, what's wrong with Bob Dylan? "Blowin' in the Wind" *says* something. But the Beatles? "I Wanna Hold Your Hand"? They'll be forgotten in two years. I mean – priorities? There's going to be a war in Vietnam. They're already talking conscription. And you scream about a rock band!'

'Come with me to the rally then?' Rachel suggested slyly. 'Bring a protest placard?'

'No way!' Beck slammed her book shut and stomped to the bathroom.

Dad winked at Rachel. 'Leave it to me.'

On the way to school she met Margaret, head of the school's Beatles Fan Club. Rachel was a passionate Beatles fan, but passionate wasn't the same as crazy. Margaret was crazy.

'. . . and there's this girl, Suzette, who's going to their reception and she said she could get me in, too.'

Rachel cringed. *People like Margaret make the rest of us look like idiots.*

'So are you coming?'

'Um. Maybe. I might have rehearsals.'

But she was at her locker when Andrea, the Commas' lead singer, tapped her gently on the shoulder.

'Rachel?' Andrea was apologetic. 'Look, sorry, but Hannah's back. We won't need you at rehearsal today after all. I'm really, really sorry. Maybe you can join us next year.'

Rachel tried to smile. 'Sure. No problem.'

Damn!

At lunchtime she took her cheese-and-Vegemite sandwiches and sat with the Beatles Club under a tree. From the window of the music room, she heard the Commas playing.

Margaret looked up. 'Hey, Rachel, I thought you were with the band?'

'Hannah came back.'

'Oh, well. Meet us at the rally, then?'

Rachel said nothing.

The Saturday *Sun* had a picture of a thrilled hairdresser clutching Beatle hairs she'd cut. There was another photo of Ringo cringing while two girls kissed him. He'd recovered and was on his way to meet the others.

Sunday morning, she and Beck went to the city.

'You owe me,' Beck said as they joined the huge crowd climbing Bourke Street towards the Southern Cross.

'I owe you,' Rachel agreed. Anything to be here.

'Hi, Beck!' called someone.

Beck turned and waved. 'Hi, Jen! What are you doing here?'

Beck's friend waded through the crowd, smiling. 'Well, you know . . . When will we ever get to see them again? You?'

'Taking my little sister.'

'Yeah, sure.' They laughed together. 'Look, there's Sylvia and Barb – join us?'

Beck glanced at her sister. 'Want to come with us, Rachel?' *Please say no*, she meant.

'Nah. I'll meet you back at Flinders Street Station, under the clocks at two, right?'

Beck gave her a grateful grin and went off with her friends. Now Rachel really was alone in a mob of thousands.

Despite that, she recognised the girl slung over the saddle of a passing mounted policeman on his way to a first aid station. It was Margaret. Rachel rolled her eyes and pushed on.

The Southern Cross loomed over Exhibition Street. Girls pressed against the glass doors. Rachel wondered what would happen if the doors broke.

'Look!' someone shrieked. 'They're coming out onto the balcony!' At once the crowd went wild, pushing forward, screaming, knocking Rachel to her knees.

'Ow!'

Someone helped her to her feet. It was Mr Pearl, a young music teacher from her school. 'What a crowd!' he said. 'I didn't know there'd be this many people . . . are you okay?'

'Yes, I'm fine. I just wanted to see Ringo.' She brushed down her knees, which were slightly grazed.

'Well, he'll be on TV tonight. Going to the concert at Festival Hall?'

She nodded shyly.

'Lucky you! I couldn't get tickets, they're all sold out.'

'I didn't know you like them.'

He laughed. 'I'm a musician. Of course I like them. They're special.'

'My sister says they'll be forgotten in a couple of years.'

'Don't you believe it! We'll be singing their songs with our grandchildren.'

She smiled.

Still, she was squashed, she was out of breath and she couldn't see much anyway. Rachel decided she'd had enough. With the help of her teacher and her elbows, she managed to get to the station. The crowd was thinner here and they spotted Beck just coming out of a phone booth. Beck saw them and smiled.

'Oh, hello, Mr Pearl. Nice to see you again, haven't seen you since the Form Six formal! Rachel, I've just rung Mum and Dad. My friends live near Melbourne Uni and invited us to their place. Dad says it's fine, as long as we ring the hospital.'

'The hospital?'

'Yeah, Mum's going now and Dad is sitting with her. The baby is being born in the next few hours!'

'Shouldn't we be going home, then?' She wasn't

sure she wanted to hang out with Beck's friends for hours.

'No. Dad doesn't want to leave you by yourself and I haven't seen Jen, Sylvia and Barb in months. I'd really like to catch up. Would you mind?'

Rachel did mind, but said, 'Okay. I guess I do owe you one.'

'See you Tuesday,' said Mr Pearl. 'Tell me all about the concert and the new baby.'

The girls walked up Swanston Street towards the university. Barb, Sylvia and Jen shared a small house in Parkville.

They spent the rest of the day playing records and catching up on gossip while Rachel browsed the bookshelves. She found a book called *New Writings in SF* and settled down to read while her sister and the others chatted.

Still, she was bored. She wondered what was happening with the baby.

'Do you have a phone?' she asked the girls.

'Nope. There's a phone box on the corner, though,' said Jen.

'Good, you can call Dad for us.' Beck handed her some change and the phone number.

'Sorry, no news yet,' Dad apologised. Would the girls let you stay the night? It's getting a bit late to take the tram home, and I don't want to leave the hospital now.'

Rachel's heart sank, but she said, 'Sure, Dad. I'll call you first thing tomorrow.'

Beck and her friends were delighted at the excuse for a sleepover. Barb fried some fish-and-chips and they had dinner before some uni friends dropped in. The music became loud and the talk even louder. It was all about their studies, Vietnam and whether there would be a war, and a folk group called Peter, Paul and Mary. Rachel excused herself and found a spot on the floor to sleep as best she could with the racket going on.

It was early when she woke, cramped and uncomfortable. She slipped out of the house to go to the phone box. The staff couldn't find Dad, but took her message. She decided to go to the hospital anyway; Beck could come or not. She went back to the house, but the door had locked behind her and no one was up.

Rachel made a decision. Beck might get mad but they'd sort it later. She began to walk into town.

It was early for trams to South Yarra, where the hospital was located, and too far to walk, but while she was waiting – why not? She grinned.

Breakfast was set up in the Southern Cross dining room. She had enough spare change for tea and toast. Rachel ordered, then glanced at the next table where a man was sitting, steaming mug in hand. He looked like a Beatle at first glance. He wasn't.

'Jimmy!' A man in a suit approached him. 'Where have you *been*? We were looking everywhere for you. You *know* you have to leave early today.'

'Went for a drive, didn't I?' He had a soft accent. 'Couldn't sleep. Found this seaside place called Beaumaris.'

'Well, *please* don't disappear again. The plane won't wait for you. Have your breakfast while I get us some transport to Essendon.'

The man went outside.

Jimmy saw her looking at him and smiled.

'A bit young to be out on your own this time of day, aren't you?'

Rachel suddenly realised: 'You're Jimmy, aren't you? I'm a drummer, too.'

'And you want to know what it's like playing with the Beatles, right?'

She did, but suspected he was tired of being asked and shook her head.

'It says in the papers that this is going to help your career when you go home. Is it?'

He chuckled, a little sadly. 'Maybe. I can start a band now. But – when you've played with the best – you know?'

She nodded. She *did* know.

The other man came back. 'Come on, Jimmy, time to go. I can't waste time – the lads have a busy day.'

Jimmy rose. He winked at her. 'I wouldn't have

missed it for anything. Just so you know.'

She smiled back at him, and checked her watch. Time to go.

Dad and Beck were waiting for her in the hospital foyer. 'Where were you?' Beck demanded. 'I was out of my mind! If Dad hadn't told me when I rang . . .'

'Shh,' said Dad. 'Let's go and see your new brother.'

The baby was in his cot behind the window, red and wrinkled. Rachel loved him right away.

Then they went to see Mum. Rachel hugged her.

'Ouch!' Mum said. 'Be careful! Well? Seen your brother?'

'He's *gorgeous*, Mum.'

'He looks like Winston Churchill,' said Beck, adding, 'like every other baby.'

'Thanks for that inspiring comment,' said Mum drily. 'You know, Rachel, we might call him Richard. How's that? Ringo's real name?'

Rachel smiled, but shook her head. 'No, Mum,' she said softly. 'Call him Jimmy.'

George and the Boat

Sally Odgers

Tasmania, 1935

George pedalled along the wet road. His knobbly knees were hidden under flannel trousers, but his toes muttered a complaint at the tightness of his shoes. Water fanned up from his bike tyres and wet his legs. His mum would have said he was looking for trouble. Maybe she would have been right.

George was a working man now. He'd been dux of the school. He could have gone to high school and excelled there too, but Mum said no. High school meant train travel and she knew about trains. Broken windows, slashed seats and larrikins scrawling rude words on the floor of the carriage. Seven years of schooling was plenty. George could sit the Post Office exam.

George sat the exam. He'd topped that, too. Now he boarded with his brother Arthur, who was twenty years older.

George had a couple of hours before teatime and he didn't want to spend them with his giggling nieces. He turned off the main road and pedalled down to Mill Dam to look at the river.

The weeklong rain had stopped, and it looked as though the river had swallowed it all. It flowed merrily along, churning up smooth khaki-coloured waves.

George got off his bike and watched bits of tree glide downstream. The roaring formed a background for his thoughts, just as his brother Reg's sax sang a background at tea dances. George leaned his bike on the rail and played imaginary drums on the rounded metal pipe. He was a drummer in Reg's dance band, and they were playing at Mrs Pitts' place tomorrow. George hoped there might be buns.

His invisible drumsticks whirled into the river as he spotted a rope knotted to the rail a few yards downstream. He squelched over for a look. The rope was stretched tightly enough to twang. George put his hand on it, and felt the vibrations thrumming up from the captive boat on the other end. He leaned over the railing. The boat was a dinghy, a ten-foot flattie with upturned metal rowlocks and a pair of oars stowed tidily on the bottom boards under the seat.

George considered the river, the boat, and this unexpected opportunity. He knew how to row a boat. Mum had been angry when Reg took George out on the lake because George couldn't swim, but rowing had come easy. George was more than six feet tall and Reg said his long legs meant he was built right for rowing, 'Cause you can brace your feet, see,' said

Reg, his eyes twinkling. George had always wanted to try it again, and here was his chance.

Being tall was a bad thing when you inherited clothing and shoes from brothers who were older but shorter. You got cold ankles, cold wrists and your toes got pinched out of line. *Still*, thought George as he climbed over the rail and let himself down to stand in the boat, *there are advantages*. If he'd been a shortie he couldn't have reached to untie the rope from the rail.

The boat jittered on the river like a pony. It wanted to glide away. George sat down and pulled the oars out from under the seat. He slid them into the rowlocks and jigged them about to make sure they were secure. He barely heard them clonk above the song of the river.

George stood up again, swaying, and reached to untie the rope. It was fastened in a highwayman's hitch, so a single tug had it free. The rope slithered into the boat and his breath *oofed* out as he sat down harder than he had intended. As he grasped the oars, he realised he'd have to move fast. Already he was several yards downstream from the boat's mooring. George swung the heavy oars backwards like a bird's wings then brought them down to bite into the water. He braced his feet as Reg had shown him, and pulled his fists towards his waist. The boat responded. It didn't go *up*stream, exactly, but at least it wasn't going *downstream* quite so fast.

George swung and dipped and pulled again and felt the boat creep a few inches backwards. That was splendid, but when he lifted the oars to swing again he more than lost the progress he'd made.

'Must try harder,' said George, which was what the schoolmaster used to write on his cousin's report cards.

He swung the oars faster, churning away like the paddle steamer he'd seen at the pictures. It was splashy, but he was making headway. George whistled between his teeth as he bent to his task. He thought he'd better get the boat back to where he'd found it, tie it up and pedal off home.

All went well until one oar missed its bite in the water and skittered through the tops of the little waves. The other plunged deeply and the boat bucked and swung in a half circle. George fell sideways, cracking his head on the rowlock.

'Ow!' he said, dabbing at his face. Now he'd have a black eye and Arthur would think he'd been fighting. He sat up, and realised the boat was headed downstream again.

Well, he obviously wasn't going to get the boat back to where he'd started, so he'd better just paddle to the rail and tie up where he could.

George bent over the oars and pulled with all his strength. They acted like a brake, but he wasn't sure how to make the boat go sideways. He tried paddling with one oar, but the dinghy just spun.

By now he was so wet that a few sudden spatters of rain didn't seem to matter, but the iron-grey sky was darkening towards evening. If he didn't hurry, he'd be late for tea. George rowed as hard as he could. He could feel his heart thudding and his breath coming short. Rowing was hard work, but that wasn't all. He was getting scared.

The river seemed to be galloping along now, tossing its mane of foam like a cranky horse. George gave up on rowing, since it seemed to be making no difference, and hung onto the gunwales. Should he jump out? But he couldn't swim! (That was Mum's fault too. She said if he learned to swim he'd be off getting drowned as soon as her back was turned.) Reg said he could learn by standing on one toe in the river and paddling his arms until his legs floated up. If he ever got out of this fix, George resolved to learn.

He was wondering if he could possibly stop the boat by wrenching an oar out of the rowlock and digging it into the riverbed like a punt pole, when he saw a curved line cutting across the river ahead. It was the Mill Dam weir.

George went even colder. Either the dinghy would crash into the weir, or else it would go sliding over on the rain-swollen current. Neither was a good thing, but just maybe he could jump out and haul himself along the weir to the bank. George shipped the oars as Reg had taught him. Then he returned his hands to their white-knuckled grasp on the gunwales. The roar and swish of the river masked his galloping heart as he readied himself to jump.

This was going to hurt. If he was lucky, he'd be bruised and battered. If he was unlucky, he'd be dead; drowned or bashed to death. Mum would cry when she saw his bloated body and she'd say she'd told him so . . .

The dinghy tore towards the weir like a horse at a hurdle. George hauled a deep breath into his lungs and flexed his knees. Then, before he was ready, the bow lifted on a wavelet and slammed down on the weir.

George yelled and bit his tongue, but the boat wasn't finished yet. It shied sideways, slithered and crunched, and then jerked twice as it tried to float in the too-shallow water. Unable to complete the trip over the weir, it tipped instead. The gunwale dipped under water and before George could make a move, the boat turned turtle.

George tumbled into the water, gulped in a mouthful and choked. He flailed his arms and legs as the current slammed him against the side of the boat. Distantly, he heard a crunching crack as the marine ply splintered under the pressure. George thought he was dying, but one of his feet hit against something hard. The weir. Gasping and spluttering, he grabbed and dragged, then draped himself over the rocky lip with cold water trying to carry him off. His hands were numb but he clung to the rocks and squirmed until he was lying lengthways along the weir. A huge shape, which he realised vaguely must be the boat, lolled and crashed repeatedly beside him.

Startled to find himself still alive, George squinted along the weir to find out which bank was nearer. Then he began his slow and painful journey back to dry land.

George shook uncontrollably as he pedalled towards Arthur's house. Everything hurt and he had lost a shoe. Wearily he got off his bike and propped it against Arthur's fence. The door opened, spilling light out into the street.

'Blimey!' said Reg. 'I came over to see if Arthur's piano's in tune and find a drowned rat. What happened to you, George?'

George explained.

'Blimey,' said Reg again. 'If that was old man Tupman's flattie you did for, he won't be too pleased. Still, you got your pay. Might take a few months wages, but you can set him right.'

George sighed. He was a working man now. It was up to him to get out of the mess he was in.

'Hope you'll be up to playing tomorrer?' said Reg.

'Yes, Reg.' George examined his skinned and battered knuckles. He'd have to be right for drumming. If he didn't drum, he didn't get paid.

Reg clapped him on the shoulder. 'Chin up,

George. If I'd known you were that desperate to learn this swimming business I'd have tossed you in the river myself.'

George lifted his chin and managed a grin. Come summer, he'd be balanced on one toe in the river and paddling his arms. If he could be dux of his school and the Post Office exam, he reckoned he'd excel at learning to swim.

Child-slave Crusader

Dianne Bates

My name is Iqbal Masih. I come from Muridke, a rural village near the city of Lahore, Pakistan. In our village, my family is the poorest of the poor. Six hundred rupees is a fortune to them. It buys two goats and a pot filled to the brim with lentils. Six hundred rupees is how much my family received when they sold me.

I do not blame my family for bonding me to the cruel man. They could not afford to feed me or my sisters or pay for my brother's wedding. The day I was four years old and the city man put money into my mother's hand was the saddest of my life. The man, my owner, put me into the back of his car and we drove away. I had never been in a car before. It drove so fast. We travelled a very long way, far from the fields of my home to a place in the city. And that is where I learned my fate. I was to become a carpet weaver.

The factory is enormous compared to my family's hut, and filled with many looms. All day and half the night the sounds of carpets being made throb in my ears. Combs beat against the woven thread.

Wood clanks. Men, women and children cough. It is so dusty in this factory, so dark. A place of much sadness. A place I hate with all my being.

I am always afraid. The supervisor and the owner scold and shout. They beat me on the back and head and curse me. If I make a tiny mistake, if I accidentally cut the thread, the supervisor takes a belt to me. Like the others, I work fourteen hours a day with one hour off. I am never allowed to go outside. My fingers bleed from where the threads cut me. When I cry with pain, the supervisor puts coffee powder on it and tells me to keep working. There is no medicine when I am sick.

This is the path that God has put me on so I have to work. It is written on my head and nobody can change my life. I don't want to weave, but there is no other way. Perhaps one day I will repay the six hundred rupees and return to my family.

I sleep in the factory with Nadeem and his cousin Amin. We prepare our food here and sleep in a space between the machines. Every morning at four we get up. Today I am yawning and stretching from sleep when Nadeem whispers in my ear, 'Amin and I are leaving today.'

I look at him, much puzzled. In the six years I have been in the factory nobody has ever left the looms.

'We are running away,' says Nadeem. 'Do you wish to come with us?'

To run away! Such a thought!

'There is a freedom celebration in the city,' says Nadeem. 'Yesterday I overheard the owner speaking with the supervisor. And this morning the door is not locked. So, Iqbal, are you with us?'

I nod, and my heart leaps with joy. But also I am filled with much fear.

Crouching low, we make our way through the darkness out of our prison.

The colours of outside almost blind me. I had forgotten that the sky could be so blue. And here, too, are people who smile, who do not reach out to slap my head. Or call me names that not even an animal should be called. And such smells! My belly rumbles with hunger. But there is no time to stop. We must get as far from the factory as we can. Along the crowded streets we run, until we are out of breath.

'I wonder what this says,' says Nadeem when at last we pant to a halt. He points to a large sign strung between two buildings. I cannot read the words but later, when I have been taught, I know they read BONDED LABOUR LIBERATION FRONT (BLLF).

Nadeem asks a stranger what the sign says.

'It is a meeting today,' the man says, 'against children working in factories.'

I want to tell the man that this is Nadeem, Amin and me. But I hold my tongue. The stranger might know our factory owner and tell him we are here.

'When will the meeting be held?' I ask.

'In one hour,' says the man. 'They are giving free food.'

Free food! I can scarcely believe it.

While we wait, we walk around the nearby markets looking at fruit and vegetables, grains and spices, things that we have only dreamed about for years. At one stall a vendor holds out slices of mango. 'Try some,' he offers.

Never in all of my life have I known such sweetness! The juice dribbles from my mouth, my tongue flicks out to catch every last drop. I smile at the vendor. When did I last smile? And the vendor – bless him in Heaven – hands me a mango. A whole mango, can you imagine?

'Thank you, thank you, sir!' I say. Nadeem and Amin and I wish him bountiful blessings. We are so happy!

We head back to the meeting place. Near a raised platform there some women are cooking chicken over a fire, a smell made in Heaven. My friends and I are filled with mango, but there is room for chicken. We linger around the women and are soon rewarded with chicken pieces on sticks. It is so delicious I cannot describe the taste.

The square fills with people. Men in white shirts and western trousers are standing on the platform. There is a microphone. One of the men calls for attention.

'The BLLF is here today,' he says, 'to call a halt to child labour.'

'I am told,' says the man, 'that children are sometimes chained to looms.'

'This is true – I know!' Suddenly I hear my own voice.

People turn and look at me.

'If it's true,' someone says, 'go up and tell of it.'

Why I push through the crowd and climb onto the platform I do not know. But suddenly I am no longer afraid. I am filled with anger. Anger that so much of my life I have been chained like a dog. To a loom that I hate. Working for an owner whom I hate even more.

'My name is Iqbal Masih,' I say into the microphone. 'I am from the village of Muridke. My family sold me to a carpet-factory owner for six hundred rupees.'

That day on the platform, the day of our escape, was over one year ago now. So much has happened since then. More than I could ever have dreamed. I have been home again, felt my mother's arms around me, shaken hands with my older brother and seen the tears running down his cheeks. I have held my sisters in my arms and been astonished at how tall they have grown.

Mr Ehsan Ullah Khan, from the BLLF – a group

working for the rights of children – helped me gain a letter of freedom from my former master. It gave my family money and paid for me to be schooled. It paid, too, for doctors to treat my bad lungs and to help me grow. (I am small for my age. The doctors say this is because of crouching so many years at the loom.)

Khan Sahib has told me much of how other children are treated poorly. They are slaves, as was I. 'Twelve million bonded child labourers in our country!' he says.

I have tried to help the BLLF and Khan Sahib for their great charity. I have excelled at my studies, and I have spoken in public – many times – of my years at the loom. One day I marched with the BLLF and with the help of the courts we freed hundreds of children from their enforced labours.

Today Khan Sahib is beside me on a stage. We are in a great hall in Sweden – the largest you can imagine. Here, thousands of good men and women are gathered. I am to talk to them. For weeks I have been practising my speech. But now I am shaking with fear. It is not the fear of my owner beating me. But the fear that I will forget what I am to say. My mouth is dry.

I hear my name spoken and Khan Sahib smiles. 'Your turn,' he whispers to me.

The microphone is brought down to my height

and I begin. My words are loud, so loud they must surely carry all the way to Lahore. I tell the people about what it was like in the factory.

'In Pakistan,' I say, 'between eight and ten million children – a quarter of all those aged from five to fifteen – work in carpet-weaving, brick kilns, domestic service, small industries and agriculture.'

In the audience, people are leaning forward, listening. Mine is the only voice in this great hall. I tell how I know now that children have rights under laws. That bonded labour is illegal. I tell them how the BLLF has freed thousands of child slaves. The words I had been so scared I would forget charge out of my mouth.

'We are calling,' I say, 'for people in the West to not buy carpets made by children.'

When I have finished, the hall is still and silent. Then, like a herd of elephants stampeding, comes the thunder of many hands clapping. Khan Sahib is grinning at me. 'Good boy,' his mouth says, though I cannot hear the words.

When the speeches are finished, cameras flash lights in my face, people mill around me. Journalists ask me many questions. Then I am seated for a television interview. Khan Sahib says my picture will be seen all over the world!

'I have a surprise for you, Iqbal,' Khan Sahib says to me later. 'We have been asked to take you to America. A company named Reebok wishes to present you with an award. And you have been nominated "Person of the Week" by the American Broadcasting Commission. It is a big honour.'

To tell the truth, I do not care about awards. I am too excited. I am helping to save children from working like slaves. I am talking to people who wish to hear what I have to say. And I am going to watch cartoons on television in a hotel room with a bed as soft as silk! Such a reward one could not get even in Heaven.

'I appeal to you to stop people from using children as bonded labourers. Children need to use pens rather than be used for labour.' Those are the words I spoke when I accepted the Reebok Youth in Action Award.

America was more than I could ever have imagined. Such sights I saw! I captured so much with the camera presented to me by Khan Sahib on my twelfth birthday. And I brought the photos home with me. To show my family and friends in case they did not believe what I told them of that amazing land. Today I knock on the door of Khan Sahib's office.

'Enter!' he calls.

The sahib is alone, sitting in front of piles of papers. He puts down his pen and smiles at me.

'Yes, young sir,' he says. 'What is it you are wanting?'

I tell him that today is the eve of Easter and I ask permission to leave school to go to my family in our village.

Kahn Sahib is slow to reply. This surprises me because it is rare he denies me. 'There is a problem, Sahib?' I ask.

'In fact,' he says, 'there may be.'

I wait in silence while he gathers his thoughts.

'We are hearing words that worry us, Iqbal,' he says. 'There are men in the city they are calling "the carpet mafia".'

I have not heard the word 'mafia' before and ask what means it.

'Rich men who own factories where children work are angry that their profits are down,' says the sahib. 'Since your talks, people are not buying so many carpets. They do not want to support factories that use children.'

I shrug. 'What does this matter?'

Khan Sahib, whose face is most often smiling, looks serious. 'I worry that the men might want to kidnap you, Iqbal. Or do you damage.'

'I am just a child,' I tell my kind and wise friend. 'You know I have many threats. It is all talk.'

We speak some more. I think my sahib knows I am homesick, so he agrees to call a wagon to carry me the twenty-five miles to my home.

I shake his hand and say goodbye.

On the trip home, I am excited about seeing my family. I have not seen them in a long while. And this week, Khan Singh has told me some news I need to discuss with them. He says that the BLLF wishes me to be schooled in America. This means I can be near doctors who can help me better heal my body than the local doctors can.

'The Americans heard how smart you are,' said Khan Singh, 'passing four grades in two years. They have awarded you a scholarship to attend an educational program at Brandeis University.'

I want so much to study at university. To become a lawyer so I can fight the bad businessmen who exploit children. But then I have a problem. Going to America means I will see even less of my family. And I love my family. Very much. There are two parts of me at war as the wagon draws closer to home. Should I go to America to study and to improve my health? Or should I stay here in Pakistan with those I love?

At home, after I have eaten my mother's chicken masala and shaha korma, I talk about my problem.

'It is up to you, my son,' says Mother. 'America offers many opportunities. It is a rich land. Pakistan is poor.'

We talk and talk. But then Mother asks me to go to the market for some curry paste.

My sister Sobia is in the compound shed, sitting in

the dirt. She is not in a happy mood.

'You are too spoiled, Iqbal,' she says. She sulks because some money came from a stranger who heard my story. And now I have a bike, silver and red, with a basket at the front.

I feel like telling Sobia she ought not to be jealous. Her back is not curved from bending to a loom for fourteen hours a day. Her hands are not scarred or her fingers gnarled from tying thousands of knots every day for many years. Her breathing does not trouble her from carpet dust.

'Ah, yes,' I say. 'I am well spoiled.' And then I am cycling away, leaving Sobia alone on the track near my home.

Should I go to America? Should I stay at home? These questions worry me as I ride to the village.

Late that afternoon I am heading back to the city. Mother and two of her sisters ride the bus with me. We are supposed to get off at Baoli where I am to catch another bus for Lahore. Instead, I decide to spend the night at my mother's family house. It will give me time with my cousins Liaquat and Faryad.

The boys are bigger than I remember, and Faryad, two years younger, is taller than me.

'Cousin, you are a dwarf,' he says.

'But with a brain to be proud of,' says Mother.

My aunt hands food to my older cousin. 'Your

father's supper,' she says. 'He's working late in the fields. You will take it to him, please.'

Of course I must go, too. Off we set. Liaquat rides his old bicycle, Faryad perched on the handlebars. I shuffle along the dirt track beside them. It is so good to be with my cousins; they are such fun.

We have gone half a mile when we see shadows by the wayside.

'Who is that?' Liaquat calls out.

'Stop! Now!' calls an angry voice.

Faryad jumps from the bike and crouches low. He looks suddenly smaller than me. Small and afraid.

'What do you want?' calls Liaquat.

The man does not answer. He lifts something. Too late I see it is a gun. I hear the sound of a shot. I see Faryad writhe and fall. Liaquat, too. And then I feel a pain in the side of my chest. It is a pain like hell, hot and beyond description.

17 April, 1995

DAILY TIMES PAKISTAN

Staff reporter

The death is reported of one of Pakistan's finest, Iqbal Masih, the child-slave crusader. Aged 13, Iqbal was a bonded-debt-slave from the age of four to ten. He was one of 250 million working children in the world. At conferences he spoke many times about this terrible practice.

Iqbal was with his cousins bringing food at night for

an uncle who was watering his field. When they were half way to their destination, shots were fired. Iqbal was hit by 120 shotgun pellets and died immediately. The other boys were hit by pellets but survived. Police have charged a field hand with murder.

NOTE: In 2000, Iqbal Masih was posthumously awarded The World's Children's Prize for the Rights of the Child.

I am an Author

Doug MacLeod

Illustrations by Mitch Vane

I am an author.
Yay!

But I'm too poor to buy clothes.
Boo!

So Mum gave me some to wear.
Yay!

They were hers.
Boo!

So I bought some cheap clothes at a fire sale.
Yay!

They were still on fire.
Boo!

As soon as my clothes stopped burning, I wrote a book.
Yay!

But an ash fell from my sleeve and the book caught alight.
Boo!

The fire brigade came to put it out.
Yay!

Then they read the book and set fire to it again.
Boo!

I rewrote the book and took it to my publisher.
Yay!

But they said they were closed for Christmas, even though it was July.
Boo!

I snuck in around the back.
Yay!

But it was the wrong building and I ended up in a toilet-paper factory.
Boo!

The people in the factory loved my book.
Yay!

But for completely the wrong reasons.
Boo!

I snuck into the correct building and handed my book to my editor.
Yay!

She threw it into the street.
Boo!

My editor said she'd made a mistake.
Yay!

She threw me into the street.
Boo!

Fortunately, there weren't any cars.
Yay!

Unfortunately, I got run over by a bus.
Boo!

An ambulance came.
Yay!

It ran over me as well.
Boo!

The doctor said that all I had was a tiny little lump.
Yay!

He was looking at my head.
Boo!

He said he couldn't feel any broken bones.
Yay!

He was inspecting the nurse.
Boo!

As soon as I got better, I wrote a brand new book.
Yay!

But it was eaten by giant Martian squirrels.
Boo!

I definitely need a new job.

Free Billy
James Roy

I hate swimming carnivals. I hate them more than anything else we do at school, except maybe the cross-country thing they make us do every year.

Why do I hate swimming carnivals, you ask? It's pretty simple, really. I hate them because I'm no good at swimming. I am a truly crap swimmer. If they had a drowning carnival, I'd be the star. I'd be the guy who broke all the records, with his name all over the school newsletter:

> The star performer at this year's Drowning Carnival was Billy Clarkson. He won five events, including the all-round drowning champion, as well as breaking two school records – the fifty-metre Cough and Splutter, and the one-hundred-metre Flail and Flounder. Due mostly to his size, Billy also seemed to be performing well in the Belly-flopper contest and the Cannonball Bomb contest, until he half-drowned trying to get out of the pool.

Yep, that'd be me. I'd be famous, but for all the wrong reasons.

This year I go to the carnival on the bus, sitting by myself, as usual. The noise is insane. I don't know what they're all getting so excited about. If it was overcast, everyone would freeze. If it was sunny, everyone would burn. Today's a special kind of day – the sun's out, but it's also windy as hell, so everyone will freeze and burn. And yet everyone is still carrying on like it's the best day of the whole year.

I'm the last one off the bus, and I look for all the kids wearing red. Red hats, red T-shirts, red scarves. My house, the mighty Winston, always comes last. Every. Single. Year.

I join the Winston line and we wait until we're allowed through the pool gates, with Mr Julius counting us off, one at a time. 'Thirty-five, thirty-six, thirty-seven – spit out the gum, Dylan – thirty-nine, forty, forty-one – looking good with the face paint, Katie – forty-three, forty-four – planning to swim today, Billy?'

'No chance,' I reply.

I go straight to my usual spot, up on the hill near the fence, under the shade of the trees. No one seems to notice. They're all dipping their toes in the water and being told to get back from the edge of the pool. The water looks cold, icy, not at all inviting. Quite the opposite, in fact. I've no intention of getting wet today. And I'm definitely not taking my shirt off. Not for anything.

Finally everyone settles down and Ms Sternman begins to read the announcements for the day. I don't usually listen all the way through. I'm never that interested. I don't plan to swim in any of the races anyway. All I'm interested in is what time they open the kiosk, so I can get started on the lollies. Strawberries-and-cream, frogs, Chupa-Chups, pineapples, Milkos . . . Plus there's the chips and the sausage rolls and the pies and the Chiko Rolls . . .

'Hey, Billy.' It's Mr Julius. He's come back for another attempt. He certainly is persistent. 'Got your togs with you?'

I shake my head.

'They're not in your bag?'

I know I can't lie to him. I know that it's a school rule that you bring your bathers to the carnival, even if you don't plan to swim. Either that, or you bring a letter, and my mum wouldn't write me one of those. She worries that I don't get enough exercise as it is, so there's no way she'd help me get out of taking my togs to a swimming carnival.

'Yeah, they're in my bag,' I admit.

'Aren't you going to put them on?'

I shake my head again. 'Wasn't planning to,' I say.

Mr Julius sighs. 'Billy, you don't have to be afraid of swimming.'

'I'm not,' I reply. 'I'm afraid of dogs, and that's about it. I'm not afraid of swimming.'

'Then why don't you want to –'

'I just don't, okay?' I snap. 'The others will all laugh at me.'

'No, they won't.'

I poke around in the grass with a stick. He has to be kidding.

'Why do you think they'll laugh at you?'

Why is he trying to make me say it out loud? Hasn't he got eyes?

'Billy?'

'They call me stuff,' I tell him. 'Whale Boy and Free Billy and . . . and other names.'

Mr Julius doesn't say anything for a while. Then he says, 'Okay, Billy. But remember, if you can make yourself compete, they'll all respect you a whole lot more.' He stands up, squeezes my shoulder and walks away.

'What's the point of them respecting me if I drown anyway?' I mutter to myself. 'Who respects someone who's dead?'

The first few events take place, and it's all pretty much exactly what I expect. The first record of the day is broken by Justin Wakeman, which isn't much of a surprise, even though he's only in first grade. You see, he's part of the famous Wakeman family. There are three Wakemans at our school, plus a couple in high school and they're all great swimmers. I think their mum must be part-dolphin or something. Mermaid, maybe.

So Justin Wakeman breaks the record for the under-eights fifty-metre freestyle, and everyone cheers. A little while later it's his sister Tina's turn, and she breaks the record for the fifty-metre backstroke. More cheering. Of course. They're like celebrities. One-day-a-year-celebrities.

While Tina Wakeman's climbing out of the pool and being hugged by her friends, her big brother Henry strides by. He's in his swimmers, with his goggles around his neck and his swimming cap in his hand. His friends John Graham and Matt Hinkley are right there with him, as usual; one on either side.

I hope he doesn't see me, because I don't like him. I really don't. But of course he does see me, and stops, mutters something to John and Matt, and comes up the bank towards me. I'm partway through a tube of Crimples cheese-and-onion chips when I see Henry and his friends approaching and I put the tube down. I could do without the extra attention.

'Bill. Billy. Billy the Kid,' Henry says.

'Hey, Henry,' I reply.

'Bilbo. Big Bill.'

I know the best one is still coming.

'Free Billy.'

And there it is.

'Hey, Henry,' I say again.

'You'd be planning to swim today, wouldn't you?'

I shake my head. 'No, not really.'

'Why not? Worried you're going to sink?'

'We could roll him in,' says John, smirking.

'Or we could just bring buckets of water up here to keep him wet,' Matt suggests.

When I reply, my voice sounds a lot weaker than I mean it to. I hate it when my voice refuses to work properly. 'I'm not a very good swimmer,' I say. 'That's why I'm not going in any races today. Or ever.' I give a forced laugh. 'Why tempt fate, huh?'

'You scared?'

I shake my head. 'No, Henry, I'm not scared. I just don't want to, that's all. I'm not as good a swimmer as you,' I add, hoping that the compliment might make him be nicer to me.

'You're right,' he says. 'It's true – no one in this school is as good as me.'

'Henry was at the State Championships last week,' Matt tells me.

'He came fourth,' John adds.

'Did he? Wow,' I say. I should probably be impressed.

'That's right, the States,' says Henry. 'So, Billy-boy, definitely not swimming then?'

I shake my head once more. 'No.'

'Well, those pies aren't going to eat themselves, are they?'

'Neither are the chips,' says Matt, bending over and helping himself from the tube of Crimples. His hand disappears into the pack and comes out holding a wad of chips, which he stuffs into his mouth and crunches noisily. Then he sees Henry and John watching him and he laughs. Little soggy fragments of cheese-and-onion chip land on my face.

'Thanks so much for that,' I say.

'You're welcome.'

'Come on,' Henry says, and giggling like idiots, they wander off. I'm so happy to see the back of them.

'You shouldn't let them pick on you like that.'

I turn and look. It's Susie Nugent. She's in my grade, but I don't think I've ever heard her say anything. Ever. But now she's sitting on her towel in the shade and talking to me.

'Maybe you should mind your own business,' I say, embarrassed.

'Fair enough. Sorry. Um . . . you missed a bit, Billy,' she says as I brush Matt's chip-spatter off my face.

'Thanks. And seriously, about what those guys said . . . it's okay. It's fine.'

'No, it's not fine. They were making fun of you because . . . well . . .' She suddenly looks the other way.

'Because I'm fat. It's okay – I do own a mirror.'

'But, anyway, they're not so great,' she says. 'I mean, sure, Henry's good at swimming, and I guess we are at a swimming carnival, but what about those other two? Do you ever see them do anything apart from following Henry around like a pair of puppies?'

'Not really,' I answer. 'But at least they're not fat.'

Susie laughs. 'They're not smart, either. I was standing behind John at the kiosk before and he was trying to convince the lady that one dollar fifty and one dollar fifty was two dollars fifty.'

'Yeah, well, that doesn't surprise me,' I say. 'So what should I do? You saw them – they came all the way over here just to call me names.'

'I know,' Susie replies. 'Maybe you should stand up to them.'

'I've tried that before. It doesn't work with the cool kids.'

'Pfft. Cool? They're not cool,' Susie scoffs.

'Yeah, well, they're definitely cooler than me. Do you want some chips?' I ask, holding out my pack of Crimples.

Susie shakes her head. 'No, I can't. I'm not allowed.'

'Why not?'

'They're full of all these chemicals.' She rubs her stomach. 'Upset tummy. But I'll have one of your frogs. Even though it's the wrong colour for my team. You don't have any green ones, do you?'

'Nope, just red,' I say, tossing her one.

'There's nothing to be afraid of, Billy,' she says.

'You too? Why does everyone think I'm frightened of something?'

'Because you are.'

'No I'm not!'

'How about drowning?'

I look at the pool. Fifty metres is a long way. But I have done it before. Just not in front of the whole school.

'I wouldn't drown,' I say.

'All right, then what? If you won't go in a race, even though you know you won't drown, what's stopping you?'

'I'm not afraid of anything,' I say, and I'm beginning to get a little tired of hearing myself say it. 'Except dogs.'

'Dogs?'

'Yeah. I got bitten once, when I was little,' I tell her, pointing to a row of shiny, flat scars on my left calf. 'Eight stitches.'

Susie whistles. 'But there aren't any dogs in the pool,' she says.

I sigh. 'You know what? Maybe you're right. Maybe I should go in just one race. I mean, I'll definitely come last, but at least then no one can say that Free Billy just lay about in the shade eating lollies all day. Or that he's scared of drowning.'

Susie nods while she twists off a bit of frog with her teeth. 'Sounds like a good idea. I went in a race before and I didn't win.'

'Did you come last, though?' I ask her.

'I came fifth.'

'That's pretty good.'

'Out of five.'

I smile. She's making me feel relaxed, which is good of her. It's more than she needed to do.

'You know what? I am going to do it,' I hear myself saying. 'I'm going to enter the seniors freestyle. That's the over-arm one, isn't it?'

Susie nods. 'Freestyle, yep.'

'Good. Then that's the one I'm going in. I've got to go and tell Mr Julius. Have another frog if you like.'

'Good luck,' says Susie with a smile.

I find Mr Julius, and tell him that I've decided to swim. 'Good for you, Billy!' he says, writing my name down on his sheet. 'We'll be calling for that one in about ten minutes, so you should go and get your swimmers on.'

That's just great, I think. Just ten more minutes until I drown. Or die of embarrassment. As I head back over to my spot in the shade, I'm starting to think that this might be the stupidest thing I've ever done.

'Did you do it?' Susie asks.

I nod. 'He wrote my name down, so I guess I have to race. Can't back out now!'

'Good for you,' Susie replies. 'Do you have your goggles?'

'Goggles?' I say, frowning at her. 'I didn't bring any goggles. I wasn't going to swim, remember?'

Susie leans over, takes her own pair of goggles from her bag, and hands them to me. 'Here, use mine. At least you'll look like you came prepared.'

I hold them at arm's length. 'They're pink.'

'Actually, they're lavender. Which is closer to purple.'

I hesitate, before taking them. 'They're more pink than purple,' I say, unconvinced.

I head into the boys' toilets to get changed, and as I'm going in, I meet Henry and John coming out. They see my towel and swimmers hanging over my arm, and Henry chuckles.

'Getting ready for the big event, huh?' he says.

'No, not really,' I lie. 'I'm just going to the loo.'

He points at Susie's goggles, which are hanging from my finger. 'Do you always take those into the toilet when you go? Come on,' he says to John. 'Let's see if Matt's feeling any better.'

I'm glad they're gone. The last thing I wanted was for them to be in the room while I was getting changed. I've heard all the names, but I reckon after seeing me naked, they might come up with a few more.

I'm standing on the warm cement behind the tiled starting block at the end of lane two, with Susie's goggles on my forehead and my hands clasped in front of me. I look around. Luckily there aren't too many people interested in this race. It's close to lunchtime and it seems like most of the kids are lining up at the kiosk for their sausage rolls and chips rather than watching seven boys swim while one boy drowns.

Mr Francis has been starting all the races. He raises his megaphone. 'Okay, boys, on your blocks,' he says.

I take a step towards the block. I can almost hear the executioner's drum. Biddy-boom, biddy-boom . . . In my head I'm already composing the letter to my parents:

> Dear Mr and Mrs Clarkson, we regret to inform you that by the time you read this letter, your son William will be bobbing face down in the Speers Point Public Pool. Interestingly, every person present saw fit to laugh and point rather than save his life. May he rest in peace.

I glance to my right. Henry Wakeman is there in lane five, swimming cap in place. Beside him is John Graham. I look around for Matt Hinkley and find him right next to me in lane one. He doesn't seem very well. There's a weird grey colour around his eyes, and his face has gone pale.

I forget the drums in my ears. 'Matt, are you all right?' I ask him.

'Don't talk to me, Tubby,' he mutters. It's almost a snarl.

Apart from Matt and me, the other swimmers on the blocks are swinging their arms around, stretching, looking like they know what they're doing.

'Are you ready?' Mr Francis says.

No, I'm not ready, I want to say. I think I've made a terrible mistake.

'On your marks.'

I can't believe I'm doing this. Copying the others, I shuffle forward so my toes are dangling over the edge of the block. The water looks deep and cold. I have an awful thought: if I die today, it's no one's fault but mine. I agreed to do this. Me. I let the teasing get to me. The teasing from Henry and his mates, and the good-intentioned 'encouragement' from Susie. I've been such an idiot, and now I'm about to pay the price.

'Get set,' says Mr Francis.

Almost in automatic now, I copy the others, bending forward and reaching towards my toes. I can't remember the last time I actually touched my toes, so I just dangle my arms and wiggle my fingers.

'Billy, you might need the goggles over your eyes,' the megaphone voice says. I hear a few tittering laughs around me as I pull Susie's lavender goggles down off my forehead and into their proper spot. The band is a bit tight and it feels like my eyeballs are being squeezed and pinched right out of their sockets.

Crack! The starting pistol fires, and I glance across to see all the boys to my right dive gracefully into the water, their hands parting the surface for their bodies to slide in.

'You can go, Billy,' the megaphone voice says.

I half dive, half belly-flop into the pool, and I'm glad that I'm underwater, because I just know that if I wasn't, all I'd be able to hear would be laughter from the sidelines.

I take a moment to get my bearings, and to make sure that I'm the right way up. By some stroke of good fortune I am, so I start flailing, with my eyes squeezed tightly shut. I can feel my arms going like a paddle steamer, over and over, making a lot of splashes, but without much forward movement.

Lifting my head above the water, I take a deep breath and go back to flailing, eyes still closed. Then I remember that I'm wearing goggles, and that I don't have to keep my eyes shut, so I open them.

For a moment I'm not sure if I'm still the right way up, because I can see someone in front of me. But they aren't swimming, or even floating. They're just kind of . . . well, they're just kind of hanging. They're just hovering there in the water, towards the bottom of the pool.

I stop flailing and have a better look, and I suddenly see who it is. It's Matt Hinkley, near the bottom of the pool, and he's not swimming. He's not even flailing. He's sinking and his limbs are completely motionless.

I lift my head above the water and look up the pool. The other boys are well on their way. In fact, Henry is almost finished and I'm still within a couple of metres of the starting blocks.

Looking back down towards Matt, I can see that he still isn't moving.

'Matt's drowning!' I shout, but my mouth isn't completely above water, so it's just a kind of burble. 'Matt's drowning!' I shout again, more clearly this time.

'Billy! That way!' Mr Francis is calling to me, pointing up the pool.

'No!'

'If you don't finish, you won't get a point for your team,' he shouts back.

'Matt's drowning! He's down here!'

'No, Matt's nearly finished the race!' Mr Francis replies.

I give up. There's no time for argument. Sucking in a huge breath, I duck my head under and dive down towards Matt. He's a fair way down, slouched in the corner where the side and the bottom of the pool meet, and with all the extra buoyancy around my middle, it takes a lot of kicking and struggling to reach him. I manage to get my hands under his arms and try to lift, but he's like a dead weight. I grip again, and planting my feet against the bottom of the pool, I push up as hard as I can.

My hands slip, and Matt sinks back down, so I come back to the surface long enough to take another huge breath.

Diving all the way back down, I get hold of Matt again, and this time I somehow manage to hold on to him all the way to the top. As I reach the surface, I hear bodies hitting the water all around me as people finally realise that while Henry Wakeman has been winning a swimming race, I've been busily rescuing someone.

'We've got him, Billy,' says Mr Julius in my ear. 'You can get out. We'll take it from here.'

I climb out of the pool and someone brings a towel and throws it around my shoulders while others drag Matt out onto the concrete beside the pool. He's not breathing.

I'm at home in my room, playing a game on my Xbox. Mum and Dad already asked me how the swimming carnival went and I told them that I went in a race. They seemed very happy, even proud.

'So you got a point for your team!' Mum said. 'Do they still do that – give points for participation?'

'Yes,' I said, even though I'm not sure that you get a point if you don't finish. Would they give you a point for getting helped to the side and up the ladder, even if that did happen after you helped save someone's life?

So now I'm hiding out in my room, quietly killing some zombies.

There's a knock at my door. It's Mum. 'Billy, honey?' she says. 'There's someone out in the living room to see you.'

'Who is it?'

'Come and see.'

It's a lady I recognise from somewhere, but I'm not sure who she is.

'Billy?' she says.

'Yes?'

The lady steps forward and takes both of my hands in hers. 'I'm Mrs Hinkley, Matthew's mum,' she says. 'The school rang me, and told me what you did.'

Mum is nodding. She obviously knows the story.

'It was nothing,' I say.

'Oh no, it's not nothing!' she replies. 'You saved Matt's life. He'll be in hospital overnight, but he's going to be all right, thanks to you. So it's definitely not nothing.'

I shrug. 'He would have done the same for me,' I say, even though I'm not sure that's true. 'I just looked down and saw him on the bottom of the pool. How come he was down there, anyway?'

'Matthew's highly allergic to certain food additives. There are quite a few, but one of the biggies is MSG, like you get in some brands of snack foods, chips, that sort of thing.'

Without meaning to I wipe my face, remembering the light spattering of soggy Crimples.

'He probably shouldn't eat those, then,' I say.

'That's what surprised me,' Mrs Hinkley replies. 'Matthew knows what he can and can't eat.'

Mum smiles and rolls her eyes. 'Boys,' she says.

'Anyway, Billy, I just wanted to come here and personally thank you for what you did. And I want you to have this.' She hands me a gift-wrapped box.

'Thanks,' I say, tearing the crepe paper off. It's a box of chocolates. 'Thanks,' I say again.

'I bought them at the hospital gift shop,' she explains, and I can't work out why she's looking embarrassed. Then I see her glance at me, up and down, and I understand. 'I'm sorry, I should have . . . ' Then she mutters something about never having met me before, and something else about Matthew not mentioning something or other, and suddenly Mum is showing her out.

'Well, Vanessa, thanks so much for coming around – that was very kind,' Mum is saying, and I take my box of chocolates and head back to my room.

I'm standing out the front of assembly, holding a two-hundred dollar voucher for Trentfield's Bookshop. Mr Julius is telling everyone that Matt is still in hospital, but that he's going to be okay. He's saying that Matt had an allergic reaction to some food additives which made him stop breathing. He's also telling the school that I was incredibly brave, and that I gave up any chance I had to win that race to drag Matt to safety.

I smile quietly to myself. It looks as if I couldn't even win the drowning event, but that's okay. This time I'm happy to come second.

King of the Playground

Pat Flynn

I knocked on the door three times, sucked in a breath, and turned the knob. 'You want to see me, Coach?'

He nodded from behind his made-to-order desk. There are many advantages to being six-feet eight-inches tall but there are plenty of disadvantages, too. Shop furniture rarely fits. You bang your head on light bulbs. You can never sleep on an airplane. You forever hear, 'How's the weather up there?'

I should know. I'm three inches taller.

'Come in, Bill,' he said.

I sat down in the large green leather chair and leant back out of habit. I'd been here hundreds of times, shooting the breeze about tactics, injuries, mental strength – heck, we'd even talked about love in this office.

'Bill . . .' He looked away, lost for words.

I followed his gaze to the wall. There was a large framed photo of me slam-dunking in the last grand final series we'd won. Must have been three, no, four years ago.

'Good times,' he said.

I nodded, my face impassive but my stomach shrinking like it did in the moments before tip-off.

'I could rattle on about a lot of things.' He folded his arms and his voice became more businesslike. 'A decreasing salary cap, pressure from the board to get this team winning again, your four knee operations.'

My jaw tightened. I couldn't believe he brought up the knee.

'But I just want to say this.' Coach looked at me with green eyes that could fill a team of men with fear, but there was none of that fire now. His look was as soft as his voice. 'Your time's up, Bill.'

Even though I was expecting it, a stab of pain still hit me in the gut like an elbow. When it passed I said, 'Three.'

He looked puzzled. 'What?'

'I've only had three knee operations. And I still moved well enough to lead the team in rebounds this year.'

'You always could bring down the boards.' He spoke more firmly now. 'But for how much longer? Don't you care about walking when you're forty?'

I shrugged. The truth is I didn't, but it wasn't the smartest thing to admit. 'What if I want to play on? What can the board offer?'

'Bill . . .'

'How much?' I wanted an answer. I deserved as much.

'Maybe twenty-five. If you're lucky.'

My jaw dropped. That's what rookies get paid to warm the bench.

Coach spread his giant palms out wide. 'I know. It's an insult. But we can offer you double that if you take on another role with the club. One I know you'll be good at.'

I raised my eyebrows. This I wasn't expecting. 'What role?'

He smiled for the first time since I'd walked in. 'Assistant coach. You and me can keep working together to make this team great.'

Up until that moment I'd spent my whole athletic life telling myself 'I can'. I can make it through rehab. I can hit this free throw. I can play another year at the highest level. But Coach said it was time to ask, 'Can I?'

'You've been the best player this club has ever had,' he said, 'but now you're on the wrong side of thirty with a stuffed right knee. Your numbers are on the slide and opponents that used to fear you now ask to be matched against you. Is that how you want to end your career?'

'What opponents?' I wanted to hunt them down and shut them up.

'All of them.'

I took the job. Coach can be very convincing.

Across town there's a gym where most of the young hotshots, plus a few of the pros, hang out in the off-season and play pick-up ball. My first assignment was to do some scouting.

There were the usual gangly teenagers to check out, but Coach told me that the word was out on another guy, an American who'd been cleaning up the hotshots and the cash. 'Find out his name and his story.' He gave me a wink. 'You might even want to burn a hole in his pocket.'

He wasn't hard to find. Walking in I saw a six-foot-four black guy hit a fade-away jumper from the top of the key. He was playing one-on-one against a kid from the Emus – the Aussie under-19s team.

A local bloke filled me in on the rules. 'Laroe plays 'em one at a time, first to eleven baskets, and starts with a fifty dollar bet. When he wins, the next guy has to match the pot. Over the past three days he's won seven hundred and fifty bucks and no one's been game to bet after that. Word is, back in Chicago he's known as King of the Playground and once took ten G's off Michael.'

'Yeah,' I said. 'Michael Jackson.' I wasn't in the mood for no homeboy boasting today.

But Laroe was good. He had that ageless look about him that made it difficult to tell if he was twenty-five or thirty-five. The fact that I never saw him showboat made me guess closer to the latter. He had long arms and enough muscle to stop from being bullied, but not too much to slow him down. I wasn't the only one watching – others circled the half-court where he was hustling, admiring a good ball player.

He finished toying with the junior star and then started beating up on a state under-21s player.

If I had to use one word to describe him, it would be smooth. He had a skill I've never had, the ability to make time seem to slow down on court. No matter how much pressure he was under, either on offence or defence, he never looked rushed. It was something to see.

Especially when a nineteen-year-old put $400 down and played the game of his life. Jack Sharp was as tall as me and although he had half a foot on Laroe, I figured the American would be too smart and quick for him. But the young guy was a hell of an athlete for his size. He swatted the first jump shot from Laroe right back in his face, and found nothing but net on his first five trips to the basket.

Down 7-3, Laroe shifted gears. He picked Sharp's pocket twice in a row and blew by him with a crossover dribble to go up 9-8. But when Sharp beat Laroe with a step-through move, I knew the American was tiring. There'd been plenty of bumps and body checks and it was Laroe's fifth straight game.

Retying the laces on his red high tops gave Laroe a chance to catch his breath. He lifted his hands to get checked the ball, and when the leather hit his skin he immediately let it fly. The ball soared high and straight for over twenty feet until it made a swishing sound as it dropped through the net.

The crowd went 'Aaww!'

Sharp was worried, and rattled a hook around the rim that didn't drop. Laroe took the rebound out past the three-point line, turned, and drove back to the basket. Sharp waited for him, but Laroe didn't come. He pulled up quickly, jumped high off two feet, and feathered a backspun shot that arced like the De Triomphe.

Game over.

Waiting patiently with his $800 was the point guard for the Melbourne Tigers. Laroe took a sip of water and was back out there. The Tiger had good skills, but was too predictable. Laroe swept the wooden floor with him.

After glancing around to make sure there was no one else, Laroe scooped down to pick up his cash. But when he bobbed back up I had a fistful of hundreds right in his face. I looked closely to see a reaction, but all he did was smile and say, 'Let's play ball.'

I have always been a tough competitor, a hard-nosed dude if the opposition pushed me, but Laroe wasn't down for any trash. I tested him early, told him to get back to the ghetto just to see what would happen. What happened was he swished three straight twenty-five footers. NBA three-pointers. I decided to shut up.

Every time I had the ball I backed in nice and tight to the hoop. I wasn't the prettiest dribbler in the world, but I knew how to stop those thieving buggers from stealing my lunch. Sticking my backside out, I kept my wide body between Laroe and the ball. Besides, who was going to call an offensive foul out here?

When I found my range of less than ten feet, I shot the ball. I could put them in blindfolded over a short six-foot-four bloke from there.

The trouble was I couldn't stop him and it was hacking me off. He kept taking the kind of bombs that should have missed everything but air, but were instead sinking like the Titanic.

'Mate, you're going to make it rain soon,' I said after he hit a twenty-two footer to make it seven-all.

By this time the crowd was building up. I was fairly well-known around here and had plenty to prove to the blokes who knew I'd been given the flick from the West Melbourne Warriors. Word travels fast.

Besides, Laroe had to be nearly exhausted by now.

It became obvious when I was in his face at nine-all. His shooting arm didn't extend and the ball bricked off the side of the rim. I grabbed it with two hands, dribbled past the three-point-line opposite Laroe and returned fast to the basket. He was slow to recover so I spun by him and reversed a jam.

Ten-9.

The next play I was determined to bring my best D. I followed him closely, watching his eyes to get a jump on what he might do. While dribbling between his legs he gave me a wink, then jerked his head and took a jab step to the right. My weight automatically shifted left, but it was all a ruse, his fake catching me out as he dribbled past my right hip. I was mentally kicking myself as I followed half a step behind, deciding there was no way I'd let him have this basket easily. I'd go for the ball and if I chopped his arms off, so be it.

He seemed to sense my intention and stopped on a five-cent piece. I tried to do the same thing, but at six-foot eleven and a half, and one-hundred and fifteen kilos, it was never going to be easy. As I pulled up, my right knee crumbled. Another disadvantage to being tall is that it's a long way down. I hit the deck in a heap, and could only watch as his lay-up went through the hoop.

Ten-all.

'Gentlemen's split?' he asked, offering me my money back.

I gave him my tough-guy sneer. 'Not in this lifetime. Next basket wins.'

I've seen a lot of good players, many with skills better than me, disappear when the pressure is on. Not literally, of course, but in spirit. If things are going their way they'll shoot the lights out, but when it's 88-88 with twenty-five seconds remaining, they'd rather be on the bench than on the court.

Me, I've never understood this. The reason I play is to test myself, physically and mentally. When the game comes down to the wire and the ball is in your hands, you have the ability to stare fear in the face and defeat it. That's a high no drug will ever come close to beating. Sure, sometimes you miss and feel like a loser. But when you make it . . .

He checked me the ball and did something I wasn't expecting. Taking two steps back, he trash-talked for the first time in the game.

'You better shoot it,' he said in a throaty voice. 'Because you're too darn slow to get past me.'

I knew what he was doing – tempting me to take a jump shot from outside my comfort zone – and it annoyed the crap out of me. In my younger days I would have driven right by him and stuffed it down the basket and his throat. Now, however, I was having second thoughts. My knee was getting stiffer by the minute and I wasn't sure I had it in me to get past him one more time.

Chances were I couldn't win either way – if I shot the ball and made it I looked like a chicken, if I drove past him and missed I looked like a fool.

I took the shot. It was a twelve-footer, two feet too long as far as I was concerned. I over extended and the ball hit the back of the rim and bounced up in the air.

You could hear the intake of breath from those watching. Everyone knew it was a bad shot – what's known in hoop language as a 'brick'.

But sometimes bricks are made of gold. The

ball hit the front of the rim, bounced up high, and dropped in.

'I owe you a beer,' I said.

We went to a bar around the corner but Laroe ended up drinking water. 'Toughest part of my job is keeping in shape. Don't need to make it any harder.'

'What is your job?' I asked.

'Same as you. I'm a ballplayer.'

'What team?'

He chuckled. 'I'm not much of a team player.' After a swig of water he changed the subject. 'You know, I seen you play before. Aussie Boomers versus Northwestern College in Chicago, 'bout ten years ago. You scored a few that night but mostly I remember your defence. You played some hardcore D.'

'It's a small world.' I remembered that game. I remembered them all. 'So what's your story? You must have played college ball?'

He toyed with a short, gold necklace that hung around his neck. Jewellery is not allowed on the basketball court, but he didn't look like a guy who followed all the rules. 'Loyola, Chicago. Averaged nineteen points my freshman year. Had it all – scholarship, fans, a cheerleader to date . . .'

He paused.

'What happened?'

'Knocked the cheerleader up.' He flashed a

mouthful of white, then pulled a photo out of his wallet. 'Saturn. My little girl.'

She wasn't little at all. A cute teenager with long legs and colourful braces.

'Bet she changed things.'

'Surely did. You got kids?'

'No.'

'They'll change your life in ways you'd never guess.' He shook his head. Fingered the necklace again. 'Summer break after Saturn showed up, I played a three-on-three tournament and we won. My share was five grand. I could reject the money and keep playing college ball or find another life. Saturn had to eat, go to the doc . . . I been hustling ever since.'

'You make a living playing pick-up ball?' I'd heard of guys doing this, but had never actually met someone who did.

He shrugged. 'I get by. Some people even call me King of the Playground.'

I took a long swig. Unlike Laroe, I was drinking the hard stuff. 'I heard. Also heard a story about you taking money off the great man.'

'People talk, huh?'

'So it's not true?'

He thought for a few moments, a long index finger pressed against his lips. Then he spoke. 'One day in the off-season he came down to the 'hood, King of the NBA to play King of the Playground. He threw ten thousand dollars cash on the ground; I had to throw my car keys beside it as collateral.'

'And you won?' I tried not to voice my disbelief.

He spoke quietly. 'Had two things in my favour. More to play for and more to lose.'

If I had my time over I would've questioned him further. But right then there didn't seem to be any more to say. You either believed him or you didn't.

'Why Australia?' I asked.

'A holiday and a new opportunity all in one.' Another smile. 'Was going well until you showed up.'

I shrugged. 'We all lose sometimes.'

'I know it. You still treading the boards?'

I nearly said yes before remembering. 'I'm a coach now.'

'A coach?' He took another swig. 'That's another name for someone who can't play no more.'

My hands squeezed the glass. Although I felt like biting, I didn't. 'You could be right.'

'Oh, I am.'

We walked back towards the gym and I stopped at my car. He gave me a half-smile, his head tilted to the right. 'You want to come inside and try getting past me? 'Cause I bet you all the money in your wallet that you can't.'

I shook my head and opened the car door. Then I pulled out a basketball and said, 'Thought you'd never ask.'

When he checked me the ball, I felt the familiar

dimpled leather in my hand. As a kid I used to sleep with my basketball. Still do sometimes.

After a few beers, the pain in my knee was gone, so I tried a move I hadn't done in years. I faked left with my head and shoulder, then took off down the right side of the key. When I got to the low post I did a two-foot jump stop, faked a shot with the right hand, swapped the ball to my left, and took a big crossover step with my right foot towards the basket. Opposition crowds always howled for a travelling violation when I did this, but good referees knew better. Everything went perfectly and I launched up to complete the slam, when a hand appeared out of nowhere, seemingly from the heavens above. It swiped the ball, and only the ball, knocking it two courts away.

When I came down all I saw was a grin on Laroe's face.

'You're pretty quick for a big guy.' He patted me on the back. 'But not quick enough.'

'You want to play in the NBL next year?'

'Man, Mike asked me the same thing, except he said the NBA. I'll tell you what I told him – I'd rather be King of the Playground.'

We spent the next hour shooting hoops and shooting the breeze. He gave me a tip that improved my free-throw shooting and he even showed me a thing or two about shot-blocking. The lesson cost me

$1600, but he lit a fire inside me that I wasn't sure I could put out.

The next day I reported to Coach. 'You should sign a kid named Jack Sharp. He could take my place at Centre and do a good job.'

'Great news,' Bill said. 'And the American?'

I shook my head. 'Not a team player.'

'Did you tell him this is a team sport?'

'I'm sure he knows.'

A pause.

'Glad you're settling into your new role,' said Coach.

'About that.' I hesitated – part of me didn't want to say it.

'You want my job?' he joked.

'No. I'm quitting.'

He sat up in his chair. 'What?'

'The Giants have offered me thirty. I'm gonna go around another year. Maybe two.'

'You're going to play for the Gold Coast?' He said the words slowly, as if I were making a strange joke. All teams are rivals, but the head coach of the Giants was someone Coach particularly disliked. I suspect this was mainly because he was as obsessive, smart and crazy as Coach.

'I'm hoping the warm weather will be kind to my knee.'

Coach ran a hand through his thick, white hair. More than anyone, professional coaches know that anything is possible in life and sport. Nevertheless, this piece of news seemed hard for him to swallow.

His voice hardened. 'Always thought you'd be a one club man. Obviously I was wrong.'

I nodded. I could've pointed out that my club didn't want me to play for them anymore, but that didn't seem necessary.

We shook hands.

'Hope it all works out for you, Bill.' The way he said it revealed that he didn't believe it would.

As I walked out of Coach's office for the last time, I looked back at the wall. Back at myself when I could still jump without pain. I guess some types of pain I can put up with. And some I can't.

Strange-headed Harry

Leigh Hobbs

Strange-headed Harry
Had a head just like no other
It was absolutely unalike
His father Ike
Nor Bernadette his mother.

At school and elsewhere sister Sue
And brother Ted bemoaned it
They panned the shape of Harry's head
And publicly disowned it.

Friends were few, apart from Toots
Whom Harry loved most dearly
She only had three legs, poor thing
His perfect partner, clearly.

But Harry was no fool, you know
For at last there came the day
When Harry wrote a tell-all book
And Toots she penned a play.

Next came the movie: *Harry's Head*
'A wondrous tale!' the critics said
Harry's dome is all the rage
A classic wonder of our age.

Monies flowed in nicely, thank you
Toots and Harry made a pile
Giving lectures, signing books,
Now Toots and Harry live in style.

Harry's family changed their minds
They modified their views
Each night they see dear Harry's head
On the television news.

'Of course we always were alike!'
Say sister Sue and brother Ted
And Bernadette and Ike insist
That they adore son Harry's head.

Harry's fine, he always has been
Harry's very smart
He's utilised his special head
Which now the world calls Art!

Shoefiti
Meredith Costain
Illustration by Grant Gittus

There are shoes
hanging from the power line
at the end of our street.
High-heeled shoes
with dainty ankle straps
and peep toes –
not your plain old trainers
found in every other suburb.
These shoes are special.
Are they warding off
pigeon-toed ghosts?
Cast-offs from a stiletto-loving
tightrope walker?
A wedding invitation?
A sign from a schoolgirl
on the cusp of freedom,
bursting for release
from a life measured out
(Prufrock-style)
in tests and bells?
A prank from a bully
with no soul/sole?
Or perhaps they're
simply hanging there
dangling idly
tossed by the wind
caressed by breezes
awaiting the spirit
of their owner to return
so they can walk
high above the ground
twenty steps closer to heaven.

Michael Wagner
Various

my online emotional range

:^) :^(

it troubled him for years
then he refused to think about it

year 1. ???????????????!
year 2. ?????????????!
year 3. ???????????!
year 4. ?????????!
year 5. ???????!
year 6. ????!
year 7. ?!!
year 8. .

the mind is awake
even as the body sleeps

ommmmzzzzzzommmmzzzzzzz
ommmmzzzzzzommmmzzzzzzz
ommmmzzzzzzommmmzzzzzzz
ommmmzzzzzzommmmzzzzzzz
ommmmzzzzzzommmmzzzzzzz
ommmmzzzzzzommmmzzzzzzz
ommmmzzzzzzommmmzzzzzzz

Killer Stories
Christine Bongers
Illustration by Peter Viska

The jaws of writers run red,
from sucking
on the veins of experience;
cannibalising
their own lives
and those of others they meet.

Hungry-eyed hunters,
stalking coffee shops
and queues,
inhaling the clattering chatter
from adjoining tables
at the mall.

Preying
on juicy titbits
falling from unwary lips.
Pressing
into the folds of memory
a fluttering vein,
a stretch of white neck.

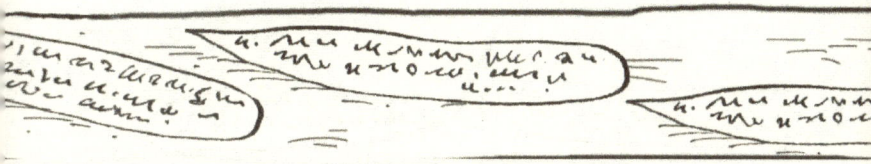

Stealing
tender morsels
that were once
some part of you
and making them
forever theirs.

Raking over
the fresh and raw,
marinating
in creative juices,
slow-cooking
till tender,
so tender
you won't even feel
the meat
fall away
from your bones.

Reducing
all that was once you,
to essence of
succulent,
spicy,
bitter
or sweet.
Creating tender morsels
on which others may feast:
killer stories that make the juices flow.

My Boy

Sofie Laguna

Illustration by Marc McBride

My boy
Did you come to me from the moon?
Your cheeks and knees are surely from the moon
Circular, mysterious.

Or did you come from the sun?
Your toes and ears are surely from the sun
Shining and necessary.

Or perhaps, my boy, you came from the river.
Your hands and elbows are surely made from water
Moving and rapid.

Or did you come to me from some other place
Beyond the moon or the sun
Or the river?
A place that contains all these things
– stars too
bright as your eyes,
But is greater than them.

My boy
Passing moon and sun, stars and river,
I think you came from a question
Floating through the universe
Dark and quiet
Until you reached the answer
Of my waiting arms.

There Are Worse Things Than Poetry

Steven Herrick

Before a poetry session I gave to Year Nine students in Melbourne, I heard one student say to his mate, 'Poetry ... what could be worse than poetry!' This is my response.

There are worse things than poetry.

Collingwood winning the Premiership.
School seven days a week, not five.
Cabbage!
Your mother finding your diary
      and publishing it on the web.
The Taliban.
The food in the school canteen.
People who think they know how you feel.
Australia being overrun by ...
      Australians.
Your girlfriend dumping you
      and taking up with your mate.
Your girlfriend not dumping you
      and still taking up with your mate.

There are worse things than poetry.

The Swans losing the Premiership.
Exams.
The smell of hospital wards.
Doing a job you hate.
Doing a job you love
      but everyone hates you for doing it.
Driving your mum's car without a licence,
      the police wailing behind.
John Howard coming back.
War, famine, earthquakes, cyclones, disease.
Your hair falling out and growing back only in your
      ears.
What we do to old people
      to the invalid
      to the unbalanced
      to the homeless.
Eating Big Macs for the rest of your life.

There are worse things than poetry.

Collingwood winning back-to-back Premierships.

Tour de Cycling

Lorraine Marwood

Illustration by Judith Rossell

My mouth is open, signalling
water, water.
I snatch a bottle from the sidelines,
see a flag like a guillotine
swinging, colours are words
shouting, banging side barriers
and the heat from the bitumen
pushes up, as my legs push down.

There's a bunch of us
wheel on wheel
backs arched, the webbing
on helmets like warriors
of sorts and we ride
our own fine light steeds,
click of many gears
as the curve of the road
dictates change of pace –
it's a sprint now
the sharp whistle warns
of points up for grabs.
School kids climb a tree
to barrack,

the police motorcycle
flashes red, blue.

My team mates have
worked around me,
we vie for space
to manoeuvre past other teams,
whirr through the corner,
up out of the saddle to push on the straight –
behind us a wheel clips another,
tyres burst,
legs
arms
bitumen scraping skin.
I'm pushing my body
through the pain barrier,
more real than the blurred
spectators. I'm alert to all
challenges, as I heave
head, shoulders, over that
finish line.
My back, my arms
release the racing curve.
I punch the air, perforate it
with my conquering sweat.

Calling Me
Gabrielle Wang

I hesitate
I wait
Only a moment
It is time for me to go

About the Contributors

Deb Abela

Having always been short and a bit of a coward, Deborah dreamed of being braver and stronger, which is probably why she writes about spies, ghosts, soccer legends and characters who battle sea monsters and evil harbour lords. She's written *Max Remy*, *Jasper Zammit*, *The Remarkable Secret of Aurelie Bonhoffen* and *Grimsdon*. She has won awards for her books but mostly hopes to be as brave as the characters inside. www.deborahabela.com.

Dianne Bates

Dianne has published 100+ books, mostly for young readers, some of which have won national and state literary awards: others have sold overseas. Her current book is *Crossing the Line*. Di has also edited a number of children's magazines. She lives in Wollongong, NSW, with her author husband, Bill Condon. Their website is www.enterprisingwords.com.

Michael Gerard Bauer

Since resigning from teaching in 2000 Michael has written a number of popular and award-winning books for children and young adults. These include *The Running Man*, *Dinosaur Knights*, *Just a Dog* and the *Ishmael* trilogy. His books have been published in the UK and USA and translated into eight languages.

Christine Bongers

Christine is a former journalist who has sunk her teeth into fiction. Her novels have been Notable and short-listed books in the CBCA awards and short-listed for the Queensland Premier's Literary Awards and WA Premier's Book Awards. Her titles include *Dust* and *Henry Hoey Hobson*. More at www.christinebongers.com.

Janeen Brian

Janeen is an award-winning children's author and has been writing full-time for over twenty years. She has had seventy-three books published and more due for release. Janeen is a 'bitser'! She writes all sorts – novels, poetry, picture books, information books – and short stories, like 'What Goes Around . . .'!

Sue Bursztynski

Sue grew up in Melbourne, writing on the beach a lot. She has written ten books, including *Crime Time* and *Wolfborn*, a werewolf novel and a CBCA Notable Book. Sue reads submissions for 'Andromeda Spaceways Inflight Magazine'. Sue's brother was born soon after the Beatles' visit. His name isn't Ringo or Jimmy.

Isobelle Carmody

Isobelle began writing *The Obernewtyn Chronicles* while still at secondary school. Since then she has established herself as one of Australia's leading writers of fantasy. Her book *The Red Wind* won the CBC Book of the Year Award in 2011 and her most recent book is a second collection of gritty, urban fantasy stories called *Metro Winds*, published in 2012. She is now working on the final book in *The Obernewtyn Chronicles*.

Margaret Clark

Margaret has written books under the names MD Clark, Margaret D Clark and Lee Striker. She has written over 100 books about relationships, friendships, and social issues under the guise of humour. Margaret's books include *Pugwall*, which was made into a TV series and The Chickabees series. Her latest book is an Aussie Nibble called *Blast Off!*

Paul Collins

Paul has written over 140 books. He's best known for *The Jelindel Chronicles*, starring the heroine Jelindel from his story in *Trust Me Too*. His latest book is *Mole Hunt*, Book #1 in The Maximus Black Files. Paul is also the Publisher at Ford Street Publishing and manages Creative Net, a speakers' agency for authors and illustrators.
Visit www.paulcollins.com.au and
www.fordstreetpublishing.com/cnet.

Bill Condon

Bill has written several young adult novels, including *Confessions of a Liar, Thief and Failed Sex God*, and *A Straight Line to My Heart*. He lives on the south coast of New South Wales with his wife, fellow writer Dianne (Di) Bates. His website is www.enterprisingwords.com.

Meredith Costain

Meredith lives in Melbourne with a menagerie of pets. Her work ranges from picture books to novels and non-fiction, and includes *Dog Squad*, *A Year in Girl Hell*, *Doodledum Dancing* and novelisations of the TV show *Dance Academy*. She plays blues piano and has too many shoes. Visit her at www.meredithcostain.com.

Gary Crew

Gary has won the Children's Book of the Year award four times and has been awarded many others including the National Children's Book Award; the Victorian Premier's Award; the New South Wales Premier's Award; the Ned Kelly Award for Crime Writing; and the School Library Journal Best Book of the Year (USA). His latest book is *In the Beech Forest* (illustrated by Den Scheer).

Justin D'Ath

Justin is the author of thirty-six books for children and young adults. His very popular Extreme Adventures are soon to become a TV series. Currently he is writing two more series for Penguin, Mission Fox and The Lost World Circus. Justin lives in Queenscliff, Victoria.

Hazel Edwards

Hazel is not a fan of graffiti, or tatts, but likes satirical cartoons. She is best known for *There's a Hippopotamus on Our Roof Eating Cake* series (now a film). Her latest YA novel is *f2m: the boy within*. It was co-written with Ryan Kennedy and was a 2011 White Ravens top 250 books internationally. As a National Ambassador for the 2012 Year of Reading, Hazel web-chats with students in remote regions and has hints for aspiring creators and e-books on her website: www.hazeledwards.com.

Corinne Fenton

Corinne has a passion for writing children's books, especially picture books, and enjoys sharing her experiences of writing and researching with children and adults. She is best known for her picture books *Queenie: One Elephant's Story*, *The Dog on the Tuckerbox* and *Flame Stands Waiting*. Visit www.corinnefenton.com.

JE Fison

Julie is a Brisbane-based writer with a background in television news and marketing. Her work has taken her around the world where she has met some amazing people (and some not so good ones), shaken hands with an orang-utan, camped with elephants and (accidentally) eaten rat soup. A family holiday on the Noosa River inspired her first fiction series – Hazard River, which is a mix of adventure and fun, with an environmental twist. She is currently working on a story for teenage girls. Visit www.hazardriver.com.

Pat Flynn

Pat lives on Queensland's Sunshine Coast. An ex-professional tennis player and teacher, he now writes realistic fiction with a dose of humour for young people. His latest book, *My Awesome Story*, is about a boy who hates writing.

Archimede Fusillo

Archimede lives in Melbourne, but travels all over Australia running writing workshops and giving author talks. With several YA novels to his credit, Archie has recently returned to his passion for writing short stories and is hoping to write another picture book so he can again work with talented illustrators.

Sandy Fussell

Sandy is afraid of polar bears, samurai swords and lava flows. So far she has written novels about the first two. Next stop, a volcano. She is the author of the Samurai Kids series, *Polar Boy* and *Jaguar Warrior*. You can find her at www.sandyfussell.com and www.samuraikids.com.au.

Susanne Gervay

Susanne Gervay OAM is recognised for her writing on social justice. Endorsed by Room to Read, Alannah & Madeline Foundation, Life Education and the Cancer Council, her award-winning books include *Butterflies* and *Ships in the Field* and the Jack books – *I Am Jack*, *Super Jack* and *Always Jack*. Visit Susanne at www.sgervay.com.

Grant Gittus

Grant is a graphic designer and illustrator who spends a lot of time designing books like this one (for money). He has written and illustrated one book about which a publisher said, 'It is hard to see who would possibly want to read a book like this . . .' Visit www.gggraphics.com.au.

Kerry Greenwood

Kerry has written fifty-eight novels, a lot of short stories and several non-fiction books. She LIKES writing and now people are paying her for it. She was born in Footscray so long ago that the Internet was called books. She lives with a registered wizard and three cats. In her spare time she stares blankly out of the window.

Phillip Gwynne

One of eight children, Phillip was raised in country South Australia. He has a degree in marine biology and has travelled the world. His first book, *Deadly, Unna?*, won several literary awards and he has written many others since, including *Nukkin' Ya*, *Jetty Rats* and *The Worst Team Ever*.

Susan Halliday

Once an English teacher, Australia's Sex Discrimination Commissioner, Board Member of the State Library of Victoria and Chairperson of the Victorian Institute of Teaching, Susan's new business card reads CHILDREN'S AUTHOR. Having written a wealth of professional material for adults, Susan has the popular Marcy series for girls under her belt and a string of child literacy projects in tow.

Jack Heath

Jack is the author of six action-adventure books. He started writing *The Lab* when he was thirteen years old and had a publishing contract for it at eighteen. In 2009 he was named ACT Young Australian of the Year. He is now twenty-six, and working on his seventh novel.

Steven Herrick

Steven is the author of eighteen books for children and young adults. His books have twice won the NSW Premier's Literary Award and been short-listed for the Children's Book Council of Australia Book of the Year on six occasions. His most recent book is *Black Painted Fingernails*.

Simon Higgins

Simon is a former police officer, prosecutor and licensed private investigator. He writes critically acclaimed adventures set in Japan, where he has trained in Iaido: the samurai art of duelling. His Moonshadow series is published in Australia by Random House and in numerous foreign countries including the US. www.simonhiggins.net.

Leigh Hobbs

Leigh is an artist and author best known for the children's books he has created featuring his characters Old Tom, Horrible Harriet, Fiona the Pig, The FREAKS in 4F, Mr Badger and Mr Chicken. Mr Chicken is at present a best seller in the Louvre Museum bookshop in Paris.

Greg Holfeld

Greg has made cartoons, comics and illustrations since he was a small boy in Saskatchewan, Canada. He has done much the same as a slightly larger adult in South Australia since 1991. You can see his work on television, commercials and short films, in books including the Captain Congo series and at www.panicproductions.com.au.

Ian Irvine

Ian, a marine scientist who has developed some of Australia's national guidelines for the protection of the oceanic environment, has also written twenty-seven novels. These include the internationally bestselling Three Worlds fantasy sequence, an eco-thriller trilogy and twelve books for younger readers. His latest book for younger readers is *Grim and Grimmer 4: The Calamitous Queen*. His latest fantasy novel is *Vengeance*, Book 1 of The Tainted Realm.
Website: www.ian-irvine.com.

George Ivanoff

Author of over fifty books, George is best known for his Gamers novels. *Gamers' Quest* won a Chronos Award and is on the reading lists for both the Victorian and NSW Premier's Reading Challenge. *Gamers' Challenge* was released in 2011. Check out George's website: georgeivanoff.com.au.

Mo Johnson

Born in Glasgow, Mo came to Australia in 1991 and began writing in 2005. Her first YA Novel, *Boofheads*, was published in 2008 in Australia and in the UK in 2009. It was a CBCA Notable Book. *Something More* was published in 2009 and her first picture book, *Noah's Garden*, was published in 2010 in both Australia and the USA. She currently divides her time between teaching English, working in her husband's Mortgage Choice franchise, and writing.

Kim Kane

Kim was born in London in a bed bequeathed by Wordsworth for '... a writer, a painter, or a poet'. Despite this auspicious beginning she went on to practise law. Five years ago Kim threw her materialism to the wind and started to write. She has written one novel, *Pip: the story of Olive* and two picture books, *The Vegetable Ark* and *Family Forest*.

Phil Kettle

Phil is an international award-winning children's author. He has written in excess of 150 children's books including *Our Australia*, *Boyz Rule*, *Get Real* and the amazingly successful Toocool series. Ford Street is publishing the latest Toocool books along with Susan Halliday's Marcy series. For the latest news go to www.philkettle.com.au.

Sofie Laguna

Sofie's books for young people have been named Honour Books and Notable Books in the Children's Book Council of Australia Book of the Year Awards and have been short-listed in the Queensland Premier's Awards. She has been published in the US and the UK and in translation in Europe and Asia.

Doug MacLeod

Doug writes for TV and novels for young adults. His most recent titles include *My Extraordinary Life and Death* and *The Life of a Teenage Body-snatcher*. One of his earlier novels, *The Clockwork Forest*, was presented as a play by The Sydney Theatre Company. In 2008 the Australian Writers Guild awarded him the Fred Parsons Award for contribution to Australian comedy. Visit Doug: www.dougmacleod.com.au.

Lorraine Marwood

Lorraine loves to write poetry. Her novel *Star Jumps*, published by Walker Books, explores the verse novel technique. It won the inaugural Prime Minister's Literary Award for Children's Fiction in 2010. Her latest books are *Chantelle's Cloak* and *Note on the Door and other family poems* from Walker. She loves capturing the poetic surprise in ordinary everyday happenings. Visit www.lorrainemarwood.com.

Marc McBride

Marc is a carbon-based life form that may or may not be currently living in Melbourne with a woman, a dog and a miniature human. He spends most of his time trawling a large garage in search of lost rubbers and pencils. Occasionally he makes pictures that are of extraordinary genius or naive incompetence and it's often difficult to tell which is which.

Sean McMullen

Sean's first young adult novel was *The Ancient Hero*; this was followed by two teenage time travel novels, *Before the Storm* and *Changing Yesterday*. Sean has fourteen adult novels

published, and his story 'Eight Miles' was runner-up in the Hugo Awards for Best Novelette.
See www.seanmcmullen.net.au.

David Miller

David has written five picture books and illustrated another ten. His books are illustrated with photographs of his dramatic, colourful 3D paper sculptures. His book *Refugees* was a CBCA Honour Book and *Snap Went Chester* was shortlisted for the CBCAs. His latest books are *Rufus the Numbat* and *Big and Me*.

Jenny Mounfield

Jenny lives in Brisbane with her husband, three grown children and one very spoilt Jack Russell cross called Leo. She is the author of three novels for kids and young adults: *Storm Born*, *The Black Bandit* and *The Ice-cream Man*.

Kirsty Murray

Kirsty enjoys the company of ghosts. She is the author of nine novels including *Vulture's Gate*, *Market Blues* and *Bridie's Fire*. Her latest novel, *India Dark*, is based on the true story of a theatrical troupe of Australian children that toured India in 1910.

Sally Odgers

Sally lives in Tasmania with her husband Darrel. Between them they write books and run a writing workshop and manuscript assessment service. Sally's interests include bothering her kids, grandkids, the dogs and people on Twitter. Big adventures include running the Sydney City2Surf. Oh, and George-in-the-story is a real person.

Wendy Orr

Wendy is the internationally published and award-winning author of *Raven's Mountain* and *Peeling the Onion*, as well as more than thirty other books, ranging from picture books to adult novels. She also had the fun of having her novel *Nim's Island* turned into a feature film starring Jodie Foster.

Oliver Phommavanh

Oliver loves to make people laugh, whether it's on the page writing humour for kids or on stage and TV as a stand-up comedian. He also shares his passion for writing as a primary school teacher. Oliver's books include *Thai-riffic!*, *Con-nerd* and *Punchlines*. Visit him at www.oliverwriter.com.

Michael Pryor

Michael is a best-selling author of fantasy for teenagers. He has published more than twenty-five novels and more than forty short stories. He has been short-listed for the Aurealis Award six times, and five of his books have been CBCA Notable Books. His website is www.michaelpryor.com.au.

Judith Ridge

Judith is internationally recognised as one of Australia's leading experts on literature for children and young adults. In a twenty-five-year career, Judith has worked as a secondary English teacher, children's editor, community arts coordinator, writer and critic. She has twice been a judge on the NSW Premier's Literary Awards, is a Churchill Fellow and has an MA in children's literature.

Judith Rossell

Judith has been an illustrator and writer for many years, with books including maze and puzzle books, picture books and novels. Most recently, she illustrated the Skoz the Dog series, written by Andrew Daddo, and is currently working on a new novel. She teaches Writing for Children at RMIT. Her website is www.judithrossell.com.

James Roy

James grew up in Papua New Guinea and Fiji as part of a missionary family, but he thinks that being a writer is probably the best adventure he's ever had. He has written twenty books, and some of them have won awards. He lives in the Blue Mountains. Visit him at www.jamesroy.com.au.

Jen Storer

Jen is a talented and exciting writer for children. Her gothic fantasy novel, *Tensy Farlow and the Home for Mislaid Children*, was short-listed for a string of awards including the Prime Minister's Literary Awards (Best Children's Fiction) and the Children's Book Council of Australia, Book of the Year. She lives in Melbourne with her partner and two teenage sons. Visit www.jenstorer.com.

Lucy Sussex

Lucy reviews weekly for *The Age*. Her writing includes genres ranging from horror crime to fiction for younger readers. She also researches early crime fiction. 'The Thieftaker's Apprentice' is based on a true case of 1752, as reported in the Covent-Garden Journal, edited by novelist and Old Bailey magistrate Henry Fielding.

Shaun Tan

Shaun grew up in Perth, Western Australia, and in school became known as the 'good drawer', which partly compensated for always being the shortest kid in every class. He currently works full time as an artist and author, writing and illustrating picture books such as *The Arrival*, *Tales from Outer Suburbia*, *The Red Tree* and *The Lost Thing*. For more information visit www.shauntan.net.

Mitch Vane

Mitch is a Melbourne-based illustrator who works in a variety of mediums but is at her happiest drawing with a good old-fashioned dip pen and Indian ink. She often collaborates with her partner Danny Katz. They have created many children's books together, including The YABBA Award-winning Little Lunch series, *Big Bad Bunnies*, and the recently released *No Thanks Hanks & other Unmannerly Tales*. Visit her website at www.mitchvane.com.

Peter Viska

Peter's cartoons have appeared in newspapers around Australia. He has since illustrated the Far Out, Brussel Sprout! series and Aussie Bite books: *The Lenski Kids and Dracula*, *Hello World It's Me* and *No Place for Grubbs*. He is the author and illustrator of *Dan Dann – the Dunnyman*. His latest book is *The Greeblies*.

Michael Wagner

Michael is the author of forty-six children's books, including the Maxx Rumble series and another about a family called The Undys. He also sings and writes songs with his band

The Grownups (available through www.grownupsmusic.com). His current book, published by Penguin Australia, is *Ted Goes Wild*.

Gabrielle Wang

Gabrielle is an award-winning author and illustrator. Her great-grandfather came to Victoria during the Gold Rush. Before becoming a children's author, Gabrielle was a graphic designer. Now she writes stories that are a blend of Chinese and Western culture with a touch of fantasy. Visit www.gabriellewang.com.

Sean Williams

Sean is the award-winning, #1 New York Times-best-selling author of thirty-five novels, seventy-five short stories, and the odd poem. His latest series is Troubletwisters, co-written with Garth Nix.

Mark Wilson

Mark loved drawing from a very early age and loved playing drums on his mum's upturned pots and pans. He also loved comics, especially *The Phantom*. He now writes and illustrates children's books like *Angel of Kokoda* and *Journey of the Sea Turtle*, and sings in the blues band, The Dodgy Chairs.

More great reading from Ford Street Publishing

50 GOOD REASONS TO READ
TRUST ME!

JUSTIN D'ATH
SALLY ODGERS
ROBERT HOOD
DEBORAH ABELA
LUCY SUSSEX
BILL CONDON
DIANNE BATES
CORAL TULLOCH
HAZEL EDWARDS
ALLAN BAILLIE
KEITH TAYLOR
JENNY BLACKFORD
MICHAEL PRYOR
SEAN MCMULLEN
GEORGE IVANOFF
CAROL JONES
DAVID RISH
JIM SCHEMBRI
SIMON HIGGINS
MEREDITH COSTAIN
KERRY GREENWOOD
RICHARD HARLAND
SOPHIE MASSON

LILI WILKINSON
SALLY RIPPIN
SCOT GARDNER
JENNY MOUNFIELD
KATE FORSYTH
SUE BURSZTYNSKI
GARY CREW
MARC MCBRIDE
ANDY GRIFFITHS
PHILLIP GWYNNE
JANET FINLAY
LOUISE PROUT
DAVID METZENTHEN
DAVID MILLER
STEVEN HERRICK
MITCH VANE

DOUG MACLEOD
JAMES ROY
SHERRYL CLARK
MICHAEL WAGNER
SOFIE LAGUNA
CATHERINE BATESON
MEME MCDONALD
SHAUN TAN
LEIGH HOBBS
GRANT GITTUS
ISOBELLE CARMODY

Edited by Paul Collins

Introduction by ISOBELLE CARMODY

www.fordstreetpublishing.com

FORD ST

RABBLE!

A story of the Paris Commune

Geoffrey Fox

Copyright © 2021 Geoffrey Fox

The moral right of the author has been asserted.

Apart from any fair dealing for the purposes of research or private study, or criticism or review, as permitted under the Copyright, Designs and Patents Act 1988, this publication may only be reproduced, stored or transmitted, in any form or by any means, with the prior permission in writing of the publishers, or in the case of reprographic reproduction in accordance with the terms of licences issued by the Copyright Licensing Agency. Enquiries concerning reproduction outside those terms should be sent to the publishers.

Any references to historical events, real people, or real places in this novel are used fictitiously. Other names, characters, places and events are products of the author's imagination, and any resemblance to actual events, places or persons, living or dead, is entirely coincidental.

Matador
9 Priory Business Park,
Wistow Road, Kibworth Beauchamp,
Leicestershire. LE8 0RX
Tel: 0116 279 2299
Email: books@troubador.co.uk
Web: www.troubador.co.uk/matador
Twitter: @matadorbooks

ISBN 9781800464254

British Library Cataloguing in Publication Data.
A catalogue record for this book is available from the British Library.

Printed and bound by CPI Group (UK) Ltd, Croydon, CR0 4YY
Typeset in 10.5pt Adobe Garamond Pro by Troubador Publishing Ltd, Leicester, UK

Matador is an imprint of Troubador Publishing Ltd

*To those who struggled, and those who struggle yet,
to make the world more just.*

Contents

Avant-propos: Empire of the World	1
I. To the future	**11**
Iron rails to the future	13
Welcome to Paris	18
Behind the red lantern	29
Manure Street	33
The scribbler	43
Stranger in the Quinze-Vingts	46
In the brasserie Glaser	59
Veteran of all the wars	66
Two communications	72
II. The rabble — That's me!	**79**
Crossing the bridge	81
A policeman's worries	88
Plebiscite	93
Ink-shitters	98
The working class	104
At the Cirque Impérial	109
Binding threads	112
Le faux mouchard	123
The house on Dragon Court	125

Moist dreams	136
Workers of the World	143
The glove-maker's counsel	150
Initiation	164
The new man	168
La Ricamarie	178
III. At war	**181**
To war with a light heart	183
The firehouse	189
Republic!	194
Beyond the barrier	200
At the Ambigu	215
The new uniform	223
On the ramparts	235
New régime in Dragon Court	242
Pigeons	252
The October protest	258
Coping	266
Assault on the palace	276
December	298
Bombs – Battles – Bindings	311
«*Vive la Commune !*»	326
IV. Insurgents	**337**
The 18th of March	339
Paris libre	368
Rue Saint Honoré, 1ᵉ arrondissement (early)	368
Rue Perronet, 16ᵉ arrondissement	372
Belleville (mid-morning)	374
Quartier des Quinze-Vingts, *12e arrondissement (just before noon)*	378
A café near the Hôtel de Ville	384

Song of liberty	386
In Versailles	397
Storming heaven	411

V. Festival of Freedom — **421**

What now?	423
Gingerbread Fair	439
Rondeau à la Mazur	456
And in Versailles…	460
Festival of freedom	465

VI. Le chant du départ — **483**

Song of Departure	485
Smoke, fire and rain	514

Note on the author — **527**
Acknowledgments — **529**

AVANT-PROPOS

Empire of the World

The Illustrated London News

Saturday, October 12, 1867. Page 1

The Paris Universal Exhibition
(From our own Correspondent)

As our readers by now are well aware, France's 'Universal Exposition of Art and Industry', occupying over fifty hectares of Paris's enormous 'Field of Mars', is far too vast for a visitor to comprehend in a single day or, yea, in three or five. The immense crowds make it sometimes difficult even to shuffle in to see the more popular pavilions, such as the reconstructed Egyptian village where a dusky fellahin offers pony rides to children accompanied by their elegantly attired mothers or nurses, or the Chinese pavilion with its costumed giant – nearly seven feet tall! – and its display of fine porcelains and tapestries, or the large Japanese pavilion, where other costumed Orientals gesture toward scrolled paintings and other works unlike any known in our civilized Christian world...

For Emperor Napoleon III, the Exposition has been a golden opportunity to show off his ambitious program of refashioning the entire metropolis of Paris, under the stern but able direction of Baron Haussmann... It is all too much, too much to take in as one shuffles through the dense crowds of this palace! …

Fortunately, thanks to the invention of a celebrated French engineer, M. Henri Giffard, since the beginning of this month visitors have been able to view the immense palace and its exhibits in the Field of Mars safely from the air. We rise by a balloon tethered to the ground by a cable, which cable is powered, for the first time ever, by a steam winch, thus assuring the passengers a safe return to the point of departure. Your reporter and our illustrator hovered for more than ten minutes at an elevation of over 50 feet in the viewing basket beneath the immense balloon, inflated with 5,000 cubic meters of hydrogen, a process one may witness for the price of 1 franc. To ascend costs 20 francs, but even at that high price M. Giffard suffers no want of eager customers. Only last week, the Empress Eugenie herself ascended, from whom we assume that the illustrious engineer did not demand his 20 francs.

See the illustration on the previous page by our Mr Warwick of the view from up high…

* * *

"Ooh! You'd never get me up in something like that!"

"Don't you worry, Blanche my dearest! At 20 francs a climb, not likely. That's not for the likes of us."

"So high! It would make a person dizzy, don't you think, Jules?"

"Pretty high."

"But then – to see all of Paris. Soaring like a bird, I'll bet we could see as far as Belleville. Aah, it takes my breath away. Twenty francs, did you say?"

"That's what that fellow over there said. In that line. I asked him. A week's wages for me, nearly two for you. On top of the franc we had to pay just to get you in here."

"But it would be wonderful. To be able to rise in a balloon like that. It should be for all of us, any person, any citizen."

"When the revolution comes. We'll have that and everything, beyond even what old Saint-Simon dreamed of. All the riches and machines and art we've seen here in the exposition, it'll all be for everybody, for every honest worker."

"When the revolution comes. Yes, that will be a heady day. But it didn't work out that way the last time, did it? We had such dreams –"

"Ah yes, those dreams. And you were so beautiful then, you were my dream, I thought you were an angel come to earth when I first saw your face through all the smoke of that gunpowder. We dreamed that the rivers would flow with chocolate, and roast chickens and sausages appear in every kitchen, and all the wine or beer that any man can drink."

"I'd settle for coal for the winter and schools where our children can learn to read and write without priests or nuns telling them lies and making them recite nonsense."

"Right. Wouldn't that be wonderful? First we'll kill all the priests, or send them out to work. And then… But come. I want you to see our bronze association's display. That's why we came here, after all."

"No, that's not the only reason we came, not the only reason for me. It is just wonderful and amazing to see this part of Paris. But it's why they gave you a free pass."

"Yes, at least that's something. An invitation by the Emperor himself, for all the members of our delegation. Something to be proud of."

"Yes, Julot, I am proud of you. Not because of the Emperor, though – what does he know about fine bronze? But your comrades in the association chose you, that's to be proud of. Why can't we have a laundry workers' association, with an exhibit gallery of our own? We could show people our modern steam tubs and the newest irons! Oh, but of course, that's women's work. Not for a universal exhibition with dukes and emperors and the like.

"Uhhh– Don't turn your head, Jules, but when she passes, take a look at that young lady, coming out of that hall we were going in, the one on the arm of that short older man, her husband I suppose, and some other gentleman. That hat. And that dress with all the pleats, too, that would be a job to iron. But that hat!"

"Oh, her. Don't worry about her, Blanche. Your bonnet looks just fine, you don't want a little hat with a veil like a bourgeoise. We're honest working people, we are. Here, this is the gallery, where those fellows with their fancy clothes and cigars and that girl you're talking about are just coming out."

* * *

"Those were some handsome pieces, eh? Amazing what a skilled craftsman can do with bronze. I'll bet you'd love that nymph pushing away the faun, right, Victorine? With her hand across her breasts. She looked just like you!"

"Oh, please, René-Pierre! Not in front of our friend Hippolyte! What will he think?"

"Oh, right! Well, Polo, what *do* you think? Are we too scandalous for my friend the police superintendent?"

"No, no. Just too frivolous."

"Oh, René-Pierre and Polo, Hippolyte. Did you see that couple? They were looking at us!"

"Yes?"

"As though *we* were the odd ones! Did you get a look at her dress, and that bonnet? Oh, I almost have to laugh!"

"And that fellow with her. A worker, obviously, with that cap, in what he considers his Sunday best. That's a fine little jacket, eh? For a working man. What do you say, Polo? What does the imperial police have to say about letting people like that into the Universal Exposition?"

"Invited by the Imperial Commission, no doubt. He may be part of the bronze workers' delegation responsible for what we just saw. Excuse me, Victorine, our friend René-Pierre knows full well, and he should have explained to you, the presence of the workers' delegations. It's because the Emperor is very concerned about the welfare of the workers…"

"Concerned to keep them on his side, you mean! With all the strikes going on."

"Well, yes, that too is a consideration. But you can't deny that they are part, an essential part, of the Empire's, of France's, industry, which is what this exposition is meant to show."

"And so, *monsieur le commissaire*, friend Hippolyte, dear Polo, you are telling us that we must tolerate this rabble among us! Ah, but you know them well! Victorine, you've never seen the *quartier* where Hippolyte reigns supreme as the 'eye of the quarter', police chief in the Quinze-Vingts. It's over in the Twelfth, on the edge of the city. He's used to the dangerous classes, deals with them every day. But to see them here, in the Champ de Mars, in the center of Paris! Such people are a rare sight in this neighborhood, and they should be.

"Look, coming out of that other hall. Those two are probably workers, too. Look, Victorine. They've got themselves disguised as bourgeois, frock coats and all, but just look at the quality of their boots, eh? And the way they walk, that wide worker's stance like they're daring somebody to try to push them over."

"Oh, yes, you're right! Like Gerôme, our comedian in 'Barbe bleue', walks like that when he comes on stage, you may not have seen him, Hippolyte. His walk is much more exaggerated, though, much funnier. They're coming out of the gallery for the book trades, isn't it? They must have been taking notes, both of them have note pads in hand. Oh, René-Pierre, I know you'll want to go in there, you so love anything to do with writing."

"Well, let's stop a moment, until those two get past. I wonder what they've been writing. That taller one, with the big beard, looks confident! Isn't that that radical Varlin? That other one, the fellow with the red hair, is nodding to us. Nod back, Victorine, politely now. After all, they must be guests of the Emperor, right, Polo?"

* * *

"Do you know those people, Rusty? You nodded to them."

"No, just being polite. The girl, though, she looks familiar. Isn't she that actress we've seen on the posters? The face in the foreground, in the chorus line?"

"Yes, could be. Or somebody like her. I recognized the man with her, the short, chubby chap with the brocaded vest. Bougainville, René-Pierre Bougainville, the journalist. Rochefort calls him '*Bagou*' because that's what he writes, just blather."

"No! He called him that in print?"

"In print. You know how Rochefort is."

"But you wouldn't write anything like that, not our 'Eugène Varlin', our polite, correct defender of the workers."

"No, no, that's not for me. Personal attacks don't advance our cause, and anyway, I've never been clever at insults like Rochefort. You know that. I hope you've got good notes on the exhibits. Even though we know the prizes will go to the ones with the richest sponsors, with that incompetent jury they've picked."

"Yes, don't worry about that. We'll have ample material for our critique. And now that our work is done, what else should we see here on the fairgrounds?"

"Yes, good idea, we can take advantage of our passes for the day. We could go see the Japanese pavilion, I hear they have amazing paintings."

"Too strange for me. It must be like another world! How about the Egyptian? They even have a sphinx! And pyramids and such. Things we've read about all our lives. But Japan – Well, let's see, let's ask that boy.

"Say, young man. You seem to be doing a fine job. And on a Sunday, too."

"Uh? Oh, excuse me, good day, *messieurs*."

"What are you doing, working today?"

"Oh, well, there's always something busted, so many people coming through here, *monsieur*."

"We're not '*messieurs*', my lad. We're workers, like you. *Compagnons*. In the bookbinders' association. Just call me Eugène, and this is Adolphe, though we call him 'Red', for obvious reasons. And what's your name?"

"M-Maurice, *monsieur*."

"No, no. Call me 'Eugène'. We'll just use first names among us workers."

"As you say, eh– Ogène."

"'*Ogène*'? Where are you from, Maurice? Not Paris, further south, I'd guess. St-Étienne? Lyon?"

"Yes, Lyon, *mes–*, eh, I mean, if you please. Just last month I came."

"I thought so. We have some good comrades there, in Lyon. And what is your trade association, Maurice? Carpenters?"

"No, no association, I just work whenever I can, whatever they ask me to do."

"And what do they pay you on a Sunday?"

"Same as any day, monsieur. It depends on how many hours. Some days I can make a franc."

"A franc!"

"Excuse me, sir, but the master will fine me if he sees me talking to you. I have to get back to work."

"Yes, of course. Fines. That's what they do when you don't have an association. Well, good luck to you, Marcel."

"Maurice."

"Oh, excuse me, Maurice. Tell you what, Maurice: first opportunity, you visit us at Rue Dauphine, number 33, any Wednesday night after eight. And now we'll let you get back to work. But remember, 33, Rue Dauphine, any Wednesday, and we'll show you how you can defend your rights. Let's go, Red, before we get this boy in trouble."

I

To the future

Let us love one another, and when we can
Join together to drink a round
Whether the cannon is still or roars,
Let's drink,
To the independence of the world!

    Le chant des ouvriers, Pierre Dupont (Lyon), 1846. Chorus.

Iron rails to the future

… *Klunkety*-klank, huff-uh-*CHOOF*, – *aaAH*-WHEEE!

A sudden jerk forward of head and shoulders signaled that Number 16 had begun grinding forward, out of Lyon, toward… toward THE FUTURE!

The man in the seat facing him pulled an imaginary watch from his worker's blouse and pronounced grandly,

"Eight twenty-eight. Right on time."

Étienne laughed with the others, a release from anxiety. Eight twenty-eight, the man said? Yes, that was what he'd seen on the schedule. But nobody he knew, except the master in his workshop, owned a real watch. Eight twenty-eight it must be then, on this Sunday morning, the First of May of this year Eighteen-Hundred and Seventy, in the Century of Inventions. And almost the seventeenth birthday of Étienne Bonin, never before away from home, and now hurtling toward Paris, toward the City of Light, of Enlightenment, of the Future. The greatest city in the world. And only twenty-seven hours away, the schedule said.

To know that it was exactly 8:28 and not just 'half past eight' seemed as wonderful as the rapid acceleration, the coach yanked into motion by the fierce iron machine chugging and wheezing somewhere behind him. The jolts and vibrations of wood against his bottom and of the window frame against his shoulder and the clang of steel on steel beneath him thrilled and jolted him with their rhythm:

Badang-badang-badangdang.
Paris-pari-Paradis, was what he heard.

Because Paris was his great *pari*, his bet on his life.

He had never thought of Paris as a real place, a possibility for him. How, he wondered, had he dared take this enormous leap?

It must have been that huge mass meeting just a few Sundays before. Funny to remember how accidental it had been that he was there. It was because of that girl from the silk mills he was trying to impress, Madeleine, Madou. His first girlfriend, sort of, he'd met her one afternoon during their strike. She and her mates, all those *ovalistes*, couldn't stop talking about it. The strike, and now the International, coming to Lyon!

He pictured himself again, that Sunday back in March, in the great circular hall of La Rotonde with thousands of workers. He'd agreed to go because it was the only way he was going to get to see her on Sunday, which was her and his one day off. But once they got to the hall, Madou kept chatting excitedly with a dozen other girls he didn't know, her co-workers from the silk mills. And comrades in their big strike last summer.

Madou and her mates were celebrating. They were all *ovalistes*, standing all day at the oval-shaped mills where they twisted raw silk into thread, in workshops across the city. It was last summer that they had struck – the first women in France or maybe anywhere to do so – and with the help of other workers including the bookbinders like Étienne, they had held out for a month, long enough to win one of their demands, a reduction in the workday from fourteen to twelve hours. The International Workers Association, *l'Association internationale des travailleurs*, had sent them 1 franc per day, and in return, the women had joined, becoming the IWA's first feminine section.

That was why Madou had been so insistent on coming to the rally, to see some of the men who had organized that support and hear what else they might have to offer. And Étienne was glad to be there, too; he had heard good things about the International and was curious to see if it could help workers like him.

Thousands of other working men and women were there, dressed in their Sunday best. Some had brought sausage and bread, and he smelled beer from nearby, and there was a lot of happy shouting, as though at a party on Saturday night.

The chatter quieted in subsiding waves as a tallish, slender man in a frock coat and a cravat just visible beneath his beard took the stage.

"That must be Varlin," said Madou.

She and her workmates started jumping up and down and repeating the name, almost shouting it.

"Varlin! Varlin! Varlin!"

The man raised his hand for silence and smiled and announced how honored he, a worker just like them, felt to be speaking in this famously revolutionary city.

Étienne joined in the shouts and applause and cheers, because he too was proud of Lyon's revolutionary tradition.

Then he introduced the other men on stage, all workers like themselves. From Lyon, Rouen, Marseille, Paris – from all over France, it seemed to Étienne, who remembered having vaguely heard that Rouen was somewhere in the north. One was a lithographer, another a clothes-dyer, another a typographer. He imagined them in their worker's blouses, sleeves rolled up, tools in hand. And then the speaker got to himself, Eugène Varlin, from Paris, 'first delegate' – meaning the top, elected authority – of the Paris section of the International Workingmen's Association, and a worker-bookbinder.

A bookbinder! Just what Étienne was preparing to become. Once he finished his apprenticeship and learned all the tricks of the trade.

He had to listen hard and missed some of the words of the men on the stage, not only because some of those words were new to him but because of their strange accents. But Varlin spoke so clearly that even despite the odd sounds in what Étienne took for a Paris accent, Étienne was sure that anybody in Lyon or workers anywhere in France could understand him.

To become a master bookbinder, knowing all the skills, to be so admired by your fellow workers that they elected you to preside at their meeting – to do all that, it would not be enough to excel in a little workshop in Lyon. To test himself and gain those skills, the real challenge would be Paris.

He had been so lost in this vision that he lost track of the words from the stage, until an unexpected phrase brought him back to the present. It was he, that bookbinder from Paris who said them, thoughts he had never heard before stated so clearly, about workers' dignity and power.

Then at the end, when the meeting was closing, that same bookbinder invited them all to join in a song that had been written by one of their own, the workers' poet from Lyon, Pierre Dupont. *Le chant des ouvriers,* the Song of the Workers.

Étienne knew only the chorus, but there were some around him who sang out all the verses.

Now on the train, the words came back to him as he watched the rapidly changing views of tall brick buildings then smaller buildings then bridges then fields and distant clusters of thatched-roof huts, the countryside rushing backwards faster than Étienne had ever imagined possible, his train speeding into the future, rushing ever forward, out of Lyon and far from the Croix-Rousse and his little workshop, out into a new world that workers like him could create…

Let us love one another, and when we can
Join together to drink a round
Whether the cannon is still or roars,
Let's drink,
To the independence of the world!

Welcome to Paris

These eight fingers waggle to salute you, Mr. Sun. I see you now, peeking over the mansard across the square. *Bonjour, Monsieur le Soleil*, you who send your rays to make these fingers glow, protruding bare from my fingerless gloves, one yellow, one red.

Bonjour, I say, *Soleil*! How good to see you smile. Now just watch these fingers toss these colored balls up into the air that your rays may kiss them. Up the red, the green, the yellow, the blue, and now the red again.

Ah, comrade Sun. Perhaps this poor *bateleur* can draw a smile and a sou or two from that disheveled bourgeois, stumbling home after a night of carousing. Look, Sun, he is barely kept upright by the painted lorette at his side, her bodice askew and her lipstick smeared half across her cheek, but she is clearly more sober than her belching companion, don't you think? He has a stupid half-smile on his face, with his hat fallen over one eye, his cravat undone and the knees of his trousers – ooh, such stains! What a fine Sunday night they must have had!

Rattatatat go my little batons on my little drum.

Good morning, good sir, and Madame. *Rattatattat*. Ah, good, yes, look up and smile. I leap, I sing, I juggle. All to wish you a very good day at the end of a very good night, good sir. *Rattatattat*. Allow me to offer you both a song.

* * *

Ah, why thank you, sir, most generous, and perhaps, in honor of this glorious day and your mistress' enchanting smile, another sou, monsieur? Ah, so kind, though, well, a franc would be even kinder. Ah, yes, why thank you once again! *Rattatatat - tat-tat.* And *Adieu, adieu.*

Mmm. The air is still cool, with that rich perfume of the morning – horse droppings still warm, spilled wine already gone stale, and – oof! *Merde.* Real *merde.* And not from horses. Tossed from one of those windows up there. Good day, Madame! How impolite. And where is my friend the ragpicker, the *chiffonnier*? Ah, there he comes! A bit late this morning, it must be nearly five.

Bonjour, mon ami!

You see, Mr. Sun, a *chiffonnier* has so few friends, that's why he almost smiles when I greet him so. Did you see that? At least I think that's a smile, clenched around his pipe. The man is probably no more than thirty, but bent over under that big basket and poking around the gutter with his long, hooked pole, he could be fifty, or a hundred!

What do you say, Mr. Sun? Oh, don't hide behind a cloud just yet. Come on. A bit of juggling may cheer our friend up. In the air, the red ball, the green, the yellow, the blue, now behind my back – he laughs! Did you hear that, Sun? And –

– Ah, how very kind, how generous. Is this for me? Why, where did you ever find this?

Look, Sun! It is a whole, almost fresh bouquet he's given me! Some drunk lorette must have dropped it during the night. But no matter, it's still clean. Mostly. And it's, it's a whole cluster of these enchanting little white flowers, like bells. Ding-a-ling-a-ling! A bouquet of lily-of-the-valley. Just the thing for this First of May – oh, I know, it's the Second already, isn't it, now that friend Sun is up again. Saint Monday. That's why the flowers look a little weary. No matter, I'll stick them in my hatband!

And now for you, my dear Pierrot – oh, not Pierrot? Crochet, then, for that hook you use? No? Achille! My, such a heroic name for one of your profession. Then for you, my esteemed Crochet, excuse me, Achille, a special trick. Ah, see! It has disappeared. Your entire bouquet. And now, a puff of my magic breath, and three little murmurs, and – whee! There it is again! Now I'll stick it in my hat, and I wish you the very best on this warm, sunny day. Mmm, mmm.

Ah. That tinkling – are my little bell-flowers really ringing? Oh, no, it's her again. Ah, yes, there she is, with her goats and their little bells. The widow Marguerite. *Bonjour, Madame!* I call her 'Marguerite' because that's the direction she's coming from, from over there, Sainte Marguerite church. And 'widow', well, because she is alone, and of a certain age.

Bonjour, bonjour! It is I, your humble servant Crépin, *bateleur* here in the Twelfth Arrondissement in all of Paris where working people live. Goats' milk, my good lady, they say that that is very good for small children, isn't that the truth? The babes drink it right from the teat, much healthier than watered cows' milk. Oh, but the good sisters at the hospital insist on nothing but donkeys' milk. What do you say to that? Well, true, a donkey's teat may be too big for an infant's mouth. No, no, we won't argue the merits, good widow. We know you have a hard enough time, with only two goats to supply your customers. Not like those rude vendors with their braying herds of she-asses, much noisier and dirtier than your little nanny goats.

Oh, but here comes some competition. I hear the song of that other milk lady, the cows'-milk lady and her son and daughter, with their cart full of their watered gray stuff.

Qui veut du LAI-ait? they sing, and sing again. Just two notes – like on my flute.

Toot-toot-toot, TOOO-oot! "Who wants some M-I-I-ilk?"

Hmm, now who is this new young lad, looking half asleep and toting that big travel bag? We haven't seen him here before, have we, Mr. Sun? We'll blast him a welcome to this quartier.

Toot-toot! Toot-toot!

Uh-oh! A clatter of hooves and steel on the cobblestones – Whoops! That was close! *Toot-toot.*

Oh, and look at that boy! There on the opposite corner, that youngster with the travel bag jumped back so violently, he's slammed his back against the lamp post, the lamp post is still shaking. And the wheels and hooves must have splashed that mud and filth on his trousers. Oh, what a face! He looks down at his pants with such dismay that I just have to laugh. Ha-ha, *toot-toot.* Oh! That caught his attention. Now he has looked up at me and blinked, as though I were an apparition. Oh, but I'm supposed to look amusing, not frightening.

A crash!

There it is, at the end of the block. That cabriolet that nearly ran us over has managed to knock over the milk cart. And there she is, the milk-lady's daughter, jumping up and screaming, waving her arms toward the offending vehicle.

Those two urchins who just rushed past are probably hoping to lap up some milk before it all spills out of those big tin barrels making such a noise as they roll back and forth across the paving stones. I'd better get down there, too. And now that youngster, the new boy with the splashed pants is running along after them. Such a lively morning!

Oh, he's dropped his bag! Well, we'll just snatch it up and put it in a safe place, right, friend Sun? Where even your rays can't reach it. Here, behind this urn in the *porte cochère*. Now let's join the commotion. *Toot-toot!*

So many people coming out now to see what it's all about. Marvelous! We're going to have an audience this morning, a bigger audience than usual in this poor quartier. *Toot-toot! Rattattattat.*

Whew, poor girl, those birch-wood shoes and her long skirt are all splashed with the grayish-white liquid of her watered milk. She looks shocked, and the way she's staring at that cabriolet, still rocking though it has drawn to a stop before the ominous stone-faced building with the red lantern – oh, my. Yes, we know that building only too well, don't we, Mr. Sun? With the lamp that says 'Commissaire de Police du Quartier Quinze-Vingts'. The local police station.

Look at her face, almost as pale as all that gray milk, but now it reddens and she opens her mouth.

"*Coquin! Escroc!*"

"Jeanne!"

Oh, that's the worried mother. Poor woman, so thin and haggard. She looks frightened. So, 'Jeanne' is the girl's name – let's remember that.

"Hush! Don't you see, that is *monsieur le quart-d'oeil*? Oh, my heavens, they'll arrest us all!"

But Jeanne just stands there, staring fiercely at the carriage. He's getting out now, that plumpish man in the frock coat and top hat, poking a shiny boot down toward the street. Yes, of course, it is our friend – forgive the irony – the *commissaire*, the police superintendent himself. He's looking back toward us now, or maybe just toward the shouting girl, looking at Jeanne as though studying her for a police dossier. His driver has stood up and is looking back, too, and now he leans over to say something to the commissaire.

"Goat's ass, pig's fart, tin prick," she screams, and then again, *"Escroc, coquin!"* My, such language! 'Pig's fart' is pretty good, I can use that.

Ah, but now her sturdy body sags and she has started sobbing, poor thing. What's good, though, is that here comes a crowd, a chance for a song, light-hearted to make them laugh again, and a bit of juggling to amuse the gawkers.

Those two ragged boys, ten or eleven they must be, are already laughing, just to look at me. Only the newcomer, that older boy with the stains on his pants, is stunned and confused. Well, it's taken him a moment, he has finally stepped tentatively toward the milk girl, Jeanne.

"Here, let me help. Oh, it's your milk, isn't it?"

"Of course it's milk, you ninny! The day's work. All this morning, milking, then filling the jugs and clack, clacking in these sabots all the way from the barrier! That *quart-d'oeil* and his rig…"

The lad looks puzzled, as though he had never heard these words. His accent gives him away as a southerner, a Lyonnais I'd bet. But surely, even in Lyon, he must know *quart-d'oeil*, the quartier's chief of the 'eye', the police. But perhaps not.

"La rousse!" she shouts in his face, exasperated. "Don't you see the red lantern where he stopped? That's his office. Where he'll drag you in if you don't watch your step."

Oh, *la rousse,* that word he seems to know. We working

folks have so many words for the officers of the law, I can always find one for a rhyme in my songs.

We've already got five or six women who've come out with their jugs to buy milk, and here come three men in workers' blouses and caps, and there's a cobbler in his leather apron, still holding nails in his teeth. And now, your obedient servant, in my most elegant costume, your friendly bateleur, with flute and drum, will deliver a song for the crowd. First, to get their attention:

Rat-a-tat-tat, rat-a-tat-tat.
La rousse ! La rousse !
The gone has never seen la rousse.
Ratatattat, rattatattat.

That word *gone* will tell them that he's from Lyon. Now I think I have some rhymes for them.

Ratatattat.

> *The milkmaid came by today, biribi,*
> *With her mother and brother and ass*
> *As they do every day of the week, biribi,*
> *That pretty young girl, my dear Jeanne.*
>
> *Though she brought us no cheese on her cart, biribi,*
> *No brébis, and no bries and no brousses,*
> *Her cart was quite full of good milk, biribi*
> *Until suddenly whizzed by the rousse.*
>
> *But she's a good girl and she knows, biribi,*
> *As everyone says every day,*

It does us no good, dear, to weep, biribi,
To cry or to weep for spilt milk.

Venait aujourd'hui la laitière, biribi,
Et sa mère et son frère et son âne
Traînant la charrette comme hier, biribi,
La très jolie fille, ma chère Jeanne.

Si elle n'avait point de fromages, biribi,
Ni brébis ni de bries ni de brousses,
Son char est chargé de bon lait, biribi
Jusqu'à –Ooo ! – est venue la brave rousse.

Mais elle est très sage, comme il faut, biribi,
Et elle sait ce qu'on dit au soleil:
Ça ne sert à rien ni ça vaut, biribi,
Pleurer sur le lait qu'est versé.

Toot-too-too-toot, toot-toot!

Thank you, thank you. And now a sou for the bateleur, my good friends? Ah, yes, thank you. And another for our brave Jeanne? Thank you, dear comrade. The good people of the Quinze-Vingts, I don't care what they say about you in the fancier neighborhoods, we know you have hearts of gold. Ah, yes, Madame, no I see it's not much, but whatever you can spare will be good, it shows the spirit and the solidarity of our quartier, of the noble and ancient Quinze-Vingts! And now, this for dear Jeanne.

But Jeanne looks so astonished when I hand her these coins! A quick smile, but then a deep frown.

"Oof! Is that it? It's something but not much."

Well, I would have expected more gratitude. I gave her nearly half. All I can do is sweep off my hat in a deep bow and see what more tricks to perform. Ah, there's that lad, the one who talks like Lyon, looking around like he's lost.

"Le Trac!"

Oh, and now there's one of those newsboys, competing for attention.

"Decree suppressing all the International!"

Decrees, orders, mandates – always something new. No concern to me. But the young fellow who can't find his bag now looks more concerned about the news than about his missing bag.

Oh, one of the men has bought a copy and he's reading out the headline, with great emphasis.

"Arrests of the leaders, the International Workingmen's Association declared illegal."

"What? They've arrested all the leaders of the International? Just in the past few days?"

There's that funny southern accent.

"Ha! I doubt it. They're too smart for that."

It's hard to make out what the cobbler is saying, with those nails still held between his teeth, but I can make it out.

"They may have caught some of them. The others will be in hiding, and we'll hear from them. That must be why the *commissaire* was in such a hurry. He drives by here every day, but his driver has never before tipped over a milk cart. The police must have all their men combing the neighborhoods for them, they think the International is behind every strike and demonstration in town. Fools!"

The boy just stares down the street toward the commissaire's carriage. He looks dizzied by the news, don't you think, friend Sun? I know you're there, hiding behind that building. But maybe you can't see him. Now he turns back to look at the milk girl, our dear Jeanne. She has begun gathering up the empty jugs and putting them back on the now-righted cart, while her old horse stands impassively. I called it a 'donkey' just for the rhyme in the song, but you know, friend Sun, it's really a well-fed but worn-out old horse. She looks like a rough, strong country girl, that Jeanne, without make-up but rather pretty – which is no doubt why that boy from Lyon keeps looking at her.

"I was going to buy shoes," she says. "Real shoes, of leather or maybe even silk, with what I earned today. All gone. *Merde!* Someday I'll have them, and some day all the rich people and the police that serve them will have to do my bidding. Look at the boots of that rousse!"

Now they've finished loading those empty cans back onto the cart and they're ready to roll away. That boy from the south looks like he wants to follow them. He must feel lost. They'll be heading back to the barrier and beyond, wherever it is they keep their milk cow, somewhere beyond the edge of the city.

That boy does look lost, standing there and staring after them. The girl is rather pretty – oh, I said that already, didn't I – which is no doubt why he keeps staring, and they are obviously country people, so will no doubt have some food, and I'll bet that boy is hungry.

He sighs and blinks. The milk lady and her daughter and son and their cart roll away and now they've turned down a side street, and the crowd that had appeared so suddenly has just as suddenly disappeared. Time for me to move on, too, perhaps to the Place de la Bastille to perform some tricks and gather a few more sous.

Oh, but first, I can't leave that poor boy so forlorn – he's looking around desperately for his bag. It's been a good joke, but I can't be cruel. He has no idea where I've hidden it.

Ah, here it is! Oh, but somebody has opened it. Must have been one of those ragged, laughing boys surely, those gamins who had suddenly appeared, and just as suddenly disappeared.

Ratta-tat!

I smile and doff my hat and bow, one arm sweeping hat to pavement, the other poised behind my back. He stares. Startled. Suddenly I stand up straight, with a sly smile, and wink and my arm swings out from behind my back and thrusts toward him – his bag!

Ha! His gasp of relief makes me laugh with joy. Oops! He has tried to embrace me. But I'm too quick, and dance lightly away, swinging my flower-decorated hat back to my head.

"Welcome to Paris!" I sing, tootling my flute before spinning around and dancing to the corner and out of sight down a side street.

Behind the red lantern

"Do you want me to nab her, sir? Insolent trollop."

Hippolyte Mireau, chief of police for the Quinze-Vingts, *commissaire*, turned back to look at the shouting girl but said nothing for a moment. It was the moment it took to compose a dossier – he guessed her to be about sixteen, a peasant judging by her dress and cap and broad stance, thus not from this arrondissement nor, probably, even from within the city limits. The milk cart and scraggly horse must have come from a dairy beyond the excise barrier at the eastern edge, the edge of this twelfth arrondissement. That older, frightened woman beside her would be her mother, the boy her younger brother. If scrubbed and trained to stand like a lady, the girl might even be pretty and caressable, or so he imagined. But he snorted and turned away. He had no time today to dally with chippies.

"No," he said sharply, and turned to the building entry, rushing up the steps, barely nodding to the uniformed *sergent de ville* at the door, and continuing briskly up the next stairs to his office above. Before even taking off his hat or finding his seat, he snatched up the stack of reports from the desk and flicked through them. Pickpockets, a pimp, another pimp, a suspected housebreaker caught with tools in hand – then he stopped to study a page more closely. A boy had been arrested with more printed copies of a satire of the Emperor, again using that ridiculously insulting nickname, '*Badinguet*'. As usual, the boy had claimed not to know who was the man who had given him the papers, just that he could earn forty centimes for delivering them to the *café conç*, the 'concert cafés' with their bawdy songsters. How they loved to laugh at authority, those drunken fools in those concert bars.

There was another pile that interested him more, in different handwriting: last night's and this morning's reports from his more political informers, his *mouchards*, on some of the many subversives undermining the Empire. Of greatest concern to the prefect, Hippolyte's boss, were the Internationalists, since their organization had just been banned. Clever chaps, supposedly with ties to foreign conspirators. But possibly more dangerous were the *Blanquistes*, more violent but purely local; that madman Auguste Blanqui had no connections nor any interest anywhere but France, where he urged setting bombs and murdering officials. But then, here was something new, on a little sect of *bakouninistes* – that Russian anarchist Bakunin was as impulsive and violent as Blanqui but with international connections. He had been meddling in France since the tsar had thrown him out.

He had been hoping to find something for his report to the prefect. But as he already knew, even in this tense time, Hippolyte's *mouchards* were disappointing. Their spelling was terrible, the handwriting barely legible, the observations disconnected and naïve. They were mostly petty criminals turned informers to avoid jail time, with no special interest in politics and little understanding of the arguments or even the vocabulary of the conspirators they were spying on. More educated men, police lore had it, would be too conspicuous to penetrate the workers' clubs, but Hippolyte hoped to find someone who could do it.

His brigadier Chardon interrupted him.

"Excuse me, sir. There's a gentleman here to see you."

Hippolyte looked up, waiting.

Chardon studied the visiting card in his hand.

"Monsieur René-Pierre Bougainville," he announced.

"Bagou? Here?"

At the name, a ruddy face surrounded by studiously tousled hair and tinted beard peered around the door frame, eyebrows tensed in a dark frown.

"Ah!" said Hippolyte. "My dear René, forgive me."

"Forgive? What? The 'Bagou'? It's what my foes call me. But no matter. They're just jealous."

"I did not mean to offend."

"Of course not, my dear *Bigorneau* – oh, excuse me, I mean Hippolyte. You see, we all have nicknames. Curious, that one. Why should a policeman be called a sea snail?"

Hippolyte turned to find his chair, sat down and at last said, "Why indeed?"

"Yes, it's a mystery. But why they call me '*Bagou*' is also a mystery, don't you think?"

Hippolyte did not answer for a long moment. But then, seeing his visitor expectant, he motioned to him to sit and then ventured,

"Perhaps because it almost rhymes with Bougainville?"

"Ah! Very good! You mean then, it has nothing to do with 'bagou' as a blabbermouth. How kind of you to say that. You are most courteous, my dear –oops, I almost said '*Bigorneau*.' Mireau, I meant. Hmm. That almost rhymes, too! But that's not what I came for."

"I haven't much time, René, I'm afraid. You've caught me at a bad moment. Please tell me what I can do for you."

"Ah, a bad moment! The International, no doubt. Ollivier's orders. Yes, then the question really is, what I can do for you."

"I beg your pardon?"

"Yes, I know that Sûreté has caught Malon. Heh, I have my sources. That's very good, and I shall congratulate the police in my next column. But the big one, the bookbinder who has such sway over them all? Eh? Any sign yet of Varlin? No? Perhaps I can help."

"Oh? Well, tell me."

"If I may suggest, perhaps we can be of assistance to one another. It would be a feather in your cap, don't you think?"

"I'm listening."

"But not here. Perhaps at supper, say the brasserie Glaser, Rue St Séverin? Let us say around eight, right? They have excellent snails – *bigorneaux*, in fact."

At that, he winked and without waiting for a response, rose and saluted by touching the brim of his hat, which he had never removed.

"Brasserie Glaser. At eight," repeated Hippolyte. "*D'accord.*"

Manure Street

Étienne lifted and examined the soiled cloth bag, expecting some further magic. It seemed lighter than it should be. Inside he found his spare shirt and socks, the bottle of eau-de-vie, the pamphlets, but not the novel by Eugène Sue… or his employment booklet! *Le livret ouvrier*, required by law. If a policeman stopped him and he couldn't present his up-to-date booklet, he could be arrested for vagrancy. And it was his only proof of employability, that he had experience as an apprentice! Without it, how could he convince any master bookbinder in Paris to take him on? He would have to go back to Lyon! But he couldn't, he didn't even have the train fare.

The purse hanging from his belt inside his pants now was much lighter, after paying the 30 francs and 55 centimes for his third-class, one-way ticket to the Gare de Lyon in distant Paris. That left him with just 5 francs 75 centines. from his savings from many weeks of folding printed sheets, pressing packs of those folded sheets of paper tightly together, then honing his knife and paring the edges for the *maître* himself to prepare the leather or parchment or cloth cover demanded by the client. Enough, he hoped, if he were very careful, for the four or five days in the great city he allowed himself to find a job. At least, he wouldn't have to pay for lodging. He was sure he could count on his cousin Maurice, whose letter had said he was prospering here. And in Paris, once he found a job, he should be able to make more than the 2 francs, 50 centimes per day that he'd been making in Lyon, for ten or sometimes eleven hours a day, six days a week.

His only hope now was to find the building of his cousin Maurice, which he knew from his letter was somewhere near the Gare de Lyon. Maurice had written that he had a good job and he must have some savings, and he might even know some binders or at least know what to do about the lost work booklet.

He looked again at this poor and narrow street with its uneven paving stones, so unlike what he had expected from the great city. He turned his face up and squinted at the letters chiseled on the corner of the building in front of him. *Rue Biscornet* on one side of the corner, on the other, *Rue du…* Surprise! This was it. Just to be sure, he looked again. Yes, *RUE DU FUMIER*. 'Manure Street'

Despite the name, he had imagined Maurice's street to be wider and in better repair – because this was Paris! And even in Lyon, people knew about Haussmann's huge demolition and reconstruction program, which was what had drawn Maurice here in the first place. But Rue du Fumier, only two blocks long and with uneven and missing cobblestones, filthy gutters and only four street lamps, was lined by façades of narrow, squat, run-down buildings. So different from homes back home on the slopes of the Croix-Rousse, where the lofts, built for weavers and their families, had ceilings high enough for their tall looms and floor-to-ceiling windows for the light to work them. The windows here were tiny and dingy, and the floors so close together that the ceilings must be very low and he imagined he might have to duck to enter a doorway.

The stink and dust made him sneeze, then he blinked and stepped forward to knock at number 9, the address that Maurice had written on the back of the envelope.

The concierge scowled hard but then, deciding that the youth before him was neither a policeman nor a bill collector, repeated, "Prost? Maurice Prost? Yes, he lives here. Attic," and motioned with his head toward the stairs.

"He hasn't been down this morning," he added, seemingly disapprovingly, and remained at his open door, watching Étienne as he mounted the stairs.

"Maurice!"

Étienne waited a moment, then knocked, surprised that the door creaked open. Inside, in the shadows far at the back where the ceiling came closest to the floor, something stirred. After the moment it took for his eyes to adjust to the gloom, he thought he recognized the figure on the bed.

"Maurice? Momo? It's me, Étienne. Momo? It's me, Étienne, Titi. Your cousin."

The figure stirred again. As the torso rose, he saw that it was his cousin, older and thinner than he remembered. Rousing slowly from sleep, not in a nightshirt but in the same soiled shirt he must have been wearing the day before. Or maybe for the whole week before. A sharp odor of sweat and urine assailed Étienne's nostrils. He glanced around and saw the chamber pot near the foot of the bed. Trousers and a vest had been dropped, with no order, onto a chair, and he saw some other clothing in a heap in a corner.

"Eh? Titi? Here?"

"You said in your letter you wished that we in Lyon could see you here, and here I am."

"Uhmm. Letter. Letter? Oh, yes, I wrote a letter. To my mother. And here you are."

Maurice struggled upright. He found a pair of pants draped over the chair and began pulling them on.

"You said things were going very well for you, that there was plenty of work."

Maurice grunted.

"Well, what did you bring from Lyon? Any food there, in that bag?"

"Uh, no. Just some eau-de-vie. You're not working today? I thought I'd have to go look for you at some construction site."

"Hmm. Work. Yes. Used to be. Ah, when I first arrived here, there was. Plenty! Four years ago, everywhere in town there was something being torn down and something else getting built. But not now."

He tugged and tugged again to get his pants where he wanted them, and then turned toward the window, gazing dreamily.

"Maurice?"

"Those were good days. I started at the big Exposition, you know, the same day I arrived! Right there on the station platform, there was a foreman looking for hands. Then, even after the exposition was over, there was still a lot of construction, demolition, more construction, more demolition. You would just show up at a worksite, any worksite, early in the morning and get hired right off, even if you didn't know anything more than how to haul bricks or drive a nail. Ah, yes, that was the time."

"And now? Your letter said that you had become a specialist, a joiner, working on floors and windows, in great demand in construction."

"Well! Yes, indeed. I did advance in my trade, after those first days. When I didn't know anything except how to work a loom, and there were no big looms here. I became a joiner, a *menuisier*, I didn't even know what that was when I got here, a specialist in finish carpentry. Doors, windows, parquet floors were especially in demand. I even learned to make fine cabinets!"

Maurice laughed. Then he gestured broadly across the room.

"There. You see? My latest construction."

Étienne looked and was surprised to see a makeshift table, two rough planks set across two joiner's sawhorses, with sheets of paper carefully laid out.

"Is this a joke?"

"'In the shoemaker's home…' Well, you know the proverb."

Étienne suddenly felt deflated. He looked up at his cousin, searchingly.

"No work now?"

"Oh, well, you're new here, Titi, and you haven't heard. The construction boom in Paris is over. *Fini!* Haussmann was dismissed in January…"

"Hauss…?"

"The baron. Don't people read the papers in Lyon? All the Empire's projects for the city, the widening of the streets, the tearing down of whole neighborhoods, the building up of fountains and parks, all that was in the hands of the baron. And all that building and destroying, all that making of wide boulevards where there used to be little streets of cramped buildings, like this one, all that brought in the big money of rich speculators, building palaces on the new avenues.

"But then the money and the credit ran out, the debts got too high, it was all the baron's fault, said the politicians and the press, the baron was booted, and with no more money pouring in from the imperial treasury, everything just stopped. In the dead of winter. And now in the spring, when you would expect things to pick up again…"

Maurice slowly shook his head, with a sad smile.

Hoping to find something positive, Étienne stepped closer to the improvised workbench to look at the mysterious diagrams and drawings and lines of notes in small, careful handwriting.

"What's all this?"

"Oh, just some inventions. What I do when there's no work to occupy me."

"You mean you're not working now? Well, I know it's Monday, Saint Monday, so a guy has a right to take a little time for himself, right?"

"Oh, sure. Actually, it's been Saint Monday for me for a long time. But tomorrow I'm sure to find something," he said more cheerily. Forced cheer, it seemed to Étienne.

"Say, did you bring any money?"

"Uh, well, not a lot. Just enough, I hope. To last me until I find a job here. That is, if I can stay with you for a few days."

"Stay with me?"

Maurice rubbed his eyes for what seemed like a full minute while Étienne, anxious, waited. Finally, Maurice twisted his face in a tremendous, comical yawn and said,

"Sure, why not? Don't know what we'll eat, though. What time is it?"

"You don't see it from here, but the sun is high. Must be a little past noon now."

"Hmm. Time for a meal. You said you had some money. I know a place. Just let me get myself together, and we'll go down and celebrate your arrival in the big city. What did you come here for, anyway? Well, let's go. You can tell me while we're eating."

They headed back toward the train station Étienne had just come from a few hours earlier, the Gare de Lyon. Above the door of a brasserie he smiled to see a crude imitation of the shield of his city, a white lion, its long tongue out and forelegs clawing the air, and the words '*Le Café de Lyon*'.

"Remind you of home? The lady runs this place, she's a countrywoman. She talks just like we do! Louise, she's called. Here, here's a place for the two of us, if these gentlemen will just scoot over a bit on the bench? Gentlemen? There we go. Thank you, comrades.

"Hey, Loulou! She doesn't see me. So crowded here today. I'll have to shout. There, she turned. Loulou, my sweet. Two of the usual, for me and my cousin, he's just come in from our home town."

"Fine. Pleased to meet you. We're busy here, as you see. Did you come to pay?"

"Oh, please, Loulou, dearest! Of course I'll settle up that pittance I owe you, those few sous. Just as soon as I can. But today, well, perhaps a little more credit, especially since it's for our dear buddy from the Croix-Rousse, he longs for a taste of your good Lyonnaise cuisine."

"Don't 'Loulou' me, Momo. It's over 30 sous you owe by now."

Thirty sous? An entire franc and a half, instantly summed Étienne. Over a fifth of all the money he'd brought with him. And did Maurice expect him to pay? Étienne looked up at the woman, who didn't appear unkind, but haggard. Then he looked at the embarrassed smirk of his cousin, whose eye he caught. Étienne signaled to him, 'No.' And Maurice shrugged and turned back to Louise.

"Well, you know, it's true that things have not been going so well these past weeks. With the baron gone, you know, everything has been very slow this spring. But it'll pick up! I'm going to see a man tomorrow morning, needs an expert floor-finisher right away! And that's good money. And you know I'm a loyal customer, Louise. Surely you can trust me for another day or two."

Louise's reply was a short, sad laugh.

"Brains or kidneys, boys?"

"One of each. Please. Very good of you. And two beers, of course."

Even though he was eating greedily, his mouth full of sautéed brains and mushrooms, Étienne couldn't keep himself from talking about what had been on his mind ever since he'd boarded that train. As Maurice calmly sopped up the kidney juice with a chunk of bread, eyeing his cousin with some amusement, Étienne talked.

"You know, I had to come! I hope you don't mind, my being here I mean. It's a long story. But mainly, I want to find a better job and become a real master binder, but – well, I don't know now…"

And he told his cousin how he had lost his worker's logbook, his only proof of his apprenticeship, which he would need to get a job.

"*Livret ouvrier*? In my work, they never ask for it. I haven't had mine updated with the employer's signature since, let's see, a big job back in November. Yes, I know it's the law, but in construction, well, if they need you they hire you, and especially in the small jobs, the work boss doesn't want to fill out any pages, usually they don't even know how to write! But it's probably different in a workshop, where the work is steady, especially in a book bindery, they must be used to reading and writing and filling out forms."

"What do you think I should do?"

"I know some people who sell them, false or altered ones. That's probably why somebody stole yours, to change the names and the description for somebody else. But they're expensive, the good ones, and you could get caught. Or you could just go to the police station and tell the brigadier you lost it, but the station chief is going to want some proof of who you are, where you live, who you work for and so on. Have you got a passport?"

"No. I never did."

"No, I supposed not. Nobody does any more."

Since the rapid expansion of the railways, the many migrants and business travelers from one city to another hardly bothered to seek the required police or mayor's stamp for travel.

The two cousins sat silent for a moment, the one hopeful, the other pondering how he could come up with a solution. To break the silence and restore his hopefulness, Étienne blurted out something that excited him.

"I heard a speaker at a huge meeting in La Rotonde, back in March. Very smart man, very persuasive – everybody cheered and applauded. He was a bookbinder, here in Paris. I want to be like him. The place was filled."

"In La Rotonde? That's a big hall. What kind of a meeting?"

"The speakers were all from something they called the *Association Internationale des Travailleurs*, the AIT. They have branches in all the big cities in France, and even London, and Switzerland and other countries they mentioned. That man I mentioned, the bookbinder, he's the head of the branch in Paris. They were urging us to join, and a lot of people, all those girls who had held out in the big silk-spinning strikes last year, they did."

Maurice looked at him, raising his eyebrows in mock horror.

"The *International*? Be careful. Well, you're very young. And I know, what they say can be exciting. I have some buddies in construction, they've been trying to get me to join.

"The International," he said again. "Dreamers, they dream about one big happy society. Look out, my young cousin from Lyon. Those guys aren't going to get you anywhere! Not in this empire, the way things are going. Not anywhere except jail, that is. Big talk, big dreams. And now look at them, running from the police."

And in a still lower voice, he added, "You want a revolution, you've got to follow Blanqui! *L'Enfermé*, the Jailbird."

He stopped for a moment.

"Well. We can continue this conversation on our walk back."

He raised a finger to one ear and nodded in the direction of the men eating at the next table.

When they were back on the street he muttered, "No dreams, just bombs! What you've got to do is stake a gamble, a big gamble. With bombs or banknotes or whatever you've got. And win!

"And win," he repeated. "That's the part I seem to have forgotten."

The scribbler

A twenty-minute walk from the Quinze-Vingts but a world away in sounds and smells and rhythms, along the newly widened streets and newer buildings of the Second Arrondissement, Alphonse-Marie Bertrand awoke to the morning street noises three storeys below his rented room. Wooden wheels sloshing noisily through a puddle, the crack of a whip and a shouted curse, the familiar squeaking of the wheels of a heavier, clumsier machine and the bell and cries of a knife grinder, *"Rémouleur, rémouleur! Repasse couteaux! Repasse ciseaux!"* and then again. These signaled the beginning of another week, another week without a writing assignment to earn a few sous.

Alphonse-Marie, in his own mind a future candidate for the Académie but for the time being still *le petit Bertrand*, twenty-two-year-old ghost writer, part-time French tutor and sometime proofreader, peered into the cracked mirror over his washbasin. Sparks of morning sun glanced from the almost-white of the collar he adjusted to get straight. He fluffed up his burgundy cravat, almost new, a lucky find among the second-hand stalls in the Carreau du Temple last week. Then with the same finger and a thumb he twisted the ends of his new, neatly trimmed and waxed mustache. He practised a wink, a raised eyebrow, and other faces he had seen in sophisticated, ironic Paris, so distant from the blunter semblances in his working-class neighborhood back in Lille, which he had left just one year ago. The fraying of his jacket would not be apparent under his cape, and with his hat at the proper impertinent angle, he fancied that he looked as though he belonged to the great city. Or that the great city belonged to him.

Thus prepared to face Paris and to scout for work, he locked the door behind him, reached for the wall with one hand and grasped the notebook and pencil in his pocket with the other and groped his way down the stairs to the street. Surely today he would find something. He had just 4 francs in his vest pocket and was four weeks behind in his rent.

Things had been going well, he remembered, with his first by-lined articles in the Paris press back in December. He was beginning to make a name for himself, he told himself again as he stepped carefully over a drunk lying across the curb. Until the day he boldly signed his full name, 'Alphonse-Marie Bertrand' to an article in *Le Petit Journal* denouncing the excesses of the Imperial family, back in January, after the Emperor's cousin, that idiot Pierre Bonaparte, had murdered Victor Noir. Since then he had not been able to publish anything at all under his own name, and no more than occasional poetry and a book review under his initials or an assumed name.

A fiacre driver signaled to him, but Alphonse waved the tired-looking horse and eager driver away – glad that at least he still looked prosperous enough to afford a ride. Fortunately it was decent weather for a walk, and he strolled with his chin high, as though he were simply enjoying the morning air. Except that the air on this particular morning and on this particular street was full of noxious odors of both animal and human waste, some of it recently thrown from upstairs windows. It was a trick to keep his chin up and his eyes down. He barely missed a fulsome puddle as he stepped from the curb to cross to the Boulevard des Italiens. Its cafés were always the place to start for news and contacts for something that Alphonse might write. That evening he hoped he would find some helpful colleague in the Glaser. But meanwhile, maybe he could persuade some workers to pay for tutoring in French. He would have to try at that worker's boarding house, across the river on the Left Bank, in the fifth, a house full of ambitious workers with big revolutionary ideas but not a clue about history or literature or proper spelling. It was 'Saint Monday,' which meant that maybe some of them had not yet bothered to go to work.

Stranger in the Quinze-Vingts

It was already his second morning, the one after his arrival on Monday, nearly six he guessed from the light, when Étienne rolled off his mat. He peed into the pot and then, after peering down and hoping that no one was passing by, tossed the contents out the window. Seeing that Maurice was still asleep and knowing that there was nothing in the attic apartment for breakfast, he set off to explore the city, thinking maybe to spend a sou on a brioche and a coffee somewhere. Or at least to get to know this quartier with the strange name, 'Quinze-Vingts' – so-named, Maurice had told him with a laugh, for its old hospital for the blind that had three hundred – fifteen times twenty – beds.

The city was already awake, and on Manure Street he passed women and men heading to their workshops and women coming back from some bakery. Street by broken street he walked, dodging one-horse cabs on a wider avenue but mostly sticking to the narrower lanes, past used-clothes sellers, a traveling tinsmith's bulky cart, ragpickers dragging their sacks and probing gutters with their hooked poles, and even a small drove of she-asses and their drovers, crying out "Milk!" – a scene he had never seen in Lyon nor could have expected in Paris, the brilliant capital of the world.

He walked, staring and marveling for what must have

been hours, starting between Rue du Fumier and the Gare de Lyon and then daring into side streets and beyond, where buildings were mostly three storeys high. He passed lots of little workshops already busy at this early hour – leather, textile, tin, boots, even a hatter with a strong smell of glue. But no book binderies. Then the sun, which he could now see from an open plaza, told him it must already be about ten in the morning. Time to get serious about looking for work. He stopped and asked a stout, mustachioed grocer where he could find a bindery. This was the first person he had spoken to in Paris all morning.

The grocer just looked up at him, frowned and grunted, "We speak French here."

Not sure he had heard correctly, Étienne tried again.

"Excuse me, I don't mean to bother you, I've just arrived here in Paris, and I thought you might help me."

The grocer glared at him for another instant, then turned to a woman who had been examining his cabbages.

"Lots of foreigners. Too many, I say. It's because we're so close to the station. They throw themselves off the train with their satchels and think they've reached the promised land, and don't even know how to speak like Christians."

The woman looked up at the grocer, then turned to Étienne, then back to the grocer.

"Oh, you're much too grouchy this morning, monsieur Anatole. Yes, the boy has an accent, but I understood him. Where do you come from, sonny? Italy?"

The question startled him. Étienne did not know what to say for a moment. Then, taking a breath,

"Lyon, Madame. I've come from Lyon."

"Oh, from Lyon, of course you do! They all come from 'Lyon'. That's the train station, silly! Everyone comes from the

Gare de Lyon. But I mean, what country do you come from?"

"Lyon, Madame. The city of Lyon. In France."

"Oh, it's a city, is it? Yes, I knew that, but I'd forgotten. Or is it a country? That's in the south, isn't it? And do you speak French there, too?"

"Yes, Madame. Lyon is in France. We speak French, just like you."

"Oh, of course you do. But not like us. A different French. Not like us at all. You see, Anatole? The boy isn't a foreigner, he's just from far away."

"Lyon," said Anatole. "I should have guessed. There's another youngster in the neighborhood from there, says some odd things, too. But that other boy, he's learned to speak almost like an ordinary person."

"And you asked about bookbinding, I think. Right, son? Well, anything about books, it would have to be over there, across the river, on the Left Bank. That's where the university is, isn't it, M. Anatole? Oh, and there are booksellers all along the river, too, if that's what you're looking for."

"Books," the grocer grunted again. "Bourgeois baubles. I don't see why any working man would spend money on a thing like that. Or have time to read one!"

He laughed at his joke. Or Étienne supposed it was a joke. He thanked them and kept walking, trying to assimilate this strange encounter as he continued, half distracted by his thoughts and half trying to keep track of where he had turned, so that he could find his way back to the house on Rue du Fumier.

It was almost noon when he was surprised to see a gang of girls and women pop out from a shop whose sign and image announced 'Gloves.' The sight of so many working girls in their dull gray smocks reminded him of the girls he would watch coming out of the silk-spinning factories back home, and of Madeleine – Madou, and he felt a pang of homesickness. He watched these girls, out on break, chattering, as three or four entered a dairy shop for lunch. This also reminded him that he hadn't eaten.

Across the river, the lady had said, was where he might find a bindery. The Left Bank. Could it be? That was where the university was, was all he knew about that mysterious territory. He hadn't expected to find working people and workshops there. But maybe, if there was a university there had to be books. And if there were books, maybe there would be a bindery. He would save that trip for another day – he had had enough strangeness for now. First he had to find his way back to Maurice's attic, but he was no longer sure just how he had come. These streets were so confusing! Back home in Lyon, you always knew where you were if you could see either of the two big hills, or the rivers.

* * *

It wasn't until late in the afternoon, after several wrong turns and a moment of desperation, that he at last found his way back to Manure Street. He had spent a few of his sous on some bread and cheese, thinking to share them with Maurice or, if any was left, to save some for tomorrow's breakfast. But when he got to the top of the stairs, Maurice was not there. He found the door unlocked so he entered and set his meager purchase on Maurice's workbench, pulled a stool over to the crooked, narrow window, and sat gazing over the mix of slate and zinc roofs. So different from the bright reds of the roof tiles in Lyon, as seen from the top of the Croix-Rousse! Here some of the gray slabs glittered in the sun, accented here and there by rusted chimney pipes, breaks in the slate creating curious shadow patterns.

It felt good to be alone, and to let his thoughts drift over the things he had seen and heard that day. How flat Paris seemed, at least what he'd seen so far. Where, he wondered, were the famous hills, mentioned so often in songs? 'Montmartre' was one of them, he recalled, and he'd heard mention of other buttes whose names he didn't remember, but they must be out at the edges of the city. He longed for the Croix-Rousse, 'the hill that works' where his family lived and all the weavers' families lived and also worked in their high lofts.

The sounds of the city were also different and thus more disturbing here than in Lyon. The many carts and wagons, carriages and even double-decker omnibuses, their creaking wheels and axles and the clompity-clomp-clomp of the horses' iron shoes against the paving stones, the cries of the vendors and their bells and horns, the bleating of milk-goats and the shouts of newsboys early in the morning, a cacophony that was urban, dense, and new to him. Even now, early evening, he heard shouts and some vehicles, probably on their way to or from the Place de la Bastille. Very different from the pulsing, crashing *bistanclaque*, bing-bang-crash, of the silk weavers' Jacquard looms, rising and falling in every weaver's loft, up and down the hill at home. And in the evenings, there would be footsteps, shouts, sometimes singing, and more singing, mostly drunken, later on. But vendors with carts and noisemakers rarely ventured up the steep slope outside his parents' flat, and the few that did moved much more slowly.

With these remembered sounds in his head and the new ones coming in through the window, he watched the shadows lengthen on the roofs and let his thoughts float free, circling in opposing clusters. First, his morning surprise at being treated as a *métèque*, an outsider too strange in speech and manner to be trusted. And then, the girls in their smocks from the glovemaker's shop, who were like and unlike his memories of other girls in smocks. Or his memory of one girl in particular, the only girl he'd ever asked to be his *petite amie*. He had not dared even to kiss her. Madeleine. So ignorant, so unlettered, so rural, but – and this seemed comical, ironical – this girl who had never traveled more than the five or seven miles from her home village to Lyon, who had read nothing and who spoke in a village accent surely more ridiculous to Parisian ears than Étienne's own, she was an *internationaliste*! A signed-up member of the International. Whereas Étienne, who not only had read books but also had by now traveled halfway across France to Paris, had yet to take that step.

What day was this? Tuesday it must be, because he had boarded the train on Sunday, arrived on Monday. If he had stayed at home, today he would have been folding or cutting or pressing pages in the bookbindery just down the hill from where he lived with his parents. After hearing the clatter of the looms on his way to work. And nobody would take him for a foreigner, nobody would have any trouble understanding him, and he'd have no trouble understanding any of them. Because everybody would be saying the same things he had been hearing all his life, in exactly the same accents and with the same gestures and facial expressions.

Well, almost everybody, because now he remembered that even in Lyon there were foreigners. A few, whom he and his friends would make fun of, the way he had been made fun of by that street clown yesterday, and maybe by that grocer today. Especially those girls the mill owners brought in from Italy, with their mix of French-Italian patois, or the other girls who came in from the villages and farms, mostly shy and unsure in their new surroundings and full of quaint rural expressions. Like Madeleine. Those were the *métèques* of Lyon, the odd strangers. Today had been the first time in his life that Étienne himself had felt like an outsider.

He picked up one of Maurice's pencils from his workbench and started a letter home. He hadn't got any farther than to write, 'Dear Maman,' and a half-remembered phrase wishing that the recipient and all her relatives were well, when he heard Maurice return. It was the last moments of sunlight. The slate and zinc roofs glowed white under the sharper angle of the sun.

"Ah, you're here!" called out his cousin. "So. I thought maybe you'd gone back to Lyon. When I got up this morning you were gone. So. Welcome back."

"*Salut*, Maurice. You knew I hadn't gone, my bag was still there on the floor. I was just trying to get to know the city, or parts of it anyway. Were you working today?"

"Did you bring any wine?"

"No. But there may be some eau-de-vie left in the bottle. And I brought us some bread and cheese."

"Hmm! Thanks. Work? No, no luck today. I thought I had a customer, said he needed his floor repaired, but when we started talking about the wage, well. Not worth my time and the materials it would cost me. We're facing a hard time, Titi. So, how was your day? What did you find out?"

Étienne told him how strange he felt in Paris after Lyon, the noise, the traffic, even the smells were different. But something had reminded him of home, when he saw all the girls in their gray smocks coming out of the shop, the glove-maker's shop, chattering and moving just like the girls from the silk mills. Maurice laughed.

"Oh, and something odd happened to me this morning."

"Hm. Yes?"

"I stopped to ask directions, and the man I asked, a grocer, he thought I was a foreigner. And a lady there did too, she asked if I was from Italy. Do I sound really foreign?"

"You sound just like all of us from Lyon, my big little cousin. But Paris, even the same words, they say them differently here. Shorter, sharper. And some of our words, most people don't use here. When I first arrived, I talked the same as you, just the same as we had always talked, all our lives. But you learn. Just exactly what did you say to him?"

Étienne tried to remember and repeated as nearly as he could the exact words.

"Oh, no! Now I see what happened."

Maurice laughed.

"Here in Paris, never tell someone you want to *bagasser*. People here don't *bagassent*, they *bavardent* when they're having a friendly conversation. And you must really have confused them when you said you didn't want to *lapider*. Maybe they thought you were going to throw stones, not that you were apologizing for bothering them."

He laughed again, and Étienne felt himself flush from embarrassment.

"A grocer, you said? Where?"

"I don't remember exactly. Pretty close to here, a corner maybe two blocks away. Monsieur Anatole, the lady called him."

"Anatole! About so tall? Round-bellied, pointed mustache? Receding hair? Uh-huh. Yes, I know him. Anatole the grocer. And he knows me, too. He's a joker. He's not even from Paris himself, but from somewhere out west, Evreux I think. I'll bet he understood everything you said. He was just having fun with you.

"So don't worry about it, Titi. There are people in Paris from all parts of France and all parts of the world, all with different accents. Even more than back home, where we just get people from the countryside and some immigrants, girls mainly, from Italy. But in Paris, there are Hungarians, and Jews, and lots of Germans, and Bretons, who are French but don't speak French, except when they do. But the Parisians, even if they understand you, they take any chance they get to humiliate you – it's their idea of a joke.

"Here's what you're supposed to do: What you're supposed to do is humiliate them right back! You're supposed to find something to make fun of about the guy's nose, or his walk, or turn around something he said so it sounds like something else ridiculous, and if you can't do it, if you can't think of something mean, or if you're too bashful or polite like most of us from the south, *touché!* – you've lost.

"But it's impossible to keep up with them, their slang, their invented words, their clever puns, *calembours*. You just have to develop a thick skin. Huh! That's why I hate the Parisians! Especially those toffs in their cravats and shiny boots, who think we're all here just to serve them. And especially when they don't pay somebody like me who does a job for them! If I didn't have my circle, my people, I wouldn't have anybody to talk to here. Well, except you, cousin long-legs.

"But you'll learn. Though you may not get the Parisian jokes – and that Anatole has a dry sense of humor. For that you really have to be here for a while. Are you sure there's no more wine? Maybe we could go out and get a bottle. You still have some money left, right?"

"You said your circle? What's that?"

Maurice searched with his fingers over his workbench, until he had clasped a booklet which he handed to his cousin. It was now too dark to read all but the largest, darkest letters, spelling out something that sounded familiar.

SAINT-SIMON.

Maurice then found a match and a candle, and Étienne was able to make out the word 'Doctrine' and in smaller letters, 'explained and annotated by B.P. Enfantin, Paris, 1854.' Had Maurice become a mystic? But then his eye was drawn to the other papers on the workbench, with complicated diagrams and numbers next to some of the lines, like construction plans, but for what kind of structure he couldn't tell.

"And those drawings you're looking at…"

"Yes? What are they?"

"Well, you don't know the work of a joiner. Nobody can know any kind of work unless you've done it, whether joining or bookbinding. Or shoemaking, or metal-casting, or the girls' work, like glove-making or lacemaking. Your hands and your mind have to be coordinated, you have to keep in mind your calculations, to judge your materials and select the right tools, the right temperatures especially with metals, or flexibility for any kind of leatherwork, or the grain and softness or hardness of the wood and just how to cut the angles, in my work. And so on. With joining, it's the different woods, their kinds and conditions and dimensions. You have to know that the board you pick up to lay will reach just where it's supposed to, and that you have the right number of boards of the right lengths even before you set to work. But once you've laid many floors, or fashioned and placed dozens of window frames or doorways, or kitchen cabinets or bookcases, selecting just the right tools for each task, examining the wood for grain and knots and age and hardness, when you've done as many of those as I have, then you can do the next one almost without thinking, or without taking time to evaluate because you see instantly what you need, and then, especially when I'm down on my knees with the right piece of wood and the proper tools in my hands, my mind goes to other things I could make with the right materials and careful calculations. And sometimes when I come home, I draw out the things I've imagined."

"And what's this?"

"That there, maybe you can't tell, because it's just a sketch and you don't see all that surrounds it, but I do. It's a barrage, to protect the city from the river's overflow."

"The Rhône, you mean?"

"Well, yes, back in Lyon, it would be the Rhône. Or the Seine here. It's really an ideal scheme, that can be adapted for wherever it's needed. And here – well, that's a canal. An idea for a canal."

And Maurice turned from his drawings and flipped through the pages of the booklet, explaining as he did so that it was this doctrine of Saint-Simon, and especially Enfantin, that had inspired him to work out the designs, both for a grand canal and also barriers to protect against flooding. All of them imaginary structures, but possible.

"That's what I really should be doing, instead of installing floors and window frames. Look, here Enfantin describes his plan for a grand canal in Egypt, to bring East and West together!"

"Then this circle you spoke of, they are all engineers?"

"Oh, no! Hardly. We have a seamstress, and a printer, and an accountant who is now trying to make a living as a candle-maker, and an old soldier with stories of Crimea and Africa, and his wife who takes in laundry. And Sophie, a glove-maker. There are eight of us now."

He stopped and sighed, then held up one of his sketches.

"I'm the only one doing these drawings. But they are a good group of people. We encourage one another. Men and women, workers mostly. You should join us for one of our gatherings."

"Your gatherings? Like a political meeting?"

"No, no, not like that. We call our gatherings that because, well, when we're all together we feel connected to each other and to the spirit of humanity. And there is a certain person there, that glove-maker I mentioned, who has become a special friend, my *petite amie*."

The sudden solemnity in Maurice's voice startled Étienne.

"*Ta petite amie*," he repeated longingly, a girlfriend. If only he could have one of his own.

"She's called Sophie, did I say that? She's the glove-maker, she may even have been one of those girls you saw this morning. And so, I'd like to have her come live with me. That is, as soon as, well, as possible."

"You mean you'll need this space, and I'll have to find another place to stay."

"Oh, but I don't mean immediately, Titi. I'm not going to throw my cousin Titi Longlegs onto the street! But when you find work and can afford a place. Which we both hope, you and I, will be soon, right?"

"Yes, of course. Soon."

They both fell silent and Étienne prepared to stretch out on his mat on the floor.

Would he ever feel at home in this huge and hostile city? Where he was treated as a foreigner, where he easily got lost in the maze of streets, where the sounds and smells were all strange and often repugnant? And worst of all, where he didn't have a job and might soon not even have a place to sleep? Because Maurice would not be able to support him much longer and anyway wanted his space to bring in his Sophie. Which reminded him again of how much he was missing that. *Une petite amie.*

In the brasserie Glaser

Hippolyte Mireau did not normally venture onto the Left Bank, but a meeting with Bougainville, he decided, could be construed as part of his duties. That is, if Bagou really did have the important information he had hinted at. But he preferred not to attract any attention to this rendezvous, given Bougainville's reputation: the journalist was capable of writing scathing satire or flowery accolades depending on who hired him, even (if paid sufficiently) rebutting himself under a pseudonym. Which was why Rochefort had called him '*Bagou*,' and why the nickname had stuck. Not the sort of practice Mireau approved of, but it was his professional duty to deal with many men, and women too, of all sorts. In the evening, then, he dismissed his usual driver, saying he preferred to stroll a bit, then walked unhurriedly to the boulevard where the big hackney carriages waited for custom. Larger and more expensive than he needed, but discreet, and if Bagou's leads proved truly useful, the extra expense would be insignificant. The driver already knew the brasserie Glaser, 40 Rue St Séverin, in the fifth. And Hippolyte sat back in the covered vehicle, out of sight of any of the curious.

It was still a bit before eight, and there were several tables still available at the Glaser. Hippolyte seated himself at an inside table that gave him a view of the terrace and the street.

Glibness was not Bagou's only fault, he muttered to himself after more than a half hour in the café. He snapped shut his watch and slid it back into his vest pocket, then looked up to see a scrawny fellow about his own age with large eyes flashing between his hat and the big beard covering half his face, followed by a younger, pudgier chap with long hair poking out from under his hat, no facial hair besides a wispy mustache, and tobacco crumbs over his vest. The older of the two greeted the waiter with a loud "*Qui vive?*" and a flurry of arms before appropriating the back of a chair at the table opposite him and making it screech loudly against the wooden floor as he pulled it back and sat down, as did his companion. These were the sort of details Mireau had trained himself to notice, even if he had no particular reason to suspect the persons he was observing.

Another quarter of an hour passed before Bougainville made his appearance. When he did, he turned toward Mireau and raised an eyebrow as salutation but stopped first at the table with the two men Mireau had just been observing. They did not appear to be overly pleased to see him, and he heard the older of the two say something like, "Oh, the usual thing, seeing what we can come up with," in answer to some question that Mireau had not heard.

Then, with a broad smile, almost a smirk, René-Pierre Bougainville wheeled his plump body toward Mireau, approached and sat down, with a hearty "Bonsoir, old chap."

Mireau cleared his throat. "You said eight," he said evenly.

"Oh, did I? Hmm. What time is it? Oh, well, a journalist's time is not his own, you know. Important matters come up."

Mireau looked at him, trying to imagine what matters of a man of letters could be more important than his police work. But he had known Bagou for years and he knew that it would require patience to get anything from him.

"You said you had some information on a man we are seeking." He lowered his voice. "A certain E.V."

"Ah, yes indeed. Very clever man, that. For a worker. A rather stilted style when he writes, but grammatically correct. And he must have many places to hide, I would suppose, with his whole web of relations, and not just in Paris."

"You know where he is?"

"Ah, well, know? Let us say rather, that we can infer where he is not, and where he might most likely be. But first, we need to establish the context, and here perhaps you can help me."

"What do you need?"

"Just how many men do you have looking for him at this moment? And where have you tried? Oh, please, Popol, my dear Hippolyte. I must have something to fill out tomorrow's column, some special news that those chaps across the way at that table don't have. You help me and I'll help you."

"At that table? You know them?"

"Oh, yes, we *chieurs d'encre*, we ink-shitters all know one another. Jules Vallès is the older one with the big beard, and that pudgy bald-faced one is called Vermersch. I thought you would recognize Vallès, he's been around a long time. Very radical, insane opinions. He's close to that madman Blanqui. But, I have to admit, as a wordsmith, he has a real talent. No rhyme or reason, but his words catch the ear, and that pulls in readers. That younger fellow Vermersch, Eugène Vermersch, he's not even from Paris. From the name I'd guess he must be from up north, Belgium or somewhere near there. A rube. He writes obscene drivel, often in verse. Like a naughty schoolboy, insulting the Emperor slyly. He also writes for

Rochefort, you know. And Vallès, you know, he's the one who put out that nasty paper *La rue* until your police colleagues shut it down last month. *La rue,* a vulgar name for a vulgar paper. I suspect that the two of them are conspiring to put out another subversive publication, so keep an eye on them!

"You see? I've already given you some information, much more than you've given me. Oh, waiter! *Garçon!* Two plates of *bigorneaux,* if you please. You do like sea snails, don't you, Polo? As an entrée, of course. And a bottle of, I think a Muscadet de Sèvre will go well, agreed? Yes, waiter, a bottle of your best Muscadet."

"Sounds to me that you don't have anything, René-Pierre. Just more of your *bagou.* As for your column, that's not my responsibility. I'm sure you can make something up. You always have."

"No, no. I do know something that may help, I do. At least tell me this: Have you posted men at their headquarters on the Rue de la Corderie? Ah yes, I thought so. How about that fellow Malon, Benoît I think his first name is. Yes, I know that Sûreté has caught Malon. Heh, I have my sources. That's very good, and I shall congratulate the police in my next column. It's true, isn't it, that Sûreté has picked him up? Has he told them anything? No, don't laugh. I suppose not. Did you know what he does for a living? He's a clothes dyer! Benoît Malon, one of the chieftains of the so-called International Workingmen's Association, a dyer, that's the sort of man who wants to overturn the empire, imagine what colorful chaos that would create. And you know? He has become a journalist, too! A common worker, a clothes dyer. Also writes for that rag of Rochefort.

"Such a sad commentary on the state of our noble profession of letters, that a common worker with his fingers stained with purple dye can actually get his words in print. Like that man you're looking for, that bookbinder Varlin. Another worker-scribbler. Fiery opinions. Like those chaps across the way."

"Someone else has joined them. Do you recognize him?"

"Oh, I think – He looks so young! Must be, or could be, that boy from Lille, what was his name? Wrote that piece about Victor Noir after he was killed, hasn't been able to get anything published since! Yes, there are far too many ink splatterers in Paris these days, at 2 sous a line it's almost impossible for any of them to make a living. Me, fortunately, I've found a niche as a theater reviewer. That way the producers pay me, whether for a glowing review of their work or to trash the competition!"

"And what if you have to review the same play twice, once to praise and the other to condemn the same work?"

"Oh, please. That would be unethical! Only one article appears under the name of René-Pierre Bougainville. The other, when I'm fortunate enough to get such an assignment, a rare treat, to squeeze out two paying articles after a single viewing, if I get to do that, it is always under a different by-line. I sometimes use the initials of one of my competitors, just to confuse everybody. You have to be clever to make a living in this trade. I doubt that that boy, whatever his name is – Bernard, perhaps? Or Bertrand, something like that – oh, yes, I remember, Alphonse-Marie Bertrand, he signed his full name, on an article against the Imperial family! The innocent child. He's too naïve to survive in this business, and not just him – no one, and certainly not Vallès, has contacts like mine for paying articles. That's the real reason they're so angry and want to overturn the system, because they haven't learned to manipulate it!

"Well, I've talked much more than I'd intended. Secrets of the trade. Now you must tell me something. And I promise I'll make it worth your while. You would really like to catch one of the biggest ringleaders of the International, wouldn't you?"

"I? That's a matter for Sûreté, State Security, not a local police chief. My bailiwick is the Quinze-Vingts."

"But that's where you'd like to be, isn't it? In the investigative branch, catching the really serious criminals? Free to roam anywhere in Paris? And for better pay than as a *commissaire* in your rundown quartier. And maybe I can help you, with a tip that should be of interest to M. le Préfet. But you must tell me something I can use. Surely your friends in Sûreté have mentioned something?"

"Malon. Yes, you were right, I have heard that he's been caught. But no, he hasn't told them where to find Varlin or any of the others. Says he doesn't know. And, I suspect, he wouldn't tell Sûreté even if he did. Unless our friends in Sûreté were to use harder methods than they are permitted now. And probably not even then."

"Oh, very good. At least that's something. I can write that up. Yes, I'll say something in my column about this dyer's 'coloration of his opinions'. Bright red, of course. And now I have a suggestion of somewhere you may not have tried, a place where you may be able to catch our man, the other one, that bookbinder who has caused so much trouble. And if you do catch him, I want to be there, to write up the story.

"Check out that workers' canteen in the Sixth. Looks innocent from the outside, but it's full of subversive newspapers. And it's one of Varlin's clever front organizations, disguised as a cooperative, to draw in workers that he can indoctrinate."

"You're going to tell me to watch La Marmite? Or La Ménagère? Sûreté knows all about those operations. And there's more than one of those workers' canteens, La Marmite. Not just in the Sixth. He hasn't been seen in any of those places for weeks."

"Oh! Well, too bad. Because those were the leads I'd planned to give you. But at least you've had a chance to memorize the features of a very dangerous journalist. That Vallès may be able to lead you to Blanqui. And that youngster who has just joined them, that Alphonse Bertrand, he may be a link for you to keep tabs on Vallès. That is, if you're looking for a new informer. I'm sure he could use the money.

"Just a suggestion, to keep in mind. If you still have ambitions to enter Sûreté.

"And anyway, we've had a chance to sample these delicious sea snails. And the beef here isn't half-bad, either."

Veteran of all the wars

Unable to sleep, Étienne rolled off the mat, pulled on his pants and boots and, leaving his cousin snoring on his cot, groped his way to the door and slowly down the stairs to the street. The gas lamps had already been extinguished, though it was still long before dawn. No moon but just enough starlight to make out the shapes of buildings and the edges of the empty street.

He had to face his terror at the thought of returning to Lyon in defeat. And having to beg or borrow the train fare to do it. And he didn't even know from whom, because it was clear that his cousin didn't have any cash. But first, to piss. Here in the dark. To piss on a Paris street seemed sacrilegious, but he had to go.

Now, where to? That Left Bank he had heard of, the mysterious area inhabited by different sorts of people, lay just over the river. That, he had been told, was where he should try his fortune. Did he dare? To defy his demons he had to go and face it.

He knew or thought he knew that the river he had not yet seen, the Seine, was to the south, probably not far. The sky glowed faintly beyond one end of Rue du Fumier, so that must be east. He turned to the western end of the rue, and there turned left onto a wider boulevard, determined to walk as far as necessary.

Hoofsteps and a creaking sound behind him caused him to jump. Then a carriage and laughter, the voices of a man and a woman behind a silent coachman, startled him. Once they had gone by, and his eyes had adjusted to the dark and the glow had become a little brighter in the sky, he could see movement and remembered the boats tied up on a basin and causing the occasional creaking sound. It was the port he recognized from his wanderings the day before, the Port de l'Arsenal, which must surely lead to the river. He noticed several bundles which he assumed were cargo until a movement surprised him and he realized that they were people sleeping, outdoors, despite the early morning chill. Would he come to that?

Soon the city would be stirring, he had already seen the shadow of a woman with a basket– on her way, he imagined, to buy fresh bread. The city could not be completely still ever, but this must be its quietest hour. The prostitutes and housebreakers and night people must have all finished their shifts, the bakers were just finishing their loaves and had not yet opened their doors, the printers and artisans and shopkeepers had not yet headed to their workshops or stores or were still pulling on their boots or maybe still sleeping like Maurice – the absence of more human activity made him feel more alone than ever.

Sooner than he expected, he came to the end of the basin and its channel to the river. To his left loomed the dark shape of an impressive bridge. He saw no one on it yet, though when he reached it he saw that it was very wide, as though for heavy traffic. Climbing on to the walkway beside the carriage lanes, he looked down over the breastwork into the water and its reflected spots of starlight, imagining how cold and dark it would feel to sink into it. This was not a plan, just an idle fantasy, an imaginary solution to his dilemma.

"Hey, you! Beanpole! Did you lose something?"

Startled, he turned. The gruff voice had come from a man with an unkempt gray beard, a flat-topped kepi and threadbare jacket that may once have been a military tunic. He had emerged suddenly from under the bridge and now shook his ragpicker's hooked staff so vigorously that Étienne stepped back and raised his arm before his face.

"Whatever you dropped, the river maid has got it now, and if you want it, you'll have to cajole her!"

At that Étienne laughed. Or rather, exhaled a yelp of relief disguised as a laugh, before he managed to say,

"The river maid?"

"But don't jump in to join her, eh? No, no, you won't be welcome in her kingdom. So whatever is bothering you, forget it! The sun will warm us soon, and whatever comes, life is better than, than that other place."

A madman?

"Ah, come on down here. You're much too young to have really suffered. Come, and I'll share my fish and even a scrap of bread and best of all, I'll share a treasure!"

Surprised by the invitation, his first from a stranger in Paris, he stepped down from the bridge and sat where the ragpicker indicated, on the low stone wall bordering the river. The ragpicker squatted by his sack and looked up at him with a sly, almost toothless grin. Étienne waited, curious and amused.

"Well? Do you want to hear it? My treasure."

"Oh, why, yes. Of course. Go ahead, if you please." It would be rude to laugh. And he was worried that the man might turn violent.

"It is the greatest treasure in the world! But it is only valuable if it is shared. It will make you rich, as it has made me. Can you guess what it is?"

There was a mystery here, about to be revealed.

"You see me with my rags and my sack, my bed here on the stones beneath the bridge and you take me for a poor man, no? Not so. I have a treasure to share, but only with those who are willing to share it. You, my boy, may be such a one. And if not, well, nothing lost if you cannot take what I lay before you. It is life itself! The treasure of experience that lets us know what truly matters, and why we are such wondrous creatures.

"All France should know these things! This, my story, is my treasure, the only thing of value I possess. But too much, too quickly, is forgotten. Or no, not forgotten, worse! Retold as lies that leave out all the most important, the burning meaning, the bone-chill, the sharp stink! Were I a writer, but I'm not."

He laughed.

"I can't spell. Nor read. Not written things, not words on paper, but I read faces and events. And I *know*. I have been there, I have felt the cuts and smelled the blood and hefted the dead weight of corpses. I, and a few others, from all the wars, we are a dwindling number. We know what no one has written yet, what our princes or our generals never talk about. So we must talk, tell our stories, to anyone who will listen. We are the veterans of all the wars."

Now suddenly Étienne wondered whether he was before a madman or an oracle. He was not going to be amused but initiated into a mystery.

"Crimea. You have heard of our glorious victories, no? Glorious! The sticky blood of Russian hussars, the fumes of black powder, the screaming of the horses. Screaming, screaming horses. That's some of what they leave out, those orators. And the noise! The cannon so loud beside you, you can't hear the drums, the captain's orders, and you turn and see the Cossack lancer bearing down on you! Ask Piou-piou, he was there!

"Or you want to know about our war in Mexico! Trente-Six had stories – No, too late to ask him. Poor Trente-Six, came back with malaria. But he saw it, at Puebla. Disaster. And for what?"

"*Trente-Six*? *Piou-piou*? Those weren't their names, were they?"

The old soldier was sitting now and looking down at his feet. Étienne was trying to absorb this new version of the war in Mexico, which had always confused him. It was supposed to have been a series of scenes of French valor but ended so badly for France.

The old soldier poked his broken boot with the end of his staff.

"*Trente-Six*. Thirty-six nails in the soles of our boots. That's why we called him Thirty-Six, the only name we knew for him. He's gone now, but he left me his story to tell. Like Piou-piou, he's still alive, or was, if you find him he can tell you about the gore and mud, the arms cut off and the legs blown away, the loss of half his company in a stupid charge, and all the other glory of our great victories in Crimea.

"*Piou-piou* – that's the sound of bullets whizzing past your ears."

He looked up suddenly, confronting Étienne's gaze with wavering eyes, squinting hard.

"Ah, the wars! Fighting for the glory and honor of France, for *la Patrie*. That was what I wanted. Me and my fellows, hungry and young and unschooled, looking for excitement and steady pay and regular meals. When I was your age. How old are you, son? Ah, you will probably want to join the army for a life of adventure. The army. And then you can just hope they send you to some real theater of war, where there's another army to fight back. Like in Crimea. There were some real battles there. Against real fighters. We really did 'em in. All those Russian soldiers, and our boys too, on the battlefield, but our side won! Or Italy, where we were defending the Pope, we never knew why, why for the Pope and not for Garibaldi, but those were our orders. And we licked the Austrians at Solferino, we did!"

"You were there?"

"The army was there. And I, Achille Lefebvre, after twenty years promoted to *caporal fourrier*, quartermaster, a stripe on my sleeve and a squad of men to lead, I believed I *was* the army of France. All the wars of Boustrapa, our emperor, Napoléon le Petit, Badinguet they call him now, the little nephew of the grand Bonaparte. Glorious battles all, or almost all.

"Almost all. Except Africa, where they sent me and my squad.

"So be proud that you are French, my boy. An heir of the *Grande Armée* of the Grand Napoléon. Not of Boustrapa, the little Napoleon today, but the Great Napoleon of my father's time."

And that was his treasure? But the man was rambling, drifting in and out of excitement, seeming to drowse and then straightening suddenly to speak of *gloire* and something dark and awful that he knew from Africa, 'caves' and 'smoke' and 'children'. Étienne made out little from his mumblings. And then again, more loudly, the old soldier shouted, "La Grande Armée!"

Two communications

Préfecture de Police, Ville de Paris
12e Arrondissement, Quartier des Quinze-Vingts

Confidential to M. Joseph Marie Pietri, Prefect

Paris, 6 July 1870

M. le Préfet,

I have the honor of submitting to Your Excellency this report requested by you, on all those activities within the *quartier* of the Quinze-Vingts and the Twelfth Arrondissement generally which may represent a danger to the integrity and stability of municipal order and of the Empire.

To begin on a positive note, I am pleased to report that, despite the interruption of urban renovation following the dismissal in January last of Baron Haussmann, and the resulting idleness of many workers in the building and related trades, the increase in common crimes such as market theft, housebreaking, and other larceny has been only moderate. Assault and violent crime continue to be a problem, but, as you will see from the attached statistical table, these have not been significantly greater than in the year previous

– unlike, I may add, the situation in certain other, more peripheral arrondissments, beyond the scope of this report. You will note from the attached table, however, that there has been a marked increase in the number of unregistered prostitutes detained in this *quartier*, particularly around popular drinking establishments on our easternmost streets. Many of these women, we believe, actually proceed from the neighboring eleventh and twentieth arrondissements, with their greater proportion of working-class families. When stopped by our officers, these women, some in their late thirties and even older, claim to be new to the trade and profess ignorance of the requirement to register and submit to the monthly medical examinations, and thus may become a serious menace to public health. Whenever possible, these women are fined and confined in jail overnight, but this system is not entirely effective, as we have neither enough *sergents de ville* to detain all the infractresses nor adequate cell space. I therefore renew my petition, for you to transmit to the government of M. Ollivier, for funds to hire as many as fifteen to twenty additional uniformed officers to cope with this problem in addition to all their other duties.

A more serious problem is that the forced idleness of a large part of the laboring population, first noted two years ago but now more widespread, coupled with resentment over the increasing rigor of disciplinary measures in our larger industries, have contributed to a marked increase in general rowdiness and to displays of disrespect for our institutions and for the Emperor personally, especially in the café-concerts and other drinking establishments. As the Government of M. Ollivier is well aware, even in the absence of the agitation and possibly treasonous activities of the International Workingmen's Association, there remain in the city conspiratorial groups eager to recruit candidates from among the brutish poor for dangerous acts of violence. We continue to be particularly watchful of the followers of Auguste Blanqui, who himself remains at large, presumably somewhere in Paris, and also the many Proudhonists, some of whom may also collaborate with *Blanquistes* in the preparation of violent acts. We have also detected subversive literature, calling for the overthrow of our entire system, printed by followers of the Russian Bakunin.

Aside from the direct influence of such well-known agitators, our plainclothesmen report strong Republican sentiment in declarations and particularly songs in the popular concert cafés or *caf'conç*, particularly by imitators of the notorious Mme. Bordas, whose rendition of the extremely insulting *La Canaille* very nearly provoked a revolution during Victor Noir's funeral last January. The *chanteuses* are aware that they are subject to heavy fines or imprisonment for subversive lyrics, but nevertheless persist, knowing that our men may hesitate to take action, to avoid being discovered and possibly subjected to physical abuse, as has happened on more than one occasion. These songs are repeated with timely variations, but they are not entirely improvised, and we have even confiscated printed versions of some of them. Almost all contain very insulting references to our Emperor, continually referred to as '*Badinguet*', and to his Empress and family or to the Government of M. Ollivier, which out of modesty I am reluctant to quote here to Your Excellency. However, these printed sheets are now in our archives for Your Excellency or any other of our authorities to consult. We have so far been unable to discover the true identities of their authors, who naturally hide behind pseudonyms.

We will continue to exercise vigilance over these '*caf'conç*' and other manifestations of anti-Imperial sentiment. As for the best police strategy for countering this tendency, may I suggest identifying some capable songwriters of our own, to turn the focus of protest songs away from our Emperor and focus instead on the dangers of foreign elements. The recent tensions with the King of Prussia, much discussed in the Monarchist and Bonapartist press, suggest that this may be an effective approach.

> With no further information to report, I remain
> Your faithful and obedient servant,
>
> (signed)
> Hippolyte-Louis Mireau
> Commissaire,
> Quartier des Quinze-Vingts, Twelfth Arrondissement

* * *

A large, unflattering caricature of Empress Eugénie and the Emperor's head of government, Émile Ollivier and this article filled the front page of a never-before-seen newspaper called La Sonnerie, *which listed its editor as a certain 'J. Vingtras'.*

The Holy Oil of a Spanish Lady in the Garden of Ol(l)ives
by our correspondent from Lille

Just this past week our distinguished Head of Government, M. Oleaginous Fruit Tree, announced a fatal blow to subversion by his suppression of the International

Workingmen's Association. And, indeed, the leaders of that association which so frightened that gentleman are now in prison at Mazas or in hiding, and their leaflets and agitation have not disturbed the good bourgeois of Paris nor any other part of France since his decree. But, mysteriously, the protests against Fruit Tree's government and the strikes against employers continue, accumulating even greater force, extending far beyond our capital, while the fragile scaffold beneath the Emperor's throne trembles more violently than before. It is in this dire moment that our Spanish dame has burst upon the scene, waving a censer of holy incense and demanding a new and more Catholic monarch for the throne of her native land.

Amazingly, despite the fumes of incense and the laying on of sacred olive oil, the Empire is assailed by renewed strikes by bronze workers, shoemakers, and even laundresses in Paris and surrounding areas, and a whole wave of strikes in other cities, from coal miners in Lille to the steel workers of Le Creusot and especially in Lyon, where the strike of silk-weavers has paralyzed industry for nearly a month. How is this possible in the absence of the International? Could it be that the general economic crisis and the fall in exports and thus in the profits of the big industrialists, which has spurred them to lengthen work hours and impose new and more onerous fines for all manner of supposed infractions, is contributing to the unrest? And all that in combination with the Empire's use of military force in support of those employers and the harsh repression of the striking miners at Le Creusot, is proving more subversive than all the rallies, leaflets and posters.

However, the Government seems to entertain a different

theory. The Emperor appears to have concluded that he can improve the economy and win back the support of the laboring populace by demonstrating French primacy in Europe. That, and the influence of his pious Spanish Empress, must be why he is meddling in the Spanish succession, insisting on his Catholic candidate for the throne of that picturesque and backward country! So far the only result has been to increase tension with the King of Prussia – who would prefer a Protestant – over an unnecessary and ridiculous issue. No doubt Badinguet hopes this tension will distract the workers from their bellies and fatigues. And of more immediate concern to His Royal Highness, help persuade them to vote 'Yes' on his duplicitously worded plebiscite.

II

The rabble – That's me!

In the old French city
there lives a race of iron,
whose soul burns like a furnace
that bronzes flesh with fire.
Its sons are birthed on mats of straw,
their palace but a crumbling shack.
That's the rabble!
Fine then! That's me!

Dans la vieille cité française
Existe une race de fer,
Dont l'âme comme une fournaise
A de son feu bronzé la chair.
Tous ses fils naissent sur la paille,
Pour palais, ils n'ont qu'un taudis.
C'est la canaille!
Eh bien! J'en suis!

First verse of *La Canaille*, 1865.

Crossing the bridge

"Come one! Come all!"

Rat-a-tat-tat, rat-a-tat-tat

"The mighty Hercule Taureau, Hercule, I say, Hercule will display his strength and lift your spirits! You there, rushing across the bridge, tarry but a moment to see this great wonder!"

Rat-a-tat-tat rat-a-tat-tat

Étienne had let another day pass in indecision, but now he was finally determined to cross the bridge to the Left Bank, to escape the fate of the old veteran and make his fortune on the other side. He passed close enough to hear the bateleur say to his confederate,

"I told you, my mighty friend, that we would have a grand crowd here on the Pont d'Austerlitz this morning. And so we do! If only we can get enough of them to stop long enough to watch you perform."

Rat-a-tat-tat! Toot-toot, toot-toot!

"Gentlemen! Gentlemen! Workers! Bourgeois! Mesdames! Stop for just a moment and you will see something that will amaze you and improve your day. Hercule here will match any man in feats of strength. Does any man dare?

"You there, with that cart full of, what is it you're pushing? Bronze works! Such cunning, shiny sculptures. What must this

weigh, this cart loaded with enormous pieces? You doubt that the mighty Hercule can lift it? You underestimate the great bull. He will crouch, like that, yes, very good, Hercou, there you go, yes, he crouches to get between the wheels and–

"*Look! Look, everyone, see the mighty Atlas holding up the world, no, it is our very own Hercule Taureau holding high a wagon loaded with a foultitude of kilograms, a hyper foultitude, a gadzillion or more kilos it must be!*

"*Careful now, my dear Hercule, a sudden drop may break the axle. And you, dear lad, surely this feat is worth a sou or two.* Toot-toot!

"*Very good, thank you, thank you. And thank you, too, monsieur. Oh, and Madame, how kind!*"

Étienne was not quite sure but he thought that it was the same busker he had encountered just days before, or someone very like him, now accompanied by the sweating, grinning giant who waved his arms to beckon challengers. Beyond these two street performers he saw an enormous structure set on a narrow island in the middle of the river, a castle, or no, it must be the cathedral, the famous Notre-Dame. The sight of the cathedral and the drumming of the *bateleur* added ceremony to his crossing of the bridge.

But then his gaze was interrupted by a broadsheet thrust before his nose.

"Take it, and vote 'No'!" said the boy before rushing off and disappearing into the crowd on the bridge.

He stuffed the leaflet into his shirt and, anxious to get away before the busker and his buddy noticed him – to make more jokes at his expense – hurried across.

Now for the first time on the fabled Left Bank and clutching the forbidden leaflet under his shirt, he felt near to panic. Alone, in new territory. He stared at the fence with the sign 'Jardin des Plantes', not clear what that meant, and then looked back to the river where he saw the booksellers' stalls along the quays. Books! Something familiar.

Trying his best not to sound like a foreigner, he approached one of the vendors and asked, as politely and clearly as he could, where he might find a bindery. The man squinted through the smoke from his pipe, then in a gesture so sudden it startled him, waved to his right and said, "Bunch of them, over there. In the Sixth."

Unsure what he meant, Étienne merely nodded and thanked him, and headed in the direction of the wave. Soon he spotted a sign with white letters '5e arr' above the name of the *rue*, 'CUVIER'. Oh, of course! If this was the Fifth Arrondissement, the sixth had to be next. Little by little, he was going to get to know the geography of Paris.

And more than the geography. Having passed another sign that said Sixth Arrondissement, he stared open-mouthed at ornate medieval façades of buildings on the blocks further from the river. But nothing that looked anything like the only bindery he knew, in Lyon.

He entered another narrow street and, after looking up and down at the many signs advertising 'Hats' and 'Wines', 'Haberdashery' and even 'Sculpture', he was surprised to spot one on a second floor announcing *'Reliure'*.

He had not expected to find a binding workshop so high up – his shop in Lyon was on street level, designed for walk-in trade. He climbed the two flights of stairs and found another surprise: the space beyond the open door of 'Engel Reliure' was enormous! He could see thirty or forty workers, all seemingly very busy, some bent over tables, others operating enormous presses, and further back the caps of women who must be sitting and working at sewing frames. No one seemed to be waiting to attend to a customer or a messenger or a prospective worker like him.

He stood there, just inside the entrance for several minutes, taking in every detail he could and unsure what to do until at last one of the men took notice of him and asked gruffly but not unkindly, "Well? What are you looking for?"

"Nothing. I mean, well, could I speak to the boss?"

The man just jerked his head in the direction of a slight, balding man standing and supervising another man carefully cutting a large piece of leather. Étienne thanked the worker and walked over.

Their conversation was brief. He tried to explain, over the noise of machines and the distractions of the man glancing around to the various workstations, that he had three years of apprenticeship.

"Let's see your work booklet."

"I don't have it. It was stolen…"

And with that the maître raised his arm so suddenly that Étienne stepped back. The gesture ended with a flick of the hand, as though brushing away something unwanted, and the man turned back to overlooking the tasks he had been overlooking before.

Dejected, Étienne shuffled back toward the stairs, where the same worker who had first spoken to him signaled him to approach.

"Lost your work booklet? Happens all the time. But you know, sonny, it probably wouldn't have helped. The only way to get a job here is if they know you. Where were you working last?"

"Lyon."

"Lyon? That won't help! Well, good luck to you."

And down the two flights of stairs to the street, which now seemed even more hostile than before.

This giant bindery was so unlike his little workshop back home, where the six workers kept busy but not frantic. And Paris was so unlike Lyon. Where he had had friends, and family. And even, well, not a girlfriend exactly, but at least what he'd thought was a potential relationship with a girl who was keen on the International.

Stumbling along, back toward the bridge he'd crossed early this morning, and hungry – it was well after midday, he realized, and he hadn't eaten all day. He had just a few coins left, too few to last more than, well, how long? And bread and everything was more expensive here. How long could he go without eating? If he didn't find a job soon, he may have to find out. He tried to laugh at his predicament.

"Hey! What're you smiling about, you young vagabond?"

The voice startled him. It came from a mustachioed man under the big cocked hat of a *sergent de ville*, belly thrust forward in his dark frock coat and his hand on the pommel of his sword.

"He must be another one from that gang!" called out a second policeman, taller and thinner than the first one but also with mustache, sword and all the rest.

The shorter, stouter man stepped directly in front of Étienne.

"Where are your buddies, scoundrel? Left you behind? You're not even from this quartier, are you?"

"No, sir. I'm from Lyon, Terreaux quarter. On the Croix-Rousse."

"Terreaux? Lyon? Then what are you doing here, spreading your foul propaganda, you and all your buddies? You want to boycott the plebiscite? Cry out, *'Vive l'Empereur!'*"

"But I don't have any buddies. I'm not trying to boycott anything."

"Shout it!"

"Shout it out, like this," said the other *sergot*. *"Vive l'Empereur!"*

"Sir? I was just walking, peaceably, back to the Quinze-Vingts. I'm just visiting here."

"Hah! 'Visiting.' Show me your passport!"

"I don't have one."

"They never do. Leave him be, Régi. He's not one of them."

"You, boy. Did you see them? Five or six men, ordinary workers, handing out leaflets against Sunday's vote?"

"No, sir. I didn't see anybody handing out anything. Oh," it suddenly occurred to him to say, "unless it was that group of workers I saw talking and laughing just back there, along that street behind me."

"Oh yes? So you did see something!"

The stout sergot slapped him across the face, so hard it stung.

"Now shout it."

"Vive l'Empereur," ventured Étienne, without emphasis.

"Bah! You're not even old enough to vote."

The same sergot thrust his sword back into his scabbard with a loud 'click' and then shoved Étienne in the chest, almost throwing him off balance.

"Let's go, Louis. Down that street he said. See if we can catch them."

And they left Étienne alone, as they pursued the non-existent group of workers he had described. He rushed to turn the next corner, anxious to get away from men in cocked hats, dark coats and sabers at their sides.

He had wanted to slug that mustachioed *sergent de ville*, and he burned with rage at himself for not having done it. Rage for not returning the slap or the shove but especially for the humiliation, of being made to cry out for the Emperor.

Damn them! He wouldn't let that happen again.

And what was that plebiscite they were so worked up about? He hadn't paid much attention because, as that sergot had noted, he was still too young to vote, but if it was so important to those police then he was certainly on the other side – whatever it was.

Then he remembered that he still had the leaflet from this morning, hidden under his shirt. He would study it as soon as he got back to Maurice's attic, and maybe Maurice could explain to him what it was all about.

A policeman's worries

This was a delicate moment, Mireau feared. The Empire was in an especially precarious position. The wars in Italy and Mexico had not brought the expected glory to the Empire. Baron Haussmann had finally been dismissed in disgrace and construction had practically stopped in Paris, and this with all the other economic troubles of the past few years had led to greater tensions with the workers' organizations, to the degree that not only iron workers and tailors and printers and bronze workers were calling strikes, but in Lyon there had even been a long strike by women in the silk mills. The scandal last January, when the Emperor's cousin shot that journalist, had nearly caused a revolution. The Emperor himself was not in good health, and now there were even rumors of possible hostility with Prussia.

Mireau, when he permitted himself, could understand and perhaps even share the concerns of the Republicans, their general disillusionment with the Empire that was his employer. Empathy was perhaps too strong a word – he could not allow himself to flag in his duty to defend the Emperor. But, as was well known and even an article of faith throughout the police corps, knowing the opponent made one a better police officer. Yes, surely the Empire needed reforms if it were to survive. But one had to move cautiously, or else the whole structure might collapse. Hippolyte had made his whole career under the Empire and was expecting a promotion to sub-prefect or possibly even to work in the Sûreté. But if the Orleanists should come to power and try to restore the Old Regime, or even worse, the Republicans on the Left or, more chaotic yet, the anarchists or communists – well, Hippolyte could be left without a job or pension.

However, he could not afford to fret over all these disastrous possibilities. His only concern should be to keep order in his quartier. In Hippolyte's opinion the handful of working-class intellectuals of the International were hardly the biggest threat. With or without them, the strikes would continue, and the *têtes brulées* – the hotheads – were mostly followers of Blanqui. Now, once his transfer to Sûreté was approved, perhaps he could do something more effective to counter all the subversion. Meanwhile, while waiting for the paperwork and for the prefect to find him a replacement, he would have to fulfill his functions as the district police chief of the Quinze-Vingts.

These were the thoughts going through his head when Bougainville – '*Bagou*' – appeared at the door of his office.

"Bonjour, Polo. Why so glum?"

"Oh! You startled me. How did you get in here?"

"Why, your man, the sergeant, the tall one with the side-whiskers."

"Chardon."

"He recognized me from my last visit, and when I told him we had an appointment, he waved me in. I thought maybe you needed some cheering up. These are perilous times."

"Yes, indeed."

"The Emperor unwell, Favre and that young Gambetta

rousing the republicans, even the Orleanists think they smell an opportunity! And then of course, the dangerous classes, still dangerous."

"You needn't remind me."

"Things are changing, Polo. The Empire has lasted twenty years, and we've had a good run, you and I. Me, with the literary journals and newspapers, and you, why, a steady rise through the ranks and now, if things should go on the way they have up to now, poised to become sub-prefect! But–"

"But?"

"Cigar?"

"No thank you. I prefer my pipe."

"Yes, the Empire has been able to provide us good tobacco from all our colonies. And many other things. But things are not going to go on the way they have, I fear."

"There will always be a need for police."

"Hah! Don't be so sure. If, God forbid, we get a republic? They say 'republic,' but it's anarchy they mean. They use that word 'commune', very frightening. As though we were going back to the days of the great Revolution, the chaos of 1792. No king, no emperor. No laws to obey, *ergo*, no need for police.

"Oh, don't make such a long face! Maybe nothing like that will happen, maybe the Emperor will hang on long enough to leave the throne to his little son as he plans. But I wouldn't count on it. It might behoove you, I tell you confidentially, to consider some other way of making a living. Just in case. Some business."

"Business?"

"I've been thinking that you would be good at managing theaters. Yes, I mean it. With all your knowledge of human character."

"Ridiculous. Police work is not theater."

"No? Surely you see a lot of actors in your line of work! Well, you should think about it. I have a theater in mind, I'm sort of a partner in it, and we'll be needing a manager. Someone who can impose discipline. And I immediately thought of you."

"I can't believe you're serious. Police work has been my life."

"Or perhaps some entirely new venture in the colonies. There are fortunes to be made in cotton in Algeria, or even farther, all that opium or silk in Cochinchina."

"You're daft. Paris is my home and always will be."

It would not be wise to let Bagou know yet of his impending move to Sûreté. He didn't even want his own sergeants to know about it until it was an accomplished fact. Bad for morale, and bad to reveal anything more than absolutely necessary about the city's secret police operation.

"Well, think about it," continued Bagou. "I do know of a possibility in the theater business, that's why I mentioned it. As for me, I'm planting articles in papers of all tendencies, or almost all, including even the republicans. Theater reviews and poetry criticism. Nothing political, so as not to take a stand until we see how things are going. Because, whatever happens, it won't hurt to have editor friends in all camps.

"But as I said, I came to cheer you up, take your mind off your policeman's worries for a night. I invite you to the theater. My little friend Victorine is performing, and I have tickets. A delightful comedy. At the Ambigu, tonight."

"Tonight? Impossible. The plebiscite is tomorrow, you know that. I have to prepare my men. We're expecting protests, you know, and they could be rowdy."

"Ah yes, a man of duty above all. Well, perhaps Saturday next then. She will be repeating her performance. It is really quite an amusing spectacle."

Hippolyte nodded, ambiguously.

"And I can introduce you to just the man, boy really, a person who can be your eyes and ears on the rabble rousers. And that place I mentioned to you, in the Court of the Dragon."

Hippolyte raised his head, now alert. If Bagou was offering him a *mouchard*, an informer, he must already be aware that Mireau would be working on larger issues beyond this district. These journalists! Bagou must have been putting together lots of hints, or perhaps he found some loose-tongued operative in the Sûreté, or maybe none of this – maybe it was just a guess, but if he was just working on hints, Hippolyte's showing interest in the offer of an informer would be another, stronger one.

"Saturday a week, then," he assented, gruffly. "A good laugh at the theater might be just the ticket. At the Ambigu, then."

Plebiscite

Sunday morning. Church bells from nearby Sainte-Marguerite, sunlight hitting the roofs but not yet striking the narrow streets and alleys. It was exactly one week since Étienne had left home and Paris streets were still strange to him, but if he followed the crowd, he thought he would be sure to find the borough hall, the *mairie*. Already there seemed to be a lot of bustle on those streets, clusters of men arguing on street corners since the taverns were all closed.

Maurice had told him to expect to see some activity around the polling stations. Étienne had shown him the leaflet, which argued against abstention but to vote 'No', and Maurice had just swung his head ambiguously and shrugged.

"It's a trick," said Maurice. "If you vote 'Yes', you're saying you approve the Emperor's reforms. If you vote 'No', you're saying you'd rather keep the Emperor without the reforms. So any way you vote, you're saying you approve of the Emperor."

Maurice laughed. No, he told Étienne, he didn't plan to vote. He didn't even want to go near the voting station, the borough hall. But he had given Étienne a rough idea of where to find it.

And he did. Outside the hall stood two police officers in their dark frock coats and bicornes, one on either side of the open door, while other sergots stood alert nearby as a small crowd of men filed in. There were two larger crowds of men standing only a few meters away, with no apparent intention of going in to vote. Then one of the groups, five or six men, two of them in frock coats like bourgeois and the others in workers' blouses and caps, started chanting, *"Votez non! Votez non!"*

The other group of about the same size then answered, louder, *"Abstention! À bas l'empire!"* The two groups kept shouting at each other, but without any apparent anger – theirs was a tactical difference, either voting "No" or refusing to vote meant opposition to the emperor.

But then one from the abstentionist crowd jumped in front to stop a man about to enter the *mairie*. One of the policemen suddenly came up behind him and swung his club, and Étienne, seeing in a flash the scowling grin of the sergot who had shoved him just days ago, without thinking jumped in and grabbed the club before he could swing again. He stood there for a moment, amazed at his own action, but then other protesters ran up, and so did other sergots. Étienne, with a new surge of confidence, bumped hard against one of the policemen, so hard that the policeman fell on his back on the street. Then somebody grabbed Étienne's sleeve. He jerked it away thinking it was another one of the police officers, until he heard the man next to him shout, "Run!"

And he did, when he saw more police coming, clubs in hand. And so did the man who had told him to run. Around the corner and into an alley, where the other fellow, barely loud enough for him to hear, said "We're clear. Slow down. You're pretty fast, too fast for me."

His new companion was a few years older than Étienne and at least ten centimeters shorter. And he was panting.

"Come," he said at last, when he got his breath. "We need to talk."

Didier, he introduced himself, tinsmith. And Internationalist.

Although on voting day the cafés were all supposed to be closed, Didier knew a place where – giving the right signal of a rap on the door – they could get a beer and talk. When Étienne told him he was an apprentice bookbinder, Didier nodded approvingly.

"Bookbinder! Then you must be an Internationalist, too."

This jump in logic puzzled Étienne, but he didn't want to disappoint his new friend.

"I haven't actually joined," he admitted. "But I did hear Varlin at a meeting."

"Oh, yes, if you've heard Varlin then surely you're one of us. Haven't joined yet? We'll get you in. We can use a fast-footed young chap like you. We're going to have more run-ins with the police, that's for sure. Where are you working?"

Étienne described his situation.

"No job? No money?"

And that's not all, Étienne admitted.

"No work booklet. I think it was stolen."

Didier looked thoughtful.

"We can maybe fix that."

The café owner found a pencil and a scrap of paper for him, and Didier took some notes after asking Étienne where he had worked and names of bosses. Then he put the paper away and asked him about politics in Lyon, and what he felt about the Empire. This put Étienne on alert. He didn't really know much or anything about the current political situation in Lyon, so he tried to satisfy Didier by talking grandly about the old history, the weavers and their battles with the silk merchants and the city authorities and the militia, back before he was born. Didier just looked at him, his head slanted and his eyes ironic.

"Uh huh. *Bien*, you're young, but still. Bookbinder. The bookbinders here are some of our most active men. We hear about a lot of strike actions in Lyon, there's even talk about forming a commune. I thought you might know something about that?"

"I was in a small shop. Just three of us, sometimes four, and a girl who stitched pages."

"But you had heard about the International."

Étienne nodded.

"You know that there's talk of a war coming up, with the Prussians. Germans. What do you think about that?"

"Why, I'm French! We've got to defend France. *La patrie*."

He wasn't sure where this was going, but he thought that 'defending the homeland' had to be the safest sentiment in existence.

Didier smiled.

"Ah, yes. *La patrie*. The homeland. Is that what they taught you in Lyon?"

After a while, he looked up and called to the owner, to give him back his pencil and pay for the beers.

Then he smiled and said he would talk to some people.

"Do you think you could find your way to Rue Larrey, in the Sixth? There's a place there called 'La Marmite'. You know the Rue du Jardinet, after you come to the end of Boulevard Saint-Germain?"

"I know it! I walked by there last week."

"Well, you turn on Rue Larrey, you step into a courtyard and then…"

Didier drew him a little map, with hashmarks for a stairway.

"Up on the first floor," he said. "Very well, if you can be there on Tuesday – yes, because then I'll have a chance to set things up on Monday. You come on Tuesday then, around twelve noon, and I can introduce you to some *compagnons* – our partners."

Ink-shitters

"Not bad, my young ink-shitter," said Vallès. "We created a bit of a stir with this last piece of yours. Too bad so few people could read it before the police started confiscating copies. Even Vermersch liked it, that bit about 'holy oil.'"

"Vermersch liked that?" Alphonse was thrilled by the compliment. "Actually," he admitted, "I was imitating him. No one can be more mordant than he."

"No one? We'll see."

Vallès' face remained bent over the paper in his hands, but his eyes rose to meet Alphonse's and one eyebrow rose even further. After a moment he looked off into the distance and inhaled before saying, solemnly,

"For this number, I'm going to write the lead article myself. Mordant? Perhaps. But that's not enough. This situation has become too serious for simple satire. It will require something that youngsters like you and especially that romantic hothead Vermersch have no patience for. A reasoned, logical argument. I'm going to devote the whole issue to it, and we have to hurry. From the noises made by his ministers, our little Badinguet is about to hitch on his sword and play at being his uncle, Napoleon the Great."

Despite Vallès' solemn tone, Alphonse had to laugh at the image.

'Badinguet.' The nickname was wrapped in myth. Supposedly, when the young and ambitious Louis-Napoléon, with no more political capital than his surname Bonaparte, had failed in another of his attempts at a *coup d'état* and been imprisoned, he had escaped disguised as a workman with borrowed papers from somebody supposedly named Badinguet. Whether true or not, the nickname was an insulting reminder to the Emperor of his humble and ridiculous beginnings.

"He's never been in combat," Vallès mused, "and with his bad health and his hemorrhoids, I don't think he can even ride a horse. It would be funny, if this were comic opera. But we're on a bigger stage, and real people are going to get killed. Defending an empire that shouldn't even exist. And that he wants to prolong with yesterday's duplicitous plebiscite. The only way to say no to the Emperor was to not vote at all."

"Or to foul the ballot," Alphonse jumped in eagerly. "I've heard some men say they wrote *'Merde à Louis-Napoléon'* instead of marking either *'Oui'* or *'Non'*."

"Not very clever, but it makes the point," Vallès grunted, with a laugh. "In any event, we've already said what we had to about it. It was enough to just quote the International, 'to vote in the plebiscite is to vote for despotism here in France and war beyond.'

"It's the possibility of that 'war beyond' that has me worried," Vallès continued. "And over what? Over who is to rule Spain? Madness. It's another of Badinguet's maneuvers, as you wrote. Like this plebiscite. But this may be his last one. After the fiasco in Mexico. And all those troops killed fighting Garibaldi in Italy. And before that, Crimea.

"I'll take this on, I should have it ready this afternoon,

I already have this whole sorry history pretty well thought out. But I'll need something more, to fill the other pages. Vermersch says he's too busy right now, because he's starting his own paper with two other boys his age. Do you know them? Humbert and Vuillaume. Such ambition! None of them is much older than you. You're not planning to start your own newspaper, too, are you?"

"With what funds?"

Alphonse laughed, surprised at the suggestion. Though he liked the idea.

"No, not now anyway," he said at last.

"Good. Then I'll need something from Alphonse-Marie Bertrand – or should I say, 'Our correspondent from Lille'? You tell me how you want to sign it. But can you get me something by tonight, something related to this war frenzy?"

"Yes, I think so. I know our friends in the International are planning a declaration against all this anti-German stuff. I can say something about how they're getting signatures and why they're doing it, and we can quote as much as we need from their manifesto, maybe even the whole thing."

"That would be good. Something signed by workers. This wild anti-foreign propaganda is a huge distraction. Earlier this morning I went to see my German tailor, I owe him for this vest and coat, to ask him to extend his credit for another week, and he just waved me away, said he was afraid he was going to have to close shop – his customers have disappeared, and he and his compatriots have been hearing all this 'Don't buy German' talk."

"Did he extend your credit?"

"Not that he had any choice. I couldn't pay him! I'm hoping that sales of this next issue will help me pay some debts – though if we quote something by the International, our newsboys are going to have to be dodging the police. I may need to find something else to fill the page – one of your little satirical essays, perhaps. If we have decent sales, I may even be able to pay you something at last! By the way, how are you making your living these days? Still tutoring in French spelling and grammar?"

"Yes, but I've only got one new pupil now. Another bookbinder. A chap named Jean-Pierre. It seems that all these workers dream of becoming journalists."

"So now you're tutoring a bookbinder. French spelling and grammar, indeed. You're right, they all want to be journalists, those workers! If they only knew! Those dyers and shoemakers and carpenters and metal workers, they imagine it would be easy to sit back at a desk with a pen in hand – Hah! It would be so much simpler for me to make a living at almost anything else. If I were any good with my hands, I mean. Well, get me that copy by eight tonight, something, but better not quote the International. Or at least, don't mention the name. I'll be at Schmidt's, you know that brasserie. Poor Schmidt! With a name like that, he may have to close up shop soon, too."

"But I've just received another, surprising offer," Alphonse said, with some hesitation. "Unconscionable, but the money is tempting."

It was time to tell Vallès of what had happened at the Café de Madrid.

Though he could hardly afford it, Alphonse had ventured there for the thrill of seeing the faces of some of the famous journalists, republicans mostly – that is, anti-imperial – who were known to hang out there. From the caricatures he easily recognized Gambetta, gesticulating in animated discussion, and then he saw another arm, gesturing to him. To Alphonse.

To his surprise, it was Bougainville, the scribbler that Rochefort and Vallès both called '*Bagou*'.

Surprised, Alphonse had stepped over and nodded. Bagou then gestured to him to sit down and offered him a Pernod. And then, after some chitchat about the difficult trade of scribbling, he had made his amazing proposal.

"*Mouchard?*" exclaimed Vallès, almost laughing. "Is that what he said? Though he didn't use that word. He wants you to become an informer for the prefecture? Does he know your opinions? Has he read any of your revolutionary pieces?"

"Yes, I think he has," Alphonse told him. "I'm sure he has, because he told me, in a low voice as though it were a great confidence, that he has always believed that a man's opinions should never stand in the way of his making a good living. I don't think he really believes in opinions or believes that anyone holds them seriously."

"And does he know you've written for me?"

"Yes, he mentioned that, and that's why he thinks I'll be a good candidate for the job. Because he thinks I already know all the most subversive journalists. And he knew I needed money."

"And you said?"

"That I'd have to think about it."

"Ha!" cried Vallès, as with sudden inspiration. "I think you should take it!"

"Take money from the police to betray my colleagues?"

Vallès laughed.

"To betray the police! You tell them whatever you want in your reports, keep them busy with false leads, and meanwhile you can let all of us know when there is a real mouchard spying on us. That's marvelous! You can take money from the police, to turn the police into fools!"

Alphonse's laugh was a gasp of relief.

"Do you think that's possible? I had thought of doing something like that, which is why I didn't say 'No' right away. Could the prefecture be such fools, not to detect the fraud?"

Vallès half-closed his eyes and smiled and nodded. "You're a clever lad. You'll think of some things for your reports to keep them busy."

"Weren't you going to pay me something for my article?"

"Yes, yes! Of course. For this last article and the next one. After we sell enough papers. Let's say 5 – no, 7 francs. Good? For the two articles, more if sales go well. And tonight's dinner will be on me."

Vallès laughed.

"And once you start collecting your salary from the police prefecture" – at this Vallès could not keep from laughing – "why, then, you can invite me to dinner."

The working class

Excited and nervous, Étienne found his way to Rue Larrey too early for La Marmite to open – he guessed from the sun that it was around eleven, and Didier had said to come by at noon. It had been a long walk, the longest stretch on Boulevard Saint-Germain. He had tried to make mental notes of the façades as he passed, but couldn't concentrate. He heard hammering, metallic banging from a workshop, and another sound that he guessed was some sort of press. He barely saw the few people that passed by him, so full was he of his apprehensions about this coming encounter with Didier and his *compagnons*. He wandered up and down the little street, tensing as he thought back to his encounter with the police just days ago, in this same neighborhood. He waited as unobtrusively as he could until he saw some men enter a courtyard and continue up the stairs that Didier had drawn on the little map of the workers' canteen. He took a deep breath and followed them up.

It seemed to Étienne that everybody in La Marmite was in a foul mood, some discouraged and others angry and demanding some aggressive action. He noticed that some had visible bruises on their faces. He knew that the plebiscite had caused an uproar. He'd seen a newspaper and heard groups of men talking, so he knew that Paris and all the other big cities, including Lyon, had voted 'No' overwhelmingly, but with all the rural votes, the Emperor's 'Yes' had won by a huge margin. Abstention, which was what Varlin's International advocated, had not been big enough to cause embarrassment.

He looked around for Didier, fearing that maybe he was still too early. The tables were just beginning to fill with workers and their plates and soup bowls. He wondered if he should step up to the serving counter himself, thinking that in the worst case, if Didier didn't show up, he could at least get a meal for 10 sous.

"Ah, my *gone*!" he heard then. And turned to see Didier studying him.

"So you did make it. I was afraid you might not show up. Here, get yourself some food and come over with us, at the table back there – see? Where that big fellow in the blue cap has just raised his wine glass, see, he's greeting you! Go get your plate and come back. Here, I'm paying for it."

From the variety of caps and aprons, he saw that there were workers from many trades, all mingling without distinction and several of them passionately discussing politics. Didier introduced him to Claude and a fellow he called J-P, both of them binders. J-P looked hard at Étienne, a half-smile on his face.

"You've come from Lyon, Didier tells me. Fine city. Lots of strikes, tough ones."

"Yes. Last year it seemed there was a new one every week, and one of them went on for months."

"Ah, yes, those girls, those silk-spinners. What do you call them?"

"*Ovalistes*. Very hard job. Fourteen hours a day at their ovals, standing all day, no breaks, six days a week, for less than a franc and a half a day."

"My! Did you hear that, Claude? Didier? And they were just young girls, weren't they?"

"Mostly. My girlfriend was one of them. She was fifteen. From a village outside Lyon, a peasant girl like almost all of them. A lot of the others, peasant girls too, had been brought in by the owners from Italy. They didn't know anything else. Most of them don't know how to read, or even what country they're in. But they got together and found somebody to write a letter for them, a very polite letter to the bosses, asking for more pay and shorter hours."

"We saw it, it was printed in our workers' press here. And they managed to go on strike! We heard there were thousands! The first time in all of France, or in the whole world, such a big strike by women! And they were just girls!"

"Well, there were some of them who were older, even thirty, they'd started as girls and just kept working as long as their lungs held out. The dust, you know."

"It must have been very tough for them, staying out a whole month, no wages, turned out from the barracks of the mill owners."

"But there was a lot of support in our neighborhoods, some families took them in, and some of the café owners let them eat for free."

"We sent them funds from Paris. The International, I mean. And our members in other cities, everybody, every true Internationalist gave whatever he could spare."

Didier broke in.

"A strike fund. We voted for it. The International provided a franc a day as long as they were on strike."

"And they won!"

"Well, they did win shorter hours, ten instead of twelve. But the mill owners wouldn't raise their wages."

"But still they won something. And they joined the International! Varlin was so proud, it was the very first time we had a women's section!"

Étienne perked up.

"Varlin, you said? The bookbinder? I *heard* him. He came to Lyon. My girlfriend, Madeleine, one of the *ovalistes*, got me to go with her to the rally."

He realized that he had just made an impression on his listeners, so he went on.

"That's when I decided to come to Paris. To be a bookbinder like Eugène Varlin."

"And to join the International!" said Claude, with a laugh.

Étienne stopped, mouth open, and looked at the faces of the men around him. Would that really be possible? For a mere apprentice? But seeing their enthusiasm, he just nodded.

"Very good," said J-P. "If you're going to be one of us, a comrade, we will have to help you out. That's what comradeship means. Solidarity."

Étienne nodded again, too dazed to say anything.

"You need a job, Didier has told us. As a binder's apprentice."

When Étienne told him he had lost his work document, Claude just nodded and then stood up, saying, "Just a moment. Let me talk with Nathalie and some of the others."

"Nathalie?"

"Yes, she's a bookbinder herself. She should be able to come up with a solution."

He came back only a few minutes later and said he thought they could solve that problem. But it might take a few days.

"And as soon as you make your first wages, we'll welcome

you into the International Workingmen's Association," added Didier, in what Étienne took as a smile of triumph. Not daring to refuse, he just nodded again, and thanked them.

"I can let you know on Friday, I think."

"Friday?" he asked, forlornly.

"Or Saturday at the latest. Is that too long for you? Have you got a place to stay?"

Étienne nodded.

"Money to eat?"

He shrugged, with a sad little smile. It would be too embarrassing to say how little he had in his pocket. It would be as though he were asking for a handout, and that – that would be unbearable.

"Well, we can't let you starve. Hang on. Don't go away, I'll be back in a minute."

He sat there, looking around. The dining hall was almost empty now, everybody or almost everybody gone back to work. He felt strange and out of place, still hearing the echoes of conversation in accents unlike those he was used to, in a dining place that was not a café or a bar but, they had explained, a 'cooperative', owned by the same people who ate in it, like – he supposed – a very big family, but without any father or mother in charge.

Claude returned with a young woman, the same one, he was pretty sure, who had been ladling out the soup when he had got in line.

"Étienne from Lyon, meet Mathilde from Rouen," he said. She gave a little bow and Étienne nodded toward her.

"She says she could use some help here. Especially from a strong young man not afraid to lift some crates and maybe sweep up. Might that be you?"

Étienne nodded. With a big sigh of relief.

At the Cirque Impérial

Sitting in the theater, surrounded by Bagou's noisy claque, Hippolyte was reminded of his crude police spies. The paid clappers and booers filling the upper banks of seats knew no more about the dramatic arts than his *mouchards* did about the theories and concepts debated so hotly by Proudhonists, Blanquists, and that new crowd of Internationalists they were supposed to be spying on. The only way to make sense of their reports was to question his informants directly, paying as close attention to their faces and gestures as to their incomplete sentences and sputtered *argot*.

But Hippolyte Mireau held a higher opinion of the intelligence and education of the enemies of the Empire. He had met some of them, in interrogations and less official encounters. And in the radical press he had seen articles of surprising sophistication and clarity, some signed by that bronze worker Tolain, especially, and more frequently lately, by that bookbinder Varlin, or that sharp-tongued schoolteacher-journalist Vallès, who may be the most dangerous of them all. Dangerous articles, dangerous, dangerous, seductive of the working class, especially of the simpler souls, but not only them, written in a language that workers could grasp. And he had heard that Varlin fellow defend himself in court, clearly and with as much conviction as he displayed in those articles he signed in those rabble-rousing newspapers.

No, the kind of mouchard that Hippolyte Mireau needed was not a common lock-picker or a thug, but someone from the ranks of those revolutionary workers' clubs, somebody who understood their language, a man who not only could quote Proudhon or Blanqui but who also had callouses on his hands or some other proof of a real trade.

His thoughts were interrupted by a loud cheering and clapping of the rough men sitting in the rows behind him. The piano played a loud march, a sort of parody, Hippolyte thought, of the Prussian anthem. And then appeared a tall, belly-bulging figure overdressed in mock elegance, a big mustache bushy at the center and with long points at the ends, and a monocle. He strode ponderously to center stage, where he clapped a helmet on his head, a gilded helmet with a high spike from which fluttered a miniature Prussian flag with its black wing-spread eagle. The crowd around Hippolyte booed, laughed and stomped, some of them loudly clapping sticks and tin cans together.

The helmet-donning was the signal for the dancing girls to burst onto the stage, five of them in a wild chahut-cancan, lifting their legs to reveal up to mid-calf emerging from their voluminous skirts as they pranced and whirled around the fat Prussian. Their white skirts flicked up and down with each kick, their bosoms near to bursting from red and blue bustiers –a patriotic tricolor. The Prussian monarch slobbered as he lurched toward one girl after another, failing to catch any of them, while the crowd around Hippolyte stamped and shouted in raucous hilarity.

Then the leering, dizzy monarch straightened, tottering, and the dancing girls paused as five young male dancers pranced onto the stage, each in a different costume. A peasant with a broad-brimmed hat and a satchel of seed corn at his waist, a demurely dressed and hatless clerk, a foppish dandy in frilly waistcoat and goatee, perhaps meant to be a student, a worker of some sort in his rough blue blouse and cap, and finally a soldier in red pants and dark blue military tunic. After a couple of spins with the girls, and a pair of menacing gestures toward the now wide-eyed 'king', the dancing circle paused, with the soldier and one of the girls center front. The orchestra of piano, horns and drums now struck up another march. At the first strains of it, pandemonium broke loose, the paid claque cheering loudly, other sectors of the audience booing and stamping their feet. Only the first few chords were necessary to identify the piece as the hoary *Partant pour la Syrie*, the unofficial anthem of the Emperor Napoleon III. And the dancer in the center began to sing, but the words were not 'Departing for Syria' but 'Departing for Berlin.'

Now Hippolyte recognized her. She was Bagou's *maîtresse*, the sprightly Victorine. He had had no idea she could sing.

Fine. Good for her. This was, he thought, her début in a solo role. He could be happy for her and see why Bagou was pleased. But yet he felt disturbed by the enthusiasm of the theater crowd, especially but not only the paid claque, for 'Departing for Berlin'. The Prussian king on stage was a foolish clown; the real Prussian king in Berlin could be a different matter.

Binding threads

"Just show up at this bindery—" Claude had scribbled the address on a piece torn from a newspaper. "It's in the sixth. Give me a day to work things out. Monday, at about a quarter to six. We start early. Meet me at the street entrance, and I'll introduce you to the *contremaître*, and we'll get you started."

As agreed, Étienne had met Claude at the entrance at a little before six in the morning, and they had come here, up one flight of stairs to what must be one of the biggest binderies in Paris. Étienne's lack of a stamped work booklet had not been a major problem for M. Perrin, the foreman, because they had a rush job and Perrin accepted Claude's assurance that the new boy could do the work and said they could arrange the papers later. And he directed Étienne to a bench with a hammer and stacks of printed sheets.

This shop was nearly as big, or maybe as big, as the one he'd been turned away from last week. He hadn't actually counted, but it looked like there were at least thirty workers, men and women, the men operating big presses or trimming pages or, the more experienced ones, cutting and applying various leather bindings. The women, or girls really, mostly no older than Étienne, had to be the *brocheuses* sewing the pages for both the expensive and the cheapest bindings. He spotted three of them sitting at sewing frames much bigger than the one in his old workshop back in Lyon.

Claude had told him that the shop had jobs ranging from pamphlets of the Church to luxury bindings in expensive leather covers with gold-stamped lettering and gilded page edges, as well as popular novels and volumes of poetry in simple bindings of stiffer paper.

Thud!

Feet together and standing close to the bench, steadying a thick section of printed sheets with his left hand, Étienne lifted the hammer and then dropped its iron head hard against the stack of paper to compress it. This was the simplest and most mindless of all tasks in this bookbinding workshop, far below what he believed he could do. He intended to become a skilled, trusted master of the craft. But he was the new boy, and this was what the foreman, the *contremaître*, had assigned him. It was a task that felt familiar in this strange new place, a simple, repetitive act –

Two or three such blows, sometimes four to get the sheets properly compressed, and then he would put that signature aside and pick up and place on the bench the next one. He would have to repeat these operations until he had pounded all of them, in this case something more than twenty signatures, 320 pages he calculated, which would then be ready for the next step, which would be for some other worker to press all those signatures in a stack in the big press behind him in the corner. But Étienne was not yet trusted with the press.

* **

It had not been a trick, as Maurice had feared. There really was a job. And his days of doing odd jobs at La Marmite had been like a school for him – overhearing the conversations, picking up newspapers and the many pamphlets to find out better what they were talking about, he felt he was entering a new world of knowledge. The articles he saw and the pamphlets were mostly about politics, including debates about issues that were not always easy for him to understand, but the conversations were wide-ranging, with many jokes and terms, maybe slang, maybe regional, or sometimes technical that were new to him. But the strongest sense he got was fraternal. The people there, the workers men and women, who came to eat, and sometimes to smoke and sing or to sit in the room where they could read the newspapers, as well as the people working there – Mathilde, Édouard the chief cook, Nathalie Lemel were the most constant – they all felt themselves to be part of a common cause, a brotherhood and sisterhood that he wanted to join.

Nathalie was clearly the center of the operation. It struck him that such a small person could exercise such authority. It wasn't just that she was more mature than he, he guessed her to be about forty. No, it wasn't that. That authority of hers, an energy she seemed to radiate, was respected by the older workers too, men and women. When, in the evenings, she read aloud some article she had selected from the workers' press, her voice affirmed the analysis and the workers all muttered their approval. At other times, the men often looked to her to settle their arguments, and after hearing her usually terse, always uncomplicated responses, they would generally take the matter as settled. Or if, to save their pride, they said it was not worth disputing with a woman, they didn't say it in her hearing. The women workers who came to eat, the seamstresses and clothing makers and *brocheuses* from the binderies, who usually sat at separate tables, deferred to her as their natural leader.

The little woman's great authority, Étienne came to believe, as he watched her revise work schedules and make sure he and everyone else in the place knew exactly what to do, must come from, first, the fact that she always seemed absolutely sure of herself, and secondly, because of her reputation as being very good at her trade, which was bookbinding. As everyone knew, she was managing the Marmite out of political commitment, as something that she together with Eugène Varlin had founded as a way to advance the struggle.

Étienne's tasks, carrying crates of food up the stairs to the big kitchen, hauling out the garbage, and scrubbing the big *marmites* they cooked the stew in, had not been onerous or probably even necessary, but they let him feel that he was earning his keep and not just accepting charity for the meals he consumed there. Now, finally, he didn't need that support, because he was really here, earning his wage, hammering sixteen-page signatures in a real book-binding shop. It was much bigger than his old shop in Lyon and with bigger and better and newer machines. He raised his head a moment to glance toward Claude, who was the one manipulating that big press, completing the compression of book pages for which Étienne's pounding was merely the first step. The press was much bigger and newer than the one he had known in Lyon, but the mechanism was similar and he was sure he could manage it if only the foreman would let him. But, he told himself again, he was the new boy, and with an odd accent, so this was where he had to start.

The hammer was simply a hammer, like a carpenter's except with a shorter handle and rounded edges on the face to avoid tearing or marring the paper. Each blow he thought of as his reply to the thoughts he imagined must be in those pages. Thud! Yes! or Thud! No! – depending on the title and whatever he may have heard about the author or the book. Because, unlike what he had managed in the small shop back in Lyon, here he was not going to have an opportunity to read any of those pages, the foreman had already warned that he would fine or even fire him if he caught him lingering over the print, especially when there was a rush job.

This act of pounding represented a kind of completion. It meant that he had already checked that the ink was dry, the pages in order and with no notable smudges, and each section neatly aligned. Then the hammering, gently and precisely so as not to damage the paper, and finally the insertion of any illustrated pages too delicate for hammering. And then the press, where they would be left for two hours or more while he continued to the next batch of page bundles, the *cahiers*. And then some other worker would pull the book out of the press and saw the slits across the back for the cords, before passing the compacted pages to one of the girls at the sewing frames, the *cousoirs,* who with needle and thread would sew the pages, section by section, *cahier* by *cahier*, around the cords.

Euh! Watch it!

He had been thinking about that girl, the one sitting at the sewing frame nearest him, and he had let the hammer turn slightly, denting the pages, and nearly mashed his fingers!

'Rose', he had heard her called. He had been watching her all morning but was too shy to say anything to her.

Having completed one stack of book sections, he picked up the first signature of the next book to work on and, without even thinking of what he was doing, read out the title page: "Erckmann-Chatrian, *The Conscript of 1813*, fourth edition."

And she, the book-stitcher he had been eyeing, laughed.

"Do you always read aloud?" she asked him.

His face warmed and he looked up for the first time directly into her eyes. Mocking eyes, bright, playful. And terribly exciting.

He didn't know how to answer such a question. Yes, of course, he wanted to say, is there any other way? But he just stared at her, his mouth open.

"Erckmann *and* Chatrian," she said. "That's not one name, the way you said it. They are two writers, they work as a team. Haven't you read *Le Blocus*?"

He shook his head, maybe too vigorously. She looked as though she was about to say something more, but the foreman looked their way, and she quickly went back to her task.

He let his thoughts pass again over all that had happened in the past few days. Maurice had complained about his bad luck, but what surprised Étienne was that his older cousin, more experienced and far better acquainted with the city, had such bad judgment. After being fired or quitting his job, it wasn't clear which, he had borrowed 40 francs from some people he knew only by nicknames and had placed it all in a betting pool with the wine-seller, hoping – he said – to duplicate his fortune and set up his own woodworking shop. And he lost. And those men with ominous nicknames – 'Béquilleur' and 'Astic' sounded the most menacing – were insisting on payment. Étienne considered himself lucky to have found this job so quickly, and he now could afford the modest meals for the two of them, but there was no way he could get together 40 francs to give to Maurice. Nor would he want to, especially if, as Étienne suspected, Maurice was planning to gamble it all again. He was anxious to move to another place, and it might be possible. Claude had mentioned a lodging house full of Internationalists, where Claude and his friend J-P slept and took their morning meals.

For the rest of that morning, as he brought down the hammer on the pages of *The Conscript*, which he supposed must be a romance of the long-ago Napoleonic wars, he felt the thudding of the hammer differently. He was touching, beating gently, something connected to her, to the *jolie camarade* with the ironic laugh and pretty eyes. To Rose, to whom he still had never said a word.

"All right, all of you," announced M. Perrin, the foreman. "Time for your break. Be back in exactly one hour or, I say this for our new man to be sure he understands, if you're one minute late you'll be docked a half-day's wages. Now, on with you."

He looked for Claude, in the crowd of workers now all standing and heading for the door, most with parcels under their arms. Étienne joined the crowd, trying to maneuver closer to Claude and then, to his surprise and confusion, finding himself elbow to elbow with Rose, who was chatting with two other book-stitchers, both a little taller than she.

"Oh, here's the new boy!"

"Is that the one who reads aloud?"

"He's not really a boy, he's a tall parrot!"

"Look! He blushes."

"What's your real name, M. Long-Bird?"

Étienne stretched tall, raised his head and straightened his shoulders as the crowd tightened while approaching the door.

"Étienne Bonin," he said, as he tried to elbow his way closer to Rose. But she was already on the arm of another young man, shorter but burlier than Étienne, who turned to him with a laugh.

"'Crane' would fit you better. Or 'Stork' maybe. You've flown a long way from your home pond. Did you get lost?"

Then he laughed again and rushed with the three girls down the stairs.

By this time Claude had caught up to him.

"Who was that fellow, the one with the big shoulders and the big mouth?" Étienne asked him.

"Oh, him? With the girls? He's all right. His name is Antoine, we call him Toinou. Good worker, and a revolutionary too, but not one of us. He's a Blanquiste."

Étienne knew from his readings in La Marmite that that meant a follower of Louis Auguste Blanqui, who seemed to command respect but was viewed skeptically and as an object of some of the jokes he had been hearing at La Marmite. Toinou however must have a much more favorable view of him. To Étienne, the disputes among Internationalists, mostly Proudhonists but now including some Blanquistes, were all too new. There was so much he was going to have to learn to navigate in his new world! Down on the street, Claude suggested following their co-workers heading toward the river.

"On sunny days like this, it's a pleasure to be outside for a bit on our break," he said. "Here, I brought some bread and cheese and sausage we can share, and if that's not enough, there are always vendors on the riverbank. If you've still got a few sous."

Étienne had been eyeing the group a few steps ahead of them, the three girls and Toinou. But when they got to the river, he saw more activity. He and Claude had caught up to the other group, and he asked, of Claude but loudly enough for the others to hear,

"What are they doing? All those women on the boats?"

"Those? The same as always," said the tallest of the girls.

"What we would probably be doing if we didn't have our jobs in the bindery. Not Toinou, though. No men there. That work is too hard for men to do."

"Oh yes there are, there are men working the boats," Toinou objected. "See, that older fellow with the pole, and the younger one, maneuvering the boat along the pier?"

"That's not much work, and they're not even needed. Probably somebody's unemployed husband and son who don't have anything else to do, so they hang out with the women. The women are doing everything," said the other, shorter girl, Louise.

It was Rose who spoke up.

"Yes, Cécile is right, that is probably what we would be doing if the bindery hadn't had need for us. And if we hadn't learned to read. Washing and bleaching, in the river water. My mother used to work on one of those laundry boats, and I would have to come and help her, like that young girl you see, over there, she can't be more than ten or eleven, pulling those shirts out of the water, see her?"

"Maybe that's what you *should* be doing," said Toinou. "Instead of bending over sewing frames all day. Those women get to chat, not like in our workshop. And they can laugh and splash each other! They look like they're having a good time. And for the younger ones, working outdoors, on the river, they can flirt with the bargemen."

"Oh, Toinou, you don't know anything about it! It's pleasant enough on a day like this, but in winter, or when there's a rainstorm, it's pretty miserable. My mother was glad to find a place in a new indoors laundry nearer our home. But indoors or outdoors, it's very hard work, and hot, and you can get scalded from those boilers, and those big boilers on the boats are especially dangerous because the boats can rock in bad weather and the deck gets slippery and sometimes a laundress, tired after many hours, slips and falls against one of them. And ooh! The burns! I've seen them."

"My mother, too. She still works the boats sometimes, but only in good weather. But the hours are long, as long as the daylight, and the pay is barely enough to stay alive."

Étienne had been listening intently. It was all new to him, this life, the laundresses on the river, the whole scene. He looked to Claude, who just smiled and raised an eyebrow as though amused. Then he raised his head abruptly, in a sign that it was time to go, and Étienne rose with him and they turned back toward the bindery.

When they had walked far enough that he thought they were out of earshot of their comrades still at the water's edge, he mentioned to Claude his need to find a cheap place to live, somewhere near the bindery if possible.

Claude stopped and looked at him, seeming to scan him from head to foot. Then he sort of half smiled, and nodded.

"Could be," he said. "I do know a place. The one I mentioned. We'll talk tomorrow."

That gave him something to think about all afternoon, as he continued his simple tasks of beating and trimming pages. There might be a place for him, closer to work and outside of that depressing attic with Maurice.

But it was to that attic he had to return when the day's work was done. On the long walk, past the quais and to the bridge and then to the Right Bank and the twelfth Arrondissement, he was thinking of many things – of all that he had learned during the week helping out at La Marmite, and about his new job, and the girls on the sewing frames, especially Rose. And whether a boisterous Blanquiste would be a serious rival.

It was still light when he got to No. 9, Rue du Fumier.

The concierge looked at him quizzically as he approached the stair up to the attic.

"Good evening," Étienne said to him.

The concierge grunted and said, "You going up there now?"

"Yes, I was going to. Why?"

The concierge just shook his head, then nodded.

Dubious about what he thought was a snicker on the concierge's face, but without any alternative in mind, Étienne climbed the stairs.

Le faux mouchard

Could he really do this? Alphonse asked himself as he walked toward the Place de la Bastille. Had his adored Jules Vallès been joking, or did he really think this would be a good idea? Yes, he did need the money, but this was not the role he had imagined for himself in coming to Paris.

'Role', had he just said 'role' to himself, in his inner voice? He had to laugh. Yes, that's what this would be, a role in a comedy – or possibly a tragedy– in the theater of life. He, an idealist who had read Proudhon and other radicals, who identified with his father's generation of '48, who could recite reams of revolutionary poetry, he would be playing a police informer, a *mouchard*. A comedy indeed, of which he himself would have to be the playwright, making up the script as he went along.

That part amused him, pleased him, the part about being a playwright. Because he was a writer, or aspired to be, aspired to be one of the great ones, and the writers he most emulated were at once poets and novelists and playwrights. Victor Hugo, just to name the greatest of all, in his estimation. *Hernani*, he had heard good things about – though he'd never seen it performed.

But if Alphonse's comedy were discovered?

No, no, Vallès had assured him, the police were too

obtuse, and he was too clever, and he had a knack for making up stories.

It was a lot to think about as he dodged puddles and crossed all the way from the Second to the Twelfth Arrondissement, over on the eastern edge of the city, working-class territory. Where he had an appointment, thanks to that sleazy Bougainville, with the chief of a quartier with a quaint name, 'Quinze-Vingts'.

Vallès had said he should just make up things, as he did in his little satirical pieces. Ridiculous things, to keep the police busy and distract them from the real doings of the associations. And of course, in the police's eyes this supposed 'work' would justify his participation in as many political club meetings and rallies as he wanted. Alphonse would be gathering material for his own, serious writings at the same time he was carrying out this masquerade.

Past the Place de la Bastille and now into that remote quartier. Odd that he had not been sent to main headquarters of the Police Prefecture, but to such a humble commissary. But Bougainville had wanted to send him to a particular friend of his, the *commissaire*.

What would this local police chief be looking for, that Alphonse could give him? He did indeed know several men, and even a few women, dedicated to overthrowing the Empire. But he wasn't about to turn them in. Well, he would think of something. First, let's meet this *commissaire*, M. Hippolyte Mireau.

The house on Dragon Court

Claude's proposal of the workers' lodging house in the sixth had both excited and frightened Étienne, making him postpone any action. But after his uncomfortable night trying to sleep along with the clochards on the banks of the Port de l'Arsenal, he was ready to overcome his fears. Fortunately, it had been a warm night, and one of those clochards had extended to him, generously and with a big smile, some rags and pages of newspaper to serve as a mattress. The bank of the estuary was probably better than that spot under the bridge that he would have had to share with the mad ragpicker, the veteran of all the wars.

He knew Maurice wouldn't be expecting him so early, because all those days last week when he was scrubbing pans and doing other jobs at the Marmite, he wouldn't get back to Manure Street until nearly midnight. But yesterday, after his first day at the bindery, he had returned just after seven, and he had even brought a little money in his pocket and a satchel of food to share with Maurice. He had found the door locked, which was unusual, but he had a key Maurice had given him so he opened it and – And there they were! The two of them, humping on Maurice's mattress!

"Hey! What is it? Who's there?" Maurice had shouted, and Étienne just shut the door and locked it again and slowly descended the stairs. Well, at least he had his package with a chunk of bread and cheese and a few sous left over from his last days at the Marmite, but not enough to pay for a room anywhere he knew of.

So he had ended up settling himself down on the borrowed newspaper and, after sharing the food he had brought with the man who had given him his makeshift bedding, and wishing goodnight to him and the others bedded down, some on paper, most on rags, he could look up at the stars and think about Claude's proposition.

A boarding house for workers, workers all more or less identified with the International. And including at least one other bookbinder besides Claude. It would be a way to get himself 'bound' into Paris, or at least into the working-class movement he had heard described at that rally back in Lyon, the idea that spurred him to travel to Paris. But – would they really accept him, a mere apprentice, still new to their world? All those authors Claude had mentioned. He had barely recognized even the names. Proudhon was the only one he remembered hearing of in Lyon. "Property is theft." And Blanqui, a name he'd first heard in Paris as somebody important, but what did he stand for? And some German names, Marx and some others. The only Internationalist he had actually read was Eugène Varlin, and that in just one short newspaper article. Could he last in such a crowd?

And then there had been the surprise when Claude mentioned *'la présidente'*. A woman at the head of this association? Claude had just laughed at his surprise.

"You'll see," he said.

Étienne was eager but nervous. So nervous about fitting in, being accepted by the older workers, and puzzled and anxious about *'la présidente'*, that he might have put off the move yet another week. But tonight's experience, joined with his memory of the stench and the heat in Maurice's attic, and of the night when, drunk and shouting, Maurice had staggered in and stumbled over Étienne on the pad on the floor, had decided him. And at the first rays of sun this Sunday, 10th of July, Étienne gathered himself up and went back to Maurice's attic apartment for his bag of possessions and left his cousin Maurice collapsed on his bed fully dressed, loudly snoring.

It was rather a long walk, but by now a familiar one because it was near the bindery, across the Seine and into the Sixth. He quickly found the passage and then the *Cour du Dragon* – the fierce dragon that Claude had described, carved in stone and spreading its wings over the gateway into the little courtyard or alleyway, made him laugh with relief that he had found the right place.

He pulled the cord at the house number he had been given, expecting Claude or one of the other men he had mentioned to answer the door. But the person who opened was a woman, hardly older than his big sister, Clotilde, and disconcertingly attractive, in a simple gown and apron and abundant wavy dark hair bursting from her little white cap. He felt confused and looked down at his feet.

"Oh, good morning, young man," she said. "And who might you be?"

When he didn't answer right away, she added, "Well, you don't look like a bill collector. Not on Sunday, anyway. Then you must be Claude's friend, no? The one he told us about. Étienne is it? From Marseille?"

He nodded, then shook his head.

"Lyon."

"Oh! Lyon! Much better. Claude said Marseille, but he

doesn't know the south. It's all the same to him. Lyon is better! That's where I come from! Or very near there, in St-Étienne. Like your name. Please excuse me. I was expecting somebody else, and I wasn't really expecting you so soon. But that's fine, especially since you're from Lyon. Claude said you were young, but *so* young! Full grown, though. My, you're tall! Well, say something. Don't you know how to speak?"

"Oh, yes, of course. Pleased to meet you, Madame. But, I, I just wanted to say hello to Claude."

"To say 'Hello'? And that bag you have in your hand?"

He felt his face grow warmer and bit his lip.

"Come," she said, taking him by the sleeve and leading him up the stairs to the first floor.

Once across the threshold, the stinging air of *eau de javel* hit his nose, the same disinfectant his mother used. It reminded him of home and cleanliness, a relief after the stale odor of sweat and urine in Maurice's place.

"Claude said you might be a little shy. So far from home. You and I should get along just fine, you don't talk much but when you do you sound just like the people I lived with all my life before I came to Paris. But come in, bring your bag. Claude isn't here now, nor are any of the other chaps, but I'll show you your bed and explain how things are here. You have come to stay, correct? Have you had breakfast? No? Well, we'll take care of that. But first come with me. Oh, I am Angélique, by the way. But don't call me 'Ange', I'm no angel. See? No wings, no halo. Just an ordinary white cap. 'Lique' will do for a nickname. That's what they call me here. And I'll call you Titi."

She laughed, and Étienne laughed with her. She actually did seem like an 'angel' to him, so pretty and bright-eyed and gentle.

First she took him to the central room, with a long table

and benches on either side and a stove and coal bin with pots, pans and a basin hanging on the wall in the back. Next she opened the door to a long, narrow room on the side with six narrow cots. Étienne noted that five of them seemed inhabited or at least claimed with bags or boxes beneath them and the bedclothes tucked in more or less carelessly, some with garments hanging from nails in the wall beside them. The remaining one, near the door, appeared unclaimed and unmade but with a neatly folded sheet over it.

"You can sleep here," she said, taking his bag from him and placing it on the empty cot. "That is, after you meet the other men and we all vote. But from Claude's description, I don't think there will be any problem."

There were items of men's clothing hung on hooks by each cot. There was also a table in the corner with a wash basin on it. Everything was much neater and cleaner than Maurice's heap of clothes and books and kitchen things. And it smelled clean.

"We had six associates when we started" - she didn't say 'boarders' - "but, well, you know, Claude must have told you what happened. It was too bad, but we now have space for one more."

Then the bell rang.

"Oh, excuse me. That must be Alphonse."

She trotted lightly down the stairs and soon returned with a thin, not very tall young man, only a couple of years older than Étienne, with a narrow, waxed mustache that, Étienne thought, failed to make him look mature. Despite the July heat, the chap had on a dark jacket and cravat.

Angélique stretched out her arms in a gesture toward each of them.

"Alphonse-Marie Bertrand, meet Étienne - eh, Étienne?"

"Bonin," supplied Étienne. "Étienne Bonin. Pleased to meet you, Monsieur Bertrand."

"Charmed."

"Alphonse is our *plumitif*, our pen-pusher. I call him 'Scribou'. You don't mind that nickname, do you, my dear scribbler?"

"My precious Angélique, no man can take offense at anything that comes out of such a pretty mouth."

"You see, Titi? That's why he's a scribbler. He always has the right words! Some of our associates are studying with him. That's why you've come, right, Alphonse? He helps them correct the spelling and the phrases in our posters and our leaflets. And," she added, turning to the newcomer, "Étienne here is a bookbinder!"

"Apprentice bookbinder," Étienne corrected.

Alphonse smiled and cocked his head, running his eyes up and down Étienne as though appraising him.

"Bookbinder, bookbinder. Very honorable profession, young man. Anything to do with books and writing is honorable, very honorable indeed. Some of your fellow tradesmen have even become notable journalists, at least in the workers' press. But where are the others, my dear Lique?"

"Ah! With that poster you helped Jean-Pierre edit. Well, if you're going to paste posters on the walls, it's best to do it early Sunday morning, before the second shift of police is fully alert. They should be back soon, our chaps. Meanwhile, I suppose you boys will want some breakfast?"

Étienne was breaking another piece of bread when he heard a big, gruff voice shout something like "Ho, Lique-Lique! Well, is he here yet, that boy?" and then a stout, very broad, heavy-bearded man suddenly appeared.

"Ah, Alphonse! You here! Good morning. And this, this

must be the new boy. The one Claude spoke of? So you did come. Claude said he thought you would. Pleased to meet you, sonny. I'm Luc. And you?"

Étienne took his thick hand.

"Étienne," he said. "Pleased to meet you, sir."

"Ah, Titi! I have a cousin, Titi."

"Étienne," Étienne repeated. "My name is Étienne."

"Right. Étienne. Well, Titi, welcome to our little house! Lique-Lique has surely explained everything to you, right? Sharing the rent and the cost of food, we save money and have good company. And Lique is another worker, except instead of paying into the fund, she holds the place together. And that's a real job, right, Lique?"

He laughed.

"And here comes – oh, it's our book paster, Claude! Claude, come in here, here's your young friend, already here. Our new comrade. 'Étienne' he prefers to be called, like Saint Étienne the martyr with all the arrows in him!"

"That was Saint Sébastien, the one stuck with all the arrows," Angélique corrected gently. "Saint-Étienne is a city, the one I come from."

"Oh, well, if you say so. I never paid much attention in church. Whoever that guy Étienne was, if he was a saint it must have been for something. But we're not especially fond of saints here, eh, Titi?"

Before Étienne could answer, he heard Claude's voice.

"Well, good morning," said Claude, with a big smile and a laugh. "I see you had no trouble finding the place, eh? Getting to know your way around Paris. That's very good."

Immediately behind him came Évariste, Jean-Pierre, and Hilaire.

"How did you get here ahead of all of us, Luc?" asked this

last man, Hilaire, a tall redhead with a scraggly beard and a crooked smile. "You ducked out before the fun began."

"I told you it might be dangerous," said Luc. "I was up on that corner nearer the prefecture, and I heard the horses and, well… Did you get all the posters up?"

"Some, anyway," said Hilaire.

"I had to toss my last ones and make a run for it, but I'd pasted up four by then. And yours, Luc?" asked Évariste, a small, wiry blond fellow in a jacket and loose-fitting pants. He was the only one who still had his cap on, on top of matted, sandy hair.

"Well, you know, my legs. I don't run as fast as you fellows, so when the *rousse* showed up, I just rolled them up under my coat. And walked away, as casually as I could. There they are, in the vestibule."

"Well, then show one to our new friend," Hilaire commanded.

Luc stepped into the vestibule and brought back and unrolled a poster which he began to read out in a big voice. First was a quote from an anonymous 'correspondent from Lille' about the Empress and the government.

Luc pointed a finger toward Alphonse, who responded with a little bow.

"That's all very fine, but now read the last part. This is our statement," said Jean-Pierre. Luc continued:

"'Workers of France! Let us join hands with the workers of Germany! Let workers' blood not be shed to preserve the riches of the bourgeoisie!'"

"That will bugger the *jean-foutres* with their war talk!"

He held up the poster for Étienne to see. The last sentence was printed in the biggest letters.

"Pretty good, huh? I don't mean the printing, rather

sloppy, it was a hasty job by our friend downstairs, but the words! Our man Jean-Pierre put those together, with the help of our scribbler friend here, of course. And thank you very much! Especially for that last part, right, J-P? J-P, that's our man Jean-Pierre, he's our intellectual! Been studying French, taking regular lessons with *le petit Phonse*. You don't mind our calling you that, do you Ti-Phonse?"

"Look out, Luc, or he'll start calling you 'Lucane', you big bug! Stag beetle!" one of the others – Étienne wasn't sure which, maybe Hilaire – said with a laugh.

Alphonse just shook his head.

"'Phonse', if you like. I prefer 'Alphonse-Marie', or simply 'Bertrand', if you please."

Luc went on.

"Started on grammar with Angélique, J-P did – you know she used to be a school teacher. And now he's studying with the very chap who wrote that article we quoted, the anonymous 'correspondent from Lille' – and here he is."

He waved toward Alphonse.

"Yes," added J-P, "but then, for the proclamation at the end, our comrade Angélique still had to correct the spelling. As she always does. Don't know what we'd do without her."

"We'd look like illiterate fools, that's what," said Hilaire.

Angélique laughed.

"No, that's not true. Jean-Pierre is learning fast. He may not have shown it to you yet, but he's working on an article that might even get published. Our young bookbinder here, Étienne, take note. If you want to write, not just bind books, our man Alphonse-Marie could be a good teacher. Read out that last sentence on the poster, J-P."

"'For workers to take command of our destiny, we must be able to express our thoughts clearly and forcefully.'"

J-P's voice had become suddenly solemn, interrupting the smiles and laughter of the others.

"Ooh! That sounds just like Varlin!" said Luc. "That's something he might have said!"

"It's something he did say, in *La Marseillaise*. I just quoted it. I can show you, I've kept that issue."

"Ah, we miss him, don't we, boys? And you too, Lique-Lique."

Luc pressed his hand to his heart and inclined his head, with a half-grin to show he was only half-joking.

Alphonse invited Étienne to sit in on the next lesson he had scheduled with J-P, and then excused himself, saying he had an important assignment that evening.

Besides Claude, from the same atelier where Étienne was working, Jean-Pierre was another bookbinder but in a smaller, specialized shop. Hilaire was a chemist in Javel – where Angélique's bleach, *eau de javel*, came from – which he explained to Étienne was a long walk away, in the Fifteenth Arrondissement, so he had little time for study. Évariste was a tinsmith, and Luc worked in the Marais, a shorter walk but on the other side of the river, on the right bank, in a factory recovering precious metals from broken or discarded jewelry and other objects.

In the evening, by the flickering of an oil lamp, Luc pulled out a deck of cards and began snuffling and shuffling, saying, "It's Sunday night and I don't think any of you boys is thinking of going out, right? So, unless you have a heavy date somewhere" – he stopped dramatically for a wink and a nod all around him – "we'll have a round of sizette. We need six players, three against three – Angélique, are you in?"

"No, not tonight. Show the new boy how you play, he'll be your sixth."

Luc raised an eyebrow and appraised the newcomer.

"It'll be a slow game then, but he's got to learn. All right, boys?"

And Étienne, teamed with Claude and J-P – "the three bookbinders," announced Luc – was introduced to a game he had heard of but had never before played.

Moist dreams

"Mii-*iiilk*."

The two-syllable call from outside startled Étienne awake.

"Mii-*iiilk*, who wants milk." And again. And again.

Then, nearer, another voice. Or two voices, a woman's and a man's, then a door closing. Étienne blinked. Light streamed through an opening above and behind him, more light than had ever entered Maurice's attic. Daylight! What time must it be? And where was he?

He had had the strangest, most delicious dream. But no, it couldn't have been a dream, he really was on a bed, a very narrow one but still a bed, and not a mat of straw on the floor of Maurice's attic on Manure Street. And there was a sheet over him. Or partly over him. And under the sheet, nothing. Or rather, just his shirt, and then the sheet, now askew, draped over his long legs. And no sign of the other, the being who had brought him here, the spirit who had lain beside him, who had done things, had guided him into her – and then again, and again. How many times? Yes, yes! Until he was exhausted. But no, it was no dream, but it had really been…

Cloti! No, no, it couldn't be, not Clotilde, not his own sister. The shame! But maybe someone who reminded him of her. Oh, yes, Angélique, that was her name. A woman, not a girl, but a woman, older than Cloti, twenty-three or even twenty-five he guessed, and probably – or so he imagined – more experienced in, well, that sort of thing. Or was it that girl in the bindery he'd been thinking of, that Rose?

He heard a man's grunt and opened his eyes. But whoever his imaginary night-time visitor had been, she was not here now. Beside his cot, he saw only his pants hanging from a nail, and on either side, other men pulling on their clothes. He tried to retain the image of what he now knew had been just a dream. Just? But what a dream! The gown that he remembered seeing her slip over her nakedness, after she had already done what she had done with him. He had imagined all that? The gown, the gown in his dream seemed familiar. Yes! It was that frilly thing he's seen on his sister. But no, not his sister!

He began to be aware that his dream had been made of things he hadn't dared speak, sensations he had only wished for. And her pressing herself to him as he shivered with delight. Until, until nothing. Nothing he could remember. He half-closed his eyes, seeking to return to that moment.

But then he snapped them open again. It must be nearly six, or even later. On Monday, here in the Sixth Arrondissement, and just a few minutes from his atelier. He had already learned that his Paris foreman did not tolerate any tardiness, not even on Monday. He had seen another worker fined a half-day's wages for showing up less than a half hour late.

He jumped up, grabbed his pants, shirt and vest, and after some hunting, his well-worn shoes. No time for breakfast, if there was any to be had. Fortunately, his workplace was very close, that had been one reason – the other reason, besides the money problems with Maurice and his desire for fellowship – for moving to this place.

He opened the door to the dining and cooking area. If anybody had eaten anything this morning, it had been cleared away. They'd all left. Or almost everybody.

"Hallo?" he called.

A bearded chin poked into the room where he was lacing his shoes, followed by Luc's broad, meaty shoulders.

"Ah, so there you are, *mon gars*! Pierrot! Oh, no, not Pierre – Titi! That's it. Titi. Who would rather be called 'Étienne', now I remember. Good morning, young fellow. How was your night? Ha, ha, pretty exciting dream you must have been having, right? You woke us all up with your moaning! Claude tried to shake you awake, but you just thrashed around, like you were still in your dream, so he just left you."

He laughed and sighed.

"Is she here?"

"She? Angélique? Was that who you were dreaming about? Oh, my! Well, dream on. And no, she's not here now, she went down to buy milk, like every morning, as soon as the milk lady gets here. With her daughter. Cute thing, that milk-lady's daughter. If you want to have more than wet dreams, take a look at that one! She's closer to your age, and just getting ripe! But say, aren't you going to be late for work?"

"Yes, I'm afraid I am. Everybody else has gone then?"

"Well of course, they all have jobs, where the owners are strict. Not like my boss. If I show up a little late on a Monday, all's well. He knows that he needs me, to pick out the best pieces. And since I'm his best worker, he leaves me be."

"Well, that's good luck for you. Not the case in the bindery. I've got to run! See you tonight?"

"Right. We'll see you tonight, back here. Around half-past six. We'll be having a meeting. Now hop to it, sonny!"

And Étienne, without answering, bounded down the stairs, stopping only briefly in the passageway out from the court to piss, the smells telling him he wasn't the first, before hiking up his pants and running to work.

* * *

At break time, Étienne decided he would finally dare to address that girl, Rose.

"Uh, *excusez-moi* –" he started, addressing her with the formal '*vous*'. She looked up, startled but smiling.

"I was wondering if we could talk a little about those authors you mentioned the other day, on Saturday."

"Authors!" said a male voice just behind his shoulder. It was that same fellow who had spoken up to Perrin. Toinou again. "If you want to talk about books, you have to read *l'Enfermé*, 'The Locked-up Man.'

This interruption threw him off stride. It had taken him all morning to decide on his phrasing and practise it, but still he thought his voice had squeaked a little on the word 'authors'. But, 'The Locked-up Man'?

"Blanqui!" the fellow clarified in a sharp, pointed tone.

Blanqui! He had heard of him, of course, and that he had spent years in prison. *"L'Enfermé."*

"Well," the girl he'd been eying said, looking around at the other young women observing her.

One of the others then cut in.

"Come on, Rose. We've got to go, that Perrin isn't going to give us any extra time. You can talk to your new friend some other time. Such a gentleman! He says '*vous*'. My, such manners!"

Rose laughed. The other two girls crowded between her

and Étienne, with that loud, bulky Toinou right behind, and they started down the stairs, leaving Étienne behind. But before they descended, Rose did turn and give him a sweet smile.

Étienne felt a hand on his arm. It belonged to one of the other workers, a man a little older than Étienne.

"Let's go, buddy. Don't worry about those girls, they're playing with you. It's the way they do. I've been after that one, Louise, that brunette, with the crooked smile?"

"The shorter one?"

"Right. But the other one, that Cécile, she's all right, too. But neither one of them will give me the time of day. And that younger one, that Rose, the one you've been trying to get close to – yes, I've been watching you. Don't waste your time! She's too smart, talks about books, I can't keep up with her. But Louise, now, I think she really likes me but she won't let on, not with those other two around her all the time."

Étienne sighed.

"Well, come on. They're going down to the river, I suppose. You and I, let's head over to the Marmite. Hey, Claude, are you coming? You know that place, don't you?"

* * *

The other little group had gone only a few paces when Toinou turned and, with a wave, grunted "Adieu."

"Oh, Toinou! Leaving us already? Another meeting? Well, we'll see you back at the shop."

Cécile turned and smiled at her two workmates.

"There he goes again. Such a busy boy! Off to meet his comrades. Too bad, it's nice sometimes to have a man around. And he speaks so well."

"Aha! Our Cécile is falling in love!"

"No, I'm not, Louise, and you know it! Anyway, that Toinou is too busy for us. With his head full of politics, he hardly notices us girls. But you, Louise, why are you treating Albert so cruelly? He would be a good catch, and he obviously has got a crush on you."

"Oh, Albert. Yes, he is all right I suppose. For some girls. But he's not my type."

"Your type? Such a picky girl! He's a gilder, making top wage in the bindery. And he's, well, maybe not as handsome as Toinou, but he's not bad looking, not really. And very polite. And what about the new boy?"

"The tall one with the funny accent? He's just a child!"

"Oh, pardon me! I forgot about your advanced age."

"Twenty-three. Same as you. But that boy looks like he's sixteen, or maybe seventeen at most. Maybe he'd be right for Rose. Just your age, my little flower! They'd be a cute couple, don't you think, Céci?"

"If she could just get him to speak up. He seems awfully shy. What do you say, Rose? He's had his eye on you. You haven't said a word. But you look kind of dreamy."

"I don't even know him," Rose said. She had scarcely been paying attention to her workmates' banter until she heard her own name, linked to 'the tall one with the funny accent', and then…

"Oh, look! She's blushing!"

Yes, she knew it was true. She could feel the blood rushing to her face. How embarrassing!

"Don't worry, my little rosebud," Cécile said soothingly.

"Loulou and I will work on him. But let's get on down to the riverbank, we don't have a lot of time to scarf down this sausage I brought before we get back to the shop. Which reminds me, Loulou, speaking of the shop, Perrin, our foreman, maybe he would be your type. Mature enough for you? Hey, don't throw that at me!"

Workers of the World

It was the next day, Tuesday, 12th July, just at the close of work and Étienne knew he was supposed to go somewhere, but Cécile and Louise had trapped him in some chitchat that he could hardly follow but that centered on the attractions of their youngest co-worker. Which he could hardly deny.

"Come on," said Claude, pulling on his arm. "They'll be waiting for us at the club. Leave those girls – I know it's hard to break off your pleasant conversation, but we've got important things to do!"

"Oh, and will you girls be all right?" Étienne said to Rose and her companions. "I mean, do you want us to accompany you?"

"Titi, come on!" insisted Claude, pulling again.

"No, no, thank you," said Louise. "We'll be fine. And here's Antoine, he'll protect us. You go the same way as we do, don't you, Toinou?"

Antoine just grunted assent.

Claude grasped his arm and hurried him down the street. As Étienne rushed with Claude toward their meeting, he tried to look back.

"I don't know what's got into them, all of a sudden those girls seem to want to talk to me all the time, making little jokes and nudging me."

"Nudging?"

"Right, toward, well, that young one."

"They've got you all hot and bothered. Well, keep your pants on. Albert said you were almost panting whenever he mentioned Rose, so he kept bringing up her name, just to watch your face."

Claude laughed, while Étienne kept wondering just what sort of threat this 'Toinou' might represent in his plans for Rose.

Quickly they reached a great arched door between massive pillars, with elaborate relief carvings in the stone façade.

"Claude, what is this place?"

"School of Medicine. I told you. Come on, they're already about to start."

Inside, there were already tens of people, maybe even fifty Étienne guessed. Mostly unknown to him, but he recognized Hilaire and Évariste, who saw him and waved. And Jean-Pierre, J-P, standing a little apart, in conversation with a smallish, blond young man in a frock coat who looked out of place among the men and women in workers' shirts and blouses. Then he recognized him, it was that journalist, Alphonse something. Claude, with Étienne close behind, stepped over to J-P.

J-P greeted them with a hearty handshake and the journalist said, "Hello, Claude. Who's your friend?"

"Oh, why this lad is our new house-mate. But you two have already met! Titi, you remember my French tutor, Monsieur Bertrand."

"Alphonse," the journalist corrected, extending his hand. "Yes, now I remember. I'm glad to see you again, Claude, and – oh, excuse me, what was your name, young chap?"

"Étienne. Pleased to see you. I remember, you're the one who helped J-P on that poster."

"Oh, he didn't really need much help. A little spelling difficulty."

Étienne thought the journalist looked embarrassed.

"That was nothing," said Jean-Pierre. "I asked him to come to look over the letter we're supposed to sign tonight, just to make sure we don't look foolish when it's published."

Alphonse just moved his head from side to side, waving his hand as though to say, 'It's nothing.'

"Well, tell them what you told me," said J-P to the slight young man in the frock coat.

"It's quite all right, your letter. Some things might be phrased differently, but there's really nothing wrong with the way it is stated, I mean from a journalistic point of view. Maybe the Emperor's police will have a problem with it," he said with a little laugh.

"Well, I should hope so! A big problem, if he wants to start a war. That was the whole idea of the letter, right, J-P?" said Claude.

"Anyway, I understand it has already been approved by other clubs, so it will have to stand the way it's written. Isn't that right, Jean-Pierre?"

"Approved by the other clubs? I don't know about that. But it's the draft of the IWA leadership, Camélinat and Theisz. After a lot of debate. But we can still ask for changes if you see something wrong with it."

Alphonse just smiled and shook his head.

"I think Camélinat must have already shown it to somebody. It is in quite proper French. I suspect Rochefort or somebody from his paper worked on it, from the style."

"Bertrand here is very meticulous about grammar and

such, so if he says it's all right, then it must be all right," J-P announced.

Somebody called the meeting to order and a heavy, older man Étienne didn't know was introduced as a printer and a proud revolutionary from '51. The revolutionary veteran, an intense, hyper-alert look in his eyes over a gray-streaked beard, rose to the lectern and, stumbling over some of the bigger words, read out fiercely the letter addressed 'To the workers of the world'. Then he looked up and glared defiantly at the audience until other voices broke out. "Hurrah!"

"Yes, comrade, that's the way to say it."

The text was approved, and even applauded but then someone shouted a question about how to get the message to the German workers, a problem Étienne hadn't considered until then.

"*Citoyenne?*" said the chairman, turning to the little woman seated behind the speaker, who sprang up to her full but modest height – to Étienne's surprise it was Madame Lemel, Mère Nathalie, whom he knew from La Marmite. She spoke clearly, firmly, unembarrassed by her Breton accent.

"The International is truly international," she said. "We have members among the German workers and comrades among the journalists. In Germany and other countries, too. They will translate the letter and see that it reaches workers' circles in Germany, and in Hungary and Switzerland and the Netherlands and everywhere!" she announced.

But the printer who had read the letter voiced a caution – that everyone should know that, by signing, he would be openly identifying himself with a banned organization, the International Workingmen's Association. That caution gave Étienne a thrill. This was his first opportunity for a bold act of defiance and his identification with the cause of the International. When his turn came, he picked up the pen and wrote boldly, *'Étienne Bonin, relieur.'* Yes, *'relieur'*, bookbinder, for this historic occasion, even though he was still an apprentice. Because soon, he was sure, that was what he would be, a fully-formed professional.

It was already dark out, and the chairman thanked the crowd and adjourned the meeting, to cheers – "Vive la République!", "No war with our worker brothers!" – and the first verses of a rowdy satirical song, about Badinguet and his hemorrhoids and the folly of war. And then the crowd quickly dispersed – everybody was going to have to get up early and get to work the next morning, whether printers or bookbinders or woodworkers or shoemakers or anything.

Back out onto the street with Claude, J-P, Hilaire and Évariste, Étienne felt exhilarated. He had committed a revolutionary act, and these were his comrades. He wanted to prolong the sensation, so when they came to a café all lit up and resounding with another version of the song ridiculing the Emperor that they had just been singing, he proposed stopping for a drink. Claude reminded him that they had to start work especially early the next morning, but Étienne looked so disappointed he relented and the two of them stepped into the concert café while the others left them there and continued walking back toward the Court of the Dragon.

The place was noisy with laughter, shouts in the middle of the verses, and the clatter of glassware on marble tabletops. The pipe and cigar smoke flavored the air and produced a gauze curtain that made the bosomy singer and her thin, mustachioed violinist accompanist mysterious. Claude found places, crowding in with three other men at a table, and Étienne – not knowing what to ask for – accepted a tall glass of some very harsh wine, and laughing, attempted to join in the chorus. And then – there was another glass, some conversation he could barely follow, lots of laughter, more songs, maybe still another glass, he wasn't sure, then suddenly cooler air. He was outside on the street now.

He tried to head back into the café but someone or something had latched onto his arm and pulled him back, and together with this other being, like some four-footed animal they walked along the dark streets, the cobblestones rough under the thin soles of his boots. They had gone some ways when he suddenly recognized a space they were passing through, the passageway under the dragon's wings. That reminded him of something. Something, something good that he wanted. Yes, Angélique! He was going to impress her with his political maturity, his actually signing a declaration of the International. This was the way to the house where she lived. Or was it Rose he was going to see? Oh, well, no matter. At least it wasn't Madeleine the *ovaliste*, but a woman, that's what he needed to celebrate, a real Paris woman. He wanted to dance, but whoever it was who held his arm restrained him and steered him toward the building door, then up the stairs – aa, up! aa, up again! one step at a time – then the door to the flat. There was a candle glowing in a niche in the little vestibule, and Étienne turned to see what it was that had been holding him. He knew that face. Ah, yes, it was his friend Claude, his work companion, his drinking comrade. How good of him.

"Time to get you to bed, young fellow. We start work early tomorrow."

And Claude started to push him toward the common bedroom. But no! He remembered. He had imagined that this would be his night with a woman. Maybe the chanteuse from the concert café. The raunchy songs, his day-dreaming about that co-worker Rose, the wine, his taking the big step into manhood of signing that letter, this had to be the night of his reward. Whoever she was, she must be behind that other door, in the back of the dining and kitchen room. He turned and headed toward it, against the pulling. With a lurch, he got to the door. It was locked. He knocked. He knocked louder, annoyed at that person pulling on his shoulders – Claude it must be, but Claude was supposed to be his friend!

"Rose!" he called.

"Hush!" said Claude. "There's no Rose here. That's our Angélique's room! You'll wake her."

"Angélique! It's me, Étienne."

Other hands now grabbed his shoulders, his waist, pulling him back.

"Angélique! Rose!"

"Hush!" another man told him. Not Claude, a different voice. Évariste, maybe.

Then Étienne, not knowing why, started to sob, as someone pulled off his jacket. He felt a wet cloth pass over his face, and then he was lying flat on a narrow bed, and several familiar male voices buzzed around him, saying things to each other that sounded very distant. But it was comfortable now to lie stretched out, and the voices were soothing, and he drifted off.

The glove-maker's counsel

The morning sun shone so fiercely through the big east-facing windows of the bindery that Étienne had to squint and blink to keep track of what his hands were doing as he ran the trimming plough over the page edges in the laying press, the razor-sharp blade cutting through more ragged edges at each stroke. He worked mechanically, almost without thinking, unsure even of how he got here and who had dressed him. Or had he ever undressed last night? He thought of that when, mimicking the other men, he took off his vest and rolled up his shirt sleeves against the mid-July heat. He passed his forearm over his brow to brush his damp forelock out of his eyes. How had he got to work this morning? He didn't really remember anything after the song in the *café conç*. One or more of his new comrades must have got him up and hustled him to the atelier on time – yes, now he had a dim memory of his feet on the stairs, and someone pushing him. And a hoarse voice. Someone – Évariste? Hilaire? – saying they were going to have to talk with him, later, after work. "We," the voice had said, meaning everyone in the house, he supposed.

There was a pulsing ache behind his eyes, and a turmoil in his stomach, made heavier by a sense of shame. Shame for what, he wasn't exactly sure. For drinking so much, or for being too young and from too far away to know how he was supposed to behave, here in his new circle.

Somehow, foggily, the morning passed, the books got trimmed, the knife got sharpened, more books got trimmed. Today he felt too embarrassed to face the crowd in La Marmite. He didn't feel himself to be the kind of man he wanted to be, to become. Calm, sober, competent and above all articulate, like Varlin. All he could manage was to try hard to focus on his work.

"Tonight. We're going to have to talk with you. Tonight," echoed in his head. What could that mean? It couldn't be good. What would happen to him if he lost their support, those men in Angélique's boarding house? Back to Lyon? His mother would be glad to see him, and maybe Madeleine, but what could he tell his friends? He wouldn't have to tell them anything. They would know. That he had lost his bet, his bet on Paris. On his new life.

Ugh! He wanted to vomit. But no, he'd hold out. And meanwhile keep his head down, looking at nothing but the trimming plough and the ragged pages as he moved the plough back and forth.

So focused was he on this mindless, repetitive task, or so distracted by his self-recriminations, that when break-time came, he was surprised. He looked up to where Claude was working but Claude, his only real buddy here, turned away. The girls at the sewing frames were gathering their things and chatting. Rose's eyes turned toward him momentarily, but now it was Étienne who turned away. As he shuffled, slouching toward the door, one of the other sewing girls – Cécile, was it? – looked back at him and laughed.

"Hey, Titi!" she called. He hated that childish nickname, especially today, when he felt so childish. And he was surprised that she even knew his name. Or maybe she always said 'Titi' to boys she didn't know, like saying 'Little one,' *'Petit'*.

"If you're not rushing off to La Marmite, you can come with us to the river. Toinou is coming, right?"

Toinou, he noticed, was standing very close to Rose. Too close, Étienne thought.

"La Marmite? So our *péquenaud* from down south hangs out with the Internationalists!" Toinou laughed. "I thought he'd have more sense than that!"

Étienne felt his face warm. *'Péquenaud.'* How could anyone call him a bumpkin when he was from the second largest city in France!

"Calm down, Toinou," said Louise. "You're so impatient."

"Do come with us, Étienne," said Rose. He was glad to hear his proper name, not 'Titi'.

"No, no. Thanks, but I…"

"Oh, come on," said the other girl, the taller one, Cécile. "If you haven't brought anything, there's a vendor down on the bank with croûtes and cheese. It will be good to have another guy along. Keep those obnoxious bums from pestering us."

She and the shorter, darker one – Louise, he remembered – giggled.

Étienne just stared at them. He couldn't find words, and here in Paris, without words a person was a defenseless lump. It wasn't just his accent that embarrassed him, it was his lifelong lack of practice at – what was that word? A fencing term. *Repartie*. That was it. The ability to strike back with a fast retort. At least he had thought of the name for it, for what he lacked!

But the girls and Toinou were already headed down the stairs. And Rose had grabbed Toinou's arm. Étienne headed down behind them, and then turned in the other direction.

* * *

Back at work, after aimless wandering without a bite to eat during the lunch break, his hunger pangs were more than tolerable, they felt welcome – a self-chastisement he deserved. He was wrong to be here, in this crowd of clever Parisians who saw him as a rube. He had behaved very badly the night before, he somehow knew, even though he didn't really remember just what he'd done, except the drinking, the loud singing, and then some sudden excitement before he had passed out. Coming to Paris had been a big mistake. He was sure. Or no, he wasn't really sure, he wasn't sure of anything.

Now, back in the bindery, the hours passed, more quickly than he wished because he was half-dreading the return to Dragon Court. He felt a strange excitement mixed with foreboding and an improbable, unfounded optimism – foreboding because of that stern and disapproving voice last night when he had been so drunk, and a giddy optimism he tried to cling to, about learning to be a Parisian, a Parisian bookbinder no less, gaining the skills, the language, the words, charting his own new course.

When the workday finally ended, Claude turned and left without a word to him, which was unusual but suited him because he wanted to walk these few blocks alone with his thoughts. Understanding his problem and calculating its dimensions should be, must be, the first step for overcoming it.

He had purposefully walked slowly, not wanting to catch up to Claude who, he assumed, was going the same way. Once past the dragon's wings, he climbed the stairs and pushed open the door, to see his comrades – all five men, but with no sign of Angélique – seated at the dining table. Two or three faces turned toward him, hard and unexpressive. Claude and Luc were looking in other directions.

"Hello, fellows," he said, trying to elicit a smile.

It was Hilaire who answered. After heaving a deep sigh.

"Well, young man," said Hilaire. "We've been waiting for you. What do you have to say for yourself?"

"What do you mean?"

"He means last night, boy," said Luc with a snort that could have been a laugh. Or not.

"Last night? Oh, yes, I guess I got pretty drunk, didn't I?"

"If that was all there was to it! We all get drunk, now and then," said Luc.

"No. That's not the problem. Or not the whole problem," said J-P.

"But he's right about that. He was plenty drunk!" Luc found this remark of his quite funny.

"The problem," began J-P…

"The problem is you offended Angélique. Lique-lique. And that we can't have. This whole operation, this whole boarding house depends on her," concluded hyperenergetic little Évariste.

"Oh, but I didn't mean, I mean, I never, I couldn't do anything to offend, I mean, I didn't mean to, to Angélique? What did she say?"

"That's the whole problem," said J-P. "She hasn't said anything. Nothing! Not a word this morning when she set out our breakfast, and then she disappeared."

"Disappeared?" repeated Étienne.

"She's gone. She's not here."

"And when she comes back, if she comes back, we have to have a decision ready, about what to do about you. To make sure she stays. We need six men here for this club to work smoothly, to meet expenses, but if need be we can get by with five, everybody paying a little more, until we find a new man." That was J-P talking.

Étienne stared, open-mouthed.

"But, I, you know, the *caf'conç'*, I'd never had so much liquor, but I would never… I *love* Angélique!"

"We all do, sonny," said Luc. "And that's why we're going to have to take steps to protect her."

"Titi, brother Étienne, we must ask you to go out for a couple of hours while we decide what to do," said J-P. "While we wait for Angélique. She hasn't taken anything from her room, so she has to come back. We think. We hope. Leave us now, and come back, say, in two hours or so."

"Leave? My things?"

"No, don't take anything now, wait and we'll see. And then if need be, you can pick up your things to go wherever you're going to go."

Étienne looked to Claude, whom he considered his closest friend here – the one who had introduced him to this house and to the atelier where they worked. Claude did not look up at him but kept staring at the wall across.

Slowly, feeling suddenly tired and sensing his eyes watering, Étienne turned and headed back down the stairs. And then, where to? In this city he barely knew. Too late for the Marmite, he guessed – and the crowd there might not be welcoming, either. To the only other place he knew, then. To Rue du Fumier and his cousin Maurice.

* * *

On the long walk back across the Seine to the Twelfth

Arrondissement, Étienne went over and over in his mind the most memorable scenes and incidents of his weeks in Paris. All the awkward moments, the things he had done or said wrong, the few moments of satisfaction he had not known how to prolong. Did he really belong here?

He could easily imagine what his life would have been like had he remained in Lyon. More tensions with the owner of the workshop, possibly becoming unbearable, more pointless drinking with companions while grumbling and swearing about the fate of working people in a system made for the rich, daydreaming of another world but with no plans to get there, and his own inevitable succumbing to the eternal frustrations of routine, reducing his ambitions to those imposed by his city and his trade.

And maybe a continuing romance with a sweet but barely literate girl, Madeleine with her peasant's speech and prejudices, who would expect nothing more from him but bread on the table and two or three or maybe a dozen children to carry on the tradition of submission to richer and more powerful persons, accepting as fate or God's will the precariousness of poverty.

She was so unlike perky Rose, the folio-stitcher. Rose, he imagined, had read books, and knew people who were going to change the world. She, always with a quick retort spoken in the cadences of Paris. If he could win her! That would be proof that he had become a real Parisian. But for now he could hardly speak to her, he would get so flushed with embarrassment.

Maybe Madeleine the peasant girl, the barely literate *ovaliste*, would not be such a bad match. She would not intimidate him, and she didn't play clever word games to catch him up. He could laugh at her ignorance and her country ways, but she was smart enough to join with the other girls and women in their big strike last year. And she wouldn't be intimidated by him and his book knowledge, either. She was sure of herself, of her loyalties to her co-workers, of the proper way for a girl to speak and dress and think. Maybe she didn't need to learn anything, certainly not anything that could be found in a book or pamphlet.

Or maybe he was underestimating her. Because he remembered again that it had been Madeleine who had dragged him to the rally where he had heard Varlin and the other speakers from the International. And where he first imagined coming to Paris. Traveling far from her and all that stilted life, far from his little world on the Croix-Rousse, where the limits were clearly marked and seemed impossible to breach. Madeleine the *ovaliste* had already achieved her version of liberation, by escaping her village and reaching the big city of Lyon, which to her must be what Paris was to Étienne.

With these confused thoughts, he approached the home of his cousin, his fellow Lyonnais. There he would hear the familiar accent, maybe even speak about things he really felt. And maybe even find a place to stay if he could not return to Dragon Court. He wanted to put off as long as possible the taking of another train, this time from the Gare de Lyon in Paris back to Lyon, which would be the confession of failure.

It was still light out when he reached number 9, Rue du Fumier. The lamplighter would not reach the neighborhood for another hour – when he had first arrived, Étienne had marveled to see street lamps everywhere, even in this part of the Twelfth Arrondissement. The concierge looked surprised to see him, but then nodded and gestured with his head toward the stairs up to the attic.

At the top of the stairs, the door was closed and, to his surprise, latched. "Maurice," he called, and knocked. "Are you there? It's me, Titi."

In his mind he had become Titi again, the boy from Croix-Rousse, not the proud Parisian Étienne.

He had to knock and call again before he heard a voice, a woman's voice, questioning, and then Maurice.

"Who's there? Is that Titi?"

"Yes, it's me."

More voices, a woman's squeal, rustle of clothing, some furniture scraped along the floor, footsteps. And the door opened.

Maurice's broad face looked sleepy. His shirt was half in, half out of his trousers. Half a head shorter than Étienne, he turned his head to look up at his eyes.

"Hello, Maurice."

Maurice nodded and grunted. Then suddenly, as though just remembering where he was and who was at his door, "Come in!" and he stepped out of the way.

The shape of the attic was the same, same walls, the same sloping roof and the same narrow window, but different. Orderly. Nothing heaped upon the floor, the sawhorses and planks of the workbench now pushed up against the wall, papers and books on it in neat piles. And there was an odor of cleanliness. And in the shadows at the far end, the figure of a woman. A young woman, he guessed, slender and not very tall.

"Sophie, come meet my cousin Étienne. He's going to be a bookbinder!"

Sophie took a step forward into what remained of the daylight from the narrow window. She was in a work-frock. Her hair, capless, formed wild, dark waves around her pale face. Étienne guessed her to be twenty, or twenty-two at the most. He couldn't make out her eye color. Étienne bowed his head toward her, and she extended her hand.

"Pleased to meet you."

"So, what brings you here tonight? I thought you'd be with your compagnons over in the Fifth, is it?"

"Sixth, in the Sixth Arrondissement. Further over."

Sophie lit a lamp and gestured for him to sit, and she and Maurice also found stools. Sophie was a glove maker in a workshop nearby, Maurice explained, and another member of Maurice's Saint-Simon circle. She seemed to Étienne very sweet, gentle and shy.

"How are things going in your workshop? Swimmingly, I trust?"

Without waiting for an answer, Maurice told him he still had not found work in his trade and Sophie's earnings were barely enough for bread and rent, and he was even thinking of selling his tools for cash – but Sophie reacted strongly.

"No! That, never! We've talked about that. And look, cousin Étienne, some of the things Maurice has been able to do with those tools. There, on the table."

At that she got up and pointed, bringing the lamp with her to illuminate some small, elaborate wooden models of constructions Étienne didn't really understand.

"See? Dams, a bridge, here's a barrage against flooding, little models of what could be big, important projects. He's really an engineer, my carpenter Maurice."

Maurice smiled and nodded.

"All right. We keep the tools. But if something doesn't turn up in the next couple of weeks, I don't know. I do have another idea, something I might have to do. But tell us what's going on with you, cousin. Something brought you here, for this unexpected visit."

And he told them, as clearly as he was able, what had happened. About how embarrassed and afraid he was that he might have lost the support of his compagnons back in the cooperative boarding house. He thought his job was still safe for the moment, but he couldn't be sure, because for that too he depended on support of the others.

"Well," said Maurice, "I'd like to say that you could stay here for a while, but now, with Sophie…"

He turned toward her. She didn't say a word but looked first at Maurice then at Étienne, seriously, as though thinking, calculating something.

"No, that's not why I came here," Étienne lied. "I just needed to talk to someone, to someone from home. And you're the only one I know. Besides that lady who runs the bistro over by the train station, and I don't really know her."

"Loulou? She's all right. You could talk to her if you need to. She knows a lot of people we know back in Lyon."

"Maybe I will. Because, well, if I can't go back to that house on Dragon Court, and if things don't go well in the bindery, I'm thinking I'll have to go back home to Lyon."

"What?" reacted Sophie. "Oh, you men! Always ready to give up. Aren't there any lions in Lyon? Here's Maurice talking about selling his tools, which would mean to lose everything he's worked for, and you, cousin Étienne, are you going to just give up after coming all the way here to become what you want to be? Because Maurice has told me your story, your dreams. No! That's not the way to do things, to just give up at the first little obstacle. Listen to Saint-Simon! It's what we learn in our circle. You have to fight for what you want!"

Étienne was surprised by her strong reaction, but Maurice just smiled and nodded. He seemed not at all surprised.

"Well, then what do you think I should do?" he asked her. "What would your Saint-Simon say? I haven't read him."

"Neither has Sophie," Maurice said. "But she understands the doctrine."

"I don't read well. There was no school for girls like me, but I do read a little, and I listen to the others in our circle. And I can tell you, first you have to step back and see what it is you're facing. They haven't actually told you you can't come back, have they?"

"No. But they're talking now, to make a decision."

"Then you don't know whether you have a problem or not," Sophie said sharply. "First you have to decide if you really want to keep living there or not. And if you do, what you have to do is go back there, explain as best you can how things happened, and if you're sorry, say that you're sorry."

"And if they have any doubt, tell them about your loyalty to the association," added Maurice.

"Or else, find someplace else to sleep, or give it all up, Paris and all your ambitions and go back home. Is that what you want?"

"No!"

"Then, go back to your house on, where was it? Serpent? Oh, I remember now, Dragon Court. What a funny name!"

"And I've been listening to her too, Titi. I do have another plan, so I won't have to sell my tools. Though Sophie is opposed."

"Yes?"

Sophie let out a huge sigh.

"It's a terrible idea. Let's hope we don't get to that."

"Think of it as a last resort. But it might not really be so bad," said Maurice. "Sophie doesn't like to hear this, but it may be all right. All this talk of war with Prussia? They're going to need skilled carpenters in the engineering corps. In the army, I mean. The salary is small, but steady. And I could send almost all of it back here to Sophie, because the army will cover all costs, and we could save for when I get back. And have a family."

"If you don't get killed," said Sophie. "Or kill other men. Which would be almost as bad."

"Germans. Enemies of France."

"Men. Human beings, like us. You don't want to be a killer, I know you don't."

"No, you're right. I don't want to be a killer. But I think I could get a spot in the engineering corps, to build things. And defend France while I do it. No, you're right, I don't want to kill anybody, but sometimes a man has no choice. To defend the homeland."

Étienne remembered the letter he had signed.

"They're our brothers, too, those German workers. Those German workers made to fight for the King of Prussia, they have more in common with us French workers than either of us have for their king or our emperor."

"But if we're attacked, Étienne, we'll have to fight for France."

"For the empire, you mean. For Napoleon and the whole apparatus of this system that keeps us poor."

"I don't want him to go. It scares me."

"Oh, Sophie! Don't be so worried. It will all be over in a couple of weeks. Our forces are so much stronger! We'll march into Berlin, and then, Titi, maybe we'll be able to free those German workers you both care so much about from their Prussian king. And then, if we want, we can turn to free ourselves from our emperor."

"War can't be good for anybody," Étienne offered. "We

should get rid of our emperor first, then there won't be any need for war."

"Hmm! Lots of luck. You and Blanqui and the proclamations of the International, against the police and the army and the Mobile Guard. Go ahead! You saw what happened in the plebiscite, right? Overthrow the Emperor! With all that support he's got from the rurals."

They were silent for a minute.

"You think I should go back, right? To the house, I mean. They said to give them a couple of hours. I guess it's time."

Sophie nodded. Maurice half-smiled and shrugged his shoulders.

"Good luck, Titi."

"Yes, cousin Étienne, good luck and have courage. And if it comes to the worst, we can make room here for a night, no matter what Maurice says."

Étienne smiled sadly and thanked them and left the apartment.

Initiation

Back at Dragon Court, he found the street door unlocked, went up and – hesitantly – knocked on the door to the loft. J-P opened and, with just the trace of a smile, told him that Angélique had returned and wanted to speak with him. Three or four of the men seated around the dining table looked up as he stepped in, Luc as usual looking amused.

"And so the boy's returned," he said. "We've been waiting. But we'd better let our president tell you what we've decided. Lique!" he called out. "He's here."

She came out of her room and sat at the head of the table, motioning to Étienne to take a chair. Yes, she told him, their association (meaning mainly she) had decided they needed his youthful energy and could forgive his transgressions. Especially since drunkenness in times of excitement like these could be seen almost as a virtue.

"But for now, it's late, and all of you men have to get up to go to work tomorrow. If you please, gentlemen, you may retire now. Except our new boy, Étienne, for a moment."

When the two of them were alone at the dining table, she said, "You're a bright lad, but new to Paris and to the movement. But if you are really going to be useful to the cause of workers' rights," she went on, "I urge you to keep studying, to be able to write and speak well, for the revolution. Like J-P is doing."

He had the impression that there was more that she wanted to say. She seemed about to speak, but then thought better of it and just shook her head, slowly, with a distant smile. After a moment, she seemed to have made a decision, and said,

"The boys – the men, I should say – said you were shouting something when you pounded on my door."

"I was drunk. I'm sorry, I, I shouldn't, I drank too much, I know."

"You were shouting a name. A girl's name. 'Rose.'"

"Oh!"

"You were, weren't you? And who is she? Someone you knew in Lyon?"

"Nnn, no. I mean, was I really shouting that?"

"Tell me who she is. Tell me about her."

And Étienne did, haltingly, with sighs and much blushing. That she worked in the same shop, that he could hardly keep his mind on his work, looking toward her, thinking of her.

"Tell me, Étienne, Titi, have you had girlfriends before?"

Well, not really, he told her. That there was a girl back in Lyon, that he had sort of talked to. That he'd even gone to a big rally with her, that she was the one who got him to go to the rally where he had heard Varlin.

"And then?"

"Then?"

"What else did you do, you and she?"

Étienne shrugged.

She smiled.

"It's late, and you have much to learn. I see it's time for you, too, to get to bed."

She rose and took his hand.

"Come," she said.

***

In the morning, as he stepped out into the kitchen and dining area, closing behind him the door of the private bedroom which he had entered for the first time last night, and only vaguely aware of where he was, a movement startled him. Then he heard a laugh and recognized it as Luc's. Then someone else – Hilaire, possibly– stepped over to pull Luc's sleeve.

"Well, he might at least tuck in his shirt," Luc said, and laughed again.

At first Étienne saw the men only vaguely, without for the moment distinguishing individuals. His body, remembered pressures and shocks and bursts of warmth, told him that this time it had not been a dream, but – his first woman! Something tingled more deeply and intimately than anything ever imagined, a whirl of sensations filled his consciousness so completely that it enveloped all that he now saw before him.

And then he realized that, indeed, his shirt was askew, half in, half out of his trousers, and that he had thrust only one arm through his vest.

As he stood straight and tried to arrange his clothes, he saw with new eyes his compagnons, his comrades, now transformed into a choir celebrating his sudden coming of age, his manhood. Not a choir of angels but of a more heroic category of beings, *ouvriers,* workers of the world, silently singing his entry into the better world they were about to make.

He stood there, only half-aware of the heads around him, some nodding, one of them humming.

Another of the phantom choir members turned into

tangible, physical reality by pressing a hand on his shoulder. Évariste, his mouth close to Étienne's ear, whispered, "We need to talk."

This startled him and made him more acutely aware of where and with whom he was. Those around him, his housemates, had momentarily paused in their preparations – pulling on boots and vests, smoothing hair, straightening clothing – to glance at their newest associate.

"Well, we have to get to work soon," announced Évariste, quite unnecessarily.

"And here's our *présidente*. Good morning to you, Madame Présidente!"

"Good morning to you, Monsieur Tinsmith," Angélique answered gaily as she closed the door behind her.

"And to all my fine gentlemen," she continued with a gentle, laughing smile.

"I'll get your breakfast together in a moment. Étienne, run down and get our bread loaves, will you? Here are some sous, you know where it is."

"No time for me, Lique. This stale bread will be good enough for now," said Évariste. "I know how my foreman gets if I show up a little late. I've got to rush."

Before turning to go, he touched Étienne again on the arm and said they should talk. In a low voice, he said he wanted to share something with him, something about Angélique.

"We'll talk this evening, after work. In the bar across the street, Adolphe's. Right? There are things that you should know, my boy. Things that she probably didn't tell you. Around seven?"

Étienne nodded and ran down to get the bread, with Évariste close behind him.

The new man

It took longer than it should have, getting the bread, mostly because with his head so full of overheated impressions, Étienne got confused and had turned down the wrong street before he found the bakery they preferred. When he did finally get back, only Luc was at the table, waiting for his breakfast.

"You're going to be late, young man. All right for me, my boss is tolerant, but yours –"

At that, Étienne, grabbed a chunk of the bread he had just brought and bounded down the stairs again. And after stopping more briefly than usual in the passageway to piss, he ran.

The bindery was only two blocks away, but after running up the stairs to the first floor he felt his chest heaving. Most of the workers were already settled into their various tasks except for two or three carrying piles of folios toward one job or another. He straightened up and tried to appear as though he hadn't rushed, as though perhaps he had just finished one job and was walking toward another – but he was sure the foreman had noticed his late appearance. Just then Claude stepped over to him and said, loudly enough for the foreman to hear,

"Oh, good, were you able to get that tool I needed?"

With his back to the observant foreman, Claude pulled out of his own pants pocket a pointe knife which he thrust into Étienne's hand before stepping to the side, so that the foreman could see the tool in Étienne's hand.

"Well, sorry to make you lose time looking for that," he said. "Now we can both get to work. But you're ready now for another job, I've spoken with Maître Perrin. Right, *maître*?"

He turned to say this directly to the thin, fortyish man in shirtsleeves and vest with pencils, ruler and knives of various shapes bulging from his vest pockets. Perrin was in fact not the *maître* but merely the *contremaître*, the foreman. The true *maître*, the owner of this and other businesses, was rarely seen here. Perrin merely grunted.

"Put him on that, Claude," he said, nodding toward the trimming table where one of the other workers had just set down a pile of books.

"Show him how you sharpen your knife, you have a trick for him to learn."

Actually, Étienne considered himself perfectly capable of keeping the blade sharp at just the proper angle, but he let Claude show him his way of holding it against the grinding stone.

"Thanks," he murmured softly.

* * *

Sharpening, trimming – it must have been nearly an hour before he looked up and around, until he found the sewing frames. Ah, there she was, that girl called Rose. A girl, a woman. One who was not a dream, but was right there, not more than two meters away from where he stood. Would she be like Lique-Lique? A girl's body, a young woman's like hers, had to be the same in many ways. Its roundnesses, its openings, the sense of skin and muscle responding to his touch. That woman-ness.

Back home he had caught glimpses of his sister dressing. Her legs, anyway. And he had, with other fellows, watched the working girls from the silkworks, dressed up as best they could to walk the fashionable streets on Sundays. He had watched how they moved and tried to picture their legs and hips beneath the clothes.

But last night, last night his dream had become reality. The reality of womanness. Warm flesh, muscle. Pulsing. He had been embracing and been embraced by a female, a real individual woman who was at the same time, for him, an imagined composite figure, made of those childhood glimpses of his sister, other glimpses of the girls from the silk mills, of fantasies he'd read or that his fellows back in Lyon had talked about.

And here across from him sat another female, this young Rose – younger than Angélique, closer to his own age, and certainly not as experienced as he imagined the mistress of Dragon Court. She, this book-sewer Rose, she must be, she had to be, he thought, as virgin as was Étienne himself. She had seemed so much smarter than he, when she had laughed at his ignorance of those authors. But he was not so ignorant, he told himself. He knew other authors. And in La Marmite and from his new comrades in Dragon Court, he had been learning surprising things about politics too.

This time he would dare to speak to her. But first, to trim these pages without letting the knife slip. First to get through the hours, and the paper trimming and the smells of newly printed pages and glue, the noise of the presses, the calls and comments of the other workers, until the midday break.

Summer work here, as in most workshops in Paris, was from six to six, but here at least they were supposed to get breaks at midday, an hour with permission to leave the premises, and a shorter break usually around four, when they could go outside to pee or just sit down and smoke for a bit.

Mystery. The idea that Angélique had a story intrigued him all morning as he worked trimming pages, stealing glances at the girls at the sewing racks. They were all attractive, he thought, but if he could choose, he wanted Rose. Maybe just because she had been the first to speak to him. Or maybe because, something about her, the laughter in her eyes, the fact that she seemed to know about books.

He would, he would speak to her. Today, he promised himself. Practising what he would say and glancing at the clock. The maître had installed the tall ornate clock in a corner, supposedly to regulate the work and break hours – but more than once Étienne had seen Perrin walk over to it, unlock the window and push the minute hand back, once by almost twenty minutes. For the midday break, he would just have to wait until the foreman pulled out his personal watch from his vest pocket and announced, "Time, *Mesdemoiselles et messieurs*" – his own little irony. No blue blouse could normally expect to be called '*monsieur*', nor a gray-clad grisette '*mademoiselle*'. According to Claude, Perrin was not really a bad man, but a former laborer himself, uncomfortable in his middle position, controlling the workers for the profit of the owner. If you talked to him the right way, he could be sympathetic, forgive some minor fault. Or agree when Claude had suggested that Étienne be given some more interesting job than the one at first.

The announcement of 'Time' came when the clock in the corner still said a quarter to twelve. "Be back here by twelve thirty, all of you. We have a lot of work this week, and more will be coming from the printer this afternoon."

"But M. Perrin, we're supposed to have an hour," protested Toinou. "That's what the agreement says."

Perrin looked at the clock and took a step toward it, as though he were going to adjust the hands again, but he stopped.

"Very well. Get back when this clock says twelve and three quarters. Not a minute later!"

So, Étienne supposed, the manipulation of the clock hands would occur after all the workers had left. No matter. Even forty-five minutes might be enough for what he planned to do. He saw Claude coming over to him and waved for him to wait, as he stepped quickly over to the sewing frames and found Rose.

This time he ignored Toinou and said directly to her, using the more intimate *tu*,

"I wonder if you would like to accompany me to a workers' canteen I know. A place where we can eat and we'll be out of that hot sun."

"Well," she said, looking around at the other young women observing her. "My friends and I were going to go off to sit outdoors, by the Seine. But you're right. It is terribly hot today."

"It's quite close."

She nodded.

"La Marmite, do you mean? That's the only workers' canteen I know of."

He took it as a good sign that she had addressed him as '*tu*', more normal among young workers.

"I've heard of it, and I've heard good things about it. From my father. I've never been in there, though."

She smiled, considering the idea.

"Yes. And they have good food, and good people there. Workers like us. It's a cooperative, and I'm a member, so I get a special price. I invite you."

"Invite me? No, please. If you've brought nothing, I can share what I brought from home. It's only dark bread, I'm afraid, but the cheese is good, and there's even a sausage."

"No, really. Thank you, but I would be very pleased if you come with me. We can get a good meal and talk in a very nice place. Save your sausage for later."

She looked around again at the two other young women still watching this interaction.

One tossed back her head and said, "Well, just give us your sausage. Cécile and I will have no trouble giving good account of it."

Rose laughed and handed her the small wrapped parcel.

It was still a little early for the workers' midday meal when they got there, so Rose and Étienne were among the first at the counter to fill their plates. She asked what was in the soup, smiled and told the woman serving that it smelled very good – though as far as Étienne could see it was just ordinary leeks and beans and milk. But it was plentiful, and the loaf of bread that came with each plate was half-white, not the cheaper rye, and the pot of wine he knew would be quite acceptable. He addressed the man taking the money with ostentatious familiarity, although he had only seen him once before and didn't know his name. The man twisted his head and gave him a questioning look, then glanced at Rose and nodded as he took the 5 sous for both.

"This place was founded by Eugène Varlin," Étienne announced, as they found places at one of the long tables. He was prepared to impart a lesson about the bookbinder's association and the International.

"Yes, I know," she answered, surprising him. "And that woman over there, is that Nathalie Lemel?"

"Yes. That's Madame Lemel. I mean, Nathalie. You know of her then?"

"Oh, yes, and I've been hoping for a chance to meet her."

Étienne looked at her with his mouth half opened, his prepared speech halted at the lip.

"You must introduce me. She has done so much for us. I mean for the girls in the binderies, we stitchers at the sewing frames like Cécile and Louise and I, and especially the *brocheuses* who have to work at such a fast pace on those cheaper bindings. We've been meeting with the girls from another shop, and they've told us that *la Bretonne* – that's what we call her, but it's affectionate – they say that she has been encouraging them to formulate their own demands, for the men to include when they negotiate with the owners."

"Oh. Yes, she would do that. She's a member of the International Workingmen's Association, you know," he said, seeking to assert some advantage of knowledge.

"Oh, is she? Well, yes, she would have to be. They say she's worked closely with Varlin. My father even has mentioned her. Well, he talks a lot about the International."

"Your father?"

"He's a bronze chaser, a *ciseleur*, he makes things like kitchen fixtures and basins, and even some fancier figures, candelabras and clock fixtures, for the bourgeois. I even have one little piece he did."

She suddenly reddened and, smiling, lowered her eyes.

"Really?"

"A small thing, but lovely. A little bronze rose bush, for my name-day last year. My fifteenth. And he also brought a little statue to Maman, for some anniversary, not a wedding anniversary exactly, but an anniversary of something important to them. When they met, I think, I don't know, I think it was their twentieth. He has to sneak these things out of the shop, of course."

She laughed at this bit of mischief. Then she suddenly looked up and said, "Oh, there's Zépherin!"

"Who?"

"There, talking to that other man, who must be another bronze worker. Those two in their work-blouses. Zépherin Camélinat has been to our house for supper more than once. He used to work in the same shop as my father, but now he must be in some other place. I've heard so much about the International and Varlin, from him and from my father, I hope to meet him some day. Varlin, I mean. But they say he's gone, out of Paris for now."

"I *saw* him. I heard him speak in Lyon," said Étienne eagerly, glad at last to have this advantage of the girl.

"Oh, really? You saw him? What a thrill. I've even heard that he is a good dancer. But you wouldn't know that, would you? He's tall, isn't he? Like you. That's what they say."

"Well, yes. I guess so. Not a giant, but, yes, he must be about my height, maybe a little taller. He was standing on the podium, so I couldn't really tell. It was at a rally, back in March. For the International. He was presiding. There were silk workers mainly in the audience, and iron workers from nearby and a few bookbinders like me. Varlin's own profession. That was one thing that made me want to come to Paris. I want to become a bookbinder, a really good bookbinder, like him. I'm trying to learn all the different skills of the trade."

She smiled.

"That's good. I'm sure you will. Oh, look. Zépherin has seen us."

She looked up and Étienne turned to see a man with carefully trimmed beard and hair and a very bright smile striding toward them, his rough blue blouse dancing around his knees. Étienne guessed him to be at least thirty, an age commanding respect.

"My little Rose! How good to see you! I haven't seen you in here before, ever."

"No, it's my first time. I just came here with my co-worker, with, eh –"

"Étienne," said Étienne, extending his hand. "Étienne Bonin."

The man nodded and said, "Camélinat," smiling more formally as he took the proffered hand.

"And how is your father, Rose? We haven't seen old Jules for weeks now."

"Oh, he's been very busy. But he's well, thank you. And he speaks of you often."

"And your mother? Still wearing herself out at the laundry?"

"Still. But what are we going to do? The family has to eat."

"And things at the bindery? Are you girls getting organized? We've got a group of the men, already signed up –" He stopped and looked at Étienne.

"Oh, you can talk here, he's with us," Rose assured him. "He was just telling me about Varlin. He saw him in Lyon."

"Oh, really? You saw Eugène? Lyon? That must have been back in –"

"March," said Étienne. "He spoke at a rally for the International in La Rotonde, the big hall in Lyon."

"Yes, now I remember. He was doing a lot of traveling. Good thing, too, that he happened to be out of Paris when that arrest order came. Well, he'll be back. And you, young man, have you joined us yet? The International?"

The question startled Étienne. Could he? Would they accept him?

"I'm still an apprentice," he said apologetically.

"Well, then, perhaps we can give you a discount on dues. I'll speak to our comrades. Clemence, you said?"

"Bonin. Étienne Bonin."

"Sorry. Bonin. I was thinking of another young binder. We'll get you signed up, Bonin. Étienne. We need to get as many of our supporters together as possible. It looks like we may be heading toward a difficult time, with all this war talk.

"But you'll have to excuse me, I've got something to discuss with those chaps at the next table. And Rose, tell your father that we're hoping he will join us for a meeting this week, soon."

He smiled again and turned and walked back, as swiftly as he had come.

"Fine man," said Rose. "But what time do you suppose it is? We're going to have to get back to the shop."

"Mmm. Right."

He hastily swallowed what was left of his wine, mopped up the bottom of his soup plate with the last chunk of bread and, following her lead, rose to go.

La Ricamarie

They did manage to get back in time, but just barely, before the boss had a chance to complain. And the afternoon went much more happily for Étienne. He glanced toward Rose only once or twice, feeling much less nervous about those glances than before. Once he caught her eye and she smiled back, quickly.

But the work day finally ended, and he remembered his appointment with Évariste.

He found him at the bar.

He knew that Évariste was also from near Lyon. More precisely, from Saint-Étienne south-west of the city, as Étienne should have guessed from his speech and certain facial gestures. What he hadn't known was what Évariste now told him, that Évariste had worked with Angélique's husband in the coal mines.

"Husband? She had a husband? A coal miner?"

Étienne had not until now imagined any of this.

"Oh yes, he was a coal miner, like me, but a handsomer, bold fellow. Joseph Ducrin was his name, Jojo we called him. Cleverer than me, too, cleverer than any of us. Good talker. We all liked him. He was the one who got our gang to strike. In La Ricamarie."

Évariste paused, watching his own finger slipping along the rim of his wine glass.

Étienne gaped and waited expectantly. He had heard of what had happened at La Ricamarie. All Lyon had heard.

"He was one of the first ones killed when the soldiers opened fire."

Étienne gasped. La Ricamarie. He had heard of that massacre, only a year ago.

"That was when I left, just days after the shooting, and came to Paris with all I had, the little I'd been able to save. No more La Ricamarie, no more coal mines for me. And here I found comrades and joined the International, almost as soon as I got here. They were the only ones who seemed to care about what was going on, the people who read *La Marseillaise* were practically the only people in Paris who had any idea what had happened at La Ricamarie. There and other places.

"When I got here I had to learn a new trade. Above ground. I'm still learning some tricks. Tin-smithing is not all easy, but at least it's above ground."

"And Angélique? When did she come here?"

"About a month after I did. In the fall. We brought her. She couldn't stay there, couldn't stand it. The memories. And after the massacre, she lost her job. The head of the school found out she was the wife, the widow really, of a radical and said they couldn't keep her. And besides all that, she had a miscarriage. There was nothing for her there."

"A miscarriage? And then she came to this house?"

"Some fellows I had met through the International, including Hilaire and Luc, single men like me, were already looking for a place where they could share the rent. And I suggested we bring Angélique, that we'd need a woman to keep house and all that. And I knew from her ideas that she would fit right in with a bunch of socialist workers. So…"

"You wrote her to come?"

"Better than that. We went down there, Hilaire and me, he wanted to get out of Paris. He'd never seen that part of the country. It's a long train ride!"

"I know."

"Well, we persuaded her to come. Hilaire, mostly. He's a good talker. Took some talking, because she didn't see herself as a housekeeper. She's a school teacher! She reads books! Keeping house for five or six men, that wasn't anything she'd ever imagined herself doing. But we talked to her about the workers, and I said she'd be carrying on what her husband Jojo had been trying to do. Helping workers who were building a movement. She cried a little when I said that, then she straightened up and looked around her house, a shack really, and said she'd come. The boys had given us enough money for her train fare. And for ours, Hilaire's and mine, of course."

Évariste fell silent, staring into his wine. And Étienne just sat back and tried to absorb all this new information. A widow, widow of a coal miner who had been a workers' leader.

"And pay attention to what she says about learning," Évariste added. "Like I told you, she used to be a schoolteacher and in her heart she still is. And, last night…"

Étienne looked up, embarrassed. A schoolteacher! He should have guessed.

"You mean, I should think of, of what happened last night, as a lesson?"

Évariste's eyes flashed and his lips puckered, suppressing a grin.

III

At war

To war with a light heart

On Monday, 19th July, the Emperor's chief minister Ollivier announced that the Empire was declaring war on Prussia 'with a light heart' – because of the Prussian king's refusal to satisfy France's justified demands.

"Over what?" Étienne asked that night at supper in Dragon Court.

"Over who should be the next king of Spain!" answered Luc, with a guffaw.

"And over the perceived insult, when the Prussian king refused to receive the French envoy. It's a duel of honor," explained J-P, more seriously. "Except that instead of two men with swords or pistols, their king and our emperor, they'll be sending whole armies."

Étienne sat back and looked around at the faces at the table.

It was Hilaire who noticed his disturbed look, and said with an ironic smile, "Yes, it will be men like you and me, and others like us from Germany, ordinary working men just wanting to get by and raise their families, killing each other to salvage the pride of the King and the Emperor."

He laughed. But it was a shallow laugh.

There was a moment of silence, broken by Angélique.

"Oh, you men!" She stood up so abruptly she knocked over her own wine glass.

"No, not us, Lique, you know we've all been doing everything we can to stop this madness. But the crowds are cheering, 'To Berlin!' they're shouting."

Angélique rushed from the table to take refuge in her room. The men looked around at each other, J-P shaking his head and saying "We'll have to see what we can do now."

Nine days later, Étienne and his co-workers learned from the papers, Napoleon III himself arrived at the front, in Metz, near the German border, to take personal command of his armies – not on a warhorse but in an imperial carriage. And then on 2nd August, French forces attacked in Saarbruck across the German border, causing the Prussians to withdraw. *Le Figaro*'s large-print headline read 'VICTORY'.

In the bindery, foreman Perrin could hardly contain his excitement over two big orders from the top political authorities. The first was from Minister Ollivier himself, the binding of 300 copies of a book of his essays, enough for every member of the legislative body.

Then the bindery had received the second big order, from Empress Eugénie and the Imperial palace: a luxury vellum binding with ample gilding of Volume I of *The Imperial Policy as set forth by the Speeches and Proclamations of Emperor Napoleon III* – over 500 pages, 200 copies, some 25,000 printed sheets hauled up to the bindery workshop in boxes now stacked in a corner, all bearing the imperial seal, the first 200 out of a print run of 6,000, the remainder presumably to have cheaper binding to be sold to the general public.

By then the news of the success at Saarbruck was followed only days later by more troubling news of a French reverse at a place called Wissembourg. Perrin was visibly worried.

* * *

The foreman's enormous pleasure over the order from Her Imperial Majesty had caused Étienne and Claude to laugh, in the wine shop when they got off work. Especially because, as they remarked to each other, the workers trimming, hammering, pressing, binding and gilding these pompous works were all fervent anti-imperialists. Practically the whole shop were republicans of some sort, from the *Blanquiste* Toinou at the extremely violent edge to the more hesitant Proudhonist, a scowling, serious man who usually operated the big press, and of course Claude and Étienne who considered themselves Internationalists.

"What about the girls?" it suddenly occurred to Étienne to ask.

"The girls? What about the girls? Do you doubt that they have political views?"

Claude's wide-eyed surprise was so theatrical that Étienne imagined it was feigned. Étienne just looked at him, trying to imagine a reply.

"Just kidding, my boy. That Cécile, the one hanging out with Toinou, she's redder than any of us! And I'll bet the others are, too. Cécile and Louise and that other one, the pretty one you've had your eye on, that Rose. You've heard her, in her quiet, sly voice, the jokes about Ollivier, and Badinguet and that whole crowd."

Then on Monday came the news of terrible defeats, also in Alsace. The French military disaster at Froeschwiller-Woerth caused the Empress, regent in the absence of the Emperor Napoleon, to dismiss Ollivier and name a new head of government, General Charles Cousin-Montauban, called 'Palikao'.

When they got back to the house on Dragon Court that evening, Étienne and Claude found Angélique nearly in hysterics and Luc and Hilaire holding her shoulders and trying to soothe her. She was calling out "Palikao!"

"Palikao," Évariste reminded him. "He was the general in command of the troops who murdered her husband at La Ricamarie."

* * *

The following Saturday as they came down the stairs after work, Étienne was surprised to see Sophie. She had been waiting for him, she said, and needed to ask him a favor. She had remembered the name of the bindery where he had said he worked and had ventured here on her own.

Maurice had written her a letter but she could barely make it out and didn't dare show it to just anyone. She begged Étienne to tell her what it said.

He led her to a table in the wine shop and drew the single sheet from its envelope. It was dated 3rd August, today was the 13th.

'My dearest Sophie,' the letter began.

Étienne skipped down a few lines before reading aloud from Maurice's cramped handwriting.

"Just as I told you would happen," Maurice had written, "I have been assigned to a sappers' unit. That means building things, especially out of wood. Just what I do best. There are many big trees here in Alsace, some so old and twisted that one of the men in our unit didn't want to cut them down. But we are carpenters, and cutting them down is what we do. We have been building bivouacs, trenches and pontoon bridges.

"I am happy working at my trade, and we're going to stop those foul Prussians in their tracks and beat them back far from French territory, and from here in Mars-la Tour…"

Étienne stopped. But too late; he had already pronounced that name, a place name he had seen in the newspapers at the Marmite on their meal break.

It was in Alsace. Did she know what was happening there? Should he tell her? The papers were reporting fierce combat, at exactly that place, heavy French losses. Deaths, prisoners.

Yes, Sophie did know. Her loud intake of breath, to suppress a shriek, made Étienne sit up and look at her. Then he looked down again at the letter, but she was trembling so hard that he wasn't sure she even heard the closing.

'With nothing else to say to you for the moment, I embrace you very strongly. Until our victory when I can embrace you again.'

He reached across the table to grasp her shoulders, steadying her.

It was some moments before she gathered her strength and, attempting a smile, rose. Suddenly erect, chin raised and eyes turned toward something distant above and behind Étienne, something he supposed may be as far as an imagined Alsace, she turned her face toward him and said, "Thank you, cousin Étienne. And goodbye" before walking steadily and firmly, out of the wine shop and onto the street. Étienne continued sitting there, his gaze continuing to follow in her direction even after she was out of sight.

He could only guess what she might be thinking. Or where she might be going. And as he continued to stare in the direction she had gone, unfocused on anything really before him as his imagination whirled around his own condition and where he was and how he got here, and his recent memory of signing the letter to the German workers.

As a Frenchman, he felt bound to defend the homeland, with all his strength and grit. Like his cousin Maurice had been doing, and he hoped, was still able to do. But, as an associate and almost a member of the International, he was bound to oppose the Empire in the name of the Republic. How could he defend one and not the other?

The firehouse

Ah, Hercule, I'm so glad I could persuade you to join me here on this beautiful Sunday afternoon. Here in La Villette. Although we don't usually perform here, do we? But these workers' neighborhoods have always given us a chance to garner a few sous, sometimes even more than in the fancier districts, eh, Hercou? At least on Sundays, always good for our merriment.

The purses won't be as full as in some quarters, of course, but on a sunny summer Sunday the men and women – just look at them! – they've doffed their work clothes and are gussied up in their Sunday best, strolling about and looking for entertainment, some amusement to take them far from their dreary workdays.

And from the terrible news from the war. You have a cousin there, don't you, Hercou? I hadn't forgotten. Well, let us hope he and all our brave soldier lads are safe, and let's not talk about that. Our job is to lift the spirits with songs and magic, and with your feats of strength! And today, a special mission, for which we have already been paid a little sum. Just to make a bit of noise and distraction here, by the firehouse, at the right moment, while those chaps do whatever it is they plan to do at the firehouse. You and I don't need to know what it is they're up to, but it should be exciting, they promised me. And we should make a lot of noise when it happens. Meanwhile let's see if we can gather a few more sous from our innocent audience.

"Ladies and gentlemen, I have itching powder for sale! ... Let's say you're visiting the wife of a government minister, you're enjoying a delicious coitus interruptus. Then the minister appears and you throw my powder..."

Ratatat! Boombiddyboom!

"That's right, only a few sous, try it out on your friends in the wine shop! Or when you're up to some naughty tricks. What? Sure, here you go, sonny. But don't let your momma catch you!

"And now, our good Hercule will lift these tots right to the sky! Whoosh! Oh, see how they laugh! But that is nothing. Now, my friend Hercule, perhaps you can show us how you can also lift with your other hand this fine gentleman, the children's father you must be, correct, dear sir? No, don't be concerned, our mighty Hercou will raise you with just one hand – yes, just sit there, if you please, on his open palm – and your two little boys with the other. There you go! Ooop! Look at that!"

Boombiddyboomboom!

Uh, oh. And there they are, finally! A whole crowd

of them, those young gentlemen we've been waiting for. Well, 'gentlemen' is a figure of speech. There he is, himself, old whitebeard, the jailbird, and those boys, I can see that they're clutching something under their shirts, pistols I'll wager. And now we're supposed to make more noise. Hold high that barbell, Hercule, while I…

Ratatatatat! Baboombaddyboomboomboom!

– A shot! Uh-oh, that fireman has fallen. And here comes running a police officer. A lone sergot against that whole crowd of ruffians. The ruckus has begun!

Hercou, quick. Time for us to make ourselves scarce.

* * *

Monday's papers reported the assault. Étienne didn't trust *Le Figaro,* but someone else in the atelier had a copy and shared the news.

"Around forty men, with pistols and daggers, attacked the fire station in La Villette! it says. Sunday afternoon, around four."

Three dead, including a little girl, three years old, shot in the stomach, and many wounded, the paper said.

"The first person killed was the fireman who opened the door and refused to let them in. They burst in anyway, and grabbed some rifles and cartridges before fleeing the police, according to the article."

"Firemen? Why would anybody attack the firemen? Unless –"

"Because they're soldiers and because there were weapons stored there."

"Look. It says here that the attackers – 'the murderers' is what the reporter calls them – it says they offered pistols to the bystanders, urging them to join in the revolt, to cries of 'Treason! Long live the republic!' But nobody joined them. And when more soldiers and police showed up, they ran."

"Did they catch any of them? The police, I mean?"

"Let's see. Yes, it says some of them were caught, the paper says. And one of them, it says, had an English passport but didn't speak English, but spoke French with a German accent."

"Prussian agents!" concluded one of the younger workers.

"That's what *Le Figaro* would like us to believe. But shouting 'Long live the republic'? And handing out weapons to neighbors? That doesn't sound like the Prussians. Where's our Blanquiste comrade?"

Toinou had not shown up at work on Monday. Or Tuesday. Meanwhile, Étienne had been hearing incomplete and contradictory accounts of the attack on the fire station in La Villette. He and his co-workers were increasingly convinced that it had been the work of the *Blanquistes*. Blanqui himself apparently had escaped, again, but his friends in the atelier wondered what had happened to Toinou. Everybody was very nervous.

Back at the house on Dragon Court, the men and Angélique argued about Blanqui and what was the best way to oppose the Empire without betraying France, arguments which left Étienne confused. Luc, and more tentatively Hilaire, seemed to admire Blanqui for his boldness. But the fact that the attempted insurrection had failed so miserably, and the little girl killed, brought condemnations, especially strong from J.P. and Claude – but then Étienne looked at Angélique's stern face as she said "Audacity!"

And watched her nod when Luc remarked, in his sly voice, "Yes, but remember, *mes braves camarades*. That firehouse was a military post. In the Emperor's war."

Again, Étienne wondered, what was the most honorable, the most courageous way to oppose the Empire without betraying France? And what had happened to Toinou?

Republic!

"Disaster!" screamed a news boy, running from corner to corner, waving three or four papers excitedly – *Le Constitutionnel, Le Figaro, Le Petit Journal,* and some other sheet. It was a Sunday morning, a day that Étienne had planned to spend with Rose.

"A great disaster!! The Emperor taken prisoner!"

What? It had finally happened! Étienne and others snatched the first paper proffered by the ragged, snot-nosed boy. Étienne had grabbed *Le Constitutionnel*, Sunday, 4th September 1870.

"Twenty centimes!" the boy demanded.

"Right. Here, take it! Hey, this is my paper, I just bought it, grab your own! Wait, I'll read it aloud, for everybody.

PARIS, 3 SEPTEMBER

PROCLAMATION
Council of Ministers

PEOPLE OF FRANCE!

A great disaster has struck the homeland. After three days of heroic struggles sustained by the army of Marshal MacMahon against three hundred thousand of the enemy, forty thousand men have been taken prisoner.

General Wimpffen, who had taken command of the army in replacement of Marshal MacMahon gravely wounded, has signed a capitulation.

This cruel reverse does not shake our courage. Paris is now in a state of defense, the country's military forces are organizing themselves; within a few days a new army will be before the walls of Paris, another army is being formed on the banks of the Loire. Your patriotism, your unity, your energy will save France.

"Forty thousand men taken prisoner?! That's MacMahon's whole army!"

"And what about the Emperor?"

"What? Oh yes, the Emperor. Here it is, down at the bottom: 'The Emperor has been taken prisoner in the struggle.'"

"Prisoner! Taken prisoner, by the Fritz. The Emperor!"

"Here, I'll read it:

"'The Emperor has been taken prisoner in the struggle. The government, in accordance with the public authorities, is taking all the measures required by the gravity of these events.'"

Shouts. Waving of fists. Hands grabbing for the paper. Cries of "*République! République!* To the Tuileries! Chase out the Empress! She has to go too!"

"*République! République!*"

More and more heads crowding close, cloth caps and top hats, a pink bonnet, elbows and a small pale hand in a lavender sleeve darted out and clutched the newspaper, pulling it from Étienne's hands.

"To the palace! The Palais Bourbon!"

* * *

Étienne would have to abandon his plan to spend the day with Rose, beginning at the Jardin des Plantes. They had heard the rumor of something big yesterday, Saturday, when they were working at the bindery, a commotion in the street and news of an emergency meeting of the senate. But they hadn't expected anything this big! And now, the Emperor a prisoner! This was no time for Sunday strolling.

Rose would understand, he told himself. In fact, she might never forgive him if he didn't join the crowd running to the Palais Bourbon. She might be headed there herself.

"*Vive la République!*" he joined in shouting.

The palace was only a short walk from Dragon Court, but he'd never been near it. He wasn't aware of the time, in all the rush and shouting of the crowd which kept swelling as they walked and waved their arms and hooted and called, "*République!*" He had become part of the flow of the crowd, filing through the security force of uniformed police, gendarmes on foot and others on horseback, soldiers gripping their rifles but seeming unsure of what they were supposed to do.

"Look, that's Palikao!" called out a man next to Étienne, pointing to a mustachioed, elaborately uniformed man on horseback.

"What's happening?"

A man in front of him turned to tell them, "Someone said that Favre declared that Louis-Napoléon Bonaparte and his dynasty were deposed from power, but the deputies don't all agree, and they've been in there for hours."

"We're here to make sure that they declare the end of the Empire! And we won't let them out until they do!"

The dense crowd, mostly men in workers' blouses or shirt sleeves and vests, others in jackets, the few women mostly bareheaded and with light jackets over their Sunday dresses, pressed up against the grill at the base of the great staircase, which was guarded by gendarmes. The crowd shifted impatiently, with clusters of animated conversation, eager for news. The sun had already passed its peak when at last they saw some men emerge from the hall and stand at the top of the steps, waving handkerchiefs and hats to the crowd down below. Shouts from around Étienne answered them: "Down with the Emperor!", "*Vive la République!*"

People were throwing their hats in the air, others were climbing up onto the pedestals of the statues. On the knees of a big statue of a long-bearded man, sitting on a sort of throne and peering into the distance, a guy in worker's blouse was sitting and smoking his pipe. Another crowd was in excited discussion around the tall statue of a helmeted woman holding a spear.

Suddenly Étienne became aware of movement ahead of him and he shuffled forward. The guards had opened the gate to let in someone, more deputies he supposed, along with a column of guards, and those at the head of the crowd pushed their way in. Étienne flowed with the crowd, past the gate and up the many stairs and then through the columns holding up the great marble triangle announcing '*Corps Législatif*'. He found himself inside the domed senate chamber, and pushed toward one of the seats still available in an upper tier. He stared, amazed to be here, in the semicircular gallery of the legislators of the Empire. He let his jaw drop open as he sat, awed by the columns, the marble, the marble relief sculptures, the light from the dome over the bright red of the velvet seats and the carpet, glimpsed between the figures of men in black waistcoats speaking and jostling around the massive lectern with marble reliefs of two naked men who seemed to be arguing about something. A head of thin white hair bobbed up from behind the lectern, and a short arm in black sleeve gesticulated. The voice of the man who had just taken the space ahead of him startled Étienne from his trance.

"*Hush!*" came other whispered voices, "they're debating!"

"Thiers, see him? Little Thiers, with that funny tuft of hair! He's answering Gambetta, says we don't need to throw out the Empire, what we need now is an emergency government until we get him back."

"What does Gambetta say? Let's listen."

Back and forth, these men Étienne had never seen before but whose names he knew from the press and from discussions in the Marmite and in Dragon Court, Jules Favre, Adolphe Thiers, Léon Gambetta and others, kept arguing. The one pointed out to him as Gambetta was calling for the end of the Empire, the smaller, older man with the funny hair wanted, it was hard to hear just what, oh, yes, there it was, a 'committee for national defense'.

"A committee!" snorted the man at Étienne's elbow. "A committee of what government? By whose authority?"

It was for the young apprentice a fascinating spectacle, especially in this splendid domed and glittering space, but disturbing and frustrating because it seemed to be going nowhere. Then, after what seemed a very long time, someone declared a recess. He was surprised to note how stiff his arms and back had got when, with the others in his row and the rows below, he stood up and began to file out to take some fresh air.

"Listen to Gambetta!"

A much taller, younger man with a thick brown beard had leapt to the space behind the lectern, crying *"Déchéance!"* A new word to Étienne, but the men in the audience began applauding wildly.

"*Déché*…? What's that?" he asked, tugging the coat of the well-dressed man who had grabbed his shoulder in the excitement.

"*Déchéance*, of the Emperor! Gone!"

"It means *chute*," the man at Étienne's other elbow translated. Downfall!

"No emperor, no empire. That means, why that means we will be a republic! Like back in '48."

"Or '92, when our grandfathers abolished the monarchy," came a louder, deeper voice behind Étienne.

Suddenly he heard another shout from the tribune, that man Gambetta it must have been: "To the Hôtel de Ville!" The shout was taken up by the crowd, which started pushing toward the exits.

Étienne joined the crowd rushing to the Hôtel de Ville. Such joy! Workers and well-dressed bourgeois, and even some noisy Blanquistes waving rifles and pistols, the police had disappeared from the streets. Shouts of *"Vive la République!"* At the Hôtel de Ville, a big red flag of revolution stood beside the Tricolor at the front of the assembly hall, filled with men shouting and congratulating each other. One young fellow kept singing, over and over, the 'Marseillaise'.

When Gambetta took the floor, there was a sudden change, some of the men loudly hushing the other. Étienne could not make out exactly what Gambetta and that other opposition deputy, Jules Favre, were saying, but from the reaction and shouts all around him he knew that the Republic had been declared!

Beyond the barrier

The Empire was no more, but the war went on – to Étienne's and everyone's dismay. Now that the Prussians had defeated and even arrested the Emperor, why didn't they just go home?

Like his housemates in Dragon Court, Étienne felt deeply discouraged by the bad news from the battlefront. And the losses and sufferings of the men, his cousin among them. Who at last report, in his letter to Sophie, was in Alsace – site of some of the earliest and greatest French disasters. Was Maurice a prisoner now? Or even alive?

The Prussians had continued advancing, inflicting defeat after defeat on the French armies which had once been so confident of taking Berlin. Now it looked as though those armies might be unable to hold the enemy back from Paris itself.

"As long as there are kings and emperors there will be wars," Claude muttered into his soup.

"Fought by working stiffs like us! Bleeding for them and their treasures and their pride," Évariste replied sharply.

"But something has changed, on our side. We are a republic now!" Angélique reminded them.

"Yes," Étienne jumped in, eagerly grasping what might be the only sliver of good news.

"Which means that now we workers are obliged to defend

it," he went on, racing to get the words out. "You, Évariste, and Claude, and Luc, and J-P, and me, all of us. To defend the French republic, because it's ours, we won it."

"You want to take up arms? More killing?" interjected Angélique, shaking her head.

"Until the Fritz get a republic of their own!" said Évariste, with a sarcastic laugh at the improbability of it.

Imperial decrees and banishments had suddenly become dead letters.

On the 5th September, just one day after the proclamation of the Republic, Victor Hugo himself had come back from Guernsey, after nineteen years of exile. Other returned exiles included some journalists Étienne had vaguely heard of – Delescluze, Pyat, both famous for their vituperations against the Emperor – and were said to be starting new newspapers. Even Louis-Auguste Blanqui had come out of hiding to launch another newspaper fiercely attacking the new government.

Most important to Étienne was news of the return of Eugène Varlin. The founder and leader of the bookbinders' association and the head of the Paris section of the International, the man who had inspired Étienne's journey. He had returned from Belgium where, Jean-Pierre and Luc told him, he had been staying only at the insistence of his comrades, to avoid the Emperor's arrest order. And Varlin had joined the National Guard, which must mean that he saw no contradiction between internationalism and defense of the republic. That then must be the patriotic *and* the internationalist thing to do!

Varlin was the very personification of all Étienne aspired to be, professionally as a bookbinder and even more importantly as a part of the struggle for the liberation of the working class of all lands.

He too had to sign up for the Guard.

In response to demands from trade associations and the rowdy political clubs, the new government was permitting, though not enthusiastically promoting, the creation of new National Guard battalions. And there was one being formed in his quarter, Saint-Germain-des-Prés in the Sixth. There shouldn't be any problem about his age – he would be eighteen in May, which was just months away. Wouldn't Rose be impressed! As a Guard he would have a smart blue tunic with kepi and brass buttons, the prestige of a patriot, and pay of 30 sous per day. A franc and a half. No great luxury, but very handy now that there was less work in the bindery and talk of its shutting down.

But at La Marmite, when Nathalie Lemel heard Étienne talking about his plans, she called him aside. Before he did something like that, she said, and submit himself to military discipline, if he wanted to make a sacrifice for the Republic, there was something he could do for her. And for the Marmite and the Ménagère. And for all the workers and their families who depended on them.

Étienne held Nathalie Lemel in the highest regard, approaching awe. He thought of her as the truest, steadiest voice of the International, almost like dealing with Varlin' himself.

Madame Nathalie, as he tended to think of her (though she laughed at him whenever he addressed her as 'madame'), had been paying close attention to the news, and was especially concerned that, as the Prussians drew closer to Paris itself, there would be problems getting supplies, especially food, from the countryside. If Étienne was ready to take risks to defend the Republic, she wanted him to perform this service first: to fetch an especially large order from the farms beyond the city limits, outside the excise barrier. Quickly, because the risk would be greater if the Prussians got close to the city's protective forts. Their troops were approaching from the north and west, but so far, the farmland just to the east, beyond the barrier of Vincennes, should be clear.

"A bright, bold lad like you should be able to get through any enemy patrols. The problem will be getting through and coming back with a wagon-load."

Nathalie knew of a farm that was especially close, just beyond the excise barrier. Was he up to the challenge?

Was he!

"Absolutely! Just show me where it is, I've never been out that way."

The stern little woman laughed at his burst of enthusiasm.

"Don't worry about finding it. If we do this, you will be going with a person who knows the way."

She paused. Étienne anxiously waited.

"Rose Durand. I think you know her."

Astounded, Étienne just held his breath.

"Very bright, capable girl. Devoted to the Republic. She's been helping out here in the evenings. She heard me worrying about running low, and said she would go out to get what we need. She did it once before, last month, when things were still quiet in the area. Just she and the teamster who has always made that trip.

"But now I think it would be better if you too went with them. There may be a lot to carry. And it will be good to have three people. When I heard you talk about joining the Guard,

I thought that our tall young man Étienne might be just the person.

"Of course, we'll have to ask Rose if she agrees to go with you. And if you can wait to join the Guard."

Étienne let out his breath and looked for a chair to collapse into.

"Right," he said. "I'll do it. If Rose agrees."

* * *

Nathalie's worries had been well-founded. Before they could get organized, even before Étienne had a chance to discuss this with Rose, just five days after the proclamation of the Republic the papers reported that Prussian armies had surrounded Paris and all its subordinate villages and forts. Even though the farm they were supposed to go to was very close to the city, closer than any reported Prussian troops so far, the risk could not be discounted.

Rose, who had been helping out at the Marmite, joined the discussion, and together the three of them – Nathalie, Rose and Étienne – worked out another, bolder idea. And riskier. But necessary. With the encirclement of the city by the enemy, getting supplies for the food cooperatives had now become more urgent.

"And now we have another problem," Nathalie explained. "Jacques – that's his name, I don't think you know him – says he isn't willing to venture his team and wagon into what might be enemy territory. He's not old but he's not young either, and, well, he seems rather, uh…"

"*Froussard? Péteux?*" Rather vulgar terms for 'cowardly'.

She laughed.

"I would say nervous about safe-guarding his property."

"Disinclined to risk," said Rose. Impressing Étienne by the unexpected elegance of her phrase. He knew she was a reader, as such expressions reminded him.

"But if you two are willing, we might still be able to do it. The people at the farm should be able to loan you a cart to carry things back to the barrier, and then you can reload them onto Jacques' wagon. He's a good man, generous, glad to help out, but, well, as I said, not a man for adventures."

Étienne drew his head back and looked at her, his whole face drawn into a question mark. And then at Rose.

"But – Rose. I mean, Rose, are you willing to venture out there? I mean, it could be dangerous, for a girl!"

Rose sat very straight and looked at him, her head cocked slightly to one side.

"Yes, yes indeed," said Nathalie. "She is a girl, as you say. A young woman. A very young woman, but pretty mature. Right, Rose? And you, Étienne, do you think she can't do this because she is a woman?"

"No, no. She can do it, of course she can. Of course you can, Rose. I know you, Rose. And I know you are very smart, smarter than me maybe."

"Thank you!" said Rose sarcastically.

"And I know she cares about doing whatever she can for the Republic. But you said it may be dangerous, and maybe strenuous. And, well, what will your parents say, Rose? Your father, I hear he's a tough man."

"Yes, you should talk with them," said Nathalie. "Not just with Jules – I know him, he's been to meetings here, and he is sometimes gruff, but he's a bronze worker, that's the way they are. He doesn't have a lot of words, but he's a good man. And also Rose's mother, you'll have to talk with her. Have you met Blanche Durand? No? There is a strong woman!"

Rose herself was convinced, and in fact this whole mission had really been her idea, Nathalie explained.

"But I thought she should have a man to accompany her, just in case there is any trouble. And because it is always good to work in pairs."

"I know you're a fast runner," Rose said to him. "Well, I am too. And if they do try to stop us, we'll just outrun them."

"But to get the supplies here," Nathalie continued, "I'm thinking that if you can't get a wagon from the farmers, you'll have to make several runs, on foot, with sacks filled with as much as you can carry."

"No, no!" said Rose. "It's one of the farms just outside the barrier. The one where the milk wagon comes from in the mornings? They have a wagon. They can loan it to us, as far as the barrier."

"And do they have a horse?" asked Étienne. "The milk wagon, you say? Is that the wagon that goes into the Twelfth? To the Quinze-Vingts?"

"I don't know about that. We see them, we used to see them before the war, in the morning here in the Sixth."

"Does that farmer have a daughter, about Rose's age?"

Nathalie said yes, she knew the family. The mother and her daughter and son, the daughter sixteen, the boy two or three years younger, usually arrived in the Twelfth Arrondissement early in the morning to peddle milk in the neighborhoods around the Place de la Bastille.

"Do you know her?" she asked. "Her name is Jeanne."

"No, but I think I saw her, or somebody like you describe, I don't remember if I heard her name, on my first day in Paris."

But Étienne announced that he would go alone, and Rose could wait at the barrier.

"Alone? No, I'm going, with or without you!" said Rose sharply. Then, turning to Nathalie, she added, "Étienne doesn't yet know Paris, or how to talk to the rural people."

"Yes," said Nathalie, after a moment. She smiled. "Yes, a woman would be good. There are things we women can handle better. Rose is a very bright girl, and may be just the right person to deal with our soldiers and National Guards at the barrier, in case they put up any objections. But you'll have to talk it over. And, I expect, with her parents."

And so, on Saturday after work, Rose and Étienne met near La Ménagère and took the omnibus as far as it went into Belleville, on the hills to the east where Étienne had never been.

It felt familiar, though. A hill of working people, rather like back home. Lots of working-class families, men in caps and blue blouses and women in gray shifts returning from work, the chatter not really all that different from what he had known back in Lyon.

There was excitement in the air, the people, mostly men and women returning from work, seemed agitated, talking about the new republic and what it might mean. It was a short climb to the Durand house.

"Maman!" called out Rose. In the doorway appeared another woman about the same age as Étienne's mother, late thirties he guessed, sturdy but lean, with a cap and an apron and, at the sight of Rose, a big smile.

Blanche Durand continued smiling, but with a lifted eyebrow before nodding knowingly as Rose introduced them.

"One of my co-workers at the bindery, Maman."

Yes, yes. More nodding.

"Well, come in. What brings you two here at this hour?"

From which Étienne understood that Rose was not expected to get home so early after work.

"Is Papa here?"

"With some of the men in the tavern, another meeting, I imagine. There's a lot happening now, and you know your father has been elected captain of his company in the new National Guard battalion."

Blanche invited Étienne to enter, following Rose, and she asked him about his work, and where he lived. A cooperative of working men? That intrigued Blanche, as an unfamiliar but sensible idea, given the price of rent and the poor wages of workers. Étienne had the sense that she was looking him over, that her questions were not really about specific information, but just to get him to talk. She noted his non-Paris accent, of course, he knew she would, and asked him to repeat some words. But she didn't seem offended. Rose waited patiently, watching her mother's reactions to her friend.

Étienne was nervous under this interrogation, though at least Madame Durand did not seem hostile. He smiled and fidgeted, until at last Rose's father appeared.

He was a broad-shouldered, heavy-footed man of – Étienne guessed – maybe forty, and in a foul mood, scowling and looking ready to throw something. Until he suddenly noticed Étienne and stood up straight to his full but modest height and asked his wife,

"Who's this?"

"A friend. A young comrade, a worker from the book bindery where Rose was working. He wants to do something for us, for the Republic."

"I hope so," answered Jules. "We're going to need every effort to save this new Republic. Are you in the Guard yet, young man?"

"Étienne," he introduced himself. "No, not yet, but I'm planning to join."

Rose broke in, eagerly.

"Madame Lemel, Nathalie, has asked him to do something."

"Nathalie? *La Bretonne*?"

Jules seemed to relax at that reference.

"Good woman, that. Whatever she asks must be important. But get it done quickly, young man, whatever it is, because we will need you in the Guard! If only this stupid government would let us do what we know how to do."

"You're angry, Julot. Tell us what's going on," said Blanche.

Almost barking and sputtering, Jules Durand began a long diatribe. These new Guard battalions were supposed to contribute to the defense of Paris against the Prussians, who were still getting closer. Jules himself had been acclaimed captain of a company in the new batallion in Belleville, and he and his men were all ready to confront the Prussians. But this new government of National Defense was not doing any better a job than they had been doing under Napoléon, the unlamented 'Badinguet'. Because the war was still being run by the same generals making the same mistakes. And because, despite the shortage of men in the army of Paris, they didn't trust the working people of Belleville and Ménilmontant to do the job for them.

"True, as they say, I am only a worker, a worker like you, young fellow, but older and more experienced and a veteran of political conflicts. And I know a thing or two about combat. Isn't that right, Blanche?"

"We both do, Julot," she answered.

"We are all workers here, men…"

"… and women," interrupted Blanche.

"Yes, men and women, working people without much schooling, but we can tell when something is right or wrong. And now we have a real intellectual here, a university professor and a firebrand, who can explain things and is ready to act. And we've elected him commander of our battalion. With our smarts and muscle, and his brains and audacity, we'll show Paris what we can do."

"A university professor?"

"Yes. Or he was. Very smart chap, young but with a lot of experience in revolts. Flourens, his name is. Gustave Flourens."

"And tell him, Jules. Tell this boy how you were elected captain of your company of National Guards, almost all the men here in our neighborhood."

"Yes, and I'm grateful to them and it's a big responsibility. It's because of that that I've had to be an energetic and attentive participant in the debates in all the meetings of the Guard, so you see, I'm in a position to critique the mistaken strategy of this Government of National Defense."

Étienne had been listening very attentively, which seemed to please the older man. And what pleased him most was that Étienne planned to join the National Guard.

"But first, Papa, Étienne has agreed to take on an important mission, to help supply the city before the Prussians cut us off completely. That's why I brought him here, to meet you. Because I'm going with him."

Jules sat back and looked, wide-eyed, at his daughter.

"You're doing what? What is this about?"

It was early on the next Sunday morning, before the heat reached its zenith on this 21st of August, that, with the reluctant assent of Rose's father and the more enthusiastic endorsement of Blanche, Rose and Étienne climbed onto Jacques the teamster's wagon, to ride from his stable in the Sixth Arrondissement, through the Fifth and then over the bridge to the Twelfth, and on east to the Vincennes Barrier, the 'Barrier of the Throne' as Jacques called it. The teamster was friendly enough, but taciturn, responding to questions mainly by grunts around his clenched pipe. Étienne did manage to extract from him an acknowledgment that he knew the barrier they were headed to, and had crossed it many times.

"And are the tax collectors tough there?" Rose asked him. She too had been through that excise barrier with an earlier load for the Ménagère and the Marmite, and had managed to get through with a smile and fluttering of eyelids and a fee rather smaller than might be expected for a full wagon. She thought that if the same man was still in charge of the collectors there, that would be a good sign – though he may not be so forgiving seeing her accompanied by a young man.

"Hmm," grunted Jacques. "We know each other. And I've brought something for them. Things they don't get from the countryside."

"What?"

"Tobacco, some good cigars. Big ones. And a jug of something very potent."

When they got there, the three men standing outside the customs house just smiled and waved them through, but Jacques reined in just past the barrier.

"I'll wait for you here. Not forever, though. Be back by three. I don't think we'll have any problem with the excise men."

"Come on," said Rose, climbing down to the trail. "It's not far. I know the way."

This was the first time since Étienne had arrived in Paris that he had stepped outside the city. And, except for his train ride from Lyon, it was his first time outside of any city. The air smelled different, the noises were only of birds and their own footsteps along the dirt road, the crunching of leaves. He felt uneasy at first, but he didn't dare show it, not when he was supposed to be the strong man protecting this girl. Who didn't seem to need protecting, which also made him a little uneasy. He wanted to take her arm, but didn't dare. But he could dream of a life with her, he as master bookbinder and she, well, a bookbinder too, if that was what she wanted, or anything. She seemed capable of anything she set her mind to.

Sooner than he had expected, they reached a fence where Rose announced, "This is the place."

She called out, and a girl appeared, a girl about the same age as Rose he guessed, but broader and in a thick skirt, wooden shoes, apron and a bonnet from which strands of red hair escaped.

"We're here again, Jeanne."

"Uh-huh. And with company. Somebody new."

"Yes, his name is Étienne. He has agreed to help me, because we weren't able to get a wagon this time. That is, we had to leave our wagon back at the Throne. We were hoping we could borrow your wagon just for that short distance."

Jeanne considered, as though calculating. Étienne was also calculating. He wasn't sure, but he thought this might be the same milkmaid he had seen the first day he had arrived in Paris, the one whose cart got overturned.

A voice came out of the farmhouse.

"It's all right, Maman," Jeanne called back. "It's that girl from the Marmite. I'll take care of it."

Then turning back to Rose, she said,

"The wagon was not part of our deal."

"Oh, but it's only that short way, from here to the barrier, where we have another wagon. If you can come with us, it will only take maybe a half an hour."

"No, can't give you the wagon."

"Oh, Jeanne, dearest! If we can't use the wagon, we can't carry the goods. That means we won't be able to pay you anything, because we won't be able to buy your eggs, your cheese, your flour. And you must have beans harvested, too."

"Lentils."

"We're prepared to pay, just like last time."

"No, more than last time. It's war time. Everything is more dear."

Rose and Jeanne stepped away from Étienne and conferred for several minutes. Then Étienne remembered something. He had seen this girl before.

"Hey, Jeanne!" he called. "Remember me? The day the cop turned over your cart, in the Quinze-Vingts? You said you wanted some real shoes."

Jeanne looked up, startled.

"Shoes?"

She looked down at her muddy sabots and shuffled her feet, as though trying to hide them.

"Yes. We can get you some," he promised. He had no idea how to fulfill such a promise, but he was sure that in the great city of Paris one could get anything, and he had seen many shoemakers' shops.

"No," said Rose, cutting in. "I don't know when we can get back here. But look, Jeanne, if you like, why you can take these, and give me your sabots."

Jeanne and Étienne looked down at Rose's feet. Étienne

was seeing them for the first time; until now, he had always been drawn to Rose's eyes, not her feet. They were encased in low-heeled boots laced to just above her ankles. Unremarkable but serviceable, ordinary, working-girl's shoes.

"They're not silk," Jeanne complained.

"No, of course not! But they're leather, real leather. Mauve, a good color for you, and I think they should fit."

"I've never had real shoes."

In the end, she agreed. She would help Rose and Étienne fill her wagon and accompany them to the barrier, and when they arrived, she and Rose would exchange footwear. Étienne was impressed by Rose's dealing.

Jeanne's old horse moved slowly, and the three humans had to push the wagon to free it from some ruts, but they returned to the excise barrier in time, well before three according to Jeanne, who was accustomed to telling time by the sun.

Now with Jacques' help, they transferred the load from one wagon to the other. The girls exchanged shoes for sabots, and Rose counted out the money for Jeanne, who was more excited about her shoes than the coins.

"Like a lady!" she said. But then she took them off.

"I don't want to get them dirty. And also, they are a might tight, but they'll do. They'll do nicely."

Étienne looked back to see Jeanne, barefoot but with a springy step, leading her horse and the now empty wagon back to her little farm.

Jacques had been right about the tax collectors at the barrier. With their cigars and the pot of liquor Jacques had given them, they just waved the wagon on through.

At the Ambigu

The bright lights were nearly blinding after so much gloomy news. And the crowd hardly like anything he was accustomed to. Hippolyte had to blink as he followed the usher through the dense crowd filing into the big, domed hall, and then – unused to such a venue – over-tipped him. He had not spent an evening in a real theater for many, many years. Not since – no, let's not think about her, old story, the one time in his life when he had seriously considered marriage, which would not have helped his career. Forget it. In any case, this was his first time ever in the grand Ambigu-Comique. Impressive, with its rows upon rows of seats and its multiple galleries, one above the other, its many chandeliers, the painted marble columns, the statuary and the adornments in what looked like gold and silk.

And, he had always supposed, with far more famous and more expensive talent than the music halls or concert cafés he was used to. Quite a coup for Bagou's mistress to get billing here, so young and hardly out of the rowdy, raucous and blatantly inelegant Cirque where he had seen her performance just months ago!

Hippolyte tried to settle himself in his seat in the first gallery, compliments of Bagou, as other noisy patrons crowded past him. He could see many more customers here in this gallery and below in the mezzanine and, little by little, filling the boxes – in one of which, he knew, Bagou would be seated.

However, settling himself was not easy. He realized he was fidgeting, that his starched collar irritated him, that the dress coat that he hadn't worn for nearly a decade was too tight, and, he feared, after looking around at the others, his cravate was too formal and outdated for this crowd. Although perhaps it didn't matter; he was surprised at how inattentive to their dress and hair were several of the men, and even some of the women, seated in his row. Had fashion been overthrown along with the Emperor?

But here he was. A night out, away from police worries. But not completely. He could hardly keep his mind off all that was happening outside the theater, all that would require adjustments and improvisations after years of habit.

Hippolyte, who had built his life and career in the institutions of the empire, now had to consider how to preserve them in this new 'republic'. He had a new police prefect, Émile de Kératry, whose first order has been to change the name and uniforms of the former *sergents de ville*, now to be called *gardiens de la paix publique*, a sign of more troubling changes to come. This ridiculous change of name and costume of what had been the regime's most sober, serious force of order amounted to treating the police as players in a comedy, a comedy called 'La République'. And even he tonight, a *commissaire de police* no less, had got himself up in an unfamiliar costume. The whole of Paris had been turned into a *théâtre comique*, playing a bizarre farce.

Worst of all, to his mind, was the blatant hypocrisy, the sudden and unapologetic reversal of loyalties all around him. Elegant shops and the theaters that had proudly announced their loyal services to the Emperor, his Royal Highness, now took every opportunity to make fun of the poor man they called 'Badinguet' or 'Napoléon le Petit' or worse. Including here, in this famous Théâtre de l'Ambigu-Comique which, he was sure, must have been graced by the the Emperor's and the Empress Eugénie's presence on more than one occasion.

Outside by the entrance, he had seen a horrible *trompe d'œil* caricature of the now-deposed emperor. Looked at one way, it showed 'Badinguet going to war!!!' Turning it upside down, it became 'Badinguet coming home from war!!!', where the hugely exaggerated mustaches became long furry ears and the ridiculous bonnet the snout of a donkey. This, for the man who had for nearly twenty years held France and the Empire together in peace – well, relative peace, if you didn't count Italy or Mexico – and unprecedented prosperity, with its enormous technical and industrial development and prestige, an example to all of Europe and carrying French culture to the benighted savages in its colonies around the world. And now all of that was threatened.

Meanwhile, to protect his own livelihood and better his pension prospects under the new Government of National Defense, Hippolyte had again been angling for a transfer to Sûreté, closer to the prefect and with better pay. But as his contacts in the prefecture reminded him, for such a move he would need to draw the prefect's attention to his investigative capacities, with sharper and more actionable reports of any signs of discontent of the populace.

He had considered approaching Bagou for contacts in the new régime, although he didn't really trust the sly scribbler. But then, without his asking, Bagou had sent him a would-be informer, that foppish young journalist. The lad had not been much help so far, but at least he was literate.

A welcome contrast to the usual *mouchards*. Hippolyte had been surprised to discover how much the young man seemed to know about the various subversive doctrines, whose arguments had at first seemed mystifying not only to him but, he was sure, to the entire police structure. Though these conversations hadn't led to any arrests yet, the *commissaire* had paid close attention. The boy's summaries of arguments in the political clubs and in the leaflets and articles might prove to be helpful. Because the problem confronting the police now was that, with the sudden change of regime, they were going to have to redefine what was subversive – opposing the Emperor who had surrendered his sword to the Prussian king could now hardly be considered a crime.

For this redefinition, the young journalist's briefings provided orientation. Hippolyte had already incorporated some of what he had learned from Alphonse about the doctrines of Blanqui and Proudhon and the International and that mad Russian, Bakhouinine, couched as his own discoveries, in a first report to the prefecture and to the chief of Sûreté. He could see how some of the arguments of those radicals could be seductive to semiliterate workers with dreams of some sort of perfect society, a society where there would be multiple benefits for the likes of them and no real obligation to strain themselves with labor. Pipe dreams, but soothingly attractive. One had to understand the enemy in order to defeat him, to come up with counter-arguments.

In any case, his young informant, Bertrand, seemed perfectly satisfied with the envelopes Hippolyte passed to him when they met, 20 francs a visit, not too high a price even if nothing much came of it. The prefecture had a budget for informers, and if he ran short of funds, Hippolyte would gladly cease the services of some of his sleaziest mouchards.

So much to worry about, so much had been happening, all for the worse, just in the past few weeks. He needed a change of scene and mood. The new political situation was not the only thing, the continuing war was also going very badly. Very badly. It was all simply too depressing. Which was why, at the persistent urging of Bagou, he had accepted this invitation. Bagou's mistress Victorine had a role in tonight's spectacle, which would be quite a contrast, he imagined, to the one he had seen her in at the outset of the war when everyone was expecting a quick and easy triumph in Berlin.

Well, he would see, he thought as he settled himself into a seat on the side in the first gallery of this immense theater. And he prepared himself to sit through yet another recital of Victor Hugo's *Châtiments,* the scathing satirical verses about the Emperor that seemed to have become suddenly obligatory for performers everywhere in the city. Hugo's royalties for tonight's performance, according to a sign at the entrance to the Théâtre Ambigu, would go to purchasing cannons for the defense of the city – at the request of the great poet himself. Hugo, Victor Hugo. Hippolyte really had no firm opinion of the man, knowing only that he had been a declared enemy of the Emperor and thus not an author that Hippolyte had ever bothered to read. But these days, one couldn't help hearing references to his works. Donating his royalties for cannons for defense against the Prussians. Yes, that sounded useful, at least. But listening once again to Hugo's insulting rhymed drivel did not.

Hippolyte found it especially distasteful that the same comedians who had performed so exuberantly for the Emperor were now, with just as much fanfare and glitter and apparent enthusiasm, lampooning him.

A fanfare from the orchestra announced the

commencement of the show, and the crowd, a full house as far as Hippolyte could see, settled from roaring bedlam into a more subdued buzz of voices and coughs. Then out stepped a deep-voice actor with exaggerated flairs and gestures to recite, yes, once again, a dozen verses from *Les Châtiments.* Hippolyte heard laughter and applause coming even from the bourgeois seated in the more expensive boxes.

Actually, Hippolyte had to admit, some of Hugo's satirical digs were clever, including some he hadn't heard before – possibly improvised by the actor, or his director. Nevertheless, he still thought it would be unbecoming for him to bring his hands together to applaud. These were attacks on the man he had loyally served for nearly two decades.

When at last this recitation came to a close, with a deep bow and wide grin from the actor, Hippolyte settled back in his seat, nodded to those who nudged him while chuckling and making other loud noises, and waited to see what Bagou's coquettish mistress would present. Although he could not forget that he was a police official, here he was disguised as an ordinary bourgeois gentleman and should play the part. More theater, perhaps (he tried to console himself) he should think of this as practice for undercover work if he should get into Sûreté.

Next the orchestra broke out again in another loud, spirited air more suitable for a *café-conç* than for such a theater – though Hippolyte knew he might be mistaken, maybe this was what always happened in the Ambigu, despite the elegant surroundings.

But unlike the Cirque Impérial, here there were no acrobats, no jugglers or clowns, but, after the second fanfare, a troupe of a dozen or more young figures pranced onto the stage, the men in pseudo-military costumes, the buxom young women in flouncy tricolored skirts and tight bustiers just like those he remembered from that earlier performance of Victorine's.

After much humming from the crowd on stage and then a loud chorus from 'La Marseillaise', complete with drum rolls, bugles and cannon-like noises from the orchestra, the vedette of the evening stepped forward in a brilliant blue dress with a tricolor sash, in high-heeled boots and an enormous fore-and-aft general's hat. From that sash hung a huge fake saber clanking against the stage floor as she bounced forward. Hippolyte braced himself, knowing what was coming.

It was, as he had expected and half-feared, Victorine herself in a starring role, performing *'Le Sire de Fisch Ton Kan'*. That was the way it was spelled on the program, but *'Fiche ton camp'* is what everybody heard – meaning 'The Lord of Get-the-Hell-Out', or 'Run for Your Life', its refrain emphasizing the Emperor's ignominious surrender to the Prussian king.

As Victorine belted out those lines, to loud applause and spontaneous accompaniment and hooting and laughter from the crowd at each repetition of the refrain, she waved her enormous saber:

He was a famous capitaine
Who looked out for his skin,
For his skin!

Hoots and laughter.

And when his saber bothered him,
To his foes he gave it with a grin,
Such a charming grin!

Wild applause.

And such a deep embarrassment. For Hippolyte personally, for the police, for all of France. And the worst part, it was true. Hippolyte felt sick and anxious to leave. And saddened that so many of his compatriots were laughing and cheering at the spectacle.

The new uniform

On Monday Étienne went back to the bindery to say his goodbyes to Perrin and his remaining co-workers. Louise and Cécile were still at the sewing frames, Albert was finishing a job gilding bookcovers, and one or two others he recognized were still coming in to work, but they didn't seem very busy; with no new jobs coming in, Étienne supposed that the others were either looking for other jobs or, more likely, had already joined the National Guard. Perrin seemed sad to see him go, or maybe he was just sad to see the workshop so void of work. He had not been a bad boss, but hardly up to what Étienne needed to learn his craft. Whatever he had learned in these past four months had been from watching and practising on his own, with no more than friendly tips from Claude and other more experienced binders. Four months was hardly enough to learn all the skills and to feel himself fully competent to set up shop for himself, but with more time and a better master, he was sure he could himself achieve his goal– but not now, not with the country and the republic calling and the workshop falling apart.

Then on Tuesday he finally got over to the mayoralty of the Sixth to sign up for the National Guard, saying he was nineteen. He could have said twenty or even thirty because the mayor's adjunct barely glanced at him as he filled out the form. They were taking anybody who wanted to serve, it looked like.

He felt excited when they handed him the folded bundle with the uniform jacket and trousers, with the kepi balanced on top. And then they handed him a voucher to be issued a rifle. Just wait till Rose could see him! And her father and mother, too, who would surely be pleased to see him in the uniform of this great people's militia.

He rushed back to Dragon Court to try it on. The sleeves and the pants were short, the tunic uncomfortably tight around the chest and the kepi a bit too snug, but they'd have to do. He hoped he would be able to exchange his package with another, shorter and more slender recruit – Évariste, maybe. But he wasn't home, and Étienne wasn't even sure if he had signed up. But all this was of little consequence. Ill-fitting or not, it was handsome and a symbol of a big event in his life, that he was now in the *Garde Nationale*. It meant he was now a man, and also a patriot, ready to fight for his country and the republic. He stroked the light fuzz on his cheeks and chin, impatient to grow a beard, but that too would come. He would turn eighteen in May.

Since neither the tunic nor the kepi bore a numeral, he wasn't sure which battalion he should report to; there were two forming in his neighborhood. But Claude told him that he and Jean-Pierre had already joined one that was going to assemble in nearby Saint-Germain Square, so he would too. He joked with the two of them that they could form a whole bookbinders' battalion, because there were so many binderies in the Sixth, but J-P solemnly told him no, they would have to fight shoulder to shoulder with men of the most varied trades. Well, of course! thought Étienne, he knew that; he had only meant it as a joke. Sometimes Jean-Pierre was just too serious.

Hilaire hadn't joined up yet, but said he was looking for a battalion closer to his workplace in the Fifteenth, which suggested to Étienne that he wasn't planning to stay long in their house on Dragon Court. Then he found out that Évariste had signed up with some pals of his in the other battalion in the quarter, a couple of blocks away. The group was breaking up. And Luc – well, he had excuses. His legs. And he said he still had all he could handle with his work schedule, and 30 sous was not enough for him to give up his job.

Thirty sous a day, a franc and a half, was less than even Étienne's apprentice wage of 2 francs 15 centimes, and a full franc less for Claude who was a qualified binder. But it was enough for a single man to live on, for bread and wine and bed. Married men would receive another 75 centimes. But with the war and all the mobilization, that wasn't a major consideration. Especially since it didn't look as though the bindery was going to be able to keep operating for long anyway. And regardless of the money, joining up was their duty as Frenchmen and Internationalists. The bindery, if it survived, was just going to have to get along without them.

As he headed out with Claude and J-P on Wednesday for their first day of training, the three binders saw another poster from the Central Committee of the Twenty Arrondissements, a pink one this time, with a long list of signatures and posted on all the most prominent walls. The committee's red poster the week before had simply pressed for a united defense and other preparations for the expected Prussian siege. This one was bolder, calling openly for the formation of a Paris 'commune', the replacement of the police by 'magistrates… assisted by the National Guard', and other things: elections of all civil officials, freedom of press, and, as before, a rationing system to face the coming siege.

"Vive la commune!"

Étienne had been hearing the phrase more and more insistently, sometimes said quickly and slyly with a knowing wink or the raising of an eyebrow, as though invoking some mystical power, the way in his boyhood Étienne and other boys would sometimes mutter 'Mother of God'. He was not sure of exactly what it implied, but he laughed as he pointed to the line about the National Guards as the new police power. He had not forgotten the fat cop who had humiliated him a couple of months ago, making him shout '*Vive l'Empereur!*' Or the one he had had to run from, after stopping him from beating a protester at the plebiscite back in May.

They assembled with the others for their first drill, not all of them in full uniform. J-P had been right, of course. They were men of all trades, even some who looked like office clerks and others he recognized as local shopkeepers. After standing at attention trying to look military and marching in step, more or less, at the shouts of a National Guard corporal, they had their first experience loading, aiming and firing their rifles. Étienne had heard of the famous chassepot, but he and the others had been given older rifles, the ones with the little 'snuff box' cover over the breech that you had to lift to pop in a cartridge. Then, aim – at the outline of a Prussian helmet painted on a wooden crate a dozen meters distant – and *Fire!*

What a start! – the sudden noise, the heat by his cheek, the sharp odor. And then, fumbling at first trying to reload. But Étienne was good with his hands and he quickly got the hang of it, more quickly than some of the others.

They were at it for what seemed like hours, though he was too excited by the experience to feel tired until after the last cartridge, when the corporal gave the order, *"Rompez!"* – which at first no one understood, and the corporal had to explain. It meant 'Break ranks. Dismissed. Go home', until tomorrow morning. That was when he suddenly felt exhausted. But happy.

But just what was going to be their relationship to the regular army, he wondered? He had begun to hear complaints that army officers had countermanded orders in Guard battalions, and that army sergeants were even trying to recruit some of the same men as were joining the Guard. They did draft some who had no choice, because they had drawn a 'bad number' in the draft lottery, but they got very few volunteers because of the army's reputation for harsh discipline and its seven-year commitment.

Joining the Guard was an entirely different proposition, an act freely entered upon, and which could be freely abandoned when it no longer suited one's needs, and where a man felt free to discuss and dispute commands. They were not a mass to be commanded *bon gré, mal gré,* 'like it or not', by more or less incompetent officers, but a workers' militia, of free men governed not by the whip but by their spirit, joining together to ensure their own freedom.

Each battalion was supposed to consist of eight companies of 120 to 125 men, four of them 'sedentary', meaning that the men could go home except when summoned to duty. But because of his youth and because he was single, Étienne was assigned to one of his battalion's four 'war' companies, which could be mobilized for longer periods and even be called on to fight outside the city walls. That was fine with him. He was anxious to get to war. But at least at first, while they were getting organized, the distinction between 'sedentary' and 'war' companies was vague and theoretical. For now, he and J-P and Claude were going to continue to live in Angélique's boarding house.

The sorry condition of the army was of concern to René-Pierre Bougainville, writing for the conservative papers. He had been talking to some officers, even to some close to General Jules-Louis Trochu himself, who had assumed the presidency of the new Government of National Defense. Trochu enjoyed some popularity with the crowd that had called for the Republic, mainly because he was the one general known to have criticized the poor preparation of the army prior to the declaration of war on Prussia. But he was a very cautious and politically conservative man, rumored to favor the restoration of the 'Orleanist' royal lineage of the Old Régime. It was Trochu's distrust of the National Guard – Bagou was convinced – that had been the reason that he had ordered General Vinoy's 40,000-man army to return to the capital, instead of remaining in the field to confront the Prussian armies.

"Our good Trochu is more afraid of the Bellevillois than he is of the Prussians," Bagou remarked in one of his late suppers with his old friend Hippolyte Mireau. "But he still had to expand the National Guard. From what I've seen, the Army of Paris, even with Vinoy's reinforcements, is in poor shape to defend the city. And getting those rowdy workers into battalions, under the command of an army general, may be the only way to keep some control of them."

"But wouldn't Vinoy's men be better deployed keeping the Prussians away from Paris, rather than sitting here inside our walls, waiting for them?"

"No, we're going to need those 40,000 here. We'll need every man we can get under arms once they start attacking our ramparts. It's the Prussian cannons I fear. They have steel ones, with longer range and bigger shells than those bronze guns you and I and all our citizens have been paying for in those subscriptions. But we do have the advantage in our infantry. Our chassepot, far better than their clumsy rifles. I hear that all the time from men who've been in the battles."

"Rifles against cannons. Is that Trochu's idea? Hardly seems fair, does it? It would seem to me to make more sense to use those riflemen to attack in the field, before the enemy gets to bring his cannons in range against our walls."

"Oh, Polo, neither you nor I is a military man. We have officers who have graduated from Saint-Cyr, men who know military strategy! We have to trust them, those gentlemen. The question is whether we can trust those new, undisciplined workers' battalions in the Guard. And bringing Vinoy's army back into the city may be the best way to keep Paris safe from those most radical Guardsmen, and from revolution."

"I thought we were trying to keep it safe from the Prussians."

"Well, of course. That too. Both things."

After refilling their glasses, Mireau and Bougainville sat in silence, having broached a delicate theme that, Mireau thought, should be embarrassing to his long-time drinking companion. He decided to change the subject.

"The other big topic I read in the papers is the influx of all those families trying to get away from the war, seeking safety behind our walls."

"Yes, annoying and inconvenient. There are families doubling up, making room for their country relatives, even in my neighborhood! But let's talk of something else, something more cheerful. What did you think of Victorine's performance last week?"

"Insulting the Emperor?"

"Polo! Please! It's the times, it's show business, and everybody is making fun of old Badinguet now. I meant, what did you think of her singing, and that little sashaying she does at the spicy verses?"

"You seem to care a lot about her."

"I've made her! Her contacts, set up things with the theater managers and directors, pulling her up from a sorry fate as just another poor grisette to now, on her way to becoming a star. And it's good for me, too. To attract attention with a glittering young bauble on my arm."

"A bauble. Yes, she's attractive enough. Does she have anything inside that pretty head?"

"Oh, Polo! You're impossible to cheer up! Things aren't that bad, you know. Our ramparts are very solid, very strong. And from what I hear, chances are good for your transfer to Sûreté. And life goes on here, in Paris."

"I'll drink to that."

* * *

Rose was heading home after finishing her work in the Marmite for the day. It was a long walk from the Sixth all the way to Belleville in the Twentieth, and the last stretch was uphill, but she was cheerful, singing to herself and almost prancing as she reached the hill. She was looking forward to seeing Étienne, who had said he had something to tell her and would meet her at her parents' house. He was kind of shy, that boy, maybe that was one of the things she liked about him – so different from that aggressive Toinou and other Paris boys she knew. Shy but clearly competent, at many things. When she was still at the bindery, she had seen how carefully and with what concentration he had observed the other workers and had been improving his skills of cutting, pressing, and all the others. And on that little journey they had taken beyond the barrier, it was Étienne who had thought of offering that girl shoes. Without that idea, they might never have succeeded in transporting all they needed. She was also impressed that he had dared to sign the International's letter to the German workers, back when that was to take a real risk.

"So," she thought as she neared the house, "if he has something to say to me, it must be – well, I don't dare think what it might be. Let's see if he has the courage to say what he wants to a girl, to me. I know he has courage for other things."

What she hadn't expected was to see him there before she got home, and in a tight National Guard uniform. Standing by the road, just a few meters from her house.

"What's this? You've done it, then. Joined the Guard. This means you've left the bindery?"

"Yes. For now, anyway."

"But you wanted to be a binder. You were set on it. And you were so close!"

"Yes, I still do. But, well, there's not much work there now, and defense of our city, our Republic, is more urgent. You know that."

"Uh-huh. But you had dreams of becoming a first-class bookbinder. Like Eugène Varlin, you said…"

"Like Varlin. Yes, like him. Though I've still got a way to go before I get up to his skill level. But you know what? He is now in the Guard himself! Eugène Varlin, Commander of a battalion, in the Sixth. If I'm going to be like him, this is what I have to do."

"I like your uniform. Brand new. But a bit snug, isn't it? You're straining the buttons on that tunic."

"Yes, and the pants are a little short. But say, those shoes!

Where did you get those? And what did you do with that girl's sabots?"

"I've got them under my bed. I'm keeping them, as a keepsake of our adventure. These are some old ones my mother lent me, until I get myself a new pair. I haven't had time yet."

She stopped to replay the scene in her memory, the exchange of shoes with Jeanne the milk girl. But then she heard Étienne's voice.

"You know, we made our trip just in time. I hear that that's where the Prussians are closest now, near the Vincennes barrier. I'm going to find a way to get out there, we have to stop them!"

"Ooh, you sound just like my dad. Can't wait for a battle. Is it true? That they're out there, near that barrier? I just hope that girl Jeanne and her family are safe."

Another pause.

"But you said you had something to say to me."

She watched him shuffling his feet and looking first at the ground, then to left and right as though worried that somebody might be listening, or maybe just so as not to look directly at her. She waited, her heart beating a little faster. It was his move now, she couldn't help him any further, he had to take the next step, to say whatever it was – she had an idea, but she couldn't be sure – whatever it was he wanted to say.

Finally he blurted out,

"You know, I think it's time for me to get out of that house at Dragon Court. And, well, I'm now in the Guard, a man, and I should be independent, and I'd like, I was wondering –"

He took a deep breath.

"Would you come live with me?"

Her eyes opened wider. She gasped to suppress an

embarrassed laugh. It wasn't a totally unexpected proposition. But he was asking more than she had anticipated, and sooner. And the implications –

She had been thinking for some time about becoming independent, moving out of her parents' home, out of Belleville. She had got deeply engaged with the other women, and some men, too, but mostly women and girls, through the Marmite and the Ménagère, and these activities and contacts had made her think of different ways she could lead her life.

But the timing of this, and Étienne's shiny and too-tight new Guard uniform, and so much that had been happening all around her, the people she had got to know at the Marmite and the Ménagère, and all that was going on in Paris – she needed to catch her balance.

But only for a moment, after which she had decided and asked, simply,

"Where?"

Étienne's head jerked up, his mouth agape and his jaw moving. She knew that he knew that she had just said 'Yes'. The fact that he seemed so unprepared for the desired answer made her want to laugh! She felt like a fencer. After his tentative attack, riposte, and she had caught him off-guard.

"Uh, where? Oh, well, I haven't found a place yet. I mean, I haven't really been looking, yet, but I just think it would be a really nice idea, the two of us. I mean, if you're willing."

She laughed and cocked her head, laughter in her lips and eyes.

"Yes?" he asked, for confirmation.

"We'll have to talk about it. This is a big decision, I need to think a bit. And we would have to find a place, but I think I have some ideas. But listen, Titi, not a word to my parents, not yet. Not until we have it all decided. Agreed?"

He nodded. He grinned, delighted and embarrassed. He started forward as though to embrace her, but she stopped him with a gesture, simply raising her hands as though pushing him away.

"Not here. Not on the street. Come with me then. Let's go in."

On the ramparts

Two days later, Étienne – his uniform adjusted by Rose's mother's friend and neighbor, Henriette – was again on his way toward the Vincennes barrier, this time with his buddies Claude and J-P. The three of them, rifles in hand, like Dumas' *The Three Musketeers*.

"*Les trois relieurs!*" Étienne exclaimed, laughing. Claude laughed with him, and even J-P gave an approving grunt.

They had heard, among the many rumors, that Vincennes was where the action would be, on the city's ramparts at the eastern edge of the Twelfth Arrondissement, and that was where they were going, even though it meant not reporting to their home battalion that day. And not collecting their 30 sous.

"What's more important? Our 30 sous, or stopping the Prussians?"

Who had said that first? None of them was sure, because each had said something like that. More than once, because the fact was they were concerned about losing a day's pay.

Also, Claude was fretting about what they would do when they got there. Étienne reassured him, insisting that, because they still didn't have numerals on their uniforms, they could just join in with whatever Guard battalion was on the ramparts. Nobody would be able to tell that they didn't belong, the battalions were mostly so new that the officers probably didn't even know all their men. J-P wasn't so sure, but he too was itching to get into action.

They had drawn their rifles from the armory in the mayoralty early in the morning, but instead of reporting to their assigned assembly spot, the three of them had pooled their few coins to hire a cab to take them to the eastern edge, to as close as possible to Fort de Vincennes. The cab driver joined in on their enthusiasm, and apologized for charging them anything, but he had no choice, because one had to prepare for hard times, but, for the homeland, he would charge them just half price.

Two francs! Two whole francs, which sounded pretty high! But they weren't going to argue, they just wanted to get there as quickly as they could.

"Got to stop the Fritz!" said the driver. "Yes, you boys are doing the right thing. If I was younger –"

No need to finish the thought.

It was going to be a long ride. Étienne knew it, and warned his friends, because it was the same journey he had taken in a much slower wagon only a little over a week before. Action! He was going to go into action! To fire at real enemies, instead of a cartoon painted on a plank. They had their rifles. The cartridges they were going to have to cadge from the forces already out there.

The driver was taking a different route from Étienne's earlier trip, along the river and through the Fifth, through some streets Étienne hadn't seen before. It was Saturday morning, and people were milling about. They saw other National Guard units and also some groups of soldiers with cannons and a smaller piece with a crank at the back.

"What's that?" Étienne asked.

"*Mitrailleuse,*" the driver called down to them.

It turned out that he was an army veteran, and claimed to know those machines.

"It looks like a cannon but it's really a bunch of rifle barrels, twenty-five, all inside that bigger tube. You can fire one after another, as fast as you can turn the crank."

The driver laughed.

"You should have seen those Arabs fall! Boom-boom-boom-boom-boom!"

This talk made Étienne think back to his conversation with Rose's parents just two days ago. He had been nervous, too anxious about what not to say, his and Rose's secret, to be able to make conversation. And he was more than a little embarrassed when Blanche, Rose's mother, held up a blanket and ordered him to take off his uniform and wrap himself in the blanket until her neighbor could let out the seams of his tunic and try to lengthen the pants and sleeves.

It was the mention of cannons that made him think of Rose's father, Jules. The older man had been very pleased to see Étienne in National Guard uniform, laughing hugely at how poorly it fit, and laughing again when Étienne huddled behind the blanket, raised like a curtain, to take it off. While he sat wrapped tight in his blanket, Rose's dad repeated what he had no doubt told his family dozens of times, boasting that in his foundry they now were no longer just making washtubs and trinkets for the rich, but were casting cannons, people's cannons, paid for by subscription of ordinary workers like Jules himself and like Étienne! The laugh was shorter, ambiguous, almost a snort, when he added that he and his compagnons in the foundry had themselves paid a part of the very cannons they were molding.

"You wouldn't think the bosses were going to donate

their production, would you? Out of patriotic duty. It's us the workers, make the sacrifices!"

And Jules' crew engraved the initials of their foundry on top of each piece, because they were proud of their work. And wanted to let the artillery men and the people know where such fine cannons came from.

Good for those bronze workers! thought Étienne. A direct contribution to the struggle. But what could bookbinders do to support the war effort? Besides joining the National Guard, and throwing themselves into battle? Which was just what he had persuaded his companions to do.

At last their carriage got close enough to the ramparts for the trio of bookbinder-guardsmen to jump out and run to where they saw other men in uniform, some army men with their red pants and kepis but mostly National Guard, all in blue, like them. Étienne had been right, the men up on the ramparts were glad to have them, and the corporal running up and down the line, handing out cartridges was ready to hand each of them a bunch. Until he looked at their rifles.

"Not these," he said. "These won't do, they're for… You'll have to wait."

At this, Étienne took a closer look at the other men on the ramparts and their weapons. He could see at least three different kinds of rifles, each one requiring a different size and kind of cartridge. He even saw some men with rifles they had to load through the muzzle. And near to them, another Guard with the stripes of a sergeant on his sleeve was firing and reloading with what seemed like uncommon rapidity. That, he concluded, must be the famous chassepot.

At last the corporal came back with cartridges for Étienne and Claude and J-P's *fusils à tabatière*, snuff-box rifles, but he had only a dozen for each of them. The three of them then joined the others all firing in the general direction of the Prussians, firing and reloading and firing again, and again, until they had to call out for more cartridges.

But all the men were firing wildly. Some faster than others, depending on their type of rifle. Firing at what? Off in the near distance, some kilometers away, there was smoke and thundering noise, cannon fire surely, but the Prussian cannons weren't directed at them, at least there had been no impacts on the wall where Étienne's group crouched. The action, the smoke and noise, was aimed at what must have been French forces around a church in some small town. Creteil, somebody said it was, eight or nine kilometers away.

This went on, firing and firing, for a very long time. The different caliber rifles made different noises, a terrible, joyous din. It was the first time any of these guardsmen had had a chance to shoot at the enemy, and they fired and fired, no matter that they had no particular target, they just fired in the direction where they thought the Prussians must be, because that's where the smoke and the bigger cannon noises were coming from. Until, after what must have been hours, somebody – a colonel, Étienne supposed – shouted "Halt!"

"No more cartridges! Corporal, you idiot, what are you doing, handing out ammunition to these madmen! And you fools, you're not hitting anything! You haven't been hitting anything all afternoon!"

Several of the men protested. "But they're still out there! We have to keep shooting!"

There were a few more shots, as some of the men tried to use up their last cartridges. But the colonel, or whatever he was, was right. They hadn't been able to hit anything, even the chassepots didn't have the range, and certainly not the rifle that had grown hot in Étienne's hands. But it had felt so good to fire!

Finally, at dusk, the men were dismissed. The army men would be going back to their barracks, the other national guards must surely be men who lived nearby, but the three weary bookbinders had no option but to walk, all the way to the Place de la Bastille, carrying their rifles, no longer virgin and now not just filthy with powder but also become very heavy. When they got to Place de la Bastille, they approched an omnibus – the other passengers made way for them, the fare-collector refused to charge them, and men patted them on the backs of their now-dirty tunics. "Our heroes!" someone shouted, and others took up the cry.

"Tell us about it! You let those Prussians have it, didn't you boys! How many did you get?"

All the sudden attention was embarrassing, and what could they say?

"Yes, we really let them have it!" Claude answered. All three climbed up to the upper deck, to much applause. They were just hoping to relax a bit, but there were more congratulations up there, and very curious people. Étienne saw the powder marks on his two companions' uniforms and then looked down at his own. What a mess! What a day.

"We really let them have it!" Yes, that sounded all right, it didn't really mean anything so it wasn't really a lie. And maybe, just maybe, their firing had helped keep the Prussian infantry from coming closer to the walls. If that was what they had intended to do.

"Good for you boys! Let's keep the Fritz back home! Keep those Prussians away! Let them know what Frenchmen are good for!"

Right. And more of the same, from other passengers, and

some admiring glances from young women, working girls mostly but even some bourgeoise ladies pushing aside the veils on their hats to smile at them. They hadn't hit anything, they knew, all three of them, but nobody else on the omnibus could know that. It had been their first day of action, and they had had a lot of practice firing and reloading, which had to be useful. And it felt good, even if a little strange, to be called a hero.

Fortunately, the omnibus they had boarded was one that crossed eventually to the Left Bank. It was dark now, but by the gaslights Claude was able to make out something he recognized and signaled to the conductor to stop.

"This is as close as we're going to get," he told the others. "We'll have to walk from here."

New régime in Dragon Court

Such shouts on Sunday morning! From the sergeant when the three binders showed up for their company's assembly with their rifles in hand and their uniforms badly soiled.

"You men! You despicable laggards!" shouted the sergeant as soon as he saw them. "You're here in the National Guard to defend our homeland! Not to make fun of it! You were supposed to be here for drill yesterday. Not to pick up your rifles and then disappear! Maybe you don't care about missing your pay for yesterday, but let's see how you feel about the fine! Three days' pay!" barked the sergeant.

" And tell us, say it out loud if you dare, just where did you three no-goods go with those rifles of the National Guard?"

"To Fort de Vincennes, sir!" answered Claude.

The sergeant stepped back, his scowl turning into a grimace of incredulity.

"You were where? Doing what?"

"All three of us," said J-P. "We were defending the ramparts against the Prussians."

"Vincennes! The battle!" shouted out one of the other men.

Then they all started shouting.

"It's in all the papers! The Prussians attacked Montmesly!"

"Mont what?" "It's part of Creteil. Just outside our walls, near Vincennes." "A French victory!" "At last!"

The sergeant looked bewildered as the men kept talking, excited and even laughing. Then he bellowed,

"You men deserted your ranks to go clear across to Fort de Vincennes, all the way on the far side of the city? With your rifles?"

"Yes, sir," said Étienne. "It was my idea, I confess it. I thought we should help our comrades holding back the Prussians there. I told my friends that I had heard that they were massing for an attack out there, and we…"

The other men started cheering.

"Action! Real action. You saw real shooting!" "Just give us a chance to have at those Prussians!"

And more and more shouts, and laughter. The shopkeepers, several shoemakers, a bakery assistant, some fellows that Étienne thought looked like typographers, some tinsmiths including one not in uniform at all but in his blouse and cap as though ready to go to work even though it was Sunday, a couple who might be carpenters, and others whose trade Étienne had not yet guessed, all breaking ranks to surround the three bookbinders, begging for details of the battle.

The sergeant shouted to return to ranks, to no effect, and then paused until his company of fifty-some untrained, undisciplined, unmilitary, but very enthusiastic workers and tradesmen and clerks, some in full National Guard uniform and some not, quieted enough for him to make himself heard. And then he shouted again, as firmly as he could.

"Attention! If we all get back into order, into your ranks, we'll let these Guardsmen tell us what they saw."

For an eye-witness report of an actual confrontation with the enemy, the company quieted down a little more, though still buzzing in low-pitched conversations up and down the line.

"You there! Bonin, is it? Front and center! It was your idea, you said. Now tell us. How close did they get, those Prussians? What did they look like? And what did you do?"

So Étienne, at his orders, stepped forward, wondering what he could say. Was it true that there had been a French victory? That was good news, if it was true.

"Why," he said, coming up with the only thing he could think to say, "we just shot and shot, the way you showed us, Sergeant Pons. Fired and reloaded, and fired and reloaded. On the ramparts, with men from some other battalion, shooting at the enemy."

At the mention of his name, the sergeant smiled broadly.

Then after a moment's pause, Étienne thought to add, more loudly, "We kept them away. They didn't dare get near our walls, those Prussians!"

Several of the men applauded.

And then the company calmed down somewhat, but still in good spirits. Their drill after Étienne's report was unusually brief. After a few marching paces and rehearsal of commands, the sergeant insisted and repeated with special emphasis that the men clean their rifles thoroughly – he had shown them how – and then he marched them all back to the mayoralty to return their weapons. And, pulling Étienne, Claude and J-P a little aside, but close enough and loud enough for the others to hear, he told them that there would be no fine and they would collect their 30 sous today along with the others after handing in their rifles. But for their 'irregular absence' of the day before, a serious offense, that was one day's lost pay.

"Never again are you to be absent without orders!" he stated loudly. Then he raised a hand as though he were about to pat each of them on the back, but then he restrained himself.

It was only after they had broken formation and left the mayoralty that Étienne and his buddies managed to see a newspaper. It was true, the papers were reporting a successful French engagement around Creteil, against Prussian artillery – but no mention of the National Guard on the ramparts by Fort de Vincennes.

As they walked back to their flat on Dragon Court, they joked about the reactions of Sergeant Pons and the surprise and enthusiasm of their comrades in the Guard company – even Jean-Pierre laughed. But when they got up the stairs to the loft, they found another drama.

No one, probably no one in all of Paris, had experienced the fall of the Empire with more emotion, and more mixed emotions, than Angélique. She felt suddenly released, and guilty all at the same time. Released to think, to feel, to desire things that she had had to suppress for a very long time. And guilty for, she knew not what, that she had not lived the kind of life she had been supposed to live. But had she had any choice?

She had been suppressing these feelings since the massacre at La Ricamarie, the murder of her partner, her common-law husband, Joseph, Jojo, over a year ago. A year, three months and one day ago, 16th June, 1869. Angélique had kept track, she could even have calculated the minutes, not since the shooting, because she hadn't been there to see it, but since she heard the news, the disaster. And then, as though in a coma, or dazed, trying to survive because she was bearing a new life inside her, a life that was to be the only continuation of something of Jojo – but it was too much for her, she was too ill, and the baby despite all the attention of the midwife was stillborn. It was a boy. Her last tie to Joseph Ducrin and to La Ricamarie, to all of Saint-Étienne.

What would she have done if Évariste had not suddenly appeared and urged her to come to Paris? Her husband dead, their child too, her school and only livelihood shut down by the local clergy and the mayor's council for being too 'radical' – her little school had admitted both boys and girls, coal miners' and other workers' children, teaching them history and geography as well as writing and arithmetic, without any reference to the Virgin and that Savior they loved to talk about while they beat down the workers.

Why had she accepted? Paris! Den of iniquity, in the eyes of those clergy and town councillors. A place she knew only as a name. But what alternative had she had?

But the really disturbing part of Évariste's proposal was that she abandon teaching, the only skill she had and the only work she loved, to become a drudge, a housemaid to a half-a-dozen men! But with her own room, and with great respect, the coal miner turned tinsmith promised her.

What made it seem bearable was that Évariste, and according to him all the other men as well, were committed to the same ideals for which she and Jojo had fought and for which Jojo had died. They were all, he said, committed to the International, which she had heard of even in Saint-Étienne and which she and Jojo had admired. And, seeing no other option, and anxious to get out of Saint-Étienne, she had agreed, barely mumbling 'Yes'.

Their arrival had been in September, just one year ago. A full year, in this strange town and with these unfamiliar duties. She had coped. It was awkward at first, dealing with the men – Évariste and Hilaire had assembled four others, one of whom soon dropped out, but Luc and Claude and that dour, serious Jean-Pierre had continued. And then they had recruited that boy, the young bookbinder's apprentice, brought in by Claude and endorsed by J-P. And it was true, they treated her with respect. Almost, she thought, the one funny thought when she reflected on all this, they treated her almost with fear. She had been so stern, and they felt so dependent on her for those little things that men are so bad at, silly, stupid routine things like cooking – she hated it, but had learned to do it competently – buying, cleaning. Laundry, she made clear, they would have to handle themselves, bundling up their dirty linen and their work clothes and trudging them over to the laundry just a block away.

That thought reminded her of what she had seen at that laundry. She had been the one to find it, the men had no idea until she told them. There she saw more women, eight or ten, some looking older than they probably were, some very young, in the steam and half dressed in all the heat from the tubs, hands and arms bright red from the heat and the soap and the lye. And she had also peeked into other work places where women were sewing shirts, or making gloves, or another one producing men's and women's hats, and except in the laundry which was entirely a women's world, those other working women were all working under the stern vigilance of a man, subject to fines for lateness or absence regardless of whether they had a sick child or some illness of their own, working long hours for very little pay. She had also met and talked with some other women she had met at the bakery, very early in the morning, women who were hurrying to work in one of the palaces of the rich. Cooking, cleaning, shopping, seeing to the whims of their bourgeois patrons. And she had thought, "They are no better off than I, in fact they are much worse. Then I surely have no right to complain, no right to demand anything better than this, my work in this house in Dragon Court. But still…"

She knew she was an attractive young widow and in a house full of single men, which would almost inevitably create sexual tensions. The men had always treated her with respect, but occasionally – usually from Luc, but also once or twice from Hilaire –she would hear some *calembour*, a clever play on words which allowed the speaker to pretend he hadn't meant the more suggestive interpretation. She would smile, to let him know she got it, and turn back to whatever task she had been doing. They all had girlfriends somewhere, she was pretty sure, so their tension around her must not be unbearable. All but Luc, who didn't go out much at night. And that new boy, Étienne, whose tensions had got so great she had first to quench his fire and then direct his passions to a more suitable target, the workmate that he really desired but was too shy to approach.

As for her feelings, she had gotten used to sleeping alone as her best option under her circumstances. Her memory of her late husband was still too fresh, and none of the men in her house was remotely as attractive to her as that memory. Except, in an odd way, the youngest of them, Étienne, who could almost be a younger, thinner and more naïve version of Jojo. And that accent! Almost like hers and Jojo's. But she wasn't looking for a relationship, not now, anyway. But it had been fun, that night, to teach such an eager pupil.

A year now in this house, in this work so unlike what she had prepared for. And she had endured, quite well in fact, and had made friends with some of the women in the neighborhood and even beyond, when she had ventured to a club meeting nearby. But now, the fall of the Emperor and the end of the Empire, and almost immediately the proclamation of the Republic, had changed everything.

And maybe now she would be able to do what she was

meant to do. The Republic must mean Liberty, Equality, Fraternity, or it didn't mean anything. That workers, men and women, could take charge of their own lives, reach their full potentials, pursue what they most desired.

And Angélique could be a teacher.

It was already happening in some of the arrondissements. Over in the Eleventh – she wasn't sure just where that was, somewhere in the eastern part of the city – the new mayor had banned the clergy from the public schools. And he and his adjuncts were going to make education obligatory and free of charge! For girls and boys. And elsewhere, even without the backing of the local mayor, she had heard that new private schools were opening – financed, she didn't know how, but open to the children of workers' families. And that was what she wanted to do.

She had already told Hilaire and Évariste, and Luc – who was very observant – had guessed before she had said anything, though he hadn't worked out all the implications. Her three bookbinder associates, however, were still in the dark. They had been away all Saturday, and hadn't returned until after Angélique and, she assumed, the others had already gone to bed, their heads too full of their new roles as National Guards for them to have noticed anything in the little remarks and gestures of the past two weeks. She wanted to tell them herself, before Luc blurted something out. Good. She could hear them now, laughing and talking as they came up the stairs.

"Gentlemen," she greeted them as they came through the door. "Our honored *Gardes nationaux*."

Claude and Étienne took deep, laughing bows. J-P nodded, with the suggestion of a smile.

"Our heroes of the Republic," she added.

"It's true, Lique-lique! You don't know the half of it!

We were at Vincennes Fort yesterday, firing at the enemy!" exclaimed Claude.

"Really? What was happening at Fort, what?"

"Vincennes. It's in the papers. Not our part, that didn't get reported, but the battle at Montmesly," Claude continued.

"That's part of Creteil, a town just a little way beyond the barrier of Vincennes," J-P explained.

"I don't think we hit anybody but at least we shot at them," said Étienne. "To make sure the enemy didn't get close to our walls."

"Oh. Well. Very good, boys. Good for you."

"Have we got anything to eat?" asked Claude, grinning and making mock panting noises.

"I was going to tell you," she replied, "but you weren't here yesterday. There are going to be some changes here."

"Changes?"

"I am not going to prepare more meals for you. I am assuming other obligations. There still is some food here, we have some bread from yesterday and vegetables and some other things, I think there's a pork bone in the pantry. Hilaire said he knows how to make a stew, he should, you know, he's a chemist."

"He makes that smelly javel stuff you use to clean!"

"He knows other things. What I'm saying is, you men can take your meals elsewhere, the Marmite is close by, I know that you already know that place. Or if you want, you can do what I've been doing. You can buy the wood and bring it in for the stove, haggle with the grocers here on the street or, better but a little farther, at the market on Rue Lobineau. It sometimes takes quite a while to fill your basket with what you need, and you'll have to learn to make a list. I can tell you the best times to avoid the crowd.

"But don't worry, my new plans won't affect your sleeping arrangements. We are going to have a new tenant, or associate, but she won't be in your way or your space. She and I will be sharing my room."

"She?"

"Yes. Her name is Noëlle. I think you'll like her, though it doesn't really matter whether you do or not, she'll be here to work with me. She and I have agreed to start a school together. Here. On weekdays in the mornings, we'll be using this space which has been our dining room."

This was a lot to take in for *Les trois relieurs.*

Pigeons

In the next days, news reached Paris of further stunning French defeats: the fort, artillery pieces and entire army corps lost to the Prussians at Toul on 23rd September, then an even larger surrender at Strasbourg on the 28th. And on that same day, according to reports reaching Paris two and three days later, there had been a short-lived declaration of a 'Federation of Communes' in Lyon, spurred by the Russian hothead Bakunin! It appeared that France was falling apart, from the pressure of the Prussians on one side, and revolutionaries – foreign and national – on the other.

Closer to home, the Prussian armies had completely encircled Paris on the 18th September, and by the 27th, they had succeeded in cutting off all communication between the city and its provinces. With the loss of contact by telegraph or rail, the government in Paris now depended on carrier pigeons, balloons, and occasional couriers slipping through the enemy lines for news that was always incomplete, unreliable and too late for effective response – if there had been anything the authorities in Paris could do to aid the French armies far afield. The commanding generals of those corps still in the field were left to improvise their own salvation, unable or perhaps too confused or too frightened to coordinate and come to the aid of other divisions.

Nevertheless, protected by Paris's walls and its ring of forts, life in the elite cafés and restaurants continued with its usual hubbub, as though denying an unacceptable and unaccepted reality. The restaurateurs and shop owners who had foreseen the loss of their usual sources of food and fuel had stocked up. In the drinking spots around the Place de la Madeleine where Alphonse sat, sometimes alone or sometimes with some other journalist, sipping a drink and nibbling before excusing himself and moving from one café to another, he watched and eavesdropped, sometimes jotting down some observation or remark in his notebook. A half hour or so in the café and ice cream shop Imoda, for starters, then on to the Durand, or to the Grand Café or the Americain on nearby Capucines, and then to yet another.

More than once he overheard a bewhiskered bourgeois in top hat and silk vest proclaim some ingenious, if impossibly complex, scheme to revert the harassment of Paris and send the barbaric Germans back to their primitive homeland – a scheme that, Alphonse calculated, would necessarily require Alexandre Dumas-worthy risk-taking by bolder, younger gallants. Other men, in a variety of uniforms, would sometimes reply with denunciations of the dishonorable and unchivalrous tactics of the Prussians, their unfair use of deadly long-range cannons, the ferocity of their Uhlan cavalry.

"French technology is the most advanced in the world," cried out one of those belligerent bourgeois.

"And of course, as for unhorsing those Uhlans, French valor and audacity has never been questioned, not since Jeanne d'Arc and the Song of Roland, the spirited fervor of '89 and the Grande Armée," replied a younger man, also in civilian dress, in a tone that to Alphonse's ear sounded like irony.

Mostly though, the men in uniform sat wordless and glowering, sometimes pounding a fist on the table or simply emptying one glass after another. Infantry officers in red pants, shiny boots and chevrons, with ribbons and gold or red curlicues on their sleeves signaling rank and regiment; cavalrymen in spurs and sashes, straddling their chairs as though on horseback, their sabers sometimes dragging to the floor and tripping the harried waiters; navy infantry in white pants and jaunty blue berets with their red pompoms, some already in a drunken stupor; and even, in one café, some Zouave officers dressed as Moorish chieftains in billowing red pantaloons and turbans while bent over their card game.

After sufficient observation, Alphonse would stand and settle his bill and, enjoying the brisk autumn temperature and the chance to stretch his legs, walk up the hill to the more popular, that is, cheaper cafés around Montmartre. Or on other days, he might head to the Café de l'Europe near the School of Medicine, to sample another sector of opinion.

In Montmartre the uniformed men were mostly National Guards of two varieties, the *gardes mobiles* – the '*moblots*' – and the *sédentaires*, local men from the neighborhood. The *moblots* were from the provinces, young men deemed fit to serve but whose draft number had permitted them to choose the Mobile Guard rather than the much stricter, longer-term army. Many were Bretons, immediately identifiable when they sat together, conversing in their own language – not a problem for the commanding General Trochu, who was himself a Breton and spoke their language. The *sédentaires* or local National Guards, in contrast, were all volunteers and very local, their slang often peculiar to a particular neighborhood or alley. In conversation, they often left Alphonse mystified, especially in the working-class sectors in the northernmost, eastern and south-eastern arrondissements. They were generally good-natured, though, and Alphonse supposed that they were trying out strange words on him as a kind of joke. But he was learning, and making a list of the new expressions.

In the Fifth Arrondissement, around the university, uniforms were scarcer, and there he listened to students with stylish foulards and carefully unkempt hair debating with one another or with long-bearded scholars and litterati.

After going the rounds from quartier to quartier, café to café, Alphonse would head back to his room – now paid up – to write up his notes.

He was spending more time than ever in the cafés, including the more expensive ones, with two objectives. First, to try to understand, from all the rumors and indiscretions, what was really going on in the war and in local politics. This was partly for his own satisfaction and also for an article on 'Paris in wartime' that he planned to submit to Félix Pyat's new paper, *Le Combat*. His other objective was to capture enough café gossip to fill his reports to the police, since *Commissaire* Mireau's payments were financing his new café habit.

It was ridiculous, he knew, but he imagined that he and the commissaire had a tacit understanding which each was careful to avoid making explicit. Hippolyte Mireau was no dummy and could see full well that Alphonse Bertrand's reports were utterly useless for catching any subversives.

This had become obvious in their conversations, and the local police chief had several times surprised Alphonse by the subtlety of his questions when Alphonse had sought to explain some arguments of Blanqui or Proudhon. Mireau would reply by summing up an argument from a work that the young Louis-Napoléon Bonaparte had written in 1844, long before he had proclaimed himself emperor: *On the Extinction of Pauperism.*

Alphonse didn't know that text and had been surprised at how close the young Bonaparte's ideas, as explained by *Commissaire* Mireau, had been to Saint-Simon and to demands still heard in the radical press and the speeches in the political clubs.

On one occasion, the commissaire had dropped an ironic reference to the ignorance and illiteracy of most of his informers, encouraging Alphonse to think that he tolerated the young out-of-towner simply because he enjoyed the interchanges with someone well read. And perhaps, Alphonse imagined, because this particular commissaire did not regard the suppression of reform as his greatest priority. But then, Alphonse couldn't really tell what the commissaire was thinking. At least, he felt sure that he had not so far said anything to endanger Jules Vallès or any of the other radicals he knew.

For the article Alphonse was preparing for *Le Combat,* he wrote that the sudden cutting off of communication, not only with the provinces but also with London, Rome, Milan, or Moscow and the rest of the world, had been an especially painful blow to the intellectual class which saw itself as the vanguard of world culture, and of course it was painful to the holdings of the financial elite that had interests everywhere on the globe. Overcoming such depressing isolation was seen as a challenge to French ingenuity.

Alphonse's article would celebrate what now seemed the most dramatic, and therefore most French, solution. On Friday, 7th October, interior minister Léon Gambetta had risen from Paris by balloon, heading toward Tours in the south, still in French hands, where he had announced his plans to organize a counteroffensive.

With him he carried a crate full of pigeons to inform Paris of his expected successes.

The October protest

Bugles and drums resounded through the quarter, calling the battalions to form.

It was a call that Étienne and his fellows had been waiting for ever since that day he and Claude and J-P had rushed to the ramparts, so eager to fire at the Prussians.

Now, on Saturday, a day after Gambetta's departure and nearly a month after that other Saturday that had been Étienne's first and only experience of firing at the enemy, he was more than eager to answer the call of the posters that had appeared that morning, to rally at the Hôtel de Ville to demand the formation of the Commune. All citizens were summoned, but especially the National Guards.

"Vive la commune!"

By now, after months of discussions with his comrades and speeches in the clubs, Étienne had formed a clearer idea of what that meant. Or at least, what it meant to him.

First of all, 'Commune' meant the people's election of the mayor of all Paris and the mayors of its arrondissements, and their right to recall them, instead of appointment by the Emperor or, now, the self-appointed military-civil cabal calling itself the 'Government of National Defense'.

But it was something more, something far more ambitious that the phrase suggested now and that the orators on street-corners and in the clubs were openly calling for. The original 'Paris Commune' had been the revolutionary government that had held power under Robespierre from 1792 to 1795, proclaiming a new world of social justice, of liberty, equality, fraternity. All of that sounded very good to Étienne.

So on that Saturday, 8th October, Étienne buttoned his tunic, grabbed his kepi –now with '84', his battalion number, sewn on – and ran down the stairs and over to the broad brick square of Saint-Germain-des-Prés. Claude and J-P were already there, in the front rank of their company and just behind the band of brass and drums. Most of the others from the battalion's eight companies had already taken their places, while others were rushing to join. They would be something like 1,500 if they all showed up, and today, with the excitement running through the quarter, Étienne had no doubt they would.

He and the men around him smiled or laughed while some, glancing up at the tall tower of the church, even crossed themselves – whether in jest or devotion or, as Étienne supposed, a mix. The battalion was overwhelmingly anticlerical, but that didn't mean that higher powers did not exist. The men were mostly in uniform, or at least some part of the uniform, some with added adornments such as a bright red scarf, a yellow bandolier, or another hat or cap instead of the numbered kepi. A few had brought heavy hammers from work and even, in one man's hand, an iron lever detached from what must have been a printing press – the rifles were still in the mayor's armory.

At a signal from the commandant, the bugling and the drumming ceased and Commandant Bixio announced that his men were to march in good order and without arms – those who had brought tools as weapons were to stash them in their belts or leave them behind – to demonstrate their peaceful intent, and that the will of the people was to turn the capital into a self-governing Commune. Because only by electing their own men, men they knew, true republicans and honest fighters, could the people properly defend Paris and thus the French republic in this dire hour.

"*Vive la République! Vive la Commune!*" he shouted, and the men in unison repeated the cry.

"*Vive la République! Vive la Commune!*" To the bugle, tuba, trumpet and French horn and the rhythm of the drums, the column set out with brisk step, singing the verses of the *Chant des girondins*.

"*Vive la République! Vive la Commune!*"

"To die for the homeland," they sang to the rhythm of their marching band.

Étienne Bonin now knew that he had found his place, in Paris and in life, and it was in this line of men, marching for change.

* * *

Back in the house on Dragon Court, in the middle room of the three, Angélique and her new friend Noëlle listened to the band, loud at first, gradually fainter as the battalion marched from the nearby square. They looked at each other for a moment, feeling the excitement but unsure of what it portended, before bending over the table again to plan what they considered an equally urgent project.

The two young women had met only the week before, at the club in the School of Medicine. Angélique had begun going to those meetings when she decided she needed to hear the debates that the men in her house were arguing about. Noëlle had gone with a more specific purpose.

As Angélique would learn later that evening, Noëlle, a tall brunette with a nervous laugh and an easy smile, was twenty-three, two years younger than she. She had been teaching in a school in Soissons until just days earlier, when on orders from the mayor she and other residents fled to Paris from the approaching Prussians. For the past nights, Noëlle had been sleeping in the crowded apartment of a very conservative and very religious aunt, and was hoping to leave as soon as possible. She had gone to the club as soon as she had heard of it, from another poster on the walls, hoping to meet people who shared her values – republican and definitely nonreligious – and to scout for other lodging and a livelihood, teaching or anything.

When she discovered that Angélique had also been a school teacher, her enthusiasm quickly broke through the other's reserve.

After about a half an hour, Noëlle remarked that the speeches had become very repetitive, and Angélique, after a moment's hesitation, nodded, and before the meeting ended the two slipped out into the autumn chill – "It's going to be a harsh winter," remarked Noëlle – and ducked into the nearest café, where they talked for hours.

Angélique was more than ready for a change in her life, and responded quickly to Noëlle's proposal to join forces to found a school. And for that, at Angélique's invitation the angular, vivacious young woman from Soissons had come to the house on Dragon Court to plan their ambitious project.

* * *

In the plaza in front of the Hôtel de Ville, Alphonse was observing and taking notes for the article he had promised to write for *Le Rappel* when the first National Guard battalion marched up, its band playing loudly. There was already a crowd of civilians gathered there, and when the guardsmen showed up, their cries of *"Vive la Commune!"* were joined by cries of *"Vive la Garde nationale!"* even louder.

He stayed in the plaza, now in front and now to one side or the other of the imposing edifice, for the whole drama, as different battalions marched up, and then a squad of *moblots*, those out-of-town mobile guards, who took up defensive positions under the command of the police prefect himself, Kératry.

After that first battalion with its banner and its enthusiastic band, more Guard battalions arrived, some of them with their rifles. But now he heard contrary shouts! Not just *"Vive la République!"* which was a sentiment everybody seemed to share, but even from some groups *"Down with the Commune!"* It was the counter-demonstration.

He had to elbow his way from one spot in the dense crowd to another, trying to find a position to see into the inner courts of the Hôtel de Ville. At one moment it looked as though there might be a violent confrontation, especially when Kératry and the *moblots* stationed themselves in the inner courts of the Hôtel de Ville as though to defend it by arms from the pro-Commune Guards and people. But then, nothing happened but more shouts and occasional arm-waving.

Hours and hours he stood there, scribbling notes, listening to occasional bursts of song, shouts and complaints, until at last Trochu appeared and another general, Tamisier, managed to quiet the crowd, proclaiming that defending against the Prussian enemy was the only priority for all the people and all the guards, and that for that reason elections would have to be postponed yet again until the end of the siege. Postponed again!

And then the heavy rain sent everybody looking for cover, drowning the demonstration in the sharp October chill.

Alphonse had taken advantage of his time in the cafés to meet Albert Barbieux, editor-in-chief of *Le Rappel*, who then introduced him to one of his star correspondents, Charles Hugo. What a thrill to meet this son of France's most famous poet! That had been just days ago. Whether it was because of his enthusisasm or his comments on current politics, or simply that he was young, available and willing to work cheap, Barbieux had proposed that Alphonse write the lead article on the demonstration expected on this Saturday. And here he was, on a real assignment from a paper he admired. This would be a test, he knew, to see if he might be charged with future articles in that strongly republican, anticlerical paper that carried the prestige of the Hugo name.

Alphonse-Marie Bertrand could not have been more thrilled. He felt he was about to become an important writer, a *belle-lettriste*. And not just another hack like that gossip columnist Bougainville, the one Vallès and Rochefort called '*Bagou*' and who had set up his ridiculous engagement as informer for that local police chief Mireau.

Because that was the other big turning point for Alphonse related to today's demonstration. Just the day before, Mireau had informed him – rather rudely –that his services would no longer be needed.

It was no surprise, really, but a major change in his situation.

He had known that Mireau would be more than displeased that he had not given him names of the ringleaders of today's protest, nor even of those who had placarded the walls with posters calling for it – in fact, Alphonse had never given the police chief any useful information, and it seemed that Mireau was no longer satisfied with the mix of literary and political discourse that at first had seemed to amuse him.

Alphonse was relieved to drop the charade of a *mouchard*, even though it meant he could no longer afford to spend so much time and money in the expensive cafés. But he had used that time well, and his new connection with Barbieux might be his professional as well as his financial salvation – though this first piece would appear anonymously, and earn him less than a franc.

With or without his services as a *mouchard*, the police and the government authorities had won the day today. There had been no revolt, only a confused rumbling, and then the rain.

And – thought Alphonse as he nibbled absent-mindedly on the butt of his pen – the important thing is to have this piece written and corrected in time for tomorrow's paper.

* * *

It was already dark when the three soaking and bedraggled guardsmen, Étienne, Claude and Jean-Pierre, returned to the house on Dragon Court, in a foul mood. There they found their new housemate, this woman Noëlle, hunched with Angélique over the table, but no sign of dinner. Something was cooking, though. Some unusual, not unpleasant but unidentifiable aroma wafted from the stove. It was Hilaire, brewing something in the big iron marmite.

"We were worried!" Angélique said.

"They were beating the call to arms all across the city!"

Noëlle added. "We thought it must be a major attack by the Prussians."

"No," said Claude. "But that's what they wanted those other Guard battalions to think. They got them to come armed, as though they were going to the ramparts."

"What happened?"

"Nothing. No elections, no commune," muttered J-P. "The same bastards still in charge. For now, anyway. And then the rain, and it was over."

"Au hasard de la fourchette?" inquired Claude, sniffing at the pot on the stove. The 'luck of the fork' – as in the poorest dining halls in Paris: whatever you speared for a sou, whether meat or vegetable or something more mysterious, was yours to eat.

"Mutton and turnips," answered Hilaire. "Enjoy it, it may be the last meat you get for a long time."

Coping

Hilaire's caution had been exaggerated, but only slightly. Food had grown scarce, but one could still find meat of some variety. Of just what variety – it was better not to ask. And something looking like bread to mop it up with. Black usually, of unknown vegetable matter, hard and with a strange taste, but baked like normal bread. Étienne saw this as another test of his resolve as a defender of Paris.

When he saw Rose in the Marmite, where he was now eating regularly and she had been working since the bindery closed, she confessed that she had felt queasy, even sorrowful, the first time she had watched the cook skin a large dog. But soon she too, she said, was skinning and butchering any animal the kids brought in and had learned to make a palatable sausage like the one he was eating. Dogs of any size had become scarce, unfortunately, but the pursuit of rats and cats had become a sport and a sort of contest for the youngsters in the quarter, who knew they would be rewarded with some tasty scrap and took pride in the hunt, bragging of their catches.

Most of the hunters were boys, except – she laughed when she told him –a fleet-footed twelve-year-old, Titine, who gave her a wicked, saucy smile whenever she appeared in the kitchen waving the dangling corpses of her prey.

Her description made Étienne queasy too, and he stared again at his plate. Nevertheless, he was too hungry to be picky and took another bite of his sausage as Rose went on. For the adults, she said, it was not a sport. In Belleville, Blanche and her neighbors stood in long lines for cat, dog or rat meat. Or horse meat, when they were lucky. The National Guard had been demanding a system of rationing, to give everyone a chance at what food there still was, but the system was not yet in place, the twenty mayors and the Government of National Defense seemingly unable to come to any agreement. Meanwhile, the rich had their own suppliers, who reserved their stock of delicacies and wines for the higher-paying clients.

* * *

Since mid-September, Rose had been working in La Marmite on Rue Larrey in the Sixth Arrondissement and La Ménagère nearby on Saint-Jacques in the Fifth, and was very happy about the convivial atmosphere with the other women there. She was more determined than ever now to get out of her parents' house, not only to be closer to her new worksites but also because of tensions in her parents' neighborhood – the men in the Guard company were now keeping their guns at home and she feared that if they got hold of a pot of 'blue wine', cheap, dark stuff that could turn a drinker blotto, they might storm down the hill to shoot up the Hôtel de Ville, or do something worse. People were angry, first of all at the government, for the shambles of its defense against the Prussians, and then as a spillover of emotions, at each other.

She told Étienne she had found a small apartment on a street about midway between the Marmite and the

Ménagère. The place was small, two tiny rooms up two flights from a narrow street, dark and with noisy neighbors. But it would be an escape, independence, for both of them. And cheap – 10 sous a day, or 3 francs, 50 per week. The two cooperatives, in their most recent joint assembly, had voted to pay their workers the same as a National Guard, 30 sous a day, so with Rose's and Étienne's combined income, and if they continued eating at the Marmite, they could afford this independence.

To economize, Étienne could give up smoking cigars, a new habit he had picked up only in imitation of some men who had impressed him in his battalion.

He was still sleeping at Dragon Court, but it was time for him to leave. It wasn't just that Angélique was no longer shopping for and preparing food, or even that she and her friend were bringing in children who were sometimes impossible to control; he'd caught two one morning, eight or nine years old, in his sleeping area and rummaging through his bag. But what made him most uncomfortable was that the whole atmosphere, the mood of the place, had changed. It no longer felt like a men's club. Only he, J-P and Luc remained of the old gang, Luc because he was too lazy to move, J-P out of what seemed to be a sense of responsibility toward Angélique's new project.

But the real, most important reason Étienne jumped at Rose's proposal was the simple, primitive, shivering of his body whenever he dreamed of embracing her. Which was most of the time, more often even than his fantasy of a full dinner with pork or beef. He had been dreaming about her, about Rose, about pressing himself against her body, about all the sensations of entering and joining a womanly body, sensations that he had only recently discovered.

Étienne too felt some responsibility, and left as much as he thought he could afford, 2 francs, which covered more than a week under the old arrangement, and said goodbye to them all, Luc, Jean-Pierre, Noëlle, and, most wistfully, Angélique. He was grateful to her, for her lesson in love and other things, but he had a more attractive prospect, with a woman of his own. Another step toward becoming the man he aspired to be.

* * *

From almost anywhere inside the city walls, one could hear the cannons thundering and snapping almost constantly, much too close on almost all sides. Some of those cannons had to be French, from batteries atop the walls, but the bigger, louder ones had to be from the Prussians. They gave Rose and Étienne the impression that the war must still be going badly. Rose told him, half-believing, half-laughing, that her father contrasted the rude, coarse, deep roar of the Prussian steel guns to what he called – half-closing his eyes– the higher, sweeter pitch, almost singing, of the bronze beauties that Jules Durand and his workmates were casting in the Broquin & Lainé foundry.

Étienne tried but failed to distinguish the loud noises, sometimes close enough to cause buildings to vibrate.

* * *

Paris was too tightly surrounded to receive food or fuel or even news beyond the tersely coded messages on the thinnest paper, folded tight and banded to the tail-feather of a pigeon. Whatever army dispatch did reach the high command in

Paris, its news was almost never filtered to the press, which could only mean that it was bad. Or, as Étienne imagined, a call for help that Paris couldn't give.

Still, there remained one great promise, echoed and magnified in the pro-government press: The powerful Army of the Rhine, more than 170,000 infantry in seven army corps and nearly 2,000 cannons and thousands of cavalry, commanded by famous and proven generals and marshals and under overall command of France's most highly decorated Marshal, François Achille Bazaine, was poised in the northern fortress of Metz to deliver a blow that would force the enemy to withdraw his troops from the siege to defend the German homeland, and thus relieve Paris. The very name of the courageous and glorious Bazaine struck fear in Teutonic hearts, assured an article signed R.-P. Bougainville, in *Le Figaro*.

Between his tours on Guard duty, much of it building barricades against a possible Prussian breakthrough into the city, and his evenings and nights happily cuddling with Rose and getting to know her better, Étienne was spending more of his time at La Marmite, where he was also close to Rose and where he tried to keep track of what was happening in the city and in the war beyond its walls. He would glance through the newspapers there, but mostly he stayed talking with and listening to the other workers, many of them now in National Guard uniform. Tinsmiths, shoemakers, carpenters, iron workers, bookbinders, workers in almost all trades, lingered or wandered in and out, their shops almost all closed with the siege.

It was a few days after the protest at the Hôtel de Ville that he spotted Hilaire and Évariste at one of the tables. After laughter and embraces, they bought him a pot of wine to celebrate his union with Rose, and even called her out of the kitchen for a toast.

The three comrades, especially Étienne, lamented that the 8th October demonstration had failed, but – Évariste insisted – the fact of such a mass of National Guards and civilians, demanding the Commune, had shaken the military command, the police, and the appointed mayors. As evidence, he said, only two days after the protest, police prefect Kératry had resigned and was said to be preparing to leave Paris by balloon. This unelected and besieged 'Government of National Defense' was looking very fragile.

Varlin had now gotten into a dispute because of the big protest, they told him, knowing that Étienne had a special interest in his hero. In the confusion and the rain, Étienne hadn't even been aware that Varlin had been there, but now it was in the papers and Hilaire said he had seen him, at the head of his battalion. Eugène Varlin, as Étienne already knew, had been elected commander of another battalion in their own arrondissement, the Sixth. He had led his men to the rally and he and most of them had cried, "Vive la Commune!". But some, even in his own battalion, had shouted "Down with the Commune!".

They had got the idea that holding elections was somehow going to aid the Prussians instead of strengthening the defense against them, because that was what the government was saying.

The fact that there was so much confusion even among the Guard battalions, declared Évariste, who was now closer than ever to the thinking of the International, showed how important it was for the International and the workers movement generally to redouble their work of educating their people. The failure of the October protest, along with

Angélique and Noëlle's new school project, had definitively split up the group at Dragon Court. Évariste had moved into a furnished room on Rue Corderie near the Internationale, where he was helping out with correspondence and other matters. Hilaire had also left Dragon Court, for a place closer to his chemical factory. And they told him that his buddy Claude – surprise, surprise! –had moved in with Cécile, the girl from the bindery that Étienne and Rose had thought had such a crush on Toinou. Which reminded Étienne that he hadn't seen Toinou, once such a prominent presence in the bindery, since the Blanquiste attack on the firehouse, back in August.

* * *

Partly out of curiosity, but also because he had left some pamphlets there, Étienne went back one evening to the old place. He was also hoping to see Luc and J-P if they were still there.

It was Noëlle who answered the door. She didn't recognize him at first, until Angélique saw him and called his name. She was embarrassed and very apologetic, but then she had hardly seen him before he moved out, and he wasn't in National Guard uniform then. She was all right, he supposed, obviously energetic, but nowhere near as pretty as Angélique. And she was almost as tall as he, which he thought was too tall for a woman. And she talked so nervously and excitedly.

Luc and J-P had not moved out but they were not there just then, Angélique told him. The two men were even trying to help out with the new school: J-P had brought in some paper from his bindery for the children's exercises, and Luc had been arranging furniture and had even brought in some child-sized benches – God knew where he'd found them. But they were contributing much less to the common fund now that Angélique was no longer providing meals or cleaning services. How she and her new comrade Noëlle were going to eat and feed the children they hoped to teach was a mystery – but they seemed confident that political pressure would force the local mayor to follow the example of the mayor of the Eleventh, and devote funds to compulsory lay education. That was another reason to demand elections, Noëlle said, and should be a good argument for mobilizing women, especially, to demand them. Since the women, she thought, were far more concerned about their children's education than were the men.

These were new ideas to Étienne. He himself had not had much schooling, beyond basic reading and what he had been able to pick up in his apprenticeship. But teaching children, especially teaching them the republican values of liberty, equality, fraternity, sounded like something that he, as an Internationalist, should support. And he imagined that his hero Varlin would agree.

While they were talking they heard footsteps on the stairs, and J-P and Luc came in together, very surprised and very pleased to see Étienne. They had brought food which they offered to share with him as well as with Noëlle and Angélique – but they hadn't brought much, and he thanked them but refused, even though he was a little hungry.

Sitting on the little benches that Luc had found, J-P between mouthfuls began asking Étienne about his new life, outside the Dragon Court. He smiled wistfully when Étienne described how he had gotten together with Rose, and that made Étienne ask if he had a girlfriend.

Jean-Pierre smiled again and moved his head in a way

that said neither yes nor no. But then, he said, he had another question. How did Étienne feel about leaving his bindery?

"It was what I had to do," Étienne answered. "The call of duty. And, you know, there wasn't much work there any more."

"Do you miss it?"

"Yes. Yes, of course I do. I was really getting better, at a lot of skills."

"Would you like to continue, to develop that trade?"

"Yes, but now, well, with the war…"

"I have a job you may be able to help me with."

"Binding? Really?"

J-P nodded. Étienne's heart was racing.

Jean-Pierre had become dextrous enough in almost all the skills required that, like other bookbinders before him, he felt confident that he could set up his own independent shop now that his old bindery was closing. He had collected most of the necessary tools, and thought he knew where to acquire a good-sized page presser and a page-slicing frame – with so many binderies in the neighborhood idle, it shouldn't be difficult to 'relieve' one of some machinery.

Most important, he had an interested potential first client: a group, actually, with very advanced ideas, and with money. Enough to pay for good binding and even, possibly, for him to hire an assistant. One woman in particular, the president of this small group of thinkers, someone Étienne may have heard of, but whose name for the moment he wouldn't mention. This lady had sent for him, she said, because of his reputation as an Internationalist and an advanced thinker; she obviously had been asking around, in workers' and intellectuals' circles.

But the work she required, a large edition of well-made

but inexpensive copies of a tract, was too big for J-P alone to complete as quickly as her association wanted. He had been thinking that he would need an assistant, someone who also had advanced ideas and would not be afraid of this project. An Internationalist ideally. And he thought it would be better to have someone young, willing to learn rather special techniques, for a very modest wage. And thus he had thought of Étienne, but didn't know where to find him.

"And now, here you are."

"Yes. Here I am. When can we start?"

Assault on the palace

'In the clubs and rallies, bigger and bigger crowds are shouting now for the Commune and all-out war,' wrote Alphonse for the front-page column of miscellany, '**The talk of the ramparts**', in *Le Rappel*.

These unsigned notes earned him only a few sous, but they established him in his own mind as a real, working Parisian journalist, and he hoped would lead to bigger things and a by-line. His brief note continued:

'One of the arguments heard most frequently in crowds of National Guards is their desire to join in assaults with the army to break through the city's isolation and weaken the enemy. So far there have been only a few timid probes of the Prussian lines, all by regular army alone, without enough men or support for any lasting gain. And the battalions of the National Guard have not been called on, even though they all are eager for action.'

* * *

René-Pierre Bougainville also had pen in hand, having turned from his usual, well-remunerated beat as drama and spectacle critic (or booster) to more political matters, now that editors seemed impatient with anything else. R-P.

B. was certain that, with so much bad news, any good news about the war would give him prominent front-page space in one of the good, solid bourgeois papers such as *Le Siècle* or *Le Monde* or even *Le Figaro*. Especially after Félix Pyat's rabid *Le Combat* had published the scurrilous rumor, denied vigorously by the government, that Bazaine was negotiating for surrender; if that were true, it would mean a total disaster for the French defense. The loss of an entire army, the nation's greatest fighting force still in the field. Impossible.

Fortunately his contacts in the military command gave Bougainville a headstart on his competitors to report on any nearby military success. Rewriting and embellishing an early draft of a communiqué from the government, he reported the glorious news that the Army of Paris had broken through the Prussian lines, chasing their troops entirely from the village of Le Bourget, just a few kilometers north of the city wall.

The government communiqué was too terse, so he felt free to add details of his own invention about hand-to-hand fighting of a brave sword-wielding sergeant against a Prussian lancer, the ecstatic relief of a village peasant woman seeing the red pants and determined visages of her liberators, and – this was the highpoint – a skirmish before the altar in the village church. Bougainville had never visited Le Bourget, but he knew it must have a church, always a good setting for dramatic action, in this case the savage and impious cruelty of the Teutons versus the nobility and piety of the French.

'This grand victory', he asserted in his final paragraph, 'is the definitive proof of the superiority of French valor, as continues to be demonstrated by the valiant, glorious Bazaine.'

He was pleased with his draft, and disappointed that Victorine merely nodded and mumbled "Mmm mmm" when she read it, failing to appreciate its poetic values. Ah, but what could one expect from such a one as she?

However, because of some comment he had heard from Rochefort, who was of course himself a journalist but also a member of the government, he had hesitated to present his beautifully crafted report to his first choice paper, *Le Siècle.*

He should have hesitated longer, because when it did appear new events made it seem ridiculous.

First, the government belatedly acknowledged that Pyat's report about Bazaine's surrender was true.

And second, after hours of Prussian bombardment and no reinforcements from Paris, Le Bourget had been retaken by the enemy with heavy French losses. This he learned from the other newspapers, most glaringly in *Le Figaro.* There, sitting in the Glaser with his article spread out before him on the table along with other papers he had just purchased, he threw down his copy of *Le Figaro* and ordered another drink.

* * *

In Belleville, the news of the surrender of Bazaine's huge army was dismaying but remote. It was definitive proof of what Jules Durand and the people around him had been saying for weeks, that they could not depend on this 'government of national defense' to defend them – they were going to have to take matters into their own hands. The loss was a tremendous problem for that government, knocking out its last remaining prop, the claim that if everybody stayed in line, obeying the authorities, without elections or other drastic changes, all would be well.

But Belleville, or at least the people Jules was acquainted

with, had more immediate concerns than that mythical, distant Army of the Rhine, and Metz – where the devil was that, anyway? Very far away, north-west somewhere.

The battles of Le Bourget struck much closer to home. Jules and Blanche knew people from that village, and if they ever saw the list of casualties, they might even recognize some names. They had been both excited and fearful at the first news of the assault by French forces. The sudden loss had been disheartening and infuriating, especially since – in Jules' unshakeable opinion – the disaster could only be due to incompetence or even treachery by the government, in not preparing for nor giving enough support to those poor lads sent to slaughter.

As if all this had not been enough to set him off, this morning another news item, unexpected but not, given what he thought of the government, surprising, made him nearly explode. One of the men in his foundry told him, it had appeared in the paper under the headline 'PRUSSIA AND M. THIERS', which at first he didn't understand.

"Thiers?"

"The old guy! Adolphe Thiers. He was president when we were kids, when Louis-Philippe was king. A royalist then and royalist still."

"Oh, right. And he was named minister of something in this government, no? What does it say, that paper? You know I don't read a lot."

"Yes, Thiers was named foreign minister, and he has been traveling to the royal courts of Europe to beg for help. And what do you suppose he's doing now? Back in Paris? Here, I'll read it. It's in *Le Rappel*, this morning."

* * *

'M. Thiers returns, it is said, to Paris. How was he able to cross the Prussian lines? Is King Wilhelm being polite to our diplomacy? Here is what some are supposing. And some are even saying: Prussia wishes to negotiate.

A wish to negotiate? It's possible. Prussia is running out of men and money. Her entire male population has been launched into France. Deserted are her cities and deserted her countryside : no more industry, no more commerce.

She would like to negotiate. But in what way? On what 'bases'? as the diplomats say. What sort of deal can she propose to us? Just one. Always the same: the cession of Alsace, the cession of Lorraine. The destruction of our fleet. Several billions in indemnity: ruin – dishonor.'

* * *

"That means surrender."

Jules could hardly believe in such treachery. Or, yes, unfortunately, after the other events of these past few days, he could believe it, that those scoundrels in high places had been sacrificing workers' lives just, just for what? To keep themselves comfortable.

"Exactly. It means giving up, everything. To Bismarck and the Prussian king. Or 'kaiser' as he calls himself now."

"Then what was all that talk of 'all-out war' and 'fighting to the very end' about? Is that what this government is planning to do? 'Negotiate', when the armies are all lost, Alsace and Lorraine are already occupied, the only thing left to offer to the Prussians is Paris itself. And these cannons we've been casting? Turn everything over to the enemy? Never!"

"Flourens is assembling the men. That's what I came to tell you. We're going to take power. Not like last time, parading outside the Hôtel de Ville and shouting. This time we're taking our rifles, and we're going to take it over. Flourens has said that, and when Flourens says something, he does it. You have to get your company of National Guards together, we're heading down there right after noon."

"Down there?"

"To the Hôtel de Ville. But this time, to take power."

* * *

When Rose went down early in the morning to get some bread, she saw new posters on the walls around their apartment on Rue Mignon. There was already a crowd gathered despite the rain, and she had to push her way through to read one. 'Armistice', it said in bold letters. It was signed by Jules Favre, 'acting minister of foreign affairs', and promised peace, a resupply of food and prompt elections once the government had reached an armistice.

Armistice!

Surrender is what that meant to Rose. And to the others clustered there on the street. She almost forgot the bread but, after she'd turned back to get it and had clutched the hot, black, unpalatable loaf under her cloak, she rushed back and up the stairs.

"Titi! They're saying 'Armistice'. The government plans to surrender!"

* * *

Even before his cab reached his commissary, Mireau had seen the posters, printed and pasted up suddenly and without advising the police, at least at his level. When he read them he knew that there would be trouble. Any police chief would have told them. He knew the mood, especially in his quarter. He talked with people every day and had abundant reports of what was being said in the clubs and wine shops. The common feeling, especially after the crashing disappointment of Bazaine's unexpected and ignominious surrender, followed by the elation and then crashing disappointment of Le Bourget, was that there had to be 'war to the utmost' as the hot-heads put it. War to avenge the nation's honor, and especially to avenge the boys killed at that village in a senseless attack with no backup. And all the other boys and men killed in this cruel war.

Any mention of armistice, of negotiating instead of fighting against the enemy, was going to stir passions against the government even stronger than those of just weeks ago at the Hôtel de Ville. He had better get over there, now. With a few of his best men.

* * *

Very early in the morning, Noëlle heard shouts and commotion on the street and ran down to see what was happening. There was a cluster of people, gesticulating and jabbering, and it took her a few moments to comprehend, especially because the poster was hidden by all the bodies. She heard someone shouting to demand that someone else tell him what that meant, 'Armistice'. The thin bespectacled hat maker from the shop across the street answered, "It means negotiating for peace with the King of Prussia."

That caused even louder buzzing of the dozen or so people, crowded as close as possible to the wall because of the rain.

"And 'revictualing'? What's that?"

"They're going to let the food get in if we give them peace!" the hat maker answered.

"No!"

"But food would be good. Real bread again!"

"Bread at the price of liberty. 'Armistice' means peace on Prussia's terms," came the gruff voice of the hatter who, oddly enough, was the only other person bare-headed in the rain. Noëlle was now aware that she had run out without a shawl or anything to cover her head.

This was appalling news, she thought, that the government was seeking to make peace under such conditions. The hatter was right, the enemy's conditions they would have to be. She rushed back upstairs to tell Angélique, and rouse J-P and Luc, because this was something the men would have to handle.

* * *

In the crowd in the square in front of the imposing but oddly incoherent, very broad façade of the palace of the city, the Hôtel de Ville, Alphonse spotted that foolish older journalist Bougainville. He was one of those pushing to try to get past the mobile guards and into the building.

Alphonse pulled his cap down and stepped back and away from the open umbrellas to take a better look at the huge building. Some parts of it much older than others. He had an interest in architecture, and he wondered how someone more knowledgeable than he might describe it. A hodgepodge, surely. It must have been enlarged and reshaped many times over the centuries, each time by a different architect and different styles, with columns and statuary and that huge central tower as though each successive architect had sought to outshine, to out-embellish his predecessors. He had yet to get inside it, but he had heard that it had many inner courts, and illustrations from the Second Empire showed dazzling, intimidatingly vast ceremonial halls, including a ballroom with a huge horse-shoe staircase where the ladies in *Le Monde Illustré* were shown posing and coyly peering from behind their fans while their uniformed escorts applauded.

That was not what would be going on in there today, however.

Some of the crowd seemed to him to be merely curious, but others were shouting and some had brought signs: 'No armistice', 'Long live the Commune', 'Down with Thiers'. That last one seemed odd, since Thiers was not the chief of government. But he was the one identified as the chief culprit of the armistice.

Alphonse saw Vallès, braving the rain under a big black hat, and worked his way over to his side.

"What do you think is going to happen, Jules?"

Vallès snorted and smiled, a sly, laughing smile.

"Something big, when Blanqui gets here. He's commanding a battalion now, you know."

"Of National Guards?"

"Clemenceau appointed him."

"In the Eighteenth? Montmartre? That's where Clemenceau is mayor."

Vallès nodded.

Alphonse tried to imagine this. The ancient firebrand, no longer the *Enfermé*. the Locked-up One, but out on the streets at the head of 1,500 armed men primed to turn his words into action.

Around noon, the rain let up a little and the crowd, which had largely dispersed, regrouped, now joined by several companies of National Guards. In all – Alphonse guessed, because he couldn't find a high enough perspective for an overview – they were three or four thousand men and a number of women, not all of them under umbrellas. Trochu came out onto the staircase and tried to give a speech. It was hard, almost impossible to make out what he was saying. Arago, the man Trochu had appointed mayor of Paris, hauled out a chair and climbed up on it to continue the discourse, almost as inaudibly as Trochu. He climbed down and another man, one of his aides, took over, and this time Alphonse made out the words 'universal suffrage' – so at last they were promising elections. But it seemed to be too late for this crowd. They were shouting, "Vive la Commune! Vive la République!"

* * *

Bougainville discovered that he could bluff his way into the palace. When stopped by one mobile guard demanding a password, he found his way to another entry and, when necessary, pronounced in his voice of greatest importance the name of some functionary who supposedly had summoned him. 'Favre' usually worked, but 'Arago' would do if the guard hesitated. He avoided saying 'Trochu' because the name of the top man would have sounded suspicious and he might be held up while the guard sought orders from some superior. It helped enormously that he was so familiar with the intricate passageways and odd connections of the building, which was more like a combination of very different buildings joined by sudden and unexpected corridors utterly unknown to these Breton *moblots* who had never been inside the place before and who, by the way, barely even spoke French. Bagou had learned a few phrases in their language, enough to make out some of their mutterings to one another, but not enough for him to speak to them, because they were very touchy and might think they were being mocked.

He had gotten into the Throne Room itself by around 4 p.m., where all the important government figures – Trochu, Favre, Arago among them – were gathered and conferring and squirming and gesticulating around the elegant old conference table, wider than the dance floor in a typical concert café. And there he was when in burst Flourens, Gustave Flourens with his big beard and shining eyes and, more importantly, some hundreds of men with rifles and the uniform of the National Guard. Now this would be something to write up for the papers! Flourens, son of a famous scientist and himself a professor of science, leaping up on top of that grand table in his shiny boots and his colonel's uniform, waving his arms and a pistol toward all the dignitaries seated around it and declaring that they were all under arrest!

His riflemen, the famous *'tirailleurs de Belleville'*, had obviously forced their way past the nonplussed Breton *moblots* who were supposed to provide security to those distinguished leaders, and now those dignitaries in their riding coats and cravats and with their long rhetorical phrases were all under arrest. General Trochu the first among them.

This Flourens, what a character! Loud, energetic. His balding cranium offset by that big, bushy beard. Bougainville had heard about his exploits, that he had somehow been involved in an anti-Turk revolt in Crete, of all places, and involved in riotous protests that had got him jailed and then exiled during the Empire, and he was only thirty or something like it.

There was more noise and confusion, many voices, with

Flourens, up on top of the table, seeming to act as a theater director.

Bougainville watched, fascinated, as this young intellectual, supported and cheered by his gang of Belleville thugs who probably couldn't even read, declared that the old government of national defense was no more. Dissolved. By order of the people – the people being here represented exclusively by his Bellevillois roughnecks with their rifles, sabers and pistols. Hardly regulation equipment for the National Guards, Bougainville imagined – although he didn't really know if the National Guards these days had any regulations that anybody paid attention to.

It took some time for voices to calm enough for Flourens to pull out his list and read the names of the people he wanted to name to head the new government of Paris. Which would necessarily then be the government of France, or what was left of it outside of Prussian hands. But no, he didn't say 'government', what Flourens was proposing was what he called a Committee of Public Safety – the term used by the dictatorship to 'save' the revolution of '89. And there he stood, with his list in hand, as though he hadn't known the names by heart, especially since his own name was the first, and then Blanqui and the others, mostly journalists, even that wild man Félix Pyat. And Rochefort and Victor Hugo were on it as well.

Much shouting and confusion, other men jumping up on the table, and on other tables in the other halls, shouting out other names and demanding the government resign.

It was late in the afternoon, and Bougainville hadn't eaten anything since eight in the morning, and there was no place for him to sit, and the discussions didn't seem to be coming to any conclusion. The term 'Committee of Public Safety' aroused a lot of protest, voices shouting that they didn't want to replace one dictatorship with another. And someone had prepared yet another, very different list of names for the new government. Then Flourens commanded that the crowd gathered in the Throne Room divide into various commissions, in the other halls, the mayors over in one of the many rooms of the palace, some other commission in some other hall, and so on to work out the intimate details of the new proposed government.

Someone – not Flourens, Bougainville thought, but somebody apparently speaking for him – gave the order that nobody should be allowed to enter or to leave. It was Blanqui! The Old One himself. Bougainville had seen him only once before, but he recognized him from the caricatures. The real Blanqui was himself a caricature, Bougainville thought, imagining that as a colorful phrase to use, unless of course this revolutionary government actually succeeded in taking power. In which case he would have to treat this little man politely, this famous insurrectionist with that ferocious stare under his long white hair, his jaw thrust forward through the equally white beard, and a voice that you had to bend very close to hear.

Whatever Blanqui's order had meant to him, what it must have meant to the various national guards supposedly keeping, or actually disturbing, order, was not to let anyone leave or enter the building, because men had been entering or leaving the Throne Room, the Council Chamber, the Governance Hall, and the various other offices constantly, looking for the commission they were assigned to or carrying some message to one of the other groups or just to find out what was going on in the other rooms. Total confusion. Amusing, it would be, if the fate of France were not at stake.

Bougainville noticed some movement over in the corner where Trochu, Favre and the others had been held at gunpoint, and then – Trochu wasn't there any more. Bougainville looked again, but it seemed that the crowd around Flourens had not even noticed. He pulled out his watch. It was already a quarter past eight. Time for him to escape also, and find something to eat.

* * *

It was cold and still raining outside the gates of the building where Étienne and his company were, they supposed, guarding the new-formed government of the Commune of Paris, sometime after nine at night, when some men from another National Guard company came over to ask what they were supposed to be doing.

"We're here to make sure they arrest the members of the government," said the sergeant of Étienne's company.

"But no! That's not right. It's those people of the commune that we're supposed to arrest."

"What? Who gave you those orders?"

"Who ordered you?"

Tension and amazement on both sides, the two groups in similar uniforms clutching their rifles and staring at each other, until one of them from the second company laughed.

"The truth is we don't know what is going on! And it's cold and wet, and we haven't had any dinner. Have you guys eaten?"

"No. You just got here, but we've been here for hours, waiting for them to resolve something."

"Brrr," said one of the men from the other company. "Let's see if we can find some wine."

At last, a proposition they could all agree to.

But at that hour, at that place, there was no wine to be had. And even though neither group was sure what it was supposed to do, or which was the government they were supposed to obey, they all had orders to be there.

They joked about the disputes inside over lists of candidates, various versions of which had been copied and thrown out the windows for the crowd below to see.

One thing they had heard from a guard who had been inside was that when Flourens was asking for names of candidates, one National Guard in the room had shouted "Gambon!"

And another had answered, "And his cow!"

And a third, "Let's nominate both!" To great hilarity.

But Flourens, at least according to the story, had taken out his pencil and in all seriousness added the name to his list, the name of a farmer and *député* from Saint-Étienne famous for protesting the seizure of his cows when he refused to pay taxes for weapons because of the army massacre in La Ricamarie.

'Gambon's cow' had become a rallying cry for readers of Rochefort's *La Marseillaise*, and a running joke in the Guard.

And after the jokes, the two opposing groups of National Guards were all agreed about the stupidity of building barricades inside the city instead of attacking the Prussians outside it.

But it was getting too late, and it looked like at least the main question had been settled. The new government was in place, and elections would be held in a few days. This had been promised and apparently sealed, as the men stationed for hours before the grill had learned from other guards who had popped out of the building to brief them, and from the papers that fluttered from the windows. In twos and threes, or singly, or in larger groups, they saw guards leaving the building, giving them a friendly but weary wave or embrace, before they headed off. Étienne looked at J-P beside him, and the two of them looked for Claude, but he was no longer around. J-P said he was going to stick around a little longer, who knew for what. Étienne said goodbye and began his walk toward home. And dry clothes. And dinner of some sort.

* * *

It was already after two in the morning when Hippolyte Mireau, at the head of a group of mobile guards along with his 'guardians of the peace', entered the Caserne Napoléon on the Rue de Rivoli, just east of the Hôtel de Ville.

General Trochu had wasted no time since his escape from the palace, and had rallied mobile guards and several National Guard battalions – more than sixty of them – from the bourgeois western arrondissements. He had probably slipped out in the same manner that Mireau and his men were planning to slip in. The Caserne, or barracks, was connected by underground passages to the Hôtel de Ville that it had been built to protect.

The battalions Trochu summoned to rescue his government were now formed across the plaza before the main façade of the Hôtel de Ville, facing other National Guard battalions that had been brought to topple that government. But at this late hour, there were far fewer of these than there had been. Trochu's battalions also occupied the relevant portions of the Rue de Rivoli, with the entrance to the Caserne.

Mireau could only guess what Trochu had told the commanders of those battalions now supporting him. Their men were probably as ready as the others to acclaim a new government with popular elections, which was what they would have understood as a commune. But not a 'Committee of Public Safety', which sounded like a dictatorship of half a dozen or more self-appointed men, especially if the men at the top included such as Blanqui and Flourens.

Quickly and quietly, the policemen of Hippolyte Mireau, accompanying an entire batallion of Breton mobiles, emerged through the basement kitchens of the Hôtel de Ville and with rifles ready and charged, climbed up the stairs and disarmed the first surprised '*tirailleurs de Belleville*' they encountered. The surprise could not be long sustained. Once aroused by the noise, the drowsy *tirailleurs* and other National Guards sprang to alert and men in and out of uniform, mobile guards, national guards and police, were aiming rifles at each other.

But it was over, Mireau knew that. And, it seemed, even Blanqui realized it. All that he and Flourens were able to secure, after all those hours and commotion, was a promise from Favre that there would be no reprisals. That all would be forgiven, and forgotten, and – one more thing, an important concession – there would be elections to the mayoralties, soon.

* * *

It wasn't until Étienne woke up just before noon the next day that he learned what had happened, in very sketchy fashion, from Rose who had been talking with the neighbors. It left him in a strange state of daze and rage – made more acute by hunger, though hunger was not what hurt.

The news grew more shocking and more unacceptable as Étienne heard more details when he got over to the Marmite, from the stories from other National Guards who had actually been inside the building with their companies and then by scanning the lengthy reports in *Le Rappel*, *Le Figaro*, and the most curious, and most contrary to the others, in Blanqui's paper *La patrie en danger*. Which he read, at least partially, and discussed with the other men in the reading room there, while waiting, in his daze and rage, for Rose to finish her duties in the kitchen.

Rose had been equally upset, but not dazed. She had her work to do. Étienne didn't know just what she was doing in the kitchen in the back of the Marmite, but he thought he detected an almost forgotten but appetizing odor.

But that could not distract him from the overwhelming problem. He could not understand, and he could not accept, not just morally but in his consciousness as a real event, as something that had really happened, that, first, he and his fellows in the Guard battalions, along with the mass of citizens shouting and waving signs outside the Hôtel de Ville, had been part of a force spearheaded by such brave and dramatic leaders as Flourens, Blanqui, Ranvier that had really and truly seized power!

And second, that in the course of a few long hours, they had lost it. Totally. That he and they, all them who had been such an unstoppable force, had let it all slip from their grasp.

That the Government had been overthrown, totally, its leaders held at gun point, was confirmed not just by some of the men he knew, but even by the bourgeois newspapers. And that a new revolutionary government had been proclaimed, with immediate elections and a council to govern the city as a Commune. *Le Figaro* presented such a vivid image of

Flourens, his sudden appearance, the elegance of his colonel's uniform and high-glossed boots and his gestures, that he sounded like the hero of a dramatic opera.

All the witnesses and newspapers concurred that this was real, that this had happened. And that the names of that provisional government, pending results of the elections, included the notoriously pro-Commune advocates, Flourens, Ranvier and Blanqui. Which was what he too had known, from the shouts of joy from inside the palace and the notes thrown down from the windows with lists of candidates for the new government.

And that was where things stood when, after hours and hours guarding their post, following the order to keep anyone from entering without other orders from the new leaders, assuming that with no further sign from them that those inside were just working out the details. Until finally, tired, soaked and hungry, but elated, he and others felt that they had done their duty and drifted home. They had won, his battalion and all the others had achieved their objective in marching to demand change.

And now, everything had been turned upside down again. It had been a real revolution, in the geometric sense, the whole 360 degrees, and Trochu and his accomplices were back on top where they had been, in charge, and there would be no Commune. The papers also confirmed that General Tamisier, speaking for the government, had promised Flourens that there would be no reprisals, so that the mobiles and soldiers backing him, and the *tirailleurs* of Belleville and other Guards who had been demanding the Commune, didn't start shooting each other inside the palace. But people were saying that Trochu had announced orders to arrest Flourens, Blanqui and the others. There would be elections, but just for the mayors, not to replace the Government of National Defense.

The aroma from the kitchen came stronger. It smelled like, or almost like, roasting beef. What's that? he asked. And the other men around him explained, grinning and with their mouths watering. During the confusion on Sunday, when the army didn't know which authorities were in command, some of the National Guards had located the stable with some army horses, no longer in service, lightly guarded by a few army hostlers for the dining pleasure of their superiors. And those fellows, those National Guards and workers, had unfettered one, a fattish one, and spirited it off while those soldier stableboys were otherwise occupied. Or paid off. Or, quite possibly, in sympathy with the revolt. Thus this Tuesday, and perhaps tomorrow too, the Marmite would offer a more substantial, meaty dinner.

That was good news, but not good enough to compensate for the terrible disappointment, the failed revolt.

"It's because they were all Blanquistes," was Évariste's opinion.

How was that? Étienne wanted to know.

"Their whole tactic, the only thing Blanqui has always taught them, is to take power! Not how to keep it."

J-P had joined them.

"Blanqui," he repeated.

"That reminds me, Titi: I saw an old friend of yours there. Said he knew you, from the same workshop."

Étienne looked at him, his face expecting an explanation.

"Toinou, he goes by. Antoine something, he was a bookbinder before the war, and when he found out I was one too, he asked if I knew a tall kid from Lyon named Bonin."

"Toinou. I haven't seen him since… Was he with Blanqui?"

"He said he was waiting for an order from Blanqui that would permit him to get into the Hôtel de Ville."

"Then he was part of Blanqui's battalion?"

"There was no battalion, no battalion under orders of Blanqui. Blanqui came on his own, with just a couple of followers, when he heard that his name was on the list for the new government. That's what Toinou told me."

"All bluff and no battalion, then." Évariste was laughing.

"Don't underestimate him. Blanqui doesn't need a battalion. He has legions who hang on his words, and some of them do command battalions. Flourens and Ranvier both, for example."

"How could they have held on to power? What should they, what should we have done different?" Étienne asked him.

"It was too early, there hadn't been enough preparation," J-P answered. "We were only some of the battalions, already convinced that we had to have the commune. We didn't have any agreement with all the Guard battalions, no plan. And then, even those battalions that were with us, when they heard those names, Flourens and Blanqui, especially, they, or their commandants, decided they couldn't support the take-over. And then Trochu slipped out, somehow, however he did it, and was able to rouse almost half the battalions in Paris to oppose the other half. Plus he had the army, and the mobiles, on his side."

"And the people?"

"Divided, as always. And fearful."

"Then what do we do now?" Étienne asked, genuinely perplexed.

He hadn't noticed Nathalie, behind him, until he heard her voice.

"We keep fighting the Prussians," she said firmly. "And at the same time, work to win over all the working people, in all the Guard battalions and in the army and in the workplaces too. So that next time, when we take power, we know how to keep it and to use it, all of us. The way we do in our trade associations. Everybody, men and women too, gets to speak and everybody understands the stake we have. That's the only way."

The three men were silent after that, until Évariste nodded and said, "Amen."

December

Ah. December already. Only the sixth of this last month of this fatal year, but already so, so cold. Button up, my good man, and tighten that scarf. You make me shiver just to look at you. No, just kidding; I was shivering already. And you, madame, what are you doing out in this cold? Scavenging for food, no doubt. Or firewood. I hope you find it quickly so you can get back inside, your coat looks much too thin for this cruel weather. But first, before you rush off, hear me, and perhaps we can warm your ésprit.

Yes, come, come closer, all of you, dear friends. Citoyens. My comrade Hercule has found a bit of fuel for the fire here in this can. Come, gather as close as you can, face to the fire and backs to the wind. It's going to be a, shall we say, unusual holiday season here in the city of light, the capital of pleasure and luxury that we remember. In Christmases past, after the midnight mass, you would sit around the stove, with perhaps some modest meal, the children's shoes set out for little gifts of sweets.

And then in the taverns filled with delicacies and drink, Hercule and I would juggle, sing and perform our amazing tricks to great merriment. This year Christmas, only weeks away, is set to be more modest, all the more reason for us to endeavor to lift spirits in these trying times. Have you been reading the newspapers? No? Yes, I know, who has 2 sous these days to spare for a paper. Two sous, that's two bowls of soup, which will do you much more good than the bad news in this cold weather, right. Just in these last weeks, the capitulation of Verdun, the losses at Thionville, and then, just days ago, the last day of November, Champigny. Disaster, and then on Sunday, oh, what we thought could never happen, the fall and capture of Orléans after its long and courageous fight. But here in Paris we shall hold out. Right, citoyens? Yes.

But to cheer you up, for those of you who failed to get seats for last week's free concert at the Opera, Hercule and I shall offer you, also for free, a sample of that performance. Can you believe it? There, in the Opera, by popular demand, the crowds cheering and repeating his name, M. Massy himself rose from the audience at the intermission to sing the 'Marseillaise'. And we can be sure that many in the crowd, if they remembered the long-forbidden words, must have joined in, if only in hushed tones. Imagine, the 'Marseillaise', banned for the twenty years of Empire, sung by a great tenor in no less a hallowed spot than the Opera.

And now, my friends, we too shall dare, because we do know all the verses, to warm your hearts if not your frozen toes and fingers. That concert was to raise money for the cannons that have kept us free from the Prussian onslaught, and may our little concert also merit a donation from you good patriots crowded around.

Hercule, the drum, please.

"Allons, enfants de la Patrie..."

* * *

Alas, the municipal elections on 5th November had not resolved the important problem for Angélique and

Noëlle in Dragon Court. The man who won in the Sixth Arrondissement was the same mayor who had been appointed by the Government of Trochu, Hérison, and he was no more willing now than before to support free, lay public education against the opposition of the clergy. Unlike the mayor of the Eleventh. But at least here, and throughout the city, the protests had accomplished something: rents had been suspended 'for the duration of the siege', so that was one less thing for the two teachers to worry about.

Their new little school now had twenty pupils, but only half of them had parents willing or able to pay the 3 francs per month they had calculated as necessary to feed themselves and provide the pupils with sustenance. To Angélique's surprise, Jean-Pierre insisted on making a small weekly payment despite the municipal rent suspension, and had shamed Luc into doing the same, saying that they had a moral commitment as Internationalists to the education of the future workers of the world. It was very little, barely enough for fuel to stave off the bitter cold, but the two young teachers were so enthusiastically involved in their care for the children that they, especially Angélique, disregarded their own hunger. J-P felt he had to watch them, because whenever he was able to bring in a little food, they were likely to slip it to the children.

* * *

Alphonse wanted to get a letter to his mother back in Lille, he was thinking more and more of home as the Christmas days approached. The carrier pigeons were available only for military use, but it was still possible – though not cheap – to send a letter out of Paris by balloon.

Would it reach his mother? He wondered what happened to the mail of balloons that fell into Prussian hands. Perhaps, with their famous efficiency, the Prussian army clerks would simply forward any mail they found to their addressees. Or perhaps not. It would all depend on orders from their superiors.

But still he had to write.

> Dearest Mother,
>
> I hope that you are well and that you, and all our family, are eating well and keeping warm in this harsh winter. I have not stopped thinking of you, constantly, and were I a believer, I suppose I would be praying for you. But such is not our family's tradition.
>
> I have been desperately awaiting news from you and from our city. Most of what we learn here of the north is of the triumphs of our Prussian neighbors. Is Lille still part of France and of our new republic?
>
> I hope that you receive this missive, and that it gives you cheer to know that your son is alive and beginning to fulfill the great ambition that I have had since learning my first letters. I have begun writing for some important republican newspapers, and thanks to the influence of you and of Papa, may he rest in peace, I am mentally prepared for the revolutionary events developing strongly here. I have even met Charles Hugo, the son of our famous poet, and have written also for Jules Vallès, well known here and, I think, even in Lille. I am enclosing a copy of one of my few signed pieces. It is very short, I know, but I feel that it is a good start for my career in letters.

We must have patience. This terrible situation cannot and will not last forever. We still have hopes of Gambetta, that the armies he has raised in the south may win, despite their recent defeats. Paris is still strong, resisting despite the cold and hunger, and the German newspapers we have seen, because it is much easier for news to get into the city than out, show us that they too are suffering from this war, because of the casualties, the tremendous costs in armament and supplies, and the absence of their young men from their farms and factories. Peace will come, and then I hope that I can again embrace you.

Your loving son,

Tiphonse

He blotted the manuscript and, feeling the stiffness in his legs and fingers, bent over the stove to nudge the last bit of too-green wood and revive the sputtering flame.

He had not really decided whether to try to send his letter or not. The next balloon scheduled to depart from the Gare du Nord would not leave until 11th December, at night to make it more difficult for the Prussians to shoot down. Thus he had a couple of days to decide whether to send it. Or to keep it for some future memoir of the siege he hoped to write. If, unlikely as that seemed, his letter actually reached his mother, she would hardly find it encouraging. Except to know that he was alive, or had been at the time of writing.

Now to try to sleep, bundled in his vest and coat under a blanket and with his once-prized burgundy cravat wrapped to warm his head.

* * *

Mireau was glad to have fuel for the stove in his office. Dry, mature wood had become too scarce and expensive for ordinary civilians, but army and government installations, police offices and commissaries such as his had priority in such supplies as remained, and in whatever new wood could still be obtained from the half-denuded parks. But, regardless of the stove, he was too restless to remain in the commissary. He had always needed to get a sense, personally, of the mood of the people on the streets of his precinct, by walking, talking and observing. And he refused to let the weather impede his long habit.

He saluted his uniformed men as he passed them, and tried to give a word of cheer. Their patrols were limited now, not only because it was too cold to stay outside for long but also because there were certains streets and alleys they preferred to avoid, unless in a sizable group. Their new uniforms, ordered by that incompetent Kératry before he took off in a balloon, were supposed to resemble those of the army and the National Guards –a kepi instead of the bicorne and a tunic instead of the long, flaring frock coat – but the resemblance was not close enough to fool people in the neighborhood. The *rousse* were still the *rousse*, and defiance of authority, meaning especially the police, had become much more frequent and bolder, even violent, in these tumultuous days since the end of the Empire.

Mireau was, as always, in civilian clothes, and wrapped in his cloak and with his hat pulled down because of the cold, he expected to pass by anonymously. Or, if recognized, to experience less overt hostility than his uniformed officers. Partly because of his greater authority and partly because – in his own view – he had always endeavored to be fair. But as he approached a small gang of urchins trying to make a fire of a pile of rags, one of them looked up and sang out *"Vingt-deux!"* – 'Twenty-two', their code for police. They tensed, prepared to run, but he just looked at them sternly and turned away. And then he heard them laughing, quietly, carefully behind him.

Few people were out, and those that were, scavenging for food or fuel he imagined, were in too much of a hurry to chat. There was not much for the police to do these days. Ordinary petty crime, or at least such of it as came to his attention, had practically disappeared. Police sometimes had to intervene to stop brawls in the lines of people with their ration coupons outside the butcher's or the grocery shop, though even there, his 'peace guardians' had to let the uniformed National Guards step in. Their authority was more respected and often they knew the people in line much better than did his men.

How would this end, this siege and hunger and cold? Paris had never been like this, it had never, as far as he remembered, even been this cold. The gods of weather must be allies of the Prussians. And never had the government, and thereby, the authority of the police, felt so precarious. He almost regretted having fired that useless journalist pretending to be an informer. He could have invited him into his warm office and at least have had someone to talk to. But he knew that was a silly idea. He suspected, more than suspected, that that young man had in fact been a sympathizer of the rebels he was supposed to be spying on. But the discourse had been amusing.

By five o'clock it was dark and he turned back to his commissary, where he still had a small supply of relatively good, ground coffee and all the appropriate apparatus to brew it, for boiling the water, infusing the brew, pressing, etc. He had become quite expert at this, and the process could keep him occupied for at least an hour, which would take another lonely hour out of the waiting for the siege to end.

* * *

Étienne had not had guard duty today. The companies rotated their turns patrolling, so today his group had been free, and now in the evening he had come to hang out at the Marmite, where he could crowd onto a bench near the fire while waiting for dinner time. The people in the kitchen, Rose included, had learned to prepare a salami tasty enough that you would never suspect what sort of animal it was made of. Last night they had soup and pigeon, which hadn't been half bad. Though the bread, as usual these days, contained more wood shavings than flour.

He had spent a good part of the day with Jean-Pierre, who, after a long delay and several evasive answers, had finally told him what his project was all about. It had been a surprise, and he didn't know how to take it. He was anxious to get a chance to talk about it with Rose, who always had sensible ideas and who was learning things from the more experienced people she was working with, especially Nathalie, and should be able to help him clear his head. Because it was something he didn't feel comfortable talking about with all the rough guys crowded around him near the fire. No, it was not a guy thing.

So instead he tried to chat with them about politics, which mayors they thought could be trusted and which ones had said the most foolish things, according to what they read in the press. Some of the men were playing jacquet, which required them to sit around a table for their board and dice and the stacks of checker pieces they called 'ladies', a little apart from the fire. Étienne preferred to stay closer to the fire and besides, he had never really learned the game, the rules seemed complicated.

After the meal, which was nearly adequate but not memorable, he lingered, fingering the newspapers, making conversation with the few others who were still around, until at last Rose was free and he could accompany her to their apartment. But first, he drew her into a corner, at the end of one of the dining tables. The remaining people saw them with their heads together and respected their privacy.

Rose was tired, her hair was a mess and she had spots on her sleeves where the apron had not protected her. She seemed to be glad to sit down before bundling up for the walk of several blocks to their apartment. He watched her stretch her shoulders back and pull the scarf off her head before she turned to look directly at him. He felt confused; he needed some confirmation about what he was doing with J-P. Rose was seldom confused. She was doing just what she had chosen to do, and he was sure that she had no doubt about why it mattered. And besides, as she had said to him often, she was learning all the time.

But Étienne, well, he knew something was bothering him tonight. He fidgeted.

"Well?" she asked him.

"You know J-P, Jean-Pierre," he said at last. "I know you haven't seen him much, but I think you would like him. He's a really good book binder."

"Yes?"

"Lambert is his name. Jean-Pierre Lambert."

"Yes? What about him? You were going to do some project together, weren't you?"

"Right. That's what I wanted to talk to you about. It's a strange project. But a good chance for me to learn some more skills."

"Strange?"

Now came the hard part for him to say.

"It's for an unusual client. A woman, a lady. A rich lady, she must be. And there's a man working with her on it. It's to bind attractively but economically a large number of tracts, about 120 each, for a society. An association."

"Well, that's an unusual opportunity, now that almost all binding work has stopped. That sounds very good. But something is bothering you. Is this lady a royalist? Or a Bonapartist?"

"No, no. Nothing like that. I think she must have very advanced views. That's why she sought out Jean-Pierre, she knew he was in the International. But, well, I have had a chance to read some of the pages and it's, well, not what I'd expected."

"I'm tired, Titi, and it's late. Tell me whatever you want to tell me, and let's get home and to bed."

"Yes, yes. Of course. The society is called the Association for the Rights of Women."

Rose sat up and looked at him with new interest. He went on, "The tract is about women being equal to men. Having the same rights, earning the same pay for similar jobs, even controlling their own finances and everything."

"And that seems strange to you?"

He squirmed.

"Do you think women don't have the same rights?" she insisted.

"No, no, I don't mean that. Of course you do, but – about equal rights and equal pay, I don't know what I think. I've never thought much about it before. But yes, I suppose so. Those girls back in Lyon, they struck for more money and shorter hours, and we, almost every working man I knew, thought they deserved it, but they were doing work that was only for girls and women. You couldn't compare their wages with what I was getting in the bindery, or a steel worker, or anything."

"Étienne, tell me. Are you in favor of equal rights for men and women or not? Or are you one of those Proudhonists who thinks you have to protect us girls by keeping us out of the workforce? Or is it that you think I'll think that you're less of a man if you do this?"

He shook his head slowly before looking up at her.

A Proudhonist? No! But, well…

"Would you?"

She laughed.

"Of course not, silly."

"It, it just seems, well, I don't know. J-P has no worry about it. You know, he talks a lot about the rights of you girls and women. But, that lady, the one with the money and the radical ideas, and us, J-P and me, working for her."

"We'll talk about it tomorrow, Titi. Let's go home."

He nodded and tucked her shawl around her shoulders as he stood.

* * *

Christmas. Time to celebrate, despite all the problems of this cold, cold winter of 1870.

The noted writer had availed himself of his contacts in high circles to secure a reservation, in the names of Man-of-Letters (not 'journalist', a poorly respected trade) M. René-Pierre de Bougainville (the '*de*' was his own recent invention) and the Noted Actress Mlle. Victorine Martin, for the gala dinner on the 25th December at the exclusive Café

Voisin. The fête would be expensive but he considered it an investment, a way to ingratiate himself further with the men, and their influential ladies, who were certain to continue to control money, appointments and publishing opportunities, everything that mattered, once this war and siege were past.

The expense was not merely the price of the dinner, which was many times what he had paid for any previous fête. There was also the matter of wardrobe, his and Victorine's. New everything, from boots to vest and coat to neckwear, cane and hat for him. And of course for her, a gown more voluminous and elegant than any she had ever worn, not counting the showy but fragile costumes for the stage. And a bit of jewelry, which fortunately he already owned, inherited from his mother.

He had learned, it was in fact an open secret, what were some of the things on the menu: consommé of elephant, ragout of kangaroo and other exotic animals sacrificed at the zoo, along with the more usual, in these last months, wolf and cats and rats, prepared as delicacies by one of Paris's most renowned chefs. All rather amusing, but he supposed that kangaroo or antelope properly prepared would end up tasting rather like more ordinary venison, say, or veal or pork or other nearly forgotten meats.

Victorine had smiled and nodded as he read to her this list of exotic meats. After rats and cats and street pigeons, none of this seemed strange. But she screamed with excitement when she heard "Peas in butter." Butter! She would die, she said for a taste of butter.

But the most prized item was the last, the promised dessert, Gruyère cheese. Ah! and she fainted. Or nearly. Or was faking, as the actress she was.

Bougainville had laughed, but her outburst made him

genuinely worried. What might pop out of the mouth of this young wench, what crude slang or grating accent from her slum origins around Rue Saint-Denis, to betray her elegant disguise and Bagou's own pretensions? But he had already paid, and he could not very well show up without his winsome mistress on his arm.

Bombs – Battles – Bindings

A shadow and then – an explosion and I'm hurled against a wall! On the Rue d'Assas where Hercule and I had just set up to perform. Oh, what a graceless posture I find myself in, sprawled out on the street. And then, uh-oh – I have to clap my hands over my ears, that woman's scream is so shrill! And men's shouts, curses, warnings or maybe just incoherent yelps. Ah, but there at last I hear a familiar sound, Hercule's loud grunt, thank the gods, he sounds unhurt.

Oh, thank you, Hercou! You lifted me too suddenly for comfort, made me gasp, but – whew, good! – I can stand. My left legging is torn and bloodied and my drum is smashed, but that's nothing – a great hole has suddeny appeared in the street just before us, and there's a little crowd, four of five people clustered around the woman, must be the one who screamed, and a man next to her tumbled onto the pavement. I should rush over to see if I can help but – anothering flickering shadow! This time I saw it just in time to jump back against the wall before the second explosion, this one not quite so close.

"It's an earthquake!" someone shouts.

"They're shelling, you fool!"

That's another voice. Oh, it's mine! I shouted that. I must be terribly rattled, I didn't even realize that I was speaking.

"It's the bloody, murderous Prussians."

"Monsters! This is the city, not the battlefront! We have women and children here."

There's a national guard in uniform, his kepi askew, he has just run into the intersection. He's waving his rifle at the sky, as though to shoot down – what? The incoming mortar shells? Now he's looking around in all directions, he seems unsure where to go or what to do. Others are running. Ces putains de Prusscos! *Hercule has lifted the wounded woman and now he's looking at me, wondering what to do.*

"That way!" Oh, that was my voice! There's an open doorway. Nothing we can do for that lady, and anyway there are two national guards looking after her.

It's time to run, Hercou, à foutre le camp.

* * *

The explosions had brought a sudden halt to the guard company's drill as all the men clutched their rifles tight to their chests and looked around to see where the danger was coming from. It was Thursday, 5th January, the eve of the Epiphany, and Étienne had been day-dreaming about the *gateau des rois* his mother would be preparing for the holiday, with beans or a Christ figure hidden in the cake, back home in Lyon.

That first noise could have been anything, an omnibus turned over by a collision, some nearby scaffolding collapsing, but the second one popped those illusions and made them know it was an attack! Prussian artillery of the sort he had heard at a distance, when his battalion had been sent as reinforcements to that fort to the west, but neither he nor anyone in Paris had expected to hear it just blocks away, from the direction of the Jardin du Luxembourg.

"Cannon?" asked the man next to him.

Étienne nodded vigorously.

"Mortar shells. For destroying buildings. Very near."

The next day, Friday, 6th January, Epiphany, a poster printed on red paper appeared on the walls of the city, calling for a universal levy of the National Guard to assault the Prussians and break the blockade. In the name of 'The great people of '89, who destroyed the Bastille and overturned thrones', it demanded

> General requisition
> Free rations
> Attack *en masse*
> Power to the people!
> Power to the Commune!

> Signed by 'The delegates of the Twenty
> Arrondissements' – the shadow Commune.

* * *

Later that day, the Government of National Defense pasted its own white posters over the red ones of the 'Twenty Arrondissements'. Étienne did not bother to read the government's whole text, which seemed simply to repeat what it had been saying over and over for the past month: That those arguing for a change in government were working on behalf of the Prussian enemy and that the Government of National Defense was committed to fighting to the final consequences and would never surrender!

And will never let us fight, thought Étienne.

* * *

"Oh, Bagou — . Excuse me, I should say M. Bougainville, Man-of-Letters. How was your gala Christmas dinner at the Voisin?"

"A disaster. But that's not why I came to see you. Did you see the red posters yesterday?"

"Yes."

"And that long list of signatures?"

"One hundred and forty."

"You counted them? Well, of course, you're the police. And all of those names, men completely unknown."

"Not all. Jules Vallès was there. And Malon, from the International. The others, we know them. Or our colleagues in Sûreté do, and they will find the others. They will be arrested."

"Vallès? Yes, he's known, certainly. He's probably the one who wrote the damned thing. But Varlin? No? Anyway, something has to be done. Even if you do arrest all of them, they're expressing something I've heard in snatches of conversation all over the city. People are demanding action to end this siege. The government is going to have to do something. If we don't get crushed by the Prussians, we'll get crushed by our own rebels here within the city."

"Yes, it's a worry. But tell me, my good man: What did you mean, the party was 'a disaster'? I thought surely you must be having a grand feast. Elephant, kangaroo. Even butter. From kangaroo milk, I suppose."

"Stop laughing. It's not funny. And I don't want to talk about it."

"Hmm. Kangaroo, must be tough."

"Look, Polo. *Commissaire* Mireau, should I say? Or

Inspecteur? If you're heading to Sûreté, that is. I saw a café that's still open, in the Place de la Bastille. We can walk there. Hard to get a cab now, with all the disruption from the bombing. I'll buy you a drink and we can find something else to talk about. This bombing is making me nervous. We can talk about other things. Your new police prefect, for example, and what you think Trochu might do. The price of firewood, which is really becoming impossible. And if anybody still has rabbits to sell, better than pigeons. Things that matter. Things we can maybe do something about, because this siege and this bombardment, it's beyond us."

"Calm down, my friend. And you'll tell me about your big night at the Café Voisin?"

"Only if you tell me what's happening with your application for Sûreté."

Mireau smiled and shook his head.

"No. Rabbits and firewood, then, and other things. I'll get my cloak."

* * *

The bombardment continued, sometimes heavier, sometimes more spaced, for days, especially in the quarters of the Left Bank, but also other areas on the northern and western edges of the city: Porte Maillot, Porte d'Orléans and Porte de Saint-Cloud. The targeting of residential and other civil buildings, and even a hospital, and the killing and wounding of civilians were taken as new outrages – though it was hardly the first time such things had happened. Napoleon (the first Napoleon, the great one) had bombarded Vienna, the British navy had bombarded Copenhagen, and more recently, Lanza had bombarded his own city of Calatafimi in Sicily when it was taken by Garibaldi, and the French themselves had bombarded Veracruz as recently as 1863. But for the ordinary civilians of Paris, and especially the troops of the National Guard, inured though they were to the many months of war, bombarding Paris was considered cowardly, unchivalrous, despicable. Omnibuses were re-routed, people scurried on the streets to reach shelter, and nerves as well as bombs were exploding, especially in those areas most vulnerable. In Étienne's company and throughout the Guard, the demand to go out in force to still those Prussian batteries and seize the high ground was becoming irresistible. If they weren't ordered to attack the foreign enemy soon, most of the battalions were ready to turn to depose their timid government, again, as they had two months ago, but this time for good.

Finally came the order, from General Trochu to the army generals and, now for the first time, the commandants of the guard battalions, to form for an assault beyond the walls. They were to form early in the morning of Thursday 19th January. The precise objective was a military secret – the Prussians were assumed to have informants inside the city. In Étienne's company, it was assumed they would be heading to one of the high points used by Prussian artillery, which could be either to the west or north of the city walls.

Étienne was up and dressed by 4:30. Rose straightened his tunic and, before handing him the cape which would be his only protection from the cold, she embraced him, hard and tight as she could. His heart was beating fast and so was hers. He was not afraid, he was eager. She was afraid, for him. But determined. She knew he had to go, that this was what he and all his company, all his battalion and all the other battalions, had been waiting for. And she knew, without anyone having told her, that her father would also be heading out this morning with his battalion, in what would be a very great force. Infantry, some cavalry – the best horses had been saved from slaughter – and cannons on caissons, but mostly men like Étienne, on foot, with rifles in their hands.

She followed him down to the street and watched him go, hurriedly, even, she thought, enthusiastically. To war. With his backpack and his canteen and his rifle. She hesitated as she watched him until he turned a corner, out of sight. She stood there still, wringing her hands, in a rare moment of doubt: Should she go back upstairs, where it was warmer? And what would she do there? It was very early. Too early to start work at the Ménagère. And did the Ménagère need her that morning, need her more than… ?

Her moment of doubt was brief, as always with Rose, scarcely a minute. She did know what she had to do. She had to go up to Belleville to support her mother, who must also be terribly anxious.

First, though, she would run back upstairs for a blanket to put over her coat and then get over to the Ménagère – she had a key – to see what food she could gather to take to her parents' home.

* * *

In the first-floor flat on Dragon Court, Noëlle and Angélique were also worried. Luc and Jean-Pierre had both been up and stirring while it was still dark, and the two young women knew that this was going to be a day of agitation and concern.

Luc was not one of those mobilized for battle. His rheumatism made him too slow, but he had got up in solidarity with J-P and to help him get his things together. Luc was always ready to lend a hand, he was good with the children, too. Jean-Pierre was another matter. Younger and still apparently healthy and vigorous, though very thin now with the poor diet, he was an officer. His Guard company had elected him lieutenant, no doubt – Noëlle supposed – because he was always serious and focused in that rowdy crowd of volunteers.

They had just celebrated his twenty-eighth birthday, which made him three years older than Noëlle and two more than Angélique, Noëlle had discovered when they had a little celebration. He had been embarrassed by the attention, more so when Noëlle presented him with a birthday present. A two-fold present, really: her much-worn copy of Lamartine, *Nouvelles Méditations Poétiques*, with certain verses marked in pencil for special attention, and a sheaf of some fifty pages of neatly hand-written verses, also titled 'Meditations', but with the name 'Noëlle D'. on the first sheet. For 'Dubois', she confessed shyly when he asked her – no one had asked her her surname until then, and she had hidden it deliberately. She did not dare compare her poor verses to Lamartine's. Signing 'Noëlle' was her way to remain virtually anonymous, it was such a common name. It was like signing 'Everywoman' or 'Anywoman'.

Jean-Pierre had frowned, his usual expression but this time especially concentrated, as he turned the pages and read the first verses in her manuscript. Those of Lamartine he merely glanced at, as something he was already familiar with. Then, after reading four of five of her pages, he looked up and astonished her, truly astonished her, by proposing to bind them! Her poor verses. He had just the right materials for a handsome cover of percaline, that he hoped would be as lovely as the meditations it enclosed.

She had gasped at this proposal, and rushed forward to

kiss him – amazed at her own audacity. Then, of course, she stepped back, feeling her face redden.

Noëlle knew that she was not a beauty, certainly nowhere near as lovely or graceful as her new friend Angélique, but she had feelings, deep feelings. And this young man, this young bookbinder Jean-Pierre, had looked at her in a way that made her know that he had feelings too.

He had reached into a pocket of his blouse and, after fumbling a bit to find it, handed her a little ball of twine.

"Ficelle de reliure," he said. Binding cord. "To remember this night."

Angélique had laughed and said, "So now you two are bound."

Which made Luc laugh, too, and Jean-Pierre look up, first at Angélique then, longer, at Noëlle.

And now he was gone. Luc had gone downstairs with him. It was still dark. And Noëlle sighed. Deeply. This would be a long day, an anxious day.

Angélique stepped over to embrace her. And soon, they both were crying. Then laughing, when Noëlle pulled out the little ball of twine which she had kept in her pocket since that night. A nondescript thing, worth scarcely a penny in the market, but infused with deep sentiment. Then she and Angélique, still embraced, sobbed again.

* * *

Despite the long march westward in the cold, dark early morning, through the westernmost districts and on beyond the city walls, Étienne and his battalion-mates were in good spirits. Unleashing the National Guard to join with the army to break the siege was what Guard commanders had been demanding for months. Étienne was especially glad to be with J-P, who had been elected lieutenant in his company, and Claude; the *trois relieurs* together again! But unlike that day on the ramparts of Vincennes, they would be face-to-face with the enemy. Étienne was so excited he wanted to sing, but the orders were not to make noise as they marched. But keeping this whole mass of men silent, most as excited as he, was not really possible. If their shouts and laughter and shouted jokes woke up the neighborhood, well, so be it.

Claude began whistling the refrain of the revolutionary hymn, '*Chant du Départ*', while others around them kept repeating the words:

The Republic is calling us

To conquer or to perish.

A Frenchman must live for her,

For her a Frenchman must die.

Yes! The Republic was worth dying for. If it came to that. But better to live and to conquer, as they should, there were so many of them, Guard and army together for the first time, eager to break the siege. Étienne was maybe a little frightened, but above all thrilled to be on his way for his first real combat test.

It wasn't until nearly seven in the morning that Étienne's and other battalions, now proceding as quietly as they could, finally reached the outskirts of Buzenval. And surprised the enemy and in the first hours of combat, driving the Prussians from their stronghold on the heights of Montretout.

* * *

Back in Paris, the first reports in the press were of victories, the National Guard and army together pushing the Prussians back from the little town of Buzenval and from its neighbor, Chanzy. But later, a dispatch from Schmitz, the major general in command, struck a more worrisome note:

A thick fog completely conceals from me the course of the battle. The officers carrying orders have great difficulty locating the troops. This is very regrettable and it makes it difficult for me to control the action as I had done until now. We are fighting in the dark.

Another dispatch that same day at 8:40 p.m., signed by General Clément Thomas, the National Guard's commander, reported:

Nightfall alone has put an end to this day's bloody and honorable battle. The conduct of the National Guard has been excellent. It honors Paris.

Despite initial successes, the advance troops received no reinforcements or other support, while the Prussians regrouped and brought in units from afar. Étienne's company had been part of the force that had taken, then lost, then retaken the fortified artillery placement on Montretout four or five times through the night.

He was tired but alert when J-P, early in the morning, tried to rally his men in the face of another Prussian counterattack. Étienne was just behind him and saw him fall to a cannon shell. Only minutes after the company had received Trochu's order to retreat.

J-P! Jean-Pierre! His instructor, his model of how to be a master binder! Of all the men in his unit, bold and determined Jean-Pierre had been his example, not only as craftsman but as a leader, a man who, more than any of the others around Étienne, understood and believed in what they were fighting for. Dead.

Étienne returned from the battle exhausted, saddened and enraged, late in the morning of the 20th. The sortie beyond the walls of Paris to retake Buzenval had turned into a disaster, as would become clear to all in the city over the next few days.

The press reported over 4,000 National Guardsmen slain, a total disaster. Paris had lost its last chance to break out of the Prussian siege, and the National Guard had lost all faith in its military commander, Trochu.

One of those slain was a young National Guard lieutenant, Jean-Pierre Lambert, bookbinder.

Étienne's deepest sadness was for his lost comrade and all the other men lost, but he also lamented the opportunity lost – they had been winning, was his impression, having taken many casualties but they had seized the high ground and were expecting the arrival of more men and artillery to hold it. But none came, from their side. The enemy had time to draw in more contingents of Prussian infantry and artillery, which sealed the defeat of the Parisian forces, guards and soldiers together.

And this was why he was angry. So angry that despite his exhaustion, Rose had to restrain him in his rage and desire to take revenge. Not on the Prussians; they were the enemy, doing what they were supposed to do, just men following orders. Étienne wanted revenge on the Trochu government that had abandoned them, as he saw it. And, he was sure, the other men did too.

He was lucky, he supposed, that he was only bruised, and his hands burned slightly from repeated firing. His other bookbinder buddy in the company, Claude, and many others had been wounded, but Claude had been able to walk with the support of Étienne and another man from the company. They had had to struggle to keep together in the dark, through the woods where they were fired on by Prussian sharpshooters, until they managed finally, just after daybreak, to get back to the city walls.

"But J-P, your friend?"

"Dead. Dead, dead, dead."

Rose sighed, then said,

"My father came back. He was tired too, of course. And I suppose he must have been angry, but not like you. Because, I think, he wasn't surprised. He had suspected the whole assault was a trick, that Trochu didn't really want the National Guard to have a victory. And he got all of his men home, even the wounded. My mother was so relieved to see him. I just left there an hour or so ago. What time is it now?"

"Time? Who cares? I don't know."

"Your friend J-P. He was your teacher, too."

"I loved that man. We used to laugh together, though he had a funny sense of humor. He really knew how to bind a book. He was showing me some tricks I'd never known, about cutting and trimming, just right. And he did covers too. Not a practised soldier, though. Even I knew better when the cannons started again. Brave but not sensible. He should have ducked, I shouted at him, but it was too late. And now— "

"He was still living on Dragon Court, wasn't he? Do they know?"

"No, no they probably don't, unless Claude has told them. Because he used to live there, too. But Claude can hardly walk now. Maybe I should go there, someone should tell them. Angélique, and anybody else who's still there."

"Yes, I think you should. But not right now. You have to rest."

* * *

It wasn't until the next day that Angélique, Noëlle and Luc got the news, from Étienne, that all three feared. Especially Noëlle. Étienne was surprised to see her lift her face as though looking at something beyond the roof of the apartment, and pull from her pocket a ball of twine, a ball that Étienne recognized at once as *ficelle de reliure*, binding thread.

He didn't know what to say, mumbled a goodbye and hurried out of the apartment and down the stairs to the street. Thinking of binding, binding books and binding people. And of his now lost tutor, J-P. And the job that they had left unfinished, of binding tracts that would advance a cause that had meant a lot to him, to J-P. And so to Étienne also, because Rose had also thought it was such a good idea.

* * *

Later that same day, the 21st January, one day after the return from the battle of Buzenval, a handful of National Guards, including Jules Durand and selected men from his company in Belleville, raided the Mazas prison near the Gare de Lyon and liberated Gustave Flourens, to reinstate him as mayor of the Twentieth arrondissement, the arrondissement of Belleville and Ménilmontant.

And the next day, Sunday the 22nd, delegates of the Guard and others from the radical political clubs – including Durand and Étienne Bonin and most of his battalion along with many civilians, including Louise Michel in National

Guard uniform – massed outside the Hôtel de Ville, demanding to take it over and to conduct the defense of Paris and of France on their own.

General Trochu meanwhile had been forced to resign in the wake of the Buzenval disaster. Someone, presumably his replacement as military chief, General Vinoy, ordered the Mobile Guards inside the Hôtel de Ville to open fire on the protesters, killing five and wounding tens more. The protesters withdrew to regroup, but did not surrender.

But it was all too late to save the so-called Government of National Defense. Or 'of National Defeat', as Rose's father had begun calling it. In the next few days, Paris learned that Vinoy's ministers had been negotiating with the Prussians. The commander of the Army of the East, General Bourbaki, had attempted suicide, and news reached Paris that the steel-town of Longwy, one of the last French hold-outs in the north, had capitulated.

Finally, on Saturday, 28th January, the Government of National Defense signed the treaty to end the war, which the government called an armistice. The terms were those dictated by Prussian King William and his chancellor, Bismarck: cession of Alsace and Lorraine, reduction of French armed forces to a minimal level, and indemnities to the Prussians of five billion francs to be paid in three years.

Étienne, Rose, the Central Committee of the National Guard and the political clubs and all the radical newspapers called it capitulation, and betrayal.

"Vive la Commune!"

"Vive la commune!"

To get a clearer picture of what that slogan meant, since that first night in the École de Médecine he had listened in at one political club after another. He had gone the first times with Hilaire or Évariste wherever there was a speaker they especially wanted to hear, other times with Claude. The excitement of the crowds was contagious. But then, feeling more confident, he had begun visiting other clubs on his own, to hear new people, hoping for some new insight. To clarify his doubts. He had so far never spoken at one of those meetings, but he listened closely, almost compulsively, hoping for guidance to reconciling two conflicting imperatives: opposing the government while defending the homeland against the Prussian invader.

And one night, at a club in Belleville, he had spotted Rose, back before they had got together. She was with her father, in his Guard uniform. That was what had encouraged him to speak to her, that day back in October, when he went up to Belleville in his brand-new too-small Guard uniform.

The surrender of the Emperor and the declaration of the Republic in September should have ended Étienne's moral conflict, patriotism vs. revolution, because defending France would henceforth be the same as defending the Republic. But, as that red poster had spelled out, the new Government of National Defense had been no improvement over the Empire – the scandalous unfairness of the rationing during the great hunger, the continuance of officials of the old regime in their posts, and especially their military incompetence and finally, the climax, the abject surrender to the Prussians in preference to continued defense of the city by the people's National Guard.

This was not the republic Étienne and the other workers had been calling for. Just what that republic would be like, he wasn't sure, but it would have to be the creation of the workers. And the name for that republic must be the Commune.

La Commune, he gathered, meant more than good common feeling, and something much more than the simple municipal administrations known as 'communes' that he had known around Lyon. Just what the speakers meant remained vague, but it would be a new social order, without king or emperor or bosses. Or priests, as many of the speakers insisted – despite the fact that most of those clubs met in churches, 'borrowed' for club meetings from their priests, who would then have to clear out scraps of leaflets and other debris before officiating at their now sparsely-attended masses.

* * *

"Commune! They're calling for the 'commune'! Do they have any idea what that means?"

Hippolyte Mireau seemed genuinely concerned, more so than René-Pierre had ever noted. He would, as usual in such circumstances, try to calm his interlocutor with a joke or at least a lighter tone.

"But my dear *commissaire*, whatever are you fretting about? It's just café talk, a bunch of happy, drunken revelers."

"No, it's not just the drunks. It's widespread, in all the club meetings, even in the press, in the reports of their meetings. My men are informing me every day. '*Vive la Commune*,' they shout. They want to overthrow our Government of National Defense and install – anarchy! The rule of the rabble! They think they can defend the city better than our generals."

"Tradesmen and ragpickers, defending the city. What a joke! And defending the city? Now? After the armistice?"

"A joke, is it? Tell me, René-Pierre Bougainville, distinguished man of letters and history buff, what does the phrase 'Paris Commune' sound like to you?"

"History buff? No, please. Not for me, those past, dead events. I always write about the immediate present, and the possible future."

"'Pericles', you wrote in your column, two weeks ago. You said that our General Trochu was like that ancient Greek hero, defending our city from the barbarians."

"Oh, yes, well, that was an exception. I needed to flatter our man at the top. That was just before he resigned. One has to do that sort of thing in my line of work, you know, to make sure to keep my contacts talking to me. And 'Pericles' was the only name of a statesman-hero I remembered from the lycée. Almost the only one I could think of at all, since one doesn't dare mention a 'Bonaparte' these days."

"Let's not go back to ancient Greece. But to our own history, in our own grandfathers' time. The commune. Surely you learned something about that in your lycée."

"In history? Oh, yes. You mean during the Revolution. Mmm, Robespierre. I remember the names. And Saint-Just. And, let's see, there was Danton. And Marat."

"And don't forget Hébert, the journalist. Like you."

"Hébert?"

"And also named René, like you. Jacques-René Hébert. He published *Le Père Duchesne*, that daily inciting the masses to ever more violence."

"Ah, the power of journalism!"

"*That* Paris Commune lasted just two terrible years. The Terror. Terror, death by guillotine, was official policy. All the men you mentioned had their heads cut off, one after another. All except Marat, murdered in his bathtub. And Hébert the journalist was the first to go."

"Oof. You frighten me."

"That was the Paris Commune. Murder, guillotine, mob rule. And now they want to bring it back."

"Calm down, Hippolyte. We won't let them, will we? Those café hotheads. I mean, the police, your police, won't let them, and we still have the army, the Prussians are leaving us some armed men here in the city. And the National Guard, if we can trust them, but the army and your police will surely keep them in line. After all, this is the nineteenth century!"

"The National Guard," Hippolyte said with a snort. "The men in those battalions have been the loudest calling for the Commune!"

"Yes, I've heard some of the army generals, and colonels and even captains, say they don't really trust the National Guard. Even when they were supposed to be fighting together against the Prussians. But you worry too much, Hippolyte. You know what they're saying, at the top? The men around Vinoy? If the revolutionaries really do look like they're about to take over, our leaders can call on the Prussians to come in and restore order."

"Call on the enemy? You're crazy! You had better not let anyone else hear you."

"No, I won't. This is just between you and me, what I've heard. The men around Vinoy, now that he has replaced Trochu, and maybe even Trochu himself, have been prepared to do it. Better the Prussians than the Bellevillois, they say. They are severe, those Germans, but at least they are civilized. And some of their officers even speak good French."

"Better the foreigners than the *canaille*, you're saying."

"That's what I'm hearing."

"René-Pierre, let's go get a drink."

* * *

The cold, dry air combined with the monotonous cadence of her neighbor's lament was making Blanche shiver. She pulled her shawl more tightly around her. It was still February, and the brutally cold winter had barely relented. At least the siege was over, and she had been able to offer her guest a cup of real coffee and some cheese that wasn't bad. She had hoped the coffee would help calm her neighbor, but Henriette was very nervous.

"And that's why I worry about Louis. Please don't take offense, Blanche, please, but I fear that your Jules is a bad influence."

At the mention of her husband, Blanche stiffened, eyes wide open, and looked again at her neighbor.

"A bad influence? How so?"

Louis and Jules worked together in the foundry, Broquin et Lainé, just a short walk down the hill from their houses. Louis was also a member of the National Guard company, where Jules had been elected captain. He was not one of Jules' closest friends, as far as she had observed, but the two men seemed to get along well, at cards and in the tavern where several of the bronze workers could always be found.

"You have to understand," Henriette went on. "We're not old Bellevillois like you and Jules, we weren't born on this hill."

"But you've been living here for, what? Five or six years, no?"

"But I mean we weren't here in the old times, before this became part of the city."

"That was ten years ago. When the barrier came down, and Belleville became part of Paris. Some people here thought that would be very good, we could carry goods into the city freely, without paying the tax. But we could see, Jules and I and some of our friends, the real reason was to control the population here. Those men who began to run the city after Napoleon took over, they were afraid that we would do again what we did in '48."

"That's what I mean, that's what I'm worried about. I know, I know about you two, because Louis has told me what Jules told him. That you and he met on the barricades in '48. With rifles! But we weren't even here yet! And I was only twelve years old, and Louis was only fourteen then. I mean, we are not old revolutionaries like you two. And I'm scared!"

"That's true, we did meet on the one big barricade, the one we built to fortify the customs house at the barrier. We were just sixteen. Ah, the excitement!"

"Oh, excitement! Terrible word, I hate that word. And dangerous. You could have been killed."

"A lot of our friends were. But we were fighting for a cause. And it looks like we are going to have to fight for it again."

"That's what I mean! That's why I'm frightened! And Louis, why, I think he'll do anything Jules asks him to. They all will! The men in the foundry, I mean. I don't know what it is he's got, his enthusiasm it must be. And he always seems to know where he's heading, just what to do. And now he keeps talking about 'the commune'. I don't know what that means, 'the commune', except that it sounds like revolution."

"What does it mean, 'the commune'? You mean, what will it be like? We won't know until we get it. But I think what they're talking about, the National Guard committee and all the others, is the same things we were fighting for in 1848. An end to the kind of wage slavery you and I have been suffering, Henriette. You in that corset factory, me in that hot laundry. And the constant fear of being thrown out of work and starving. And maybe even schools for our children. If it hadn't been for Rose, I wouldn't even know how to read the little that I do, and how she learned, well, mostly on her own. Oh! There she is.

"Hello, Rose, what have you been up to?"

"Hello, *Maman*. Good morning, Henriette. I've just come from La Ménagère. So much is happening now!"

"Tell us."

"There's talk of forming a women's association, to support the Committee of the Twenty Arrondissements. Nathalie proposed it."

"A women's association? That's politics, my child. Don't you agree, Blanche? I mean, it's men's work. We don't want to get into that!"

"Excuse me, Madame Henriette. I know now, since I've been working at the cooperatives, at La Marmite and La Ménagère, that politics *is* women's work. We're the ones who prepare the meals, wash the linen, sew the clothes, heal the sick, care for the children, without us the men can't be free to do anything."

"Yes, that's true. And that's why we have to stay out of politics. We have much too much to do without going to meetings, arguing about who is to govern…"

"No, no. What Nathalie says, that's Nathalie Lemel, she's in charge now of La Ménagère, she has organized strikes, she knows what she's talking about. It is our responsibility, she says, to take part in the decisions that affect us, and our families, most directly. Schooling, for example. We need schools for our children, and we can't have schools without funding, and that's politics. That's a political decision, and we have to be part of it. Don't you think so, Maman? You've always talked about how women and men must struggle together."

Blanche smiled at her daughter, and nodded. Then she looked toward poor, frightened Henriette. To calm her neighbor and friend, she said,

"No, don't worry, my dear. Rose doesn't mean voting or holding office or anything like that. But we have to be there to support them, and to share with them our ideas, so that when they vote, they'll vote for the things our families need. Isn't that right, Rose? You are talking about a women's support group, to help our husbands and the other men, not to take over from them, right?"

Rose looked back at her mother, clearly unconvinced but silent.

"Well, then, I suppose that's all right," said Henriette. "I do influence Louis, I know. But I'm afraid. Your husband, Blanche, your father, Rose, that Jules Durand, well – he has some very radical ideas. There has been so much war, so many boys killed fighting, and in the bombardment even women and children. I just hope – oh, well, spring is coming! Like that song says, 'the time of the cherries'. And now that at least the siege has ended, and the bombardment, I hope we can just live in peace."

Blanche smiled at her neighbor Henriette reassuringly for a moment, before turning a bigger, complicit smile to Rose.

* * *

Mireau was feeling discouraged. He would put on a brave face, as always, but things were really not going well. The armistice, the impeding mass assembly of an uncontrollable city population, and his own lagging transfer.

The armistice was a deep embarrassment, especially after those duplicitous assurances of Trochu and those men of the parties of the Left who had promised 'total war' to defend the new republic. Given the level of organization and agitation of the Paris populace, and especially the proliferation of arms that the National Guard had not surrendered, one didn't need to be a police chief in a proletarian quartier like the Quinze-Vingts to predict serious trouble.

In the past, that bourgeois left had been able to channel the concerns of the working masses. But not now. Famous republicans like Jules Favre had in the end preferred surrender to trusting the armed people in their National Guard to continue that defense. Capitulators, *capitulards* the people were calling them, for docilely accepting all of the enemy's demands. including the hastily organized elections to a new national government. Elections held under conditions of Prussian occupation of half the country and which, as the Prussian king no doubt hoped and expected, had given monarchists and the extremely conservative rural landowners the overwhelming majority. Leaving Paris, Lyon and other cities that had voted just as overwhelmingly for far more radical representatives as islands of republicanism.

Paris was in danger of become a fiefdom of Prussian King Wilhelm, who had now declared himself Emperor, with a ceremony in the Palace of Versailles. The shame!

The coming anniversary of the revolution of '48, would surely be a riotous demonstration.

* * *

The demonstration around the July Column in the Place de la Bastille, beginning 24th February and lasting for three days, was in fact huge. A hundred battalions of the National Guard were there for some or all of that time, more than half of all the battalions in Paris, including bourgeois battalions as well as those from the working-class sectors of the city, to celebrate those days in 1848 when a mass rising had forced the abdication of King Louis-Philippe and the creation of the Second Republic.

But it was not any of the uniformed Guards who took part in the murder of forty-six-year-old Bernard Vincenzi on the 26th, which was the work of wilder, undisciplined elements in the dense crowd. As one of Sûreté's undercover men, he had been recognized, beaten near to death and thrown into the canal of the Arsenal, where exalted rioters threw stones until it could not be determined whether he had died of drowning or lapidation.

The mass rally and speeches and shouting of slogans were not merely an enormous venting but also a clear demonstration that a truly massive revolt was waiting to burst through. France had been conquered, France had submitted. But not Paris. The police thereafter did not dare enter certain neighborhoods, and not only in Belleville or Ménilmontant.

Less than a week later, on 1st March, Prussian troops paraded on the Champs Elysées by agreement with the government of conquered France. The Prussians were blocked from further entry by a wall of closely massed National Guards and citizens.

IV

Insurgents

The 18th of March

"Soldier! Prost! Wake up!"

A gulp of air. Eyes wide open barely distinguished shadows. He had escaped! He had again eluded those Prussian lancers and the blood and fear and the screaming men and horses that had pursued him almost every night since that terrible day in Alsace.

But to where? It was dark and cold here, colder and darker than in the prisoner-of-war camp.

And that voice, it was French!

Maurice Prost, formerly sapper in the 1st Corps of the Army of the Rhine, and before that a carpenter-joiner in Paris, and before that… no, too long ago. He sat up to let the whirling images and memories connect in some coherent pattern as they sought to make contact with the new surroundings. The movements of other men reaching for their boots, the smell of mildew, of mud and sweat, the dampness in the air told him he was in an army bivouac. The flickering kerosene lamp and rapid shadow play, that it was not yet dawn. The lack of rooster or other animal noises, just the rustle of the men and their grunted swear words, that they were not in some northern farmland, and that they were being ordered for some action. No, he now remembered, he was no longer a prisoner of war, that had been almost two weeks ago. Nor could he have returned to the 1st Corps, nor to any part of Marshall MacMahon's Army of the Rhine, because – of this he was certain – that army no longer even existed.

In the prison camp in Metz he had suffered many discomforts, but after the chaos of the first weeks in the open air and hardly any rations, the men had at least slept on cots inside a shed with walls and a roof, not this bedroll on the ground in a mildewed tent. As he pulled on his boots, he recalled how, unexpectedly, he and the others had been mustered and herded onto a train and delivered like cattle all the way – hours in a crowded wagon – to the Île de France and then to Paris itself. Then it must be that he was again under French command, not Prussian. And was there still an army of France? And now he remembered, they were camped in the Jardin du Luxembourg, no less! A place that he, as a worker, had never dared enter. But they were in the mud.

Boots on, tunic tugged down, some mud knocked from his red trousers, his blue kepi clapped onto his head over his tangled, unwashed, overlong hair, he tried to remember the number of this new, makeshift regiment – 67th? – and the name of the officer in command of his company, Leroy, Lefevre? No. Ah, yes, Laurent. Newly promoted to captain, the rumor went. Then this was probably his first command.

He shuffled out of the tent to join the men shivering in the rain for their turn at the latrine. A light moved past the line – a lantern with a candle. He looked up to see if he could find any stars, but it was too cloudy and the rain made him turn his face down again. He felt cold and his cloak was thin and none of the men had had enough to eat for days. But at least it had stopped snowing.

"Must be midnight! Why have they got us up so early?"

"No," said the man behind him. "I'd say it's nearly three already. See those stars?"

"You must be from the country, you sound so sure."

"Voisins, that's near Claye. Wine country. And we had some cattle, too. You have to be up before sunrise to take care of them all."

Pissing, elbow to elbow with half a dozen other men, Maurice wondered if he was the only man in the company who had ever even been in Paris before. On the platform where they had disembarked, he'd seen a man who said he was from Paris escorted outside by a guard, whereas others were told to report to 'Army of Paris'. Then when they got to him, he gave his old address in Lyon – so that they would let him stay in Paris and, if the army gave him some free time, to reunite with Sophie.

"Hurry up, you sluggards. Rifles and canteens and extra cartridges. Get all your gear together and line up in formation. On the double!"

Rifles and extra cartridges? The war is over, we're in Paris, there are no Prussians here, so who are we supposed to shoot? He shivered at the only possible answer.

* * *

As his column marched out of the park, Maurice recognized the neighborhood even under the scant light of the gas lamps.

"We're passing near the Sorbonne," he told the man next to him.

"Quiet, you!" called out the sergeant in an exaggerated hush. "We don't want to wake up the neighbors."

In the flickering light of a streetlamp, he could just

make out the gray rump of the horse ahead of them, where their Captain Joseph Laurent was practising sitting as tall as possible in the saddle, no doubt – Maurice was convinced – to demonstrate a confidence he couldn't really feel. The hastily reorganized army was desperate for officers, and Laurent's mustache and his distant relationship to the colonel had been enough to earn him this sudden promotion, so went the scuttlebutt.

Not only was their commander inexperienced, but this whole regiment had never before operated together. They were remnants of various defeated and decimated divisions, nearly half of them former prisoners of war, with no military memory of anything but defeat. Except maybe the sergeants, who looked like veterans who may have tasted a victory in France's wars in Africa, or the Crimea, or Italy, or even Mexico – though that one had ended badly too. Maurice imagined that the army hoped this operation would turn them into a fighting unit, and that the operation would be simple enough for such a haphazard company. He had an idea what their mission must be, though no one had told them: retrieving the lightly-guarded cannons from only half-awake sentries, those undisciplined workers in National Guard uniforms. Newspapers smuggled into the camp had spoken of repeated, and so-far failed, attempts to seize the Paris cannons in the daytime, but by marching before dawn and in greater force they should catch the National Guard unawares.

The column crossed one bridge without incident, then another, and was now near the Hôtel de Ville. Tramp, tramp, tramp, boots on cobblestones. But now, what was that other sound? Bells?

"Hey, you!" he heard a sergeant shout. "Get those goats out of the road. Army coming through!"

He glimpsed under a gaslight what looked like a small woman in many layers of clothes, and then the whole column stopped as the captain's horse backed up and swayed. And then a loud Thwack! of a rifle butt, and a moan. And another voice, an older man, crying out,

"Leave her alone, you *cul-rouge battu,* you whipped red-pants!"

"Sergeant! Stop that man!" ordered the captain, struggling to bring his horse under control.

"A rioter?"

"He's just a filthy ragpicker, my captain."

"That's right," came the hoarse reply. "I *am* a ragpicker, and with pride. But I too was a red-pants like you, but not a defeated one like your pack. In Crimea I was, in an army that knew how to win! And we didn't pick on old ladies. We fought the Russians!"

"Catch him, Sergeant! And stop him from shouting!"

But the chiffonnier had dropped his bag and run away, and from up the street they heard him yelling, "It's soldiers! Wake up! Sound the tocsin! Soldiers have come! They're coming for our cannons!"

Just then the column passed the Hôtel de Ville, where they were joined by two other columns of two or three hundred men in dark blue tunics and, Maurice supposed, bright red pants, though the colors were hard to make out in this pre-dawn. What he could see more clearly was that each had a rifle on his shoulder. A church bell was ringing furiously, whether alerted by the shouts of the chiffonnier or just the noise of the march.

All these columns of silent, marching men, three or four now, each with its captain on horseback, had merged into an improvised regiment all under the overall command of an officer whose red kepi identified him as a colonel. They kept trudging, trying to ignore the increasing sounds of church bells and shouts.

After a long march and when it was already light, they reached a spot where the road rose steeply between houses, farms and taverns.

"What is this place?" said the man next to him, the same farm boy he'd talked to an hour or more before.

Maurice looked up at the windmills near the top, a long climb up the mountain and beyond the jumble of little buildings.

"It must be Montmartre," he told the peasant.

"Where they've parked the cannons!" gasped the boy from Voisins. A sergeant shouted at them to begin the ascent.

* * *

Standing in the rain outside the town hall of the Twelfth, Hippolyte Mireau heard a distant church bell waking the neighborhood and began to feel uneasy. The whole point of this pre-dawn mission was surprise! He held his watch up to catch the streetlight, nearly five. The troops should already be here. He had spent the night, very uncomfortably, in his police commissary, and had been standing here in the cold drizzle since a quarter past four with his fifteen *guardians of the peace*, waiting for the troops they were supposed to lead to the Rue Basfroi, where National Guardsmen had hauled a dozen cannons. That army company should have been here by now, he thought again. Morning was breaking, and already he heard the creaking axle and clomping hoof steps of a milk cart pulled by a tired old horse. And there again was that peasant girl, he had seen her before, the dairy girl, she used to come before the siege. She and her horse came alone this time, without her mother or brother.

"Hey, missy, how about some milk for my men?" he called out.

Hot coffee would be more welcome, but at least a little nourishment should improve his policemen's spirits. Now, where were those damned soldiers? The lighter it got, the less likely they were to catch the National Guards by surprise. And he had heard that church bell ringing.

The girl looked up at him, hesitant, unbelieving that he was serious, but he reached into his purse and showed her some coins and she ladled out milk into a big tin cup and carried it to the line of policemen, who stamped their feet and snickered but managed to say things like "Thank you, sweetheart."

* * *

Rose's mother burst into the hut breathless and breadless before Rose had finished dressing – Blanche had as usual gone out to fetch a loaf at first light.

"Soldiers out there!" she announced, waking her husband and Rose's younger brothers. "Scores, hundreds of them. Whole companies. With rifles."

"Soldiers? Armed?" said Jules. "In Belleville?"

"A whole column, I saw forty or fifty, and more coming up behind them. Heading up to the Buttes, it looked like."

"The cannons! They're after the cannons!" said Jules, suddenly sitting up.

"Of course they are! We've got to stop them," Blanche said firmly. "Rose, you're not going to work today. You're coming with me. We have to stop those soldiers."

"That's man's work," protested Jules.

"This is the people's work," she answered. "All of us. And you know it, Julot. It won't be the first time we fight together."

He laughed.

"No, you're right about that. Ah, we still remember '48, don't we? Come on, boys, you too."

"Where to?"

"Why, Buttes de Chaumont is our area."

"No," said his wife. "Montmartre is where the most cannons are. Let's go."

"Woman! The Buttes' cannons are important too. But if Montmartre's where you're heading, well, all right. Let me get my rifle –"

"And your trousers, big boy. Not those, you silly, the blue ones with the stripe from your Guard uniform. Over there, on that nail behind you."

"Oh, right. Where's my tunic? And I have to gather the fellows in our company."

"Fine. You do that. But Rose and I are not going to wait. You catch up to us when you can. At Montmartre, *mon capitaine*."

Jules, still pantless, stood at attention and saluted, laughing only slightly, but Blanche was already out the door, with Rose close behind.

* * *

Over in the Sixth Arrondissement, the bells at Saint-Sulpice and more bells from another church, then shouts in the street had awakened Étienne before the sky was quite bright. Hurriedly he climbed into his uniform and grabbed the rifle he had ready in a corner of the tiny bedroom. Without even thinking of breakfast, he ran down to the street and then to their agreed-upon assembly point on Rue Taranne. Étienne wasn't even thinking of what he was doing, if his unit was rushing, he wasn't going to be left behind. Not for this adventure!

Thirty or forty of the hundred or hundred twenty-five of their company were already there, including their elected captain, a tinsmith they knew as Philippe. Dozens of men from other companies kept arriving, milling until they located their group and their captain.

"Well, where to, Philippe?"

But Philippe just stretched his neck and looked around.

"Where do we go, Philippe? Don't just stand there!"

"We have to wait for orders. Our commandant, of the whole battalion."

"Place des Vosges," someone shouted. And Claude picked up the cry, adding, "That's right, it's only a half hour from here and where the cannons are."

"Right. The cannons!"

The men stamped their feet impatiently. They were excited, but not angry – rather the opposite, all in good spirits, glad to be doing something together. To take action after so many frustrating weeks, of the French defeat, the Prussians' parade, the ridiculous and intolerable demands of their new, defeated government. Someone started humming a love song but was quickly interrupted by other men demanding something more martial.

"Wait. Where are the other companies? and our battalion commandant?"

"The Saints-Pères company has already started out, I heard their drummer."

"Look, here comes a runner now. Hey, it's Aloïs. You coming from the commandant?"

"Wait. Catch my breath. Yes. Our commandant says to start out now. All eight companies. We can meet up at Place des Vosges."

"That's what I said!"

"Oh, right. Well, men – Did somebody bring the banner?"

"Forget the banner. We've got to get there before the soldiers do."

"Right. Ready?"

"Ready!"

And so Philippe, the company captain, repeated the order firmly, as though it had been his own idea.

"In formation, men of the National Guard. We go to defend the cannons in the Place des Vosges! Pépin, sound the drum! Pépin, have you got your drum? Sound, oh, I don't know. *Le rappel!*"

"Hey, Philippe, you're supposed to say, *En avant!*"

"*En avant!*"

* * *

René-Pierre Bougainville splashed water onto his face from the marble-topped wash stand in a corner of his bedroom and looked around, from the heavy six-drawer dresser with brass fittings to the wide bed with its padded leather headboard. Atop the dresser a pair of bronze putti clutched a clock by Raingo Frères. Across the bed sprawled a naked Victorine, her left leg draped over her right and a thumb in her mouth. Bougainville pulled the sheet over her – it was chilly and damp this morning. Victorine stirred and said "Uuf!" and went back to sleep. The clock said nearly five.

Wrapping a robe around his nightshirt, Bougainville stepped to his writing desk and picked up the sheets he had written last night. 'A GLORIOUS VICTORY of REASON over Mad Rebellion' was his proposed headline. So confident was he of his sources that he had already written a description of events that were yet to occur.

Here he had an edge over the other pen-wielders, because of his excellent contacts in the army and the police. He knew how many would be going up to the heights of Montmartre, in the northern Eighteenth Arrondissement, that there would be another column also in the heights, but at Buttes de Chaumont in the Nineteenth, and another on lower ground closer to the center, to get the cannons at Place des Vosges and the nearby Place de la Bastille, in the Fourth. Those two army captains he had plied with wine and a fine meal only last night, Robert and Laurent, had been especially informative. Robert said he saw this operation as a chance to restore order before it occurred to the Thiers government to do something drastic and foolish, such as to restore the Orleanist monarchy, but Laurent was brash and unconcerned, saying he didn't care whether they had a republic or a king, the important thing was to crush the rebels. A paragraph about each of them would serve to fill out his article. He would add details after hearing from them at the celebratory gathering with those two and possibly other victorious captains and majors, scheduled for nine this evening at the Saint-Séverin. And he might get more details after talking with another good source, Mireau. He should be able to tell him what happened at the little artillery park on Rue Basfroi in the Eleventh.

This would be the article to make the by-line of René-Pierre Bougainville shine brightest among the journalists scrambling to please the new government of M. Thiers. Fame and repute that, he hoped, would bury forever the odious nickname '*Bagou*'.

He considered for a moment rushing to the Place de la Bastille to see the excitement for himself. For the delight of seeing the surprise and astonishment on the faces of those foolish National Guardsmen, caught in their sleep next to their cherished cannons! But then, with spirits so animated, there might be some shooting. Very distasteful, possibly even dangerous to a civilian like him. And besides, it was raining. Not hard, but still unpleasant on a chilly March morning.

Really, he decided, there was no need to hurry. He didn't really need to see anything for himself. He could, as he had done many times before, repeat or invent whatever eyewitness accounts he needed to please his readership.

* * *

In his tiny room in Belleville, Alphonse-Marie Bertrand was startled awake by voices and running feet and then a church bell, much too early for a Saturday. He had changed lodgings several times since the beginning of the siege, always looking for something cheaper, until finding this space with a worker's family on the hills of Belleville. The man of the family, Louis, worked in the nearby bronze foundry and like most of the workers he knew in the neighborhood was in the National Guard, whether out of enthusiasm for the defense of Paris or for the 30 sous a day. The wife, Henriette, had had a job in a corset factory before the siege closed it down, and now was struggling to make a little money by sewing at home, so they were glad for the extra income, slight as it was, from the young journalist's rent.

They had also had a soldier billeted here when Alphonse arrived, a chap younger even than Alphonse and from some western village. It was cheaper for the army than having to build new barracks. But that army boy, and the others here in Belleville, had been suddenly withdrawn just days ago, unhappily, it seemed, because they had made friends with the families and the close-knit neighborhood must have reminded them of the villages they had left behind. Or so Alphonse had surmised in his latest article, poetic and lyrical, which he hoped to see published soon in Rochefort's paper. Like those soldiers he too was an outsider in this working-class neighborhood, from another world because of his clothes, his accent, his manners, but the family he was lodging with had accepted and vouched for him – "A scribbler, yes, but telling *our* story, for our papers".

This sudden early morning tumult, and the sudden departure of the twenty or so soldiers earlier in the week, must signal another attempt to seize the cannons. The neighborhood had been expecting something like this for days, since the earlier frustrated attempts by small companies of soldiers. Just this week Alphonse had visited most of the places where the cannons had been hauled and had written an unsigned article on them for what turned out to be the last issue of *Le Père Duchêne* before the police closed it down. The cannons and *mitrailleuses* were only lightly guarded, just one or sometimes ten or fifteen men in National Guard uniform standing or sitting nearby. And, as he had noted, they had been parked without their powder charges, so they couldn't be fired. Alphonse and anybody who was interested had been able to walk around them and see the names and symbols embossed, most with the mark of Broquin et Lainé, the big bronze foundry where Alphonse's host Louis and many others in the neighborhood worked. He had seen dozens of cannons nearby on the Buttes and the largest collection, scores of them, lined up on the heights of Montmartre, looking menacing even though their bagged charges were stored safely away, Alphonse hadn't been able to find out just where.

Hastily dressed and with notebook and pencil in hand, he ducked out the low door and into the drizzle, where he saw Louis in his Guard tunic and kepi arguing with Henriette. She, already dressed, scowled at him and pushed him back just as Alphonse interrupted.

"Hey! Good morning to you! Up already? Where are you heading?"

"Montmartre," answered Henriette.

"No, you're not!" shouted Louis. "*I'm* going there. No place for women!"

Montmartre! That's where he had to go, too. This would be a story!

* * *

By the time Étienne's company reached the Place des Vosges, there was already a huge crowd. Women and men, some of the men in National Guard jackets and caps and the blue trousers. And then, when the crowd briefly opened, Étienne saw a company in the red trousers of the army, marching or rather shuffling out of the square behind an officer on horseback. Without the cannons.

"Catch them!" a woman shouted. "They're headed to the Place de la Bastille. We stopped them here."

Separated from Étienne's company by men and women in civilian clothes was another group in National Guard uniforms. Their captain worked his way to Étienne's company.

"So there you are. Good. Now we're all here, our whole battalion and the others from the Sixth," he said loudly.

"Our whole legion, almost. And lots of men from this arrondissement, the Fourth."

The men from the Fourth, he said, would be staying here to secure the site, but the Sixth's commandant Marcel had decided that all four companies should continue to the Bastille, following the troops who had already given up trying to take the cannons from Place des Vosges.

"Given up? Already?"

"Their captains and even their major didn't want the men to fire into the crowd, and the women, they kept shoving themselves between the soldiers and the cannons. Some of those ladies even embraced them, the soldiers I mean, and the soldiers just stood there, smiling and looking embarrassed. There aren't many cannons here, anyway. Those fellows in the Fourth dragged most of them over to Place de la Bastille. Just in the past two days."

Relieved, Étienne and the others in his company shouldered their rifles and continued on toward the Bastille, surrounded by cheers from the crowd. Someone started singing 'La Marseillaise', and soon he and the other Guardsmen joined in, almost skipping as they walked. He had never known such excitement since he first came to Paris!

* * *

Maurice now found himself up at the top of Montmartre, his company now mixed with others and surrounded by a swirl of civilians. The only thing clear was the order cried out by the captain and repeated by the sergeants, "Secure the cannons." It had been easy for the first hour or so, there were only about forty National Guards and they had been disarmed without much trouble, except for that sentry one of the units had killed. But now, how were they to do anything with all these people in the way? Maurice, now teamed with another soldier he didn't know, had dragged this cannon away from the others and swung it around to attach it to its caisson and hitch it to the pair of horses nervously stamping amid all the noise and shoving. If they could only get the horses close enough and in the right position. But then, the mob of people from the neighborhood had showed up, pressing around them, and some youngster maybe twelve or fourteen had snuck in beneath the flailing arms and cut the harness. Maurice tried to obey the sergeant shouting at him and was trying to move the cannon manually. But –

"Hey, lady! Look out, please!"

There were two of them, a woman he guessed to be around forty, not tall but very determined, and a girl.

"Excuse me, madam, but we've got orders to…"

Maurice could have pulled his arm free with an effort, but that would be abrupt, rude against a lady, especially a French lady, one of the people he was supposed to be defending. The girl with her, not much over sixteen he guessed, had latched on to the other soldier. Maurice looked around, hoping for orders, or at least clues as to what to do. Similar scenes were all around him, soldiers engulfed in a swarm of women's arms and bodies, bonnets bobbing up and down alongside the regimental kepis.

The girl called out a name.

"Émile!"

The other soldier, the one working with Maurice on this cannon, jerked his head up.

"Émile, what are you doing? Look, *Maman*, it's Émile, who was staying with Henriette and Louis next door."

"Uh, I don't know –," mumbled Émile. "You, you are?"

"I'm Rose, Rose Durand. Daughter of Jules. You hardly saw me, because I had to go to work so early. But you'll remember my mother, Blanche."

"Oh, Madame Durand. Yes, of course. Pardon me, I didn't recognize you."

Maurice just stared, amazed and confused by this new situation, one hand on the cannon but no longer trying to pull away from the woman whose name he had just learned.

"And what is your name, young man?" she asked.

Maurice looked to Émile who was looking at Rose.

"Eh?" Blanche said again. "And where are you from?"

"Maurice, madam. Maurice Prost. From the sappers' company of the First Corps of the Army of the Rhine."

The other soldier, Émile, looked at him with exaggerated mock surprise.

"Well, to tell the truth, the Army of the Rhine isn't any more. Now I'm in, uh, it's the new 67th regiment I think. Émile, is this the 67th?"

"No, that's not what I meant, soldier. What *place* are you from? Not Paris, hmm?"

"Lyon, madam," was all he had a chance to say before he felt another shove. There were more people trying to separate him from the cannon.

"You can't take our cannons! We paid for them!" This was a man's voice, accompanied by a strong shove. Now the girl spoke,

"He's right, we paid for them. And my father was one of the men who made them! To defend us from the Prussians!"

Amidst all the din, these words reverberated most strongly in Maurice's head.

"To defend us from the Prussians."

That was right, Paris had defended itself, and defended itself still. The Prussians were still outside the walls. Whereas Maurice's army, the famous Army of the Rhine, had simply dissolved, surrendered, been torn apart, died. But Paris, Paris had defended itself. And now the remnants of his wretched Army of the Rhine and all the other defeated French armies wanted to take away the cannons that had kept this part of France free.

At that thought, he let his arms drop, and the woman's grasp on one of them relaxed, becoming almost a caress. He turned to see the man who had shoved him and saw that he was in National Guard uniform. The man opened his mouth in a wide grin and reached forward and hugged him.

"Brothers!" he cried. "Soldiers and Guardsmen, brothers for France!"

* * *

Bastille was even more tumultuous than Vosges. There seemed to be lots of soldiers there, and officers, some dismounted next to their horses and talking animatedly with the civilians around them. In one company, all the soldiers had stuck ramrods into their rifle barrels, to show that they weren't going to shoot. Étienne heard somebody give a whoop of joy and then heard a shout about 'breakfast'. One of the army captains waved, and turned and said something to his sergeants, and Étienne, curious about this unexpected behavior, watched the officer as he dismounted and stepped easily, calmly, toward one of the cafés on the edge of the square.

Some soldiers came over to Étienne's group with friendly gestures, and one of them said, "Guess it's like the major said, the captains can go get some breakfast and so should we. We've been up since three, and they haven't given us anything to eat! We're starving. Aren't you guys, you Guardsmen, you coming along? A cup of hot coffee would be really good!"

"Sure. But, what is this all about?" Claude asked him. "We're all Frenchmen. The war is over. Why did you all have to come for our cannons?"

"Beats me," said the soldier. "Nobody tells us anything. Except to give us orders. March! they said. We got up at three in the morning! And we haven't had anything to eat or drink. I told you that already, didn't I? Hard to think of anything else. The last thing we want to do is fight other Frenchmen. Think we can get some coffee and maybe a baignet over in that place, over there?"

Claude laughed, and Étienne, feeling released from tension, laughed much louder. Then stopped and looked at the others, all older, and felt himself blushing. Claude looked at him, a silent laugh on his lips, then turned to the soldier.

"Something to eat? Of course you can! If you've got a few sous. And if you don't, we'll help you. Right, Étienne? Hey, Philippe, what do you say? We're going with these fellows to get something to eat. What regiment are you with, anyway?"

Then louder, "Hey, Philippe, you hear me? That's all right with you, right? Well, we elected him and we could unelect him, so he has to say yes."

"You're joking! No? You *elect* your officers?"

"You bet. Our company captain *and* the commandant of our whole battalion. And all our battalions together in our arrondissement, we choose our general!"

"You lucky dogs," said the soldier. "We don't get to elect anybody, certainly not our officers. They just gave us a new one the day before yesterday, Robert, Captain Robert is his name. Well, at least he seems to be a decent guy, he told us not to shoot. And now I don't know where he went – over to one of the cafés, I'll bet."

"Hey, Philippe!" shouted Claude again. "I said we're going to get some breakfast with these fellows, our friends in the army. The army of France."

"Yes, sure," said Philippe. "I heard you. I'll be along in a few minutes."

* * *

The expedition to Rue Basfroi and Place Puebla was even more of a disaster than Mireau had expected. By the time his *agents de paix* and the soldiers got there, the whole neighborhood was aroused and had already constructed at least one barricade, so that Mireau had to lead the troops through some tortuous side-streets and an alleyway he knew to get around it and continue – they were not about to begin an open attack on a barricade, their mission was simply to recover cannons, not start a civil war.

But it was too late, and impossible to get the cannons. Civilians, some of whom Mireau recognized and many others he suspected were not even from the neighborhood, were not only awake but all gathered in a boisterous crowd protecting the cannons. There was even a street clown he had seen before, rattling on his drum and singing 'La Marseillaise' to the amused accompaniment of several in the crowd.

Mireau was appalled but not entirely surprised. He had known it would not be as easy as the army high command had assumed, and the bungling and late start of this operation had doomed it. The army captain, an inexperienced and uncomfortable-looking man named Sapin, very foolishly ordered his men to fire on the crowd, and the troops – mostly young, dispirited boys with no idea of what they were supposed to do, here in Paris – lifted their rifles as though to fire, but when one of them turned his upside-down rifle butt in the air, the others imitated him. There were cheers from the crowd, including especially the dozen or so men in National Guard garments. The captain shouted again and drew his pistol, but two men pulled him off his horse and some of his own men had trained their rifles on him. One of the National Guards intervened, and the captain was allowed to pick himself up, straighten his tunic and his decorated cap. And, then reconsidering, he slowly remounted and issued a new order.

"Men! Do not fire. We shall protect the lives of these people."

"*Citoyens!*" shouted someone from the crowd.

"*Citoyens et citoyennes!*"

There was that rebel language, from the Revolution of '89. '*Citoyen*', a person with rights. To Mireau and no doubt to the captain, the word summoned lurid images of the guillotine and sans-culottes demanding the heads of rulers and wealthy merchants. The cry was repeated, until at last the captain himself picked up the word – which, Mireau imagined, must be distasteful to him.

"Indeed, yes, my dear *citoyens*. We ask you –"

"And *citoyennes!*" shouted a woman.

"Citoyens and citoyennes, in the name of the French army I declare that we have completed our mission of reconnoitering and now all we ask of you good people, *citoyens et citoyennes*, is that you allow us to withdraw. In good order. Men! Soldiers! In your ranks!"

Mireau and his police officers observed. The National Guardsmen and all the civilians stepped back and most of the soldiers obediently reassembled in their ranks, but there were a few who stood apart, and even some who had got into animated and apparently friendly conversation with men and women in the crowd.

It took less time than Hippolyte had feared for Captain Sapin to determine that he had had enough and begin leading his troops, those who continued to follow, back the way they had come, no doubt with the intention of returning to military headquarters. Mireau just let them go, to find their own way through the labyrinthine streets. He had another mission. In his jacket he had folios with a list of the names and supposed addresses of men he was supposed to arrest, presumed leaders of the subversion in the National Guard.

He stood still for a moment, contemplating the excited crowd, now including seven or eight men in army uniform. Deserters, to be arrested and shot according to military law. But that was not his job. Especially since those soldiers were armed and surrounded by excited supporters. And since he had only fifteen more lightly armed police officers, of doubtful reliability, under his command.

In one of the little bars off to the side of Place Puebla he saw a fire going in a brazier. Mireau stepped over to it, withdrew the sheets of paper from his jacket and dropped them into the fire.

* * *

Alphonse was young and healthy, but still by the time he'd reached the top of Montmartre following Louis and the other men in that National Guard company, he was out of breath. He looked around at his companions, wondering if he was the only one gasping – the other men were mostly older, but they had moved quickly and eagerly, their excitement overcoming any fatigue in the long, steep climb. Up here on the plateau where most of the cannons were, there were other men in the tunics and kepis of the Guard, but most of those he saw were not in uniform. There were at least as many women as men up at the top, and lots of children.

He heard shouting and cursing and turned to see a boy with a knife running from an army sergeant. What happened? Oh, now he saw. The kid had cut the traces of a horse that had been attached to a *mitrailleuse*. The sergeant hurried back to where he had been, seeing that there was no chance of catching the boy who had now merged into the crowd.

Then he heard more shouting, even louder than before, and looked up to see an officer on horseback waving his pistol at the mob surrounding his horse.

"It's that general! Get him!"

"That's the second one. Two generals in one day! Did you see old Clément-Thomas? He showed up in disguise, dressed as a civilian!"

Surrounding the general were soldiers holding their rifle butts up, ostentatiously refusing orders to fire on the crowd. Alphonse then lost sight of the general on horseback, whose name he learned was Lecomte.

What he had expected to be a battle had turned into a kind of festival. National Guardsmen and soldiers were embracing, and some of them in little groups were abandoning the flat area with the cannons, heading a little down the road to the taverns. Even some of the women he saw heading into the taverns.

The cannons and *mitrailleuses* now were clearly going to

be safe. That is, they were going to stay in the hands of the people, the people of Paris.

Something seemed to be happening a little further up the hill, around one of the humble village houses. Alphonse looked to Louis and the others he had come with, and one of them raised a fist in a gesture of approval or perhaps of victory. Alphonse worked his way through the crowd until he saw Jules Durand, the captain of another Guard company from Belleville.

"What's going on?" he asked him.

"They've locked up those two generals in the garden behind that house."

"What are they going to do with them?"

"Well, they should wait for one of our officers to take charge. For a military tribunal, as our code says. Due process. I'm just a company leader, I can't take on that responsibility. We need somebody from the Guard's central committee. Look at that crowd, they're furious."

"They're mostly soldiers, it looks like."

"Right. Lecomte's own men have got him locked up."

The crowd was shouting and there were shuffling feet and the sound of a caisson being overturned when suddenly Alphonse heard two rifle shots, then three or four more.

"Uh-oh," said Jules. "Let's see what's happened."

* * *

It was nearly noon when Bougainville finally ventured outdoors, and the scene was not at all what he had expected. Here in his western arrondissement, the most bourgeois section of the city, he had expected to see people celebrating the final humiliation of the rebellious units of the National

Guard, which were almost all in the east. But the noises he heard sounded more menacing.

All the stores had closed, which seemed very odd for a Saturday. And there were orators on street corners, haranguing small crowds with cries of "Treason!" directed, not at the rebel Guardsmen and their allies but at the new government of Adolphe Thiers, for surrendering to the Prussians and for sending troops into the city to seize the cannons. He stopped to listen to one of them, but he couldn't believe what he heard. No, they could not have dared to assassinate two generals of the army!

He came across a barricade that must have been erected just that morning. There were men with rifles behind it, some of them in parts of National Guard uniform and some just in their worker's blouses and caps. And others in French army uniforms! This is what frightened him most, soldiers together with rebel guardsmen. It was a soldier with insignia of the 113th regiment who wouldn't let him pass until he joined them in shouting, *"Vive la République!"*

Personally, Bougainville didn't care one way or another whether France should be a republic or a monarchy, as long as that rascal Bonaparte didn't come back. In that, he had agreed with that Captain Laurent he had talked to last night, the one with the waxed mustache and the jaunty air, who told him about the coming operation on Montmartre. Now, how had that gone, he wondered?

"What do you hear about the cannons on Montmartre?" he asked a gentleman, as decently accoutered – that is, obviously not a working man – as he.

"Oh, disaster! Haven't you heard? That's where they killed all the generals and ran the army out!"

"What?"

"No, no," said another man who had overheard them. "Only two generals. And the army has withdrawn in good order, to fight another day."

"Killed two generals? The savages! What do you mean, 'withdrawn'? The army was supposed to restore the cannons to the rightful government!"

This second man just laughed and waved toward a crowd that was singing and cheering.

"They're cheering!" said Bougainville.

"Yes. They're cheering on the army. Their departure, I mean. You can't see them from here, but I was just down on that corner. The people are cheering and booing, cheering that the soldiers are marching out of the city, catcalls for their generals."

"Is that true? The army withdrawing?"

"And from what I hear, after leaving all the cannons and *mitrailleuses* just where they were. Paris, it seems, is about to become independent."

"No! The army cannot leave the city to that rabble! It would be treason even to suggest that!"

"Look. Here comes a column now. Heading for the Versailles gate, it looks like. Do you see any cannons?"

No, there were no cannons being hauled by the scores of men in bedraggled uniforms, some without their kepis. The men on foot all looked exhausted, stooped and dragging their feet. Their major sat up fiercely on his horse, a dark scowl on his thickly mustached face, paying absolutely no attention to the troops behind him, as though embarrassed by their presence. Bougainville thought he recognized him, and since he didn't give the appearance of really being in formation, he stepped toward him and called out:

"Major! Fournier? Is it Major Fournier?"

From high upon his horse, the major turned his scowl unwelcomingly toward his importuner.

"I'm the journalist Bougainville, Major. René-Pierre Bougainville. I write for *Le Figaro* and *Le Journal de Paris*. I need to ask you: Have you come from Montmartre?"

The major's left eyebrow registered the occurrence of a thought.

"Bagou?" the major snorted. And laughed.

"There is no Montmartre, scribbler. Write that. Montmartre has been consumed by Hell."

And he turned sharply away, spurring his tired horse to give a brief spring forward. But then reined in, so as not to get too far ahead of his bedraggled troops. They looked like rather less than a full regiment to Bougainville, and there were gaps in their ranks as they continued their dispirited shuffling down the avenue.

There would be no celebratory dinner in the Saint-Séverin brasserie tonight. He wondered where he could find those two captains he had talked to, Robert and Laurent. Or any other army officers. How could such a large military mission have failed? Had all the columns failed? Entirely?

He wandered, on foot, through the neighborhoods, walking from west to east. It was impossible to find a cab, and even the omnibuses were not to be seen. He trudged toward the Hôtel de Ville then on toward Place de la Bastille. Any further and he would find himself in truly hostile working-class territory. As it was, he had had to pass through several barricades and repeat, as he had at that first one, that he was loyal to the republic. The Place de la Bastille was one boisterous party, with drums and singing and lots of drunken workers, it seemed to him. Not his crowd. He decided to turn back toward what he assumed would be the safer

Palais Royal. If he dined in the Frères Provinciaux, the most securely bourgeois restaurant he could think of, he could get away from the celebrants of what now appeared to have been a disaster for the forces of order.

Dinner was especially solemn. He saw three or four other diners, men he recognized but who barely acknowledged him as he passed to follow the waiter to one of the many empty tables, where he sat alone. The noise from the street, shouts, loud singing, drums beaten furiously penetrated this usually very quiet dining room. His waiter was as efficient as ever, but unusually silent, his face betraying no emotion except a quick jerk of the head at an unusually loud banging sound nearby.

Bougainville wasn't even aware of what he was eating, barely touched anything but the wine, lingering for what must have been hours. He left a generous tip after the noise outdoors seemed to have died down and stepped out into the street.

He must have stopped somewhere else on his way home for a drink. He didn't really remember, but somehow he had got a little drunker than he had been. He waved away the women in the shadows offering their services and stumbled home. As he drew nearer to his apartment, he thought again of the article he must write for the next day's paper. 'Montmartre a Hell' He laughed at the irony of how the day seemed to have turned out.

Victorine was not in the apartment. Not in bed, not in the sitting room, not there at all. He didn't know whether he should be surprised. He lit a cigar to make himself more alert and sat down to write a new draft of tomorrow's article.

He had nearly finished when he heard a noise at his door, and two voices, a man's and a woman's. Then the door closed and he saw it was Victorine. Whoever had accompanied her to this point had been left outside. Bagou looked up at his clock. It was nearly 4 a.m.

"And where have you been, young lady?"

"Oh, René-Pierre! You know. Such an exciting day. Such partying! I was with some of the nicest, politest National Guardsmen you ever saw. So shy! But so brave. Did you know what has just happened, maybe half an hour ago? The whole government has departed! Carriage after carriage, with everyone important, heading for Versailles!"

"The government fleeing? And you were partying with the National Guard?"

"Oh, René-Pierre! They were so nice. And they really wanted to dance."

"*Putain!*"

Paris libre

Rue Saint Honoré, 1ᵉ arrondissement (early)

The bright sun and somebody shaking his shoulder told Étienne that the night had ended and that he had fallen asleep on the street, his kepi crushed under his head and his guardsman's tunic twisted around him. Slowly he sat up at the foot of a crude barricade that he vaguely remembered helping to build, along with five or six other guardsmen, by grabbing chairs from the corner cafés to pile atop the paving stones. Laughing and paying no heed to the protests of the cafés' owners.

And then drinking and singing and dancing, to drums, bugles, an accordion, even a squealing bagpipe *cabrette*, jaunty tunes interrupted from time to time by the more solemn chorus of the *Marseillaise*, or *La Canaille*, or even the angry plaint of the *Chant des Ouvriers*. Singing, Étienne and others laughed at their own insolence, with no policeman to stop them from playing the forbidden tunes. After several long swigs of cheap wine, Étienne surprised even himself by an exhibition of steps and leaps he'd seen in the cheap cabarets, the *goguettes* of Lyon.

As he lay there in the sun, eyes closed, he thought back to the strange, exciting night that had ended that wonderfully exhilarating day. And then that girl, that woman he should say because she was at least three or four years older than he. In the red gown, stunningly attractive. Not like Rose, but from another world, the world of show business and expensive clubs. She had singled him out, to his great surprise, young, and awkward as he knew he was. He was expecting her to make him the butt of a joke. But her laugh was friendly, and she said – at least, this is what he understood– that she would teach him to dance like civilized people, the Paris way.

Then after a first bounce to the music, and another one, at the climax of a chorus she lifted one leg so high, and her skirt opened so wide, that he glimpsed – everything!

He almost fell backward from her sudden motion and his fright.

But then, not at all sure of the cues and not quite in balance, doing what he thought she wanted, he lunged toward her, arms open to embrace. But she pushed him back, hard.

"Quiet now, *mon grand beau garçon*," she said.

Was she joking? "My tall handsome boy." No woman had ever called him that before. Handsome. Could it be true?

Now, embarrassed, confused and encouraged, all at once, he said, "I beg your pardon, mademoiselle. I meant no harm. I just thought…"

"*Mademoiselle?*" she laughed, and then with a big sweep of her arm, "And now you're begging my pardon! With that, oh, so sweet, southern accent! Young man, you are just too exceedingly polite!"

And she laughed again.

She was making him extremely nervous, this elegant, perfumed woman with large black-rimmed eyes, green eyelids and a teasing pucker of red lips. Another guardsman stepped over and shouted.

"Is that, is that Victorine? Victorine Martin? You look just like her. No, it is her! Look, fellows, it's the girl in the posters!"

She just smiled, neither denying nor confirming, and danced and drank with others during the night, but always coming back to Étienne, as though they had some understanding.

She kept him torn between desire and fear for hours, until at last they were interrupted – to his great relief. A commotion up the street caused the gay music to stop and made them all look up.

There they saw mounted men with drawn sabers pushing their way through the revelers, opening a path for a string of three closed carriages, one after the other, that rumbled cautiously over the broken street, jouncing over its missing paving stones, in the direction of the gate to Versailles.

"That will be Thiers himself in that biggest carriage," said a man near Étienne, as though he could possibly know who was behind the drawn curtains in that or the other carriages.

"Then the old man is up late," said someone else.

"Or early!" cried another voice. "He's got to look after his chickens. It must be nearly four in the morning!"

"Oh," cried Victorine, grabbing Étienne's arm. "Can it really be that late? Then I really must go."

And Étienne, as polite as always, and hoping to make up for any offense and also reluctant to give up this excitement, offered, or even insisted, on escorting her on what turned out to be a long walk westward, through other noisy streets until entering a posh arrondissement with wider streets and bigger, more substantial houses, almost palaces, streets with gaslights all ablaze but no signs of partying, and certainly no barricades. And most surprisingly for such a bourgeois neighborhood, no policemen, as Étienne was sure there would have been on any normal night.

After a reeling walk past dozens of street corners, they reached the door of a large brick building of three floors, where this woman in red, this pulsating package of temptation, stretched up on tiptoe to kiss him quickly on the cheek before slipping inside, and Étienne, after mumbling "Goodnight," turned around, to begin his walk back to more friendly territory. Somehow, in a half-drunken daze, he found his way back to the barricade he remembered helping construct. And there he had fallen asleep, feeling safe and surrounded by his comrades.

And now it was morning, maybe seven or later. Étienne got himself up and straightened his tunic and swung his crushed kepi onto his head and waved to his barricade comrades, and then, still woozy, began working his way through the streets and across the first bridge over the Seine to the Left Bank, and on toward home, where he hoped to find his Rose. After his sensations last night, he really needed her embrace, to finish with her what that Victorine woman had got him so excited about.

"*Vive la république!*" came a shout from behind another makeshift barricade.

"*Vive la commune!*" he shouted back.

Was he really a "beau garçon"? He laughed at the idea and imagined its implications. He wondered if Rose could see him that way.

And then another thought: Had they really defeated the government in their defense of the cannons? Had they won, finally? After the siege and all the disappointments, had they really been joined in their revolt by the very soldiers sent to suppress them?

Yes! He laughed. And had he really been dancing with a beautiful actress whose picture was on theater posters all around town? Yes again, he congratulated himself.

He remembered that fierce dragon curled above the entrance to the courtyard where he used to live, and imagined that it was laughing *with* him, not *at* him. He decided that it was his secret ally, *un beau dragon*, just as he was a *beau garçon*.

And he remembered that he had a woman now, a real woman of his own. The actress had been fun, and exciting, but he didn't need her. As he started up the stairs to the apartment and his cot, he forgot that he was sleepy. But not too sleepy to embrace his Rose. Who must have her own story of the day and the night before.

But his Rose, his woman, was not there. Now, besides feeling frustrated, he was worried. But also very, very sleepy. He stretched out, collapsed, on their bed without even unlacing his boots. Wondering where his Rose could be.

* * *

Rue Perronet, 16ᵉ arrondissement

A chatter of birds outside his window woke Bougainville. He blinked and lifted his head from his writing desk. His big clock now told him it was already past seven.

Victorine had ignored his angry outburst last night and simply thrown herself onto the bed, still in her red party gown, and René-Pierre had neither energy nor conviction to say or do anything more. He had known she was a flighty thing, that grisette. And ungrateful. It was he who had rescued her from what was sure to be a life of poverty, after hearing her sing one night in a *café-conç*. It was he who had guided her into the theater, with his contacts with impresarios and theater managers. She had been useful to him as an amusing adornment, good to have on his arm when he appeared in public, and she had indeed attracted attention and comments on his good taste and seductive abilities.

But she was not what he needed now, in these turbulent times.

So turbulent he didn't know what he needed. He faced the impossible task of writing an article on events he couldn't comprehend and refused to accept. How to start? He had only the vaguest idea of what had happened yesterday. Only that it had been the end of something.

His career would depend on this article. Not just the words but more than that, the tone, the angle. He would have to be cautious not to offend, but whom should he avoid offending? If the revolutionaries really were in charge, he dared not insult them, not yet, but he certainly could not afford to offend Thiers and the army! He would as always be ambiguous and cautious, but he should not be so cautious as to appear neutral and thus useless. His policy had always been to be on the winning side, ever alert to the shifting of forces, aligning himself by implication more than direct statement, always leaving himself room to twist and realign as necessary.

But, which was the winning side today, and which might be tomorrow? The Government? The good, bourgeois battalions of the National Guard or the other battalions, those of the murderous rebels?

It was much too late for an article to appear in today's paper. But for Monday he must surely have something.

If only he could talk to those two captains, Laurent and Robert, and other officers, but they, it seemed, must have gone to Versailles. He would have to take the train there. If it was still running. Or perhaps he could find his old friend the police chief of the Quinze-Vingts, if he was still in town.

Bougainville knew he was considered an opportunist, that was part of what was implied by that odious nickname they had given him, '*Bagou*'. No matter; in his mind, opportunism was just another name for realism, especially for a man trying to live by his pen. His problem now, as always, was to identify the right opportunity.

* * *

Belleville (mid-morning)

Alphonse-Marie Bertrand awoke, startled when some noise broke the spell of his furious, joyous dream. He felt that he had been winning a race, excited and exhilarated, far ahead of the bad people pursuing him and laughing at them. It took him a moment to realize where he was, on his narrow cot in – where was this? A woman's voice, familiar, made his scattered impressions fall into place.

Yes, now he remembered, he was in Belleville. In the midst of a revolution. He was lying in the back of the house of a bronze worker and his wife, Louis and Henriette. In Belleville, no less! Famous Belleville, the very center of revolutionary fervor.

The Fates were on his side. He had come to Paris with no more idea than to bring his pen to where there were the greatest number of newspapers.

Then he had found this lodging simply because it was the cheapest he could find.

And now his perch was perfect, a room in a bronze-worker's house in Belleville, this famously revolutionary working-class quarter. On high ground with easy access to the center. With some of the most active National Guard battalions and, as he had seen yesterday, the most vigorous and determined revolutionary women.

He could hardly believe what was happening. Revolution; *Le monde à l'envers* – The world turned upside down.

Rather than a foot race as in his dream, what was happening around him was more like a mass stampede. An upheaval, greater than 1830, or '48, the year he was born. Maybe as great as the Big One, the Revolution of 1789, the end of the Old Regime. Or greater even, because this was the nineteenth century, century of lightning-fast movements of men and ideas by rail and telegraph and even balloon, of industry, scientific miracles like photography, art. And again, like those other great revolutions, this one was happening in Paris, the very center of the modern world.

And here he was, Alphonse-Marie Bertrand, *le petit Phonse* as he had been called, a smallish young man from a small city on the northern fringe of France, here in Paris, the very center of the vortex, to record and celebrate these world-transforming events for all humanity. Instead of being just another ink-shitter spilling out words for 2 sous a line, he would be the author of an epic to be remembered for generations! A verse drama worthy of Victor Hugo. He would call it *Le chant à la liberté*.

And also, here was that perky girl he had seen many times and would really like to get to know better. And as he had learned yesterday, her father was a company commander in the Guard.

* * *

In the house of that perky girl, next door to the little house of Henriette and Louis where Alphonse had just awakened, Rose was already up and about. As she had been since dawn. She could feel the excitement in the air in Belleville, a cautious but joyous excitement. A most welcome break in the tension and the anger and the frustrations of the months of the siege, defeats, and then the humiliation of watching the enemy Prussians parade right on the Champs-Élysées.

Now, after their victory, the victory of people like her and like all her neighbors in Belleville and Ménilmontant, Rose herself felt happier and more alert than she had in months. And eager to get back to Rue Mignon, to her Étienne. Was he all right? She thought he must be, there had been so little violence on Montmartre, except for that sad shooting of the generals, but she had no idea what had happened with his battalion. She knew he must have marched with them, and she hoped that battalion, too, had had great successes in guarding the cannons.

Up here in Belleville, the worried faces were gone and she even saw some neighbors smiling and laughing. She watched two men she knew greet each other and embrace, congratulating each other, she supposed, for yesterday's victory. One of them, a locksmith, was still in his National Guard tunic, unbuttoned and with a non-regulation red scarf knotted around his neck. She watched the two of them exchange tobacco, laughing before interrupting their chat with curses and obscene gestures against 'that traitorous government', which was her view also. A government that had tried to steal the people's cannons, including cannons her own father had forged! And, worse than the attempted theft, the government's raid had caused the deaths of some Guardsmen and civilians, including the brother of one of her closest friends, and that older sentry everybody was talking about who had been guarding the cannons on Montmartre when the first troops arrived. And there must have been other casualties.

But despite the deaths, people were celebrating and remembering how the soldiers, up and down the line, had refused orders to fire on the people. Rose was especially pleased to hear her own mother sing again, for the first time since before the beginning of the siege. Her father had been in a serious, determined mood this morning, and had dressed himself carefully in his dark blue Guard tunic, which meant to Rose that this must be a very special day for him, too. He had kissed her, and his wife, and then with a sly smile that seemed to say that he was up to something, had started down the road to town, with Louis their neighbor and two or three other men from the neighborhood.

She waited until Blanche had paused in her singing, and dutifully asked her if she needed help preparing their Sunday meal. But Blanche said no, that wouldn't be necessary today, her Jules had come home safely, and she knew she was anxious to get back to her boy down in the city. Jules had gone off with Louis, Henriette's husband – as Rose already knew – so she would be eating with their neighbor Henriette, in Henriette's kitchen.

So Rose did not have to wait any longer. And she wondered if she should try to carry out the impossible mission that the soldier had given them yesterday. Not Émile, the soldier they knew from before, but the other one who said he was from Lyon.

He had asked Rose to carry a message to his *petite amie*, to tell her that 'Momo' had survived, and that he would find her and to make her his woman. The nervous young soldier had searched for something for Rose to give his lady love, some token, and finally tore off the insignia from the front of his kepi with the number of his old regiment. "Tell her it is from Maurice, no, from Momo," he repeated, "and that I love her and will find her."

* * *

Quartier des Quinze-Vingts, 12e arrondissement (just before noon)

For only the third time in his entire career, Mireau had spent the night in his commissary. Those two earlier nights had been just in the last year, first in September when news came of the fall of the Emperor and the proclamation of the Republic, and he was expecting trouble. The second time had been after the mob had seized the Hôtel de Ville on that last night of October, which was real trouble, revolution. That night he hadn't really slept at all, just left his things at the commissary and rushed with his men to assist the Mobile Guards who were assembling to retake the Hôtel de Ville. After that he had thought to leave blankets and a pillow here, just in case. And last night, for the first time ever, he had had an empty jail and an entire cell with its narrow cot, rather than the mat on his office floor. But he had hardly slept.

When he and his men had finally returned from their failed mission the day before, Mireau had been startled to see thirty or forty National Guardsmen in the street in front of the police station, shouting and waving their rifles at the stout sergeant standing before the door in his new uniform of a *gardien de la paix*, very similar to that of the Guards. Mireau was surprised by the crowd, because he had imagined that all the National Guards would be occupied by the defense of their cannons and had not imagined an assault on the police.

The policeman guarding the door was Dussardier, one of Mireau's biggest and steadiest men, fortunately. He had one hand on the handle of the revolver in his belt, the other holding a club behind his back. His belly and chin were thrust forward and legs wide, braced to repulse an attack.

Mireau, despite weariness from their march, lunged forward, interposing himself between the company of Guards and his lone sergeant, and bellowed.

"Guardsmen! Citizens! Which of you is in charge here?"

Holding his rifle in his left hand, at the ready but not pointing at anybody, he had scanned their faces. Many were familiar to him, and he knew the names of several. He stood alone before them, with only the sergeant, Dussardier, behind him. Seeing that the dozen policemen who had returned with him were a pitifully inadequate force if there were to be a combat, he gestured for them to remain where they were. Police and National Guards stood eying each other warily.

After a moment, a scrawny red-haired man in the dark blue tunic and kepi of the Guard, rifle in hand, stepped forward and announced,

"I. I, Édouard Garnier, engraver, am the elected captain of this company of the National Guard. We demand that your prisoners be released."

"Very good, Captain Garnier. Congratulations on your election," Mireau said calmly.

Garnier grinned and waved his head from side to side. He looked unsure what to do next, Mireau thought. He would try to keep him off balance. But the men behind him reminded Garnier of his mission.

"The prisoners! The prisoners!"

"The prisoners," repeated the engraver Garnier. "We want you to release all your prisoners."

"Oh? And which prisoners are you interested in? The house-breakers, the cut-purses or the assassins?"

"The political prisoners!" shouted the captain.

Mireau half-turned his face toward his sergeant behind him.

"Brigadier Dussardier, how many prisoners are we holding at present?"

"Just two, Commissioner. One drunk and disorderly, and another one, also disorderly, who was in a brawl the night before last and injured a man with a bottle."

"Anyone arrested for political offenses?"

"No, sir. If they have any political opinions, they've kept them to themselves. One of them was singing a rowdy song about the Emperor, though."

This caused a laugh among the guardsmen. Mireau was silent for a moment, studying their faces. They were in a celebratory mood.

"We already chased the army away!" shouted one. "We're not afraid of the police!"

Now Mireau laughed.

"No, nor should you be. You men of the National Guard and we of the Paris police have the same mission, to keep peace and order in our city. Isn't that right, Captain Garnier?"

The guard captain seemed startled by this question. Then he found his answer.

"Our mission is to defend the republic!"

"Then we are of the same mind, my good man, for that is our mission also, the mission of the police and of the National Guard. The police are defenders of public order, and now in these changing times, that means defending the republic.

Therefore we must work together. And if you, Captain Garnier, are prepared to accept the responsibility, I will release these two prisoners to your custody. To keep a watch on them so as not to create any new disorders. Agreed?"

"You're going to release them?"

"If you accept the responsibility," Mireau replied sternly.

"Release them to us!" shouted the men.

Mireau nodded, and turning to Brigadier Dussardier, with another gesture of his head, said, "Go unlock their cells, my man."

The face-off with those Guardsmen had been tense, and the situation was bound to become more difficult. No messenger had yet reached him with any orders, but he feared that all the Paris police might be withdrawn. To Versailles. Still, until such order came, it was his duty to defend this quartier. He had just ordered one of his men to fetch some breakfast and was considering whether to talk to the mayor of the arrondissement, and whether there might be a chance to work with some of the National Guards, when the journalist René-Pierre Bougainville appeared in his office.

This was a surprise, but not unwelcome. He must have news of what was happening in other parts of the city.

Bagou was clearly agitated, perspiring but oddly euphoric.

"What a day that was yesterday, eh? But the strange thing, this morning after all that rioting the streets are calm and the cafés are open, almost like any normal Sunday, though some of them have pretty damaged furniture. The barricades we saw yesterday have mostly been dismantled, and I didn't have any trouble hailing a cab, though it had to go slowly around some of the rubble. Even the omnibuses are running. Just like, or almost like, a normal Sunday."

"And what brings you here, René-Pierre?"

"I was worried that I wouldn't find you here. I didn't see any police officers anywhere – a café owner told me that the new prefect ordered them to withdraw to Versailles. But then, I'm not really surprised to find you, *Monsieur le commissaire*, in your police station, at your post. Always on duty, my good *quart d'oeil*. But you'll be leaving soon, I suppose?"

"This is my city. Where I was born, where I have lived all my life. And this quartier is my responsibility."

"But you will have no support."

"Well, we'll see."

"Anyway, I'm glad I found you. I really need some information to make sense of all that happened yesterday. It seems that everything went badly on Montmartre, at the Place de la Bastille and everywhere else I've heard about. How did it go for you and your men yesterday? You were heading to the Rue Basfroi, weren't you? Did you get the cannons?"

The commissaire snorted as though at a joke and raised his eyebrows.

"No? That was what I was afraid of. So now that the government has failed to assert its authority, what happens next? And what are you going to do?"

Mireau told him sketchily only the main point, that the populace had so firmly defended their cannons that the army captain in command of the troops decided to withdraw. No lurid details about the captain being unhorsed, and nothing about that list of subversives he had been charged with arresting. Instead, he told him of his plans to meet with the district's mayor and that he had already spoken to a local Guard captain, a bronze worker.

"A captain in the National Guard? Do you know what those people are up to? You can't trust the National Guard! They've taken over the Hôtel de Ville! There were armed men at the doors, some kind of assembly they were having. They're probably still there.

"Bronze? And your man you said is a bronze worker? Those fellows are especially dangerous. Lots of radicals in the foundries."

"Engraver. He's well respected by his men, which is why they elected him. He has promised his cooperation in keeping order."

"But they're the pirates, those National Guard rebels! Savages! They've murdered at least two generals!"

"Murdered? Two generals? Where did you hear that? How do you know?"

"It's all over town! It will be in the papers tomorrow. In Montmartre, I think it was."

Mireau just looked at him for a long minute.

"All the more reason for the police, and this commissaire, to remain in place. The mayors, and I and my men, the few remaining, are the only government authority left."

Bougainville shook his head.

"You mean the only ones who can hold back the rebel units of the National Guard. Which is damned near all of them, at least here in the eastern districts, it seems."

"And you, René Pierre? Perhaps you can file a report on conditions here. The government of the National Assembly should be kept informed."

"A report? Yes, maybe. But if things go on as they have, and you and the mayors don't manage to bring some order in the next few days, we may all have to head for Versailles. Yes, really. It is a dreary thought, I admit. Well, we'll see. It's something to keep in mind."

* * *

A café near the Hôtel de Ville

"Hey, Julot, don't look so disappointed. Just because they voted down our proposal. You've got to admit, things are moving very fast! We've got Paris, and the rest of France is bound to rally to our side, no matter what that new government of Thiers tries to do."

"I don't know about that. I agree with Jules, and so do you, Didier. We all voted with Jules. We have the men, we could strike now and do away with that cabal of landowners and monarchists and sycophants in Versailles."

"Yes, we could, that's pretty clear. We've already seen that the troops they've got aren't going to fire on other Frenchmen, I agree with you, Gustave. And Jules, of course. We all agree. But you heard their argument, that's it not up to us in Paris to decide for all of France."

"Ridiculous. If not us, the working people of the biggest and most important city in the country, then who should take the lead? Who do you want to do the deciding?"

"I know, I know. I was just repeating what they said, those lawyers or journalists or whatever they are. And they talk so fine, they had a lot of the workers convinced."

"Now is the time to strike. You know that, Didier, and you, Gustave. Before those clever politicians and their allies have a chance to get their defenses together. We've got to persuade all the battalions, especially the ones with workers like us. I know, I've been through insurrection before. He who hesitates is dead."

"Calm down, Jules. There's still time. And we're going to have elections to our Commune. Then we'll be a real government, and we can make responsible decisions and call on our comrades in all the other cities to support us!"

Jules Durand smiled at last, studying the faces of his companions, Didier the locksmith, Gustave the printers' devil, and Louis, his neighbor and coworker in the foundry, who had not said a word since they had left that assembly of the Guard's Central Committee. Not surprising, that silence and the uncertain comments of the others.

They were all having to cope with an entirely new situation. The Central Committee itself, for the Guardsmen to run their own affairs, had been invented only two and a half weeks ago. And it was just four days ago, three before yesterday's confrontation with the army, that the delegates at the big National Guard rally in the Vauxhall, including Jules, had disavowed the general named by the Thiers government and voted to name Giuseppe Garibaldi as their top commander!.Too bad that Garibaldi had turned them down, Jules thought. The new man they had elected, Lullier, talked a good fight but he had refused demands that they march on Versailles and do away with that shameful government once and for all. A bad decision, in Jules Durand's mind.

He lifted his glass, studying it for a moment, before declaring, with an ironic smile,

"To the Commune!"

Song of liberty

What was driving Bougainville to distraction was that people seemed to be going along as normal, even better than normal. How could this be, with no uniformed police, the government fled to Versailles, and not even any of the soldiers that during the siege had been everywhere, at their posts and barricades and interrupting street traffic with their maneuvers? Almost the only uniformed men to be seen now were those National Guards, with or without rifles, some just strolling around, and a few men in army uniforms, mingling with the mutinous Guards in diabolical fraternization. This was terrible! Who now was going to catch the crooks, the thieves, the murderers? Because it was the thieves and murderers who were now in charge!

Something had to be done, and Bougainville sincerely hoped someone would do it. It was not for him, of course, to take up arms against this mob. Which was not just a huge gang of pseudo-soldiers, their uniforms awry and their kepis askew and chewing or smoking or spitting or drinking, and laughing, especially at ordinary, properly dressed civilians such as he. No, it was not just them. It was also the general working and especially the non-working populace, ragpickers and bums, men and boys and, worst of all, the harridans who had bubbled up out of their filthy slums in unprecedented numbers into the most elegant avenues and parks of Paris, nasty, foul-mouthed wenches, young and old, in this city that had always been famed for its beauties and the courtesies of the fair sex.

They were contaminating everything, these rebels. Even his Victorine, who he now saw reverting to her slum origins in speech patterns and attitude. After all his efforts and expense. He should have known, he had seen the signs, when she had laughed so uproariously and rudely at the Christmas party, singing her bawdy songs and spilling wine all over that general and his lady! And then, when the mad mob took over the city, dancing all night with one of them. In a street party with those mutinous Guards. She is just one more of them, that disgusting rabble that calls itself 'the people'. As though they alone were people.

* * *

Alphonse had also noted that the ordinary routines of life were resuming, almost as they had been before the war and the siege. Or better. He had been able to write these observations in *Le Rappel*, where he suggested that people seemed happier now, not just that the bombing and the food shortage were over, but also that they no longer had the Empire pressing down on them, with its heavy-handed clamping down on protest or even any rowdy fun. The people were in a new, freer mood: workers headed toward their recently re-opened workshops with a light step, sometimes humming or singing, bakers still worked through the night to prepare fresh bread for the break of day – now without wood shavings mixed in the flour – shopkeepers stood outside their shops beckoning clients, and the crowds in the wine shops, mostly but not exclusively men, could be heard laughing and sometimes breaking into song before going back to arguing over politics. Even the omnibus drivers had mostly resumed their scheduled routes, as more of the streets damaged by Prussian bombardment were being repaired by men in blouses happy to get back to work. All this activity with no officials to inspect or fine for infractions, no *agents de paix* to interfere, no higher authority whatever to settle disputes – except the National Guard, which was to say, the people themselves. The Commune, once in place with its elected councilmen, would establish order, an order in which every man – and every woman, too, Alphonse supposed – would feel and be free.

On the eve of elections to the Commune Council, Alphonse tried to sum up the busy, breathless week. Breathless not just for Paris, but for the world, because Paris was Europe's banking hub, the heart of a global empire and – Alphonse had no doubt – the way-maker of humanity's entry into the modern age.

So much was happening so quickly. It was only a week ago, on Saturday 18th, that the people had routed the army and the government. On the next day, the National Guard had given itself a new commander and proclaimed city-wide elections to a Commune, originally scheduled for the following Wednesday, 22nd – impossibly rushed. Many, especially in the most bourgeois arrondissements around the city center – the First, Second, Third and Ninth –and also in the even richer western Sixteenth feared chaos, mayhem, disorder. They were convinced that their property would be seized and wasted, their streets and homes would be unsafe, rowdies, rapists and thieves unchecked. Some saw no hope and prepared to flee – the trains were still running to Versailles, no one knew for how long, and from there they might escape to some other more tranquil place. Many of those enemies of the commune, though, were determined to hang on, calling on their mayors to assert their scant authority and to call back the government now in Versailles. And among them, some urged their sons to take up arms against the rabble in the rebellious National Guard units, who –they were convinced – would flee in panic at the first sign of serious resistance.

Meanwhile, on Monday after the Saturday insurrection, the mayors of a dozen arrondissements had traveled to Versailles to negotiate a peaceful accord between the city and the government, and – though the papers didn't say this directly, Alphonse inferred it – the National Assembly delegates had scorned and laughed at their pretensions. The government of Thiers and the rural majority in the Assembly had made it plain that they did not deign to negotiate with savages and assassins, the murderers of army generals, led by drunkards and foreign agents stirring the urban rabble to revolt. That was how *Le Gaulois*, for one, described it.

Then came an event that Alphonse had witnessed. On Tuesday a gang of fancy-dressed bourgeois, calling themselves 'The Friends of Order', had marched through the fancy neighborhoods, brandishing weapons and shouting slogans and demanding a boycott of the elections. And again the next day, but then when a Guard patrol blocked their path on the Boulevard des Italiens, some of them started firing. And then so did the Guards. The result: Two dead and seven wounded among the Guards, and fifteen dead and about ten wounded among the protesters. And elections postponed to the following Sunday, tomorrow.

The second confrontation Alphonse had written up, and a report in the press carried his by-line. It had been amazing, he wrote, to see those aristocrats, 'so contemptuous of our common people that they thought they could intimidate our National Guards by their bravado and shotguns'. After that, more of those rich folks in the most affluent quartiers packed up and fled the city – to their country villas, one supposed. Good riddance.

* * *

Bougainville had not himself witnessed the confrontation, though he had seen the gang of excited bourgeois men and boys, mostly young men, waving sword-canes and rifles and marching toward a National Guard post on the Rue de la Paix, as they shouted "Down with the Commune! Long live the Assembly! Hurrah for the party of order!"

He had sensed that there would be a confrontation, very likely with gunfire, and had decided that it was his duty, as a journalist, to stay away. After all, a dead man or a seriously wounded one could hardly write great prose.

He was right: there were shots, a dozen or more. He waited a few minutes, to be sure that things were calmer, and cautiously approached. He saw some weapons scattered on the street, and two or three guards carrying a body of a man dressed as a bourgeois, he could only imagine what indignities they had in mind for that poor corpse.

His note on the affair, which he sent to *Le Gaulois* now hastily relocated in Versailles, was headlined 'THE ASSASSINS', and included what he considered his best most portentous lines:

'Paris is in the hands of a horde of brigands.'

'All the legal authorities have abandoned it to those drunken scoundrels...'

* * *

Étienne was spending much of his time in rallies of the National Guard and in the political club nearest him. Rose was also getting her head filled with revolutionary ideas, some from the men who frequented one or another of the Marmite's four canteens in different working-class neighborhoods of the city, and even more from the women she worked with in the kitchens and in the Ménagère. She and Étienne were convinced that this was the moment to unite all their countrymen, that the Paris Commune would be the heart of a great federation of communes in the radical cities of Marseilles, Lyon, Toulouse and others.

A poster pasted on walls in the Sixth Arrondissement, including one right in Dragon Court and another near Étienne and Rose's place on Rue Mignon, announced the reopening of Étienne's old bindery, and called for the workers to return. He considered it, for a moment. But then he thought no, he had nothing more to learn from old Perrin, if he was still in charge. And the activities of the Guard – not just forming and drilling, but now constant meetings and discussions – hardly left him any time.

* * *

Over the next week Alphonse returned to the Durand home half a dozen times, to listen to Blanche's colorful accounts of her life and stories about the neighborhood and how it had changed.

Some of what the good lady said he couldn't really follow, partly because of some odd Belleville expressions, her way of swallowing syllables and leaving sentences uncompleted, as though anybody listening was supposed to understand her references to things and people from long before his time. She wasn't ancient, this woman, not even quite as old as Alphonse's mother, and he could still see traces of the beauty she must once have been. But she was of a different generation, a radically different political generation that had lived the revolution of '48, and had a different way of seeing the world. He sometimes thought she was laughing at him.

One incident he almost understood, because she referred to it more than once, although she half hid her words as though embarrassed. He gathered that she had met Jules at a barricade in the revolution of '48, when both were teenagers, fifteen or sixteen they must have been. 1848 was the year Alphonse was born, the year of revolutions across Europe. Even in Lille, according to his father's accounts.

He enjoyed these conversations, especially for the colorful expressions for dialogues to enliven his epic *Le chant de la liberté*. He had at first been hoping to catch the attention of her attractive daughter, whom he had seen only a few times. That girl always seemed to be in a hurry – she had some sort of job 'in the city', her mother said.

Belleville had been part of Paris for over a decade, but Blanche still spoke of it as a village just outside the city.

And then, as though not giving it any importance, she mentioned her daughter's boyfriend, a nice young *Fédéré* down in the Sixth – the term now used for those National Guards who had rallied to the support of the Commune, because there were some who had not. Perhaps he should become one if he wanted to get a girlfriend up in this revolutionary neighborhood. Oh, well, he was sure to find someone, he thought, to share his opinions and his bed in these revolutionary times. And if not here in Belleville, where? Meanwhile, he would continue gathering anecdotes of Belleville and taking notes.

* * *

Meanwhile, in what Blanche called 'the city', in the neighboring Tenth Arrondissement, spontaneous gatherings in political clubs and on street corners and plazas were all calling for the 'Commune' – which could mean many things. Events in Paris and far beyond, Alphonse believed were proving that the rising of the common people was unstoppable, its tremors spreading across France. Especially in its largest cities, and especially in the south. Communes had been proclaimed in Marseille and Lyon, in Narbonne and Saint-Étienne, and then in Toulouse, even before Paris. But now at last, Paris would elect the leaders of its Commune tomorrow, Sunday, 26th March.

What that 'Commune' would be like, in this city, surrounded by Prussians and with its government in flight, could only be determined by practice. The revolutionary violence of the communes of 1789 and '92 was not what Blanche or anyone else he had talked to in Belleville wanted, but there were other elements in the city and some candidates for the Commune's council who might be ready for that. Some of the Blanquistes, for example. And that fiery editor Pyat had seemed bloody-minded in his articles. A system of equality and wealth-sharing that would allow all citizens to live in material comfort, and a free school system independent of the clergy, were the aspirations most loudly voiced in those clubs and rallies. To realize them would require a municipal government independent of the monarchists and rural landlords dominating the National Assembly in Versailles, which was opposed to all those things.

He was so excited by this prospect he thought he must put this great experience in verse, for his epic 'Song to Liberty'.

* * *

Sunday, 26th March, in Belleville, Jules Durand was up earlier than usual and with more than usual excitement. He and his company would be the security detail of National Guard at the mayoralty of the Twentieth. He knew who his candidate would be, a worker like himself and one he knew personally. The Twentieth Arrondissement, Belleville and Ménilmontant, because of its large population could elect five councilors. And he had pretty much convinced Blanche of which men he should support. She of course could not vote, but his vote would be for the two of them. They had debated, because he wanted her to believe he had made the right choice.

Flourens had to be one of them, he was convinced. She knew personally the shoemaker Trinquet, and liked him, so Jules added that name to his list. Ranvier, because he had been in the take-over of the Hôtel de Ville. The others he wasn't sure of.

She had prepared his breakfast and felt proud to be part of this process, through her husband. But their daughter had surprised them this morning, as Jules was straightening his tunic and preparing to march out to the mayoralty. She had come up to their place very early, after a heated discussion with Étienne.

"Why is it just the men who are voting?" she asked, the same question she had asked Étienne. "Isn't the Commune going to be for the *citoyennes* too, as well as the *citoyens*?"

Jules frowned hard as he tried to think how to answer her.

"The Commune will be for everybody," Blanche interjected. "That's what 'Commune' means. In common, for the common good, for everybody."

"Then why are only men going to make all the decisions?"

Jules didn't know how to answer. Neither had Étienne, which disappointed her, because Rose had more hope for him. He obviously had not read very much of that tract from the Association for the Rights of Women that he had been supposed to be binding, before J-P's death.

But Rose had; at her insistence, he had brought a packet of the unbound pages home. But even that association wasn't advocating voting for women, which seemed to her the obvious next step. Now with the Commune, when everything would be possible.

Neither man, neither her father nor her young partner, had ever really thought about this question before. Rose wondered if Jules, once he did consider it, might not realize that this daughter of his, and certainly Blanche, his long-time partner in everything, would be very reliable decision-makers, certainly wiser than some of the loose-tongued, wildly gesturing men they knew who were candidates.

"That's just the way it is," he said at last. "Women have never voted or held office, here or any place I know of. And there must be a good reason."

"Yes?" said his daughter. "And what might that be?"

He shook his head and, after a moment, said, "But you do have influence. You females have tremendous influence! On us men. Your mother knows this, certainly, the influence she has on me. And it's influence without all the risks, the insults, the shoving, the brawls we men have to face."

Jules seemed satisfied with his answer. But Rose looked doubtful.

Blanche at last joined in.

"That's true, Julot. But still, I hope our Commune will pay attention to the issues we women know best. That's why I think it would be good if we could participate directly. Women's work, family care, schooling. Not just by trusting husbands and boyfriends, who get distracted."

"Or drunk," added Rose.

"Don't worry," Jules answered. "We'll look after those things. You women will make us do it!"

* * *

Étienne, in the Sixth, had no doubts about his vote. The first name he was going to mark was 'Varlin, Eugène, bookbinder'.

In Versailles

Amant de la ville, et bon vivant. This was how Hippolyte Mireau liked to imagine himself in his ideal life. Lately though his life as a *bon vivant*, partaking of the *gaieté parisienne* of theater, cafés, and all the other excitements of Paris, was a memory more than a reality. Though still hale at forty, he was no longer a frantic youth desperate to bed every *cocotte* who seemed available; sometimes, in fact, an occasional night alone in his bachelor apartment with his pipe and books was a welcome respite. But there was another more important reason: with all the turmoil of the past two years, his official duties had rarely left him a night free either for cocottes or contemplation. But at least the possibility had always been present in Paris, the liveliest and most exciting metropolis on Earth, as fantasy if not always reality. Even in the past grueling months, he had made occasional escapes to the theatre or cafés and nights with sophisticated women which had brought him moments of laughter and even relief from the tensions on the job.

But that was yesterday. Before a messenger had brought him orders to withdraw from Paris, the only city he knew.

It took some time and a bit of shoving for Hippolyte Mireau, traveling alone with only a small satchel of personal belongings, to insert himself into one of the crowded wagons. All the trains to Versailles from the Gare de l'Ouest were packed, and as he had expected, National Guardsmen came through each wagon before the train could depart, questioning the men, nodding politely to the women, and demanding to look through any luggage. Mireau could see that they were looking primarily for men in the army, he supposed either to detain them or recruit them to the cause of the Commune. Mireau had been careful not to include anything identifying him as a police official in his bag, and probably because of his age and embonpoint was not taken for a soldier, as were some of the other men he saw pulled off the train. The National Guard riffling through everybody's luggage were not thieves, he was glad to see, but very determined to spot anyone politically suspicious – that is, not supportive of their new 'commune'.

As he stepped down from the train onto the crowded, chaotic platform with the sign 'Versailles', he felt a moment of near panic, or at least deep disappointment. How long would he be stuck in this backward encampment of the overprivileged, this collection of palaces like museum pieces in disrepair and the crumbling barracks of a dead regime, this monument to all that was stale, rigid and anti-cosmopolitan? It was a sudden exile from all that he had known all his adult life: The Empire had disappeared, the city he loved had fallen into the hands of an uncultured mob, and the government now commanding him that was of uncertain duration or direction.

He had been in the Paris police for almost as long as there had been an empire, since shortly after that day in December 1851, almost twenty years ago, when Louis-Napoléon had declared himself 'Napoléon III'. Young Hippolyte, a fervent Bonapartist almost from birth, had fired a small pistol toward a gang of young bourgeois who were protesting the coup, shouting 'Long live the Constitution'. That was in the Second Arrondissement, on Boulevard Poissonnière, he remembered. He had at least winged one of those youths, he thought, and the brigadier-major of the police at that location recruited him to the force on the spot.

Despite having no rich friends or relatives to push for him, he had risen on his merits through the ranks to his position as *commissaire* of a marginal and thus uninfluential working-class quartier, and had assumed that would be as far as he could rise. But the sudden fall of the Empire, and the perceived new threats from rebels within, combined with the improvised defense against the Prussian enemy, had shaken the whole police structure, creating vacancies and new needs. And now that Hippolyte had been pulled out of his quartier, he felt sure that he would be offered a position as *inspecteur* of the Sûreté, the fabled investigative police. A far greater challenge, very risky in these turbulent times, but with a wider liberty of action, better pay and a bigger promised pension. But so far he was without any precise instruction as to what was to be his mission in Versailles.

For this Hippolyte had given up his modest but comfortable bachelor apartment, with its familiar bed, his books and pipes and the portraits of his parents on the wall and the tinted likeness of his great uncle in the uniform of a Hussar *chef d'escadron*, a hero in the army of that first and greatest Napoleon, a heroic uncle dead before Hippolyte's birth but revered by him. And his other most accustomed things – the battered tea kettle, his well-worn slippers, trivial things perhaps but things that made him feel that the place was his. To be lodged in this barracks in Versailles, in a former stable appropriated by the Paris police in exile, where he felt little better than a teenage recruit in the army.

He had not yet unpacked his satchel and was sitting on the army cot in his cell-like room when an orderly informed him that a 'M. Bougainville' had asked for him.

He should not have been surprised. Bagou, with his sources in the police and army, must have known of the general order of the prefect for all police to depart from Paris, and would easily have found out where new arrivals were housed. Hippolyte sighed, stood and straightened his cravate, snatched up his hat and cane and stepped out to see the journalist.

"Ah, my dear Polo. Welcome to Versailles, the new capital of free France!"

"Oh, really? Where is that? Free France, I mean."

"Polo, Polo – all is not lost! This is the launching point from which we shall retake Paris, and then free France."

"From the Prussians? Or do you mean from the Parisians?"

"From both! If by Parisians you mean that rabble of beggars and ragpickers with their foreign leaders who've taken over the city, we take care of them first. And then, with Paris restored to order, we can pay the reparations, which we must do to free France. For then the Prussians will leave. But the first order of business is to free Paris. Versailles is the vanguard of the new, free France."

Hippolyte merely nodded. He was not at all confident that it would be easy to oust the armed 'rabble' nor was he happy thinking about the onerous war damages demanded by the Prussians.

"Come! It's nearly lunchtime, and I can introduce you to someone whom you will be glad to meet, one of our saviors. That is, if you don't have another appointment."

"Lunch, you say? Is there anywhere decent to eat in this town?"

"Oh, well, of course, it's not Paris, but the man who runs the place we're going to was a sous-chef at the Tortoni until last week, or so he says. In any case, it will be more appetizing than the officers' mess you'd get if you stayed here. Oh, don't look so down in the mouth, my friend! There is life in Versailles, if you know where to look for it."

As they walked, dodging army carts and even a platoon of mounted grenadiers in streets too narrow for such traffic, Bougainville proceeded to tell his friend that he had been in Versailles for a week already and had thoroughly scouted the resources. The most important was the National Assembly, the de facto government relocated here from Paris and led by Adolphe Thiers, with all the ministries and officials that that implied. And of course it was also the headquarters of the high military command, more sources for Bougainville's reporting.

The rebels in Paris had taken over the plant and printing facilities of the government's *Journal officiel*, he exclaimed.

"But of course, you knew that. The scoundrels! Pretending to be a government, using the real government's seals and equipment to publish their obscene decrees and news of further outrages."

But, he continued, the National Assembly here in Versailles has already mounted its own, authentic *Journal officiel*, so now there were two. And Bougainville was hoping to get something in that, but meanwhile he had other dailies to write for, including some still published in insurgent Paris.

"In Paris?"

"Yes. But I don't know for how long. Those outlaws masquerading as law in the city are sure to try to close down all the opposition press. But here's our restaurant.

"Ah, there you are, Captain. Allow me to introduce you.

Captain Laurent, Joseph Laurent, I believe. Right? A captain in what is in the process of becoming the new French army. He was on Montmartre on the 18th. Captain, meet my good friend, Hippolyte Mireau of the Paris police. He has just arrived in Versailles today."

The captain was a slender man of maybe thirty, a bit shorter than Hippolyte, but he held his head tipped far back so that he appeared to be looking down on him. Hippolyte extended his hand, and after some hesitation – Hippolyte wondered if the captain wasn't expecting a military salute – the captain accepted it, and all three men sat down.

Hippolyte's practised eye took in the excessively groomed mustache, the tipping back of the head, the suggestion of a smirk, and the captain's repeated movement of his eyes around the small dining salon as though watching himself being observed. A *poseur*, Hippolyte concluded. The captain made some sarcastic remark about the restaurant and its poor offerings and then fell silent.

Hippolyte wondered why they had been brought together, when Bagou explained.

"Captain Laurent has confided in me that he and other officers are facing a serious challenge now in this conflict, and I thought that a man like you, with your experience, Hippolyte, may be of some help. And the captain thought it was a good idea, correct, Captain?"

Laurent nodded.

The problem, it turned out, was that Laurent didn't trust the men under his command. The fiasco of 18th March had been a great embarrassment, as soldiers of the line refused to obey orders to fire and had even fraternized with the rebellious National Guardsmen. What he wanted was to weed out the most doubtful elements in his regiment, those who might secretly – or even openly – sympathize with the insurgents, because the day of reckoning would be coming soon.

"Then why don't you simply separate those you think are unreliable from the rest?" Hippolyte asked, although he thought he knew the answer.

Bagou tried to explain.

"Our captain is well trained in the arts of war and certainly quite effective in command of disciplined troops. But the mix of men in this new regiment, with scarcely any military experience beyond a month or so before falling prisoner, men barely literate, simple villagers confused and, we must admit, dispirited – well, they're hard for him to talk to."

Laurent's was a newly-formed regiment, composed of the remnants of other commands, including many who had until recently been prisoners of war of the Prussians. And Laurent, it appeared, had not even learned the surnames of his platoon leaders.

"That's why I suggested that he meet with you, that with your trained police eye you would be able to separate the laggards from the men most fit to serve. And thus perform a patriotic service to the cause of liberating Paris from the hoodlums who have taken it over and are doing such damage to our nation. And to our Chief of the Executive Power."

Captain Laurent seemed distracted, more attentive to the other diners who might be admiring his uniform than to either of his table companions. The conversation with such a disdainful companion was hardly agreeable and the meal, thought Hippolyte, though adequate in quantity, was hardly up to Paris standards.

Laurent seemed to have contempt for all civilians, including even a police official nearly ten years his senior, and also for the men under his command. His apparent deference to Bougainville, Mireau surmised, must be because the journalist had written a paragraph mentioning him favorably after the disaster of the 18th March, and might be expected to do so again.

Mireau considered Bagou's proposal, apparently assented to by Laurent, to sound out his troops. And after a moment and a sip of not very good wine, he agreed that that might be a good idea. It might help him foresee what Versailles, or at least its army, was planning in its confrontation with Paris. And if, as Bagou had suggested, his investigations were seen by Thiers' government as a useful service, that should serve Hippolyte in reestablishing his career and securing the position he had been seeking in Sûreté.

"If Captain Laurent will grant me liberty to interview whichever of his men seem to me deserving of attention, I would be honored," he replied.

Laurent's eyebrows went up and his mouth twisted into a mock smile.

'Deserving of attention'. Yes, indeed, and some of them certainly have been. Five days in stockade and fifty lashes for those who were the first to upend their rifles on Montmartre!"

Now it was Hippolyte Mireau who raised his eyebrows, but he made no oral comment.

"Of course!" continued Laurent. "Talk to any of them you like! And let them know what scoundrels they have been, and that they'd better obey their commanders! If there is any doubt, my sergeants can point you to the ringleaders of dissent, or let us say, those who are least enthusiastic about saving our country from those villains who have seized the capital."

Then, in a louder voice, so that all in the little restaurant could hear him, he went on.

"We, the army of France, will march in there despite their famous city walls and that ring of forts they've got, and we'll show those traitorous insurgents in that befouled and corrupted city that submission will be their only alternative to death or worse!"

This speech startled Mireau, though he allowed himself to display no emotion. His city, Paris, 'foul and corrupt'? And given the mood he had seen in Paris, not just in the Quinze-Vingts, he silently shuddered to think how many would face 'death or worse' before they would submit, if they would submit at all to a direct aggression.

"Do not be surprised, *monsieur*," said Laurent, addressing Hippolyte directly for the first time and emphasizing ironically that civilian honorific *monsieur*.

"But you are talking to an officer of the army of France, and all Frenchmen should know, that is my conviction and how I and other loyal officers see our mission.

"Or almost all of us, not like some other officers I know who are still talking of parlaying with the rebels and the masses who follow them. 'We're all Frenchmen', says – well, you know who I mean, Bougainville. Hm! 'All Frenchmen'.

"'All Frenchmen', as though those who have betrayed our legitimate government and have murdered two generals still had the right to be considered French! Especially since their leaders, half of them or more, are foreigners. Poles, Italians, the scum of Europe. And the ignorant fools who follow them, drunk on their own lunatic cries of 'Commune' herding like sheep to the slaughter. Well, slaughter they shall get!"

Mireau held his face expressionless before this saliva-spewing peroration. He was reminded of one of his earliest interrogations, of a rapist and serial murderer of prostitutes who proclaimed that all prostitutes or potential prostitutes must be killed to purify society. One just had to let such excited subjects rant on, waiting for them to subside.

Laurent at last did subside, then he laughed sharply and pulled out a handkerchief to mop his brow.

"There!" he said, as he rose from the table. "The army will see to the bill here. And you, *monsieur* of the police, may begin as soon as you like. Tomorrow. We must get those troops in shape for a serious confrontation."

He nodded to Bagou and turned to walk out of the restaurant, holding himself erect as though on parade.

"Who is that other officer he referred to?" Mireau asked Bagou. "The one who said 'We're all Frenchmen'?"

"Oh, I know who he means. That's another recently commissioned captain, a good man. And one who has seen much more action in the war than Laurent, who, just between us, managed pretty well to stay out of danger as a sub-lieutenant up in, where was it exactly? Not Alsace."

"Yes? And this other officer? Is he here in Versailles, too?"

"Robert? Oh, yes, he's here. I thought of introducing you to him, too, but Captain Robert is different. He seems to have good rapport with his men, and has even managed to learn most of their names. Or so I was told by one of his lieutenants. It's a brand-new company, so he didn't know any of them until a few weeks ago. He doesn't want an outsider talking with them."

Mireau nodded and thought about this. And then excused himself, to report to his new chief.

Thiers had named General Vinoy as the prefect of police. A man with no police experience. It was a short walk to his headquarters.

***

General Vinoy was unavailable and had left no orders for *commissaire* Hippolyte Mireau – his aide did not even find his name on a list he hastily scanned, nor – more disappointingly – any mention of a pending reassignment to Sûreté. Mireau then left a note with his name and the number of the officers' barracks where he was housed, and said he would return the next day to see if he should receive any new orders.

The next morning he was at the perimeter of the encampment of the 67th Regiment before eight. After some negotiation with the guard – as he expected, no one had been informed that he would be coming – another officer appeared, and pointed him toward the tents of Captain Laurent's company. There he found a Lieutenant Mercier, a stout man whom Mireau guessed to be about his own age, forty.

"A veteran, I see," said Mireau, his eyes and eyebrow signaling the scar running from above the man's left eyebrow to his cheek.

"Mexico," answered the lieutenant, touching the scar.

"But this is newer," he added, tugging at the scarf knotted around his neck and revealing a portion of another ugly, purple scar. "Alsace. Are you an army man?"

"No. Police. I've been assigned to sound out the morale of the troops here. Beginning with the men in Captain Laurent's company."

"Morale, you say?" Mercier laughed. "A bit down, I'd say. But they'll do as they're ordered. Come, there's a bunch of them in this tent. Men!" he shouted to them.

"We have someone here who wants to talk with you. By orders of Captain Laurent. Give him your full attention and courtesy. Whatever you're doing, suspend it now. This is official government business."

This was not what Mireau had been expecting. He would have preferred a more discreet entry, to observe the men quietly and engage a few in conversation. He began by asking the ones nearest him where they were from, if they had family back there, what it was they most missed from civilian life. Hoping that way to break the tension. Then, gradually, unobtrusively, he would sound them out about what they thought about Paris, and about their mission. It was a little different from his usual interrogations, where he was used to isolating the individual of interest, impossible in this tent this morning. Any man who spoke knew that his comrades were listening, and might snort or chuckle or cheer at any remark. Still, they permitted him to assess the mood.

It was not going to be easy under the circumstances to get a sense of what the men really thought, but he was quick to improvise when necessary. He had greeted a knot of some fifteen soldiers, some of whom were doing laundry and others cleaning or repairing their kit. He told them that he was there on behalf of the government, and wanted to become acquainted with the brave lads who had defended the homeland.

This was met with grunts and snorts, Mireau could only guess why. 'Brave lads' probably sounded to them like hypocritical flattery, though he hadn't meant it that way. Or perhaps they were unhappy about their failure to 'defend the homeland', which had just capitulated.

"And are prepared to continue to do so," Hippolyte continued nonetheless. No response. So he decided to change tack.

In as friendly and unthreatening a tone as he could

manage, he asked one after another where they were from, what life was like back there, whether they were married, and – the most optimistic query he could think of – what they imagined themselves doing after they got out of the army.

He heard names of towns he hadn't known existed, and others that he knew vaguely were in regions far from the Île de France. As for their plans for life after the army, just thinking about this brought smiles to some of their faces. None of them said 'Re-enlist'. Mostly, they hoped to take up again whatever they had been doing before the war. There were farmers, mechanics, one who wanted to be a stage-driver.

"Are any of you here from Paris?"

"You mean the city of Paris? No, no! The closest must be Jeannot here. He's from Rambouillet, right, Jeannot? That's just a half-day's ride from Paris."

"We had some, in our old regiment, fellows from Paris, but they were cut from the new regiment when we got back here. After the prison camp."

"Well," Mireau persisted, "but some of you know Paris, don't you? That is, you've visited the city, I mean before your last military operations, on March?"

The men were reluctant to speak to this, but a sergeant told him that, yes, about half of the men had been housed in the eastern quarters briefly, for a couple of weeks. But none of them really knew the city.

And what did they think of Paris? What was their opinion of the people? This question was met by embarrassed shuffling.

"Do you know what is going on there?"

No, they didn't. They hadn't seen any Paris newspapers since they had been marched to Versailles, after the 18th March.

Nevertheless, he had been surprised to spot what he thought was a familiar face, a young man he was sure he had seen in his very own quartier, in the Quinze-Vingts.

"And that fellow over there, you know him? Isn't he from Paris?"

"Prost? Why, no! He's from somewhere south, Lyon maybe."

Yes, maybe he was mistaken. This chap was a lot thinner than the one he remembered. But Mireau had doubts; he knew that he had a very good memory for faces.

* * *

That evening, back in his room in the barracks, he took out his notebook and pen to sum up what he had learned, and to prepare a more formal report for General Vinoy. He saw no point in presenting anything to Laurent.

Storming heaven

Such a festival, this celebration of the declaration of the Commune, so long anticipated! All through the city. Or almost. Even the weather has been collaborating, sunny and warm this Tuesday. Right, Hercou? Yes, I see you chuckling.

Almost all through the city, I should say, because just a couple of hours ago, when you and I traveled from the festive Sixth Arrondissement into the Sixteenth, we saw only glum faces. Hercou, you hadn't wanted even to try there, but you know me, I'm very curious, and I wanted to see how those bourgeois were reacting after the elections they had boycotted and that noisy, bloody confrontation their youth had had with the National Guards last week. So I tried out some scandalous verses, rather obscene I confess, yes, Hercou, sorry to embarrass you. Verses about that typographer Bergeret who commanded the Guard there when the shooting broke out, but all I got were some snorting grimaces and a few sous. But you and I already know that the richer the neighborhood, the less princely the emoluments, even for fine street artists as entertaining as us.

Jaw-droppingly impressive houses they have, palaces really, on those streets near the Bois de Boulogne.

But then a short walk, or a prance really because, to revive my spirits, I went with dancing step, up to the Batignolles, in the Seventeenth. What a difference! Pure joy. And then, after an hour or so and exhausting our repertoire of songs and tricks, over to Montmartre in the Eighteenth. And that was a happy, jumping, continuous party! People laughing and dancing and asking us for more and more songs. And generous with what coins they had, if only centimes. And there you were, Hercou, lifting the ladies – with the permission of their escorts, if they had them, you are also so polite, big fella – and bouncing children in the air, and lifting heavy objects until even you got tired, while everybody, even the older ladies, was dancing to our songs. Then you beat on that huge drum that the army had abandoned in Montmartre, to accompany me on my tooter as I was making up new verses to the old tunes. And the kids running around with the kepis left behind by the soldiers they had routed, and some of the men were waving canteens that the army had abandoned, the day of the cannons.

Canteens now filled with that famous wine of Montmartre, the wine that makes you piss. To piss on that poor, stupid government in Versailles, I sang. 'Diurétique' for the wine was a perfect rhyme for 'despotique' for Versailles, in my dythyrambique about the struggle, and even those who didn't know those words laughed and imitated my gestures and got the sense.

But it's growing late now and Hercou, you and I shall head down toward the center, around the Hôtel de Ville, where we expect to find a mix of glum bourgeois and elated working people. I must see those faces, too. And even if some of them are as stingy as the bourgeois further west, at least we now have some weight in the purse you're carrying, my comrade, for both of us.

* * *

In Belleville, people were also singing and drinking and dancing in celebration. And for Blanche and Jules Durand, a sense of enormous relief. Like their neighbors, they were glad that the victory of 18th March had been consolidated with a Council of the Commune, men voted into office and who could be voted out whenever the people felt betrayed or neglected.

Yes, that was very good, but, in speaking with each other, Blanche and Jules were more cautious. Especially Blanche, whose caution was quieter than his. Jules was pacing up and down in their tiny kitchen, his nervousness kept him from sitting still. They had already lived through a revolution, and knew how hard it would be to hold on to this victory.

In 1848, the joyous freedom they had felt at the barricades at the overthrow of the King and the creation of the Republic, for the first time since the brief First Republic in their grandparents' time, had led first to the presidency of Louis-Napoleon, and then his declaration of himself as Emperor Napoleon III. And then nearly twenty years of rule by the rich, the growing inequality, repression and violence against strikers, the continued stranglehold on education by the clergy, and no improvement in the lives of the growing working class in all the east and north and south of Paris. All of these things, reversals of the slogans the *sans-culottes* had fought for in 1789 and the youngsters Blanche and Julot had taken up again in '48: liberty-equality-fraternity.

This time it could be different, because far more of the working class had been mobilized, and now were armed. And because the men they had elected in this Twentieth Arrondissement, Flourens, Ranvier, Trinquet and Bergeret, were men that Jules, at least, believed they could trust. But the forces arrayed against them were also formidable.

Not the government in Versailles and its poor army. That army, Jules was more than confident, would be no serious obstacle. Those soldiers would be happy to collaborate once again against the reactionary assembly once the armed people finally agreed to march to Versailles to throw them out. The army would surely join them, join the *Fédérés* of the Federation of the National Guard, as they had on the 18th March.

But then there were those Prussians, their army and their cannons. Would they permit this revolution to succeed?

* * *

Down on the left bank, Rose and Étienne in the Sixth Arrondissement had danced all morning, with each other and with their neighbors to celebrate the event. Rose had to laugh at her partner's energetic leaps and turns, while she tried to respond with what Étienne considered a rather modest *chahut cancan*, happily revealing up to mid-calf of her unstockinged legs.

Early in the morning Étienne had pointed out to Rose that same bateleur he had seen on his first day in Paris, accompanied now by a hulking strong-man displaying muscle in sleeveless jersey and tights and fierceness with an enormous, pointed waxed mustache. The strong man didn't do much except flex and toss some children in the air, while his skinny partner in colorful costume tooted and sang songs that were hard to make out in the noise of the crowd. But then other musicians appeared, with louder instruments, including some brass and a drum from Étienne's own battalion and even the rustic cabrette and an accordion, and the bateleur and strong man disappeared.

"We have the Commune! We have the Commune!" Étienne and others shouted.

"And now?" called out one of the dancers.

"To Versailles!" came the chorus of voices.

* * *

Alphonse was joyous about today's events, but still, even after weeks of sleeping in Belleville, he felt out of place among those workers chatting about kinds of work he had never known, whether in the big bronze foundry or the slaughterhouses up in La Villette. After joining some of his neighbors in a pot of wine and smiling and laughing, pretending to comprehend jokes that sent his fellow celebrators into gales of laughter, he shrugged and grinned and slipped away. He was beginning to doubt that Belleville was really the best place for him to find a female partner, and headed down the road toward the more familiar Place du Château-d'Eau. And from there, on down to the big celebration in the square before the Hôtel de Ville. All along the way, he saw people strolling and obviously taking this Monday off from whatever work they normally performed.

When he got to the crowd in front of the Hôtel de Ville, he saw a journalist he recognized, watching and chatting in a group gathered around a pair of musicians, accordion and bagpipe. Lissa – his name was really Lissagaray, but nobody called him that – was in a very happy mood, smiling broadly when Alphonse greeted him, though Alphonse suspected that he really had no idea who he was. Alphonse told Lissa that he had read a recent article of his, and said that he too was a journalist and had written about the 31st October. At this Lissa stepped back and looked at him again. He was starting a new newspaper, he said, and maybe young Bertrand could be a contributor.

They both had noticed one young woman whose feet were twitching, obviously eager to dance. This might be the one for him, Alphonse thought. And with Lissa's encouragement, he tapped her on the shoulder and invited her, by gesture of his head and a sweeping bow, to join him in some steps.

And that, of course, led to an attempt at conversation, over the wild cheering as each of the newly elected councilmen was sworn in.

"On to Versailles!" shouted someone near them.

"Yes! We'll take heaven by storm," thundered the orator on the steps of the palace.

More cheers. Alphonse joined in, half-amused by the Bible reference, but anxious to get his new acquaintance apart from the crowd.

Tugging her elbow and gesturing, with his hand as though feeding his mouth, he got her to nod and smile. And then, a late lunch at one of the cafés a couple of blocks off the square, where, tired but excited, he could finally hear her and make himself heard.

Her exuberance, he found, was a thin cover for deeper worries. Their talk progressed from the day's events, to how wonderful it could be to have a commune, and then to how each had gotten through the months till now. She had not had work since the beginning of the siege, when her factory had closed, and she had been surviving, barely, by taking on little sewing jobs to do at home. And she had had a boyfriend, long ago, she confessed, turning her head away from him and seeming to look away to a great distance. But he, poor dear, she added abruptly, in a sharper tone, had gone off to war. She had begged him not to go, but that young man was thinking, as so many did at the beginning, that it would be a short adventure. Was he still alive? She didn't know and couldn't know, and feared the worst. But anyway, she said, trying to brighten up, that had been so long ago. Months and months. And now, well, now was now. But – and she suddenly turned morose again – was the war going to begin again, this time a civil war?

Her name was Sophie. And she seemed impressed when Alphonse told her of his writings for the papers and of his plans. Or at least she said, "Very good" and "Good for you." She knew Prosper Lissagaray, she said – Lissa, she said, knew everybody – and she thought it would be very good that Alphonse might begin working for him.

Alphonse began to feel that he was on to something.

He wasn't the man she had been waiting for, and she wasn't the girl he had been dreaming of, but, in these hard times and after all the troubles, one had to make the most of what one had. Or what she had, which included a little place over in the Second Arrondissement, not far from where Alphonse had lived when he first got to Paris and where he had met with Jules Vallès and other journalists and had made his first professional contacts.

He could say goodbye to Henriette in Belleville, he thought, leaving her a franc or two – no, one should be enough. She might be sorry to see him go, but not terribly. She would probably be glad to recover that little corner of her house, which had previously been her workspace. And he could be with a young woman who seemed to understand him and even praise him, and whose speech was more familiar, and who would be happy to be eating better with the income, modest though it was, that he hoped to count on from his journalism.

* * *

The day came at last, after weeks of build-up of enthusiasm for storming Versailles, heated again by news of Versailles' attack on the Fédéré outpost at Courbevoie, 2nd April. Men began gathering in their battalions that Sunday night, and Étienne and his battalion had formed by midnight.

Three great columns of hastily trained, variously armed, enthusiastic Fédérés set out that morning. One commanded by Jules Bergeret, together with Flourens, on the right, another under Émile Eudes in the center, another by Émile Duval on the left. Of all these new generals, only Bergeret had army experience, as an infantryman. None of them had ever commanded an army, but they had all four demonstrated their bravery in the days before 18th March and afterwards, and that was all that counted. The three columns had not bothered to deploy scouts, and took with them only a small number of cannons. Taking Versailles, for many tens of thousands of high-spirited Fédérés facing soldiers who had already shown that they sympathized with them, would be little more than a promenade.

Étienne's battalion was to be part of Bergeret's column. They assembled just before midnight, and reached the Pont de Neuilly around 3 a.m., Monday, 3rd April, on their way to Versailles. A long walk, but a spirited one, the men all eager to do away with the reactionaries in Versailles.

Bergeret arrived in a calèche, its team driven by another guard, which started some murmuring among the men who had been walking for hours from the various gathering points of their battalions. Claude, though, laughed but was not surprised – he had already heard some things about this typographer Bergeret, an army veteran who didn't know how to ride a horse.

The men were tired but happy. They had no scouts and only eight cannons in their column, but they were convinced that that night they and the other columns would be in Versailles and would have chased the rascals out.

They continued marching in the first light, approaching the fort atop Mont Valérien, which the men all assumed was theirs, when suddenly a projectile exploded in their ranks, a mortar shell containing its hundred or more steel fragments and killing, maiming and dispersing the column.

"Treason!" some shouted. They had all believed that the fort was in the Commune's hands, and that any soldiers they encountered would not fire. Another shell hit, and Étienne and the men around him began running through the fields.

* * *

Jules' battalion had no better luck. They had reached Rueil, where they were surprised by the fierce resistance and attacks, by cavalry and artillery. It was clear that they were not going to advance, and that the only way to save their army was to get back to the safety of the Paris walls as quickly as they could. Jules was part of a small group that held off the Versailles cavalry, with rifles only, long enough to let their comrades make their retreat. Then and only then did he and the men with him make their run. It was true that the Versaillais counter-attack had been stumbling and probably half-hearted, but with their artillery and cavalry, and their organization and relative discipline contrasted to the Fédérés' brave but uncoordinated struggle, they had an overwhelming advantage.

* * *

By noon, news reached Paris that the torrential attack on the government in Versailles had run into unexpected trouble.

Alphonse now knew it was time for him to take up arms. He hastily enrolled in the 92nd in the Second Arrondissement, one of the battalions summoned to answer Duval's call for reinforcements. He was new to the Guard and had never fired a rifle, but if one of the generals of the Commune was in trouble, he was ready to make whatever sacrifice was called for, and he reported to the assembly point.

But instead of being rushed to the front, he and the others – all strangers to him until now – were sent to Place Vendôme to endure patriotic speeches and conflicting orders and then simply to wait, without food or bedding, on the stones until past midnight.

Determined to do his duty, Alphonse stayed there in the cold night, sitting pressed against another man for warmth, catching himself or grasping the other when one of them dozed off. When around 2 a.m. they got the order to move on to the Place de la Concorde, they were many fewer, and with the bustle to the new location more men slipped away in the dark. To their homes, Alphonse supposed, which was where he wanted to be. The Place Vendôme was really close to the apartment where he had left Sophie. Cold and tired and hungry, and especially tired of what seemed like pointless orders, he too simply slipped away.

* * *

It wasn't until the next day and the days after that that Paris learned the full extent of the disaster.

V

Festival of Freedom

What now?

We must, we must go out again, Hercou.

Please, don't look at me like that, like you've lost, oh, I don't know, whatever. Everything. It's not true. You and I are still alive. And the Commune is, too. Yes, it is. Wounded but alive. If ever our Paris needed a little spirit, some chuckles at our jokes, a little song to lift the hearts, it is now.

Please, Hercou, please. Oh, even your mustache is drooping. We can't have that!

We won't go into the Sixteenth today, I promise you. I know you hate that. Over there they must be celebrating this tragedy, the great victory of their National Assembly over our brave men, and I couldn't stand to see that. But maybe up in Montmartre? Or Belleville?

No? That would be worse? No time for fun and jokes, you say. Or so I read your gestures. Well, maybe you're right. I don't feel like going out alone. Not today. People will not be welcoming frivolity today, and we're no good at doing dirges.

Let's see what we can find to eat. Excuse me, I'm crying.

* * *

As she gathered what news she could, in snatches, of how great had been the losses, Rose was deeply affected, saddened by the deaths especially but also by the failure of the great liberation adventure. But she could see that Étienne's reaction was stronger, more self-damaging. He had grown more and more morose. As though, having lost a battle, he felt that everything was over.

Articles in the press were contradictory, especially between the papers in Paris and those, like *Le Figaro* and *Le Gaulois*, that had moved to Versailles. Those Versailles papers, of course, reflected the views of the National Assembly, very hostile to what they called the 'assassins' and 'degenerates' of the Commune. *Le Rappel*, the Hugo family paper, still based in Paris, was much friendlier, but didn't have the kind of detail she wanted. And then there were panicked reports from survivors, none of them knowing anything beyond what they personally experienced, but often believing and repeating the wildest tales. Étienne had not wanted to say anything about what had happened, but she had managed to get out of him that there had been a bombshell and then another from the fort high on Mont Valérien, which they had thought was in friendly hands.

Le Gaulois, dated the 5th and having reached La Marmite on Larrey Street two days later, declared, rejoicing,

"Flourens killed, Duval executed, Henry a prisoner, there is hardly anything left of the insurrection but the generals Cluseret, Bergeret and Eudes. We think that in short time the same fate will fall to them."

Henry, she knew, must be Lucien, the young painter, very revolutionary and popular in the Fourteenth Arrondissement, where he had been voted chief of his battalion. She had seen him eating in the Marmite in that neighborhood, one of the four cooperative restaurants Nathalie and her comrades had set up in the city. That was sad, that he was taken prisoner, but the deaths of the two generals, Flourens and Duval, if true, were especially grievous.

There followed a florid description of Flourens, supposedly hiding out from his own men who had accused him of treachery and trying to disguise himself, until he was discovered. No word in the article of how or by whom he had been killed. Not true, was what she had heard at the Marmite, either about any problem with his men or the disguise, which everyone assured her was a ridiculous invention, but they did believe that he had been killed. And Duval, too.

Whatever and however it had happened, the loss of those men was hard. But not the end. She would have to get her Titi out of his terrible mood.

What he felt must be embarrassment, or worse, shame. Shame at having run – though he had not been alone, he had done it with all the others, and there really wasn't anything any of them could have accomplished if they had stayed there, with no cannons to fire back and hardly any other support. And no guides, and not even a clear plan. Rose was very, very glad that he had run and made it home. But he, her man, her young partner, wasn't glad.

But meanwhile, she had to get to work. If only he would get himself over to one of the Marmites, maybe the one up in the Batignolles where he might see his hero Varlin, or over to that place on Corderie Street where the International had its headquarters, to talk to people, to comrades. But he wouldn't listen to her, just sat there, looking very sad. Or angry. At himself, she supposed. He would have been proud to stand and die there. For nothing. He had wanted to be a hero.

* * *

Alphonse had conflicted feelings. He knew he hadn't deserted, but he felt rather that his whole battalion had been deserted by the men who were supposed to order them into action but couldn't make up their minds how or when, or even if. They, all those men stomping their feet and ready to go out and fight, had dithered away the whole night, wasting energies and the high morale they had started with. He had nothing to be ashamed of, but he was sorry he hadn't got into the action.

Now he felt that he needed to understand how everything went wrong, how what had seemed like an overwhelming force of men, so full of spirit, could have lost so miserably. After all, he was a journalist, and a journalist is supposed to find out things.

Sophie had just sighed and shaken her head. She had no idea how it had gone so badly, but wondered about the leadership. Had they even made a plan? she asked. And anyway, why had everybody been so anxious to attack Versailles? She didn't really care about those people, over there.

"They attacked us first!" Alphonse reminded her. "In Courbevoie, on Sunday, just before our men went out. Killed dozens of our men and took a bunch of prisoners, before we'd done anything to them."

She just shook her head and looked down, then she raised her face to look somewhere far beyond Alphonse.

"We wanted the Commune to make our lives better. I just wish they would get the factories open again. I liked my job, it was hard and we didn't make much money, but I was independent and had friends there."

Well, yes, he admitted. The Commune would have to do that, to get production going again.

"But first it has to defend itself."

She hummed, pensive, then said she had got the impression, from what she was hearing and what people told her was in the papers, that those generals of theirs had not even had a clear idea of the terrain. And those men, the bulk of the force, had gone out in the dead of night, with no scouts. It didn't make sense. And not knowing that that fort was in enemy hands.

No, it didn't, and Alphonse's experience when he volunteered to go out that afternoon, that didn't make sense either. Was somebody in the Commune council or the National Guard federation trying to sabotage them? No, he didn't dare think that. But something had to be done.

He had talked about it to Lissa, who encouraged him to try to find out, because things had to be better organized if this Commune was going to succeed. He decided to try to talk to the military experts, if there really were any. Bunch of amateurs, it seemed so far. And he would write up what he found, so that they could do things better. There was this Polish chap just named to head the cavalry, or part of it. Maybe he could get to him. They'd said at least he had military experience.

* * *

Angélique was silent. So silent, she worried Noëlle. What had happened the past two days was like Buzenval, but that had been against the Prussians. These were Frenchmen killing other Frenchmen, all because of some stupid debate between the generals on each side. It was as though Versailles had assumed the burden of the war that the King of Prussia had finally abandoned. Or not abandoned, because he'd won everything he asked for.

The children were noisy and full of questions. Some of them were asking when their fathers would come back, and this, this was a hard question to face. Because Noëlle and Angélique could not know if those fathers were ever coming back.

But if things were going badly on the military front, Angélique, and Noëlle with her, were both more convinced than ever that they had to win a victory on the home front, bringing up children who would grow up not to be monsters, not easily manipulated by propaganda, but caring, honest people. Incapable of imagining a civil war.

The two of them had an appointment in the mayor's office this afternoon. Luc, meanwhile, was going to clean up the place, after the dozen children had had what was surely their most substantial meal of the day. Now more than ever, they would argue in the mayoralty, the Commune had to devote resources to educating the next generation.

* * *

Blanche was greatly relieved that Jules had made it home. Late on Tuesday, weary, unhappy, but fiercely proud that all but three of the men of his company had also managed to return. The losses, he said, had been terrible. Flourens, Duval, Bergeret – they were all good men, he said, but they should have had more cannons, they should have had scouts to give them warning, they should have known that that fort was not secure.

Henriette was also greatly relieved. She had suffered a terrible anxiety attack, waiting and waiting after the first news reached their quartier of troubles in the attacking expedition. Louis had come back, with that Jules Durand who, bless his heart, was a gruff man, and stubborn, but he did look after his men. Louis was sleeping now, finally. He hadn't even been wounded, just bruised from falls while running after their final defense, a defense that had permitted more of their comrades to escape. She would let him be for now, let him recover, poor dear, and she would try to sit and talk with her neighbor Blanche who had a wonderfully calming way.

But Blanche was not entirely calm this afternoon. As she assured Henriette, who now seemed almost giddy, so happy that that ordeal was past, that she was going to do everything in her power to see that her husband, Jules, did not go off on any more far-flung military adventures. Versailles was there, and it was going to stay there, and what he and she and all of them had to do was make the best of what they could, here in – and this time, she did not say Belleville – in the city.

It may have been because of Rose, her work down in the Ménagère and the Marmite, in all the Marmite's locations, four so far and they were talking of setting up others, even one in Belleville. Blanche found herself thinking of herself not just as a resident of her former village, her quartier, Belleville, but as part of the whole of Paris, all twenty arrondissements. A person, a *citoyenne* no less, a woman with rights guaranteed by this city.

That was world enough for her. Versailles could look after itself, stew in its own juice of corruption. She and Jules, and Rose too, she hoped, would be content to stay and work right here, in this great city.

* * *

In La Ménagère, Rose had been closely observing Nathalie Lemel. She admired the older woman and wanted to learn from her, especially how to deal with and talk to workers, but she did not want to emulate her completely, because of her Breton accent, her sharp tongue when provoked and, especially, her unhappy marital history.

She knew that she was too young to understand everything and was impatient to grow up. Because it was necessary, she believed. In this time of crisis, she was going to have to assume far greater responsibility than any sixteen- or seventeen-year-old in a quiet village, or in those big houses she had seen especially in the western part of the city, but also in the center, on the great avenues near the Hôtel de Ville. But grow up how?

Her mother was one model, a strong model, a very good woman, but, Rose thought, an imperfect model, now that she had seen other possibilities. Blanche was nearly illiterate and ignorant of many things, but wise in practical ways. And she had developed a very good, strong, comradely relationship with Rose's father Jules. Who could be a lot to deal with, sometimes. Those were all good qualities, but not enough. Not all that the times and Rose's own ambitions demanded.

And then she had met Élizabeth Dimitrieff – an exotic young woman, hardly older than Rose herself but so much more worldly and self-confident, so stunning and attractive to men that she sometimes had to impatiently dismiss them. From that magical, distant place she knew only from fairy tales, Russia. And Élizabeth had been in London, and now she was here in France, in Paris. To Rose, this dark-haired, bright-eyed beauty *was* the International.

Moreover, the Russian talked about texts and philosophies unknown to Rose, and she was very exotic, because of course she was foreign and her French was not always completely comprehensible but whatever it was she was saying, she knew so much. Rose wasn't sure that Nathalie always understood her, but they got along wonderfully, this older bookbinder and the foreign girl young enough to be Nathalie's daughter. And with gestures and expressions from another world. Rose secretly adopted her as an impossible ideal: she want to 'be' Élizabeth Dimitrieff, elegant but not haughty, with her knowledge of international labor struggles and her attractiveness and self-confidence.

In the little apartment she had found on Rue Mignon, Rose had been sure there was a mirror. She practised doing her hair up on top of her head, the way that Russian girl wore it. But —

The Russian would not be a useful example for dealing with Étienne. She had told Rose that she had married a man she didn't love simply because it was the only way in Russia that she could escape her father's control and travel. And she seemed proud of having done it. Whoever that husband had been, he wasn't around and apparently had no interest in being near her, but Rose didn't really understand those Russian customs.

For a marriage partnership, Nathalie was not a good example either. Rose didn't know the details, but her marriage to Lemel must have been pretty awful, and she was raising her children on her own. She got along beautifully with the men in the Marmite, though, but as far as Rose could tell, she didn't have an intimate partner.

What Rose wanted was the Russian girl's elegance and worldly knowledge and Nathalie's skill and ease at organizing workers. But for working out how to live with her moody Étienne, Blanche, her mother, was the only model available. Except for some characters she had read in novels, none of them working-class girls like herself.

When Rose learned, only days after the defeat of the great assault, that Élizabeth and Nathalie had joined to create 'The Women's Union for the Defense of Paris and Care of the Wounded', she was more than enthusiastic to participate. This would be the perfect opportunity to practice her new sense of herself, and the new association would be the perfect response to the disgusting triumphalism of that bloody-minded, reactionary regime in Versailles. They would get women active and counter any sense of defeatism in the Commune.

Also, as Élizabeth had tried to explain to her, in many big words and analogies – Rose had had to ask Nathalie to explain again, because she didn't always understand the rapid speech and peculiar accent of the Russian – it would be the way to make sure that women and their rights and their needs were not forgotten in this new world of liberty they were creating.

Nathalie had shown her the announcement in the Commune's own *Journal officiel*:

Patriotic *citoyennes* are requested to meet today, Tuesday, 11th April, at 8 p.m., 79 Rue du Temple, in Larched Hall of the Grand Café of the Nation, to take the definitive steps for the formation of committees in all arrondissements, for the purpose of organizing the women's movement for the defense of Paris, in case the reaction and its gendarmes should attempt to seize it.

We seek the active participation of all *citoyennes* who understand that the salvation of the homeland depends on the outcome of this struggle, who know that the present social order carries within it the seeds of misery and death, for all liberty, all justice, and who, knowing that, acclaim the reign of labor and of equality, and who are ready, in this moment of supreme danger, to combat and die for the triumph of this revolution for which our brothers are making their sacrifice.

Hou-la-la! She had to read that out to her mother.

She would get her mother involved, too, and all women. And, after seeing that Étienne had at least begun to stir and was meeting with some other men around his age, she rushed off to Belleville.

It took her more than an hour, part way by omnibus but most of the way on foot, to get from her workplace in the Sixth to the heights of Belleville in the Twentieth. Her mother wasn't home, but she saw her father talking to some men on the street nearby.

"No, I don't know where she is right now. She hasn't been still for a minute, your mother, all this week. Not since we got back, from, you know. The assault. I don't know who she's talking to, but she's been going all over the neighborhood. Oh, do you know these men?"

No, except for their neighbor and Jules' workmate, Louis. The others were all strangers to her, but they seemed to be very attentive to Jules. They each nodded to her very courteously and mumbled their names.

"You men must have a lot to talk about," she said, preparing to excuse herself.

"You had better believe it!" said her father.

"Your father here, our chief Durand, miss, he's got some good ideas. After what happened last week."

"Oh?" Rose was now genuinely curious. Her father looked at her a moment, then at the little group of men around him – there were five of them – and then back to Rose.

"Well, my girl. You're a woman now, I should say. You're part of this," he told her. "Part of this struggle. I was telling these men, and they agree with me, that it's time to stop trying to save the whole world, or even the whole of France, by ourselves. Until we secure a base right here, in our neighborhoods. That's what I've been saying. We are going to build barricades, like we did in '48, and like some of our neighbors have been doing ever since, ever since the day of the cannons."

"You mean, just defend the neighborhood? Nothing else?"

"Missy," said one of the other men, she hadn't caught his name. "What Chief Durand is saying, and we agree with him, is that of course France is important, terribly important. And, and even other places, beyond our country, if we set the example. But we won't be able to help them unless first of all we defend ourselves."

The others all made mumbling sounds of assent. And Rose nodded. She wasn't about to argue the point. Not with her father in this mood.

* * *

Blanche returned home rather late in the afternoon and was surprised to see her daughter there. She had been participating in a political club and organizing women workers, especially in the laundries and clothing factories, which was why she hadn't come home there earlier as Rose had expected.

Her daughter looked very surprised, too, but Blanche told her, no, it was something she had always wanted to do. But the hours in the laundry hadn't permitted her to talk much with any women besides the few working with her, and she had persuaded some of them to get involved, too.

"And what have you been up to?" she asked her daughter.

Rose took a deep breath and showed her the page from the *Journal officiel*.

"I've been helping Nathalie and a new girl, a foreigner but really involved in our struggle, to organize this meeting," she told Blanche.

Blanche squinted at the page and held it a little away from her.

"*Citoyennes*," she repeated in a low voice. "I like that. But the print is too small. Is this about the meeting tonight?"

"You can read! And you knew? I mean, about the meeting?"

"I don't read well, you know that. But the meeting, that's what we were talking about, my friends and I. Some of them new friends, some women I've just met in the past few days. From here in Belleville, and Ménilmontant, and some from La Villette. We heard about it from someone, I don't know her name, a girl much younger than you, said that someone named Élizabeth sent her up to Ménilmontant. Not everybody is free to go tonight, but I think there may be as many as fifteen of us going down there. Rue du Temple, is it?"

"Yes. In the Marais. I can take you there."

"Oh, very good! I haven't been down there since, since Jules took me that day we went to the Universal Exposition. That was three, four years ago.

"But first you come with me, to where we've agreed to meet the women I've been organizing. And then we'll all go down there. But wait, I'm going to have to change. "You look fine. But what have you done with your hair?"

* * *

Down in the Second Arrondissement, Sophie had also decided to attend the inaugural meeting of the Women's Union for the Defense of Paris and Care of the Wounded, because it seemed like a patriotic thing to do even though, from the announcement, it didn't sound like it was going to address her most urgent problem. Which was getting back to work. Her Petit Alphonse, as she called him, was out somewhere – a joke, because Petit was her own surname. 'Phonse was doing what he called 'investigating', so there was no reason for her not to go to the meeting that night. She wished she had someone to go with her, but maybe she would see some of her old friends there.

She got out her light blue, going-out dress. It was old and faded, but still the best she had.

* * *

Étienne was left alone that night. Rose had told him that she wouldn't be home till late, and he had grunted that that was fine. And really, it was fine with him, because he wanted the time. He had been back to the house on Dragon Court and had found the work that J-P had left: piles of sheets of printed paper, his cutting tools. He had somehow even acquired a complicated little machine for the *endossure*, the rounding of the backs of the books – much smaller than what they had used in the bindery, but it would do just fine for a small number of carefully finished volumes. Under the bed, what had been Jean-Pierre's bed, he found several samples of different cover materials. And two manuscripts.

Luc watched him with approval and admiration, because he really had no idea of the bookbinder's craft, and Étienne seemed to be going about it with confidence and concentration, which Luc recognized as values for any worker. He had offered to bring in some fancy metal pieces that he came across in his work, but Étienne had just smiled tightly and shaken his head, no need for them, "But thanks."

Luc did help him set up his workspace, though. He piled up the now-unused cots to make room and set up a table for the young binder. He was very curious to observe this process. He had never seen a bookbinder work, and it seemed very intricate, with many steps.

Étienne stopped when he pulled out another sheaf of papers from under J-P's bed. Luc watched him staring at the pages and stepped over to see what they were.

"Oh, that's where that got to!" he said.

Étienne looked up at him, his face forming a question.

"That's, look at it, the lines don't all go to the edge of the page, that's poetry."

"Yes," said Étienne, "but what's it doing here?"

"What does it say, on that top page?"

"'Meditations'. And then down below, in smaller letters – what is this? Oh, yes, it's a name. 'Noëlle D'. Noëlle? Is this hers?"

"Wait. I'll tell her. I think she's in the next room." And Luc went out to find her.

When she saw the yellow sheets with her handwritten verses, Noëlle paled, then sighed. And finally pulled herself together to say, "He must have forgotten it."

Étienne, understanding that this was something important even though he didn't know the story, decided to say something to improve her mood.

"No, not forgotten. Jean-Pierre had put these pages in a very special place, a privileged place. Next to these other stacks of paper. It must mean that he was intending to give this a very special binding."

Noëlle looked at him, let out the air that had inflated her lungs, and then reached into her pocket and pulled out a ball of twine.

"If you are going to bind it, you must use this."

He recognized the ball as binding thread.

Gingerbread Fair

WHEE-OOO!

Oh! Did I scare you? No, please, just laugh. That was a happy somersault, a leap of joy for our great festival. We can't let those nasty Versaillais – ooh, no, did I say something wrong? Yes. You're right. Let's not pronounce their name. Those dreadful meanies just outside our gates, but we won't let them in! And we won't, we won't, we won't let them ruin our wonderful festivals, our great Fair of the Hams last week and now this most splendid display of talent, of arts, and of merchandise, our joyous, super-joyous Gingerbread Fair!

Come one, come all, and we shall perform amazing leaps and turns and our mighty Hercule – that's him, right there, grinning, take a bow, Hercou! Yes, our mighty Hercule Taureau will lift you up so that you feel that you are flying, flying far up into the sky!

Oh, yes, the sky. A bit cloudy, is it? Well, let us remember what our grandmothers used to say back in the country, 'April rain brings in the grain' – Pluie d'avril remplit le fenil. *Sing it with me!* Pluie d'avril – *Yes, that's it, very good!* – remplit le fenil. *Oh, I am so proud of you good people, especially these youngsters, how loudly you sing. Keep it up, and Hercou and I will include you in our act! You like that, you little rascal?*

But hurry, hurry, before the clouds break, though a soaking can only do us good. No? You look doubtful. So hurry, hurry while the sky is still clear, and drop a few sous into this upturned drum. Every centime, yes, I said every centime, Hercule and I will donate to the fund to support the widows and orphans of the brave men who have fallen, and those who may be falling now to keep our city free so that we might celebrate.

Yes, you heard me right, Hercule Taureau and your servant, Crépin the bateleur, are dedicating the whole proceeds, the entire purse, every sou and centime, and even every franc, to this noble cause. For the orphans! For the widows! For the men who have kept us free!

Ten or twenty sous, or whatever you can afford, please, and Hercule Taureau and I, your humble servant, will demonstrate great feats to lift your souls and hearts!

* * *

Alphonse stared at the gaudily dressed bateleur and his hulking partner, amazed and not sure whether he should be delighted. This was his first time in Paris's famous Gingerbread Fair. Last spring, when he was newly arrived in Paris, he was so caught up with trying to become a serious writer and with his lessons to half-literate workers and other odd jobs as proof-reader that he had missed it.

Now he marveled at the streets filled with bright-colored signs and drawings, musical noises, street artists like the two he had just seen and vendors of the most varied things and barkers summoning crowds into tents promising splendid sights. The fair spread out over a vast area of the Twelfth Arrondissement. As far as he had seen so far, though, there was no sign of gingerbread. But maybe that too was on offer at some stand nearby.

It felt strange, but perhaps it was good, he thought, that

people insisted on celebrating their traditional festivals, high jinks, dances and foolery even in the face of bloodshed and destruction just outside the walls. Maybe they wanted to ignore the mayhem and danger, or to deny that it was a reality. At least, those who were not yet widows or maimed. How complicated is the human psyche!

Notebook in hand, Alphonse dodged a carousel and turned down one of the other streets filled with vendors and hawkers, still wondering if anyone was really selling gingerbread. He hadn't had a taste of that since childhood, back in distant Lille.

Alphonse had busied himself these past few days, visiting as many points as possible on the sides of Paris exposed to the hostile government only twenty kilometers away. And he was worried.

Perhaps he was overly pessimistic. The five forts to the south were still holding, and the sturdy walls and moat would be further protection if the army of Versailles should try to enter. He had not yet ventured out to any of those forts, but he had talked with men who had been and it was clear that the bombardment out there was much more exhausting and dangerous, with many more wounded.

The Prussians, on the eastern edge of the city, had promised to remain neutral, or so the papers said. They were happy, he supposed, to see Frenchmen shoot each other while they waited for whoever won to make the payments they had demanded. On the other sides of the city, cannons were firing almost constantly. For the artillery men he had talked to in quick snatches between salvos, it was their welcome opportunity to fire back at an army that they felt had offended them personally, as well as to defend the city they felt was theirs.

* * *

Taking Rose's suggestion, Étienne had spent the day over on Corderie Street, where both the International and the National Guard committee had set up their headquarters. He needed to talk to somebody, and fortunately he found his old housemate Évariste, taking a cigar break outside the offices.

"Book-paster! Great to see you! I thought maybe we had lost you. You were in the expedition with Bergeret, weren't you?"

"Hey, Solder-man," he answered the tinsmith, but his joy at seeing him suddenly turned dark at the reminder of that day. "How'd you know?"

"Our friends here in the Federation. National Guard. I knew your battalion number, and I could check and saw that yours was one of those with his column. Must have been awful. I was one of the guys at the gate, to make sure they didn't get through, those troops from the Assembly. Glad you made it. To fight another day."

"Another day. And the day after that. Is this ever going to end?"

The little tinsmith laughed.

"When we win. When those royalists and hangers-on and plutocrats and landlords get tired of banging on our walls and realize that the Commune is here to stay. They must be terribly frustrated, to see that life here is going on almost normally, here behind our forts and walls. Those men who had been running everything before 18th March, all the heads of municipal departments, they did as much damage as they could before they fled. Did you see it in the *Journal officiel*? You should read that, get the real news. Those bastards who fled with Thiers burned records or ripped them up and destroyed equipment. And yet, look at us, the street lamps still get lit when they're supposed to; the omnibuses are making their normal runs, almost like before the Prussian bombardment, and their horses and coaches are properly maintained; our hospitals, still mostly staffed by nuns but now with more students assisting a smaller number of doctors, they're doing a magnificent job in caring for the sick and especially all the wounded who keep coming in, especially from those forts just south; and the garbage still gets picked up and the septic tanks emptied, and the worst of the bomb-damaged streets are – though slowly – getting repaired."

Évariste paused and smiled, evidently pleased by his little summary.

Étienne nodded, and asked if there was some place where they could talk. He had lots to tell him about their old lodgings, the school they had started, and maybe he'd even tell 'Riste about his own, personal binding project. He was genuinely glad to see his skinny little comrade so proud of the corporal's insignia, even on a tunic too big for him.

"Sure. They won't miss me for an hour."

In the wine shop, Étienne told him about Angélique's school, with the new girl Noëlle, another schoolteacher. And the death of J-P. But Évariste already knew about that.

Évariste must have seen how Étienne was so obviously depressed, because he was making an effort to rally his spirits. He was now an adjunct, the main office secretary of the International, and saw the leading figures constantly and read every declaration enthusiastically. Thus when Étienne mumbled something about not knowing what the devil they were fighting for, he had his speech already formulated. It spilled out of him spontaneously, as what he knew to be true and was eager to tell to anyone who would listen.

"We are remaking the world, my friend. This Commune, here in Europe's greatest city, this is only the beginning! We have created a new model of direct democracy. Paris is not going to be the capital of France, oh no, not just that. It is going to be the starting point and center and model for a whole federation of Communes, all across this country and beyond. And look what we have already done here, right here in Paris."

Étienne looked at him, his face a mixture of surprise and expectation, waiting for his fervent Internationalist friend to elaborate.

He didn't have to wait. Évariste seemed almost in a rapture as he continued, gripping the wine glass he had slammed down onto the table, "Look what is happening now in industry!"

Workers now had proved themselves to be enthusiastic about the new order, Évariste told him. That German guy, Frankel, a jewelry maker, elected to the Commune from the Thirteenth, he was one of the International's men, and he was the Labor Delegate, the man in charge of reorganizing industry. Very bright guy, a real Internationalist and a socialist, too. Workers, men and women, running their own shops, so proud. Proud, Évariste said, to demonstrate how well they could do their jobs without bosses watching and disciplining them. And in some places even delighted to teach their new directors, sent in by the Commune, just how things should work.

Then he mentioned another name, Albert Theisz, a bronze carver and long-time organizer of the bronze workers' association. Étienne had heard his name before, from Rose's father who was in that association. He had taken on the job as director of the postal service after the departing postmasters had destroyed metal postmarking seals, records and everything else they could that night, that famous 18th March, when they sneaked off to Versailles. Theisz had never worked in a post office, but he was so good at organizing and respecting workers that he quickly learned from the old hands everything he needed to know and appointed good veteran postal workers as assistants. And that was why the mail was still delivered, punctually, all across the city.

But, Évariste added, leaning across the table and dropping his voice to a conspiratorial tone, getting anything out or in from beyond the city walls was more difficult. But not impossible, thanks to the ingenuity of the spirits liberated by the Commune, he said with a wink.

To slip letters or parcels past the Prussian soldiers on the northern and eastern edges, or, worse, past the Versaillais all along the south and west, required ingenuity, duplicity and sometimes bribery or menace. But these were all highly developed arts among a certain class of Parisians, mostly men well known to the police of the old regime, and who now offered their services, glad to have the opportunity to put their skills to patriotic use.

This struck Évariste as particularly funny.

"And you know who's running the police now? They're all Blanquistes! What a joke. One of them working for the Commune's police prefecture is a bookbinder, like you. Maybe you know him. Antoine something. They call him Toinou. Big fellow."

"Toinou? In the police?"

"Our revolutionary Commune police. Nothing at all like the old force. Their job is to protect us from the counterrevolution. Because you know, there are spies everywhere, and certain Parisians working against us."

"Toinou. I had no idea. I thought the Commune had abolished the police."

Évariste half-closed his eyes and smiled at the young bookbinder's naïvety. Then he just nodded and refilled Étienne's glass.

"Tell me, have you seen Angélique? How is she, now that almost everybody has left that place?"

* * *

In Jules Durand's bronze foundry, as he told Blanche when he got home that night, since the owners had abandoned the plant and had fled the city, the workers had replaced the old management with their own elected committee. And of course, Jules was part of it, along with their neighbor Louis and three others.

They were still working at a steady, even accelerated pace, with no supervision but their own, producing the famous cannons they all were so proud of, embossed with the symbol of the foundry, plus new artifacts to meet a new demand. Elaborate bronze belt buckles with battalion numbers had become suddenly popular, required by men suddenly elevated by vote of their neighbors to undreamed of rank in their National Guard units. Blanche laughed when Jules raised an eyebrow and cocked his head in that ironic way of his, to tell her how these brand-new lieutenants, captains and even colonels wanted things to make their rank as conspicuous as possible. He could understand it, he said, up to a point; he too was proud to show off his National Guard tunic with his captain's insignia. But some of these demands were ridiculous. Elaborate stirrups for those few who knew how to ride a horse, and whose rank gave them that privilege, and sabre pommels and other military adornments.

He raised his hands and lifted his eyes skyward in mock adoration when he reached his punch line, "And would you believe, some of these new officers even bring in their own sketches for the designs."

True, bronze artwork had been a specialty in Broquin et Lainé, with real artists, but this –

He gestured with his hands to show the size of the belt buckle demanded by one new colonel. And Blanche could not help laughing with him.

* * *

Alone in the house after the kids had gone and Luc had accompanied Noëlle to shop for tomorrow's lunch, Angélique picked up the copy of the collection of essays that Étienne had put aside to measure for binding. She had always liked reading, poetry but also history and geography, which she could use in her teaching.

She turned the pages very carefully, afraid to damage them, and read a page at random. It was different writing from what she had expected, very serious in tone, the vocabulary in some places beyond her, the phrasing elegant. Some sentences read like poetry. And she was especially impressed that the author had a woman's name, Maria, Maria Deraismes.

But reading this would require some effort, and her mind was wandering to other matters. She put the sheets back where she had found them and sat down back in the common room, what had been the dining area when all those men lived there.

Sitting in one of the comfortable reading-and-thinking chairs that Luc had brought in from somewhere, she was thinking of Noëlle, who reminded her of herself in the days before she had married Joseph. She had been watching her and could empathize with her feeling that J-P's death had left her widowed. An imaginary widow, because she never really had had a relationship with Jean-Pierre. Angélique was sure that he had scarcely noticed Noëlle before that night, their surprise birthday celebration for him, when she gave him her manuscript as a present. But he had said something that she took as a compliment on her verse and she must have felt a connection. And ever since, and especially since they learned of his death, she had seen Noëlle reaching into the pocket of her apron to rub that ball of twine. That ball of twine that, just the other day, she had practically commanded Étienne to use in his binding of her poems.

Poor, sweet Noëlle, feeling as lost in Paris as Angélique had felt in her first months. A sort of widow in her own mind. Whereas Angélique was a real widow, of a real marriage. And maybe it was because of that, that she had had a love partner, a husband in fact if not by law, that she felt free of the anxiety for a relationship that she sensed in Noëlle.

What she found especially curious, even amusing, was the relationship she saw developing between Noëlle and Luc, a shy flirtation, still very tentative but undeniable. Luc had always been the joker in the house, hard to take seriously, but maybe the joking was always a way to mask deeper feelings. They were a rather funny looking couple, she thought, smiling to herself. Noëlle so tall, taller than Angélique, as tall as J-P had been though not quite as tall as that long-legged Étienne. And Luc, well, not a midget exactly, but much shorter, and squat. And probably a dozen years older than Noëlle. But around her, instead of joking he behaved with elaborate courtesy, and he had gone to a lot of trouble to set up the space the way he thought she would want it for teaching the kids. He was good with the kids, too, like a funny uncle.

He had even offered, and Noëlle accepted, to accompany her to that meeting about women's support for the Commune. Angélique had not gone with them; she was glad to have some time for herself to read again some poetry, to think, to plan the lessons for the school next day – and also, she thought it would be good for Noëlle and Luc to have some time together without her.

As Luc told her the next day, he had accompanied Noëlle up to the door of the hall where they were meeting, and then had waited, probably in some wine shop or maybe just walking up and down the street, an hour or more to walk her home.

Noëlle had come back full of enthusiasm, especially because, she said, she had met someone she saw as an older, more advanced version of herself, another tall, plain-looking schoolmistress but full of conviction and experience and especially devoted to free education. Louise, her name was, Louise Michel.

When Luc heard that, he was impressed.

"The Red Virgin, we call her in the International," he said. "The Blanquistes call her that, too. Because she's full of radical ideas, and she's not anybody's wife or mistress."

He applauded this new contact of Noëlle's.

Noëlle had mentioned another proposal she had heard that night, one that intrigued Angélique. The new association was organizing women to serve in the ambulances, which meant field hospitals each with a tent and cots and surgeon and nurses, bandages and tools, to set up near the ramparts or wherever there was fighting to care for the wounded. Angélique was not a nurse, but she was good at caring for people and could be part of the medical team under fire. She remembered Jojo and that bloody day at La Ricamarie. If only they had had such an ambulance –

Jojo had been an impetuous man, a man with whom she had shared many things, practical as well as in the realm of ideas. Joseph Ducrin, Jojo, miner and revolutionary and so much more.

He was no reader, but he listened to and commented on things she read, and they had agreed on most things. Including having a child. She knew that he was taking a great risk, but she did not try to stop him. Because she knew how important the strike was to him, to act on what they both agreed was urgent and necessary.

But no, it would not have been possible, not there on that day, to set up such a service. Not in front of those rifles and that bloody general Palikao. Not without armed men to protect it. But now, now that the workers were armed, she could help save other men. It would be her vengeance against bloody generals like Palikao, life against death, and a tribute to the values she and he had shared.

* * *

When Étienne saw Rose that evening, she told him something else her father had told her, something she thought would especially delight him because it involved his hero.

Hmm? he asked. By now there were lots of heroes in the Commune.

The committee coordinating the work in the foundry had questioned some of the new demands from new Guard officers, she explained, thinking they took time and energy from more important production, including the cannons and also bed pans, pitchers and other objects for the military ambulances, as well as ordinary household goods such as sinks and faucets. Demand for these things was as great as ever, greater maybe since more workers had the means to set up households. At Louis's suggestion, the foundry's governing committee had sent a query to the two Commune chiefs in charge of finances. Jourde and Varlin. In reply they received a letter saying not to accept any such requests without specific authorization, and that the Commune would not pay for them. Signed, E. Varlin.

"Varlin? Eugène Varlin? The bookbinder?"

"He and Jourde are the ones in charge of finances for the whole Commune."

Étienne had to stop to assimilate that image. Varlin had been elected to the Commune council, the governing body of their city, and had also been elected by the Guards to command his battalion. And was the man in charge of finances! If a worker-bookbinder could rise to such responsibilities, there was no limit to what a bookbinder-worker like Étienne could aspire to.

"But I see you never even asked me what we women did in our big meeting."

Now he felt embarrassed. This Rose, his Rose, loyal and supporting of him all the time. And she was right, he hadn't given a thought to what she might be doing in that meeting. Women's matters, girl stuff it would be. Then he thought again of those books he was setting out to bind, a collection of essays on women's rights.

"No, really, Rose, I do care."

Or at least he thought that he should care.

"It's just that I had other things on my mind. Tell me about it."

"No. Not now. Oh, one thing that might interest you. I met a girl there, somebody whose name I had heard before, and she said she knew you. Sophie. She was there to see if we could help her organize her old work-mates to re-open the glove factory where she used to work."

"Sophie? She knew me?"

"And I had heard her name. One of the soldiers on Montmartre, on 18th March, asked me to give her a message. His name was Maurice. Maurice Prost."

"Maurice! He's my cousin. Then he's alive."

Étienne's face took on a startling, rapid change of expressions. First, a look of relief.

"Alive!"

And then dismay, as he went on:

"But in the uniform of the army of Versailles."

"Oh, no!" muttered Rose. She watched him as he closed his eyes tight and shook his head, shoulders tense.

"I thought you might know him, because he said he was from Lyon. But your cousin! No."

She kept looking at him for a moment before adding,

"Yes, it's both good news and sad, sad that he's in that army. But he behaved very properly that day on Montmartre. Very polite, he seemed reluctant to be pulling on a cannon. And he even allowed one of our Fédérés, in Guard uniform, embrace him.

"But Sophie told me she has a new boyfriend, and now wants to throw herself into the work of organizing her industry. And we're going to help her do it."

* * *

Alphonse was glad to see Sophie excited about her new project. She had located several of her former workmates and they were going to re-open the glove factory. Not just to produce fancy-dress for bourgeois gentlemen and ladies, she said, but for real workers, like those artillerymen who were keeping the city safe, and the men who harnessed the horses for the omnibuses, and a thousand other needs for gloves that had been neglected in the old days. The laundry workers, for example, women who always risked scalding on the hot cauldrons.

Moreover, she added proudly, they were going to run the shop themselves, without any man to tell them what to do and how to do it. Or to fine them, or pressure them for certain special favors – she didn't need to explain to Alphonse, who reddened with anger or embarrassment at the thought of what she and other girls like her had had to endure. The glove girls, well, girls and women because they weren't all young, had got together and petitioned the Commune Council, and Frankel, the Commune delegate for labor had actually congratulated them on their initiative and had ordered a locksmith to open up the closed shop. Even though he was a man, Sophie said with admiration. She and her coworkers had found a mess there, machines broken and tables overturned, but Sophie was sure they could get the factory going again in just a few days.

Her mention of the artillerymen needing gloves gave Alphonse pause. Yes, they certainly could use them, and earplugs too, though nobody used them. And he doubted that many of them would bother with gloves, they got so impatient when firing. But it would be good, because he had seen the burns on some of their hands from the hot cannon barrels.

He was worried by many things he had seen, not just on the ramparts but also in the ranks of the battalions. Half of the problem was that there were hardly any men available who had real command experience in the military, and the battalions were taking their notion of democracy to such extremes that they were electing as officers the guys they liked best for whatever reason.

The other half of the problem was that, once they had selected their officers, they didn't bother to obey them if they disagreed, of if they thought they had something more important to do, or if they just got tired of duty. As a result, though there was plenty of individual courage on display, individuals sometimes competing to show how bold they were, there was hardly any discipline or strategy beyond holding the forts and walls. Some battalions were spending days, even a week on exhausting duty, with no relief because a battalion from some other sector didn't want to go that far, and their elected chiefs couldn't force them. This was especially a problem for the battalions in the southern arrondissements, the Thirteenth, Fourteenth and Fifteenth. Poor zones, with working-class families, the area that had already suffered most from the Prussian bombardment during the siege, and now the areas the Commune depended on to staff the forts to the south that were under fierce attack.

There were those veterans of the French army, Cluseret and Rossel, but they each had got so impatient with the lack of discipline that they had gotten into huge quarrels with the men in the Commune Council.

There were some commanders, though, who inspired more confidence in that rough mass of working men. Whether by personal example of bravery, or for wise and considerate treatment of their troops, or, in some few cases, by demonstrating tactical skill in battles with the Versailles. Four or five that Alphonse could name. Maxime Lisbonne, Napoléon La Cecilia, Émile Eudes, among them, and also the foreigners, especially two Poles, veterans of the insurrection against Russia. Alphonse thought they would make a good subject for an article. He liked their names: Wroblewski and Dombrowski and all the other '–skis'. Names that sounded to him like some strange poetry from another world.

Wroblewski he discovered was at the moment in Gentilly, south of the city walls. With his troops. Walery Wroblewski, he wrote in his notebook. He had been named commander of the cavalry for the left bank. Jaroslaw Dombrowski, he knew, had been named commander of the 11th legion of the National Guard, which meant all the battalions in that arrondissement, the Eleventh, on the right bank. Because the ferocious attacks of the Versaillais on the forts in the south had been much in the news, he decided to try to find Wroblewski first. He found some Fédérés from the Thirteenth who were scheduled to head down there.

And so, for the first time since arriving from Lille almost two years ago, he ventured outside Paris, in a calèche with two young workers and their sergeant, through the Gentilly Gate. Into the air outside the walls.

It was wonderful, frightening, stimulating. Outside the carapace, as though escaping a prison but entering an unknown world of danger.

Rondeau à la Mazur

The ride in the open carriage to Gentilly was a thrill for Alphonse, despite the intermittent showers. He was happy just to get outside the fortifications and into the countryside.

The Fédérés who had offered him a ride had given him one of the two forward-facing seats in the calèche as a courtesy, so he could get a good look at the fields and trees. It had been a long time since he had last breathed country air, with its rich smell of greenery and newly turned soil, or heard bird calls other than the courting gurgles of dingy, strutting pigeons.

He was seated next to the sergeant, a burly, fair-haired fellow of about thirty, polite but a bit distant. Alphonse supposed that he didn't know what to make of his passenger, in civilian clothes and clutching a notebook. The younger National Guards in front of him, he learned from their conversation, were leather workers from this area. One had a peculiar accent and said something to the sergeant in a foreign language. The sergeant answered him very briefly in that same language, then told him,

"Let's speak French. For our guest here, who probably doesn't know Polish. Is that right, friend?" he added, turning his face to Alphonse.

"Polish?"

"Marek here – or 'Marc' you would say – was just asking how long I thought it would take to get there."

Marek nodded.

"Paul, there, he's a Frenchman all right, from right here in Gentilly. But since he's joined us, he's picked up a lot of Polish words. Right, Paul?"

"*Poprawny!*" said Paul, as though on command. Or something like that.

"But that's about all I know," he added. "And 'Tacky yes'."

"*Tak jest,*" corrected the sergeant.

"That means 'Yes sir'. They've all learned that by now!" he added, laughing. "All the men in my company."

"Do you have a lot of Poles in your battalion?"

"With General Wroblewski in command, they've flocked to us. General Dombrowski, over on the other bank, he has attracted a lot, too. But we're mixed. We have some Germans, too. And there's a Belgian, I think. A metalworker. But most are French, workers from the tanneries. Good group of men."

The one called Marek started humming a little tune as the calèche bounced along.

Alphonse was surprised to learn of so many Poles here, but then he thought about it, and it made sense. The only Poles he had heard of in Paris were artists or musicians, but the great majority must be ordinary workers.

"And you, Sergeant, what were you doing before the siege?"

"In Poland, I was a schoolteacher until the insurrection made me a soldier. But the Russians were too strong for our forces. Here, I am working in the same tannery as these too. Such is life, it takes its turns. And now, I am back in the insurrection! Not against Russians, this time, but against the same inequalities."

Marek started humming louder, what sounded like a little folk melody, maybe a country dance.

The calèche rolled into the town, and the sergeant called up to the driver to stop in front of a modest little house.

"Here is the general's headquarters," he said. "We'll be continuing to our camp. Best of luck to you, comrade! And write the truth."

A thin, blond man in what he took to be a captain's uniform standing at the door stopped Alphonse with a gesture.

"Good day, Captain." Though not in uniform, Alphonse saluted.

"I'm a journalist, Alphonse-Marie Bertrand, here to interview General Wroblewski. For the *Cri du peuple*."

Which was a little lie, or a stretch, because he hadn't even told Vallès he would be venturing here, south of the walls. But he thought he could probably get Vallès's paper to print his story.

At the name of the paper, the captain smiled and said, "That's very good. But wait. The general is not to be interrupted now. Do you hear that?"

Yes, he did hear. A piano. Not a tune he was familiar with, but very well played.

"Is that General Wroblewski playing?" he asked.

The man nodded and smiled.

"It's practically his only relaxation. He has been riding all day, over to Vanves, then over to Issy. Checking on the fortifications, talking to the men. When you speak to the war delegate, tell him, tell the whole Commune, we need more men. Urgently. And cannons. There, you heard that? Cannon fire from over there, must be by Fort Issy, ours or theirs. It goes on all day."

"I hope I can speak with the general. Excuse me, what is your name, please?"

"Dombrowski."

"General Dombrowski?"

"That's my brother, Jaroslaw. He is in command of the entire 11th legion. I'm Théophile. Colonel Dombrowski. The general, that is, my brother, asked me to come talk with our countryman, Walery. General Wroblewski, that is. Military matters. But I have to return to Asnières. The general will be waiting for my news on this front. It is not good. And I think your interview of our friend Wroblewski will have to wait for another day. If ever. He is terribly busy. But for your article, I can give you some information. Do you know how to ride?"

"Uh, no, not really. I mean, I never have."

The blond colonel shouted something to some Fédérés nearby, and they brought over another little carriage similar to the one he had come in. Théophile Dombrowski posted another man at the entrance to the house, where Alphonse could still hear the piano, tied his own horse to the back of the carriage and instructed the driver.

"What is it he's playing?" Alphonse asked.

Théophile half-closed his eyes and said, "*Rondeau à la Mazur en fa majeur*. By Frédéric Chopin. Lovely, isn't it?"

Alphonse had never before heard anything like it, so he couldn't really say. But, seeing the colonel's pleasure at the music, he agreed.

"Yes. Yes, very lovely."

Who, he wondered, was Chopin?

.

And in Versailles …

Hippolyte's transfer to Sûreté was going to have to wait and might never happen with things in such turmoil. The whole prefecture of police was now, in effect, subsumed under the army, and the only important task for the new prefect was to assure the reconquest of Paris. Then, we would see. We would see whether the police could again become an independent organization, dedicated to preventing disturbances and violence instead of seeking to provoke them. Whether it made sense for him to continue in this institution to which he had dedicated his life.

He was not happy about this situation – nobody was – but that was how things were, and he would just have to make the most of the new demands and the new limitations. The prefect now was a general, Louis Ernest Valentin, neither a lawyer nor a career police official like his predecessors. And the only thing he cared about was that the troops be in fighting shape for the final assault on the city. Thus Hippolyte's task, as head of a small team of investigators, was to feel the pulse of those hastily assembled regiments and remove those elements without a sufficient degree of hostility to Paris. The high command's greatest fear was another humiliation, like the one 18th of March.

Hippolyte's team of police investigators included two of

the men who had been under his command in the Quinze-Vingts, Chardon and Poirier, and two others whom he had, patiently, tried to train. Their mission was to purge any soldiers found to have ties to Paris: relatives in the city or girlfriends or other connections, or who had merely said anything that sounded favorable to Paris or to the Commune. He himself had continued visiting the troops, listening in on conversations, interviewing sergeants and corporals who he thought might be closest to the men, making lists and decisions.

On more than one occasion, soldiers had been found reading one of the forbidden newspapers, pro-Commune papers smuggled out from Paris. The men caught with Rochefort's *Le mot d'ordre* said it came every day, with the woman who sold them wine. And Vallès' *Le cri du peuple* was for sale openly in Meudon, the town where Eudes' column had been defeated, that terrible day when those hordes from Paris were marching on Versailles. That terrible, frightening, fateful day just two weeks ago, 3rd April. Ten thousand men or more, just in that one of the three attacking columns.

That day was a horror that sent tremors through the commanders in Versailles, but it turned out to be much worse for those 'communards', as the Versailles papers had begun calling their foes. The army was still a mess, feared to be unreliable. Facing three separate columns with huge numbers of men with blood and vengeance on their minds, shouting and singing. Most of the army units were so undertrained, so ragtag, so confused about their mission that in several places they had refused to fire on the approaching columns. Their officers had to threaten them with revolvers and still many of them dropped their arms and tried to run. Some units disbanded in panic the first time they were fired on, and almost all the regiments reached their battle stations understaffed because so many of their men had hung back.

But fortunately other units, under better command and discipline, had held and fought ferociously, the cavalry especially, and artillery. As he knew from the press and what he had heard from some officers, the Versailles commanders had been surprised at how few cannons the enemy had brought on their expedition. It was as though those exuberant workers from Paris thought they were going on a picnic. Some of them didn't even have munitions for their weapons, as was discovered when they were taken prisoner. What saved Versailles against the Parisians, despite their huge advantage in numbers, was that the Paris militias were even more disorganized. It was the failure to organize a serious assault, rather than any skill or special courage on Versailles' part, that had won the day against the *communards*.

Hippolyte was uncomfortable with that *-ard* suffix, which was belittling, as in *bâtard* or *clochard*. He understood it as a response to the insult of the government as *capitulards*, 'giver-uppers', for their surrender to the Prussians. But in police work it was always wiser to take your opponent seriously, and in his reports, he had carefully used the more neutral term *communeux*. But then just yesterday, he had seen *communard* used proudly in one of the most rabidly pro-Commune papers which, as a police official, he was privileged to read. It seemed that they wanted to turn the insult into a badge of honor, like their red flag.

The government troops had been cut off from all news except from the terse announcements read to them by their officers, lest pro-Commune articles and opinion pieces in the general press corrupt them. But the soldiers scoffed at the circulars issued by the high command, dismissed as more stupid army propaganda, while they were anxious to know what was happening, in Paris and in Versailles, that was going to affect their lives. Which was why they so eagerly grabbed any Paris newspapers that came their way, whether from village women selling wine or any other means. Finally, to meet the demands of officers and men for information, the Assembly had agreed to distribute two Versailles papers to them: *Le Soir* and *Le Gaulois*.

No danger of a pro-commune slant there, Hippolyte chuckled to himself as he picked up one of Bagou's recent articles for *Le Soir*. This one was full of gossip about the supposed shady past of some of the leading figures of the Commune – that one of them had been a beggar just before 18th March, another, Rigault, now the Commune's prefect of police, supposedly had made a fortune selling fake passports. This made Hippolyte sit back.

It was obvious to him that someone must have given René-Pierre Bougainville access to confidential unconfirmed and uninvestigated police records, mere notes on claims by the police's network of informers. As he knew from long experience, upon investigation such allegations often proved to be wild exaggerations if not entire inventions, which was why they had to be kept confidential. But somebody in the prefecture was informing Bougainville, because from some of the details, he thought that Bagou was not himself just making the stuff up but had read something he shouldn't have. This crisis was corrupting even the police, the institution in which Hippolyte Mireau had had the greatest confidence.

Next he picked up *Le Gaulois*, hoping for news on the war. There he found another piece signed 'R. de B'. Could this be another of the signatures of René-Pierre Bougainville, or 'de Bougainville' as he now liked to call himself? It claimed that the village of Asnières, which that Pole Dombrowski had seized by a surprise attack only a week ago, had now been retaken by National Assembly troops. Perhaps it was true or, as he suspected, just more propaganda to make the Versaillais side feel good.

His eye was drawn to another mention of Asnières in the next column, clearly by a different journalist. He read,

> *The brother of General Dombrowski must have been disapproved of by the Commune because he has been replaced by another Pole.*
>   *General Okolowitz replaces Colonel Dombrowski, the general's brother, in command of Asnières.*
>   *It is decidedly only foreign chiefs who are in command in Paris. Together with the Poles we have Colonel La Cecilia, who must be Italian. And so it is that Paris is in the power of the insurrection, but the insurrection is in the power of the foreigners.*

Hippolyte reflected on this a moment. And wasn't it true, he wondered, that the government of the National Assembly was in the power of the Prussians? Foreigners everywhere. Which had never been a problem for cosmopolitan Paris. But that was then, when Paris saw itself as the leader of progress in the world, and welcomed men, and even women, from all parts.

And besides, he happened to know that Colonel Napoléon La Cecilia was French.

Festival of freedom

The Guard battalions were divided into eight companies supposed to have about 125 men each, four of them 'sedentary' companies which meant the men continued living at home, and 'four war companies' which could be summoned for duty anywhere, on the ramparts or outside. Being under twenty and without children, Étienne had been assigned to one of his battalion's four 'war companies' which also included some volunteers considerably older, men eager to fight. Their sergeant was in his mid-twenties, a welder by trade, whom they all loved.

At their assembly in the afternoon of Monday, 1st May – the anniversary of his arrival in Paris – Étienne's company was told to prepare to be sent the next morning to relieve the exhausted garrison in Fort d'Issy, vital to the defense of the city.

As he packed his gear that morning, he was excited to be going into action. Especially, he was determined to redeem himself for his panic on that great sortie just a month ago. And everybody in Paris knew how important it was to defend those forts, Issy, Vanves, Montrouge, Bicêtre. The loss of any one of them would weaken the others, and it was their cannons and their riflemen that had so far prevented the enemy from getting closer to Paris's long southern wall.

Rose was terribly anxious about this assignment. She wanted to go with him, but to do that she would have needed an appointment as a *cantinière*, in charge of the military food supply, or as a nurse. But this had come up so suddenly she hadn't had a chance to apply. Her absence from the city would have been a problem for her work with the women's union, which was counting on her, but if it had been at all possible she would have accompanied her Titi to the battlefront.

But it was not. She made sure he had a good breakfast, and after he marched off very early to his company's rallying spot, she prepared herself, mentally and practically, to keep herself as busy as she could. So as not to fret. How long would he be gone? There was no way of knowing. And would he come back?

Best for her to get off to work. Immediately, to stop thinking about what could not be helped.

The Marmite on Larrey Street was no longer her exclusive workstation for hours every day, but now just one of several places, including the *marmites* in the other arrondissements and some trade association headquarters, where she was supposed to meet with workers to help them organize themselves to run their own shops. They were all from workshops with a majority of women, sometimes with a few men workers, too, who had to be persuaded to cede authority to whomever the majority elected.

There had been some giggling and guffawing at first about calling the forewoman *'maîtresse'*, because of course 'mistress' had that other connotation. Rose laughed with them and told them, as Nathalie had told her to do, that they should call their forewoman *'déléguée'*, the feminine of the Commune's term for the person in charge. For example, Eugène Varlin was the *délégué* of finances, Léo Frankel the *délégué* of labor and so on. That seemed to satisfy everybody, and gave a new, official-sounding dignity to the little group in charge in each shop – the elected *déléguée* would coordinate but she wasn't supposed to run things without consulting the others. Those were the rules.

The other problem was the supply of raw materials for production. This also kept Rose busy, trying to coordinate between, for example, the cotton manufacturers and the women in the clothing workshops.

This traveling from one end of the city to another, from laundries to a glove factory to workshops making trousers and tunics for the National Guard, and her meetings with all those different groups of women, helped Rose keep from worrying about Étienne and the other men facing the cannons to the south. But it was hard. She had to make a special effort to laugh a little even when she hadn't really been paying close enough attention to understand one of the women's jokes. The women she met with were usually in very good humor, and sly jokes and singing broke out once they had set up their committees. Some of those women, some she knew who were making the most outrageous jokes, were also trying not to collapse with worry over husbands or sons on the ramparts or in the forts. And some, the silent ones, must be trying hard not to think about some loved one recently killed.

Oh, if this war would just end! They were accomplishing so much in Paris now, the freedom and confidence she shared with all these women was exhilarating. Just exactly what she needed. Paris would be an entirely different place once the hostilities had ceased. If only those armies would let them be.

* * *

Sophie's glove factory was one of the workshops where Rose had helped set things up. It was Sophie who had solicited the Women's Union's help in re-opening and organizing the shop, but she had declined to become the 'deleguée'. Sophie Petit did not want to run anything, she just wanted to get back to work, to earn her own money and thus feel herself free and independent.

Outside of work, her relationship with Alphonse was comfortable and comforting. He was not a bad man. Maybe even a good man. Not a lot of laughs, though. She still missed that Maurice, the finish carpenter with the wicked sense of humor and that nicely naughty way of making love, that poor, wild boy who had so foolishly marched off as a soldier. With his funny Lyonnais accent that he would sometimes exaggerate for laughs. She had marveled at his intricate drawings and what she thought of as his playful little constructions, though he took them very seriously. Part of what made him interesting was his lust for adventure. Which, alas, must be why he volunteered for the army even though, as she had told him, he almost surely could have avoided service if he had wanted to. Foolish, charming Momo.

But here she was with Ti-Phonse as she called him, and he would do. He was kind and considerate, though usually focused on something far away. Lovemaking with him was not exciting, but it was comforting to feel a body next to hers after so many months of living alone, and a way of warding off anxiety.

'Phonse was spending most of his time, even evenings, somewhere else, not with other women, she was confident – he wasn't that type – but when he wasn't on duty with his Guard company he'd be off on one of what he called his investigations. He had got himself into one of the sedentary companies, so if he went up on the ramparts it was because he wanted to and he could come home whenever he wanted. Not like those men he talked about, out there for days, even weeks now, with no relief. Riflemen and especially the artillerymen who so impressed him.

Well, good. If their cannons kept the Versaillais away, then life could go on more or less peacefully here in the Marais.

When they got together and Alphonse had some wine, he loved to talk about his excitement at living this great revolution. That was fine, too, thought Sophie.

Yes, let those men all make their glorious revolution. She was content to be making gloves and collecting wages and living here quietly. And seeing her coworkers also settling into a good routine, but it would be better without all this agitation and cannon fire around them. Revolution she could leave alone. Especially since, as was obvious to her now, it inevitably meant war.

* * *

On Rue de la Corderie in the neighboring Third Arrondissement, Évariste continued to be one of those most enthusiastic about their revolution. It was so much more exciting than mining coal back there in Saint-Étienne. Which reminded him of his old workmate Jojo, Joseph Ducrin, and the kinds of changes he had dreamed about back there.

Thinking about Joseph Ducrin reminded him of Jojo's widow. He hadn't seen Angélique now for, it must be more than a month. He wondered if she was still in that house on Dragon Court. It was close to Larrey Street and the Marmite, so he could go and try to see her after lunch.

The Marmite was as busy and crowded as ever, but now most of the men eating and talking there were in National Guard uniform, as was he. Even the women, some of them now dressed as *cantinières*. It was a fetching costume, he thought. The same colors as the National Guard, but with a skirt and a cute little bonnet. And the girls – there was one in the full uniform – seemed so proud.

At the table he talked with some of the guys, who were mostly repeating to each other how strong the Paris fortifications were and that those enemy-of-the-people cannoneers were bound to get tired of pummeling our walls. Uh-huh, maybe so, he thought. If they were really confident, they wouldn't have to repeat it so often.

He noticed that some of them had battalion numbers which meant they were supposed to be on duty – he had been keeping track of those numbers and their assignments, through his comrades in the National Guard's headquarters which was in the same building as the International where he was working. Absenteeism of men in some of the battalions, maybe in almost all of them, had become a significant problem. He'd been hearing about it a lot lately. But he wasn't anyone to discipline those men. And reporting it wouldn't do any good, either; their captains surely knew who was missing, and would have to take whatever action they could. Usually just a mix of scolding and encouragement, the Guard didn't permit any severe punishments. This wasn't like the army.

The food was good, good enough, anyway, as always, and now, after relieving himself – the place to do it was downstairs, in a little house in the court – he was ready to see if he could find Angélique.

When he got up the stairs to her place, he heard children's

voices and he had to knock hard, two or three times, before he heard footsteps.

"'Riste!" said Angélique, delightedly.

"Hey, Lique, what's going on?"

"Good, good. Everything is good. Come on in, it's play time for the kids."

And there was that other girl, the one who arrived just before Évariste had left Dragon Court. What was her name?

"You remember Noëlle, don't you?" Lique said.

He nodded and even bowed a little, with as friendly a smile as he could manage.

"Together we are really making this work," Angélique went on. "She's been a big, big help. And we are now getting a subsidy from the mayor's office."

"Which means from the Commune."

"Yes, of course, that's where the mayor gets the money. And we can provide lunch for the children, and we have some books."

This was something that really pleased him, made him feel that they were accomplishing something real in this Commune. Seeing all those children, boys and girls, now able to read their first letters. And without a priest or a nun in sight. A real education, not indoctrination. If only he had had such an opportunity when he was little. He had learned how to read, finally, but he hadn't had much help. The Commune was really something worth fighting for, he told himself again.

* * *

Victorine had made the very deliberate decision to remain in Paris when René-Pierre decided to leave for Versailles.

He hadn't exactly invited her to accompany him, but she could have persuaded him to take her if she had wanted. But Versailles? What was there for an artist to do there?

Thanks in good part to René-Pierre's contacts, though, and also thanks to her own native talent, she had got a start with small roles in some of the theaters. Now she was determined to make it, to really make it. A lot of singers and actresses had left the city suddenly after 18th March, or were maybe hiding out somewhere, so that left more opportunity for her. She knew she had a seductive manner, she had seen how she could arouse lustful glances with her walk and her eye movements, and she also had, she thought, a pretty good voice. There were dramatic roles she would die for, if only she could get an audition, and that might be possible now. She was tired of the concert café scene, with all those drunken National Guards and their rude belches and obscenities, and their cigars and pipes smoking up the place. So far, her night at the Ambigu just after the proclamation of the Republic had been her biggest performance. Her only one in a really respectable theater. But it had just been a silly farce. She knew she could do more. If someone made a theater piece out of George Sand's *Consuelo,* that would be a perfect role for her.

Meanwhile, she was making enough money from the concert café acts to survive comfortably, here in the Fourth Arrondissement, and she had her lovers, including some with theater connections, and something, some good dramatic role, was bound to turn up. She didn't really miss René-Pierre at all, or that big apartment he had had in the snooty sixteenth with all those rich bourgeois. Those people, she knew, hated the Commune and couldn't wait to see it overthrown or crushed under foot. Here, in the center of the city, there was more of a mix of people, some very conservative and very opposed to the Commune, some enthusiastically embracing it, and most just doing like she was, making the most of the new opportunities without taking any unnecessary risks.

Her chance would come. She looked carefully through the newspapers, especially the *Journal officiel*, for all the announcements related to the theater and the arts. There was a big change coming in the Conservatory, now that the old man – he must be truly ancient, that director, Auber – was ill and bound to be replaced. The culture pages of the *Journal officiel* were full of news showing that the Commune was doing everything it could to promote new opportunities in the arts, and her chance had to come very soon.

* * *

Étienne came back, finally, to Rose's enormous relief. He had been gone a week, and she found him at home on Tuesday, 9th May. The Commune had now survived for over a month and a half.

Étienne's news was not good. Fort Issy had been totally destroyed by the bombardment. The men had been sleeping, very poorly, in the tombs of the Issy town cemetery, covering themselves from the rain as best they could with tarps and branches. Their cannons, that had for long kept the Versailles army back from the city walls, were of little use when the few artillery men who had survived had no more cover. No more support from Paris was arriving, food, cannons, or men, and the nearby fort at Vanves, whose cannons had helped save Issy up to then, had also fallen that same day, 8th May. The order had finally come to evacuate, which the entire garrison did at night. Louis Rossel, the War Delegate and one of the Commune's few experienced commanders, posted the disastrous news without authorization and then resigned the next day, 10th May, clearly frustrated by the lack of support by the Commune Council. The Commune now had no experienced military man as war *délégué*, supreme commander, and with the fall of the forts at Issy and Vanves, the way was clear for the enemy trenches and fortifications to creep ever closer to the city.

Titi was exhausted and wounded but only slightly. A bullet had gone through one calf muscle, his hearing had suffered, probably only temporarily, from the blasts of mortar explosives, and his right eye looked very bad – the constant firing, holding his rifle's 'snuff-box' against his cheek, had filled the eye with gunpowder and left the area around it bruised and burned. But he was going to get better, she was sure of it.

It had been hard for him, she knew, and there had been some very scary moments, but she saw him more content than at any time since the failed sortie in April. He had faced a major challenge and had been up to it.

* * *

Up in Belleville, news of the fall of the two forts had given Jules even more incentive to push his men to build barricades at the entrances to the quarter. It was going to be 1848 all over again, he was convinced. This time they, the workers in Belleville and Ménilmontant and La Villette and all the other working-class quarters would have to hang on to their independence. Barricades were the only means he knew to do it.

His wife, meanwhile, had been organizing her laundry, which now had a lot of work to do with all the blood and mud and gunpowder-stained uniforms. He knew she was working especially hard, but she seemed happy. And so were most of his men, in the foundry, still making more cannons and much else.

The news on Thursday that General Wroblewski had managed to retake both forts, Vanves and Issy, gave him some encouragement, but he knew that wasn't going to be enough to keep the Versailles army from trying to come up here to Belleville. Barricades were the only answer.

* * *

More bad news. Wroblewski's successful recovery of the two ruined forts had been very brief. His men had been forced to withdraw after two days of heavy shelling, which meant that the Versailles army could now use those forts' positions to train its own long-range cannons on the city walls.

But the walls were strong. Surely they would hold. Or so the papers said. And so did the leaders of the Commune, especially the new War Delegate, Charles Delescluze. At sixty-two, he was one of the oldest of the elected members of the Commune, a respected radical journalist regarded as rigidly honest but with absolutely no military experience. The enemies of the Commune, especially in the richer western arrondissements, must be terribly frustrated to see that old radical now in such a powerful position.

This at least was the opinion of Évariste, which Étienne took to be the more or less official view. But, as Évariste had also told him, there was no longer a single official view. The Commune council had now split; in response to the evacuation of Issy, the majority had voted to form a Committee of Public Salvation, taking its name from the one that had brought the Terror during the Great Revolution eighty years ago. Évariste called it a 'Blanquiste' idea, but there was no telling what Blanqui might say; he was still in a Versailles prison, incommunicado. One of the chief figures in the minority was Varlin, who Évariste knew was Étienne's special hero and the head of the Paris section of the International. As Évariste understood it, what he and the others in the minority – Malon and other Internationalists – feared was a dictatorship by a cabal of politicians interfering with military and social decisions they didn't really understand.

It seemed like the men elected to run the Commune were spending as much energy fighting each other as they were defending the city.

* * *

On Tuesday 16th May, Étienne and his whole battalion, accompanied by Rose and many other women, joined the crowd to watch and celebrate the toppling of the great column in the Place Vendôme – which turned out to be simpler than people had expected. The column wasn't really made of solid bronze, cast from the cannons seized by Napoleon I from the Russians and Austrians after the battle of Austerlitz, but was simple bricks with a bronze coating. It made a satisfying crash, though, and everybody smiled and applauded and shouted revolutionary slogans. Rose and Étienne even got their photograph taken, posing by the rubble.

But the truly big event was scheduled for the weekend: as announced in the *Journal officiel*,

> *Sunday, 21st May, Place de la Concorde, a grand festival will be presented by the musicians of all the*

battalions of the National Guard of Paris for the benefit of the widows, orphans and the National Guards wounded in defense of the Republic. Various patriotic pieces, performed by 1,500 musicians together, under the direction of citoyen Delaporte.

The musicians of *all* the battalions. Everyone except for the Guards manning the ramparts would have to be there. Too bad they were all playing together; Étienne was sure that his battalion's band was one of the best, but mixed in as part of 1,500 musicians, no one would ever notice. Anyway, he and Rose would be there.

He had splurged and bought two 1-franc tickets for best views – the 2-francs price for the terrace seats would be too extravagant, but the 50 centime seats would be too far back. Étienne didn't recognize the names of most of the composers on the program, but that didn't matter. It would be a lovely evening with Rose, and the price would go for the best of causes, for the wounded, the widows and the orphans.

That Sunday, the weather was lovely. Cannon shells were hitting too close to the Place de la Concorde, though, prompting the National Guard committee to move the concert to the safer Tuileries garden. Posters were put up to that effect, and men were posted on the street to advise concert goers of the change. An annoyance, but nothing to worry about, they said. The Paris defenses were impregnable.

Now that they were going to be in the Tuileries instead of Place de la Concorde, he wasn't sure where they would be, but with 1-franc tickets, they were ushered to fairly good seats toward the back of the garden. Étienne was sorry that he and Rose hadn't taken the opportunity to attend the earlier concerts that the Commune had held in the 'salle des Maréchaux'. He could hardly believe that such ordinary workers as they could be seated here in the courtyard of such a splendid palace.

The crowd was huge. The musicians were superb. Or at any rate, very loud. The battalion orchestras were most energetically blowing their horns and beating drums and cymbals and sawing at their fiddles, performing a grand selection of classic pieces, all entirely new to Étienne but impressive. With arias from operas and dramatic readings and the declamation of revolutionary poetry by the revered Victor Hugo. The whole show gave confidence in the robustness of Paris culture despite the civil war, the cannons that could be heard in the distance seemed merely to provide punctuation, as though part of the performances.

Victorine and her date were also there, seated several rows further forward and closer to the center. Victorine smiled and nodded at the people around her, even though she didn't know them, fussed with her hair, and tried to remember the name of the man who had brought her – Gaspard, was it? Yes, she thought that was it. Nice, eager young fellow who worked as an assistant in one of the theaters. She smiled again when, in a brief moment of relative silence after the overtures, he said loudly enough for the patrons around them to hear that she should be the one declaiming the verses of Hugo. But the theater directors still saw her as a concert-café chanteuse, which was their mistake, he said. Such gallantry! She warmed to the thought of being invited to perform on such a vast stage and squeezed his arm, and was about to say, "Oh, Gaspard –" when, just in time, she remembered that Gaspard had been that older choral director she had been with last week.

At the close of the concert, after two hours of music, the

master of ceremonies, a National Guard colonel, mounted the stage beside the orchestra director and announced that the performance would be repeated on the following night, but at the Opera. Wonderful, thought Victorine!

The Opera, now there was a hall where Victorine could really show off her talent. She wasn't on the program yet, but she would be one day soon, she was sure of it. Yes, the Commune had a lot to celebrate. It had survived now, for two whole months, and was still going strong. The voices of the chorus and the orchestra confirmed it.

The same officer continued, in a commanding voice,

"*Citoyens,* Monsieur Thiers promised that he would enter Paris yesterday. M. Thiers has not entered. He will not enter. I invite you for next Sunday, 28th, here, at this same place for our second concert in benefit of the widows and orphans."

* * *

Rose's parents had not joined the crowd in the Tuileries. They had heard the cannon fire during the day and were both worried, especially Jules, who had become unusually nervous. He spent most of the afternoon inspecting the barricades, not only on the narrow streets leading to their house but also at other strategic corners in Belleville and Ménilmontant.

Most of them he found entirely unguarded. True, everything seemed calm here on the hillsides, and the chiefs in the Commune had been reassuring about the strength of the city's defenses, but he and Blanche had vivid memories of that other revolution, '48, and the deadly fire at the barricades. At the few barricades where he saw someone standing or sitting, keeping watch, it was either an old man, some old enough to have seen that still earlier revolution in 1830, or a few boys twelve or fourteen, eager to get into battle.

Perhaps he shouldn't worry. It had been months now, and the Versailles army had not been able to breach the walls. Perhaps. But it had been a long siege, the second long siege since December, and the battalions were weary. And there were still those Prussians, just outside the walls to the north and east. No telling what they might do.

To help him calm down, Blanche had suggested that they stay home that night and do something special, something they hadn't found time or energy to do in too long a time. And Jules, getting her drift, didn't want to wait till evening.

The neighborhood was unusually quiet, probably because so many of their neighbors had gone to the grand concert. And Blanche and Jules made love almost as they remembered doing it twenty years before.

* * *

A little before noon, a messenger had brought Hippolyte Mireau the order he had been expecting for over a week. He and his squad of twenty hand-picked policemen, *gardiens de la paix*, in their dark blue military-style uniforms and armed with chassepots, assembled in the transport lot to be taken by army carriages to the army post just outside the Point du Jour, barely a dozen kilometers from Versailles.

This south-east corner of the ramparts was the most exposed section of the city's fortifications, jutting out from the wall toward Versailles. Versailles' forces had bombarded it especially heavily for weeks. And had almost as incessantly been fired upon by the Fédérés' artillery mounted there.

But there had been a lull in the firing from the Fédérés, and just this morning army scouts, alerted by a civilian inside the city, had discovered that the ramparts there were unmanned. However the troops and especially their commanding officers feared some sinister trap, and hesitated. Better to send in the police, the generals decided. The police would be more familiar with the city, was their voiced argument. That the police were less likely than the soldiers to flee in panic or to refuse to advance against other Frenchmen was the real, unvoiced, reason. Or so Mireau was convinced.

For that or the other reason it would be Hippolyte Mireau and his squad of police who were to be the first forces from Versailles to breach the wall and enter Paris since the beginning of the civil war. To clear the way for the Army of Versailles and the reconquest of Paris.

He barely noticed the trajectory, so concentrated was he on this momentous act and checking to see the determined faces of his men. And then they were there, before the battered walls at the Point du Jour. Hippolyte checked his watch. It was just after 3 p.m. on Sunday, 21st May.

It was a strange, eerie sensation, to look up at the still imposing ramparts at Point du Jour and not hear a shot, or a shout, or anything at all beyond the fluttering wings of a gray pigeon perched on the broken rim of the high, thick wall. The bird cocked its head to stare with one eye at Mireau and his blue-uniformed *gardiens de la paix*, oblivious as was Hippolyte himself to the larger mass of red-trousered soldiers lined up in ranks behind them.

Mireau turned to look at the general on horseback behind him and nodded sharply. Upon receiving an answering nod, he raised his right arm to point toward the wall and the city beyond. He then swung his left hand holding the rifle in a wide arc forward. The command to his men. As they rushed toward the ladders that the army engineers had propped against the wall, the pigeon fluttered up and off toward the city, as though to spread the alarm.

VI

Le chant du départ

Song of Departure

(Refrain)
The Republic calls on us
May we conquer or perish
A Frenchman must live for her
For her a Frenchman must die.
A Frenchman must live for her
For her a Frenchman must die.

Song of Departure

The long-awaited breakthrough of the city's walls had been surprisingly easy. It was now clear that the Saint-Cloud gate had been wide open and undefended for days, but the generals, fearing a trap, had kept their troops outside until now, continuing to fire explosive mortar shells at the now completely ruined rampart.

But now, in the hours since Mireau had signaled the 'All clear', the entire 4th and 5th corps had slipped in, nearly 30,000 men, wary of ambushes. They had encountered very little resistance at first, and so far had been able quickly to overwhelm the pockets of National Guards they met. The first Fédérés they encountered had been so surprised at the sudden appearance of so many red-trousered troops that they hadn't even fired. Those who had fired and tried to hold their position were quickly surrounded, shot if they didn't immediately drop their weapons.

Among the hundreds of National Guards taken prisoner in the first hours was an entire company from the Javel chemical factory, just across the river on the left bank in the Fifteenth. Their captain, a tall, thin redhead whose men called him Hilaire, had given the order to cease firing only when he saw that they had been completely surrounded by an entire regiment. He had stared in open-mouthed astonishment, then indignation as he and his men were forced to drop their weapons. His look turned to proud defiance as an army sergeant, ordered by his own captain, ripped the National Guard captain's insignia from his tunic before snatching off his kepi, which the sergeant tucked into his shirt as a trophy. These prisoners, including three badly wounded who had to be carried by their comrades, would join others to be marched later to the new prison camps that the Versaillais were going to have to build.

And behind the infantry, the artillery units rolled in their cannons on their caissons. And then the cavalry, *chasseurs à cheval* and *dragons* ('dragoons').

Hippolyte and the high command were aware that this was happening while the battalion orchestras were performing for the crowd in the distant Tuileries, having read the announcement in the Commune's *Journal officiel*. A lucky break, this coincidence, that the discovery of the undefended rampart occurred while so many of their opponents were distracted by their entertainment. Here in the Sixteenth Arrondissement, near the Bois de Boulogne, the fanfare from the concert could not be heard. And, he supposed, since the Versailles cannons had gone momentarily silent, those seated in the Tuileries must have remained oblivious to the Versailles incursion. Good. The later those communards reacted, the better.

It was not until late in the afternoon that Dombrowski appeared, leading a column in an attack to drive the army back. It was a lightning attack but undermanned and, for once, the astute Pole had misjudged the timing and struck too late – too many troops had already entered and installed themselves with *mitrailleuses* and cannons in what had been the bulwarks of the Fédérés. The soldiers and artillery repulsed that counterattack causing many casualties, Dombrowski presumably among them, though his body had not been recovered – probably, the high command assumed, withdrawn by his comrades in their hasty retreat.

The colonel on horseback next to Mireau was delighted at this first victory over his prime foe. The blond Pole in his austere, undecorated uniform taunting his enemies, whether on foot behind a parapet or astride his black horse, had assumed a mystical power in his imagination. More even than that other Pole, Wroblewski, or the several French commanders, all to be taken seriously but none as dramatically insolent.

Having taken few casualties, accidental injuries as much as bullet wounds, the army quickly spread through the streets of Paris's affluent westernmost district, where the civilians seemed overjoyed to see the Versailles troops. Or at least, those women who came out to present flowers to the officers and even to embrace the men.

Things would become much tougher as the army tried to advance further east, into the working-class districts, Hippolyte was certain. But at least the reconquest was underway.

That night he and his policemen camped in a neighborhood park, while most of the troops who had fought that first day went back to their own camp back outside the city walls. Those troops would be given a day's rest, to be replaced tomorrow by fresh soldiers, so as not to endure too much strain. Versailles had no shortage of men now, with the release of the Prussian prisoners of war and the drafting of new troops from the countryside. Hippolyte's policemen, however, would not enjoy such a rest. They and other police would have to continue on the job: scouting and then the dangerous job of inspecting the houses in the conquered blocks, looking for weapons or dangerous individuals.

Some of the higher-ranking officers, Hippolyte had observed, had accepted invitations from, or perhaps had forced themselves into, some of the most elegant mansions of the district and no doubt were celebrating this first day's success with better wine and food than was available in the officers' mess.

* * *

As they walked home that evening after the Tuileries, Étienne remarked that it was unusually calm. The cannon fire had stopped entirely for the moment, which seemed unexplainable but welcome. The sky was clear, the spring weather delightful. All the way back to their apartment across the river, Étienne kept repeating in his mind the assurances they had heard from the stage that the city's defenses would never be breached. Wishing that he could believe it, but at the same time remembering the terrors he had seen and lived through in the terrible destruction of the fort at Issy.

Rose, still hearing in her mind strains of orchestral music, reflected on all the things she, with others in the Commune, had been able to accomplish. Especially important to her was the Women's Union, and how much she felt she had grown by joining in those efforts led by those two amazing and so different women, the worker Nathalie and the foreign aristocrat Élizabeth. The excitement she had seen in the other women, working women, taking charge of their own industries. They had begun something very big and important here in Paris.

Sensing her partner's unease, she grasped his arm as they

crossed the Pont Royal and continued along the river toward the Sixth. The barricades they passed were mostly half-built, chest-high affairs that would no doubt be built higher and stronger if real danger appeared. But for now all was calm. Little groups of men and women were lingering and talking on the streets, enjoying the air.

But still Étienne was nervous. After they had climbed up to their little apartment, she invited him by look and gesture to embrace her. And soon they lay together, flesh to flesh, bone to bone along their narrow, lumpy bed. Only then did she begin to feel secure and endeavored to bring him into her so that he too would feel secure. She had been careful not to let him see that she was as nervous as he.

But here, tonight, with her Titi's arms around her and his long legs held tightly between her thighs, her womanhood embracing his manhood within her, she enjoyed a thrill that blotted out the fear, completing her union with this other, beloved being.

He, stretched out on their narrow bed and clutching her as tightly as he could without hurting her, imagined her as a beam within the maelstrom, a floating fragment to which he was hanging on for survival against the tremors and currents of bombs, bullets, cries and fears, his enduring memories of the battles at Issy, of his hours up on the ramparts, but also of his shameful panic in that terrible failed expedition back in April. By hanging on to her he felt safe, removed from danger and anguish, if only for the moment. He felt energy from her body surge into his, and his he felt must be flowing into her, giving them joint power greater than that of either of them alone.

The Commune would survive because it was theirs, he believed. It was something they had created – all of them, all working together, because that was what 'commune' meant. And here, in this narrow bed, this young and generous and loving woman, and this equally young and energetic, impulsive nervous man, had solidified their own indestructible commune. And with this dream they could sleep.

Until just before dawn, when an explosion only blocks away startled them awake. The war continued. He clutched her once again, then released her and sprang to his feet to don his uniform.

* * *

The explosion also awoke Hippolyte, on his uncomfortable army cot under a tent. He had not been this close to the cannon fire before now, and it was a bit of a shock. He knew it was very early, and he wanted to go back to sleep, but more explosions followed, fired, he knew, from nearby but their shells landing somewhere near the defenses of the Fédérés.

Instead, between blasts, he thought over yesterday's events, and what they might mean for today and tomorrow.

The officers he'd taken supper with were more relaxed than they had been at the start of the day. Repulsing that attack by Dombrowski, and probably killing him, had left them almost confident now of easy success. But the ordinary soldiers, he knew, were still uneasy.

It had been his job to interview them, to get a sense of the variety and contradictions of their half-formed political opinions and their mixed feelings. Many were farm boys, newly recruited and prone to believe the wildest myths of the great city. Most of the others were former prisoners of war, released by the Prussians to let Versailles rebuild its army –

but not one big enough to restart the war against Prussia. To excite them against the Parisians, the Versailles press had insisted over and over again that the Commune was the work of foreigners, supposedly – according to *Le Gaulois* in article after article – in the pay of those same Prussians.

At the beginning almost all of the common soldiers, whether peasant recruits or army veterans, had been extremely reluctant to fire on other Frenchmen. Which explained the debacle on 18th March. Even weeks after that fiasco, after drilling and haranguing and purging the troops of possible Commune sympathizers, when they had to stop the Commune's legions from pushing towards Versailles, nearly a third of the infantrymen had lagged far behind or found other ways to avoid combat. Firing into the air, some even running away at the first shots.

But the army as a whole had won the day, thanks mainly to its artillery and cavalry, and that had changed things. That first taste of victory had given the soldiers confidence. And some of them at least believed the accounts in the *Gaulois* and the *Soir*, the only papers they were permitted to read, feeding them stories of supposed atrocities by the Commune. With nothing about the violence on the Government's side, which Hippolyte knew about because he had the rare privilege of reading the Paris papers, full of news of chilling massacres of Fédérés who had surrendered, stories he had been able to check out with his sources in the officer corps and which were not always exaggerations. But he assumed that on both sides, the violence went far beyond what might be necessary in combat. Emotions were raw.

However many of the soldiers, especially the older ones, were skeptical of the atrocity stories and paid little attention to them. There was something else driving them to want to crush the Commune: time. After weeks of war and the slow, grinding advance against the outer forts and villages, they just wanted to go home. And they blamed the Commune for keeping it going. Crushing the Paris insurrection, by whatever means they had to, had become an urgent, personal desire for those men.

Also, they were soldiers, all of them, trained to obey orders. Reluctant or enthusiastic, they would do as they were told, at least when under the eye of a corporal or an officer.

By around ten that Monday morning, after inspecting his men to make sure they were ready, he and his brigadier, Chardon, accompanied several officers to inspect the ruined shed that had been Dombrowski's command post in La Muette. The walls were full of holes, and the crumbling space had been emptied of any sensitive documents. The general and his aides had clearly decamped in a hurry.

Greater numbers of army troops had by now flowed in, through the blasted gates of Passy, Auteuil, Saint-Cloud, Sèvres, Versailles. Pouring into Paris. The edge of Paris, the rich western edge of the great city. And so far, with little difficulty. The officers in command now had no doubt that they would wipe out the resistance easily and quickly.

Hippolyte hoped that they were right, but decades of police work had conditioned him to be skeptical, especially of situations or conclusions that appeared too easy. Depending on the advance of the army, his police would be required either to scout for ways around barricades or, in those sections already subdued, to conduct searches for dangerous communards, anyone with a rifle or a National Guard uniform or with signs of gunpowder on his hands.

* * *

Some time around noon the Commune's chiefs in the Hôtel de Ville must have realized that something serious had happened in the western districts. Posters appeared calling all citizens to arms and bravely declaring that the spirit and bravery of the people would quickly expel the enemy because mighty Paris could never be defeated.

By then, the renewed cannon fire and the call-to-arms drumbeat could be heard throughout the Sixth Arrondissement. It was time to spring into action.

Étienne and Rose had been up since that early cannon blast before dawn. Taking time only for a quick embrace, they rushed downstairs, where the first thing they saw was a group of women, older men and children building up the barricade that yesterday had been barely chest high. The boys and girls were scraping up dirt and bringing it in wheelbarrows to patch the holes in the growing, neatly ordered pile of paving stones, bed frames, scraps of other furniture and even mattresses.

Étienne reached down to scoop up a paving stone to add to the pile and Rose lifted another one, before they turned to look at one another again. With his look of concern and eagerness, no words were necessary. She knew he had to rush to his company's assembly point. She watched him running to Saint-Germain, rifle in hand. She, in her *cantinière* uniform, then hurried toward the Ménagère for victuals to take to the barricades.

As he ran, he passed other groups building barricades at major intersections in a frenzy of panic and elation. Panic, because the danger was ever nearer. Elation, at least in some faces, because they believed this would be the long-expected and decisive battle, the one that if they won, would make their Commune at last secure.

About half the men of his company were already in the square. Some talking excitedly, some tensely quiet and looking defiant. Étienne heard talk about the number of enemy troops, suspicions that treason must have let them in, and a loud discussion about the cannons, which battalions would get how many and where to place them.

"How many do we have in the legion?" he asked Claude. The legion meant the dozen battalions in the Sixth, about 10,000 men if everyone reported for duty.

"In the whole legion? Who knows? Must be hundreds," Claude answered. "Last I counted, we had about a dozen in our battalion."

"No, we should have at least sixty!" interrupted one of the other men. "Because our section of the Sixth is really vital!"

"You know what? Every other battalion commander, just like ours, is going to fight to get the good ones, the big ones."

This from still another of the Guards.

"And where are the artillery men to man them?"

Funny. Or not really funny, just disappointing. It struck Étienne that all this should have been worked out before, how many cannons they had and where best to place them and who would man them. But, as everyone knew by now, in this ultra-democratic pseudo-army they could never fight as a legion, or even as a united battalion, but each company was going to fight as best it could, improvising its strategy independently.

And maybe it didn't matter. The only thing that mattered now was to inflict enough damage on the invaders to make them run back in defeat. As the rebels had tried to do in '48, as Rose's father, Jules, liked to recount.

Étienne's company, with Claude and the others, was assigned to the barricade at Croix-Rouge Street. And, to his amazement and delight, he realized that the man giving orders was Varlin. Étienne had known that he was commander of a battalion in the Sixth, but he had never before been so close. He elbowed Claude and shouted "Hurrah!" He felt – not confidence, because he knew that there was no assurance of surviving or beating back the Versaillais – but a sense of dignity, knowing he was doing the right thing, with this chance to fight alongside the man who more than any other exemplified his ideals, as tradesman and leader in the struggle for a fairer world.

They were joined by other Fédérés fleeing from the neighboring Seventh Arrondissement, which was now almost completely occupied by the enemy, they said. They had seen men who had surrendered being summarily shot, the newcomers told them. That meant that they had no choice but to resist or run, and if they ran they would almost surely be shot. And there in front of them appeared the mass of enemy troops, firing and trying to set up their cannons as Étienne and his fellows did their best to pick them off.

They had been firing for hours and it was already noon when a very young girl found Étienne. She was dressed as a miniature *cantinière*, in a uniform that was like his, but with a flared blue skirt and tailored tunic with space for breasts that the child did not yet have. But, though she couldn't have been more than twelve or thirteen, she really was a *cantinière*, carrying a basket of food, wine, and gauze and alcohol for wounds. She had been asking at the barricade until she found him.

"Citoyen Bonin? Étienne Bonin?" she demanded.

"Yes, that's me." He thought he recognized her.

"Titine? Rose's helper in the Marmite?"

"Citoyenne Rose Durand has given me a message for

you. That you are not to worry about her, that she is with a company from the Women's Association. They are heading to Montmartre."

She handed him and the men next to him some bread and wine, before standing on a fallen paving stone to peer over the barricade and shout, *"Vive la Commune, fils de putains!"*

Then she ducked down as bullets whizzed over her head and said "I have to catch up to them. Good luck, comrades." And off she ran.

Étienne barely had time to worry about Rose or what might be happening up on Montmartre. His chassepot was hot in his hands from all the firing, but then the enemy soldiers broke into some nearby houses and began firing on them from the upper floors. Then the heavy cannons they had rolled in blew away a great section of their barricade, killing or disabling at least a half a dozen men. The cannons swiveled to point to the section where Étienne was firing next to Claude. There was nothing the survivors in his company could do but run to try to find a stronger point to defend, further east. He grabbed Claude's arm – knowing Claude couldn't run as fast as he – and they headed toward a bigger, stronger barricade with cannons, in the Fifth near the river.

* * *

Not far from that barricade on Croix-Rouge Street that Étienne, Claude and the others had just abandoned, Noëlle had gathered a dozen of her students who, along with a few adults, had piled up another ramshackle barricade on Rue du Dragon before the entrance to Dragon Court. A company of Versailles soldiers had rushed by, but seeing they were only women and children, had ignored them as their captain shouted to them to hurry on, they had more important points to take.

Noëlle shouted after them. She had somehow got hold of a rifle, an old cavalry carbine, muzzle-loaded, and with the help of one of the boys, she had got it loaded and took a shot at the departing soldiers.

"Stop that!" cried Angélique. "Our job is to keep these kids safe."

"And save our school," answered Noëlle. "They want to destroy everything. Everything we've done. These monsters will be worse than the Prussians in Soissons."

Then another company of Versailles troops spotted them and especially the red flag that Noëlle had planted on top of their pile of rubble, paving stones and broken bedding. This time the troops opened fire. Noëlle lurched to protect one of the children and was hit.

Luc gasped when he saw her fall and hurried to her side, keeping low to avoid the gunfire. She smiled at him and said, "We must stop them. We must. Stop them or die, because they want to take away everything that we have won."

He tried to hold up her head. Angélique, in her nurse's uniform and with her basket of supplies, tried to staunch the blood.

"Is that Luc?" Noëlle asked.

"Yes, I'm here. I'm with you, my beauty."

He was choking back tears.

"In my basket. The book. You have to save the book."

Not sure he understood, he found a book in the basket of food and water she had brought from their flat.

"You must save it. It is the Commune," she said, with a fading smile. "It is our work. And J-P's. And all of us."

More soldiers had by now taken an interest in their humble, child-defended barricade and Luc, clutching the book, looked around desperately.

A hand grasped his arm.

"Come on. It's too late for her. I know a place."

He didn't recognize the man's voice, but a glance told him he could only be a ragpicker, in his worn and ancient army tunic. A new volley of shots frightened him and he let himself be guided by this stranger, running and shuffling back into Dragon Court and into a narrow passageway he hadn't even known existed.

* * *

Victorine had slept late after the concert and woke up in a strange bed, the bed of… Gaston, or was it Gaspard? They'd been singing and drinking until late that night, and now, here she was. He really had a fairly nice voice that Gas– pard? A rather rough manner in bed and a hairy torso, but that hardly mattered. The important thing, what had drawn her to him, was that he said he was an old friend of *Maestro* Daniel, the new director of the Conservatory. Where Victorine was going to have to go tomorrow – Tomorrow, was it? Or today? She stopped to think. The concert had been on Sunday, so this must be Monday, 22nd, and Maestro Daniel's call for artists to come for the re-opening of the Conservatory was 23rd. Yes! Tomorrow, Tuesday. Then she had a day to prepare. For her big chance to perform the kind of role she had been dreaming of.

Gastro or whatever was still half-asleep. She kissed him on his forehead and said she had to rush. She was going to get dressed and made up for her role as an Oriental princess, and the hair alone was going to take her most of the day. She dressed hurriedly in last night's red concert-going gown and ran out to the street to get to her own rented room, where she had already collected all she needed for her costume.

There was a great commotion, though, before she could get there, more even than in the past few days. Some citizens insisted that she help construct a barricade. She didn't want to damage her nails, but she could hardly refuse to lift a paving stone. A barricade on Rue du Temple! Who would have thought it? This was like a scene from a tragic opera, just the thing for Victorine Martin!

Or maybe she should find a more dramatic, a more theatrical name. 'Victorine' was fine, it sounded like victory. But 'Martin'? Awfully plebeian. Well, she'd think of something.

She found another barricade on the corner just outside the place with her rented room. And so many armed and excited people! Something must be about to happen. Oh, this was so dramatic! She loved it. But now she would have to get herself together for tomorrow's audition, as she saw it. That maestro with the Spanish name, Francisco Something Daniel, hadn't actually said it would be an audition, but it would be her chance to catch his attention.

She would recite some favorite verses. Lamartine, perhaps; everybody by now had heard enough Hugo.

* * *

Place Blanche, where Boulevard Clichy was joined by five other streets near the foot of Montmartre, would be an obligatory crossing point for troops seeking to attack the Commune's most important fortress, Montmartre, the highest point in all the city, from which the Fédérés' cannons could strike wide areas of the district and beyond. Here people from the neighborhood and many others had erected an especially formidable barricade, and here was where Rose found herself, in the company of more than a hundred women, a half a dozen men – mostly older – and numerous children. Including Titine, who arrived panting and proudly told Rose she had delivered her message.

Rose was not a riflewoman but a *cantinière*, a provider of food and drink to combatants. In her uniform she looked almost like a National Guard, at least from the blue tunic up, and now she thought that she was going to have to act like one. The sounds of cannons, *mitrailleuses* and rifles, and the shouts and bugle calls, signaled the approach of the forces set to destroy the Commune.

The women, many of whom she recognized from earlier Women's Association meetings, had no shortage of rifles. Someone told her they had got them from the mayor's office in the Eighteenth. A boy and a girl disputed the privilege of showing her how to load and fire one, the girl finally imposing herself as tutor. Had that girl actually fired one? Well, no, she answered, but she had watched and knew how it was done.

Rose saw her mother behind the part of the barricade blocking the street heading most directly up the hill. She ran over to embrace her. Blanche looked fiercely proud.

"This is what we had to do in '48," she said. "This time, we'll really show them! And look, we are all women."

"No, Mother, look, there's a man over there. And another one. And several boys."

"Fine. More than welcome. But this is a woman's company, and they'll have to do as we say. We've elected Claudine there, the tall one in the kepi, as our captain. As she says, we are to hold our fire until we see them close, or else, or else it will be a lot harder."

"Is this like the gun you used in '48?"

"No, hardly. Everything's changed. And I didn't really shoot then, just fed the cartridges to your father, Jules, and the other men. Everything's more modern. Including this big gun. But Louise, there, she showed me."

"Louise? Oh, that Louise! There she is. My partner from the bindery! Wait, I have to go greet her!"

"Go ahead. We're going to be here all night. Your father is back in Belleville, they've built a barricade on Rue du Jourdain. This is the first time I won't be by his side when we're fighting. But he's the man in charge back there, so he couldn't leave. And I had to come here, with all my women comrades from the Association. He and I agreed to defend Montmartre."

Rose hugged her mother again and then lurched over to where she had seen her former workmate in the bindery.

"Louise!"

"Rose. You look stunning in that uniform, just like a female National Guard. I should have become a *cantinière*, too, but it really doesn't matter. However we're dressed, our task is going to be to fight, not to feed the troops."

"Is Cécile here too?"

"No, I haven't seen her. She's maybe with Claude. You knew that they had got together, didn't you?"

"No! I thought she had a crush on Toinou."

"Crush, crush. Those things pass. I got together with Albert, but he was killed at Vanves."

"Oh! I'm so sorry."

"We all have a lot of sorrows. Which is why we have to keep fighting. How about you? Still with the long-legged southerner? What did you call him? Titi, right?"

"Yes, but I had to leave him in the Sixth. With his Guard company. We all have our duties in this crisis. Oh, I hope he survives."

"We all hope we all survive. But we know we won't, not all of us. I want to shoot at least one of the bastards for Albert. And another one for my older brother, and as many others as I can for all the people they've killed so senselessly. And you know? I've got pretty good aim. We have to save our cannons up on the hill."

"It's getting dark. They might sneak up on us."

"That's all right. We'll be alert. Go ask Claudine there, she's a clothes-presser or was, heading her laundry. Or Blanche – is she your mom? I saw you talking with her. She's the second in command, in case anything happens to Claudine. She'll tell you when it will be your turn to stand watch. You know how to fire that thing you're carrying?"

"I think so."

"Good. And now we just wait and watch, and maybe sing a little. At nightfall, which is coming soon, you and I can take turns sleeping. But check with Claudine first."

"I'm so sorry about Albert."

Louise said nothing but turned her face away.

* * *

Tuesday. Alphonse was not in Guard uniform, just his ordinary frayed suit as a working journalist, but he had secured a pass signed by Delescluze and another by the Commune's police prefect, Rigault, which permitted him to pass by the many barricades in the surrounding neighborhoods, all the way to the Hôtel de Ville. He arrived just as the barely breathing body of Dombrowski was carried in by his men. Dombrowski had survived the fighting on Sunday and then moved his command post to a barricade at the base of Montmartre, where he had been mortally hit on Rue Myrha, not far from the other barricades at Place Blanche and Place Pigalle. According to the men who brought in the body, the Versailles army's First Corps had entered Paris from the north, at the St Ouen Gate, supposedly neutral territory held by the Prussians, and had attacked the barricades from above.

Carefully, slowly and very gently, four tired and powder-stained men in torn uniforms carried the slight body of their general, from the entry hall and down a corridor into what, as Alphonse learned from muttered conversation, had been the bedroom of Baron Haussmann's daughter. He joined others crowding at the door as the men, all very young, lay the corpse on the blue satin bed cover, straightened the bloodied, undecorated tunic and brushed the long, sweated hair back from the general's face. One of the corpse-bearers muttered some words of what Alphonse assumed must be a poem in Polish, and another repeated, in French, a long and solemn *adieu*.

The new Versailles incursion was from the north, but the red flag could still be seen flying atop Montmartre. This meant that the Commune's cannons and *mitrailleuses* assembled there surely must enter action soon. Or such was the general opinion at the Hôtel de Ville. Outside, bombshells and rifle fire continued their racket, but no cannons roared from Montmartre.

Around the government palace itself, men were frantically building up barricades, quite late in the game. The Commune had never expected the fighting to come this close, but now Delescluze and the others in the Commune's newly proclaimed 'Committee of Public Safety' were truly concerned.

Nobody he had seen seemed to have slept except in snatches during the night. In the Hôtel de Ville itself, National Guards, exhausted from building and fighting, were stretched out on the corridors, some of them snoring, while others stirred all around them. Alphonse himself had hardly slept since leaving Sophie on Monday, and he was half-asleep on his feet. In one of the inner offices, he was startled to see a half-dozen young men who seemed not only wide awake but also unnaturally calm in the midst of the chaos, bending over papers and writing. He approached to find out what they were up to. One of them, the insignia on the shoulders of his Guard uniform indicating that he was a second lieutenant, turned to him, smiling – which also seemed eerie in the circumstances – and showed him: an appeal to the soldiers of Versailles to abandon their officers and fraternize with their brothers in the Commune, as they had on 18th March.

And how were they going to get that message out to those soldiers? Another smile, and the calm young officer said they would be sure to see the posters on the walls. Now, looking into his eyes, Alphonse saw a glimmer that made him think that the man was not really awake, not in the ordinary sense of being aware of his surroundings, but in a trance.

The officer-scribe was writing a message to the hordes to stop marauding and embrace their brothers as they had on 18th March? If that was the defense strategy, God help us! thought Alphonse.

* * *

After hours of shooting, the barricade at Place Blanche was overrun late Tuesday afternoon, attacked by troops who came from Saint-Ouen in the north. The Prussians, supposedly neutral, had let the Versailles regiments pass through. Around three that afternoon, Claudine was wounded and fell, and when Blanche raised the red flag in one hand and a rifle in another, she too was shot. Rose, keeping low, ran to the side of her mother and held her.

"Run," Blanche told her. "Run to our home, to Belleville. Stand with your father, my Jules. My time has come. Tell him, tell him I will meet him later, up there."

"Up there?"

Blanche raised a finger toward the heavens. A new volley of bullets shattered pieces of the barricade around them.

"Run!" shouted Louise. "There's another barricade at Pigalle. I got some of them! But I'm not through."

And Rose let down her mother's head, as gently as she could, and – crouching – got up and ran down the boulevard.

In her run from Place Blanche to Place Pigalle, Rose lost one of her *godillots*, the heavy, solid marching shoes issued to the National Guards, but kept running with a limping skip, holding tight to her rifle. At Pigalle, there were already a dozen corpses, women and men, with only a few people still resisting. But they had no more cartridges for her Remington, an older gun than the others. Under a new assault, the few remaining fighters were preparing to run. Rose threw down her useless rifle, unlaced and kicked off her remaining boot and ran, barefoot, as fast as she could and ignoring her bloody feet, all the way toward Buttes de Chaumont and Belleville. Where she hoped at least to see her father.

* * *

From their barricade in the Sixth Étienne and Claude, panting, running and dodging shells and skirting other barricades for what must have been a half an hour, crossed the river and ran along its edge until they reached the huge and multi-storied barricade on the Rue de Rivoli, Étienne half dragging Claude the last few paces. There Brunel – one of the few Commune commanders with military experience – was using his cannons to 'sweep' the thoroughfare of the advancing Versaillais, leaving corpses and other debris. But hardly had Étienne had a chance to rest before the enemy abandoned the impassable avenue and broke into the buildings on either side to fire down from their upper stories. To stop them, Brunel gave orders to burn those buildings. Then incendiary shells from the Versailles mortars set the Ministry of Finances aflame, adding to the enormous blaze.

And still the enemy could not advance. Étienne managed to sleep only for moments at a time, before being nudged to resume firing. Continuing now by the light of the fires, through the night, while the Versailles troops were working their way through adjoining neighborhoods to get around the barricade. Until finally, on Wednesday morning, bombarded and assaulted from all sides, the great barricade fell.

Étienne and Claude, hardly aware of what they were doing, ran and were among those who escaped. They were too tired to think but their bodies moved by reflex and a commitment to struggle, combat inertia, driven into them by the ceaseless combat until it had become a kind of instinct. Running ever eastward, to turn and fire on the approaching enemy at every opportunity.

Behind them, the victorious Versailles troops simply shot their prisoners, the dozens they had managed to trap, and threw their bodies into the ditch in front of the barricade.

At some point Claude could not continue but collapsed just as they reached the new barricades outside the Hôtel de

Ville. Étienne could not abandon him, but he knew that this was not a defensible position. Looking up at him with a look of terror and dismay, Claude said he could not, he just could not, not any longer. He struggled to his feet, threw his rifle down far from him and tore off his tunic.

He was not the first, Étienne knew. All along the way from that last, now destroyed great barricade on Rue de Rivoli, they had seen discarded kepis, tunics, canteens and anything else that would identify a man as a National Guard. If Claude could find some place to hide, someone who would take him in and give him other clothes and find him space in a basement or an attic or a closet, he might survive. Or not. But he could no longer continue running and firing, firing and running, from barricade to barricade before the ceaseless advance of the enemy.

It meant abandoning the struggle, abandoning the Commune. He knew that and was in tears. But he was exhausted and felt that he could not lift a rifle again.

"Pardon me, my buddy," he said.

Étienne embraced him, with a "*Bon courage*, and *bonne chance*." And he turned to hasten to the next site where he heard firing. Toward the Place de la Bastille, where his revolution had begun on 18th March, and where perhaps it would end.

* * *

"Chief?"

Chardon's voice broke in on police *commissaire* Hippolyte Mireau's thought as he contemplated the cadavers all around them in Place Blanche. Turning toward his sergeant, Mireau lifted an eyebrow to invite him to speak.

"Why?" asked Chardon, almost shouting. "Why this, this…"

"Killing?" supplied Mireau. "Or do you mean the resistance?"

"Women. They're almost all women."

"Nn-hnn. And old men, older than I. And far older than you. Or than any of the soldiers. And children."

"Chief. Pardon me, pardon me for asking, but I don't know, I don't know whether you've ever seen anything like this before, in all your years in the police. I've been with you for nearly seven years now, and before that, I was an ordinary *sergent-de-ville* assigned to Les Halles. I thought I'd seen everything. Vicious murders, bloody killings over small gains. Or over nothing. But this…"

This hardened police sergeant was almost crying.

"Look at that one, the little one with all the blood in her hair. Dressed like a *cantinière*, and with a rifle in her hand."

Hippolyte waited for a moment, thinking, or merely glimpsing scenes past.

"You asked me if I had ever seen anything like this. Here, in a central square of Paris. Tens, dozens of corpses. No, Eloi, the barricades of '51, which I did see, were not like this."

He remained silent, looking at but not really focusing on the small body Chardon had pointed out.

"I didn't think you even knew my first name, Chief."

Hippolyte almost smiled.

"I know my men. Or something about them. You are from Noisy, right?"

"Noisy-le-Grand, yes sir."

"Farm country. Do you have any sisters?"

"I did, Chief. But she died. When she was about the age of that one there."

Hippolyte nodded.

Why? Chardon had asked. Hippolyte did not have an answer. Something had gone terribly wrong in this modern age.

Then, straightening up and pulling back his shoulders, he said, "Well, at least our soldiers have taken Montmartre. At a terrible cost to these people."

"The red flag is still flying up there."

"Let's see how long that works to deceive the Communards. They'll be waiting for a bombardment from their side that will never come."

Chardon tried to smile. But as Hippolyte could see, his police sergeant was with difficulty holding back vomit.

* * *

As he ran with the others from the Hôtel de Ville, Alphonse threw off his frayed and sooty jacket and snatched a National Guard tunic from the ground. He didn't need another layer of clothing over his shirt in this heat from the May sun and the flames at his back, but he wanted the tunic as a kind of flag. He had almost been shot by some Fédérés when he approached a barricade out of uniform, taken for a spy even though he was waving his signed passes. Tensions were extremely high. He regretted having left this morning in civilian clothes, when he was still thinking he could be a reporter without being a combatant. He had also picked up a kepi, Number 381 sewn onto it. Not his battalion, but it didn't matter now, not today, late in the afternoon of 24th May, days after the incursion of the Versaillais, with the remnant of battalions from all the central and eastern quarters all mixed up and running from barricade to barricade.

The great palace, the Hôtel de Ville, had been set ablaze after the batteries of two corps of Versailles had crashed through its outer defenses and made it indefensible. From there it was a long run to the immense Château-d'Eau square, where Delescluze, the delegate for war – meaning chief of all the Commune's defenses – and the delegates for other Commune services were now supposedly directing operations. He slouched to the ground in the shade of the part of the barricade blocking the Boulevard Saint-Martin, one of the many converging on this square.

Why were the cannons on Montmartre still silent? Those on the high ground of Père Lachaise continued booming, sending their shells overhead to hit areas now occupied by the enemy. After all the hours of explosions, fires, rifle and *mitrailleuse* and cannon fire, and all the crouching and running and shooting, sitting here in the shade of the barricade and listening to the boom of friendly fire was almost calming.

He half-closed his eyes and tried to think, to make sense of all this chaos. Why, he wondered, were he and all those other men, and women too, and even children, still fighting, risking our lives for a cause when all could see that defeat was inevitable?

Maybe because they did not really believe the cause was lost. The Commune, yes, its elected council, its embryonic reforms, its crazy festival of freedom. All that could be, was being destroyed. But the sense of solidarity, of worker with worker regardless of trade, and even worker with bourgeois when the bourgeois was a defender of the Republic, could that last? And its aspirations of Liberty, Equality, Fraternity as they put it in the Revolution of 1789. And the same ideas in different words and languages all over the world, wherever men, and women too, he supposed, had demanded freedom, from the earliest human communities. Or was he dreaming?

He was so weary. So weary he could die, happy in the noise and agitation, content to be part of this reaffirmation of ancient and eternal principles. Yes, to the lullaby of cannonade, he was drifting, dreaming –

'Phonse! Is that you?"

His eyes snapped open and he looked to find the unfamiliar voice.

"And where did you get that kepi? 381 can't be your battalion, you were in the Second Arrondissement, right?"

"Uh – Hi. Do I know you?"

"Évariste. Évariste Joubert, the tinsmith, from that house where you used to give classes in French. Dragon Court."

"Oh, right. Évariste. That seems so long ago."

"Yes, it does, doesn't it? You were trying to get some things published in our workers' papers. Did you?"

Alphonse laughed.

"Yes, I did. Not that it matters now. And you?"

"Now, second lieutenant, working in the central committee of the National Guard. And the Commune, too. Liaison between the two committees. But now everybody's moved over here, the Commune and the Guard. We're going to hold those bastards, you'll see. Rebuild the Commune, from our headquarters now in the town hall of the Eleventh. And then push back, until we can retake Paris."

"You really think so?"

"We still have cartridges, plenty of ammunition. And cannons. And men with spirit."

"Tell me, Évariste. Why do you think all these men, the others all around us here, and all those at the other barricades, why, how can they keep fighting? It's been days now, with no rest."

"Why? Because there's really no alternative. Those bastards in the army, if they catch you, or if you drop your gun and try to surrender, they shoot you and throw your body in a ditch or just let it lie there. The only way to save yourself is to shoot first, and if they're going to shoot you, you want it to be while you're shooting back at them."

"Mm-hmm," Alphonse muttered, not really convinced.

"Or you can try to run away. Like whoever it was who threw off that kepi you're wearing. Throw away your rifle and your uniform and pretend you never fought them, and hope you can hide and survive. I've seen some men try that. Desperate, maybe not as convinced as some of us, you and me. But you know? There haven't been many of them. And you know why?"

Alphonse thought he could guess, but he asked anyway.

"Tell me. Why?"

"Because for almost all of them, maybe not you and not me, who come from other places, but almost all of them, it's their neighborhood they're defending. The barricade is right on their street. And it's their neighbors who are fighting alongside them. And to betray them would be a disgrace, worse than death."

So, thought Alphonse. Maybe that's it. This man Évariste, whom he didn't really remember but who seemed so confident, maybe understood the men better than he did. The answer to Alphonse's question, of why keep fighting when the situation is so desperate?

What he would have said, his guess when Évariste had said that, was a kind of automatism, that after so many days of firing rifles and building barricades and shouting slogans, they didn't know how to stop. And fear, because as Évariste had said, if captured they would be killed. But what Alphonse had failed to take into account, no doubt because he wasn't from Paris and hadn't really belonged all his life to any particular neighborhood here, was shame, or the deep embarrassment that would come if a man betrayed his neighbors, his family, his street. "Disgrace worse than death," Évariste had said.

Just then another cannon blast shattered a grand chunk of the barricade from Magenta, the boulevard to the north. The enemy had circled around this makeshift fortress, and were closing in.

Smoke, fire and rain

How strange the city had become, thought Victorine when she went out on Wednesday, for her second attempt to reach what she hoped would be her breakthrough audition. Strange and ugly. With smoke overhead and flames visible from down near the river. Suddenly transformed. Everything had seemed so lovely this weekend.

On Tuesday, when she had set out early for her appointment at the Conservatory, there had been commotion and noise, but that hardly mattered. She was full of excitement at the hope of being selected for the gala performance that, she was sure, would be part of the grand re-opening of that famous institution, after the war and the siege and the second war and second siege had shut it down.

But she had not been able to reach her destination on Tuesday. She had barely reached the Boulevard Sebastopol, after skirting more barricades like the ones she had seen on Monday, when intense and rapid rifle and then cannons between her and the Conservatory, just a few blocks ahead of her in the Ninth Arrondissement, frightened her and made her turn back toward her rented room in the Second. Some of those Versailles soldiers must have slipped through, she thought. They were sure to be expelled, she told herself, the impregnability of Paris was well known and had been announced once again at Sunday's concert. Some posters she had seen just this morning said the same thing. But not today. She would just have to wait until those brave boys in the National Guard, proud and handsome in their uniforms, devoted to the Commune, restored order. The audition would be rescheduled, she was sure, probably for tomorrow, she supposed. She would just have to go home to wait this out. And perhaps memorize some more verses if the director should give her a chance to recite.

After several anxious hours back in her furnished room, and only a brief outing for a meal in the wine shop at the corner, she went to bed, her own bed, alone. She tried to sleep, by reciting to herself the heroic verses from the songs she thought would please the director. And she did manage to doze. When morning came, she decided to try again.

Just as she had on Tuesday, she put on her most elegant dress, the one that René-Pierre had bought her for that Christmas dinner in the Café Voisin. It was still very early, she spent some time re-arranging her curls and elaborate braids, adorning them with bits of red ribbon and some glittering ceramic flowers. She packed her Oriental princess costume and silk stage slippers in the lovely, oversized cashmere handbag she had cajoled from another admirer, and set out again.

The trouble did not seem to be over, though. She had not got far when she heard more rifle fire. This was when she first saw the great cloud of smoke rising from the area nearer the river. And then, suddenly, the soldiers. Not Fédérés, not the Commune's National Guards, but those soldiers in red trousers, the ones the Commune had promised to expel. There was a cannon pointing toward the corner she was about to pass.

She wheeled around, to run back away from this horror. This was not the theater; these men were really shooting! She heard the shouts.

"Stop! Stop her!"

"It's a *pétroleuse*!" she heard. "She's got the makings of a fire in that bag!"

What were they talking about? Her bag, her fine, expensive costume, is that what they wanted? She stopped and turned and lifted it, to show them that it was harmless.

And she was shot. Four, five, six times.

"Very good," called out a commanding voice. "That's the third one we've got today. And stay alert, you men. There are more of them in this city. Witches they are, and arsonists, and murderesses, if they get the chance."

Though fading, in these last seconds, she could still hear a voice.

"No petrol here in her bag, Cap'n Laurent," someone called back.

"No matter. You can't trust them. They are all potential arsonists, these mad wenches. I'm going to have to shoot a dozen more at least today. Look what they've already done, those flames!"

She heard the Thud! of her bag against the street and a slighter sound that could only be her pretty slipper on the pavement. And then, the very last thing she was aware of was the silk of a gown spread over her arms and shoulders. She knew that she had at last achieved her role, princess of an Oriental kingdom, far away.

* * *

Mireau, in the course of his interviews and investigations

of the morale of the troops, had become better acquainted with Captain Charles-Arthur Robert, a clever and well-read officer, ten years younger than Mireau – he was only thirty-one – and with a rather wicked sense of humor, Mireau thought. Though this veteran of many battles against the Prussians, and more recently against Parisians, did not seem amused or even enthusiastic about his present assignment, to clean out supposed insurgents from the insurgent-ridden th Arrondissement on the slopes and hilltop of Montmartre.

Mireau had volunteered his squad of police for this zone, viewed as especially dangerous by the high command, not because he was especially familiar with the area but because he preferred coordinating with Robert rather than any of the other, more ignorant and inflexible officers he had had to deal with. Denunciations had been reaching all the Versailles forces, from fearful neighbors, concierges, and people who might have some particular grievance against an individual, pointing out people they said were especially dangerous Communards, who had built barricades or fired on troops or spoken loudly in favor of the Commune. Captain Robert, unlike some of the other officers of his rank, heard out these accusations somewhat skeptically, and had at times asked Hippolyte his opinion, which Hippolyte considered meant he had good judgment.

No doubt all or most of the people denounced had been supporters of the Commune. But very few of them could be considered dangerous, now that the barricades here had been abandoned and no one was lifting a weapon against the soldiers. There had been one case, a man pointed out as being especially active in constructing the barricades both at Place Blanche and Place Pigalle, that had made Robert sit back and – Mireau had been watching him closely – almost laugh. Yes, certainly this giant must have been useful in lifting paving stones and bigger rocks, and he seemed so good-natured he must have been delighted to collaborate in barricade construction. His hands were rough and calloused, but – they bore no signs of powder. And, upon questioning, no witness could swear that he had fired a weapon. 'Hercule', they called him, though his true name, he assured the captain, was Ovide. He smiled and frowned and seemed perplexed by the questioning and shook his head as he looked around at the soldiers. When asked about the killings, he began to cry, which surprised even Hippolyte, who had seen all manner of reactions by suspects under questioning.

* * *

Running, running, away from a horror she had to escape and toward another one she hoped to prevent. Her mother was dead, and many of her friends; her father she hoped might still be alive and could need her. Her lover too would need her, her Étienne somewhere down in the city, and she would need him. But first she had to get to Belleville.

The troops, the enemy, were approaching, somewhere behind her. But she also heard gunfire from the heights to her left, so some of the enemy must also be approaching Belleville from another angle, from the side where supposedly the Prussians were still neutral.

Running up the street toward her parents' house, she saw bits of discarded uniforms and gear, which reminded her that she was in her *cantinière's* tunic and skirt. Her kepi was now long lost. She saw no people on the street. The barricade nearest what had been her home and her parents' home was now broken as though blasted by a cannon. The door to their house was ajar, half off its hinges. Her father? Nowhere around.

She looked again at the ruined barricade. It had been made of furniture and dirt and stones. She was surprised to recognize what had been her own bed in the rubble. Her bed. Where she had slept for many years, until she had set up house with Étienne. Where she had stored her diary and other things, beneath the bed. Including, she now remembered, a pair of wooden shoes from that dairy farm beyond the barrier. Where were those?

Surprised again, she found one. Then, under some of the rubble, she found the other. Well. She had never really expected to need them, but now – much better than continuing barefoot. The soles of her feet were sore. Those wooden shoes, those *sabots*, would have been no good for the running she had been doing up to now, but now that she could stop, and even sit a moment, it was good to slip these wood things on. After first rubbing her feet.

But she couldn't stay here long. She had to find her father. Unsteadily, she stood and tried walking a pace or two in the sabots. She felt dizzy. Then a voice.

"Rose! Is that you? I thought I'd never see you again!"

It was Henriette, from next door.

"Come in, child. Come quickly."

She pulled Rose by the arm, into her kitchen.

"What happened here?" Rose asked after a minute.

"Ah, it was awful. I would have run with Louis, but he shouted at me to stay, I'd be better here than with him, and he needed to have me safe."

"Run where?"

"With your father, with Jules Durand. They fought, those men, but when they saw the size of the enemy forces, and they started coming from the other side, they grabbed their rifles and a bag of cartridges and ran off. I don't know why they hadn't been killed, there were so many troops attacking!"

"But where?"

"I don't know, but from the direction they were taking, and the noises we could hear from down there, I would guess it was to the barricades still further east. Probably to the high ground of the cemetery, Père Lachaise."

"I have to go there!"

"Not now, child, you are exhausted. And the soldiers are probably going to come back. The men, and some women too, they captured when the barricade fell, they took them over there, to that edge – you know it, that dangerous gulley you used to play in. And I heard shots. They must have thrown the bodies there, or just let them fall. And if they find you like that, look at you! That flared skirt, that tunic. They'll throw you in there too. We have to get you out of those clothes."

Rose allowed herself to be undressed, her face and hands scrubbed – "That gunpowder has to go. You've been shooting, poor dear."

Henriette found her a simple dress, too big for her, but still, useable. They heard noises, and Henriette said "Hush!" She rolled the discarded skirt and tunic into as tight a ball as she could and looked for someplace to hide it.

Barely in time. A policeman looked in the door.

"Who's there?" he demanded.

"Just us," said Henriette. "Me and my daughter."

"Tell the men to come out, with their hands up."

"The men have all gone, *monsieur l'agent*. It is just us two women. And my daughter here, she has been terribly frightened by all the shooting."

"Step outside," said the uniformed *agent de paix*.

"What have you got, Chardon?" called out another man's voice.

"Two women. A woman and her daughter. I'm going to check to see if there is any man hiding here."

"Good. I'll watch these two."

Chardon came out after a minute.

"Nobody here, Chief. But these two. And this."

He held up the ball Henriette had made of Rose's uniform.

The other man, the chief, stood looking at Rose and Henriette, as though studying them.

"Do you think they're dangerous, Chardon?"

The policeman stepped over to say something privately to his chief.

"No, you're probably right. She, that older one, clearly has not been involved in the fighting. And the girl?"

"Look at her, chief! A peasant! She's even got wooden shoes!"

"No *godillots*, then."

Rose, trembling slightly and hiding her gunpowder-stained hands under her apron, fixed her eyes on the older policeman, the one in charge. She saw his eye movements as, without turning his head, he glanced at the destruction all around them. The broken barricade, damaged façades of workers' houses, and other detritus – rifles, scraps of uniforms —

"Throw that ball of rags away, Chardon. There's been enough mayhem here. We'll leave them be.

"First let's see if we can find any men, and any weapons. And then we're going to have to move faster, to catch up with the army. Robert's men and the other units are already down there in lower Belleville."

And after a brief questioning about any men, the two women, Rose and Henriette, shaking their heads and saying they didn't know, the police – besides the two who had spoken, there were four others in the same uniform – went a little further up the hill and then turned down a street, toward Ménilmontant and Père Lachaise, Rose guessed.

* * *

It was Saturday, under pouring rain, that Étienne found himself as one of the last holdouts of the Fédérés. As he had imagined, he was back in the Place de la Bastille, now hardly recognizable as the way he remembered it from 18th March. He had been crouching and firing and reloading and rising to fire in another direction now for so many hours he had no clear idea of time, of when he had got here. He had run once, that terrible day, 3rd April, when they had marched out to take Versailles; he was not going to run again, not run *from* a battle, but run only if it were to another barricade, or another corner of the barricades erected to block all the avenues and boulevards that fed into this square, avenues of attack by the Versaillais.

Had it been Thursday, or Friday when he got here after abandoning the Rue de Rivoli, and then the now-ruined Hôtel de Ville, and then the Château-d'Eau, where, as he now knew, Delescluze had let himself be killed, leaving them with no overall commander of the Commune's, the Fédérés', now depleted remnants?

His body should have been totally exhausted, but his heart was pounding wildly. He had crumpled beside a barricade, seeking shade and maybe a moment's rest, when he heard a familiar voice.

"*Péquenaud!*" 'Rube' is what that meant. Only one person in Paris had ever called him that. Could it be?

"Toinou! You here? Still alive?"

"Still alive, and still trying to send those bastards to the devil! You were an Internationalist, weren't you? Still?"

"Mmm. Guess so. Whatever that means now."

"A fine mess you guys have got us into! If Blanqui had been in charge, well, it would be a different story. But those *jean-foutres* have got him locked up."

"I know. Since just the day before we saved the cannons."

"But here we are. I have to admit, you guys in the International have been putting up a good fight. But what a mess, this defense! Nobody's really in charge, no coordination."

"Yes, I know. But that's not the International's fault, we're not running this show."

"I know, I know."

"And like you said, here we are. All together, what's left of us. Blanquistes, Internationalists, some of us, but most of these men, I'll bet, don't belong to any bigger movement. I've seen even some bourgeois fighting alongside us."

"Well, take care, buddy. They may get us in the end, but we're going to get as many as we can first! I don't care about anything else anymore. It's just revenge. They've killed lots of my best buddies, and I'm going to get some for them."

"Me too."

But he couldn't say any more. A cannon was now blasting from another, unexpected angle. And then –

And then it was morning. Of some day, no telling which.

Étienne felt the harsh stone pressing against his cheek, then half-opened his eyes and began to work his brain to understand why and where he was. Dust and dirt mixed with the stench of gunpowder tickled his nose, along with the more acrid, rusty smell of blood. He was sprawled upon the street, face down, he realized, among debris. To lift himself he would need to move his arms. He found his left arm extended nearly straight as though reaching for something, something that had escaped his grasp. His rifle, he must have flung it. His other arm lay bent and cramped along his side, squeezed between his torso and some other hard, cloth-bound bundle. He rotated his wrist and hand and pulsed the bundle, realizing with a shiver that the cloth was the twill of a National Guard uniform like the one he wore, and that what it enclosed was a lifeless human arm. Who had been standing next to him just now, or whenever it had been, in those last minutes before, before he remembered anything? J-P? Claude? No, no, he had lost those comrades earlier. And not Jules, surely, though he imagined that he had been very near, shouting orders. No, no, that could not be, Jules would have been up in Belleville. Then he remembered dimly the last voice he had heard. "*Péquenaud*": Toinou.

He considered whether he could or should lift his head, which seemed very heavy. First he needed to lie still and gather his thoughts. He wanted to pull back from that dead arm, but it was pressed too tightly against his side. He feared turning his head to see the corpse. Could it be Rose?

Odd now, and disturbing, the near silence. Not to hear the crash of battle, nor cannon booming, nor bombs exploding, nor crackling fusillades of *chassepots*. But there! The report of a single rifle shot startled him, somewhere near, but no responding fire.

It was a sudden change, this near silence, because he had been in constant battle, day after day, in different streets, since Sunday last. He remembered someone saying it was Thursday – had that been yesterday? – and that they were burying Dombrowski, up in the cemetery Père-Lachaise. Père-Lachaise, where the Fédéré cannons had been firing up to now. Why weren't they sounding now? There had been rain, and shouts and crashes and screaming horses and even, twice, loud and spirited singing. He felt the rain now on his shoulder and back, and the wet stone pressed against his cheek, and the stickiness under his left hand that was too thick to be from water. Blood, surely, and sweat, and street filth.

Now he heard a second shot, but from a pistol, he thought. Some officer, finishing off some comrade. Then he caught scents of burning wood and cloth and what might be flesh.

Yes, then this must be Bastille, where he had taken his last stand with his rifle as the enemy advanced. The broken pavement beneath his chest and hips and thighs and arms, that also meant something, but he was not sure what. Oh, yes! Barricade. He had been defending a barricade, with Toinou and the others, all equal, no more chief of their battalion. He was expecting to hear someone shout, to order them to fire and keep firing, but then —

A voice! The barricade commander? No, some other man. The enemy. Someone in command, giving orders to someone he called 'soldier', not his name or '*citoyen*' the way Guards, the Fédérés, addressed each other. 'Soldier' could only mean the enemy, Versailles, right here! And bootsteps, starting and stopping, coming closer. If only he could reach his rifle, but he didn't know where it was and sensed that it would be better not to move a muscle until he could tell where the enemy was and where he was.

Oof! A boot struck hard against his left ribs, pushing, trying to turn him over. Now he made the effort to turn and face his foe. The silhouette of a soldier, the sun behind his head making a halo around his kepi. An angel of death with a tricolor armband. The shadow of the soldier's rifle muzzle passed before his nose, then aimed at his chest. This then, was the end.

And as in a dream, he heard his own childhood nickname, "Titi."

Was he being summoned to the afterlife? A hallucination, a message from the past, reminding him of the boy called Titi, young Étienne Bonin from Lyon, who dreamed of revolution and of becoming a master bookbinder like his hero Eugène Varlin, and who was now waiting for the dark shape of the slender soldier hovering over him to fire and add his body to the corpses he now knew lay all around him in Place de la Bastille, where his revolution had begun.

"Titi!" he heard again. "Cousin!"

His eyelids fluttered open and he tried to make out the features of the soldier standing over him. It was – no, could it be? Maurice!

He almost called out, but the soldier lifted a finger to his lips and, turning back, called out, "All dead here, my captain."

And nodded to him quickly before moving on.

Note on the author

Geoffrey Fox is an American fiction writer and essayist. In addition to *Rabble!* his fiction includes the novel *A Gift for the Sultan* (translated into Turkish as *Bir cihan, iki sultan*), the collection of short stories *Welcome to My Contri*, and scores of other short stories online and in print.

His non-fiction includes the books *Hispanic Nation: Culture, Politics and the Construction of Identity*; *The Land and People of Argentina*; *The Land and People of Venezuela*, and articles and reviews in such media as *The New York Times, The Nation,* the *Los Angeles Times,* and *The Village Voice* and in academic publications. For more information on him, see his website, **Geoffrey Fox** (https://geoffreyfox.com/) and his Amazon Author profile.

Acknowledgments

My first and foremost gratitude is to my life-partner, *camarade* and accomplice in all projects, Susana Torre, who has sustained my spirit and much else in this complicated effort to convey the power of real events through fictional characters.

Writer friends whose critical readings of drafts have been very helpful include the novelists Dirk van Nouhuys, Jan Alexander, Peter de Lissovoy, and Margaret Murray, and freelance editor Robbie Guillory.

My thanks also to José Bonifacio Bermejo Martín, now head of the Department of Museums of the city of Madrid and formerly director of the Imprenta Municipal of Madrid, who showed and explained to me the operation of the presses and cutting and other machines that would have been in use in Étienne Bonin's bindery in Paris. He also located for me a book bound by Antoine Menard, a young *communard* and bookbinder much like Étienne Bonin who, after escaping the slaughter in the last days of the Commune, found his way to Madrid, where he established himself as a binder.

In Paris, historian Eric Lebouteiller of the *Amies et Amis de la Commune de Paris 1871* (46 Rue des Cinq Diamants, 75013 Paris, France) guided my research in the association's extensive bibliographic resources.

And finally, my very special appreciation of Michèle Audin, author of books, articles and a passionate, critical blog on the Paris Commune, https://macommunedeparis.com/. Michèle welcomed me in Paris, read my drafts and, from her detailed knowledge of the personalities and events of the Commune, guided me to correct several minor errors of fact or interpretation.

Et aussi à Mlle Madeleine Doerfler, qui m'a mis sur le chemin.

For exclusive discounts on Matador titles,
sign up to our occasional newsletter at
troubador.co.uk/bookshop